vampire

Literature

# vampire literature

## AN ANTHOLOGY

edited by Robin A. Werner
and Elizabeth M. Lewis

broadview press

BROADVIEW PRESS
Peterborough, Ontario, Canada

Founded in 1985, Broadview Press is a fully independent academic publishing house owned by approximately twenty-five shareholders—almost all of whom are either Broadview employees or Broadview authors. Broadview is supported by a collaboration with Trent University, a liberal arts university located in Peterborough, Ontario—the city where Broadview was founded and continues to operate. Broadview is committed to environmentally responsible publishing and fair business practices.



**Library and Archives Canada Cataloguing in Publication**

Title: Vampire literature : an anthology / edited by Robin A. Werner and Elizabeth M. Lewis.
Names: Werner, Robin A., editor. | Lewis, Elizabeth M., editor.
Description: Includes bibliographical references.
Identifiers: Canadiana (print) 20240396332 | Canadiana (ebook) 20240396340 |
ISBN 9781554816064 (softcover) | ISBN 9781770489691 (PDF) | ISBN 9781460408964 (EPUB)
Subjects: LCSH: Vampires—Fiction. | LCSH: Vampires in literature. | LCGFT: Literature.
Classification: LCC PR1309.V36 V36 2024 | DDC 823/.0873808375—dc23

*Broadview Press handles its own distribution in Canada and the United States:*
PO Box 1243, Peterborough, Ontario K9J 7H5, Canada
555 Riverwalk Parkway, Tonawanda, NY 14150, USA
Tel: (705) 482-5915
email: customerservice@broadviewpress.com

Broadview Press acknowledges the financial support of the Government of Canada for our publishing activities.

Canada

Copy edited by Tania Therien
Book Design by Chris Rowat Design

Broadview Press® is the registered trademark of Broadview Press Inc.

PRINTED IN CANADA

# CONTENTS

1 The author has transitioned, but he still wishes to be published under the name of Poppy Z. Brite.

# A CHRONOLOGY OF TEXTS

194 Jewelle Gomez, *The Gilda Stories* (1991)
418 Jane Yolen, "Mama Gone" (1991)
307 Poppy Z. Brite/Billy Martin, *Lost Souls* (1992)
423 Toni Brown, "Immunity" (1996)
430 Nalo Hopkinson, "Greedy Choke Puppy" (2001)
201 Ibi Aanu Zoboi, "Old Flesh Song" (2004)
211 Octavia E. Butler, *Fledgling* (2005)
440 Silvia Moreno-Garcia, "A Handful of Earth" (2011)
368 Karen Russell, "The Vampires in the Lemon Grove" (2013)
445 Kazuki Sakuraba, *A Small Charred Face* (2014)

# ACKNOWLEDGMENTS

We would like to thank Christopher and Brant Walterman, Phillip Marion Humphreys, S'Heelia Marks, Michael Mechtenberg, Marilyn Lewis, Michael Bibler, Lisa Verner, Mary Rodrigue, Don LePan, and all of those who read drafts, listened to us explain, and gave us their perspectives on the anthology as it evolved. We would also like to thank all the students whose engagement with these texts motivated us to create the anthology and who continue to inspire us.

# INTRODUCTION

## What Is a Vampire?

*"There is no such creature as 'The Vampire'; there are only vampires."*
—*Nina Auerbach,* Our Vampires, Ourselves[1]

What is a vampire? A suave aristocrat with a pronounced widow's peak and a wicked grin who drinks the blood of vulnerable women? A beautiful woman who steals youth from her lovers? A ball of flame that drains an infant's life? Vampire myths are as diverse as the cultures that created them. Feminist cyborg scholar Donna Haraway insists that "vampires are ambiguous,"[2] while in his compelling critical work, *The Vampire: A New History*, Nick Groom suggests that we have "reworked the vampire into an all-embracing cipher, a cosmic vessel to be filled and refilled with endless readings and re-readings—a veritable multiplicity."[3] Yet, despite this ambiguous multiplicity, most readers have no difficulty knowing when they are looking at a vampire story.

As with most fantasy, horror, and speculative fiction, a careful reading of these tales can tell much about a society's preoccupations and anxieties. In contrast with other monstrous creatures, vampires have a unique tie to humanity. In most vampire literature, the vampire spends much of the narrative passing as human, instilling a unique brand of horror—the uncanny fear of the seemingly familiar rather than the completely foreign. Unlike so many monsters, vampires can be charming, and, whether seductive or repulsive, one of the vampire's key threats is their ability to infiltrate society. In fact, vampires can even penetrate the family home itself. Despite the array of skills and weaknesses attributed to these monsters over the centuries, they "are disturbingly close to the mortals

1 Auerbach, *Our Vampires, Ourselves* 5.
2 Haraway, *Modest_Witness* 80.
3 Groom, *The Vampire* 201.

they prey on."[1] The dissolution of the boundary between human and monster is one of the most pronounced traits of the literary vampire. Sigmund Freud uses the return of the dead as an example of the uncanny—the unheimlich—human but not human—familiar but alien.[2] Carl Jung describes the shadow aspect of the unconscious as containing "wicked blood-spirits, swift anger and sensual weakness,"[3] which David Cohen interprets as depicting the vampire as "the dark, unconscious aspect of the self that the ego tries to avoid."[4] Throughout the history of the literary vampire, the threat these monsters pose is uncomfortably close to home.

Vampires are tied to humanity by both their form and their hunger. Throughout literary history, the vampire is depicted as a parasite feeding off the human beings they so closely resemble. They hunger for life—whether blood, energy, or passion. Some readers insist that without a bite and blood, it is not quite a vampire; for others, it is the stolen life that is the essential factor. Across feeding styles and victim profiles, one unifying factor remains—vampires survive by draining the life of others. In some tales, vampires are the dead who would not stay dead and in others, they are a separate species entirely; in all, they survive at the expense of humanity. We delight in reading tales in which we are the prey.

The vampire we know today predominantly evolved throughout the nineteenth century—a period of tremendous social change and scientific advancement. The origins of Western vampire myths, however, are in the medieval folklore of Eastern Europe. Today's popular culture vampires are quite different from earlier iterations of the monster. The "supposedly authentic cases" surfaced around the same time as the witch trials.[5] There are some common features of the vampire of European folklore that clearly set these monsters apart from their literary progeny. In tale after tale, the folklore vampire appears as a skeleton or corpse more akin to what today's readers might see as a zombie. Their breath reeks. They creep through their existence, prey to an uncontrollable hunger for life.[6] The folklore vampire is rooted in the "primaeval [sic] fear" of the return of the dead.[7] Much of this folklore arose as a way of explaining the unexplainable. Critics like Groom attribute reports of vampires to everything from anemia and strokes to rabies or even porphyria.[8] Throughout European history, disease epidemics can be correlated with reports of vampires, "making them vectors and consequently part of the history of infectious diseases."[9] By

1 Auerbach, *Our Vampires, Ourselves* 6.
2 Freud, "The 'Uncanny'" 241–43.
3 Jung, "Archetypes of the Collective Unconscious" 20.
4 Cohen, *The Psychology of Vampires* 33.
5 Carter, "The Vampire as Alien in Contemporary Fiction" 27–44.
6 Senf, *The Vampire in 19th-Century English Literature* 18–19.
7 Groom, *The Vampire* 4.
8 According to the Mayo Clinic, porphyria refers to a group of inherited blood disorders that can result in light sensitivity as well as anxiety, confusion, and hallucination.
9 Groom, *The Vampire* 15–16.

the eighteenth century, vampire myths had begun to solidify with "key features being the ever-fresh corpse, the ruddiness of the skin, the grave-eating, the rising from the dead and the murderous craving to suffocate victims."[1] The roots of vampires' aversion to Christianity can also be found here. Vampires in most European folktales consume blood in a perversion of Christian communion, and the murderers and suicides who would be denied Christian burial would also be considered at risk of transforming into vampires.

It is during the Romantic era that the literary vampire is born. Today's vampire arises out of the Enlightenment,[2] and they took what would become their most familiar shape in the Romantic era. In *The Vampire Book*, J. Gordon Melton suggests, "the literary vampire of the nineteenth century transformed the ethnic vampire into a cosmopolitan citizen of the modern imagination."[3] Tied as they are to the working class and physically displaying their identity as walking corpses, the vampires of Eastern European folklore were decidedly lacking in romance. They would never have been able to court their victims in a ballroom or opera house, no matter how elegant their evening wear.

Many scholars date the origin of contemporary vampire narratives to 1816—the year without a summer, thanks to the eruption of Mount Tambora in Indonesia earlier the same year, affecting weather around the globe.[4] The same ghost-story writing contest that would produce Mary Shelley's *Frankenstein* also ultimately led to the creation of the literary vampire when John Polidori took up Lord Byron's discarded fragment and created Lord Ruthven to vent his frustration with his erstwhile employer. Polidori's 1819 novella, *The Vampyre*, creates the Western literary vampire as Byronic villain—evil yet alluring. This aristocratic pedigree brought the vampire out of the shadows and into society. The Byronic influence also tied the vampire to sexuality. Transformed from an asexual monster to an aristocratic seducer, nineteenth-century literary vampires are still undoubtedly villains, but somehow appealing ones. Whether male or female, hideous or fair, literary vampires move freely amongst the humans upon whom they prey.

In the Victorian era, vampires' hunger expands, becoming a metaphor for many kinds of power including class, gender, and race. Indeed, Karl Marx repeatedly uses the figure as a metaphor for capitalism: "capital is dead labour which, vampire-like, lives only by sucking living labour."[5] The vampire is linked simultaneously with capital and with those who exploit the labor of the masses: "the vampire is manifest capital, an insatiable arch-consumer."[6] Vampires take without compunction. Their privilege is linked to strength—physical and eco-

1 Groom, *The Vampire* 28.
2 Groom, *The Vampire* 4.
3 Melton, *The Vampire Book* xxxii.
4 Frayling, *Vampyres* 7.
5 Marx, *Capital* 342.
6 Groom, *The Vampire* 160–61.

nomic. The vampire is greed incarnate. While twenty-first-century vampires may shed their aristocratic titles, the majority remain associated with the wealth and privilege that defined them throughout the nineteenth century.

As vampire literature evolved, the vampire came to represent different kinds of power. As nineteenth-century Europe rushed to divide up the world, colonizers took their monsters with them. Throughout the world, rapacious vampires surface as metaphors for both colonizers and the colonized. The Western vampire drank from native mythologies of witches, ghosts, and fairies, recreating them in its own image. Sometimes, aspects of the Western vampire shift and change as they, in turn, are transformed by the mythologies they colonize: as Luise White asserts, "Vampires were new. Despite scattered written references and a dictionary definition, no one I ever interviewed knew any precolonial stories about whites or Africans who took blood."[1] However, J. Gordon Melton points out the witches of the African diaspora possess powers akin to "psychic vampirism."[2] The vampire in its European guise may be typically absent from African and Caribbean cultures, but monsters like witches, ghosts, and soucouyants abound. In Caribbean folklore, a soucouyant sheds her skin and as a ball of fire jettisons across the night sky to drain the life of infants. In *She Bites Back*, Kendra R. Parker persuasively argues that "African Diasporic figures like the soucouyant, lougaorou and wazimamoto" can be compared to the literary vampires of Western culture.[3] Though this comparison is fruitful, it can be a dangerously colonizing move to take non-Western folklores and uncritically group them under a Western term like "vampire." Consequently, we have chosen to focus on works by authors who specifically evoke the Western idea of the bloodsucker or vampire as part of their exploration of African, Caribbean, and Asian monsters. Thus, we hope to invite a comparison between the mythologies rather than attempting to elide them.

In the early decades of the twentieth century, vampires, both on the page and on the screen, come to represent the outsider and the other. In such early monster films as *Nosferatu* (1922) and short stories such as C.L. Moore's "Shambleau" (1933) published in popular magazines, vampires are outsiders. Essentially conventional in its gender performance and heteronormative, at least on the surface, early twentieth-century vampire literature hid from the conflicting sexual tensions of the Romantic-era tales. Whatever disruptions the vampire introduces into the narrative, the tales themselves ultimately served to reinforce the status quo. This trend continues through the mid–twentieth century as literary representations of vampires became less frequent, replaced by mass-produced horror films, such as those from London's Hammer Studios. A few interesting stories, such as Fritz Leiber's "The Girl with the Hungry Eyes" (1949),

1 White, *Speaking with Vampires* 14.
2 Melton, *The Vampire Book* 6.
3 Parker, *Black Female Vampires* xv.

Richard Matheson's "Drink My Blood" (1951), and Philip K. Dick's "The Cookie Lady" (1953), were published; however, literary vampires would have to wait for the later twentieth century to again become the fluid, boundary-pushing monsters we know today.

By the 1970s and 1980s, vampires offered an alternative to the prudence and conformity of the 1950s American Dream. Narratives begin to show the return of two distinct tropes: the folklore vampire theme of contagion and the Romantic vampire's Byronic rebellion. Even Blaxploitation films like *Blacula* (1972) and *Ganga and Hess* (1973) reflect the ways in which vampires articulated social and cultural preoccupations. As U. Melissa Anyiwo explains in her introduction to *Race in the Vampire Narrative* (2015), vampire literature "perfectly mirrors that search for identity, offering a figure on which to mirror everything we desire and fear."[1] In the late twentieth century, vampires became the consummate other.

Once the AIDS epidemic took hold, authors like Stephen King began to use vampires to explore cultural anxieties about contagion. For example, both Nina Auerbach and Sue-Ellen Case explicitly link the fear of vampires to the threat of AIDS. Once blood is seen as diseased, "blood could no longer be the life."[2] In stories such as Stephen King's "One for the Road," vampires explore cultural anxieties about contagion, and become a plague threatening public safety. Far from the life—blood now holds death.

The end of the twentieth and the beginning of the twenty-first century also saw the vampire as a new kind of rebel idol: from runaways to rock stars, socially deviant vampires become the focus of many tales and films. Carol Senf notes that a hint of rebellion is characteristic of all literary vampires, but for the anti-heroes of writers like Anne Rice[3] and Billy Martin/Poppy Z. Brite,[4] the counter-culture vampire is the center of the narrative.[5] Few heroes and certainly no victims could ever be as enticing as these monsters. Far from the repulsive undead creature of folklore, as the twentieth century moved into the twenty-first vampires *became* our desires—the vampire as sex symbol took over. These texts "present the vampire not as villain but as protagonist, less a shadowy creature of mythic proportion than a worldly being whose day-to-day existence is minutely scrutinized."[6] Vampire literature has come in and out of vogue many times over the centuries, but in the twenty-first century, popular culture has fallen in love with vampires all over again.

1 Anyiwo, "Introduction" 1.
2 Auerbach, *Our Vampires, Ourselves* 175.
3 Unfortunately, we have been unable to gain permission to include Rice's writing in this anthology; however, as the AMC adaptation of *Interview with the Vampire* reveals, her iconic characters continue to reflect both the sexuality and rebellion of the vampire in the twenty-first century.
4 Martin published *Lost Souls* under the name of Poppy Z. Brite. He has since transitioned and is now known as Billy Martin. He has requested that his work continue to be published under the name Poppy Z. Brite.
5 Senf, *The Vampire* 152.
6 Latham, *Consuming Youth* 77.

Vampires are inherently subversive creatures transgressing boundaries of race, class, and sexuality. In the last thirty years, the question "Who gets to be a vampire?" has begun to be asked by writers and filmmakers alike. Parker points out "the archetypal vampire is a tall, slender, seductive, and economically privileged white male" and asks, "what happens when the vampire is female *and* black?"[1] Writers such as Ibi Zoboi, Nalo Hopkinson, Jewelle Gomez, and Octavia Butler use their vampire narratives as vehicles for questioning oppressive systems of power.[2] Vampires in the current century occupy many positions. They are pansexual creatures who trouble the socio-political waters. They are figures of fantasy romance and demonic infection. Some harken back to old-world forms and tropes while others mock traditional systems of power. Twenty-first-century writers continue to push and problematize this uncanny creation, taking it in new and unexplored directions to challenge and enthrall yet another new age. In the works of contemporary authors, vampires operate as both protagonists and antagonists. They challenge the status quo. Clearly, the literary vampire continues to offer writers tremendous scope for reflecting on culture, society, and life itself.

In shaping this anthology, we have endeavored to emphasize the reoccurring themes that make up the more than 250 years of Western vampire literature: power, immortality, race, sexuality, hunger, and family. Each section presents a range of texts, some older, some newer—some literary, some popular—all exploring the core theme of the chapter. There will necessarily be overlaps—tales that could fit in any number of sections. After all, as Haraway suggests, vampires have "specific category-crossing work to do."[3] The texts are arranged so that they speak to one another in order to foster discussion and analysis. Within each section, texts are arranged chronologically, but it is not our intent to attempt to trace the evolution of the vampire through time. Rather, this anthology emphasizes how these texts reflect society's fears, desires, and obsessions. The focus is on the ways in which these authors use the unique monstrosity of the vampire to comment on, to critique, or even to reinforce the norms of their societies.

We have found that virtually everyone with whom we speak—every reader, every student, every colleague—has a favorite vampire. Clearly it would not be possible to include them all, but we have committed to presenting a wide array of texts. There are classics here, but there are also forgotten popular texts. There are award-winning contemporary works and cult classics. The vast majority are originally published in English, but we have included works from the US, Canada, Europe, the Caribbean, Africa, and Asia. Since so much of the history

1 Parker, *Black Female Vampires* xiii.

2 See also Anatol's *Things That Fly in the Night*, which discusses a range of black female vampires from folklore and contemporary literature to reveal how these myths and stories challenge structures of racial, gender, and sexual oppression.

3 Haraway, *Modest_Witness* 79.

of the literary vampire has been dominated by a few white male authors, we actively sought out works by underrepresented writers. From the start, it has been our goal to hold the familiar classics up against less anthologized works to explore the varied perspectives these texts bring to the theme.

So, what precisely is a vampire? What are the qualities that have made vampires such a perennial favorite? The more one reads about them, the harder it becomes to answer these questions. Unlike so many monsters, vampires appear to transcend limits placed on their existence, becoming "privileged metaphors possessing an uncanny ability to evoke the psychological and social experience—the relationships of desire and power."[1] From the start of their literary history, vampires have tapped into our psyches, tying together desire and fear, attraction and revulsion. From the beginning, these tales have been more than simple monster stories, reflecting themes of political rebellion, class consciousness, gender politics, racial divisions, and sexual exploitation. Perhaps, that is the real secret. Vampire tales remain popular simply because they are so malleable. They take on so many different meanings. These tales appeal because of their tensions and ambiguities—they speak to our anxieties about what it means to be human.

1 Latham, *Consuming Youth* 1.

# VAMPIRES AND POWER

John William Polidori, *The Vampyre* (1819)

James Malcolm Rymer and Thomas Peckett Prest, from *Varney the Vampire* (1847)

Vasile Alecsandri, "Vampire (Strigoiul)" (1886)

Bram Stoker, "Dracula's Guest" (1914)

Henrik Galeen, *Nosferatu* (1922)

Richard Matheson, "Drink My Blood" (1951)

Vampires are *super*natural monsters: whatever limits or weaknesses they may possess, they are defined by physical and psychic powers beyond the range of human beings. As they moved from folklore into literature, vampires began to take on social power as well: "the vampire has, after all, regularly functioned as a political metaphor for aristocrats, for the rich who suck the life blood and/or labor potential from the poor."[1] This metaphor remains a major aspect of popular depictions of vampires even today. Films as diverse as *Underworld* (2003), *Twilight* (2008), and *Only Lovers Left Alive* (2013) all show vampires exercising economic and social privilege. They depict vampires as courtly, even feudal. For over 200 years, vampires have been associated not only with supernatural power, but also perhaps even more significantly with the power of privilege.

In seventeenth- and eighteenth-century Eastern European folklore, vampires arose from disadvantaged outsiders, working-class suicides, or executed criminals. These early creatures were relentless but had little power other

1 Nixon, "When Hollywood Sucks" 121.

than physical strength and the fact that they rose from the dead. As vampires entered the literary realm, they came to be associated with certain additional preternatural abilities. Vampires could mesmerize victims, shape-shift their bodies, and heal from wounds that would be fatal to a human. Beyond their incredible strength, vampires could scale walls (see Illustrations, from *Dracula* p. 515), pass through closed doors, control weather, and even fly. Stoker describes Dracula as having "the strength in his hand of twenty men,"[1] and Polidori claims Lord Ruthven has "irresistible powers of seduction" (see p. 29). Of course, these superhuman abilities came with certain weaknesses, but the literary vampire has always been a formidable foe.

While some literary vampires expressed power through physical prowess, others made use of social power structures. The aristocracy and patriarchy are, of course, both systems of power, and many vampire narratives expose the tension evident within these systems. Although the older texts in this chapter were written at a time when few would question the assumptions supporting the patriarchal power structure, these vampire narratives nonetheless problematize the ideals of the system. These tales present their readers with monstrous patriarchs: Lord Ruthven, Sir Francis Varney, Count Dracula; each an aristocrat who corrupts, infects, and endangers any who depend upon them. Far from the fatherly leaders of patriarchal myth, they are defined by inhuman cruelty and power.

The first selection of this chapter, John Polidori's 1819 novella *The Vampyre*, exemplifies this dramatic shift from the vampire of folklore to the literary vampire. While Lord Ruthven's physical abilities are never quite clearly defined, his use of social privilege is obvious. He moves through British society as a wealthy, titled, and powerful aristocrat, and he uses this social privilege to prey upon women. Following Polidori's tale, literary vampires take on social, political, and economic power. Many also benefit from gendered power in patriarchal societies. Inspired by his own difficult relationship with Lord Byron, Polidori moves the vampire from the margins into the heart of British society.[2] Nick Groom argues that in transforming the vampire into a figure of power, Polidori "triggered a cultural sensation."[3] Literary vampires became embedded in the culture of aristocratic and patriarchal privilege.

Even as revolutions and reform began the long push to greater equality, vampire narratives continued to feature titled aristocrats embodying the privilege and power of the past. Nick Groom suggests that these aristocratic titles can be overemphasized by contemporary critics: "Vampires are, more usually, often oddly classless. Lord Ruthven, for instance, may be an aristocrat, but his lifestyle is not markedly lavish or luxurious."[4] We would suggest, however, that a realistic

1 Stoker, *Dracula* 241.
2 Groom, *The Vampire* 111.
3 Groom, *The Vampire* 111.
4 Groom, *The Vampire* 160.

depiction of an aristocratic lifestyle is not necessarily the point. The vampires may not live the luxurious life of an aristocrat, but they benefit from social privilege. For a middle- or working-class reader, the right to call oneself Count, Lord, or even Sir signifies the power of a secure social position. The vampires' noble titles are symbolically important for the reader. Titles are an instantly recognizable marker of unassailable and often unearned authority protecting the vampire, giving him access, and enabling him to move through society in a way that the vampires of Eastern European folklore would never have managed. From Polidori and Rymer to Stoker and Galeen, the protagonists of the stories in this chapter accord the monsters respect for their title alone. These monsters attack from within the social system of power. The power structure actually enables the monsters to prey on the vulnerable, disempowered, and dependent—particularly women. For these vampires, power comes without any responsibility. The aristocratic vampires neither protect nor lead the people under their control.

It is no accident that the majority of vampires in this chapter prey on the young women who are their polar opposites in the power systems of nineteenth- and early twentieth-century society (see Illustrations, from *Varney the Vampire*, pp. 508–09). This power differential is highlighted by the fact that the early literary vampires do not even attempt to seduce their victims. Vampires like Varney "use great physical and political power to attack sleeping or otherwise defenseless victims, giving them no opportunity to protect themselves or even understand what is happening to them."[1] The young women who become the victims in these narratives are the same women the patriarchy insists should be sheltered and protected by the patriarchal model.

The power and privilege of the vampires we see in this chapter can also be observed in their relationships with men. While these vampires may attack young women, often it is the connections between men that form the heart of the narrative plot. In "Women and Vampires: Nightmare or Utopia?," Judith Johnson observes that nineteenth-century writers use the vampires' monstrosity to explore homosocial relations between men, noting that the connections between the vampire and his companions reflect an exchange of women.[2] After all, it does not require a very close reading of Polidori to see that while women are the vampire's food, the real connection in the narrative is between Ruthven and Aubrey, the male narrator. While Dracula is the quintessence of the patriarchal vampire with his castle and his brides (see Illustrations from the 1931 *Dracula*, p. 520), both the novel and Henrik Galeen's *Nosferatu* (1922) begin by exploring his relationship with Jonathan Harker. Dracula, like Ruthven, preys on women to control men.

1 Senf, *The Vampire* 153.

2 Johnson, "Women and Vampires." For more information on the theories of homosocial bonds, see Sedgwick, *Between Men* and Lipman-Blumen, "Toward a Homosocial Theory of Sex Roles."

As we will see later in this anthology, in the second half of the twentieth and the early twenty-first centuries, power in vampire literature remains a point of tension. The trope of the older male vampire protected by his title and preying on vulnerable, innocent, young women is so familiar it has become a stereotype. In the mid-twentieth century, stories like "Drink My Blood," by Richard Matheson, further explore this idea of the connections between men and vampire literature's exploration of patriarchal authority. The fact that many twentieth-century monsters are only pale reflections of their nineteenth-century predecessors merely reinforces the tensions within the narratives.

While their supernatural abilities and their crippling weaknesses shift with every iteration, the allure and conflict generated by vampires' social power remains a major theme. Twenty-first-century films encapsulate this tension. From the suicidal ennui of the wealthy vampire protagonist in *Only Lovers Left Alive* to the wealthy vegetarian heroes of the *Twilight* saga, Western culture remains fascinated with the power and limitations of undeath. Social and economic power remain aligned with the vampire's supernatural existence. Even when films like *Underworld* openly critique the patriarch's power, his strength remains a major part of the plot, and while the film may end with the ruler defeated, another elder will always awaken to take his place.

# John William Polidori

(1795–1821)

"The year without summer" has long been known for producing Mary Shelley's *Frankenstein*, but it also led to the writing of what is widely considered to be the first literary vampire story in English. Due to the climatic impact of the Mount Tambora volcanic eruption, the summer of 1816 was cold and wet. John William Polidori was part of the famous group who found themselves on the shores of Lake Geneva. Polidori traveled to Europe as Lord Byron's personal physician, where they met up with Percy Shelley and Mary Godwin (who would later become Mary Shelley). Here, Polidori would participate in the famous ghost story competition that inspired both Mary Shelley's *Frankenstein* and his own gothic tale, *The Vampyre*. Notably, it is Polidori's imaginative conceptualization that establishes the vampire figure as a cosmopolitan aristocrat rather than a wild creature of Eastern European legend. Polidori did not intend for the manuscript to be published, but it was discovered by a disreputable publisher who credited Byron as the author. Polidori, an aspiring writer himself, had a contentious relationship with his erstwhile employer that is mirrored in the tale through the personification of Byron as Lord Ruthven. Although Polidori tried to establish authorial rights, his attempts were unsuccessful; haunted by rejection and humiliation, he took his own life at the age of 25.

## *The Vampyre*

(1819)

It happened that in the midst of the dissipations attendant upon a London winter, there appeared at the various parties of the leaders of the ton[1] a nobleman, more remarkable for his singularities, than his rank. He gazed upon the mirth around him, as if he could not participate therein. Apparently, the light

1 Colloquial expression used to refer to fashionable upper class society during the British Regency era.

laughter of the fair only attracted his attention, that he might by a look quell it, and throw fear into those breasts where thoughtlessness reigned. Those who felt this sensation of awe, could not explain whence it arose: some attributed it to the dead grey eye, which, fixing upon the object's face, did not seem to penetrate, and at one glance to pierce through to the inward workings of the heart; but fell upon the cheek with a leaden ray that weighed upon the skin it could not pass. His peculiarities caused him to be invited to every house; all wished to see him, and those who had been accustomed to violent excitement, and now felt the weight of ennui,[1] were pleased at having something in their presence capable of engaging their attention. In spite of the deadly hue of his face, which never gained a warmer tint, either from the blush of modesty, or from the strong emotion of passion, though its form and outline were beautiful, many of the female hunters after notoriety attempted to win his attentions, and gain, at least, some marks of what they might term affection: Lady Mercer, who had been the mockery of every monster shewn in drawing-rooms since her marriage, threw herself in his way, and did all but put on the dress of a mountebank,[2] to attract his notice:—though in vain;—when she stood before him, though his eyes were apparently fixed upon hers, still it seemed as if they were unperceived;—even her unappalled impudence was baffled, and she left the field. But though the common adultress could not influence even the guidance of his eyes, it was not that the female sex was indifferent to him: yet such was the apparent caution with which he spoke to the virtuous wife and innocent daughter, that few knew he ever addressed himself to females. He had, however, the reputation of a winning tongue; and whether it was that it even overcame the dread of his singular character, or that they were moved by his apparent hatred of vice, he was as often among those females who form the boast of their sex from their domestic virtues, as among those who sully it by their vices.

About the same time, there came to London a young gentleman of the name of Aubrey: he was an orphan left with an only sister in the possession of great wealth, by parents who died while he was yet in childhood. Left also to himself by guardians, who thought it their duty merely to take care of his fortune, while they relinquished the more important charge of his mind to the care of mercenary subalterns,[3] he cultivated more his imagination than his judgment. He had, hence, that high romantic feeling of honour and candour, which daily ruins so many milliners' apprentices.[4] He believed all to sympathise with virtue, and thought that vice was thrown in by Providence merely for the picturesque

1 Boredom and lethargy.

2 Deceiver—especially one who tricks people out of money.

3 This term has a variety of meanings from a lower ranking officer in the British army to a member of an oppressed population under colonialism, but in this context, it refers to inferiors who are taking advantage of Aubrey and steering him in the wrong direction.

4 A girl studying to become a woman's hat maker. Such young women were often stereotyped as overly fanciful and used as examples of the dangers of light reading.

effect of the scene, as we see in romances: he thought that the misery of a cottage merely consisted in the vesting of clothes, which were as warm, but which were better adapted to the painter's eye by their irregular folds and various coloured patches. He thought, in fine, that the dreams of poets were the realities of life. He was handsome, frank, and rich: for these reasons, upon his entering into the gay circles,[1] many mothers surrounded him, striving which should describe with least truth their languishing or romping favourites: the daughters at the same time, by their brightening countenances when he approached, and by their sparkling eyes, when he opened his lips, soon led him into false notions of his talents and his merit. Attached as he was to the romance of his solitary hours, he was startled at finding, that, except in the tallow and wax candles that flickered, not from the presence of a ghost, but from want of snuffing, there was no foundation in real life for any of that congeries[2] of pleasing pictures and descriptions contained in those volumes, from which he had formed his study. Finding, however, some compensation in his gratified vanity, he was about to relinquish his dreams, when the extraordinary being we have above described, crossed him in his career.

He watched him; and the very impossibility of forming an idea of the character of a man entirely absorbed in himself, who gave few other signs of his observation of external objects, than the tacit assent to their existence, implied by the avoidance of their contact: allowing his imagination to picture some thing that flattered its propensity to extravagant ideas, he soon formed this object into the hero of a romance, and determined to observe the offspring of his fancy, rather than the person before him. He became acquainted with him, paid him attentions, and so far advanced upon his notice, that his presence was always acknowledged. He gradually learnt that Lord Ruthven's affairs were embarrassed,[3] and soon found, from the notes of preparation in —— Street,[4] that he was about to travel. Desirous of gaining some information respecting this singular character, who, till now, had only whetted his curiosity, he hinted to his guardians, that it was time for him to perform the tour,[5] which for many generations has been thought necessary to enable the young to take some rapid steps in the career of vice towards putting themselves upon an equality with the aged, and not allowing them to appear as if fallen from the skies, whenever scandalous intrigues are mentioned as the subjects of pleasantry or of praise,

1 I.e., society parties during the season.
2 A disorderly collection.
3 Meaning Lord Ruthven is in debt and creditors are pressing to be repaid. During the nineteenth century, you could be sent to prison for failure to pay debts, so those who could afford to do so might flee the country to avoid such a penalty.
4 Here, Polidori mimics the style of a scandal sheet or gossip magazine, leaving out a portion of the address to imply anonymity.
5 It was typical for a young gentleman to go on a "grand tour" of Europe at the close of his education. The stated intent was to see the great sights and works of art, although the result, as Polidori points out here, was often more vulgar.

according to the degree of skill shewn in carrying them on. They consented: and Aubrey immediately mentioning his intentions to Lord Ruthven, was surprised to receive from him a proposal to join him. Flattered by such a mark of esteem from him, who, apparently, had nothing in common with other men, he gladly accepted it, and in a few days they had passed the circling waters.

Hitherto, Aubrey had had no opportunity of studying Lord Ruthven's character, and now he found, that, though many more of his actions were exposed to his view, the results offered different conclusions from the apparent motives to his conduct. His companion was profuse in his liberality;—the idle, the vagabond, and the beggar, received from his hand more than enough to relieve their immediate wants. But Aubrey could not avoid remarking, that it was not upon the virtuous, reduced to indigence by the misfortunes attendant even upon virtue, that he bestowed his alms;—these were sent from the door with hardly suppressed sneers; but when the profligate came to ask something, not to relieve his wants, but to allow him to wallow in his lust, or to sink him still deeper in his iniquity, he was sent away with rich charity. This was, however, attributed by him to the greater importunity of the vicious, which generally prevails over the retiring bashfulness of the virtuous indigent. There was one circumstance about the charity of his Lordship, which was still more impressed upon his mind: all those upon whom it was bestowed, inevitably found that there was a curse upon it, for they were all either led to the scaffold, or sunk to the lowest and the most abject misery. At Brussels and other towns through which they passed, Aubrey was surprized at the apparent eagerness with which his companion sought for the centres of all fashionable vice; there he entered into all the spirit of the faro[1] table: he betted, and always gambled with success, except where the known sharper was his antagonist, and then he lost even more than he gained; but it was always with the same unchanging face, with which he generally watched the society around: it was not, however, so when he encountered the rash youthful novice, or the luckless father of a numerous family; then his very wish seemed fortune's law—this apparent abstractedness of mind was laid aside, and his eyes sparkled with more fire than that of the cat whilst dallying with the half-dead mouse. In every town, he left the formerly affluent youth, torn from the circle he adorned, cursing, in the solitude of a dungeon, the fate that had drawn him within the reach of this fiend; whilst many a father sat frantic, amidst the speaking looks of mute hungry children, without a single farthing of his late immense wealth, wherewith to buy even sufficient to satisfy their present craving. Yet he took no money from the gambling table; but immediately lost, to the ruiner of many, the last gilder[2] he had just snatched from the convulsive grasp of the innocent: this might but be the result of a certain degree of knowledge, which was not, however, capable of combating

1 Card game popular with gamblers in Europe at this time.
2 Currency in the Netherlands from the seventeenth century to 2002.

the cunning of the more experienced. Aubrey often wished to represent this to his friend, and beg him to resign that charity and pleasure which proved the ruin of all, and did not tend to his own profit;—but he delayed it—for each day he hoped his friend would give him some opportunity of speaking frankly and openly to him; however, this never occurred. Lord Ruthven in his carriage, and amidst the various wild and rich scenes of nature, was always the same: his eye spoke less than his lip; and though Aubrey was near the object of his curiosity, he obtained no greater gratification from it than the constant excitement of vainly wishing to break that mystery, which to his exalted imagination began to assume the appearance of something supernatural.

They soon arrived at Rome, and Aubrey for a time lost sight of his companion; he left him in daily attendance upon the morning circle of an Italian countess, whilst he went in search of the memorials of another almost deserted city. Whilst he was thus engaged, letters arrived from England, which he opened with eager impatience; the first was from his sister, breathing nothing but affection; the others were from his guardians, the latter astonished him; if it had before entered into his imagination that there was an evil power resident in his companion, these seemed to give him sufficient reason for the belief. His guardians insisted upon his immediately leaving his friend, and urged, that his character was dreadfully vicious, for that the possession of irresistible powers of seduction, rendered his licentious habits more dangerous to society. It had been discovered, that his contempt for the adultress had not originated in hatred of her character; but that he had required, to enhance his gratification, that his victim, the partner of his guilt, should be hurled from the pinnacle of unsullied virtue, down to the lowest abyss of infamy and degradation: in fine, that all those females whom he had sought, apparently on account of their virtue, had, since his departure, thrown even the mask aside, and had not scrupled to expose the whole deformity of their vices to the public gaze.

Aubrey determined upon leaving one, whose character had not yet shown a single bright point on which to rest the eye. He resolved to invent some plausible pretext for abandoning him altogether, purposing, in the meanwhile, to watch him more closely, and to let no slight circumstances pass by unnoticed. He entered into the same circle, and soon perceived, that his Lordship was endeavouring to work upon the inexperience of the daughter of the lady whose house he chiefly frequented. In Italy, it is seldom that an unmarried female is met with in society; he was therefore obliged to carry on his plans in secret; but Aubrey's eye followed him in all his windings, and soon discovered that an assignation had been appointed, which would most likely end in the ruin of an innocent, though thoughtless girl. Losing no time, he entered the apartment of Lord Ruthven, and abruptly asked him his intentions with respect to the lady, informing him at the same time that he was aware of his being about to meet her that very night. Lord Ruthven answered, that his intentions were such as he supposed all would have upon such an occasion; and upon being pressed whether he intended to marry her, merely laughed. Aubrey retired; and, immediately writing a note, to say, that from that moment he must decline accompanying his Lordship in the remainder of their proposed tour, he ordered his servant to seek other apartments, and calling upon the mother of the lady, informed her of all he knew, not only with regard to her daughter, but also concerning the character of his Lordship. The assignation was prevented. Lord Ruthven next day merely sent his servant to notify his complete assent to a separation; but did not hint any suspicion of his plans having been foiled by Aubrey's interposition.

Having left Rome, Aubrey directed his steps towards Greece, and crossing the Peninsula, soon found himself at Athens. He then fixed his residence in the house of a Greek; and soon occupied himself in tracing the faded records of ancient glory upon monuments that apparently, ashamed of chronicling the deeds of freemen only before slaves, had hidden themselves beneath the sheltering soil or many coloured lichen. Under the same roof as himself, existed a being, so beautiful and delicate, that she might have formed the model for a painter wishing to portray on canvass the promised hope of the faithful in Mahomet's paradise,[1] save that her eyes spoke too much mind for any one to think she could belong to those who had no souls.[2] As she danced upon the plain, or tripped along the mountain's side, one would have thought the gazelle a poor type of her beauties; for who would have exchanged her eye, apparently the eye of animated nature, for that sleepy luxurious look of the animal suited but to the taste of an epicure. The light step of Ianthe often accompanied Aubrey in his search after antiquities, and often would the unconscious girl, engaged in the pursuit of a Kashmere butterfly,[3] show the whole beauty of her form, floating as it were upon the wind, to the eager gaze of him, who forgot the letters he had just decyphered upon an almost effaced tablet, in the contemplation of her sylph-like[4] figure. Often would her tresses falling, as she flitted around, exhibit in the sun's ray such delicately brilliant and swiftly fading hues, it might well excuse the forgetfulness of the antiquary, who let escape from his mind the very object he had before thought of vital importance to the proper interpretation of a passage in Pausanias.[5] But why attempt to describe charms which all feel, but none can appreciate?—It was innocence, youth, and beauty, unaffected by

1 In the limited and racist British popular understanding of Islam, Muslims believed that faithful men would be rewarded with beautiful virgins in the afterlife. Polidori uses this simplification of Islam to suggest that Ianthe is beautiful enough to serve as a model for a heavenly maiden.

2 Various religions throughout history have attempted to argue that women are without souls in order to justify their oppression in patriarchal regimes. This may also be a xenophobic reference to the fact that Ianthe is not Christian. At the time, Greece was occupied by the Ottomans. This led many to convert to Islam.

3 Several beautiful types of butterfly are associated with Kashmir. This detail further exoticizes Ianthe—associating her with the East rather than British society.

4 Slender and graceful. A sylph is an air spirit in sixteenth-century works of Paracelsus.

5 Ancient Greek traveler and geographer.

crowded drawing-rooms and stifling balls. Whilst he drew those remains of which he wished to preserve a memorial for his future hours, she would stand by, and watch the magic effects of his pencil, in tracing the scenes of her native place; she would then describe to him the circling dance upon the open plain, would paint, to him in all the glowing colours of youthful memory, the marriage pomp she remembered viewing in her infancy; and then, turning to subjects that had evidently made a greater impression upon her mind, would tell him all the supernatural tales of her nurse. Her earnestness and apparent belief of what she narrated, excited the interest even of Aubrey; and often as she told him the tale of the living vampyre, who had passed years amidst his friends, and dearest ties, forced every year, by feeding upon the life of a lovely female[1] to prolong his existence for the ensuing months, his blood would run cold, whilst he attempted to laugh her out of such idle and horrible fantasies; but Ianthe cited to him the names of old men, who had at last detected one living among themselves, after several of their near relatives and children had been found marked with the stamp of the fiend's appetite; and when she found him so incredulous, she begged of him to believe her, for it had been, remarked, that those who had dared to question their existence, always had some proof given, which obliged them, with grief and heartbreaking, to confess it was true. She detailed to him the traditional appearance of these monsters, and his horror was increased, by hearing a pretty accurate description of Lord Ruthven; he, however, still persisted in persuading her, that there could be no truth in her fears, though at the same time he wondered at the many coincidences which had all tended to excite a belief in the supernatural power of Lord Ruthven.

Aubrey began to attach himself more and more to Ianthe; her innocence, so contrasted with all the affected virtues of the women among whom he had sought for his vision of romance, won his heart; and while he ridiculed the idea of a young man of English habits, marrying an uneducated Greek girl, still he found himself more and more attached to the almost fairy form before him. He would tear himself at times from her, and, forming a plan for some antiquarian research, he would depart, determined not to return until his object was attained; but he always found it impossible to fix his attention upon the ruins around him, whilst in his mind he retained an image that seemed alone the rightful possessor of his thoughts. Ianthe was unconscious of his love, and was ever the same frank infantile being he had first known. She always seemed to part from him with reluctance; but it was because she had no longer any one with whom she could visit her favourite haunts, whilst her guardian was occupied in sketching or uncovering some fragment which had yet escaped the destructive hand of time. She had appealed to her parents on the subject of

1 This idea—that the vampire must feed specifically on young females—appears to be Polidori's invention. Vampire folklore typically does not include this restriction but many literary vampires that follow will repeat this trope.

Vampyres, and they both, with several present, affirmed their existence, pale with horror at the very name. Soon after, Aubrey determined to proceed upon one of his excursions, which was to detain him for a few hours; when they heard the name of the place, they all at once begged of him not to return at night, as he must necessarily pass through a wood, where no Greek would ever remain, after the day had closed, upon any consideration. They described it as the resort of the vampyres in their nocturnal orgies, and denounced the most heavy evils as impending upon him who dared to cross their path. Aubrey made light of their representations, and tried to laugh them out of the idea; but when he saw them shudder at his daring thus to mock a superior, infernal power, the very name of which apparently made their blood freeze, he was silent.

Next morning Aubrey set off upon his excursion unattended; he was surprised to observe the melancholy face of his host, and was concerned to find that his words, mocking the belief of those horrible fiends, had inspired them with such terror. When he was about to depart, Ianthe came to the side of his horse, and earnestly begged of him to return, ere night allowed the power of these beings to be put in action;—he promised. He was, however, so occupied in his research, that he did not perceive that day-light would soon end, and that in the horizon there was one of those specks which, in the warmer climates, so rapidly gather into a tremendous mass, and pour all their rage upon the devoted country.—He at last, however, mounted his horse, determined to make up by speed for his delay: but it was too late. Twilight, in these southern climates, is almost unknown; immediately the sun sets, night begins: and ere he had advanced far, the power of the storm was above—its echoing thunders had scarcely an interval of rest—its thick heavy rain forced its way through the canopying foliage, whilst the blue forked lightning seemed to fall and radiate at his very feet. Suddenly his horse took fright, and he was carried with dreadful rapidity through the entangled forest. The animal at last, through fatigue, stopped, and he found, by the glare of lightning, that he was in the neighbourhood of a hovel that hardly lifted itself up from the masses of dead leaves and brushwood which surrounded it. Dismounting, he approached, hoping to find some one to guide him to the town, or at least trusting to obtain shelter from the pelting of the storm. As he approached, the thunders, for a moment silent, allowed him to hear the dreadful shrieks of a woman mingling with the stifled, exultant mockery of a laugh, continued in one almost unbroken sound;—he was startled: but, roused by the thunder which again rolled over his head, he, with a sudden effort, forced open the door of the hut. He found himself in utter darkness: the sound, however, guided him. He was apparently unperceived; for, though he called, still the sounds continued, and no notice was taken of him. He found himself in contact with some one, whom he immediately seized; when a voice cried, "Again baffled!" to which a loud laugh succeeded; and he felt himself grappled by one whose strength seemed superhuman: determined to sell his life as dearly as he could, he struggled; but it was in vain: he was lifted from his feet and hurled with enormous force against the ground:—his enemy threw himself upon him, and kneeling upon his breast, had placed his hands upon his throat—when the glare of many torches penetrating through the hole that gave light in the day, disturbed him;—he instantly rose, and, leaving his prey, rushed through the door, and in a moment the crashing of the branches, as he broke through the wood, was no longer heard. The storm was now still; and Aubrey, incapable of moving, was soon heard by those without. They entered; the light of their torches fell upon the mud walls, and the thatch loaded on every individual straw with heavy flakes of soot. At the desire of Aubrey they searched for her who had attracted him by her cries; he was again left in darkness; but what was his horror, when the light of the torches once more burst upon him, to perceive the airy form of his fair conductress brought in a lifeless corpse. He shut his eyes, hoping that it was but a vision arising from his disturbed imagination; but he again saw the same form, when he unclosed them, stretched by his side. There was no colour upon her cheek, not even upon her lip; yet there was a stillness about her face that seemed almost as attaching as the life that once dwelt there:—upon her neck and breast was blood, and upon her throat were the marks of teeth having opened the vein:—to this the men pointed, crying, simultaneously struck with horror, "A Vampyre! a Vampyre!" A litter was quickly formed, and Aubrey was laid by the side of her who had lately been to him the object of so many bright and fairy visions, now fallen with the flower of life that had died within her. He knew not what his thoughts were—his mind was benumbed and seemed to shun reflection, and take refuge in vacancy—he held almost unconsciously in his hand a naked dagger of a particular construction, which had been found in the hut. They were soon met by different parties who had been engaged in the search of her whom a mother had missed. Their lamentable cries, as they approached the city, forewarned the parents of some dreadful catastrophe.—To describe their grief would be impossible; but when they ascertained the cause of their child's death, they looked at Aubrey, and pointed to the corpse. They were inconsolable; both died broken-hearted.

Aubrey being put to bed was seized with a most violent fever, and was often delirious; in these intervals he would call upon Lord Ruthven and upon Ianthe—by some unaccountable combination he seemed to beg of his former companion to spare the being he loved. At other times he would imprecate maledictions upon his head, and curse him as her destroyer. Lord Ruthven, chanced at this time to arrive at Athens, and, from whatever motive, upon hearing of the state of Aubrey, immediately placed himself in the same house, and became his constant attendant. When the latter recovered from his delirium, he was horrified and startled at the sight of him whose image he had now combined with that of a Vampyre; but Lord Ruthven, by his kind words, implying almost repentance for the fault that had caused their separation, and still more by the attention, anxiety, and care which he showed, soon reconciled him to his presence. His lordship seemed quite changed; he no longer appeared that apathetic being who had so astonished Aubrey; but as soon as his convalescence began to be rapid, he again gradually retired into the same state of mind, and Aubrey perceived no difference from the former man, except that at times he was surprised to meet his gaze fixed intently upon him, with a smile of malicious exultation playing upon his lips: he knew not why, but this smile haunted him. During the last stage of the invalid's recovery, Lord Ruthven was apparently engaged in watching the tideless waves raised by the cooling breeze, or in marking the progress of those orbs, circling, like our world, the moveless sun;—indeed, he appeared to wish to avoid the eyes of all.

Aubrey's mind, by this shock, was much weakened, and that elasticity of spirit which had once so distinguished him now seemed to have fled for ever. He was now as much a lover of solitude and silence as Lord Ruthven; but much as he wished for solitude, his mind could not find it in the neighbourhood of Athens; if he sought it amidst the ruins he had formerly frequented, Ianthe's form stood by his side—if he sought it in the woods, her light step would appear wandering amidst the underwood, in quest of the modest violet; then suddenly turning round, would show, to his wild imagination, her pale face and wounded throat, with a meek smile upon her lips. He determined to fly scenes, every feature of which created such bitter associations in his mind. He proposed to Lord Ruthven, to whom he held himself bound by the tender care he had taken of him during his illness, that they should visit those parts of Greece neither had yet seen. They travelled in every direction, and sought every spot to which a recollection could be attached: but though they thus hastened from place to place, yet they seemed not to heed what they gazed upon. They heard much of robbers, but they gradually began to slight these reports, which they imagined were only the invention of individuals, whose interest it was to excite the generosity of those whom they defended from pretended dangers. In consequence of thus neglecting the advice of the inhabitants, on one occasion they travelled with only a few guards, more to serve as guides than as a defense. Upon entering, however, a narrow defile,[1] at the bottom of which was the bed of a torrent, with large masses of rock brought down from the neighbouring precipices, they had reason to repent their negligence; for scarcely were the whole of the party engaged in the narrow pass, when they were startled by the whistling of bullets close to their heads, and by the echoed report of several guns. In an instant their guards had left them, and, placing themselves behind rocks, had begun to fire in the direction whence the report came. Lord Ruthven and Aubrey, imitating their example, retired for a moment behind the sheltering turn of the defile: but ashamed of being thus detained by a foe, who with insulting shouts bade them advance, and being exposed to unresisting slaughter, if any of the robbers

1 A steep-sided gorge requiring groups to move in single file.

should climb above and take them in the rear, they determined at once to rush forward in search of the enemy. Hardly had they lost the shelter of the rock, when Lord Ruthven received a shot in the shoulder, which brought him to the ground. Aubrey hastened to his assistance; and, no longer heeding the contest or his own peril, was soon surprised by seeing the robbers' faces around him—his guards having, upon Lord Ruthven's being wounded, immediately thrown up their arms and surrendered.

By promises of great reward, Aubrey soon induced them to convey his wounded friend to a neighbouring cabin; and having agreed upon a ransom, he was no more disturbed by their presence—they being content merely to guard the entrance till their comrade should return with the promised sum, for which he had an order. Lord Ruthven's strength rapidly decreased; in two days mortification[1] ensued, and death seemed advancing with hasty steps. His conduct and appearance had not changed; he seemed as unconscious of pain as he had been of the objects about him: but towards the close of the last evening, his mind became apparently uneasy, and his eye often fixed upon Aubrey, who was induced to offer his assistance with more than usual earnestness—"Assist me! you may save me—you may do more than that—I mean not my life, I heed the death of my existence as little as that of the passing day; but you may save my honour, your friend's honour."—"How? tell me how? I would do any thing," replied Aubrey.—"I need but little—my life ebbs apace—I cannot explain the whole—but if you would conceal all you know of me, my honour were free from stain in the world's mouth—and if my death were unknown for some time in England—I—I—but life."—"It shall not be known."—"Swear!" cried the dying man, raising himself with exultant violence, "Swear by all your soul reveres, by all your nature fears, swear that, for a year and a day you will not impart your knowledge of my crimes or death to any living being in any way, whatever may happen, or whatever you may see."—His eyes seemed bursting from their sockets: "I swear!" said Aubrey; he sunk laughing upon his pillow, and breathed no more.

Aubrey retired to rest, but did not sleep; the many circumstances attending his acquaintance with this man rose upon his mind, and he knew not why; when he remembered his oath a cold shivering came over him, as if from the presentiment of something horrible awaiting him. Rising early in the morning, he was about to enter the hovel in which he had left the corpse, when a robber met him, and informed him that it was no longer there, having been conveyed by himself and comrades, upon his retiring, to the pinnacle of a neighbouring mount, according to a promise they had given his lordship, that it should be exposed to the first cold ray of the moon[2] that rose after his death. Aubrey

1 Infection. A major risk with gunshot wounds in the days before antibiotics.

2 Polidori may have invented this vampire power of being rejuvenated by moonlight (Senf, *The Vampire* 34 and Twitchell, *Dreadful Pleasures* 111).

astonished, and taking several of the men, determined to go and bury it upon the spot where it lay. But, when he had mounted to the summit he found no trace of either the corpse or the clothes, though the robbers swore they pointed out the identical rock on which they had laid the body. For a time his mind was bewildered in conjectures, but he at last returned, convinced that they had buried the corpse for the sake of the clothes.

Weary of a country in which he had met with such terrible misfortunes, and in which all apparently conspired to heighten that superstitious melancholy that had seized upon his mind, he resolved to leave it, and soon arrived at Smyrna.[1] While waiting for a vessel to convey him to Otranto, or to Naples, he occupied himself in arranging those effects he had with him belonging to Lord Ruthven. Amongst other things there was a case containing several weapons of offence, more or less adapted to ensure the death of the victim. There were several daggers and ataghans.[2] Whilst turning them over, and examining their curious forms, what was his surprise at finding a sheath apparently ornamented in the same style as the dagger discovered in the fatal hut—he shuddered—hastening to gain further proof, he found the weapon, and his horror may be imagined when he discovered that it fitted, though peculiarly shaped, the sheath he held in his hand. His eyes seemed to need no further certainty—they seemed gazing to be bound to the dagger; yet still he wished to disbelieve; but the particular form, the same varying tints upon the haft and sheath were alike in splendour on both, and left no room for doubt; there were also drops of blood on each.

He left Smyrna, and on his way home, at Rome, his first inquiries were concerning the lady he had attempted to snatch from Lord Ruthven's seductive arts. Her parents were in distress, their fortune ruined, and she had not been heard of since the departure of his lordship. Aubrey's mind became almost broken under so many repeated horrors; he was afraid that this lady had fallen a victim to the destroyer of Ianthe. He became morose and silent; and his only occupation consisted in urging the speed of the postilions,[3] as if he were going to save the life of some one he held dear. He arrived at Calais; a breeze, which seemed obedient to his will, soon wafted him to the English shores; and he hastened to the mansion of his fathers, and there, for a moment, appeared to lose, in the embraces and caresses of his sister, all memory of the past. If she before, by her infantine caresses, had gained his affection, now that the woman began to appear, she was still more attaching as a companion.

Miss Aubrey had not that winning grace which gains the gaze and applause of the drawing-room assemblies. There was none of that light brilliancy which only exists in the heated atmosphere of a crowded apartment. Her blue eye was never lit up by the levity of the mind beneath. There was a melancholy charm

1 Smyrna was the name of a Greek port city now called Izmir.
2 Turkish sword.
3 Person who rides the left-hand leading horse of a team drawing a carriage.

about it which did not seem to arise from misfortune, but from some feeling within, that appeared to indicate a soul conscious of a brighter realm. Her step was not that light footing, which strays where'er a butterfly or a colour may attract—it was sedate and pensive. When alone, her face was never brightened by the smile of joy; but when her brother breathed to her his affection, and would in her presence forget those griefs she knew destroyed his rest, who would have exchanged her smile for that of the voluptuary? It seemed as if those eyes,—that face were then playing in the light of their own native sphere. She was yet only eighteen, and had not been presented to the world,[1] it having been thought by her guardians more fit that her presentation should be delayed until her brother's return from the continent, when he might be her protector. It was now, therefore, resolved that the next drawing-room, which was fast approaching, should be the epoch of her entry into the "busy scene." Aubrey would rather have remained in the mansion of his fathers, and fed upon the melancholy which overpowered him. He could not feel interest about the frivolities of fashionable strangers, when his mind had been so torn by the events he had witnessed; but he determined to sacrifice his own comfort to the protection of his sister. They soon arrived in town, and prepared for the next day, which had been announced as a drawing-room.

The crowd was excessive—a drawing-room had not been held for a long time, and all who were anxious to bask in the smile of royalty, hastened thither. Aubrey was there with his sister. While he was standing in a corner by himself, heedless of all around him, engaged in the remembrance that the first time he had seen Lord Ruthven was in that very place—he felt himself suddenly seized by the arm, and a voice he recognized too well, sounded in his ear—"Remember your oath." He had hardly courage to turn, fearful of seeing a spectre that would blast him, when he perceived, at a little distance, the same figure which had attracted his notice on this spot upon his first entry into society. He gazed till his limbs almost refusing to bear their weight, he was obliged to take the arm of a friend, and forcing a passage through the crowd, he threw himself into his carriage, and was driven home. He paced the room with hurried steps, and fixed his hands upon his head, as if he were afraid his thoughts were bursting from his brain. Lord Ruthven again before him—circumstances started up in dreadful array—the dagger—his oath.—He roused himself, he could not believe it possible—the dead rise again!—He thought his imagination had conjured up the image his mind was resting upon. It was impossible that it could be real—he determined, therefore, to go again into society; for though he attempted to ask concerning Lord Ruthven, the name hung upon his lips, and he could not succeed in gaining information. He went a few nights after with his sis-

1 She has not yet officially entered society. Being presented or "coming out" meant that a young woman was marriageable and would be invited to parties during the London season. Having a reliable chaperone was essential.

ter to the assembly of a near relation. Leaving her under the protection of a matron, he retired into a recess, and there gave himself up to his own devouring thoughts. Perceiving, at last, that many were leaving, he roused himself, and entering another room, found his sister surrounded by several, apparently in earnest conversation; he attempted to pass and get near her, when one, whom he requested to move, turned round, and revealed to him those features he most abhorred. He sprang forward, seized his sister's arm, and, with hurried step, forced her towards the street: at the door he found himself impeded by the crowd of servants who were waiting for their lords; and while he was engaged in passing them, he again heard that voice whisper close to him—"Remember your oath!"—He did not dare to turn, but, hurrying his sister, soon reached home.

Aubrey became almost distracted. If before his mind had been absorbed by one subject, how much more completely was it engrossed, now that the certainty of the monster's living again pressed upon his thoughts. His sister's attentions were now unheeded, and it was in vain that she intreated him to explain to her what had caused his abrupt conduct. He only uttered a few words, and those terrified her. The more he thought, the more he was bewildered. His oath startled him;—was he then to allow this monster to roam, bearing ruin upon his breath, amidst all he held dear, and not avert its progress? His very sister might have been touched by him. But even if he were to break his oath, and disclose his suspicions, who would believe him? He thought of employing his own hand to free the world from such a wretch; but death, he remembered, had been already mocked. For days he remained in this state; shut up in his room, he saw no one, and ate only when his sister came, who, with eyes streaming with tears, besought him, for her sake, to support nature. At last, no longer capable of bearing stillness and solitude, he left his house, roamed from street to street, anxious to fly that image which haunted him. His dress became neglected, and he wandered, as often exposed to the noon-day sun as to the midnight damps. He was no longer to be recognized; at first he returned with the evening to the house; but at last he laid him down to rest wherever fatigue overtook him. His sister, anxious for his safety, employed people to follow him; but they were soon distanced by him who fled from a pursuer swifter than any—from thought. His conduct, however, suddenly changed. Struck with the idea that he left by his absence the whole of his friends, with a fiend amongst them, of whose presence they were unconscious, he determined to enter again into society, and watch him closely, anxious to forewarn, in spite of his oath, all whom Lord Ruthven approached with intimacy. But when he entered into a room, his haggard and suspicious looks were so striking, his inward shudderings so visible, that his sister was at last obliged to beg of him to abstain from seeking, for her sake, a society which affected him so strongly. When, however, remonstrance proved unavailing, the guardians thought proper to interpose, and, fearing that his mind was becoming alienated, they thought it high time to resume again that trust which had been before imposed upon them by Aubrey's parents.

Desirous of saving him from the injuries and sufferings he had daily encountered in his wanderings, and of preventing him from exposing to the general eye those marks of what they considered folly, they engaged a physician to reside in the house, and take constant care of him. He hardly appeared to notice it, so completely was his mind absorbed by one terrible subject. His incoherence became at last so great, that he was confined to his chamber. There he would often lie for days, incapable of being roused. He had become emaciated, his eyes had attained a glassy lustre;—the only sign of affection and recollection remaining displayed itself upon the entry of his sister; then he would sometimes start, and, seizing her hands, with looks that severely afflicted her, he would desire her not to touch him. "Oh, do not touch him—if your love for me is aught, do not go near him!" When, however, she inquired to whom he referred, his only answer was, "True! true!" and again he sank into a state, whence not even she could rouse him. This lasted many months: gradually, however, as the year was passing, his incoherences became less frequent, and his mind threw off a portion of its gloom, whilst his guardians observed, that several times in the day he would count upon his fingers a definite number, and then smile.

The time had nearly elapsed, when, upon the last day of the year, one of his guardians entering his room, began to converse with his physician upon the melancholy circumstance of Aubrey's being in so awful a situation, when his sister was going next day to be married. Instantly Aubrey's attention was attracted; he asked anxiously to whom. Glad of this mark of returning intellect, of which they feared he had been deprived, they mentioned the name of the Earl of Marsden. Thinking this was a young Earl whom he had met with in society, Aubrey seemed pleased, and astonished them still more by his expressing his intention to be present at the nuptials, and desiring to see his sister. They answered not, but in a few minutes his sister was with him. He was apparently again capable of being affected by the influence of her lovely smile; for he pressed her to his breast, and kissed her cheek, wet with tears, flowing at the thought of her brother's being once more alive to the feelings of affection. He began to speak with all his wonted warmth, and to congratulate her upon her marriage with a person so distinguished for rank and every accomplishment; when he suddenly perceived a locket upon her breast; opening it, what was his surprise at beholding the features of the monster who had so long influenced his life. He seized the portrait in a paroxysm of rage, and trampled it under foot. Upon her asking him why he thus destroyed the resemblance of her future husband, he looked as if he did not understand her—then seizing her hands, and gazing on her with a frantic expression of countenance, he bade her swear that she would never wed this monster, for he—But he could not advance—it seemed as if that voice again bade him remember his oath—he turned suddenly round, thinking

Lord Ruthven was near him but saw no one. In the meantime the guardians and physician, who had heard the whole, and thought this was but a return of his disorder, entered, and forcing him from Miss Aubrey, desired her to leave him. He fell upon his knees to them, he implored, he begged of them to delay but for one day. They, attributing this to the insanity they imagined had taken possession of his mind, endeavoured to pacify him, and retired.

Lord Ruthven had called the morning after the drawing-room, and had been refused with every one else. When he heard of Aubrey's ill health, he readily understood himself to be the cause of it; but when he learned that he was deemed insane, his exultation and pleasure could hardly be concealed from those among whom he had gained this information. He hastened to the house of his former companion, and, by constant attendance, and the pretense of great affection for the brother and interest in his fate, he gradually won the ear of Miss Aubrey. Who could resist his power? His tongue had dangers and toils to recount—could speak of himself as of an individual having no sympathy with any being on the crowded earth, save with her to whom he addressed himself;—could tell how, since he knew her, his existence, had begun to seem worthy of preservation, if it were merely that he might listen to her soothing accents;—in fine, he knew so well how to use the serpent's art, or such was the will of fate, that he gained her affections. The title of the elder branch falling at length to him, he obtained an important embassy, which served as an excuse for hastening the marriage, (in spite of her brother's deranged state,) which was to take place the very day before his departure for the continent.

Aubrey, when he was left by the physician and his guardians, attempted to bribe the servants, but in vain. He asked for pen and paper; it was given him; he wrote a letter to his sister, conjuring her, as she valued her own happiness, her own honour, and the honour of those now in the grave, who once held her in their arms as their hope and the hope of their house, to delay but for a few hours that marriage, on which he denounced the most heavy curses. The servants promised they would deliver it; but giving it to the physician, he thought it better not to harass any more the mind of Miss Aubrey by, what he considered, the ravings of a maniac. Night passed on without rest to the busy inmates of the house; and Aubrey heard, with a horror that may more easily be conceived than described, the notes of busy preparation. Morning came, and the sound of carriages broke upon his ear. Aubrey grew almost frantic. The curiosity of the servants at last overcame their vigilance, they gradually stole away, leaving him in the custody of an helpless old woman. He seized the opportunity, with one bound was out of the room, and in a moment found himself in the apartment where all were nearly assembled. Lord Ruthven was the first to perceive him: he immediately approached, and, taking his arm by force, hurried him from the room, speechless with rage. When on the staircase, Lord Ruthven whispered in his ear—"Remember your oath, and know, if not my bride today, your sister is dishonoured. Women are frail!" So saying, he pushed him towards his attendants, who, roused by the old woman, had come in search of him. Aubrey could no longer support himself; his rage not finding vent, had broken a blood-vessel, and he was conveyed to bed. This was not mentioned to his sister, who was not present when he entered, as the physician was afraid of agitating her. The marriage was solemnized, and the bride and bridegroom left London.

Aubrey's weakness increased; the effusion of blood produced symptoms of the near approach of death. He desired his sister's guardians might be called, and when the midnight hour had struck, he related composedly what the reader has perused—he died immediately after.

The guardians hastened to protect Miss Aubrey; but when they arrived, it was too late. Lord Ruthven had disappeared, and Aubrey's sister had glutted the thirst of a VAMPYRE!

# James Malcolm Rymer

(1814–1840)

AND

# Thomas Peckett Prest

(CIRCA 1810–1859)

Not much is known about James Malcolm Rymer except that he was born in Clerkenwell, London, was of Scottish descent, and is on record as a civil engineer. Along with Thomas Peckett Prest, he co-authored the long serially published novel *Varney the Vampire* (1847), although Rymer is credited with doing most of the work. Both men were prolific popular writers, noted for their publications in penny dreadfuls. Before writing penny dreadfuls, Prest was a talented musician and composer. The two also co-authored *The String of Pearls* (1846), which is famous for the introduction of Sweeney Todd, the "demon barber." Scholars have observed that Varney is the prototype for the vampire figure in both appearance and modus operandi, influencing subsequent vampire fiction including Bram Stoker's *Dracula* (1897). Varney has superhuman strength, hypnotic powers, and attacks sleeping maidens with his fangs, leaving two puncture wounds on the neck. A noted exception is that he is able to venture out in daylight and is not repelled by garlic or crosses. Later in the series, he also comes to exemplify the "sympathetic vampire" who detests his position but is helpless to do anything about it. See Illustrations (pp. 508–09).

## from *Varney the Vampire*

(1847)

### CHAPTER I

"How graves give up their dead.  
And how the night air hideous grows  
With shrieks!"

## MIDNIGHT.—THE HAIL-STORM.—THE DREADFUL VISITOR. —THE VAMPYRE.

The solemn tones of an old cathedral clock have announced midnight—the air is thick and heavy—a strange, death-like stillness pervades all nature. Like the ominous calm which precedes some more than usually terrific outbreak of the elements, they seem to have paused even in their ordinary fluctuations, to gather a terrific strength for the great effort. A faint peal of thunder now comes from far off. Like a signal gun for the battle of the winds to begin, it appeared to awaken them from their lethargy, and one awful, warring hurricane swept over a whole city, producing more devastation in the four or five minutes it lasted, than would a half century of ordinary phenomena.

It was as if some giant had blown upon some toy town, and scattered many of the buildings before the hot blast of his terrific breath; for as suddenly as that blast of wind had come did it cease, and all was as still and calm as before.

Sleepers awakened, and thought that what they had heard must be the confused chimera[1] of a dream. They trembled and turned to sleep again.

All is still—still as the very grave. Not a sound breaks the magic of repose. What is that—a strange, pattering noise, as of a million of fairy feet? It is hail—yes, a hail-storm has burst over the city. Leaves are dashed from the trees, mingled with small boughs; windows that lie most opposed to the direct fury of the pelting particles of ice are broken, and the rapt repose that before was so remarkable in its intensity, is exchanged for a noise which, in its accumulation, drowns every cry of surprise or consternation which here and there arose from persons who found their houses invaded by the storm.

Now and then, too, there would come a sudden gust of wind that in its strength, as it blew laterally, would, for a moment, hold millions of the hailstones suspended in mid air, but it was only to dash them with redoubled force in some new direction, where more mischief was to be done.

Oh, how the storm raged! Hail—rain—wind. It was, in very truth, an awful night. There is an antique chamber in an ancient house. Curious and quaint carvings adorn the walls, and the large chimney-piece is a curiosity of itself. The ceiling is low, and a large bay window, from roof to floor, looks to the west. The window is latticed, and filled with curiously painted glass and rich stained pieces, which send in a strange, yet beautiful light, when sun or moon shines into the apartment. There is but one portrait in that room, although the walls seem panelled for the express purpose of containing a series of pictures. That portrait is of a young man, with a pale face, a stately brow, and a strange expression about the eyes, which no one cared to look on twice.

There is a stately bed in that chamber, of carved walnut-wood is it made, rich in design and elaborate in execution; one of those works of art which owe

1 Something illusory; a delusion.

their existence to the Elizabethan era. It is hung with heavy silken and damask furnishing; nodding feathers are at its corners—covered with dust are they, and they lend a funereal aspect to the room. The floor is of polished oak.

God! how the hail dashes on the old bay window! Like an occasional discharge of mimic musketry, it comes clashing, beating, and cracking upon the small panes; but they resist it—their small size saves them; the wind, the hail, the rain, expend their fury in vain.

The bed in that old chamber is occupied. A creature formed in all fashions of loveliness lies in a half sleep upon that ancient couch—a girl young and beautiful as a spring morning. Her long hair has escaped from its confinement and streams over the blackened coverings of the bedstead; she has been restless in her sleep, for the clothing of the bed is in much confusion. One arm is over her head, the other hangs nearly off the side of the bed near to which she lies. A neck and bosom that would have formed a study for the rarest sculptor that ever Providence gave genius to, were half disclosed. She moaned slightly in her sleep, and once or twice the lips moved as if in prayer—at least one might judge so, for the name of Him who suffered for all came once faintly from them.

She has endured much fatigue, and the storm does not awaken her; but it can disturb the slumbers it does not possess the power to destroy entirely. The turmoil of the elements wakes the senses, although it cannot entirely break the repose they have lapsed into.

Oh, what a world of witchery was in that mouth, slightly parted, and exhibiting within the pearly teeth that glistened even in the faint light that came from that bay window. How sweetly the long silken eyelashes lay upon the cheek. Now she moves, and one shoulder is entirely visible—whiter, fairer than the spotless clothing of the bed on which she lies, is the smooth skin of that fair creature, just budding into womanhood, and in that transition state which presents to us all the charms of the girl—almost of the child, with the more matured beauty and gentleness of advancing years.

Was that lightning? Yes—an awful, vivid, terrifying flash—then a roaring peal of thunder, as if a thousand mountains were rolling one over the other in the blue vault of Heaven! Who sleeps now in that ancient city? Not one living soul. The dread trumpet of eternity could not more effectually have awakened any one.

The hail continues. The wind continues. The uproar of the elements seems at its height. Now she awakens—that beautiful girl on the antique bed; she opens those eyes of celestial blue, and a faint cry of alarm bursts from her lips. At least it is a cry which, amid the noise and turmoil without, sounds but faint and weak. She sits upon the bed and presses her hands upon her eyes. Heavens! what a wild torrent of wind, and rain, and hail! The thunder likewise seems intent upon awakening sufficient echoes to last until the next flash of forked lightning should again produce the wild concussion of the air. She murmurs a prayer—a prayer for those she loves best; the names of those dear to her gentle heart come from her lips; she weeps and prays; she thinks then of what devastation the storm must surely produce, and to the great God of Heaven she prays for all living things. Another flash—a wild, blue, bewildering flash of lightning streams across that bay window, for an instant bringing out every colour in it with terrible distinctness. A shriek bursts from the lips of the young girl, and then, with eyes fixed upon that window, which, in another moment, is all darkness, and with such an expression of terror upon her face as it had never before known, she trembled, and the perspiration of intense fear stood upon her brow.

"What—what was it?" she gasped; "real, or a delusion? Oh, God, what was it? A figure tall and gaunt, endeavouring from the outside to unclasp the window. I saw it. That flash of lightning revealed it to me. It stood the whole length of the window."

There was a lull of the wind. The hail was not falling so thickly—moreover, it now fell, what there was of it, straight, and yet a strange clattering sound came upon the glass of that long window. It could not be a delusion—she is awake, and she hears it. What can produce it? Another flash of lightning—another shriek—there could be now no delusion.

A tall figure is standing on the ledge immediately outside the long window. It is its finger-nails upon the glass that produces the sound so like the hail, now that the hail has ceased. Intense fear paralysed the limbs of that beautiful girl. That one shriek is all she can utter—with hands clasped, a face of marble, a heart beating so wildly in her bosom, that each moment it seems as if it would break its confines, eyes distended and fixed upon the window, she waits, froze with horror. The pattering and clattering of the nails continue. No word is spoken, and now she fancies she can trace the darker form of that figure against the window, and she can see the long arms moving to and fro, feeling for some mode of entrance. What strange light is that which now gradually creeps up into the air? red and terrible—brighter and brighter it grows. The lightning has set fire to a mill, and the reflection of the rapidly consuming building falls upon that long window. There can be no mistake. The figure is there, still feeling for an entrance, and clattering against the glass with its long nails, that appear as if the growth of many years had been untouched. She tries to scream again but a choking sensation comes over her, and she cannot. It is too dreadful—she tries to move—each limb seems weighed down by tons of lead—she can but in a hoarse faint whisper cry,—

"Help—help—help—help!"

And that one word she repeats like a person in a dream. The red glare of the fire continues. It throws up the tall gaunt figure in hideous relief against the long window. It shows, too, upon the one portrait that is in the chamber, and that portrait appears to fix its eyes upon the attempting intruder, while the flickering light from the fire makes it look fearfully lifelike. A small pane of glass is broken, and the form from without introduces a long gaunt hand, which seems utterly destitute of flesh. The fastening is removed, and one-half of the window, which opens like folding doors, is swung wide open upon its hinges.

And yet now she could not scream—she could not move. "Help!—help!—help!" was all she could say. But, oh, that look of terror that sat upon her face, it was dreadful—a look to haunt the memory for a lifetime—a look to obtrude itself upon the happiest moments, and turn them to bitterness.

The figure turns half round, and the light falls upon the face. It is perfectly white—perfectly bloodless. The eyes look like polished tin; the lips are drawn back, and the principal feature next to those dreadful eyes is the teeth—the fearful looking teeth—projecting like those of some wild animal, hideously, glaringly white, and fang-like. It approaches the bed with a strange, gliding movement. It clashes together the long nails that literally appear to hang from the finger ends. No sound comes from its lips. Is she going mad—that young and beautiful girl exposed to so much terror? she has drawn up all her limbs; she cannot even now say help. The power of articulation is gone, but the power of movement has returned to her; she can draw herself slowly along to the other side of the bed from that towards which the hideous appearance is coming.

But her eyes are fascinated. The glance of a serpent[1] could not have produced a greater effect upon her than did the fixed gaze of those awful, metallic-looking eyes that were bent on her face. Crouching down so that the gigantic height was lost, and the horrible, protruding, white face was the most prominent object, came on the figure. What was it?—what did it want there?—what made it look so hideous—so unlike an inhabitant of the earth, and yet to be on it?

Now she has got to the verge of the bed, and the figure pauses. It seemed as if when it paused she lost the power to proceed. The clothing of the bed was now clutched in her hands with unconscious power. She drew her breath short and thick. Her bosom heaves, and her limbs tremble, yet she cannot withdraw her eyes from that marble-looking face. He holds her with his glittering eye.

The storm has ceased—all is still. The winds are hushed; the church clock proclaims the hour of one: a hissing sound comes from the throat of the hideous being, and he raises his long, gaunt arms—the lips move. He advances. The girl places one small foot from the bed on to the floor. She is unconsciously dragging the clothing with her. The door of the room is in that direction—can she reach it? Has she power to walk?—can she withdraw her eyes from the face of the intruder, and so break the hideous charm? God of Heaven! is it real, or some dream so like reality as to nearly overturn the judgment for ever?

The figure has paused again, and half on the bed and half out of it that young girl lies trembling. Her long hair streams across the entire width of the bed. As she has slowly moved along she has left it streaming across the pillows.

1 There are numerous references in folklore and literature to the belief that serpents could paralyze their prey with their gaze.

The pause lasted about a minute—oh, what an age of agony. That minute was, indeed, enough for madness to do its full work in.

With a sudden rush that could not be foreseen—with a strange howling cry that was enough to awaken terror in every breast, the figure seized the long tresses of her hair, and twining them round his bony hands he held her to the bed. Then she screamed—Heaven granted her then power to scream. Shriek followed shriek in rapid succession. The bed-clothes fell in a heap by the side of the bed—she was dragged by her long silken hair completely on to it again. Her beautifully rounded limbs quivered with the agony of her soul. The glassy, horrible eyes of the figure ran over that angelic form with a hideous satisfaction—horrible profanation. He drags her head to the bed's edge. He forces it back by the long hair still entwined in his grasp. With a plunge he seizes her neck in his fang-like teeth—a gush of blood, and a hideous sucking noise follows. *The girl has swooned, and the vampyre is at his hideous repast!*

## CHAPTER II

## THE ALARM.—THE PISTOL SHOT. —THE PURSUIT AND ITS CONSEQUENCES.

Lights flashed about the building, and various room doors opened; voices called one to the other. There was an universal stir and commotion among the inhabitants.

"Did you hear a scream, Harry?" asked a young man, half-dressed, as he walked into the chamber of another about his own age.

"I did—where was it?"

"God knows. I dressed myself directly."

"All is still now."

"Yes; but unless I was dreaming there was a scream."

"We could not both dream there was. Where did you think it came from?"

"It burst so suddenly upon my ears that I cannot say."

There was a tap now at the door of the room where these young men were, and a female voice said,—

"For God's sake, get up!... Did you hear anything?"

"Yes, a scream."

"Oh, search the house—search the house; where did it come from—can you tell?"

"Indeed we cannot, mother."

Another person now joined the party. He was a man of middle age, and, as he came up to them, he said,—

"Good God! what is the matter?"

Scarcely had the words passed his lips, than such a rapid succession of shrieks came upon their ears, that they felt absolutely stunned by them. The elderly lady, whom one of the young men had called mother, fainted, and would have fallen to the floor of the corridor in which they all stood, had she not been promptly supported by the last comer, who himself staggered, as those piercing cries came upon the night air. He, however, was the first to recover, for the young men seemed paralysed.

"Henry," he cried, "for God's sake support your mother. Can you doubt that these cries come from Flora's room?"

The young man mechanically supported his mother, and then the man who had just spoken darted back to his own bed-room, from whence he returned in a moment with a pair of pistols, and shouting,—

"Follow me, who can!" he bounded across the corridor in the direction of the antique apartment, from whence the cries proceeded, but which were now hushed.

That house was built for strength, and the doors were all of oak, and of considerable thickness. Unhappily, they had fastenings within, so that when the man reached the chamber of her who so much required help, he was helpless, for the door was fast.

"Flora! Flora!" he cried; "Flora, speak!"

All was still.

"Good God!" he added; "we must force the door."

"I hear a strange noise within," said the young man, who trembled violently.

"And so do I. What does it sound like?"

"I scarcely know; but it nearest resembles some animal eating, or sucking some liquid."

"What on earth can it be? Have you no weapon that will force the door? I shall go mad if I am kept here."

"I have," said the young man. "Wait here a moment."

He ran down the staircase, and presently returned with a small, but powerful, iron crow-bar.

"This will do," he said.

"It will, it will.—Give it to me."

"Has she not spoken?"

"Not a word. My mind misgives me that something very dreadful must have happened to her."

"And that odd noise!"

"Still goes on. Somehow, it curdles the very blood in my veins to hear it."

The man took the crow-bar, and with some difficulty succeeded in introducing it between the door and the side of the wall—still it required great strength to move it, but it did move, with a harsh, crackling sound.

"Push it!" cried he who was using the bar, "push the door at the same time."

The younger man did so. For a few moments the massive door resisted. Then, suddenly, something gave way with a loud snap—it was a part of the lock,—and the door at once swung wide open.

How true it is that we measure time by the events which happen within a given space of it, rather than by its actual duration.

To those who were engaged in forcing open the door of the antique chamber, where slept the young girl whom they named Flora, each moment was swelled into an hour of agony; but, in reality, from the first moment of the alarm to that when the loud cracking noise heralded the destruction of the fastenings of the door, there had elapsed but very few minutes indeed.

"It opens—it opens," cried the young man.

"Another moment," said the stranger, as he still plied the crowbar—"another moment, and we shall have free ingress to the chamber. Be patient."

This stranger's name was Marchdale; and even as he spoke, he succeeded in throwing the massive door wide open, and clearing the passage to the chamber.

To rush in with a light in his hand was the work of a moment to the young man named Henry; but the very rapid progress he made into the apartment prevented him from observing accurately what it contained, for the wind that came in from the open window caught the flame of the candle, and although it did not actually extinguish it, it blew it so much on one side, that it was comparatively useless as a light.

"Flora—Flora!" he cried.

Then with a sudden bound something dashed from off the bed. The concussion against him was so sudden and so utterly unexpected, as well as so tremendously violent, that he was thrown down, and, in his fall, the light was fairly extinguished.

All was darkness, save a dull, reddish kind of light that now and then, from the nearly consumed mill in the immediate vicinity, came into the room. But by that light, dim, uncertain, and flickering as it was, some one was seen to make for the window.

Henry, although nearly stunned by his fall, saw a figure, gigantic in height, which nearly reached from the floor to the ceiling. The other young man, George, saw it, and Mr. Marchdale likewise saw it, as did the lady who had spoken to the two young men in the corridor when first the screams of the young girl awakened alarm in the breasts of all the inhabitants of that house.

The figure was about to pass out at the window which led to a kind of balcony, from whence there was an easy descent to a garden.

Before it passed out they each and all caught a glance of the side-face, and they saw that the lower part of it and the lips were dabbled in blood. They saw, too, one of those fearful-looking, shining, metallic eyes which presented so terrible an appearance of unearthly ferocity.

No wonder that for a moment a panic seized them all, which paralysed any exertions they might otherwise have made to detain that hideous form.

But Mr. Marchdale was a man of mature years; he had seen much of life, both in this and in foreign lands; and he, although astonished to the extent of being frightened, was much more likely to recover sooner than his younger companions, which, indeed, he did, and acted promptly enough.

"Don't rise, Henry," he cried. "Lie still."

Almost at the moment he uttered these words, he fired at the figure, which then occupied the window, as if it were a gigantic figure set in a frame.

The report was tremendous in that chamber, for the pistol was no toy weapon, but one made for actual service, and of sufficient length and bore of barrel to carry destruction along with the bullets that came from it.

"If that has missed its aim," said Mr. Marchdale, "I'll never pull a trigger again."

As he spoke he dashed forward, and made a clutch at the figure he felt convinced he had shot.

The tall form turned upon him, and when he got a full view of the face, which he did at that moment, from the opportune circumstance of the lady returning at the instant with a light she had been to her own chamber to procure, even he, Marchdale, with all his courage, and that was great, and all his nervous energy, recoiled a step or two, and uttered the exclamation of, "Great God!"

That face was one never to be forgotten. It was hideously flushed with colour—the colour of fresh blood; the eyes had a savage and remarkable lustre; whereas, before, they had looked like polished tin—they now wore a ten times brighter aspect, and flashes of light seemed to dart from them. The mouth was open, as if, from the natural formation of the countenance, the lips receded much from the large canine looking teeth.

A strange howling noise came from the throat of this monstrous figure, and it seemed upon the point of rushing upon Mr. Marchdale. Suddenly, then, as if some impulse had seized upon it, it uttered a wild and terrible shrieking kind of laugh; and then turning, dashed through the window, and in one instant disappeared from before the eyes of those who felt nearly annihilated by its fearful presence.

"God help us!" ejaculated Henry.

Mr. Marchdale drew a long breath, and then, giving a stamp on the floor, as if to recover himself from the state of agitation into which even he was thrown, he cried,—

"Be it what or who it may, I'll follow it.... Let who will come with me—I follow that dreadful form."

As he spoke, he took the road it took, and dashed through the window into the balcony.

"And we, too, George," exclaimed Henry; "we will follow Mr. Marchdale. This dreadful affair concerns us more nearly than it does him."

The lady who was the mother of these young men, and of the beautiful girl who had been so awfully visited, screamed aloud, and implored of them to stay. But the voice of Mr. Marchdale was heard exclaiming aloud,—

"I see it—I see it; it makes for the wall."

They hesitated no longer, but at once rushed into the balcony, and from thence dropped into the garden.

The mother approached the bed-side of the insensible, perhaps the murdered girl; she saw her, to all appearance, weltering in blood, and, overcome by her emotions, she fainted on the floor of the room.

When the two young men reached the garden, they found it much lighter than might have been fairly expected; for not only was the morning rapidly approaching, but the mill was still burning, and those mingled lights made almost every object plainly visible, except when deep shadows were thrown from some gigantic trees that had stood for centuries in that sweetly wooded spot. They heard the voice of Mr. Marchdale, as he cried,—

"There—there—towards the wall. There—there—God! how it bounds along."

The young men hastily dashed through a thicket in the direction from whence his voice sounded, and then they found him looking wild and terrified, and with something in his hand which looked like a portion of clothing.

"Which way, which way?" they both cried in a breath.

He leant heavily on the arm of George, as he pointed along a vista of trees, and said in a low voice,—

"God help us all. It is not human. Look there—look there—do you not see it?"

They looked in the direction he indicated. At the end of this vista was the wall of the garden. At that point it was full twelve feet in height, and as they looked, they saw the hideous, monstrous form they had traced from the chamber of their sister, making frantic efforts to clear the obstacle.

Then they saw it bound from the ground to the top of the wall, which it very nearly reached, and then each time it fell back again into the garden with such a dull, heavy sound, that the earth seemed to shake again with the concussion. They trembled—well indeed they might, and for some minutes they watched the figure making its fruitless efforts to leave the place.

"What—what is it?" whispered Henry, in hoarse accents. "God, what can it possibly be?"

"I know not," replied Mr. Marchdale. "I did seize it. It was cold and clammy like a corpse. It cannot be human."

"Not human?"

"Look at it now. It will surely escape now."

"No, no—we will not be terrified thus—there is Heaven above us. Come on, and, for dear Flora's sake, let us make an effort yet to seize this bold intruder."

"Take this pistol," said Marchdale. "It is the fellow of the one I fired. Try its efficacy."

"He will be gone," exclaimed Henry, as at this moment, after many repeated attempts and fearful falls, the figure reached the top of the wall, and then hung by its long arms a moment or two, previous to dragging itself completely up.

The idea of the appearance, be it what it might, entirely escaping, seemed to nerve again Mr. Marchdale, and he, as well as the two young men, ran forward towards the wall. They got so close to the figure before it sprang down on the outer side of the wall, that to miss killing it with the bullet from the pistol was a matter of utter impossibility, unless wilfully.

Henry had the weapon, and he pointed it full at the tall form with a steady aim. He pulled the trigger—the explosion followed, and that the bullet did its office there could be no manner of doubt, for the figure gave a howling shriek, and fell headlong from the wall on the outside.

"I have shot him," cried Henry, "I have shot him."

[*The Bannerworths consult a doctor and eventually arrive at the realization that Flora has been visited by a vampire. The vampire returns and is driven off. Flora shoots at him. They fear that even if Flora has escaped, the attack will mean that she is doomed to become a vampire. The Bannerworths' family history is outlined and it is revealed that the family is in strained financial circumstances.*]

## CHAPTER XIII

### THE OFFER FOR THE HALL.—THE VISIT TO SIR FRANCIS VARNEY. —THE STRANGE RESEMBLANCE.—A DREADFUL SUGGESTION.

The party made a strict search through every nook and corner of the garden, but it proved to be a fruitless one: not the least trace of any one could be found. There was only one circumstance, which was pondered over deeply by them all, and that was that, beneath the window of the room in which Flora and her mother sat while the brothers were on their visit to the vault of their ancestors, were visible marks of blood to a considerable extent.

It will be remembered that Flora had fired a pistol at the spectral appearance, and that immediately upon that it had disappeared, after uttering a sound which might well be construed into a cry of pain from a wound.

That a wound then had been inflicted upon some one, the blood beneath the window now abundantly testified; and when it was discovered, Henry and Charles[1] made a very close examination indeed of the garden, to discover what direction the wounded figure, be it man or vampyre, had taken.

But the closest scrutiny did not reveal to them a single spot of blood, beyond the space immediately beneath the window;—there the apparition seemed to have

1 Charles Holland is a friend of Henry's who is visiting. He wishes to marry Flora.

received its wound, and then, by some mysterious means, to have disappeared.

At length, wearied with the continued excitement, combined with want of sleep, to which they had been subjected, they returned to the hall.

Flora, with the exception of the alarm she experienced from the firing of the pistol, had met with no disturbance, and that, in order to spare her painful reflections, they told her was merely done as a precautionary measure, to proclaim to any one who might be lurking in the garden that the inmates of the house were ready to defend themselves against any aggression.

Whether or not she believed this kind deceit they knew not. She only sighed deeply, and wept. The probability is, that she more than suspected the vampyre had made another visit, but they forbore to press the point; and, leaving her with her mother, Henry and George went from her chamber again—the former to endeavour to seek some repose, as it would be his turn to watch on the succeeding night, and the latter to resume his station in a small room close to Flora's chamber, where it had been agreed watch and ward should be kept by turns while the alarm lasted.

At length, the morning again dawned upon that unhappy family, and to none were its beams more welcome.

The birds sang their pleasant carols beneath the window. The sweet, deep-coloured autumnal sun shone upon all objects with a golden luster; and to look abroad, upon the beaming face of nature, no one could for a moment suppose, except from sad experience, that there were such things as gloom, misery, and crime, upon the earth.

"And must I," said Henry, as he gazed from a window of the hall upon the undulating park, the majestic trees, the flowers, the shrubs, and the many natural beauties with which the place was full,—"must I be chased from this spot, the home of my self and of my kindred, by a phantom—must I indeed seek refuge elsewhere, because my own home has become hideous?"

It was indeed a cruel and a painful thought! It was one he yet would not, could not be convinced was absolutely necessary. But now the sun was shining: it was morning; and the feelings, which found a home in his breast amid the darkness, the stillness, and the uncertainty of night, were chased away by those glorious beams of sunlight, that fell upon hill, valley, and stream, and the thousand sweet sounds of life and animation that filled that sunny air!

Such a revulsion of feeling was natural enough. Many of the distresses and mental anxieties of night vanish with the night, and those which oppressed the heart of Henry Bannerworth were considerably modified.

He was engaged in these reflections when he heard the sound of the lodge bell, and as a visitor was now somewhat rare at this establishment, he waited with some anxiety to see to whom he was indebted for so early a call.

In the course of a few minutes, one of the servants came to him with a letter in her hand.

It bore a large handsome seal, and, from its appearance, would seem to have come from some personage of consequence. A second glance at it shewed him the name of "Varney" in the corner, and, with some degree of vexation, he muttered to himself,

"Another condoling epistle from the troublesome neighbour whom I have not yet seen." [...]

When Henry found himself alone [...] he turned his attention to the letter he held in his hand, and which, from the autograph in the corner, he knew came from his new neighbour, Sir Francis Varney, whom, by some chance or another, he had never yet seen.

To his great surprise, he found that the letter contained the following words:—

> Dear Sir,—"As a neighbour, by purchase of an estate contiguous to your own, I am quite sure you have excused, and taken in good part, the cordial offer I made to you of friendship and service some short time since; but now, in addressing to you a distinct proposition, I trust I shall meet with an indulgent consideration, whether such proposition be accordant with your views or not.
>
> "What I have heard from common report induces me to believe that Bannerworth Hall cannot be a desirable residence for yourself, or your amiable sister. If I am right in that conjecture, and you have any serious thought of leaving the place, I would earnestly recommend you, as one having some experience in such descriptions of property, to sell it at once.
>
> "Now, the proposition with which I conclude this letter is, I know, of a character to make you doubt the disinterestedness of such advice; but that it is disinterested, nevertheless, is a fact of which I can assure my own heart, and of which I beg to assure you. I propose, then, should you, upon consideration, decide upon such a course of proceeding, to purchase of you the Hall. I do not ask for a bargain on account of any extraneous circumstances which may at the present time depreciate the value of the property, but I am willing to give a fair price for it. Under these circumstances, I trust, sir, that you will give a kindly consideration to my offer, and even if you reject it, I hope that, as neighbours, we may live long in peace and amity, and in the interchange of those good offices which should subsist between us. Awaiting your reply,
>
> "Believe me to be, dear sir,
>
> "Your very obedient servant,
>
> "FRANCIS VARNEY.
>
> "To Henry Bannerworth, Esq."

Henry, after having read this most unobjectionable letter through, folded it up again, and placed it in his pocket. Clasping his hands, then, behind his back, a favourite attitude of his when he was in deep contemplation, he paced to and fro in the garden for some time in deep thought.

"How strange," he muttered. "It seems that every circumstance combines to induce me to leave my old ancestral home. It appears as if everything now that happened had that direct tendency. What can be the meaning of all this? 'Tis very strange—amazingly strange. Here arise circumstances which are enough to induce any man to leave a particular place. Then a friend, in whose single-mindedness and judgment I know I can rely, advises the step, and immediately upon the back of that comes a fair and candid offer."

There was an apparent connexion between all these circumstances which much puzzled Henry. He walked to and fro for nearly an hour, until he heard a hasty footstep approaching him, and upon looking in the direction from whence it came, he saw Mr. Marchdale. [...]

"I have received a communication from our neighbour, Sir Francis Varney," said Henry.

"Indeed!"

"It is here. Peruse it for yourself, and then tell me, Marchdale, candidly what you think of it."

"I suppose," said Marchdale, as he opened the letter, "it is another friendly note of condolence on the state of your domestic affairs, which, I grieve to say, from the prattling of domestics, whose tongues it is quite impossible to silence, have become food for gossip all over the neighbouring villages and estates."

"If anything could add another pang to those I have already been made to suffer," said Henry, "it would certainly arise from being made the food of vulgar gossip. But read the letter, Marchdale. You will find its contents of a more important character than you anticipate."

"Indeed!" said Marchdale, as he ran his eyes eagerly over the note.

When he had finished it he glanced at Henry, who then said,—

"Well, what is your opinion?"

"I know not what to say, Henry. You know that my own advice to you has been to get rid of this place. [...] With the hope that the disagreeable affair connected with it now may remain connected with it as a house, and not with you and yours as a family." [...]

"I do not know," said Henry, with a shudder. "I must confess, Marchdale, that to my own perceptions it seems more probable that the infliction we have experienced from the strange visitor, who seems now resolved to pester us with visits, will rather attach to a family than to a house. The vampyre may follow us."

"If so, of course the parting with the Hall would be a great pity, and no gain."

"None in the least."

"Henry, a thought has struck me."

"Let's hear it, Marchdale."

"It is this:—Suppose you were to try the experiment of leaving the Hall without selling it. Suppose for one year you were to let it to some one, Henry."

"It might be done."

"Ay, and it might, with very great promise and candour, be proposed to this very gentleman, Sir Francis Varney, to take it for one year, to see how he liked it before becoming the possessor of it. Then if he found himself tormented by the vampyre, he need not complete the purchase, or if you found that the apparition followed you from hence, you might yourself return, feeling that perhaps here, in the spots familiar to your youth, you might be most happy, even under such circumstances as at present oppress you. [...]

[I]f I were you, I would call upon Sir Francis Varney, and make him an offer to become a tenant of the Hall for twelve months, during which time you could go where you please, and test the fact of absence ridding you or not ridding you of the dreadful visitant who makes the night here truly hideous."

"I will speak to my mother, to George, and to my sister of the matter. They shall decide."

Mr. Marchdale now strove in every possible manner to raise the spirits of Henry Bannerworth, by painting to him the future in far more radiant colours than the present, and endeavouring to induce a belief in his mind that a short period of time might after all replace in his mind, and in the minds of those who were naturally so dear to him, all their wonted serenity.

Henry, although he felt not much comfort from these kindly efforts, yet could feel gratitude to him who made them; and after expressing such a feeling to Marchdale, in strong terms, he repaired to the house, in order to hold a solemn consultation with those whom he felt ought to be consulted as well as himself as to what steps should be taken with regard to the Hall.

The proposition, or rather the suggestion, which had been made by Marchdale upon the proposition of Sir Francis Varney, was in every respect so reasonable and just, that it met, as was to be expected, with the concurrence of every member of the family.

Flora's cheeks almost resumed some of their wonted colour at the mere thought now of leaving that home to which she had been at one time so much attached.

"Yes, dear Henry," she said, "let us leave here if you are agreeable so to do, and in leaving this house, we will believe that we leave behind us a world of terror."

"Flora," remarked Henry, in a tone of slight reproach, "if you were so anxious to leave Bannerworth Hall, why did you not say so before this proposition came from other mouths? You know your feelings upon such a subject would have been laws to me."

"I knew you were attached to the old house," said Flora; "and, besides, events have come upon us all with such fearful rapidity, there has scarcely been time to think."

"True—true."

"And you will leave, Henry?"

"I will call upon Sir Francis Varney myself, and speak to him upon the subject."

A new impetus to existence appeared now to come over the whole family, at the idea of leaving a place which always would be now associated in their minds with so much terror. Each member of the family felt happier, and breathed more freely than before, so that the change which had come over them seemed almost magical. [...]

Henry, now, having made a determination to see Sir Francis Varney, lost no time in putting it into execution. At Mr. Marchdale's own request, he took him with him, as it was desirable to have a third person present in the sort of business negotiation which was going on. The estate which had been so recently entered upon by the person calling himself Sir Francis Varney, and which common report said he had purchased, was a small, but complete property, and situated so close to the grounds connected with Bannerworth Hall, that a short walk soon placed Henry and Mr. Marchdale before the residence of this gentleman, who had shown so kindly a feeling towards the Bannerworth family.

"Have you seen Sir Francis Varney?" asked Henry of Mr. Marchdale, as he rung the gate-bell.

"I have not. Have you?"

"No; I never saw him. It is rather awkward our both being absolute strangers to his person."

"We can but send in our names, however; and, from the great vein of courtesy that runs through his letter, I have no doubt but we shall receive the most gentlemanly reception from him."

A servant in handsome livery appeared at the iron-gates, which opened upon a lawn in the front of Sir Francis Varney's house, and to this domestic Henry Bannerworth handed his card, on which he had written, in pencil, likewise the name of Mr. Marchdale.

"If your master," he said, "is within, we shall be glad to see him."

"Sir Francis is at home, sir," was the reply, "although not very well. If you will be pleased to walk in, I will announce you to him."

Henry and Marchdale followed the man into a handsome enough reception-room, where they were desired to wait while their names were announced.

"Do you know if this gentleman be a baronet," said Henry, "or a knight merely?"

"I really do not; I never saw him in my life, or heard of him before he came into this neighbourhood."

"And I have been too much occupied with the painful occurrences of this hall to know anything of our neighbours. I dare say Mr. Chillingworth, if we had thought to ask him, would have known something concerning him."

"No doubt."

This brief colloquy was put an end to by the servant, who said,—

"My master, gentlemen, is not very well; but he begs me to present his best compliments, and to say he is much gratified with your visit, and will be happy to see you in his study."

Henry and Marchdale followed the man up a flight of stone stairs, and then they were conducted through a large apartment into a smaller one. There was very little light in this small room; but at the moment of their entrance a tall man, who was seated, rose, and, touching the spring of a blind that was to the window, it was up in a moment, admitting a broad glare of light. A cry of surprise, mingled with terror, came from Henry Bannerworth's lip. *The original of the portrait on the panel stood before him!* There was the lofty stature, the long, sallow face, the slightly projecting teeth, the dark, lustrous, although somewhat sombre eyes; the expression of the features—all were alike.

"Are you unwell, sir?" said Sir Francis Varney, in soft, mellow accents, as he handed a chair to the bewildered Henry.

"God of Heaven!" said Henry; "how like!"

"You seem surprised, sir. Have you ever seen me before?"

Sir Francis drew himself up to his full height, and cast a strange glance upon Henry, whose eyes were rivetted upon his face, as if with a species of fascination which he could not resist.

"Marchdale," Henry gasped; "Marchdale, my friend, Marchdale. I—I am surely mad."

"Hush! be calm," whispered Marchdale.

"Calm—calm—can you not see? Marchdale, is this a dream? Look—look—oh! look."

"For God's sake, Henry, compose yourself."

"Is your friend often thus?" said Sir Francis Varney, with the same mellifluous tone which seemed habitual to him.

"No, sir, he is not; but recent circumstances have shattered his nerves; and, to tell the truth, you bear so strong a resemblance to an old portrait, in his house, that I do not wonder so much as I otherwise should at his agitation."

"Indeed."

"A resemblance!" said Henry; "a resemblance! God of Heaven! it is the face itself."

"You much surprise me," said Sir Francis.

Henry sunk into the chair which was near him, and he trembled violently. The rush of painful thoughts and conjectures that came through his mind was enough to make any one tremble. "Is this the vampyre?" was the horrible question that seemed impressed upon his very brain, in letters of flame. "Is this the vampyre?"

"Are you better, sir?" said Sir Francis Varney, in his bland, musical voice. "Shall I order any refreshment for you?"

"No—no," gasped Henry; "for the love of truth tell me! Is—is your name really Varney!"

"Sir?"

"Have you no other name to which, perhaps, a better title you could urge?"

"Mr. Bannerworth, I can assure you that I am too proud of the name of the family to which I belong to exchange it for any other, be it what it may."

"How wonderfully like!"

"I grieve to see you so much distressed. Mr. Bannerworth. I presume ill health has thus shattered your nerves?"

"No; ill health has not done the work. I know not what to say, Sir Francis Varney, to you; but recent events in my family have made the sight of you full of horrible conjectures."

"What mean you, sir?"

"You know, from common report, that we have had a fearful visitor at our house."

"A vampyre, I have heard," said Sir Francis Varney, with a bland, and almost beautiful smile, which displayed his white glistening teeth to perfection.

"Yes; a vampyre, and—and—"

"I pray you go on, sir; you surely are far above the vulgar superstition of believing in such matters?"

"My judgment is assailed in too many ways and shapes for it to hold out probably as it ought to do against so hideous a belief, but never was it so much bewildered as now."

"Why so?"

"Because— [...] you so much resemble the vampyre," added Henry, "that—that I know not what to think."

"Is it possible?" said Varney. [...]

Varney gave a twinge of pain, as if some sudden bodily ailment had attacked him severely.

"You are unwell, sir?" said Marchdale.

"No, no—no," he said; "I—hurt my arm, and happened accidentally to touch the arm of this chair with it." [...]

"A—a wound?"

"Yes, a wound, but not much more than skin deep. In fact, little beyond an abrasion of the skin."

"May I inquire how you came by it?"

"Oh, yes. A slight fall."

"Indeed."

"Remarkable, is it not? Very remarkable. We never know a moment when, from some most trifling cause, we may receive really some serious bodily harm. How true it is, Mr. Bannerworth, that in the midst of life we are in death."

"And equally true, perhaps," said Henry, "that in the midst of death there may be found a horrible life."

"Well, I should not wonder. There are really so many strange things in this world, that I have left off wondering at anything now."

"There are strange things," said Henry. "You wish to purchase of me the Hall, sir?"

"If you wish to sell."

"You—you are perhaps attached to the place? Perhaps you recollected it, sir, long ago?"

"Not very long," smiled Sir Francis Varney. "It seems a nice comfortable old house; and the grounds, too, appear to be amazingly well wooded, which, to one of rather a romantic temperament like myself, is always an additional charm to a place. I was extremely pleased with it the first time I beheld it, and a desire to call myself the owner of it took possession of my mind. The scenery is remarkable for its beauty, and, from what I have seen of it, it is rarely to be excelled. No doubt you are greatly attached to it."

"It has been my home from infancy," returned Henry, "and being also the residence of my ancestors for centuries, it is natural that I should be so. [...] The house, no doubt, has suffered much," said Henry, "within the last hundred years."

"No doubt it has. A hundred years is a tolerable long space of time, you know."

"It is, indeed. Oh, how any human life which is spun out to such an extent, must lose its charms, by losing all its fondest and dearest associations."

"Ah, how true," said Sir Francis Varney.

# Vasile Alecsandri

(1821–1890)

Poet, dramatist, politician, and activist, Vasile Alecsandri was born in Romania to an aristocratic family. As a young man, he studied in Paris and toured Western Europe. He was a leader in the 1848 revolutionary movements in Moldavia and Wallachia and is credited with the nineteenth-century campaign for the preservation of Romanian cultural identity. To this end, Alecsandri studied Romanian folklore extensively, including the vampire figure. Interestingly, according to Romanian legend, there is a differentiation between mortal vampires, moroi, and immortal vampires, strigoi. The vampire is a theme in several of Alecsandri's works, including the dramatic farce *Doi Morti Vii* (*Two Living Dead*, 1851) and the poem anthologized here, "Vampire (Strigoiul)" (1886). Alecsandri is considered one of the most important Romanian writers in the second half of the nineteenth century.

# "Vampire (Strigoiul)"[1]

(1886)

Near the cliff's sharp edge, on high
Standing out against the sky,
Dost thou see a ruined cross
Weatherstained, o'ergrown by moss,
Gloomy, desolate, forsaken,
By unnumbered tempests shaken?
Not a blade of grass grows nigh it,
Not a peasant lingers by it.
E'en the sombre bird of night
Shuns it in her darksome flight,
Startled by the piteous groan

1 Translated by William Beatty-Kingston.

That arises from the stone.
All around, on starless nights,
Myriad hosts of livid lights
Flicker fretfully, revealing
At its foot a phantom, kneeling
Whilst it jabbers dismal plaints,
Cursing God and all the saints.
Tardy traveller, beware
Of that spectre gibbering there;
Close your eyes, and urge your steed
To the utmost of his speed;—
For beneath that cross, I ween,
Lies a Vampyre's corpse obscene!

*

Though the night is black and cold
Love's found story, often told,
Floats in whispers through the air,
Stalwart youth and maiden fair
Seal sweet vows of ardent passion
With their lips, in lovers' fashion.
Restless, pale, a shape I see
Hov'ring nigh; what may it be?
'Tis a charger, white as snow,
Pacing slowly to and fro
Like a sentry. As he turns
Haughtily the sward he spurns.
'Leave me not, beloved, tonight!
Stay with me till morning's light!'
Weeping, thus besought the maid;
'Love, my soul is sore afraid!
Brave not the dread Vampyre's power,
Mightiest at this mystic hour!'
Not a word he spake, but prest
The sobbing maiden to his breast;
Kissed her lips and cheeks and eyes
Heedless of her tears and sighs;
Waved his hand, with gesture gay,
Mounted—smiled—and rode away.

*

Who rides across the dusky plain
Tearing along with might and main
Like some wild storm-fiend, in his flight
Nursed on the ebony breast of Night?
'Tis he, who left her in her need—
Her lover, on his milk-white steed!

The blast in all its savage force
Strives to o'erthrow the gallant horse
That snorts defiance to his foe
And struggles onward. See! below
The causeway, 'long the river-side
A thousand flutt'ring flamelets glide!
Now they approach, and now recede,
Still followed by the panting steed;
He nears the ruined cross! A crash,
A piteous cry, a heavy splash,
And in the rocky river-bed
Rider and horse lie crushed and dead.

Then from those dismal depths arise
Blaspheming yells and strident cries
Re-echoing through the murky air
And, like a serpent from its lair,
Brandishing high a blood-stained glaive
The Vampyre rises from his grave!

# Bram Stoker

(1847–1912)

Abraham "Bram" Stoker was born in Ireland and attended Trinity College in Dublin, excelling in both athletics and academics, and graduating with honors in mathematics. He wrote theater criticism and worked closely with the famous actor Henry Irving at England's Lyceum Theatre. Irving is said to be one of the inspirations for Stoker's famous vampire. Stoker's imagination was sparked at an early age by the vivid stories his mother told him about the 1832 cholera epidemic. He began writing and publishing in the 1890s while venturing into vampire research. *Dracula* (1897) follows the gothic tradition of Polidori's *The Vampyre*, Rymer and Prest's *Varney the Vampire*, and Le Fanu's *Carmilla*. Stoker married noted beauty Florence Balcombe (Oscar Wilde was also a suitor). As Stoker's literary executor, Balcombe published the following tale as a separate story, but it is thought to have originally been part of the novel's early chapters before Stoker removed it to focus more centrally on Dracula.

## "Dracula's Guest"

(1914)

When we started for our drive the sun was shining brightly on Munich, and the air was full of the joyousness of early summer. Just as we were about to depart, Herr Delbrück (the maître d'hôtel of the Quatre Saisons,[1] where I was staying) came down, bareheaded, to the carriage and, after wishing me a pleasant drive, said to the coachman, still holding his hand on the handle of the carriage door:

"Remember you are back by nightfall. The sky looks bright but there is a shiver in the north wind that says there may be a sudden storm. But I am sure you will not be late." Here he smiled, and added, "for you know what night it is."

1 The Four Seasons—a hotel in central Munich.

Johann answered with an emphatic, "Ja, mein Herr,"[1] and, touching his hat, drove off quickly. When we had cleared the town, I said, after signalling to him to stop:

"Tell me, Johann, what is tonight?"

He crossed himself, as he answered laconically: "Walpurgisnacht."[2] Then he took out his watch, a great, old-fashioned German silver thing as big as a turnip, and looked at it, with his eyebrows gathered together and a little impatient shrug of his shoulders. I realised that this was his way of respectfully protesting against the unnecessary delay, and sank back in the carriage, merely motioning him to proceed. He started off rapidly, as if to make up for lost time. Every now and then the horses seemed to throw up their heads and sniffed the air suspiciously. On such occasions I often looked round in alarm. The road was pretty bleak, for we were traversing a sort of high, wind-swept plateau. As we drove, I saw a road that looked but little used, and which seemed to dip through a little, winding valley. It looked so inviting that, even at the risk of offending him, I called Johann to stop—and when he had pulled up, I told him I would like to drive down that road. He made all sorts of excuses, and frequently crossed himself as he spoke. This somewhat piqued my curiosity, so I asked him various questions. He answered fencingly, and repeatedly looked at his watch in protest. Finally I said:

"Well, Johann, I want to go down this road. I shall not ask you to come unless you like; but tell me why you do not like to go, that is all I ask." For answer he seemed to throw himself off the box, so quickly did he reach the ground. Then he stretched out his hands appealingly to me, and implored me not to go. There was just enough of English mixed with the German for me to understand the drift of his talk. He seemed always just about to tell me something—the very idea of which evidently frightened him; but each time he pulled himself up, saying, as he crossed himself: "Walpurgisnacht!"

I tried to argue with him, but it was difficult to argue with a man when I did not know his language. The advantage certainly rested with him, for although he began to speak in English, of a very crude and broken kind, he always got excited and broke into his native tongue—and every time he did so, he looked at his watch. Then the horses became restless and sniffed the air. At this he grew very pale, and, looking around in a frightened way, he suddenly jumped forward, took them by the bridles and led them on some twenty feet. I followed, and asked why he had done this. For answer he crossed himself, pointed to the spot we had left and drew his carriage in the direction of the other road, indicating a cross, and said, first in German, then in English: "Buried him—him what killed themselves."

1 Yes, sir.

2 The eve of Saint Walpurgis is held on April 30th. Tradition holds that on this night, evil beings can enter the world and attack human beings. Bonfires are used to protect communities from the evil spirts.

I remembered the old custom of burying suicides at cross-roads:[1] "Ah! I see, a suicide. How interesting!" But for the life of me I could not make out why the horses were frightened.

Whilst we were talking, we heard a sort of sound between a yelp and a bark. It was far away; but the horses got very restless, and it took Johann all his time to quiet them. He was pale, and said, "It sounds like a wolf—but yet there are no wolves here now."

"No?" I said, questioning him; "isn't it long since the wolves were so near the city?"

"Long, long," he answered, "in the spring and summer; but with the snow the wolves have been here not so long."

Whilst he was petting the horses and trying to quiet them, dark clouds drifted rapidly across the sky. The sunshine passed away, and a breath of cold wind seemed to drift past us. It was only a breath, however, and more in the nature of a warning than a fact, for the sun came out brightly again. Johann looked under his lifted hand at the horizon and said:

"The storm of snow, he comes before long time." Then he looked at his watch again, and, straightway holding his reins firmly—for the horses were still pawing the ground restlessly and shaking their heads—he climbed to his box as though the time had come for proceeding on our journey.

I felt a little obstinate and did not at once get into the carriage.

"Tell me," I said, "about this place where the road leads," and I pointed down.

Again he crossed himself and mumbled a prayer, before he answered, "It is unholy."

"What is unholy?" I enquired.

"The village."

"Then there is a village?"

"No, no. No one lives there hundreds of years." My curiosity was piqued, "But you said there was a village."

"There was."

"Where is it now?"

Whereupon he burst out into a long story in German and English, so mixed up that I could not quite understand exactly what he said, but roughly I gathered that long ago, hundreds of years, men had died there and been buried in their graves; and sounds were heard under the clay, and when the graves were opened, men and women were found rosy with life, and their mouths red with blood. And so, in haste to save their lives (aye, and their souls!—and here he crossed himself) those who were left fled away to other places, where the living lived, and the dead were dead and not—not something. He was evidently afraid to speak the last words. As he proceeded with his narration, he grew more and

---

1 In folklore, suicides are buried at cross-roads because of their tendency to rise as vampires. The cross-road confused the new vampire, preventing it from attacking its family.

more excited. It seemed as if his imagination had got hold of him, and he ended in a perfect paroxysm of fear—white-faced, perspiring, trembling and looking round him, as if expecting that some dreadful presence would manifest itself there in the bright sunshine on the open plain. Finally, in an agony of desperation, he cried:

"Walpurgisnacht!" and pointed to the carriage for me to get in. All my English blood rose at this, and, standing back, I said:

"You are afraid, Johann—you are afraid. Go home; I shall return alone; the walk will do me good." The carriage door was open. I took from the seat my oak walking-stick—which I always carry on my holiday excursions—and closed the door, pointing back to Munich, and said, "Go home, Johann—Walpurgisnacht doesn't concern Englishmen."

The horses were now more restive than ever, and Johann was trying to hold them in, while excitedly imploring me not to do anything so foolish. I pitied the poor fellow, he was deeply in earnest; but all the same I could not help laughing. His English was quite gone now. In his anxiety he had forgotten that his only means of making me understand was to talk my language, so he jabbered away in his native German. It began to be a little tedious. After giving the direction, "Home!" I turned to go down the cross-road into the valley.

With a despairing gesture, Johann turned his horses towards Munich. I leaned on my stick and looked after him. He went slowly along the road for a while: then there came over the crest of the hill a man tall and thin. I could see so much in the distance. When he drew near the horses, they began to jump and kick about, then to scream with terror. Johann could not hold them in; they bolted down the road, running away madly. I watched them out of sight, then looked for the stranger, but I found that he, too, was gone.

With a light heart I turned down the side road through the deepening valley to which Johann had objected. There was not the slightest reason, that I could see, for his objection; and I daresay I tramped for a couple of hours without thinking of time or distance, and certainly without seeing a person or a house. So far as the place was concerned, it was desolation itself. But I did not notice this particularly till, on turning a bend in the road, I came upon a scattered fringe of wood; then I recognised that I had been impressed unconsciously by the desolation of the region through which I had passed.

I sat down to rest myself, and began to look around. It struck me that it was considerably colder than it had been at the commencement of my walk—a sort of sighing sound seemed to be around me, with, now and then, high overhead, a sort of muffled roar. Looking upwards I noticed that great thick clouds were drifting rapidly across the sky from North to South at a great height. There were signs of coming storm in some lofty stratum of the air. I was a little chilly, and, thinking that it was the sitting still after the exercise of walking, I resumed my journey.

The ground I passed over was now much more picturesque. There were no striking objects that the eye might single out; but in all there was a charm of beauty. I took little heed of time and it was only when the deepening twilight forced itself upon me that I began to think of how I should find my way home. The brightness of the day had gone. The air was cold, and the drifting of clouds high overhead was more marked. They were accompanied by a sort of far-away rushing sound, through which seemed to come at intervals that mysterious cry which the driver had said came from a wolf. For a while I hesitated. I had said I would see the deserted village, so on I went, and presently came on a wide stretch of open country, shut in by hills all around. Their sides were covered with trees which spread down to the plain, dotting, in clumps, the gentler slopes and hollows which showed here and there. I followed with my eye the winding of the road, and saw that it curved close to one of the densest of these clumps and was lost behind it.

As I looked there came a cold shiver in the air, and the snow began to fall. I thought of the miles and miles of bleak country I had passed, and then hurried on to seek the shelter of the wood in front. Darker and darker grew the sky, and faster and heavier fell the snow, till the earth before and around me was a glistening white carpet the further edge of which was lost in misty vagueness. The road was here but crude, and when on the level its boundaries were not so marked, as when it passed through the cuttings; and in a little while I found that I must have strayed from it, for I missed underfoot the hard surface, and my feet sank deeper in the grass and moss. Then the wind grew stronger and blew with ever increasing force, till I was fain to run before it. The air became icy-cold, and in spite of my exercise I began to suffer. The snow was now falling so thickly and whirling around me in such rapid eddies that I could hardly keep my eyes open. Every now and then the heavens were torn asunder by vivid lightning, and in the flashes I could see ahead of me a great mass of trees, chiefly yew and cypress all heavily coated with snow.

I was soon amongst the shelter of the trees, and there, in comparative silence, I could hear the rush of the wind high overhead. Presently the blackness of the storm had become merged in the darkness of the night. By-and-by the storm seemed to be passing away: it now only came in fierce puffs or blasts. At such moments the weird sound of the wolf appeared to be echoed by many similar sounds around me.

Now and again, through the black mass of drifting cloud, came a straggling ray of moonlight, which lit up the expanse, and showed me that I was at the edge of a dense mass of cypress and yew trees. As the snow had ceased to fall, I walked out from the shelter and began to investigate more closely. It appeared to me that, amongst so many old foundations as I had passed, there might be still standing a house in which, though in ruins, I could find some sort of shelter for a while. As I skirted the edge of the copse,[1] I found that a low wall encircled

1 A small group of trees.

it, and following this I presently found an opening. Here the cypresses formed an alley leading up to a square mass of some kind of building. Just as I caught sight of this, however, the drifting clouds obscured the moon, and I passed up the path in darkness. The wind must have grown colder, for I felt myself shiver as I walked; but there was hope of shelter, and I groped my way blindly on.

I stopped, for there was a sudden stillness. The storm had passed; and, perhaps in sympathy with nature's silence, my heart seemed to cease to beat. But this was only momentarily; for suddenly the moonlight broke through the clouds, showing me that I was in a graveyard, and that the square object before me was a great massive tomb of marble, as white as the snow that lay on and all around it. With the moonlight there came a fierce sigh of the storm, which appeared to resume its course with a long, low howl, as of many dogs or wolves. I was awed and shocked, and felt the cold perceptibly grow upon me till it seemed to grip me by the heart. Then while the flood of moonlight still fell on the marble tomb, the storm gave further evidence of renewing, as though it was returning on its track. Impelled by some sort of fascination, I approached the sepulchre[1] to see what it was, and why such a thing stood alone in such a place. I walked around it, and read, over the Doric[2] door, in German:

COUNTESS DOLINGEN OF GRATZ
IN STYRIA[3]
SOUGHT AND FOUND DEATH
1801

On the top of the tomb, seemingly driven through the solid marble—for the structure was composed of a few vast blocks of stone—was a great iron spike or stake. On going to the back I saw, graven in great Russian letters:

"The dead travel fast."

There was something so weird and uncanny about the whole thing that it gave me a turn and made me feel quite faint. I began to wish, for the first time, that I had taken Johann's advice. Here a thought struck me, which came under almost mysterious circumstances and with a terrible shock. This was Walpurgisnight!

Walpurgisnight, when, according to the belief of millions of people, the devil was abroad—when the graves were opened and the dead came forth and

1 Synonym for tomb or vault.

2 The Doric style is one of the three main architectural forms of Ancient Greece and often featured fluted columns.

3 A state in what is today southeast Austria. This is also the setting of Le Fanu's *Carmilla*. Gratz or Graz is the capital city of Styria.

walked. When all evil things of earth and air and water held revel. This very place the driver had specially shunned. This was the depopulated village of centuries ago. This was where the suicide lay; and this was the place where I was alone—unmanned, shivering with cold in a shroud of snow with a wild storm gathering again upon me! It took all my philosophy, all the religion I had been taught, all my courage, not to collapse in a paroxysm of fright.

And now a perfect tornado burst upon me. The ground shook as though thousands of horses thundered across it; and this time the storm bore on its icy wings, not snow, but great hailstones which drove with such violence that they might have come from the thongs of Balearic slingers[1]—hailstones that beat down leaf and branch and made the shelter of the cypresses of no more avail than though their stems were standing-corn. At the first I had rushed to the nearest tree; but I was soon fain to leave it and seek the only spot that seemed to afford refuge, the deep Doric doorway of the marble tomb. There, crouching against the massive bronze door, I gained a certain amount of protection from the beating of the hailstones, for now they only drove against me as they ricocheted from the ground and the side of the marble.

As I leaned against the door, it moved slightly and opened inwards. The shelter of even a tomb was welcome in that pitiless tempest, and I was about to enter it when there came a flash of forked-lightning that lit up the whole expanse of the heavens. In the instant, as I am a living man, I saw, as my eyes were turned into the darkness of the tomb, a beautiful woman, with rounded cheeks and red lips, seemingly sleeping on a bier. As the thunder broke overhead, I was grasped as by the hand of a giant and hurled out into the storm. The whole thing was so sudden that, before I could realise the shock, moral as well as physical, I found the hailstones beating me down. At the same time I had a strange, dominating feeling that I was not alone. I looked towards the tomb. Just then there came another blinding flash, which seemed to strike the iron stake that surmounted the tomb and to pour through to the earth, blasting and crumbling the marble, as in a burst of flame. The dead woman rose for a moment of agony, while she was lapped in the flame, and her bitter scream of pain was drowned in the thundercrash. The last thing I heard was this mingling of dreadful sound, as again I was seized in the giant-grasp and dragged away, while the hailstones beat on me, and the air around seemed reverberant with the howling of wolves. The last sight that I remembered was a vague, white, moving mass, as if all the graves around me had sent out the phantoms of their sheeted-dead, and that they were closing in on me through the white cloudiness of the driving hail.

Gradually there came a sort of vague beginning of consciousness; then a sense of weariness that was dreadful. For a time I remembered nothing; but slowly

1 Ancient peoples particularly noted for their skill with the slingshot. Mentioned in Livy as mercenaries.

my senses returned. My feet seemed positively racked with pain, yet I could not move them. They seemed to be numbed. There was an icy feeling at the back of my neck and all down my spine, and my ears, like my feet, were dead, yet in torment; but there was in my breast a sense of warmth which was, by comparison, delicious. It was as a nightmare—a physical nightmare, if one may use such an expression; for some heavy weight on my chest made it difficult for me to breathe.

This period of semi-lethargy seemed to remain a long time, and as it faded away I must have slept or swooned. Then came a sort of loathing, like the first stage of sea-sickness, and a wild desire to be free from something—I knew not what. A vast stillness enveloped me, as though all the world were asleep or dead—only broken by the low panting as of some animal close to me. I felt a warm rasping at my throat, then came a consciousness of the awful truth, which chilled me to the heart and sent the blood surging up through my brain. Some great animal was lying on me and now licking my throat. I feared to stir, for some instinct of prudence bade me lie still; but the brute seemed to realise that there was now some change in me, for it raised its head. Through my eyelashes I saw above me the two great flaming eyes of a gigantic wolf. Its sharp white teeth gleamed in the gaping red mouth, and I could feel its hot breath fierce and acrid upon me.

For another spell of time I remembered no more. Then I became conscious of a low growl, followed by a yelp, renewed again and again. Then, seemingly very far away, I heard a "Holloa! holloa!" as of many voices calling in unison. Cautiously I raised my head and looked in the direction whence the sound came; but the cemetery blocked my view. The wolf still continued to yelp in a strange way, and a red glare began to move round the grove of cypresses, as though following the sound. As the voices drew closer, the wolf yelped faster and louder. I feared to make either sound or motion. Nearer came the red glow, over the white pall which stretched into the darkness around me. Then all at once from beyond the trees there came at a trot a troop of horsemen bearing torches. The wolf rose from my breast and made for the cemetery. I saw one of the horsemen (soldiers by their caps and their long military cloaks) raise his carbine and take aim. A companion knocked up his arm, and I heard the ball whizz over my head. He had evidently taken my body for that of the wolf. Another sighted the animal as it slunk away, and a shot followed. Then, at a gallop, the troop rode forward—some towards me, others following the wolf as it disappeared amongst the snow-clad cypresses.

As they drew nearer I tried to move, but was powerless, although I could see and hear all that went on around me. Two or three of the soldiers jumped from their horses and knelt beside me. One of them raised my head, and placed his hand over my heart.

"Good news, comrades!" he cried. "His heart still beats!"

Then some brandy was poured down my throat; it put vigour into me, and I was able to open my eyes fully and look around. Lights and shadows were moving among the trees, and I heard men call to one another. They drew together, uttering frightened exclamations; and the lights flashed as the others came pouring out of the cemetery pell-mell, like men possessed. When the further ones came close to us, those who were around me asked them eagerly:

"Well, have you found him?"

The reply rang out hurriedly:

"No! no! Come away quick—quick! This is no place to stay, and on this of all nights!"

"What was it?" was the question, asked in all manner of keys. The answer came variously and all indefinitely as though the men were moved by some common impulse to speak, yet were restrained by some common fear from giving their thoughts.

"It—it—indeed!" gibbered one, whose wits had plainly given out for the moment.

"A wolf—and yet not a wolf!" another put in shudderingly.

"No use trying for him without the sacred bullet," a third remarked in a more ordinary manner.

"Serve us right for coming out on this night! Truly we have earned our thousand marks!" were the ejaculations of a fourth.

"There was blood on the broken marble," another said after a pause—"the lightning never brought that there. And for him—is he safe? Look at his throat! See, comrades, the wolf has been lying on him and keeping his blood warm."

The officer looked at my throat and replied:

"He is all right; the skin is not pierced. What does it all mean? We should never have found him but for the yelping of the wolf."

"What became of it?" asked the man who was holding up my head, and who seemed the least panic-stricken of the party, for his hands were steady and without tremor. On his sleeve was the chevron of a petty officer.

"It went to its home," answered the man, whose long face was pallid, and who actually shook with terror as he glanced around him fearfully. "There are graves enough there in which it may lie. Come, comrades—come quickly! Let us leave this cursed spot."

The officer raised me to a sitting posture, as he uttered a word of command; then several men placed me upon a horse. He sprang to the saddle behind me, took me in his arms, gave the word to advance; and, turning our faces away from the cypresses, we rode away in swift, military order.

As yet my tongue refused its office, and I was perforce silent. I must have fallen asleep; for the next thing I remembered was finding myself standing up, supported by a soldier on each side of me. It was almost broad daylight, and to the north a red streak of sunlight was reflected, like a path of blood, over the waste of snow. The officer was telling the men to say nothing of what they had seen, except that they found an English stranger, guarded by a large dog.

"Dog! that was no dog," cut in the man who had exhibited such fear. "I think I know a wolf when I see one."

The young officer answered calmly: "I said a dog."

"Dog!" reiterated the other ironically. It was evident that his courage was rising with the sun; and, pointing to me, he said, "Look at his throat. Is that the work of a dog, master?"

Instinctively I raised my hand to my throat, and as I touched it I cried out in pain. The men crowded round to look, some stooping down from their saddles; and again there came the calm voice of the young officer:

"A dog, as I said. If aught else were said we should only be laughed at."

I was then mounted behind a trooper, and we rode on into the suburbs of Munich. Here we came across a stray carriage, into which I was lifted, and it was driven off to the Quatre Saisons—the young officer accompanying me, whilst a trooper followed with his horse, and the others rode off to their barracks.

When we arrived, Herr Delbrück rushed so quickly down the steps to meet me, that it was apparent he had been watching within. Taking me by both hands he solicitously led me in. The officer saluted me and was turning to withdraw, when I recognised his purpose, and insisted that he should come to my rooms. Over a glass of wine I warmly thanked him and his brave comrades for saving me. He replied simply that he was more than glad, and that Herr Delbrück had at the first taken steps to make all the searching party pleased; at which ambiguous utterance the maître d'hôtel smiled, while the officer pleaded duty and withdrew.

"But Herr Delbrück," I enquired, "how and why was it that the soldiers searched for me?"

He shrugged his shoulders, as if in depreciation of his own deed, as he replied:

"I was so fortunate as to obtain leave from the commander of the regiment in which I served, to ask for volunteers."

"But how did you know I was lost?" I asked.

"The driver came hither with the remains of his carriage, which had been upset when the horses ran away."

"But surely you would not send a search-party of soldiers merely on this account?"

"Oh, no!" he answered; "but even before the coachman arrived, I had this telegram from the Boyar[1] whose guest you are," and he took from his pocket a telegram which he handed to me, and I read:

1 Term for an aristocrat of feudal Eastern Europe and the Baltic, including Bulgaria, Russia, Serbia, Wallachia, Moldovia, and Romania.

> BISTRITZ.[1]
> Be careful of my guest—his safety is most precious to me. Should aught happen to him, or if he be missed, spare nothing to find him and ensure his safety. He is English and therefore adventurous. There are often dangers from snow and wolves and night. Lose not a moment if you suspect harm to him. I answer your zeal with my fortune.—*Dracula.*

As I held the telegram in my hand, the room seemed to whirl around me; and, if the attentive maître d'hôtel had not caught me, I think I should have fallen. There was something so strange in all this, something so weird and impossible to imagine, that there grew on me a sense of my being in some way the sport of opposite forces—the mere vague idea of which seemed in a way to paralyse me. I was certainly under some form of mysterious protection. From a distant country had come, in the very nick of time, a message that took me out of the danger of the snow-sleep and the jaws of the wolf.

1 Also called Bistrița. This is a capital city in Transylvania where Jonathan Harker stops on his journey in Stoker's *Dracula.*

# Henrik Galeen

(1881–1949)

Henrik Galeen was born in the Austrio-Hungarian Empire. He moved to Germany prior to World War I, and became an assistant to the esteemed theater director Max Reinhardt, a leader of the Expressionist movement. In 1922, he wrote the screenplay for *Nosferatu*, working with the filmmaker Friedrich Wilhelm Murnau. The film is a loose adaptation of Bram Stoker's *Dracula*, which was incorrectly believed to be in copyright so the title was changed to *Nosferatu*. Central to the adaptation was the change in the appearance of the vampire figure, namely the bat-like look of Count Orlock. The release of the film was mired in controversy, as Stoker's widow, Florence Balcombe Stoker, filed a lawsuit claiming that the film was based on *Dracula* without permission of the estate. The case was settled in 1925. Despite the legal entanglement, the film is considered to be a masterpiece of German Expressionist Cinema (see Illustrations, p. 519).

## *Nosferatu*[1]

(1922)

Cast:

Count Orlock, the vampire .................. Max Schreck
Renfield, an estate agent ..................... Alexander Grannach
Jonathon Harker, Renfield's clerk ............ Gustav von Wangenheim
Nina, his wife .............................. Greta Schroeder
Westenra, Harker's friend.................... G.H. Schell
Lucy, his wife .............................. Ruth Landshoff
The Professor .............................. John Gottowt
The Town Doctor............................ Gustav Botz
Captain of the "Demeter".................... Max Nemetz
First Mate ................................ Wolfgang Heinz

1 This screenplay was originally transcribed by B.J. Kuehl.

> "From the diary of Johann Cavallius, able historian of his native city of Bremen: Nosferatu! That name alone can chill the blood! Nosferatu! Was it he who brought the plague to Bremen in 1838? I have long sought the causes of that terrible epidemic, and found at its origin and its climax the innocent figures of Jonathon Harker and his young wife Nina."

BREMEN[1]
1838
MORNING

*Scene:* At the Home of Jonathon and Nina Harker

*Harker leaves for work.*

HARKER: (*presents Nina with a bouquet of flowers*)

*In the streets of Bremen, Harker walks to work.*
*An old man approaches:*

OLD MAN: Wait, young man. You can't escape destiny by running away.
HARKER: (*shakes the old man's hand and continues walking*)

*Scene:* At the Estate Office of Agent Renfield

*Renfield reads a letter.*
*The agent Renfield was a strange man, and there were unpleasant rumors about him.*
*Enter Harker.*

RENFIELD: Here is an important letter from Transylvania. Count Orlock wishes to buy a house in our city. It's a good opportunity for you, Harker. The Count is rich, and free with his money. You will have a marvelous journey. And, young as you are, what matter if it costs you some pain—or even a little blood? The house facing yours ... that should suit him. Leave at once, my young friend. And don't be frightened if people speak of Transylvania as the land of phantoms.

*Scene:* At the Home of the Harkers

1 Bremen is a city in northern Germany.

HARKER: I may be away for several months, Nina. Renfield is sending me to some lost corner of the Carpathians.
NINA: (*looks worried*)

*Harker left Nina with his good friends, Westenra and his wife Lucy.*

*Scene:* Outside the Westenras' House

*Nina runs to say goodbye to Harker.*

HARKER: Don't worry, Nina, nothing can happen to me.

*Harker mounts a horse and rides away.*

**********************

TRANSYLVANIA
*From relay to relay, through the dust raised by the stages, Harker hurried on.*

*A coach speeds along rugged countryside.*

EVENING

*Scene:* A Village Inn

*Harker disembarks from the coach and enters the Inn.*

HARKER: Dinner, quickly! I should already be at Count Orlock's castle!

*The inn patrons look away in worry.*

INNKEEPER: You must not leave now! The evil spirits become all-powerful after dark!
HARKER: (*chuckles to himself*)

*Scene:* In a room at the Inn

*Harker undresses for bed. He reads from a book left on the bedtable.*

"THE BOOK OF THE VAMPIRES
...and it was in 1443 that the first Nosferatu was born.

> That name rings like the cry of a bird of prey. Never speak it aloud... Men do not always recognize the dangers that beasts can sense at certain times."

HARKER: (*laughs and goes to bed*)

*Outside the window, a hyena prowls. Village horses scatter in fear. Village women cower in terror.*

MORNING

*Scene:* Outside the Inn

*A coach departs.*

LATE AFTERNOON

*Scene:* In the Carpathian Mountains

*The coach speeds along mountain roads.*

PASSENGER: Hurry! The sun will soon be setting.

AT DUSK THAT EVENING

*Scene:* At a crossroads

*The coach stops and Harker disembarks.*

DRIVER: We will go no further, sir. Not for a fortune! We will go no further. Here begins the land of the phantoms.

*The driver throws down Harker's luggage.*

HARKER: (*Walks away, crossing over a bridge*)

"And when he had crossed the bridge, the phantoms came to meet him."

*Harker is met by a coach which carries him to Castle Dracula.*

*Scene:* At the Castle

*Harker is greeted by the Nosferatu Count.*

NOSFERATU: You are late, young man. It is almost midnight. My servants have all retired.

*He leads Harker to sup at a dining table.*

HARKER: (*cuts finger on a bread knife*)
NOSFERATU: Blood! Your precious blood!

*Harker warily backs away.*

NOSFERATU: Let us chat together a moment, my friend. There are still several hours until dawn, and I have the whole day to sleep.

*He leads Harker to a chair by a fireplace.*

DAWN

"As the sun rose, Harker felt himself freed from the oppressions of the night."

*Harker awakens. He notes two marks on his neck.*

LATER THAT MORNING

*Harker walks in the countryside around the Castle.*
*He finds a gazebo and writes there a letter to Nina.*

"Nina, my beloved—
Don't be unhappy. Though I am far away, I love you. This is a strange country. After my first night in the castle, I found two large bites on my neck. From mosquitoes? From spiders? I don't know. I have had some frightful dreams, but they were only dreams. You mustn't worry about me. I am leaving immediately to return to Bremen—and to you."

*Harker stops a traveler and gives him the letter to post.*

EVENING

*As twilight came on, the empty castle became alive with menacing shadows.*

*Scene:* In the parlour at Castle Dracula

*Harker and the Nosferatu review legal papers.*
*The Count sees Harker's picture of Nina.*

NOSFERATU: Is this your wife? What a lovely throat! That old mansion seems quite satisfactory. We shall be neighbors.

*Count signs the documents.*

THAT NIGHT

*Scene:* In Harker's Bedroom

*Harker packs away Nina's picture.*
*He finds* The Book of the Vampires *and reads more:*

> "Nosferatu drinks the blood of the young, the blood necessary to his own existence. One can recognize the mark of the vampire by the trace of his fangs on the victim's throat."

HARKER: (*peeks out his bedroom door*)
COUNT: (*stands motionlessly at the end of the hall*)
HARKER: (*quickly closes his bedroom door, looks out the window at the river far below, and climbs into his bed*)

*Enter the Count.*

"That same night in Bremen, in a somnabulistic dream..."

*Scene:* At the home of the Westenras

NINA: (*awakens in a trance and walks out to the terrace*)

*Westenra follows.*

WESTENRA: Nina?

*Nina collapses in Westenra's arms.*
*Enter servant.*

WESTENRA: The doctor, quickly!

LATER THAT NIGHT

*Scene:* In Harker's Bedroom in Castle Dracula

*The Count advances on Harker as he lies asleep.*

MEANWHILE

*Scene:* In Nina's Bedroom in Bremen

*The doctor, Westenra and Lucy stand over Nina as she sleeps.*

NINA: (*suddenly sitting up*) Jonathon! Jonathon! Hear me!

MOMENTS LATER

*Scene:* In Harker's Bedroom in Castle Dracula

*The Count turns from Harker's sleeping body.*
*Exit the Count.*

MEANWHILE

*Scene:* In Nina's Bedroom in Bremen

NINA: (*sighs relief and returns to sleep*)
DOCTOR: A sudden fever.

> "The doctor laid Nina's trance to some unknown disease. Since then I have learned that she had sensed the menace of Nosferatu that very night. And Harker, far away, had heard her cries of warning."

THE NEXT MORNING

*Scene:* In Harker's Bedroom at Castle Dracula

*Harker awakens.*
*He rushes from his bedroom out into the courtyard and wanders into a crypt.*
*He finds the Count lying in a coffin.*

*Exit Harker, horrified.*

EARLY THAT EVENING

*Harker looks out his bedroom window.*
*He sees the Count loading coffins on a horse-drawn cart.*

COUNT: (*climbs into a coffin and closes the lid*)

*Exit horses, cart, coffins and Count.*

HARKER: (*Makes a rope from a bedsheet and climbs out window*)

*Harker falls to the ground below and is knocked unconscious.*

THE NEXT DAY

*Scene:* A cargo-bearing raft floats down a river.

"The men little suspected what terrible cargo they were carrying down the valley."

SEVERAL DAYS LATER

*Scene:* In a hospital room somewhere in Transylvania

*A nurse and doctor tend to Harker at his bedside.*

NURSE: Some peasants brought him here last evening. He still has a high fever.
HARKER: (*leaps up suddenly*) Coffins! Coffins filled with earth!

*Scene:* In a shipyard

*Sailors load crates onto a ship.*
*Tipping over one crate, they find only dirt and rats.*

*Nosferatu was en route; and with him disaster approached Bremen. At the same time, Dr. Van Helsing was giving a course on the secrets of nature and their strange correspondences to human life. The professor told his students about the existence of a carnivorous plant.*

************************

## BREMEN

*Scene:* Professor Van Helsing's Laboratory

*Van Helsing and four colleagues watch as a Venus flytrap traps a fly.*

VAN HELSING: Astonishing, isn't it, gentlemen? That plant is the vampire of the vegetable kingdom.

*Scene:* At the Sanitarium

"Nosferatu held Renfield under his influence from afar."

*An attendant enters the doctor's quarters.*

ATTENDANT: That patient who was brought in yesterday has gone out of his mind!

*Scene:* In Renfield's cell at the Sanitarium

*Enter Doctor and Attendant.*

RENFIELD: (*catches and eats flies*) Blood! Blood!

*Renfield leaps at Doctor.*
*Attendant subdues Renfield.*

*Scene:* In Van Helsing's Laboratory

*Van Helsing and colleagues peer into a tank.*

VAN HELSING: And now, gentlemen, here is another type of vampire: a polyp with claws... transparent, without substance, almost a phantom.

*Scene:* On the dunes overlooking the sea

"Nina was often seen alone among the dunes, watching and waiting for her husband's return."

*Nina sits on a bench looking out to sea.*
*Lucy and Westenra bring Nina the letter from Harker.*

MEANWHILE

*Scene:* In Harker's Hospital Room Somewhere in Transylvania

*Harker dresses for his journey back to Bremen.*

AT THE SAME TIME

*Scene:* In Renfield's Cell at the Sanitarium in Bremen

*Renfield unfolds a newspaper clipping and reads it.*

"NEW PLAGUE BAFFLES SCIENCE
A mysterious epidemic of the plague has broken out in eastern Europe in the port cities of the Black Sea, attacking principally the young and vigourous. Cause of the two bloody marks on the neck of each victim baffles the medical profession."

RENFIELD: (*laughs*)

*Scene:* In the hold of the *Demete*r

"Aboard the *Demeter*, first one man was stricken, then all."

*Captain tends to a sick sailor.*
*The Count appears briefly then fades.*

*Scene:* On the deck of the *Demeter*

*One evening at sundown, the captain and his first mate buried the last man of the crew.*

*Captain and first mate toss a body overboard.*

FIRST MATE: I am going below. I want to have a look in the hold.

*Scene:* In the hold of the *Demeter*

*First mate sees the Nosferatu rise from his coffin.*

FIRST MATE: (*rushes topside and leaps overboard*)

CAPTAIN: (*ties himself to the steering wheel*)

*The Nosferatu approaches the Captain.*

*Despite all sorts of obstacles, Harker pushed on towards Bremen. Meanwhile, driven by the fatal breath of the vampire, the vessel moved rapidly towards the Baltic.*

ONE NIGHT

*Scene:* At the Westenras' House

*Nina sleepwalks to the terrace.*
*Lucy follows Nina.*

NINA: He's coming. I must go to meet him.

"In the Bremen Harbour the *Demeter* sails into port."

*Scene:* In Renfield's Cell at the Sanitarium

*Renfield attempts to climb out his window.*

RENFIELD: The Master is coming! The Master is here!

*Renfield escapes.*

"I have long tried to understand why Nosferatu travelled with the earth-filled coffins. Recently I discovered that to preserve their diabolic power, vampires must sleep during the day in the same unhallowed ground in which they had been buried. The Count carries his coffin from the harbour to his newly-purchased house in Bremen."

MEANWHILE

*Scene:* At the Westenras' House

*Harker returns and is met by Nina.*

NINA: Jonathon! Thank God you are safe! Now I feel that I too have been saved!

THE NEXT MORNING

*Scene:* In the Bremen Harbour

*Officials search the Demeter.*
*The captain is found dead at the wheel.*

OFFICIAL: We couldn't find a single living soul on board!

*A second official discovers the Ship's Log.*

Ship's Log—Varna[1] to Bremen
24 April 1838
Passed the Dardanelles[2]—East wind—Carrying 5 passengers, mate, crew of 7, and myself, the Captain.
6 May 1838
Rounded Cape of Inatagran—One of my men, the strongest, is sick—Crew is restless, uneasy.
7 May 1838
Mate reported stowaway hiding below decks—Will investigate.
18 May 1838
Passed Gibraltar[3]—Panic on board—Three men dead already—Mate out of his mind—Rats in the hold—I fear the plague.

BURGOMASTER: The plague is here! Stay in your houses!

HOURS LATER

*Scene:* In the deserted streets of Bremen

*Towncrier reads a notice.*

"~ ~ ~ ~ ~ NOTICE ~ ~ ~ ~ ~ ~
To halt the spread of the plague, the Burgomaster of Bremen forbids the citizens of this city to bring their sick to the hospitals until further notice."

1 Varna is a port city in Bulgaria on the Black Sea.
2 Also known as the Strait of Gallipoli, a narrow body of water that forms the boundary between Europe and Asia.
3 The Rock of Gibraltar guards the entrance to the Mediterranean.

"Nina had promised her husband never to open *The Book of the Vampires*, but she found herself unable to resist the temptation."

*Scene:* In the living room of the Harkers

*Nina reads from* The Book of the Vampires.

"One can recognize the mark of the vampire by the trace of his fangs on the victim's throat. Only a woman can break his frightful spell—a woman pure in heart—who will offer her blood freely to Nosferatu and will keep the vampire by her side until after the cock has crowed."

*Enter Harker.*

NINA: (*pointing out the window to the mansion across the street*) Look! Every night, in front of me!

*The townspeople lived in mortal terror. Who was sick or dying? Who will be stricken tomorrow?*

*Scene:* At the Harkers' House

*Nina lies sick in bed.*

HARKER: Don't be frightened. I will get the professor.

*Exit Harker.*
*Nina looks out the window at the line of coffins being carried along the street. She reads from* The Book of the Vampires.

"Only a woman can break his frightful spell—a woman pure in heart—who will offer her blood freely to Nosferatu and will keep the vampire by her side until after the cock has crowed."

MEANWHILE

*Scene:* Outside the Sanitarium

*Two old women talk to each other.*

OLD WOMAN: They saw him escape. He strangled his keeper.

*Renfield runs down an alley, pursued by a crowd. He climbs onto a roof. The crowd throws rocks at him. He climbs down and runs outside of town. The crowd pursues.*

THAT NIGHT

*Scene:* In the Harkers' Bedroom

*Nina is awakened by the Nosferatu outside her window. She opens the window. Harker awakens and Nina faints in his arms.*

HARKER: The professor! Call the professor!

*Exit Harker.*
*Enter the Nosferatu.*

THE NEXT MORNING

*Scene:* In the Harkers' Bedroom

*The cock crows. The Nosferatu looks up from drinking at Nina's neck.*

MEANWHILE

*Scene:* In Renfield's Cell at the Sanitarium

RENFIELD: Master! Master! Beware!

*Scene:* Outside the Harkers' House.

*Harker and Van Helsing arrive.*

*Scene:* In the Harkers' Bedroom

*Sunlight sweeps across the buildings across the street from Nina's window. Nosferatu attempts to escape but is touched by the sunlight. He vanishes in a puff of smoke.*

*Scene:* In Renfield's Cell at the Sanitarium

RENFIELD: The Master is dead.

*Scene:* In the Harkers' Bedroom

*Nina awakens.*
*Enter Harker.*

NINA: Jonathon!

*Harker takes Nina in his arms as she dies.*

"And at that moment, as if by a miracle, the sick no longer died, and the stifling shadow of the vampire vanished with the morning sun."

THE END

## Richard Matheson

(1926–2013)

Richard Matheson defined an era with his screenwriting for the iconic *Twilight Zone* series in the 1950s and 1960s. He also wrote short stories and novels, and adapted many of his works for film. Matheson remains highly regarded in the genres of horror, fantasy, and science fiction, and was influential in the popularization of vampire fiction in the twentieth century. Like his anti-protagonist Jules in "Drink My Blood," who reads Bram Stoker's *Dracula* as a child, Matheson read the novel as a young man during army training. Stoker's novel left an indelible mark on Matheson's imagination. His masterful vampire dystopian novel *I Am Legend,* with its remarkably innovative approach to the vampire fiction genre, demonstrates Stoker's influence on his writing. Matheson has had a profound influence on later writers, including Ray Bradbury and Anne Rice, and on filmmaker Steven Spielberg. Stephen King has said that Matheson is "the author who influenced me most as a writer." Matheson is the recipient of numerous prestigious awards including the 2011 Bram Stoker Award and the 2012 Horror Writers Association Award; the Association named *I Am Legend* the vampire novel of the twentieth century.

# "Drink My Blood"

(1951)

The people on the block decided definitely that Jules was crazy when they heard about his composition.

There had been suspicions for a long time.

He made people shiver with his blank stare. His coarse guttural tongue sounded unnatural in his frail body. The paleness of his skin upset many children. It seemed to hang loose around his flesh. He hated sunlight.

And his ideas were a little out of place for the people who lived on the block.

Jules wanted to be a vampire.

People declared it common knowledge that he was born on a night when winds uprooted trees. They said he was born with three teeth. They said he'd used them to fasten himself on his mother's breast, drawing blood with the milk.

They said he used to cackle and bark in his crib after dark. They said he walked at two months and sat staring at the moon whenever it shone.

Those were things that people said.

His parents were always worried about him. An only child, they noticed his flaws quickly.

They thought he was blind until the doctor told them it was just a vacuous stare. He told them that Jules, with his large head, might be a genius or an idiot. It turned out he was an idiot.

He never spoke a word until he was five. Then one night coming up to supper, he sat down at the table and said, "Death."

His parents were torn between delight and disgust. They finally settled for a place in between the two feelings. They decided that Jules couldn't have realized what the word meant.

But Jules did.

From that night on, he built up such a large vocabulary that everyone who knew him was astonished. He not only acquired every word spoken to him, words from signs, magazines, books; he made up his own words.

Like nighttouch. Or killove. They were really several words that melted into each other. They said things Jules felt but couldn't explain with other words.

He used to sit on the porch while the other children played hopscotch, stickball and other games. He sat there and stared at the sidewalk and made up words.

Until he was twelve Jules kept pretty much out of trouble. Of course, there was the time they found him undressing Olive Jones in an alley. And another time he was discovered dissecting a kitten on his bed.

But there were many years in between. Those scandals were forgotten.

In general he went through childhood merely disgusting people.

He went to school but never studied. He spent about two or three terms in each grade. The teachers all knew him by his first name. In some subjects, like reading and writing, he was almost brilliant.

In others he was hopeless.

One Saturday when he was twelve, Jules went to the movies. He saw *Dracula*.

When the show was over he walked, a throbbing nerve mass, through the little-girl and -boy ranks.

He went home and locked himself in the bathroom for two hours.

His parents pounded on the door and threatened but he wouldn't come out.

Finally he unlocked the door and sat down at the supper table. He had a bandage on his thumb and a satisfied look on his face.

The morning after he went to the library. It was Sunday. He sat on the steps all day, waiting for it to open. Finally he went home.

The next morning he came back instead of going to school.

He found *Dracula* on the shelves. He couldn't borrow it because he wasn't a member and to be a member he had to bring in one of his parents.

So he stuck the book down his pants and left the library and never brought it back.

He went to the park and sat down and read the book through. It was late evening before he finished.

He started at the beginning again, reading as he ran from streetlight to streetlight, all the way home.

He didn't hear a word of the scolding he got for missing lunch and supper. He ate, went in his room and read the book to the finish. They asked him where he got the book. He said he found it.

As the days passed Jules read the story over and over. He never went to school.

Late at night, when he had fallen into an exhausted slumber, his mother used to take the book into the living room and show it to her husband.

One night they noticed that Jules had underlined certain sentences with dark shaky pencil lines.

Like: "The lips were crimson with fresh blood and the stream had trickled over her chin and stained the purity of her lawn death robe."

Or: "When the blood began to spurt out, he took my hands in one of his, holding them tight and, with the other seized my neck and pressed my mouth to the wound...."[1]

When his mother saw this, she threw the book down the garbage chute.

The next morning when Jules found the book missing he screamed and twisted his mother's arm until she told him where the book was.

Then he ran down to the cellar and dug in the piles of garbage until he found the book.

Coffee grounds and egg yolk on his hands and wrists, he went to the park and read it again.

For a month he read the book avidly. Then he knew it so well he threw it away and just thought about it.

Absence notes were coming from school. His mother yelled. Jules decided to go back for a while.

He wanted to write a composition.

One day he wrote it in class. When everyone was finished writing, the teacher asked if anyone wanted to read their compositions to the class.

Jules raised his hand.

The teacher was surprised. But she felt charity. She wanted to encourage him. She drew in her tiny jab of a chin and smiled.

---

1 The first quote describes the newly arisen vampire Lucy whom Dracula has turned into a vampire and who has been biting a child. The second quote is when Dracula forces Mina to drink his blood. Dracula's relationship with both women is described in language that suggests rape.

"All right," she said, "pay attention, children. Jules is going to read us his composition."

Jules stood up. He was excited. The paper shook in his hands.

"My Ambition by…"

"Come to the front of the class, Jules, dear."

Jules went to the front of the class. The teacher smiled lovingly. Jules started again.

"My Ambition by Jules Dracula."

The smile sagged.

"When I grow up I want to be a vampire."

The teacher's smiling lips jerked down and out. Her eyes popped wide.

"I want to live forever and get even with everybody and make all the girls vampires. I want to smell of death."

"Jules!"

"I want to have foul breath that stinks of dead earth and crypts and sweet coffins."

The teacher shuddered. Her hands twitched on her green blotter. She couldn't believe her ears. She looked at the children. They were gaping. Some of them were giggling. But not the girls.

"I want to be all cold and have rotten flesh with stolen blood in the veins."

"That will…hrrumph!"

The teacher cleared her throat mightily.

"That will be all, Jules," she said.

Jules talked louder and desperately.

"I want to sink my terrible white teeth in my victim's necks. I want them to…"

"Jules! Go to your seat this instant!"

"I want them to slide like razors in the flesh and into the veins," read Jules ferociously.

The teacher jolted to her feet. Children were shivering. None of them were giggling.

"Then I want to draw my teeth out and let the blood flow easy in my mouth and run hot in my throat and…"

The teacher grabbed his arm. Jules tore away and ran to a corner. Barricaded behind a stool he yelled:

"And drip off my tongue and run out of my lips down my victims' throats! I want to drink girls' blood!"

The teacher lunged for him. She dragged him out of the corner. He clawed at her and screamed all the way to the door and the principal's office.

"That is my ambition! That is my ambition! That is my ambition!"

It was grim.

Jules was locked in his room. The teacher and the principal sat with Jules' parents. They were talking in sepulchral voices.

They were recounting the scene.

All along the block parents were discussing it. Most of them didn't believe it at first. They thought their children made it up.

Then they thought what horrible children they'd raised if the children could make up such things.

So they believed it.

After that everyone watched Jules like a hawk. People avoided his touch and look. Parents pulled their children off the street when he approached. Everyone whispered tales of him.

There were more absence notes.

Jules told his mother he wasn't going to school any more. Nothing would change his mind. He never went again.

When a truant officer came to the apartment Jules would run over the roofs until he was far away from there.

A year wasted by.

Jules wandered the streets searching for something; he didn't know what. He looked in alleys. He looked in garbage cans. He looked in lots. He looked on the east side and the west side and in the middle.

He couldn't find what he wanted.

He rarely slept. He never spoke. He stared down all the time. He forgot his special words.

Then.

One day in the park, Jules strolled through the zoo.

An electric shock passed through him when he saw the vampire bat.

His eyes grew wide and his discolored teeth shone dully in a wide smile.

From that day on, Jules went daily to the zoo and looked at the bat. He spoke to it and called it the Count. He felt in his heart it was really a man who had changed.

A rebirth of culture struck him.

He stole another book from the library. It told all about wildlife.

He found a page on the vampire bat. He tore it out and threw the book away.

He learned the section by heart.

He knew how the bat made its wound. How it lapped up the blood like a kitten drinking cream. How it walked on folded wing stalks and hind legs like a black furry spider. Why it took no nourishment but blood.

Month after month Jules stared at the bat and talked to it. It became the one comfort in his life. The one symbol of dreams come true.

One day Jules noticed that the bottom of the wire covering the cage had come loose.

He looked around, his black eyes shifting. He didn't see anyone looking. It was a cloudy day. Not many people were there.

Jules tugged at the wire.

It moved a little.

Then he saw a man come out of the monkey house. So he pulled back his hand and strolled away, whistling a song he had just made up.

Late at night, when he was supposed to be asleep, he would walk barefoot past his parents' room. He would hear his father and mother snoring. He would hurry out, put on his shoes and run to the zoo.

Every time the watchman was not around, Jules would tug at the wiring.

He kept on pulling it loose.

When he had finished and had to run home, he pushed the wire in again. Then no one could tell.

All day Jules would stand in front of the cage and look at the Count and chuckle and tell him he'd soon be free again.

He told the Count all the things he knew. He told the Count he was going to practice climbing down walls head first.

He told the Count not to worry. He'd soon be out. Then, together, they could go all around and drink girls' blood.

One night Jules pulled the wire out and crawled under it into the cage.

It was very dark.

He crept on his knees to the little wooden house. He listened to see if he could hear the Count squeaking.

He stuck his arm in the black doorway. He kept whispering.

He jumped when he felt a needle jab in his finger.

With a look of great pleasure on his thin face, Jules drew the fluttering hairy bat to him.

He climbed down from the cage with it and ran out of the zoo; out of the park. He ran down the silent streets.

It was getting late in the morning. Light touched the dark skies with gray. He couldn't go home. He had to have a place.

He went down an alley and climbed over a fence. He held tight to the bat. It lapped at the dribble of blood from his finger.

He went across a yard and into a little deserted shack.

It was dark inside and damp. It was full of rubble and tin cans and soggy cardboard and excrement.

Jules made sure there was no way the bat could escape.

Then he pulled the door tight and put a stick through the metal loop.

He felt his heart beating hard and his limbs trembling.

He let go of the bat. It flew to a dark corner and hung on the wood.

Jules feverishly tore off his shirt. His lips shook. He smiled a crazy smile.

He reached down into his pants pocket and took out a little pen knife he had stolen from his mother.

He opened it and ran a finger over the blade. It sliced through the flesh.

With shaking fingers he jabbed at his throat. He hacked. The blood ran through his fingers.

"Count! Count!" he cried in frenzied joy. "Drink my red blood! Drink me! Drink me!"

He stumbled over the tin cans and slipped and felt for the bat. It sprang from the wood and soared across the shack and fastened itself on the outer side.

Tears ran down Jules' cheeks.

He gritted his teeth. The blood ran across his shoulders and across his thin hairless chest.

His body shook in fever. He staggered back toward the other side. He tripped and felt his side torn open on the sharp edge of a tin can.

His hands went out. They clutched the bat. He sighed.

He started to moan and clutch at his chest. His stomach heaved. The black bat on his neck silently lapped his blood.

Jules felt his life seeping away.

He thought of all the years past. The waiting. His parents. School. Dracula. Dreams. For this. This sudden glory.

Jules' eyes flickered open.

The side of the reeking shack swam about him.

It was hard to breathe. He opened his mouth to gasp in the air. He sucked it in. It was foul. It made him cough. His skinny body lurched on the cold ground.

Mists crept away in his brain.

One by one like drawn veils.

Suddenly his mind was filled with terrible clarity.

He knew he was lying half-naked on garbage and letting a flying bat drink his blood.

With a strangled cry, he reached up and tore away the furry throbbing bat. He flung it away from him. It came back, fanning his face with its vibrating wings.

Jules staggered to his feet.

He felt for the door. He could hardly see. He tried to stop his throat from bleeding so.

He managed to get the door open.

Then, lurching into the dark yard, he fell on his face in the long grass blades.

He tried to call out for help.

But no sounds, save a bubbling mockery of words, came from his lips.

He heard the fluttering wings.

Then, suddenly, they were gone.

Strong fingers lifted him gently. Through dying eyes Jules saw the tall dark man whose eyes shone like rubies.

"My son," the man said.

# VAMPIRES AND IMMORTALITY

Elizabeth Grey, "The Skeleton Count; or, The Vampire Mistress" (1828)

Mary Elizabeth Braddon, "The Good Lady Ducayne" (1896)

Arabella Kenealy, "A Beautiful Vampire" (1896)

Philip K. Dick, "The Cookie Lady" (1953)

What makes vampires so very alluring? Is it their supernatural power, their social position, or their eternal youth? Many vampires throughout literary and cinematic history have embodied cultural fears of aging and death. The iconic 1983 film *The Hunger* vividly depicts this fear of mortality. Much of the film's tension revolves around Miriam's failure to keep her lovers young. Miriam can give them eternal life but eventually they all succumb to a horrifyingly rapid aging process. As this film shows, the fantasy of defying the ravages of time has become one of the most enduring aspects of the vampire in popular culture and in literature.

The appeal of vampire literature is inherently tied to time. Seeing the past through the vampire's eyes, a reader can experience a kind of time travel, and the fantasy of becoming a vampire promises the opportunity to live to see future centuries. Death is defeated by the vampire, at least temporarily. In fact, extended lives become an important feature in many of the literary vampires who follow Polidori—the stories of Varney, Carmilla, and Dracula all give the reader glimpses of the past. This feature of vampire literature has grown as the genre has evolved. In some more contemporary texts, sympathetic vampires learn and grow over their long lives, but in many, the vampires seem stuck in a kind of perpetual arrested development. Longevity is more curse than blessing. These tales help us work through our questions about life and death.

A key aspect of vampire immortality is cheating death; a vampire can continue to enjoy physical life long after their natural death. We open this chapter with Elizabeth Grey's "The Skeleton Count," where the villain not only cheats death but also resurrects the object of his lust. The beautiful vampire he creates has no memory of her past existence, and, driven by instinct, she returns home to her village to prey on her former friends and neighbors. Fear of the return of the dead is a central concern of the human condition, but indefinitely prolonging life also leads to horror. In Mary Elizabeth Braddon's "The Good Lady Ducayne," Lady Ducayne has cheated death for over a hundred years at the expense of her companions (see Illustrations, p. 514). Vampire literature helps us explore our anxieties about the return of the dead, but it also offers the promise of defeating death.

Immortality in vampire literature is not just about cheating death; it is also about the allure of eternal youth. Unlike Lady Ducayne, who simply wants "a few years more in the sunshine" (see p. 134), most vampires crave more than mere existence. The vampires in this chapter, from Arabella Kenealy's Lady Deverish to Philip K. Dick's Mrs. Drew, crave the power of youthful desirability. It is interesting that so many of the stories exploring the theme of immortality feature female monsters. Youth and beauty are significant aspects of these monsters. Unlike many male vampires in our first chapter, the power that female vampires crave is directly tied to their appearance; their beauty becomes part of their uncanniness. Historically, in patriarchal societies, women have been far more likely to be valued for their youthful physical appearance rather than for the wisdom of their experience. Indeed, the beauty standards to which women are still held today continue to emphasize extreme youth. Perhaps this is what makes vampire literature so appealing. Sometimes, these beautiful monsters do not even physically attack their victims. In Kenealy and Dick, the monsters are psychic vampires—not blood drinkers. These women's narcissistic obsession with youth and beauty produces their monstrousness.

Yet the tales in this chapter do more than emphasize unreasonable beauty standards—they also reveal cultural anxieties about the gendered role of desire and power. Carol Senf suggests that narratives featuring female vampires predominate at times "when the social conditions of women are changing."[1] Just as Stoker linked his female vampires to the sexual forwardness and anti-maternal characteristics popularly associated with the New Woman of the 1890s, the tales here emphasize the vampires' selfish quest for youth and beauty as part of their monstrousness. Interestingly, the tales of both Braddon and Kenealy

1 Senf, *The Vampire* 160.

were published in the 1890s just like Stoker's *Dracula*. They also respond to the Victorian ideology that proper women were supposed to be selfless.

More than their quest for youth and beauty alone, these female vampires are monstrous because the desirability resulting from these attributes is imperative to their ultimate goal: power. They are willing to exploit others to achieve this goal. They desire beauty because it gives them power and not for the more traditionally acceptable goal of pleasing another. In her 1993 book, *Unbearable Weight: Feminism, Western Culture, and the Body*, Susan Bordo unpacks the complexities of female desirability and desire: "female 'desire' is potent and threatening in our culture, with its sexual overtones and suggestions of personal gratification and capricious self-interest"[1] The monsters we read about in this chapter defy proscriptions of gender for entirely self-centered reasons. Their own pleasure is all that matters, and any sacrifice is acceptable if it enhances their existence, undercutting the kinds of social and political power that women's movements have long sought. In many tales, both in this chapter and throughout the anthology, while immortal, the vampire's youth is fleeting. Like Kenealy's Lady Deverish, vampires must keep consuming those around them in order to remain desirable.

Vampire literature allows us to explore fantasies of eternal youth and nightmares about being unable to die. *The Hunger* continues a tradition that has existed since Ancient Greek mythology: corporeal immortality without eternal youth is torment. Beauty becomes part of what makes the female vampire so threatening. The beauty of female vampires also emphasizes the inevitable losses associated with the aging process. As Groom points out, "the dead will always rise—until death itself dies, and then vampires will be our thought experiments in fathoming the horrors (and possible delights) of immortality."[2]

1 Bordo, *Unbearable Weight* 78–79.
2 Groom, *The Vampire* 201.

# Elizabeth Grey

(1798–1869)

A great deal of mystery surrounds the life of Elizabeth Caroline Grey (née Duncan). In fact, what little we know about her may be largely fabricated. The niece of a popular actress, she was apparently married to a Colonel Grey who was a reporter for the *Morning Chronicle*. There remains some controversy over whether she actually penned the more than thirty novels attributed to her. These works represent diverse genres of nineteenth-century popular fiction from triple-decker romances to penny dreadfuls like "The Skeleton Count" (1828). Many of her penny dreadfuls were initially published anonymously, which was not uncommon for a nineteenth-century female author anxious to protect her reputation from her less savory creations. This anonymity however deepens the questions about her authorship. Vampire scholar Peter Haining attributes the tale to Grey and claims that "The Skeleton Count" is the first vampire tale published by a woman. Other scholars have questioned her authorship and attributed "The Skeleton Count" to *Varney the Vampire* author James Malcolm Rymer. Whoever the real author, this early tale of an unwilling female vampire depicts an intriguing twist on the development of the genre and offers a unique perspective on the theme of immortality.

# "The Skeleton Count; or, The Vampire Mistress"

(1828)

Count Rodolph, after his impious compact with the prince of darkness, ceased to study alchemy or to search after the elixir of life, for not only was a long lease of life assured him by the demon, but the same authority had declared such pursuits to be vain and delusive. But he still dabbled in the occult sciences of magic and astrology, and frequently passed day after day in fruitless speculation, concerning the origin of matter, and the nature of the soul. He studied the writings of Aristotle, Pliny, Lucretius, Josephus, Iamblicus, Sprenger, Cardan, and the learned Michael Psellus;[1] yet was he as far as ever from attaining a correct knowledge of the things he sought to unveil from the mystery which must ever envelope them. The reveries of the ancient philosophers, of the Gnostics and the Pneaumatologists,[2] only served to plunge him into deeper doubt, and at length he determined to pass from speculation to experiment, and put his half-formed theories to the test of practice.

After keen study of the anatomy of the human frame, and many operations and experiments on the corpse of a malefactor who had been hanged for a robbery and murder, and which he stole from the gibbet in the dead of night, and conveyed to Ravensburg Castle, with the assistance of two wretches whom he had picked up at an obscure hostelry in the town of Heidelberg,[3] he resolved to exhume the corpse of some one recently dead, and attempt its reanimation. The formula of the necromancers for raising the dead did not suffice for their restoration to life, but only for a temporary revivification; but in an old Greek manuscript, which he found in the library of the castle, was an account of how this restored animation might be sustained by means of a miraculous liquid, for the distillation of which a recipe was given.

Count Rodolph gathered the herbs at midnight, which the Greek manuscript prescribed and distilled from them a clear gold-colored liquid of very little taste, but most fragrant odour, which he preserved in a phial. Having discovered that a peasant's daughter, a girl of singular beauty, and about sixteen years of age, had died suddenly, and was to be buried on the day following that on which he had prepared his marvelous restorative, he set out on that day to Heidelberg to obtain the assistance of the fellows who had aided him in removing the corpse of the malefactor from the gibbet, and then returned to Ravensburg Castle, to prepare for his strange experiment.

At the solemn hour of midnight he departed secretly from the castle by a door in the eastern tower, of which he retained the key in his own possession, and bent his step to the church-yard of the neighbouring village. It was a fine moonlight night, but all the rustic inhabitants were in the arms of Morpheus, the leaden-eyed god of sleep, and the violator of the sanctity of the grave gained the church-yard unperceived. He found his hired associates waiting for him in the shadow of the wall, which was easily scaled, and being provided with shovels and a sack to contain the corpse, they set to work immediately. The fresh broken

1 In addition to writers who would have been part of the curriculum for any student of the classics, Count Rodolph studies more esoteric writers from the Middle Ages and Renaissance.

2 The Gnostics arose in the first century and favored spiritual beliefs over orthodox teachings and the authority of religious institutions. A pneaumatologist is someone who interprets the theological doctrine of the holy spirit.

3 A town in southwestern Germany known for its university, which was founded in the fourteenth century.

earth was soon thrown off from the lid of the coffin, which the resurrectionists removed with a screw-driver, and then the dead was disclosed to their view.

The corpse of the young maiden was lifted from its narrow resting place, and raised in the arms of the ungodly wretches whom Rodolph had hired, who deposited the inanimate clay on the margin of the grave, which they hastily filled up, and then proceeded to enclose in the sack the lifeless remains of the beautiful peasant girl. Having removed every trace of the sacrilegious theft which they had committed, one of them took the sack on his shoulders, and when he was tired his comrade relieved him, and in this manner they reached the castle. Count Rodolph led the way up the narrow stairs which led to his study chamber in the eastern turret, and having deposited the corpse upon the floor, and received their stipulated reward, the two resurrectionists were glad to make a speedy exit from a place which popular rumour began to associate with deeds of darkness and horror.

Having lighted a spirit lamp, which cast a livid and flickering light upon the many strange and mysterious objects which that chamber contained, and made the pale countenance of the corpse appear more ghastly and horrible, Count Rodolph proceeded to denude the body of its grave-clothes, which he carefully concealed, lest the sight of them, when the young maiden returned to life might strike her with a sudden horror which might prove fatal to the complete success of his daring experiment. He then placed the corpse in the centre of a magic circle which he had previously drawn upon the floor of the study, and covered it with a sheet. He had purchased some ready-made female apparel in the town of Heidelberg, and these he placed on the table in readiness for the use of the young girl, whom he felt sanguine of resuscitating.

Bertha had been, as was evidenced by her stark and cold remains, a maiden of surpassing symmetry of form and loveliness of countenance; no painter or sculptor could have desired a finer study, no poet a more inspiring theme. As she lay stretched out upon the floor of the study she looked like some beautiful carving in alabaster, or rather like a waxen figure of most artistical contrivance. Her long black hair was shaded with a purple gloss like the plumage of the raven, and her features were of most exquisite proportion and arrangement. But now her angelic countenance was livid with the pallid hue of death, the iron impress of whose icy hand was visible in every lineament.

Count Rodolph then took in his hand a magic wand, one end of which he placed on the breast of the corpse, and then proceeded to recite the cabalistic words by which necromancers call to life the slumbering tenants of the grave. When he had concluded the impious formula, an awful silence reigned in the turret, and he perceived the sheet gently agitated by the quivering of the limbs, which betokened returning animation. Then a shudder pervaded his frame in spite of himself, as he perceived the eyes of the corpse slowly open, and the dark dilated pupils fix their gaze on him with a strange and stolid glare.

Then the limbs moved, at first convulsively, but soon with a stronger and more natural motion, and then the young girl raised herself to a sitting posture on the floor of the study, and stared about her in a wild and strange manner, which made Rodolph fear that the object of his experiment would prove a wretched idiot or a raving lunatic.

But suddenly he bethought him of the restorative cordial, and snatching the phial from a shelf, he poured down the throat of the resuscitated maiden a considerable portion of the fragrant gold colored fluid which it contained. Then a ray of that glorious intellect which allies man to the angels seemed to be infused into her mind, and beamed from her dark and lustrous eyes, which rested with a soft and tender expression on the handsome countenance of the young count. Her snowy bosom, from which the sheet had fallen when she rose from her recumbent position on the floor, heaved with the returning warmth of renewed life, and the Count of Ravensburg gazed upon her with mingled sensations of wonder and delight.

As the current of life was restored, and rushed along her veins with tingling warmth, the conscious blush of instinctive modesty mantled on her countenance, and drawing the sheet over her bosom, she rose to her feet, with her long black hair hanging about her shoulders, and her dark eyes cast upon the floor. Count Rodolph then directed her attention to the clothing which he had provided, so sanguine of complete success had the daring experimentalist been, and then he withdrew from the study while the lovely object of his scientific care attired herself.

When the Count of Ravensburg returned to his study, Bertha was sitting before the fire, attired in the garments he had provided for her, and he thought that he had never beheld a more lovely specimen of her sex. She rose when he entered, and kissed his hand, as though he were a superior being, and would have remained standing, with head bowed upon her bosom, as if in the presence of a being of another world, had he not gently forced her to resume the seat from which she had risen, and inquired tenderly the state of her feelings upon a return to life so strange and wonderful. But he found that she retained no remembrance of a previous existence, and all her feelings were new and strange, like those of Eve on bursting into conscious life and being from the hand of the Omnipotent. In her mysterious passage from life to death, and from death to new life, she had lost all her previous ideas and convictions, all her experience of the past, all that she had ever acquired of knowledge; and had become a child of nature, simple and unsophisticated as a denizen of the woods, with all the keen perceptions and untrained instincts of the untutored savage.

The young girl had braided up her flowing tresses of glossy blackness, and on her cheeks dwelt color that might test a painter's skill, so rich yet delicate its hue, like the rosette tinge of some rare exotic shell, or that which a rose would cast upon an alabaster column. The young count felt himself irresistibly attracted towards the maiden, whom his science had endued with such a mysterious and preternatural existence, and she, on her part, regarded the handsome Rodolph with the wild, yet tender passion of frail humanity, mingled with the gratitude and devotion which she deemed due to one who stood to her in the position of her creator.

Thus the feelings which had so rapidly sprung up in her heart towards the only being of whom she had any conception, partook of a nature of a religious idolatry, but mingled with the grosser feelings of earth, like those which agitated in the bosom of the vestal whose sons founded Rome, or the virgin of Shen-si who was chosen from among all the women of the celestial empire to become the mother of the incarnate Foh.[1]

"Thou art gloriously beautiful, my Bertha!" exclaimed the enamored count, pressing her in his arms. "Say that thou wilt be mine, and make me thy happy slave; thou should'st be loving as thou art lovable, beautiful child of mystery!"

"Love thee!" returned Bertha, a soft and tender expression dwelling in the clear depths of her dark eyes. "I adore thee, my creator; my soul bows itself before thee, yet my heart leaps at thy glance, though I fear it is presumptuous for the work of thy hands to look on thee with eyes of love."

"Sweet, ingenuous creature!" cried the Count of Ravensburg, kissing her coral lips and glowing cheeks. "It is I who should worship thee! Thou art mine, Bertha, now and for ever. Henceforth I live only in thy smile!"

"For ever! Shall I remain with thee for ever? Oh, joy incomparable! My heart's idol, I adore thee!" and the beautiful Bertha wound her white arms about his neck, and pressed her lips to his, for in the new existence which she now enjoyed her feelings knew no restraint, and she yielded to every impulse of her ardent nature.

"Come, my Bertha," said the enraptured Rodolph, "this solitary turret must not be thy world; come with me, thy Rodolph, and be the mistress of Ravensburg Castle, as thou art already of its owner's heart."

Passing his arm around the taper waist of the mysterious maiden, Rodolph took up the lamp, and quitting the eastern turret, they proceeded with noiseless steps to his chamber, where the first faint blush of day witnessed the consummation of their desires, nor did the torch of Hymen[2] burn less brightly because no priest blessed their nuptial couch.

The presence in Ravensburg Castle of this young girl, which Rodolph, with that contempt for the opinion of the world which usually marked his actions, took no pains to conceal, became the engrossing topic of conversation in the servants' hall throughout the day, and as Rodolph had never before indulged in any intrigue, either with the peasant girls of the neighbouring village or the

1 The exact reference is not clear, but this seems to present a Chinese version of the Christian Virgin Mary and Jesus or Foh may be a transliteration for Buddha.
2 Greek goddess of marriage.

courtesans of Heidelberg, the circumstance seemed the more remarkable. But the beautiful Bertha seemed quite unconscious of the equivocal nature of her position in reference to the young count, and though her views of human nature became every moment more enlarged with the sphere of her existence, she still regarded Rodolph as a being of superior mold.

When night again drew his sable mantle over the sleeping earth, Rodolph and the mysterious Bertha sought their couch, and never had shone the inconstant moon on a pair so well matched as regarded physical beauty, or we may add as regarded their strange destiny—one gifted with almost superhuman powers of mind, yet in a few days to undergo so horrible a transformation, and far removed by that strange fate from ordinary mortals; the other endowed with such singular beauty yet doomed to the dreadful existence of one who had passed the boundaries of the grave, and returned to life!

With sonorous and solemn stroke the bell of the castle clock proclaimed the hour of midnight, and then Bertha slowly raised herself from her lover's body and slipping from the bed, attired herself in a half-unconscious state, and stole noiselessly from the room.

Her cheeks were pale, and her eyes had the wild and stolid glare which Rodolph had observed when she awakened from the slumber of the grave; she quitted the castle, and after gazing around her, as if uncertain which way to go, she proceeded towards the village.

She stopped opposite the nearest cottage, and then advanced to the window, and shook the shutters; the fastenings being insecure, they opened with little trouble, and a broken pane of glass enabled Bertha to introduce her hand, and remove the fastenings of the window. Then she cautiously opened the window, and entered the room—she ascended the stairs on tiptoe, and entered a chamber where a little girl was in bed and fast asleep. For a moment she shuddered violently, as if struggling to repress the horrible inclination which is the dread condition of a return to life after passing the portals of death, and then she bent her face down to the child's throat, her hot breath fanned its cheek, and the next moment her teeth punctured its tender skin, and she began to suck its blood to sustain her unnatural existence!

For such is the horrible destiny of the vampire race, of whom we have yet further mysteries and secrets to unfold; and such a being was she whom Count Rodolph had taken from the grave to his bed!

Presently the child awoke with a fearful scream, and its father, leaping from his bed in the next room, hurried to her succor, but Bertha rushed past him in the dark, and escaped from the house. The peasant found the little girl much frightened, and bleeding at the throat; but she had suffered no vital injury, and having ascertained this fact, he snatched up his match-lock, and hurried after the aggressor.

"A vampire!" exclaimed the peasant, turning pale with horror, as he distinctly saw, by the light of the moon, a young female hurrying from the village at a rapid pace.

The man gave chase to the flying Bertha, and gradually gaining ground, came within gun shot, just as she reached the shelving banks of the river, when he raised his weapon to his shoulder, and fired. The report echoed along the banks of the Rhine, and Bertha screamed as the ball penetrated her back, and tumbled headlong into the stream. The peasant hastened back to the village, satisfied that the horrible creature was no more, and the corpse of the vampire floated on the surface of the moonlit river.

The moon was that night at the full, and shed a flood of pearly light over the picturesque scenery of the Rhine, which, throughout its whole course, is a panorama of scenic beauty, every bend revealing some object interesting either for its historical reminiscences or legendary associations. There was the village, but now the scene of a horrible outrage—the castle, thrown into alternate light and shadow by the passing of the light fleecy clouds over the face of the moon—the town of Heidelberg, sloping from the Castle of the Palatine, and spanning the river with its noble bridge—and the Rhine, here shaded by the dark rocks which overhung the opposite bank, and there reflecting the silver light of the moon. The corpse of the vampire floated down the stream for some distance, and then it became arrested in its course by the bending of the river, and lay partly out of the water on the shelving bank.

And now commenced another scene of strange and startling interest—another phase in the fearful existence of the vampire bride! For as the beams of the full moon fell on the inanimate form of that being of mystery and fear, sensation seemed slowly to return, as when the magic spells of the Count of Ravensburg resuscitated her from the grave; her eyes opened, her bosom rose and fell with the warm pulsations of returning life; her limbs moved spasmodically, and then she rose from the bank, and shuddering at the recollection of what had occurred to her, she wrung the water from her saturated garments, and ran towards the castle at a pace accelerated by fear.

Having admitted herself into the castle, she sought the count's chamber with noiseless steps, and having taken off and concealed her wet clothes, she returned to his bed without his being aware that she had ever quitted it. The count was surprised to find that his mistress took no refreshment throughout the day, but he was led to consider it as one of the natural laws of her strange existence, and thought no more about it.

But in the village, the utmost excitement prevailed when it became known that the cottage of Herman Klaus had been visited by a vampire during the night, and his little daughter bitten by the horrible creature. All day long the cottage of the mysterious visitation was beset by the wondering villagers, who crossed themselves piously, and wondered who the vampire could have been, and the services of the priest were called into requisition to prevent the little blue-eyed Minna becoming a vampire after death, as is supposed to be the case with those who have the misfortune to be bitten by one of those horrible creatures, just as a person becomes mad after the bite of a mad dog or cat.[1]

According to the terms of the compact which had been entered into between Count Rodolph and the demon, its conditions did not come into operation until seven days after the signing of the dreadful bond, and as day after day flew on, Rodolph dreaded the necessity of acquainting Bertha with the terrible transformation which he must nightly undergo. But he knew how impossible it would be to keep his hideous and appalling metamorphosis a secret from his mistress, and he reflected that if he made her the confidant of his terrible fate it would be the more likely to remain unknown to the rest of the world. He accordingly nerved his mind to the appalling revelation which he had to make, and on the seventh day after his compact with Lucifer, he disclosed to her his awful secret.

"Bertha," said he, in a sad and solemn tone, "I am about to entrust thee with a terrible secret; swear to me that thou wilt never divulge it."

"I swear," she replied.

"Know, then," continued the count, lowering his voice to a hoarse whisper, "that, by virtue of a compact with the infernal powers of evil and of darkness, I am endowed with a term of life and youth amounting almost to the boon of immortality but to this inestimable gift, there is a condition attached which commences this night, and which I almost tremble to impart to thee."

"Fear not, my Rodolph!" exclaimed his beautiful mistress, twining her round white arms about his neck, "thy Bertha can never love thee less, and her soul the rather clings to thee more intensely for the preternatural gift which links thy destiny more closely to my own. For mine, too, is a strange and fearful existence, which I owe to thee, and therefore shall I cling to thee the more fondly for the kindred doom which allies us to each other while it lifts us far above ordinary mortals."

"Then prepare thy ears for a dread revelation, Bertha," returned the Count of Ravensburg. "Each night of my future existence, at the hour of sunset, my doom divests me of my mortal shape, and I become a skeleton until sunrise on the morn ensuing. Now, thou knowest all, my Bertha, and be it thy care to prevent the dreadful secret from becoming known."

"It shall, my brave Rodolph!" exclaimed Bertha, her eyes glittering with a strange expression, as she thought of the facility which her lover's strange doom would allow for her nocturnal absences from the castle. "No eye but mine shall witness thy transformation, and I will watch over thee until thy return to thy natural shape."

"Thanks, my Bertha!" returned Rodolph, embracing her. "The hour draws nigh when I must relinquish for the night my mortal form; come, love, to our chamber, and see that no prying eye beholds the ghastly change."

1 A reference to rabies—one of the diseases thought to inspire vampire folklore.

Bertha and her lover accordingly repaired to their chamber, and when the luminary of day sank below the horizon, leaving the traces of his splendor on the western sky, the Count Rodolph shrunk to a grisly skeleton, and fell upon the bed. Bertha shuddered as she witnessed the horrid transformation, and they lay down on the bed until midnight, the necessity of secrecy overcoming any repugnance she might otherwise have felt to the horrible contiguity of the skeleton, but when the castle clock proclaimed the hour of midnight with iron tongue, she rose from the bed, and locking the door of the chamber which contained so strange a guest, she stole from the castle to sate her unnatural appetite for human blood.

The moon rode high in the heavens on that night of unfathomable mystery and horror, and her silver beams shone through the chamber-window of Theresa Delmar, one of the loveliest maidens in the village of Ravensburg, revealing a snowy neck, and a white and dimpled shoulder, shaded by the bright golden locks which strayed over the pillow. The maiden's blue eyes were concealed by their thin lids and their long silken fringes, and her snowy bosom gently rose and fell beneath the white coverlet as the thoughts which agitated her by day, mingled in her dreams at night. Silence reigned in the thatched cottage, and throughout the village was only occasionally broken by the barking of some watchful house-dog.

But soon after midnight the silence was broken by a slight noise at the chamber window as if someone was endeavoring to obtain an entrance, and the flood of moonlight which streamed upon the maiden's bed was obscured by the form of a woman standing on the windowsill. Still Theresa slumbered on, nor dreamed of peril so near, for the woman had succeeded in opening the window, and in another moment she stood within the room.

With slow and cautious step she softly approached the bed whereon the maiden reposed so calmly, little dreaming how dread a visitant was near her couch, and then she shuddered involuntarily as she bent over the sleeping girl, and her long dark ringlets mingled with the masses of golden hair which shaded the white shoulder, and the partially exposed bosom of Theresa Delmar. Her lips touched the young girl's neck, her sharp teeth punctured the white skin, and then she began to suck greedily, quaffing the vital fluid which flowed warm and quick in the maiden's veins, and sapping her life to maintain her own!

Still Theresa awoke not, for the puncture made in her throat by the teeth of the horrible creature was little larger than that which would be made by a leech, and the vampire sucked long and greedily, for her long abstinence from blood had sharpened her unnatural appetite. Suddenly Theresa awoke with a start, doubtless caused by some unpleasant transition in her dreams, but she did not immediately cry out, for she felt no pain, and as yet she was scarcely conscious of her danger. But in a few seconds she was thoroughly awake, and her surprise and horror may be more easily imagined than described, when she found bending over her, and sucking her blood, the horrible creature that had but a few nights previously attacked Minna Klaus, and which the child's father thought he had destroyed.

Spell-bound by the glittering eyes of the vampire, she lay without the power to scream, until the appalling horror of her situation became too great for endurance, her quivering nerves were strung to their utmost power of extension, and a wild shriek burst from her lips. Even then the horrible creature did not leave its hold, but continued to suck from her palpitating veins the crimson current of her life, until footsteps were heard hastily approaching the chamber, and the lovely Theresa, whose screams seemed to have broken the fascination which had bound her in its thrall, struggled so violently that Bertha was compelled to relinquish her horrid banquet. Springing to the window, she effected her escape, just as heavy blows resounded on the door of the chamber, and her affrighted victim sank insensible on the bed.

"What is the matter, Theresa? Open the door!" exclaimed her terrified parents; but they received no answer.

Then Delmar broke open the door, and he and his wife rushed into the room and found their daughter lying insensible on the bed, with spots of blood on her throat and bosom, and the window wide open.

"The vampire has come to life again, and has attacked our Theresa!" exclaimed her mother. "See the blood-marks on her dear neck! Raise the village, Delmar, to pursue the monster."

"Oh, dear! where am I? Has it gone, mother?" inquired Theresa, as she recovered from her swoon, and gazed in a frightened manner round the room.

"Yes, it has gone now, dear," said her mother. "What was it like?"

"Aye, what was it like?" added old Delmar. "Perhaps it was not the same one that neighbor Klaus shot at the other night."

"Oh, yes! it was a young woman, and as much like Bertha Kurtel as ever one pea was like another," replied the young girl, shuddering.

"Holy virgin!" exclaimed her mother, crossing herself with a shudder. "Bertha Kurtel a vampire, and returned from the grave to prey upon our Theresa! Oh, horrible!"

Delmar hurriedly dressed himself, and catching up an axe, he hastened to call up Klaus and others to pursue the vampire, and in a few minutes the whole village was in commotion. About twenty men armed themselves with whatever weapon came first to hand, and followed the direction which the vampire had taken when chased by Herman Klaus on a former occasion. They searched every bush all round the village, to which they returned at sunrise without having found any trace of the object of their search. Delmar found his daughter somewhat faint from fright and loss of blood, but not otherwise injured by the vampire's attack. The greatest excitement prevailed in that usually quiet village, and all the morning, groups of men stood about the little street, or clustered round Delmar's cottage, conversing in low and mysterious whispers of the dreadful visitation which the village had a second time received.

"What a shocking thing it would be if a pretty girl like Theresa Delmar was to become a vampire when she dies," observed one. "And who knows what may happen now she has been bitten by one of those horrible creatures?"

"And poor little Minna Klaus," said another.

"Ah, and we do not know how long the list may be if we do not put a stop to it," added one of the rustic group. "I have heard Father Ambrose say that they generally attack females and children."

"Who can it be? that is what I want to know," said old Klaus. "Why, Theresa declares it was just like Bertha Kurtel," returned another, shaking his voice to a whisper.

"Bertha Kurtel!" repeated a youth who had loved her who once bore that name. "Bertha a vampire! impossible."

"It is easily ascertained," observed the gruff voice of the village blacksmith. "We have only to take up the coffin and see if she is in it, as she ought to be. If we do not find her we shall know what's o'clock."

"If it was not for her parents' feelings I really should like to be satisfied whether it is Bertha," remarked old Delmar.

"Feelings!" repeated the smith, in a surly tone. "Have we not all got our feelings? Are we to have our wives and children attacked in this manner, and all turned into vampires, and let other people's fine feelings prevent us from having satisfaction for it?"

"There is something in that," observed Delmar, scratching his head with an air of perplexity.

"I would make one if anybody else would go," said Herman Klaus, after a pause.

"And I will be another," exclaimed the smith, looking around him. "Now who will go and have a peep in the churchyard to see whose coffin is empty?"

Several expressed themselves ready, and others following their example the smith proceeded to the churchyard, backed by about twenty of the most resolute of the villagers, to reenact the scene which had taken place there but a few nights since. On arriving at the churchyard the smith and another immediately set to work to throw the earth out of the grave, which was soon accomplished, and amid the most breathless silence the smith proceeded to remove the lid of the coffin.

"Look here, neighbors," said he, turning pale in spite of himself. "The lid has been removed, and the coffin is empty!"

"So it is!" exclaimed Herman Klaus.

"Then is it not plain that Bertha is the vampire—the horrible creature that sucked the blood of Theresa Delmar and little Minna Klaus?" said the smith, looking round upon the throng which had been swelled during the work of exhumation by idlers from the village.

"But where is she now? that is the question," observed Herman Klaus.

"This must be investigated," said the smith. "We must keep watch for the vampire, and catch it; then we must either burn it, or drive a stake through the creature's body, for they say those are the only methods that will effectually fix a vampire."

The wondering group of peasants returned to the village, and great was the grief of the Kurtels at the horrible discovery that their daughter had become a vampire, and the youth who had so loved Bertha in her human state became delirious on hearing the confirmation of the suspicion which Theresa's assertion had first excited. The ordinary occupations of the villagers were entirely neglected throughout the day, and nothing was talked of but vampires and werewolves, and other human transformations more terrific and appalling than any recorded in the metamorphoses of Ovid.[1] Towards the evening the venerable seneschal of the Count of Ravensburg arrived in the village and had an interview with the Delmars, after which he visited the cottage of Herman Klaus, and a vague rumor spread like wildfire from house to house, to the effect that the vampire was an inmate of Ravensburg Castle.

The communication made by the seneschal to Delmar and Klaus was to the effect that, on the morning following the interment of Bertha Kurtel, a young female exactly resembling her in form, features, voice, and every individual peculiarity, had appeared in a mysterious manner at the castle, and had resided there ever since in the capacity of the count's mistress. No one knew who she was, where she came from, or how she obtained admission into the castle; and the occurrences in the village having reached the ears of the count's retainers and domestics, accompanied with the suspicion that the vampire was the revived Bertha Kurtel, the seneschal had hastened to the village to report his observations. The abstinence of the count's mistress from food was deemed corroborative of the suspicion that she was a vampire, and the seneschal's report caused the utmost excitement among the villagers. Symptoms of hostile intentions soon became visible, and in less than half an hour, more than a hundred men were proceeding in a disorderly manner towards the castle, armed with every imaginable weapon, and swearing to put an end to the vampire.

Count Rodolph and his beautiful mistress were sitting at a window which commanded a view of the road for some distance, the small white hand of Bertha locked in that of her lover, and whispering words of tenderness and love, when their attention was attracted by a disorderly mob approaching from the village.

"What can this mean?" said Rodolph, rising.

"Oh, this is what I have dreaded!" exclaimed Bertha, turning pale, and clasping her hands in a terrified manner: "your studies have caused you to be suspected of necromancy, my Rodolph, they come to attack the castle."

1 Mythicohistorical narrative poem by Roman poet Ovid detailing the history of the world. *Metamorphoses* (8 CE) is one of the most influential texts of Western culture.

"I fear thou art right, dearest," said the count: "but we will give them a warm reception. Ho! a lawless mob menaces the castle with danger: make fast the gates; bar every door; bid my retainers man the battlements to repel the attack."

"And sunset is approaching," exclaimed Bertha, with a meaning glance at her lover.

"Do thou retire, sweet love, to thy chamber," said Rodolph; "fear not for me; I bear a charmed life, and neither sword nor shot will avail against it. If this lawless rabble be not dispersed when the dread moment comes all hope will be lost, and they shall behold the grisly change. Perhaps they may be struck with a sudden panic, and we may be enabled to fly into another country."

Bertha retired after embracing the count, and shut herself up in her chamber. Preparations were immediately made to resist the attack of the insurgent villagers, who continued to advance upon the castle, yelling like savages, and breathing vengeance against the vampire mistress of Count Rodolph.

"Down with the vampire!" was the hoarse and sullen cry which rolled like distant thunder from a hundred throats, and then the mob drew up before the castle gates, and the smith struck them heavily with his ponderous hammer.

The count took an arquebuse[1] and fired at the mob, very few of whom were provided with fire-arms; one of the peasants was wounded, and with a shout of rage and defiance a volley of shot, arrows, and stones was directed against the beleaguered castle. The smith continued to batter away at the gate, aided by several stalwart fellows with axes, and though several of the mob were killed by the fire of the men-at-arms, those who were endeavoring to force the gate were protected by the overhanging battlements, and continued to ply their implements with unwearied energy.

Count Rodolph turned pale, and shuddered as he listened to the wild cries of the assailants, not from fear, for apart from his invulnerability he was inaccessible to that feeling, but from the horrible ideas engendered from these shouts, having reference to the beautiful Bertha Kurtel. Had her resuscitation from the grave endowed her with the horrible nature of the vampire? Could that lovely creature sustain her renewed existence with the blood of her former companions? Horrible! yet, had she not hinted at something of the kind when he revealed to her the horrors of his own strange doom? It must be so, then; and he shuddered violently at the appalling idea.

"Down with the vampire!" was still the menacing cry which rose from the assailants, who at length succeeded in breaking down the gates, and rushed tumultuously into the court-yard, shouting and brandishing their weapons.

Undismayed by the fire from the battlements, they commenced an attack on the doors and windows of the castle, and now they were all crowded in the courtyard, Count Rodolph thought the moment favorable for a sally. Drawing his sword, and commanding a score of his armed retainers to follow him, he

1 A form of long gun in fifteenth-century Europe.

suddenly opened a door leading into the court-yard, and fell furiously on the flank of the assailants. For a moment they were thrown into confusion, but they quickly rallied, when Count Rodolph and his little party were surrounded and compelled to act on the defensive. The ruddy beams of the setting sun were already purpling the distant hills when the peasants marched upon the castle, and as his broad disk sank below the horizon, the aspect of the Count of Ravensburg suddenly underwent a marvelous change, and much as the insurgents had wondered to see arrows glance off from his body, and their swords rebound as if their stroke fell on a giant oak, how much greater was their astonishment when they beheld him suddenly transformed into a fleshless skeleton!

"It is some device of Satan!—he is a sorcerer!" cried the stalwart smith, brandishing his huge hammer. "Come on, mates—down with the vampire!"

"Down with the vampire!" echoed from the mob, and the count's retainers giving way on all sides, as much appalled as the peasants at this horrible metamorphosis, the assailants rushed into the castle by the open door, and marched from room to room, looking in every closet and under every bed, while the terrified Bertha flew from one apartment to another, until she at length sought refuge in the highest apartment of the eastern turret, that chamber which had witnessed her return from death to her renewed state of strange and horrible existence. She had locked and bolted the door of the study, but what availed these obstacles against a furious mob, animated by their success in gaining the castle, and bent upon destruction and revenge? The door cracked, yielded, was forced open, and several men rushed into the little chamber.

"Here she is!—here is the vampire!" cried the foremost, and despite her piercing shrieks and earnest supplications for mercy, the wretched Bertha was dragged out of the study, with her long black hair hanging in wild disorder about her shoulders, and her beautiful countenance pale with overpowering terror.

"Mercy, indeed! What mercy can we feel for a vampire?" cried the peasants, and the terrified creature was dragged down the turret stairs by one or two of the boldest, for few would venture to come in contact with the dreaded being.

As they reached the foot of the stairs a volume of smoke rolled along the passage, and the crackling of burning wood told them that some of their companions had set fire to the castle.

"Now what shall we do with the vampire?" said her remorseless captors.

"Throw her into the Rhine!" suggested one.

"Tie her up and shoot at her!" said another.

"What will be the use of that?" objected a third. "Nothing but fire or a sharp stake will destroy a vampire. Let us shut her up in the castle, and burn her to ashes!"

"Yes, yes! burn the vampire!" shouted a score of voices.

"No, no!—I say, no!" cried the smith. "Let us carry her to the churchyard, put her in her coffin again, and peg her down with a stake, so that she can never rise again."

The suggestion of the smith was approved of, and the wretched Bertha was half-dragged and half-carried, more dead than alive, towards the village church. The flames were bursting forth from all parts of the castle when the lawless spoilers left it, and a red glow hung over its ancient towers; the work of destruction was rapid, and in a few hours naught but the bare and blackened walls were left standing.

On the destroyers of Ravensburg Castle reaching the churchyard, the almost lifeless form of Bertha Kurtel was dragged to the grave, which had been left open, and flung rudely into the coffin. Then a sharp pointed stake was produced, which had been prepared by the way, and the smith plunged it with all the force of his sinewy arms into the abdomen of the doomed vampire. A piercing shriek burst from her pale lips as the horrible thrust aroused her to consciousness, and as her clothes became dabbed with the crimson stream of life, and the smith lifted his heavy hammer and drove the stake through her quivering body, the transfixed wretch writhed convulsively, and the contortions of her countenance were fearful to behold. Thus impaled in her coffin, and while her limbs yet quivered with the last throes of dissolution, the earth was replaced and rammed down by the tread of many feet.

But those strange and terrible scenes were not yet ended. A young peasant of equal curiosity and boldness, and who had been engaged in the attack upon the castle and the horrible tragedy which followed it, was anxious to know more of the strange affair of the skeleton, which had been left in the courtyard where it fell, none of the villagers caring to interfere with so ghastly an object. He therefore stole away a little before midnight, and went towards the castle, where the fire was dying out, though a fiery glow was still reflected from the moldering embers of beams and rafters. He advanced cautiously through the broken gates of the castle, and shuddered slightly as he perceived the skeleton of the Count of Ravensburg still lying on the pavement of the courtyard.

He determined to watch until daylight, and see what became of the grisly relics of mortality, which a few hours before had been the young and handsome Count of Ravensburg. The hours passed slowly on from midnight to the dawn of another day, and when the rising sun tinged the eastern sky with crimson and gold, a strange spectacle was witnessed by the solitary watcher in the court-yard of Ravensburg Castle.

The skeleton rose slowly from the pavement, and assumed the form of Count Rodolph, just as he appeared at the moment preceding his transformation on the evening before. A cold perspiration bedewed the brow of the peasant, and his hair stood erect with terror, on witnessing this sudden metamorphosis. The count looked up at the dilapidated walls and towers of his castle, and shuddered violently, and crossing the court-yard, passed through the broken gate.

The peasant then hastened to the village, and reported what he had seen, which was a source of much marvel to the rustic inhabitants. The story of the skeleton count, and his vampire mistress, quickly spread all over Germany, but the villagers were no more molested by vampires, for Bertha Kurtel was securely fixed in her coffin, and no ill effects ensued from her attacks upon Theresa Delmar and little Minna Klaus.

## Mary Elizabeth Braddon

(1835–1915)

Widely considered to be one of the creators of the sensation fiction genre, Mary Elizabeth Braddon was a prolific writer. Throughout her career, she produced more than eighty novels, as well as numerous short stories, essays, poetry, and plays. Braddon was born into a family experiencing financial difficulties. By the time she was four, her mother had left her father and was raising the children on her own. At seventeen, Braddon took the unconventional step of becoming an actress to support herself and her mother. While she found modest success acting, it was in writing that she would make her name, publishing her first novel, *The Trail of the Serpent*, in 1861. By the time her most famous novel, *Lady Audley's Secret*, was published in 1862, Braddon was practically a household name. Braddon's personal life intensified the scandal of her stage career when her relationship with her married publisher, John Maxwell, became public. His wife was confined to a mental hospital, and when she died, Maxwell and Braddon married. Braddon's work remained popular well into the twentieth century and today she is seen as an important figure in Victorian fiction.

# "The Good Lady Ducayne"

(1896)

### I

Bella Rolleston had made up her mind that her only chance of earning her bread and helping her mother to an occasional crust was by going out into the great unknown world as companion to a lady. She was willing to go to any lady rich enough to pay her a salary and so eccentric as to wish for a hired companion. Five shillings told off reluctantly from one of those sovereigns which were so rare with the mother and daughter, and which melted away so quickly, five solid shillings, had been handed to a smartly-dressed lady in an office in Harbeck Street, W., in the hope that this very Superior Person would find a situation and a salary for Miss Rolleston.

The Superior Person glanced at the two half-crowns as they lay on the table where Bella's hand had placed them, to make sure they were neither of them forms, before she wrote a description of Bella's qualifications and requirements in a formidable-looking ledger.

"Age?" she asked curtly.

"Eighteen, last July."

"Any accomplishments?"

"No; I am not at all accomplished. If I were I should want to be a governess—a companion seems the lowest stage."

"We have some highly accomplished ladies on our books as companions, or chaperon companions."

"Oh, I know!" babbled Bella, loquacious in her youthful candour. "But that is quite a different thing. Mother hasn't been able to afford a piano since I was twelve years old, so I'm afraid I've forgotten how to play. And I have had to help mother with her needlework, so there hasn't been much time to study."

"Please don't waste time upon explaining what you can't do, but kindly tell me anything you can do," said the Superior Person, crushingly, with her pen poised between delicate fingers waiting to write. "Can you read aloud for two or three hours at a stretch? Are you active and handy, an early riser, a good walker, sweet tempered, and obliging?"

"I can say yes to all those questions except about the sweetness. I think I have a pretty good temper, and I should be anxious to oblige anybody who paid for my services. I should want them to feel that I was really earning my salary."

"The kind of ladies who come to me would not care for a talkative companion," said the Person, severely, having finished writing in her book. "My connection lies chiefly among the aristocracy, and in that class considerable deference is expected."

"Oh, of course," said Bella; "but it's quite different when I'm talking to you. I want to tell you all about myself once and for ever."

"I am glad it is to be only once!" said the Person, with the edges of her lips.

The Person was of uncertain age, tightly laced in a black silk gown. She had a powdery complexion and a handsome clump of somebody else's hair on the top of her head. It may be that Bella's girlish freshness and vivacity had an irritating effect upon nerves weakened by an eight hours day in that over-heated second floor in Harbeck Street. To Bella the official apartment, with its Brussels carpet, velvet curtains and velvet chairs, and French clock, ticking loud on the marble chimney-piece, suggested the luxury of a palace, as compared with another second floor in Walworth where Mrs. Rolleston and her daughter had managed to exist for the last six years.

"Do you think you have anything on your books that would suit me?" faltered Bella, after a pause.

"Oh, dear, no; I have nothing in view at present," answered the Person, who had swept Bella's half-crowns into a drawer, absentmindedly, with the tips of her fingers. "You see, you are so very unformed—so much too young to be companion to a lady of position. It is a pity you have not enough education for a nursery governess; that would be more in your line."

"And do you think it will be very long before you can get me a situation?" asked Bella, doubtfully.

"I really cannot say. Have you any particular reason for being so impatient—not a love affair, I hope?"

"A love affair!" cried Bella, with flaming cheeks. "What utter nonsense. I want a situation because mother is poor, and I hate being a burden to her. I want a salary that I can share with her."

"There won't be much margin for sharing in the salary you are likely to get at your age—and with your—very—unformed manners," said the Person, who found Bella's peony cheeks, bright eyes, and unbridled vivacity more and more oppressive.

"Perhaps if you'd be kind enough to give me back the fee I could take it to an agency where the connection isn't quite so aristocratic," said Bella, who—as she told her mother in her recital of the interview—was determined not to be sat upon.

"You will find no agency that can do more for you than mine," replied the Person, whose harpy[1] fingers never relinquished coin. "You will have to wait for your opportunity. Yours is an exceptional case: but I will bear you in mind, and if anything suitable offers I will write to you. I cannot say more than that."

The half-contemptuous bend of the stately head, weighted with borrowed hair, indicated the end of the interview. Bella went back to Walworth—tramped sturdily every inch of the way in the September afternoon—and "took off"[2] the Superior Person for the amusement of her mother and the landlady, who lingered in the shabby little sitting-room after bringing in the tea-tray, to applaud Miss Rolleston's "taking off."

"Dear, dear, what a mimic she is!" said the landlady. "You ought to have let her go on the stage, mum. She might have made her fortune as an actress."

## II

Bella waited and hoped, and listened for the postman's knocks which brought such store of letters for the parlours and the first floor, and so few for that humble second floor, where mother and daughter sat sewing with hand and

1 Found in Greek and Roman mythology, a harpy is half-woman and half-bird. The personification of storm winds, harpies were known for stealing from their victims.

2 Impersonating for humorous effect.

with wheel and treadle, for the greater part of the day. Mrs. Rolleston was a lady by birth and education; but it had been her bad fortune to marry a scoundrel; for the last half-dozen years she had been that worst of widows, a wife whose husband had deserted her. Happily, she was courageous, industrious, and a clever needle-woman; and she had been able just to earn a living for herself and her only child, by making mantles and cloaks for a West-end house. It was not a luxurious living. Cheap lodgings in a shabby street off the Walworth Road, scanty dinners, homely food, well-worn raiment, had been the portion of mother and daughter; but they loved each other so dearly, and Nature had made them both so light-hearted, that they had contrived somehow to be happy.

But now this idea of going out into the world as companion to some fine lady had rooted itself into Bella's mind, and although she idolized her mother, and although the parting of mother and daughter must needs tear two loving hearts into shreds, the girl longed for enterprise and change and excitement, as the pages of old longed to be knights, and to start for the Holy Land to break a lance with the infidel.

She grew tired of racing downstairs every time the postman knocked, only to be told "nothing for you, miss," by the smudgy-faced drudge who picked up the letters from the passage floor. "Nothing for you, miss," grinned the lodging-house drudge, till at last Bella took heart of grace and walked up to Harbeck Street, and asked the Superior Person how it was that no situation had been found for her.

"You are too young," said the Person, "and you want a salary."

"Of course I do," answered Bella; "don't other people want salaries?"

"Young ladies of your age generally want a comfortable home."

"I don't," snapped Bella; "I want to help mother."

"You can call again this day week," said the Person; "or, if I hear of anything in the meantime, I will write to you."

No letter came from the Person, and in exactly a week Bella put on her neatest hat, the one that had been seldomest caught in the rain, and trudged off to Harbeck Street.

It was a dull October afternoon, and there was a greyness in the air which might turn to fog before night. The Walworth Road shops gleamed brightly through that grey atmosphere, and though to a young lady reared in Mayfair or Belgravia such shop-windows would have been unworthy of a glance, they were a snare and temptation for Bella. There were so many things that she longed for, and would never be able to buy.

Harbeck Street is apt to be empty at this dead season of the year, a long, long street, an endless perspective of eminently respectable houses. The Person's office was at the further end, and Bella looked down that long, grey vista almost despairingly, more tired than usual with the trudge from Walworth. As she looked, a carriage passed her, an old-fashioned, yellow chariot, on cee springs,[1] drawn by a pair of high grey horses, with the stateliest of coachmen driving them, and a tall footman sitting by his side.

"It looks like the fairy god-mother's coach," thought Bella. "I shouldn't wonder if it began by being a pumpkin."

It was a surprise when she reached the Person's door to find the yellow chariot standing before it, and the tall footman waiting near the doorstep. She was almost afraid to go in and meet the owner of that splendid carriage. She had caught only a glimpse of its occupant as the chariot rolled by, a plumed bonnet, a patch of ermine.

The Person's smart page ushered her upstairs and knocked at the official door. "Miss Rolleston," he announced, apologetically, while Bella waited outside.

"Show her in," said the Person, quickly; and then Bella heard her murmuring something in a low voice to her client.

Bella went in fresh, blooming, a living image of youth and hope, and before she looked at the Person her gaze was riveted by the owner of the chariot.

Never had she seen anyone as old as the old lady sitting by the Person's fire: a little old figure, wrapped from chin to feet in an ermine mantle; a withered, old face under a plumed bonnet—a face so wasted by age that it seemed only a pair of eyes and a peaked chin. The nose was peaked, too, but between the sharply pointed chin and the great, shining eyes, the small, aquiline nose was hardly visible.

"This is Miss Rolleston, Lady Ducayne."

Claw-like fingers, flashing with jewels, lifted a double eyeglass to Lady Ducayne's shining black eyes, and through the glasses Bella saw those unnaturally bright eyes magnified to a gigantic size, and glaring at her awfully.

"Miss Torpinter has told me all about you," said the old voice that belonged to the eyes. "Have you good health? Are you strong and active, able to eat well, sleep well, walk well, able to enjoy all that there is good in life?"

"I have never known what it is to be ill, or idle," answered Bella.

"Then I think you will do for me."

"Of course, in the event of references being perfectly satisfactory," put in the Person.

"I don't want references. The young woman looks frank and innocent. I'll take her on trust."

"So like you, dear Lady Ducayne," murmured Miss Torpinter.

"I want a strong young woman whose health will give me no trouble."

"You have been so unfortunate in that respect," cooed the Person, whose voice and manner were subdued to a melting sweetness by the old woman's presence.

1 Springs supporting a carriage to provide a smoother ride. They were shaped like the letter C.

"Yes, I've been rather unlucky," grunted Lady Ducayne.

"But I am sure Miss Rolleston will not disappoint you, though certainly after your unpleasant experience with Miss Tomson, who looked the picture of health—and Miss Blandy, who said she had never seen a doctor since she was vaccinated—"

"Lies, no doubt," muttered Lady Ducayne, and then turning to Bella, she asked, curtly, "You don't mind spending the winter in Italy, I suppose?"

In Italy! The very word was magical. Bella's fair young face flushed crimson.

"It has been the dream of my life to see Italy," she gasped.

From Walworth to Italy! How far, how impossible such a journey had seemed to that romantic dreamer.

"Well, your dream will be realized. Get yourself ready to leave Charing Cross by the train deluxe this day week at eleven. Be sure you are at the station a quarter before the hour. My people will look after you and your luggage."

Lady Ducayne rose from her chair, assisted by her crutch-stick, and Miss Torpinter escorted her to the door.

"And with regard to salary?" questioned the Person on the way.

"Salary, oh, the same as usual—and if the young woman wants a quarter's pay in advance you can write to me for a cheque," Lady Ducayne answered, carelessly.

Miss Torpinter went all the way downstairs with her client, and waited to see her seated in the yellow chariot. When she came upstairs again she was slightly out of breath, and she had resumed that superior manner which Bella had found so crushing.

"You may think yourself uncommonly lucky, Miss Rolleston," she said. "I have dozens of young ladies on my books whom I might have recommended for this situation—but I remembered having told you to call this afternoon—and I thought I would give you a chance. Old Lady Ducayne is one of the best people on my books. She gives her companion a hundred a year, and pays all travelling expenses. You will live in the lap of luxury."

"A hundred a year! How too lovely! Shall I have to dress very grandly? Does Lady Ducayne keep much company?"

"At her age! No, she lives in seclusion—in her own apartments—her French maid, her footman, her medical attendant, her courier."

"Why did those other companions leave her?" asked Bella.

"Their health broke down!"

"Poor things, and so they had to leave?"

"Yes, they had to leave. I suppose you would like a quarter's salary in advance?"

"Oh, yes, please. I shall have things to buy."

"Very well, I will write for Lady Ducayne's cheque, and I will send you the balance—after deducting my commission for the year."

"To be sure, I had forgotten the commission."

"You don't suppose I keep this office for pleasure."

"Of course not," murmured Bella, remembering the five shillings entrance fee; but nobody could expect a hundred a year and a winter in Italy for five shillings.

## III

From Miss Rolleston, at Cap Ferrino, to Mrs. Rolleston, in Beresford Street, Walworth, London.

*"How I wish you could see this place, dearest; the blue sky, the olive woods, the orange and lemon orchards between the cliffs and the sea—sheltering in the hollow of the great hills—and with summer waves dancing up to the narrow ridge of pebbles and weeds which is the Italian idea of a beach! Oh, how I wish you could see it all, mother dear, and bask in this sunshine, that makes it so difficult to believe the date at the head of this paper. November! The air is like an English June—the sun is so hot that I can't walk a few yards without an umbrella. And to think of you at Walworth while I am here! I could cry at the thought that perhaps you will never see this lovely coast, this wonderful sea, these summer flowers that bloom in winter. There is a hedge of pink geraniums under my window, mother—a thick, rank hedge, as if the flowers grew wild—and there are Dijon roses climbing over arches and palisades all along the terrace—a rose garden full of bloom in November! Just picture it all! You could never imagine the luxury of this hotel. It is nearly new, and has been built and decorated regardless of expense. Our rooms are upholstered in pale blue satin, which shows up Lady Ducayne's parchment complexion; but as she sits all day in a corner of the balcony basking in the sun, except when she is in her carriage, and all the evening in her armchair close to the fire, and never sees anyone but her own people, her complexion matters very little.*

*"She has the handsomest suite of rooms in the hotel. My bedroom is inside hers, the sweetest room—all blue satin and white lace—white enamelled furniture, looking-glasses on every wall, till I know my pert little profile as I never knew it before. The room was really meant for Lady Ducayne's dressing-room, but she ordered one of the blue satin couches to be arranged as a bed for me—the prettiest little bed, which I can wheel near the window on sunny mornings, as it is on castors and easily moved about. I feel as if Lady Ducayne were a funny old grandmother, who had suddenly appeared in my life, very, very rich, and very, very kind.*

*"She is not at all exacting. I read aloud to her a good deal, and she dozes and nods while I read. Sometimes I hear her moaning in her sleep—*

*as if she had troublesome dreams. When she is tired of my reading she orders Francine, her maid, to read a French novel to her, and I hear her chuckle and groan now and then, as if she were more interested in those books than in Dickens or Scott. My French is not good enough to follow Francine, who reads very quickly. I have a great deal of liberty, for Lady Ducayne often tells me to run away and amuse myself; I roam about the hills for hours. Everything is so lovely. I lose myself in olive woods, always climbing up and up towards the pine woods above—and above the pines there are the snow mountains that just show their white peaks above the dark hills. Oh, you poor dear, how can I ever make you understand what this place is like—you, whose poor, tired eyes have only the opposite side of Beresford Street? Sometimes I go no farther than the terrace in front of the hotel, which is a favourite lounging-place with everybody. The gardens lie below, and the tennis courts where I sometimes play with a very nice girl, the only person in the hotel with whom I have made friends. She is a year older than I, and has come to Cap Ferrino with her brother, a doctor—or a medical student, who is going to be a doctor. He passed his M.B. exam at Edinburgh just before they left home, Lotta told me. He came to Italy entirely on his sister's account. She had a troublesome chest attack last summer and was ordered to winter abroad. They are orphans, quite alone in the world, and so fond of each other. It is very nice for me to have such a friend as Lotta. She is so thoroughly respectable. I can't help using that word, for some of the girls in this hotel go on in a way that I know you would shudder at. Lotta was brought up by an aunt, deep down in the country, and knows hardly anything about life. Her brother won't allow her to read a novel, French or English, that he has not read and approved.*

*"'He treats me like a child,' she told me, 'but I don't mind, for it's nice to know somebody loves me, and cares about what I do, and even about my thoughts.'*

*"Perhaps this is what makes some girls so eager to marry—the want of someone strong and brave and honest and true to care for them and order them about. I want no one, mother darling, for I have you, and you are all the world to me. No husband could ever come between us two. If I ever were to marry he would have only the second place in my heart. But I don't suppose I ever shall marry, or even know what it is like to have an offer of marriage. No young man can afford to marry a penniless girl nowadays. Life is too expensive.*

*"Mr. Stafford, Lotta's brother, is very clever, and very kind. He thinks it is rather hard for me to have to live with such an old woman as Lady Ducayne, but then he does not know how poor we are—you and I—and what a wonderful life this seems to me in this lovely place. I feel a selfish wretch for enjoying all my luxuries, while you, who want them so much more than I, have none of them—hardly know what they are like—do*

*you, dearest?—for my scamp of a father began to go to the dogs soon after you were married, and since then life has been all trouble and care and struggle for you."*

This letter was written when Bella had been less than a month at Cap Ferrino, before the novelty had worn off the landscape, and before the pleasure of luxurious surroundings had begun to cloy. She wrote to her mother every week, such long letters as girls who have lived in closest companionship with a mother alone can write; letters that are like a diary of heart and mind. She wrote gaily always; but when the new year began Mrs. Rolleston thought she detected a note of melancholy under all those lively details about the place and the people.

"My poor girl is getting homesick," she thought. "Her heart is in Beresford Street."

It might be that she missed her new friend and companion, Lotta Stafford, who had gone with her brother for a little tour to Genoa and Spezzia, and as far as Pisa. They were to return before February; but in the meantime Bella might naturally feel very solitary among all those strangers, whose manners and doings she described so well.

The mother's instinct had been true. Bella was not so happy as she had been in that first flush of wonder and delight which followed the change from Walworth to the Riviera. Somehow, she knew not how, lassitude had crept upon her. She no longer loved to climb the hills, no longer flourished her orange stick in sheer gladness of heart as her light feet skipped over the rough ground and the coarse grass on the mountain side. The odour of rosemary and thyme, the fresh breath of the sea, no longer filled her with rapture. She thought of Beresford Street and her mother's face with a sick longing. They were so far—so far away! And then she thought of Lady Ducayne, sitting by the heaped-up olive logs in the over-heated salon—thought of that wizened-nut-cracker profile, and those gleaming eyes, with an invincible horror.

Visitors at the hotel had told her that the air of Cap Ferrino was relaxing—better suited to age than to youth, to sickness than to health. No doubt it was so. She was not so well as she had been at Walworth; but she told herself that she was suffering only from the pain of separation from the dear companion of her girlhood, the mother who had been nurse, sister, friend, flatterer, all things in this world to her. She had shed many tears over that parting, had spent many a melancholy hour on the marble terrace with yearning eyes looking westward, and with her heart's desire a thousand miles away.

She was sitting in her favourite spot, an angle at the eastern end of the terrace, a quiet little nook sheltered by orange trees, when she heard a couple of Riviera habitués talking in the garden below. They were sitting on a bench against the terrace wall.

She had no idea of listening to their talk, till the sound of Lady Ducayne's name attracted her, and then she listened without any thought of wrong-doing.

They were talking no secrets—just casually discussing an hotel acquaintance.

They were two elderly people whom Bella only knew by sight. An English clergyman who had wintered abroad for half his lifetime; a stout, comfortable, well-to-do spinster, whose chronic bronchitis obliged her to migrate annually.

"I have met her about Italy for the last ten years," said the lady; "but have never found out her real age."

"I put her down at a hundred—not a year less," replied the parson. "Her reminiscences all go back to the Regency. She was evidently then in her zenith; and I have heard her say things that showed she was in Parisian society when the First Empire was at its best—before Josephine was divorced."[1]

"She doesn't talk much now."

"No; there's not much life left in her. She is wise in keeping herself secluded. I only wonder that wicked old quack, her Italian doctor, didn't finish her off years ago."

"I should think it must be the other way, and that he keeps her alive."

"My dear Miss Manders, do you think foreign quackery ever kept anybody alive?"

"Well, there she is—and she never goes anywhere without him. He certainly has an unpleasant countenance."

"Unpleasant," echoed the parson, "I don't believe the foul fiend himself can beat him in ugliness. I pity that poor young woman who has to live between old Lady Ducayne and Dr. Parravicini."

"But the old lady is very good to her companions."

"No doubt. She is very free with her cash; the servants call her good Lady Ducayne. She is a withered old female Croesus,[2] and knows she'll never be able to get through her money, and doesn't relish the idea of other people enjoying it when she's in her coffin. People who live to be as old as she is become slavishly attached to life. I daresay she's generous to those poor girls—but she can't make them happy. They die in her service."

"Don't say they, Mr. Carton; I know that one poor girl died at Mentone last spring."

"Yes, and another poor girl died in Rome three years ago. I was there at the time. Good Lady Ducayne left her there in an English family. The girl had every comfort. The old woman was very liberal to her—but she died. I tell you, Miss Manders, it is not good for any young woman to live with two such horrors as Lady Ducayne and Parravicini."

They talked of other things—but Bella hardly heard them. She sat motionless, and a cold wind seemed to come down upon her from the mountains and to creep up to her from the sea, till she shivered as she sat there in the sunshine,

1 The Regency period in England lasted from 1811 to 1820. The First Empire or Napoleonic Empire spanned the years from 1804 to 1814. Napoleon divorced Josephine in 1810. As the story appears to be set close to its publication date of 1896, that would make Lady Ducayne over 100.

2 King of Lydia who reigned from 585 BCE to 547 or 546 BCE, proverbial for his wealth.

in the shelter of the orange trees in the midst of all that beauty and brightness.

Yes, they were uncanny, certainly, the pair of them—she so like an aristocratic witch in her withered old age; he of no particular age, with a face that was more like a waxen mask than any human countenance Bella had ever seen. What did it matter? Old age is venerable, and worthy of all reverence; and Lady Ducayne had been very kind to her. Dr. Parravicini was a harmless, inoffensive student, who seldom looked up from the book he was reading. He had his private sitting-room, where he made experiments in chemistry and natural science—perhaps in alchemy. What could it matter to Bella? He had always been polite to her, in his far-off way. She could not be more happily placed than she was—in this palatial hotel, with this rich old lady.

No doubt she missed the young English girl who had been so friendly, and it might be that she missed the girl's brother, for Mr. Stafford had talked to her a good deal—had interested himself in the books she was reading, and her manner of amusing herself when she was not on duty.

"You must come to our little salon when you are 'off,' as the hospital nurses call it, and we can have some music. No doubt you play and sing?" upon which Bella had to own with a blush of shame that she had forgotten how to play the piano ages ago.

"Mother and I used to sing duets sometimes between the lights, without accompaniment," she said, and the tears came into her eyes as she thought of the humble room, the half-hour's respite from work, the sewing-machine standing where a piano ought to have been, and her mother's plaintive voice, so sweet, so true, so dear.

Sometimes she found herself wondering whether she would ever see that beloved mother again. Strange forebodings came into her mind. She was angry with herself for giving way to melancholy thoughts.

One day she questioned Lady Ducayne's French maid about those two companions who had died within three years.

"They were poor, feeble creatures," Francine told her. "They looked fresh and bright enough when they came to Miladi; but they ate too much and they were lazy. They died of luxury and idleness. Miladi was too kind to them. They had nothing to do; and so they took to fancying things; fancying the air didn't suit them, that they couldn't sleep."

"I sleep well enough, but I have had a strange dream several times since I have been in Italy."

"Ah, you had better not begin to think about dreams, or you will be like those other girls. They were dreamers—and they dreamt themselves into the cemetery."

The dream troubled her a little, not because it was a ghastly or frightening dream, but on account of sensations which she had never felt before in sleep—a whirring of wheels that went round in her brain, a great noise like a whirlwind, but rhythmical like the ticking of a gigantic clock: and then in the midst of this uproar as of winds and waves she seemed to sink into a gulf of unconsciousness, out of sleep into far deeper sleep—total extinction. And then, after that blank interval, there had come the sound of voices, and then again the whirr of wheels, louder and louder—and again the blank—and then she knew no more till morning, when she awoke, feeling languid and oppressed.

She told Dr. Parravicini of her dream one day, on the only occasion when she wanted his professional advice. She had suffered rather severely from the mosquitoes before Christmas—and had been almost frightened at finding a wound upon her arm which she could only attribute to the venomous sting of one of these torturers. Parravicini put on his glasses, and scrutinized the angry mark on the round, white arm, as Bella stood before him and Lady Ducayne with her sleeve rolled up above her elbow.

"Yes, that's rather more than a joke," he said, "he has caught you on the top of a vein. What a vampire! But there's no harm done, signorina, nothing that a little dressing of mine won't heal. You must always show me any bite of this nature. It might be dangerous if neglected. These creatures feed on poison and disseminate it."

"And to think that such tiny creatures can bite like this," said Bella; "my arm looks as if it had been cut by a knife."

"If I were to show you a mosquito's sting under my microscope you wouldn't be surprised at that," replied Parravicini.

Bella had to put up with the mosquito bites, even when they came on the top of a vein, and produced that ugly wound. The wound recurred now and then at longish intervals, and Bella found Dr. Parravicini's dressing a speedy cure. If he were the quack his enemies called him, he had at least a light hand and a delicate touch in performing this small operation.

Bella Rolleston to Mrs. Rolleston—April 14th.

"EVER DEAREST,

*"Behold the cheque for my second quarter's salary—five and twenty pounds. There is no one to pinch off a whole tenner for a year's commission as there was last time, so it is all for you, mother, dear. I have plenty of pocket-money in hand from the cash I brought away with me, when you insisted on my keeping more than I wanted. It isn't possible to spend money here—except on occasional tips to servants, or sous to beggars and children—unless one had lots to spend, for everything one would like to buy—tortoise-shell, coral, lace—is so ridiculously dear that only a millionaire ought to look at it. Italy is a dream of beauty: but for shopping, give me Newington Causeway.*

*"You ask me so earnestly if I am quite well that I fear my letters must have been very dull lately. Yes, dear, I am well—but I am not quite so strong as I was when I used to trudge to the West-end to buy half a pound*

*of tea—just for a constitutional walk—or to Dulwich to look at the pictures. Italy is relaxing; and I feel what the people here call 'slack.' But I fancy I can see your dear face looking worried as you read this. Indeed, and indeed, I am not ill. I am only a little tired of this lovely scene—as I suppose one might get tired of looking at one of Turner's pictures*[1] *if it hung on a wall that was always opposite one. I think of you every hour in every day—think of you and our homely little room—our dear little shabby parlour, with the armchairs from the wreck of your old home, and Dick singing in his cage over the sewing-machine. Dear, shrill, maddening Dick, who, we flattered ourselves, was so passionately fond of us. Do tell me in your next that he is well.*

*"My friend Lotta and her brother never came back after all. They went from Pisa to Rome. Happy mortals! And they are to be on the Italian lakes in May; which lake was not decided when Lotta last wrote to me. She has been a charming correspondent, and has confided all her little flirtations to me. We are all to go to Bellaggio next week—by Genoa and Milan. Isn't that lovely? Lady Ducayne travels by the easiest stages—except when she is bottled up in the train deluxe. We shall stop two days at Genoa and one at Milan. What a bore I shall be to you with my talk about Italy when I come home.*

*"Love and love—and ever more love from your adoring, BELLA."*

## IV

Herbert Stafford and his sister had often talked of the pretty English girl with her fresh complexion, which made such a pleasant touch of rosy colour among all those sallow faces at the Grand Hotel. The young doctor thought of her with a compassionate tenderness—her utter loneliness in that great hotel where there were so many people, her bondage to that old, old woman, where everybody else was free to think of nothing but enjoying life. It was a hard fate; and the poor child was evidently devoted to her mother, and felt the pain of separation—"only two of them, and very poor, and all the world to each other," he thought.

Lotta told him one morning that they were to meet again at Bellaggio. "The old thing and her court are to be there before we are," she said. "I shall be charmed to have Bella again. She is so bright and gay—in spite of an occasional touch of homesickness. I never took to a girl on a short acquaintance as I did to her."

"I like her best when she is homesick," said Herbert; "for then I am sure she has a heart."

1 J.M.W. or William Turner was one of the most popular British artists of the nineteenth century. He was best known for landscapes and marine paintings.

"What have you to do with hearts, except for dissection? Don't forget that Bella is an absolute pauper. She told me in confidence that her mother makes mantles for a West-end shop. You can hardly have a lower depth than that."

"I shouldn't think any less of her if her mother made match-boxes."

"Not in the abstract—of course not. Match-boxes are honest labour. But you couldn't marry a girl whose mother makes mantles."

"We haven't come to the consideration of that question yet," answered Herbert, who liked to provoke his sister.

In two years' hospital practice he had seen too much of the grim realities of life to retain any prejudices about rank. Cancer, phthisis, gangrene, leave a man with little respect for the outward differences which vary the husk of humanity. The kernel is always the same—fearfully and wonderfully made—a subject for pity and terror.

Mr. Stafford and his sister arrived at Bellaggio in a fair May evening. The sun was going down as the steamer approached the pier; and all that glory of purple bloom which curtains every wall at this season of the year flushed and deepened in the glowing light. A group of ladies were standing on the pier watching the arrivals, and among them Herbert saw a pale face that startled him out of his wonted composure.

"There she is," murmured Lotta, at his elbow, "but how dreadfully changed. She looks a wreck."

They were shaking hands with her a few minutes later, and a flush had lighted up her poor pinched face in the pleasure of meeting.

"I thought you might come this evening," she said. "We have been here a week."

She did not add that she had been there every evening to watch the boat in, and a good many times during the day. The Grand Bretagne was close by, and it had been easy for her to creep to the pier when the boat bell rang. She felt a joy in meeting these people again; a sense of being with friends; a confidence which Lady Ducayne's goodness had never inspired in her.

"Oh, you poor darling, how awfully ill you must have been," exclaimed Lotta, as the two girls embraced.

Bella tried to answer, but her voice was choked with tears.

"What has been the matter, dear? That horrid influenza, I suppose?"

"No, no, I have not been ill—I have only felt a little weaker than I used to be. I don't think the air of Cap Ferrino quite agreed with me."

"It must have disagreed with you abominably. I never saw such a change in anyone. Do let Herbert doctor you. He is fully qualified, you know. He prescribed for ever so many influenza patients at the Londres. They were glad to get advice from an English doctor in a friendly way."

"I am sure he must be very clever!" faltered Bella, "but there is really nothing the matter. I am not ill, and if I were ill, Lady Ducayne's physician—"

"That dreadful man with the yellow face? I would as soon one of the Borgias[1] prescribed for me. I hope you haven't been taking any of his medicines."

"No, dear, I have taken nothing. I have never complained of being ill."

This was said while they were all three walking to the hotel. The Staffords' rooms had been secured in advance, pretty ground-floor rooms, opening into the garden. Lady Ducayne's statelier apartments were on the floor above.

"I believe these rooms are just under ours," said Bella.

"Then it will be all the easier for you to run down to us," replied Lotta, which was not really the case, as the grand staircase was in the centre of the hotel.

"Oh, I shall find it easy enough," said Bella. "I'm afraid you'll have too much of my society. Lady Ducayne sleeps away half the day in this warm weather, so I have a good deal of idle time; and I get awfully moped thinking of mother and home."

Her voice broke upon the last word. She could not have thought of that poor lodging which went by the name of home more tenderly had it been the most beautiful that art and wealth ever created. She moped and pined in this lovely garden, with the sunlit lake and the romantic hills spreading out their beauty before her. She was homesick and she had dreams: or, rather, an occasional recurrence of that one bad dream with all its strange sensations—it was more like a hallucination than dreaming—the whirring of wheels; the sinking into an abyss; the struggling back to consciousness. She had the dream shortly before she left Cap Ferrino, but not since she had come to Bellaggio, and she began to hope the air in this lake district suited her better, and that those strange sensations would never return.

Mr. Stafford wrote a prescription and had it made up at the chemist's near the hotel. It was a powerful tonic, and after two bottles, and a row or two on the lake, and some rambling over the hills and in the meadows where the spring flowers made earth seem paradise, Bella's spirits and looks improved as if by magic.

"It is a wonderful tonic," she said, but perhaps in her heart of hearts she knew that the doctor's kind voice and the friendly hand that helped her in and out of the boat, and the watchful care that went with her by land and lake, had something to do with her cure.

"I hope you don't forget that her mother makes mantles," Lotta said, warningly.

"Or match-boxes: it is just the same thing, so far as I am concerned."

"You mean that in no circumstances could you think of marrying her?"

"I mean that if ever I love a woman well enough to think of marrying her, riches or rank will count for nothing with me. But I fear—I fear your poor friend may not live to be any man's wife."

"Do you think her so very ill?"

1 Aristocratic family who became powerful during the Renaissance. The Borgias were famous for murder by poison, especially arsenic.

He sighed, and left the question unanswered.

One day, while they were gathering wild hyacinths in an upland meadow, Bella told Mr. Stafford about her bad dream.

"It is curious only because it is hardly like a dream," she said. "I daresay you could find some common-sense reason for it. The position of my head on my pillow, or the atmosphere, or something."

And then she described her sensations; how in the midst of sleep there came a sudden sense of suffocation; and then those whirring wheels, so loud, so terrible; and then a blank, and then a coming back to waking consciousness.

"Have you ever had chloroform given you—by a dentist, for instance?"

"Never—Dr. Parravicini asked me that question one day."

"Lately?"

"No, long ago, when we were in the train deluxe."

"Has Dr. Parravicini prescribed for you since you began to feel weak and ill?"

"Oh, he has given me a tonic from time to time, but I hate medicine, and took very little of the stuff. And then I am not ill, only weaker than I used to be. I was ridiculously strong and well when I lived at Walworth, and used to take long walks every day. Mother made me take those tramps to Dulwich or Norwood, for fear I should suffer from too much sewing-machine; sometimes—but very seldom—she went with me. She was generally toiling at home while I was enjoying fresh air and exercise. And she was very careful about our food—that, however plain it was, it should be always nourishing and ample. I owe it to her care that I grew up such a great, strong creature."

"You don't look great or strong now, you poor dear," said Lotta.

"I'm afraid Italy doesn't agree with me."

"Perhaps it is not Italy, but being cooped up with Lady Ducayne that has made you ill."

"But I am never cooped up. Lady Ducayne is absurdly kind, and lets me roam about or sit in the balcony all day if I like. I have read more novels since I have been with her than in all the rest of my life."

"Then she is very different from the average old lady, who is usually a slave-driver," said Stafford. "I wonder why she carries a companion about with her if she has so little need of society."

"Oh, I am only part of her state. She is inordinately rich—and the salary she gives me doesn't count. Apropos of Dr. Parravicini, I know he is a clever doctor, for he cures my horrid mosquito bites."

"A little ammonia would do that, in the early stage of the mischief. But there are no mosquitoes to trouble you now."

"Oh, yes, there are, I had a bite just before we left Cap Ferrino." She pushed up her loose lawn sleeve, and exhibited a scar, which he scrutinized intently, with a surprised and puzzled look.

"This is no mosquito bite," he said.

"Oh, yes it is—unless there are snakes or adders at Cap Ferrino."

"It is not a bite at all. You are trifling with me. Miss Rolleston—you have allowed that wretched Italian quack to bleed you. They killed the greatest man in modern Europe that way, remember. How very foolish of you."

"I was never bled in my life, Mr. Stafford."

"Nonsense! Let me look at your other arm. Are there any more mosquito bites?"

"Yes; Dr. Parravicini says I have a bad skin for healing, and that the poison acts more virulently with me than with most people."

Stafford examined both her arms in the broad sunlight, scars new and old.

"You have been very badly bitten, Miss Rolleston," he said, "and if ever I find the mosquito I shall make him smart. But, now tell me, my dear girl, on your word of honour, tell me as you would tell a friend who is sincerely anxious for your health and happiness—as you would tell your mother if she were here to question you—have you no knowledge of any cause for these scars except mosquito bites—no suspicion even?"

"No, indeed! No, upon my honour! I have never seen a mosquito biting my arm. One never does see the horrid little fiends. But I have heard them trumpeting under the curtains, and I know that I have often had one of the pestilent wretches buzzing about me."

Later in the day Bella and her friends were sitting at tea in the garden, while Lady Ducayne took her afternoon drive with her doctor.

"How long do you mean to stop with Lady Ducayne, Miss Rolleston?" Herbert Stafford asked, after a thoughtful silence, breaking suddenly upon the trivial talk of the two girls.

"As long as she will go on paying me twenty-five pounds a quarter."

"Even if you feel your health breaking down in her service?"

"It is not the service that has injured my health. You can see that I have really nothing to do—to read aloud for an hour or so once or twice a week; to write a letter once in a way to a London tradesman. I shall never have such an easy time with anybody else. And nobody else would give me a hundred a year."

"Then you mean to go on till you break down; to die at your post?"

"Like the other two companions? No! If ever I feel seriously ill—really ill—I shall put myself in a train and go back to Walworth without stopping."

"What about the other two companions?"

"They both died. It was very unlucky for Lady Ducayne. That's why she engaged me; she chose me because I was ruddy and robust. She must feel rather disgusted at my having grown white and weak. By-the-bye, when I told her about the good your tonic had done me, she said she would like to see you and have a little talk with you about her own case."

"And I should like to see Lady Ducayne. When did she say this?"

"The day before yesterday."

"Will you ask her if she will see me this evening?"

"With pleasure! I wonder what you will think of her? She looks rather terrible to a stranger; but Dr. Parravicini says she was once a famous beauty."

It was nearly ten o'clock when Mr. Stafford was summoned by message from Lady Ducayne, whose courier came to conduct him to her ladyship's salon. Bella was reading aloud when the visitor was admitted; and he noticed the languor in the low, sweet tones, the evident effort.

"Shut up the book," said the querulous old voice. "You are beginning to drawl like Miss Blandy."

Stafford saw a small, bent figure crouching over the piled-up olive logs; a shrunken old figure in a gorgeous garment of black and crimson brocade, a skinny throat emerging from a mass of old Venetian lace, clasped with diamonds that flashed like fire-flies as the trembling old head turned towards him.

The eyes that looked at him out of the face were almost as bright as the diamonds—the only living feature in that narrow parchment mask. He had seen terrible faces in the hospital—faces on which disease had set dreadful marks—but he had never seen a face that impressed him so painfully as this withered countenance, with its indescribable horror of death outlived, a face that should have been hidden under a coffin-lid years and years ago.

The Italian physician was standing on the other side of the fireplace, smoking a cigarette, and looking down at the little old woman brooding over the hearth as if he were proud of her.

"Good evening, Mr. Stafford; you can go to your room, Bella, and write your everlasting letter to your mother at Walworth," said Lady Ducayne. "I believe she writes a page about every wild flower she discovers in the woods and meadows. I don't know what else she can find to write about," she added, as Bella quietly withdrew to the pretty little bedroom opening out of Lady Ducayne's spacious apartment. Here, as at Cap Ferrino, she slept in a room adjoining the old lady's.

"You are a medical man, I understand, Mr. Stafford."

"I am a qualified practitioner, but I have not begun to practice."

"You have begun upon my companion, she tells me."

"I have prescribed for her, certainly, and I am happy to find my prescription has done her good; but I look upon that improvement as temporary. Her case will require more drastic treatment."

"Never mind her case. There is nothing the matter with the girl—absolutely nothing—except girlish nonsense; too much liberty and not enough work."

"I understand that two of your ladyship's previous companions died of the same disease," said Stafford, looking first at Lady Ducayne, who gave her tremulous old head an impatient jerk, and then at Parravicini, whose yellow complexion had paled a little under Stafford's scrutiny.

"Don't bother me about my companions, sir," said Lady Ducayne. "I sent for you to consult you about myself—not about a parcel of anemic girls. You are young, and medicine is a progressive science, the newspapers tell me. Where have you studied?"

"In Edinburgh—and in Paris."[1]

"Two good schools. And you know all the new-fangled theories, the modern discoveries—that remind one of the medieval witchcraft, of Albertus Magnus, and George Ripley;[2] you have studied hypnotism—electricity?"

"And the transfusion of blood,"[3] said Stafford, very slowly, looking at Parravicini.

"Have you made any discovery that teaches you to prolong human life—any elixir—any mode of treatment? I want my life prolonged, young man. That man there has been my physician for thirty years. He does all he can to keep me alive—after his lights. He studies all the new theories of all the scientists—but he is old; he gets older every day—his brain-power is going—he is bigoted—prejudiced—can't receive new ideas—can't grapple with new systems. He will let me die if I am not on my guard against him."

"You are of an unbelievable ingratitude, Ecclenza," said Parravicini.

"Oh, you needn't complain. I have paid you thousands to keep me alive. Every year of my life has swollen your hoards; you know there is nothing to come to you when I am gone. My whole fortune is left to endow a home for indigent women of quality who have reached their ninetieth year. Come, Mr. Stafford, I am a rich woman. Give me a few years more in the sunshine, a few years more above ground, and I will give you the price of a fashionable London practice—I will set you up at the West-end."

"How old are you, Lady Ducayne?"

"I was born the day Louis XVI was guillotined."[4]

"Then I think you have had your share of the sunshine and the pleasures of the earth, and that you should spend your few remaining days in repenting your sins and trying to make atonement for the young lives that have been sacrificed to your love of life."

"What do you mean by that, sir?"

"Oh, Lady Ducayne, need I put your wickedness and your physician's still greater wickedness in plain words? The poor girl who is now in your employment has been reduced from robust health to a condition of absolute danger by Dr. Parravicini's experimental surgery; and I have no doubt those other two young women who broke down in your service were treated by him in the

1 Two of the most famous medical schools of the time.

2 Albertus Magnus was a thirteenth-century German Dominican friar, philosopher, and theologian. George Ripley was a nineteenth-century American transcendentalist.

3 Blood transfusion was a new and risky medical technology at the time. Blood groups would not be discovered until the twentieth century.

4 Louis XVI was guillotined in 1793, which would make Lady Ducayne 103 at the time the story was published.

same manner. I could take upon myself to demonstrate—by most convincing evidence, to a jury of medical men—that Dr. Parravicini has been bleeding Miss Rolleston, after putting her under chloroform, at intervals, ever since she has been in your service. The deterioration in the girl's health speaks for itself; the lancet marks upon the girl's arms are unmistakable; and her description of a series of sensations, which she calls a dream, points unmistakably to the administration of chloroform while she was sleeping. A practice so nefarious, so murderous, must, if exposed, result in a sentence only less severe than the punishment of murder."

"I laugh," said Parravicini, with an airy motion of his skinny fingers; "I laugh at once at your theories and at your threats. I, Parravicini Leopold, have no fear that the law can question anything I have done."

"Take the girl away, and let me hear no more of her," cried Lady Ducayne, in the thin, old voice, which so poorly matched the energy and fire of the wicked old brain that guided its utterances. "Let her go back to her mother—I want no more girls to die in my service. There are girls enough and to spare in the world, God knows."

"If you ever engage another companion—or take another English girl into your service, Lady Ducayne, I will make all England ring with the story of your wickedness."

"I want no more girls. I don't believe in his experiments. They have been full of danger for me as well as for the girl—an air bubble, and I should be gone. I'll have no more of his dangerous quackery. I'll find some new man—a better man than you, sir, a discoverer like Pasteur, or Virchow,[1] a genius—to keep me alive. Take your girl away, young man. Marry her if you like. I'll write her a cheque for a thousand pounds, and let her go and live on beef and beer, and get strong and plump again. I'll have no more such experiments. Do you hear, Parravicini?" she screamed, vindictively, the yellow, wrinkled face distorted with fury, the eyes glaring at him.

The Staffords carried Bella Rolleston off to Varese next day, she very loth to leave Lady Ducayne, whose liberal salary afforded such help for the dear mother. Herbert Stafford insisted, however, treating Bella as coolly as if he had been the family physician, and she had been given over wholly to his care.

"Do you suppose your mother would let you stop here to die?" he asked. "If Mrs. Rolleston knew how ill you are, she would come post haste to fetch you."

"I shall never be well again till I get back to Walworth," answered Bella, who was low-spirited and inclined to tears this morning, a reaction after her good spirits of yesterday.

"We'll try a week or two at Varese first," said Stafford. "When you can walk

1 Louis Pasteur was a French chemist and microbiologist known for his discoveries in vaccination, fermentation, and pasteurization. Rudolph Virchow was a German physician and writer known as "the father of modern pathology."

half-way up Monte Generoso[1] without palpitation of the heart, you shall go back to Walworth."

"Poor mother, how glad she will be to see me, and how sorry that I've lost such a good place."

This conversation took place on the boat when they were leaving Bellaggio. Lotta had gone to her friend's room at seven o'clock that morning, long before Lady Ducayne's withered eyelids had opened to the daylight, before even Francine, the French maid, was astir, and had helped to pack a Gladstone bag with essentials, and hustled Bella downstairs and out of doors before she could make any strenuous resistance.

"It's all right," Lotta assured her. "Herbert had a good talk with Lady Ducayne last night and it was settled for you to leave this morning. She doesn't like invalids, you see."

"No," sighed Bella, "she doesn't like invalids. It was very unlucky that I should break down, just like Miss Tomson and Miss Blandy."

"At any rate, you are not dead, like them," answered Lotta, "and my brother says you are not going to die."

It seemed rather a dreadful thing to be dismissed in that off-hand way, without a word of farewell from her employer.

"I wonder what Miss Torpinter will say when I go to her for another situation," Bella speculated, ruefully, while she and her friends were breakfasting on board the steamer.

"Perhaps you may never want another situation," said Stafford.

"You mean that I may never be well enough to be useful to anybody?"

"No, I don't mean anything of the kind."

It was after dinner at Varese, when Bella had been induced to take a whole glass of Chianti, and quite sparkled after that unaccustomed stimulant, that Mr. Stafford produced a letter from his pocket.

"I forgot to give you Lady Ducayne's letter of adieu," he said.

"What, did she write to me? I am so glad—I hated to leave her in such a cool way; for after all she was very kind to me, and if I didn't like her it was only because she was too dreadfully old."

She tore open the envelope. The letter was short and to the point:—

*"Goodbye, child. Go and marry your doctor. I enclose a farewell gift for your trousseau.*

—ADALINE DUCAYNE"

"A hundred pounds, a whole year's salary—no—why, it's for a—A cheque for a thousand!" cried Bella. "What a generous old soul! She really is the dearest old thing."

1 Mountain on the border between Italy and Switzerland.

"She just missed being very dear to you, Bella," said Stafford.

He had dropped into the use of her Christian name while they were on board the boat. It seemed natural now that she was to be in his charge till they all three went back to England.

"I shall take upon myself the privileges of an elder brother till we land at Dover," he said; "after that—well, it must be as you please."

The question of their future relations must have been satisfactorily settled before they crossed the Channel, for Bella's next letter to her mother communicated three startling facts.

First, that the enclosed cheque for £1,000 was to be invested in debenture stock in Mrs. Rolleston's name, and was to be her very own, income and principal, for the rest of her life.

Next, that Bella was going home to Walworth immediately.

And last, that she was going to be married to Mr. Herbert Stafford in the following autumn.

"And I am sure you will adore him, mother, as much as I do," wrote Bella.

"It is all good Lady Ducayne's doing. I never could have married if I had not secured that little nest-egg for you. Herbert says we shall be able to add to it as the years go by, and that wherever we live there shall be always a room in our house for you. The word 'mother-in-law' has no terrors for him."

# Arabella Kenealy

(1859–1938)

Arabella Kenealy was a controversial figure whose life seems to contradict her politics. A female physician in an era where such achievements were rare, she was also a eugenicist who opposed women's equality. Kenealy graduated from the London School of Medicine for Women and began her medical practice in 1888 but had to give it up in 1894 after a bout of diphtheria. After medicine, Kenealy turned to writing, publishing a successful novel and the gothic short story "A Beautiful Vampire." In 1920, she published *Feminism and Sex Extinction*, warning of what she perceived to be the dangers of the women's rights movement. Despite the conflicting ideas of Kenealy's life, her story appears to criticize the Victorian ideology that praised a useless decorative woman. "A Beautiful Vampire" contrasts its vain, conventionally feminine antagonist, Lady Deverish, with the clever, practical, working woman, Nurse Marian, who ultimately outwits her.

# "A Beautiful Vampire"

(1896)

There was a flutter indeed in the little town of Argles, when it became known that Dr. Andrew had made an attempt upon the life of Lady Deverish. Andrew was a youngish, good-looking fellow, junior partner in the firm of Byrne & Andrew, the principal doctors in the place. Everybody liked him. He was as clever as he was kind. He would take equal pains to pull the ninth child of a navvy[1] through a croup seizure as he would have done had it been heir to an earldom. Some people thought this mistaken kindness on the doctor's part—the navvy's ninth could well have been spared, especially as the navvy drank, and in any case was unable to provide properly for eight. Some went so far even as to assert that Andrew was flying in the face of Providence—to say nothing of

1 Navvy, a colloquial form of the word navigator or navigational engineer, referred to manual laborers working on major civil engineering projects like roads, railroads, and canals.

the ratepayers—when he brought this superfluous ninth triumphantly through its fifth attack of croup. Otherwise, he was as popular as a man may be in a world wherein flaws and scandal lend to tea and bread-and-butter a stimulating quality denied to blamelessness and good repute.

"The butler says he heard raised voices," it was whispered over dainty cups, "and then Lady Deverish shrieked for help, and he ran in and found the doctor clutching her round the throat."

"And only just in time. Her face was perfectly black!"

"Isn't it awful? Such a kind man as he has always seemed. Is there any madness in the family?"

"It is not certain. They say his mother was peculiar. Wrote books, and did other extraordinary things. Always wore very large hats with black feathers. Quite out of fashion, Mrs. Byass tells me. She knew her."

"What have they done with him?"

"That is the strangest part of it. She wouldn't charge him—said it was all a mistake. So he just got into his carriage, and continued his rounds."

"Gracious! Strangling everybody?"

"Oh, I believe not."

"Her throat was bruised black and blue. Old Dr. Byrne went at once and saw to her. He got a new nurse down from London. They say it was a nurse they quarrelled about, you know."

"Well, they won't get anyone to believe that, my dear."

"No, because she was as plain as could be. And Lady Deverish's groom told cook that Dr. Andrew scarcely looked at her."

"And I never heard that he admired Lady Deverish."

"Ah! Well, most men do."

"I don't see what she wants a nurse at all for. She's the picture of health."

"She says she suffers from nerves."

"If all of us who suffer from 'nerves' were to have trained nurses to go round."

"No, but all of us are not widows with the incomes of two rich dear departeds at our bankers, my dear."

Now, knowing both her charming ladyship and Andrews, I was naturally interested as to why he had put hands about her beautiful throat in anything other than loving kindness. Therefore, I made a point of drinking tea with a number of amiable and gracious persons of my acquaintance during the week following this most notable attempt. All the information I got for my pains has been condensed into the foregoing gossip, and since it was insufficient for my purposes I set about seeking more. I called early at the Manor. I did not entirely credit rumour's whisper concerning the victim's mangled throat, but I knew Andrew's muscular lean hands, if he had been in earnest, would, to say the least of it, have rendered prudent her retirement for the space of some days, so that I did not expect to see anybody but her companion, Mrs. Lyall.

"Gracious, how ill you look!" I could not help exclaiming, as she entered.

I had known her some months earlier as a buxom matron. Now she was a haggard old woman. Her features worked and twisted. She slid into a chair, her hands and members shaking like those of one with palsy. For several minutes she could not speak.

"You must have been sadly troubled," I said.

She was a mild and somewhat flaccid person, one of those plump anaemic women who give one the impression that in their veins run milk. But as I spoke her face became contorted. She struggled up and brandished a trembling, clenched hand.

"If he had only done it!" she cried passionately, "if by some mercy of Providence he had only done it!"

She was transformed—distorted. It was as though some mild and milky Alderney[1] had suddenly developed claws. She slid trembling again into her chair.

"My dear Mrs. Lyall," I remonstrated, "if he had only done it, the world would have lost a beautiful and accomplished member of your sex—and poor Andrew's career would have come to a summary and lamentable end."

"No jury would have convicted him," she protested, "*not when they knew.*" She dropped her voice and searched the room with apprehensive eyes. Then she whispered, "She is a devil."

Now I was aware that some plain and very good women are in the habit of regarding every comely member of their sex as allied in one or another way with the Father of Evil, but it was clear that some sentiment stronger than general principles was moving Mrs. Lyall.

My interest was roused. But she had come to the end of her remarks. She glanced round timorously.

"For Heaven's sake, Lord Syfret,[2] do not mention a word of this," she stammered. "I am sadly unnerved. I scarcely know what I say. Poor Lady Deverish has been rather trying." She shut her weak lips obstinately. I assured her of my discretion. I expressed sympathy, and went my way.

Byrne had nothing to tell. "Andrew will not say a word," he said. "He was over-taxed. Been up several nights. She must have exasperated him somehow. Shouldn't have thought he had it in him. He has always been the kindest of fellows."

"What does she say?"

"Laughs it off, though she don't seem amiable. Looks as if she don't want things to come out."

"You don't mean—?"

"My dear fellow, whatsoever I mean, I do not say."

---

1 Now extinct, a type of dairy cow that originated on the British Channel island of Alderney.

2 The story's first narrator, Lord Syfret, is a Van Helsing-esque character who appears in a number of Kenealy's supernatural stories.

It has always been my habit in life to take the bull by the horns whensoever circumstances have rendered this feat at the same time possible and prudent. I determined to attempt it now. Andrew, after all, was a very mild and tractable bull, despite his recent outbreak.

"I will not disguise the object of my visit," I informed him. "You know my weakness. Anything you tell me will go no further. The ball of Argles' scandal will get no push from me. But I like to probe human motive; and you must admit the situation is suggestive."

He smiled—a nervous smile. I had never seen him so careworn. He shook his head. "She has tied my hands," he said. "If they had let me I would have strangled her."

"I do not wonder you are hard hit," I adventured, watching him. "She is certainly a siren of the first water."

He burst out laughing. "Great Scott!" he said. "Is that what they say? Do they think I am aspiring to the Deverish's hand and acres? No, no; I am not altogether a fool."

At this moment somebody ran up the stairs and after a preliminary knock, burst into the room.

"Please, doctor, come quick," a pageboy blurted. "There's Lady Deverish's nurse has fallen down in the road, and they says she's dying."

The same change come over Andrew that had come over Mrs. Lyall. His face became contorted. He held a clenched fist in the air. "Damn her!" he cried, and rushed out.

Now this ejaculation had every appearance of applying to her ladyship's nurse, and would point to an amount of callousness on Andrew's part—considering the moribund condition of that unfortunate young person—whereof I am sure he was incapable. I hasten, therefore, to inform the reader that it was intended solely and absolutely for her ladyship's own bewitching self. It was as fervid and whole-souled a fulmination as I remember to have heard. It left no doubt in my mind whatsoever as to the fact of her ladyship owing her life to that timely advent of her butler. My interest was not abated. I followed Andrew out. In the next street a knot of curious persons were assembled.

"Stand back," the doctor called as we went up. "Give her air."

The circle widened, disclosing the figure of a young woman in nursing dress, lying senseless on the pavement. Her upturned face was curiously pinched, though the conformation was young, and her hair fallen loose about her cheek hung in girlish rings.

"She does not look strong enough for nursing," I remarked to Byrne, who came up at the moment.

"Strong enough," he echoed testily. "A week ago she was sturdy and robust. The Deverish takes care of that. Can't stand sickliness about her." He added half to himself, "Must be something wrong with the house. Ventilation bad or something. One after another they've gone off like this." The girl now began to show signs of consciousness. She opened her eyes, and seeing Andrew, smiled faintly. Presently, she sat up.

"When you feel equal to it, my dear," Dr. Byrne said, "we will help you to my carriage, and you can drive straight back."

"Back," she repeated wildly, "where?"

"Why, to the Manor. You must—"

She interrupted him; she caught his hand. "No, no," she gasped, "not there, never there. I cannot stand another hour of it."

"The beautiful Deverish must be something of a vixen," I reflected, seeing the expression on the girl's face.

Andrew was helping her to her feet. "Don't be afraid," he said quietly, "I will see that you do not go back."

She looked into his face. "What is it?" she whispered, with white lips. "Do you know?"

"Yes, I know," he answered, meeting her look.

I had an inspiration. Among my clientele I numbered several trained nurses. I called at the post office on my way home and wired for one. In less than two hours she was with me. I dispatched her to the Manor. "Say you have been sent from Heaven or Buckingham Palace, or any other probable and impressive source, and keep your eyes and ears open," I enjoined her, with that utter disregard for truth and scrupulousness which I have found the greatest of all aids to me in my researches.

She returned in an hour. There was anger in her eyes. The gauze veil streaming from her bonnet fluttered mane-like to the offended toss of her head.

"You did not stay long," I said.

"My lord," she returned, "I did not have the opportunity. Lady Devilish—I believe you called her Devilish—just came into the room and gave a little cry, and turned her back on me as if I'd been an ogre. 'Oh, you would never suit,' she said, 'I must have someone young'—my lord, I am twenty-six—'and plump'—I weigh ten stone[1]—'and heathy'—I have never had a day's illness. 'Send someone young, and plump, and healthy,' and she marched out."

"I suppose that would not be difficult?" I commented.

"Not at all," she said resolutely, "a little padding, a touch of rouge, and some minor details are all that are needed."

"You mean to go yourself, then?"

"Yes, I mean to go," she returned. "If there is anything to find out she may be sorry she wasn't more civil," she added meditatively.

"Would she not recognize you?"

I admire grit. I admired the uncompromising and superior disdain with which she met my question. She turned and left without condescending a word.

1 Equivalent to 140 pounds.

In fifteen minutes she came back, or, rather somebody did whose voice was all I recognized. Her disguise was perfect. Before, she had certainly looked neither youthful (despite her assurance as to twenty-six), nor plump (despite her boasted avoirdupois[1]), nor healthy. Now she was plump, and young, and rosy. She had been dark; now a profusion of rich red hair rippled from her brows. I wondered why she did not always go about disguised. She explained.

"In most houses, my lord," she said, "there are sons, and brothers, and husbands. A woman who has her living to get by nursing can only afford to sport cherry cheeks under exceptional circumstances."

When she had gone I dipped my pen in coloured ink and entered her name in my diary. Whether or not she succeeded with Lady "Devilish," she was a capable person. And capable persons are red-letter persons in a world where incompetency rules seven days out of most weeks.

## II

### *NURSE MARIAN'S STORY*

She received me with open arms. "You are just what I want," she said effusively. "I loathe sickliness. There was a gaunt, haggard creature here an hour ago. Ugh!" she shuddered, "I would not have employed her for worlds."

I may be prejudiced, but after her remark, I confess to feeling somewhat antipathetic to her ladyship. She has a curious way of staring. I suspect her of being short-sighted and shirking glasses for the sake of her looks. Certainly, I have never seen anybody so brilliantly beautiful.

Upstairs I was introduced to her companion, Mrs. Lyall. She did not strike me as being altogether sane. She has rather a grim smile.

"You'll soon lose those fine cheeks," she said the moment she saw me.

"I trust not," I returned, with some amount of confidence. (I had only just opened a new packet.) "Is Lady Devilish rather a trying patient, then?" I asked.

She broke into a laugh. "What did you call her?"

"I understood her name to be Devilish," I said.

"No, it's her nature," she retorted, looking furtively about. "Her name has an 'r' instead of an 'l.'"

Her ladyship was plainly no favourite of Mrs. Lyall's. Indeed, everybody in the house seemed to be in mortal terror of her. The servants would not, if they could help it, enter a room where she was.

From the unhealthy faces of the household I came to the conclusion that the house was thoroughly unsanitary. I determined to investigate the drains. Whatsoever there might be that was unwholesome it did not affect the mistress. Her

1 Weight or heaviness, often used humorously.

energy was marvellous. She never tired. When after a long day picnicking or a late ball, everybody looked as white as paper, she was as fresh and blooming and gay-spirited as possible. It seemed a mere farce for her to employ a nurse. But she had a fad about massage, and insisted on being "massed" morning and night.

"You don't look tired," she remarked in a puzzled way, at the end of my first night's operations. She was staring curiously at my rouged cheeks. Strangely enough I was feeling actually faint. Strong-nerved as I am, I fairly reeled.

"Whatsoever I look," I answered her, a little irritably, "I certainly feel more tired than I ever remember feeling."

I thought she seemed pleased. Certainly I had said nothing to please her. No doubt she was thinking her own thoughts.

Her engagement to be married again was announced the day after my arrival. She had been already married twice. The young man—The Earl of Arlington—was, with a number of other persons, stopping in the house. He was handsome and pleasant-looking. I was told he had thrown over a girl he had cared for and who had cared for him for years in order to propose to Lady Deverish. He did not look capable of it. But, to all appearance, he was head over heels in love. He could not keep his eyes from her. He sat like a man bewitched, and neither ate nor rested.

"Poor young gentleman! He'll go the way of the others," Mrs. Plimmer, the housekeeper, confided to me.

"You don't suspect Lady Deverish of poisoning her husbands?" I returned.

"It isn't my place to suspect my betters, Nurse," she said with dignity, "All I say is there's something terrible mysterious. Why does everybody who comes to the Manor fail in health?"

"Drains," I suggested.

She tossed her ample chin. "Why did her two young husbands, as likely men as might be, sicken from the day she married them, and die consumptive? Was that drains, can you tell me?"

I thought it might have been, but having no evidence, did not commit myself.

Mrs. Plummer tossed her ample chin again, this time triumphantly. "And why," she proceeded, "did Dr. Andrew, as kind a gentleman as walks, try to strangle her?"

I braved her scorn and ventured "jealousy."

She eyed me witheringly. "The doctor's no lady's man," she said, "and besides if he was, it's no reason for strangling them."

I was unable to find any fault with the drains. I began to grow interested. I myself felt strangely out of sorts—a new experience for me.

Lord Arlington's infatuation amounted to possession. He sat staring at her in a kind of ecstasy of fascination. He was pale and moody and obviously unhappy. I was told he had lost health and spirits markedly since his engagement. Probably his conscience troubled him about the other woman. At breakfast one morning he unwrapped a little packet which had come by post for him, without, it is to be supposed, observing the handwriting. As he undid it mechanically there dropped from the wrappings a ring, a knot of ribbon, and a bundle of letters. He seemed stunned. Without a word he gathered them together and quitted the room. I met him later pacing the garden like a madman.

Poor man! His love affair was short-lived.

A week later I was involuntary witness to a curious scene. I was sitting late one evening in the garden. Lady Deverish would not need me until bedtime, when her massage was due. Suddenly he and she, talking excitedly, came round the shrubbery.

"I have been mad," he exclaimed, in a hoarse, passionate voice. "For God's sake let me go free. They say her heart is broken."

She put her two hands on his shoulders, and lifted her face to his.

"I will never let you go," she said, with a curious ring as of metal in her voice. She wound her arms about his neck and kissed his throat. "And you love me too much," she added.

"Heaven only knows if it is love," he answered, "it seems to me like madness. I had loved her faithfully for years."

"And now you love me, and there is no way out of it," she whispered. She leaned up again and kissed him. Then with a little cooing laugh she left him.

He remained looking after her. "Yes, there is one way out of it," I heard him say slowly.

That night he shot himself.

Now, although I had known her but a fortnight, I had known her long enough to believe her superior to the weakness of being very deeply in love. Yet the night he died I was inclined to alter my opinion. He had bidden her a hasty goodbye, saying he was summoned to town. He took the last train up.

During the night I was called to her. I found her sitting up in bed, her face ashen pale, her eyes distended, her hands clasped to her head. She was gasping for breath. She seemed like one stricken; her features were picked out by deep grey lines. She did not speak, but pointed with an insistent finger to her right temple. I put my hand upon it. Then I called quickly for a light; for my fingers slipped along that which seemed to be a moist and clammy aperture, moist with a horrible, unmistakable clamminess. But when the light was brought there was neither blood nor aperture, only a curious blanched spot, chill to the touch.

I gave her brandy, and put hot bottles in her bed. She was shaking as with ague. She clutched my hands, holding them against that ice-spot in her temple till I was sick and faint. Soon she seemed better. Some colour returned to her.

"My God, he is dead!" she said, through chattering teeth. Then she crouched down in the bed, a shuddering heap.

Next morning the news came. In that same hour he had put a bullet through his right temple. She was ill all that day, nerveless and almost pulseless. She looked ten years older. I never saw so singular a change. I sent for Dr. Byrne, who attributed it to the shock of bad news. Why it developed some hours before the news arrived he did not explain. He only said: "Tut, tut, Nurse, life is full of coincidences"; and prescribed ammonia.

Next day she was better, and suggested getting up, but changed her mind after having seen a mirror. "Gracious!" she said, with a shudder, "I look like an old woman." She broke into feeble weeping. "He ought to have thought of me," she cried angrily.

She demanded wine and meat-juices,[1] taking them with a curious solicitude, and carefully looking into her mirror for their effect. But she saw little there to comfort her.

"Do you think it might be my death blow?" she questioned once through quivering lips. I shook my head. "Ah, you don't know all," she muttered.

In the afternoon she asked that the gardener's child should be brought to her. He was a chubby, rosy little fellow, whom everybody petted. "I must have something to liven me," she said. I had never supposed her fond of children. But she held her arms hungrily for him, and strained him to her breast. Her spirits rose. Her eyes brightened: she got colour. Soon she was laughing and chatting in her accustomed manner. The child had fallen asleep, but she would not part with him. When at last she let him go, I was horrified to find him cold and pallid. He was breathing heavily, and quite unconscious. I concluded the poor little chap was sickening for something. Later, I was surprised to receive a note from Dr. Andrew, whom I did not know. I dismissed him as I had done Mrs. Lyall, and probably Mrs. Plimmer, as not altogether sane. "I have been called in to attend Willy Daniels," the note ran. "For Heaven's sake, do not let her get hold of any more children."

Next day she was better. She seemed to have forgotten Arlington and talked only of her health. She asked again for the boy. I told her he was ill. She broke into a curious laugh which seemed uncalled for. "Thank goodness, I haven't lost my power," she said a minute later. But she did not explain the saying.

She was in high spirits all the morning, talking and singing and trying on new laces and bonnets. She still complained of pain in the right temple. After her massage she turned peevish, protesting that it did her no good. "If you hadn't such a colour I should not believe you healthy," she said crossly.

She had the parson's children to tea. It would amuse her, she said, to see them eat their strawberries. They seemed afraid of her, and eyed her from a distance. When she attempted to take the little one, it clung to me and shrieked. But she persisted, and it soon fell asleep in her arms. On presently taking it from her, I found it chilled and breathing stertorously[2] and quite unconscious. I thought of Dr. Andrew's injunction. Heavens! what had she done? Was she a secret poisoner? I dismissed the notion forthwith. I had not left the room a moment

1 Commonly prescribed for invalids. A thin broth made from lean cuts of meat. It was believed to build strength.

2 Noisy and labored breathing. Interestingly, this is the same word Stoker uses repeatedly to describe the ragged breathing of Dracula's victims.

during the time the child was with her, nor had it taken anything to eat or drink.

"What is the matter?" I demanded.

Her eye avoided mine. She answered nonchalantly: "What does one expect? Children are everlastingly teething or over-feeding or having measles."

Next morning I was called up at daybreak. Dr. Andrew was waiting to see me. I threw on my things and went down. He was stalking up and down the drawing-room. He stared.

"You seem to have resisted her," he muttered, looking at my cheeks. I have a long memory, and had not forgotten my rouge. He told me a wild and incredible story. He wound up by handing me a small bottle.

"Give her that dose so soon as she wakes," he said. The man was probably a better doctor than he was an actor. His manner paraded the nature of the dose. I took out the cork and smelt it. It was as I suspected. I walked across the room and emptied its contents out of the window. "Pardon me," I said, "but you are exceeding your duty."

"Is she to be allowed to go on murdering people?" he protested. "Do you know I have been up all night with that unfortunate baby? Do you know Willy Daniels is not yet out of danger? Good Heavens! if I am willing to take the consequences, how can one who knows the circumstances hesitate?"

"I have a safer and more justifiable plan," I said. "If what you say is true the remedy is simple, and poison is uncalled for. After all, Dr. Andrew, your story would sound lame enough in a lawcourt. By my plan you run no risks."

I laid it before him. He seemed interested. But he would not, after the manner of men in their dealings with women, permit me to take too much credit to myself.

"It might work," he said lukewarmly, "and as you say it would certainly be safer."

I went to my room and opened a further packet of rouge. I applied it lavishly. I began to see that the health tint on my cheeks had an important bearing on the situation. I put vermilion on my lips. Then I carried my patient her breakfast.

She seemed restored and lay in her rose-pink bed, a smiling Venus. She fairly glowed with beautiful health. I thought of that poor little sick boy. "Goodness!" I said with a start, "how ill you look!" She ceased from smiling. She leapt across the floor, her draperies clinging round her pink flushed toes. She fled to the glass. She turned on me peevishly. "Why did you tell me?" she protested. "I should have thought I looked well."

I went and stood beside her. "Compare yourself with me."

She was pale enough indeed by the time she had done so. "Am I losing my power after all?" she muttered. "Heavens! shall I grow old like other people?"

Suddenly she flung herself upon me. She pressed her lips and cheeks against my throat and face.

"Give *me* some of it," she cried ravenously. "You have so much vitality. Let me drain some of that rich health and colour."

I nearly fell. It seemed as if she were actually sucking out my life. I reeled and sickened. Then with a tremendous effort I pushed her away and stumbled from the room. Was Andrew's story indeed true? Was she a monster or merely a monomaniac?[1]

Years ago he had said she was dying of consumption. So far as physical signs could be trusted, she had not a week to live. Suddenly she began to recover. She made flesh rapidly, gained health, and came back to life from the very jaws of death. Meanwhile, her sister, a schoolgirl, whom she insisted on having always with her, sickened and died.

Then a brother died, then her mother. By this time she had grown quite strong. Since then she had lived on the vital forces of those surrounding her. "The law of life," he said, "makes creatures interdependent. Physical vitality is subject to physical laws of diffusion and equalization. One person below par absorbs the nerve and life sources of healthier persons with them. Many old, debilitated subjects live on the animal forces of the cat they keep persistently in their chair, and die when it dies. Wives and husbands, sisters and brothers, friends and acquaintances: there is a constant interchange of vital force. Lady Deverish has to my knowledge been the actual cause of death of a dozen persons. Besides these she has drained the health of everybody associated with her. And in her case—a rare and extreme one—the faculty is conscious and voluntary. She was living on Arlington. The man was powerless. She paralysed his will, his mind, his energies. She robbed him of strength to resist her. The sequel is interesting, psychologically. She being for the time charged with his vitality, his sudden death, by some curious sympathy, affected her in the way you have described. She was all at once and violently bereft of the source whence she was drawing energy. But she will soon, if she be allowed, find some other to prey on. For some years I have studied her closely. She is the archetype of a class of persons I have long had under observation. I find such power depends largely on force of will and concentration. If she can maintain these there is no reason why she should not live to be a hundred. There will always be persons of less assertive selfishness to serve as reservoirs of vital strength to her. At present her confidence is shaken, her power—therefore her life trembles in the balance. In the interests of humanity and justice she must not be allowed to regain her confidence. She lives by wholesale murder."

## III

I drank a glass of port and went back to my patient. She lay panting on her bed.

"Fie!" I said; "that was a bit of hysteria. Come now, take your breakfast."

She looked me in the face. A terror of death stood in beads on her skin. "I

1 Someone with obsessive enthusiasm for one thing.

have heard of transfusion,"[1] she said faintly; "if you will let me have some of the rich red blood run out of your veins into mine I will settle £500[2] a year on you."

I shook my head.

"A thousand," she said. "Fifteen hundred."

"I should be cheating you," I insisted, "even were I willing. The operation has never been really successful."

She broke into raving and tears.

"I cannot die," she said; "I love life. I love being beautiful and rich; I love admiration. I must have admiration! I love my beautiful, beautiful body and the joy of life! I cannot, cannot die!"

"What nonsense!" I said. "You are not going to die."

"If I could only get it," she raved, "I would drink blood out of living bodies rather than I would die."

An hour later she summoned the housekeeper. She had been cogitating with a fold between her brows; her teeth set like pearls in the red of her lower lip.

"Plimmer," she said, "give all the servants a month's wages and an hour's notice to quit. I cannot endure their sickly faces. Get in a staff of decently healthy people. These cadaverous wretches are killing me."

Plimmer left the room without a word. At the door she cast one look toward me and threw her hands up, as one who says: "The Lord have mercy on us!"

I followed, and bade her stay her hand. Whether Andrew's theories were true, or whether my lady were but a person with a mania, there was no doubt but that her convictions played an important part in the case.

I threw on my things and expended a half-sovereign[3] at the chemist's. I came back the possessor of sundry packets. These I distributed among the household with explicit directions. Her ladyship was not well; her whim must be humoured.

It is surprising what a little rouge will do. In a few minutes the servants' hall was a scene Arcadian. Even the elderly butler reverted to blooming youth. Then I said to her cheerfully:

"You are making a mistake about the servants. For my part I am struck with their healthy looks."

"Since I have been ill?" she faltered.

She lay quiet, breathing hard through her dilated nostrils. "Send some of them in," she said presently.

By the time they had gone she was as white as paper. "Good Heavens!" I heard her mutter, "I have lost my power. I am a dead woman."

Then she flung out her arms and wept. "Get me healthy children," she cried; "I must have health about me."

1 See Braddon's "The Good Lady Ducayne," page 134, note 3.

2 £500 in 1896 would be worth approximately £68,000 today (or $85,000).

3 Half a pound sterling or 10 shillings. Equivalent to approximately £67 today ($83).

Dr. Byrne, who was attending her, assented in all innocence. "Why, of course," he said; "it will be cheerful for you. Get in some cherry-cheeked children to amuse her ladyship, Nurse."

I nodded—in token that I was not deaf—not at all in acquiescence. Food and wine I supplied in plenty, but neither children nor adults. I isolated her in toto. I allowed her maids only to come near her long enough to dust and arrange the room. I have seen her fix them with a basilisk stare, straining her will. She had undoubtedly some baleful hypnotic power which set them trembling and stumbling about in curious, aimless fashion. They would seem drawn, as by some spell, to stand motionless and dazed beside her bed. Then I would turn them face about and parading their roseate tints, scold them for idleness and dismiss them. She would stare after them in a despair which, under other circumstances, would have been pitiful. The sense that her power was gone robbed her actually of power. She raved and cursed her self-murdered lover for involving her in his death.

Whether Dr. Andrew and I were justified in what we did I sometimes wonder now. Then I had no room for doubt. In face of the horrible facts it did not occur to me to question it. If that she believed were true, we were assuredly justified; if not, that we did could not affect results.

Andrew's theory of those results is that she had lived so long on human energy that food in the crude state stood her in little stead. Certainly, though she was fed unremittingly on the choicest and most nourishing of diets, she was an aged and haggard woman in a week. Nobody would have recognized her. She shriveled and shrank like one cholera-stricken. One day her dog stole into the room. She put out her hand and clutched it voraciously. I took it an hour later from her. It was dead and stiff.

How I myself, and a nurse I had called in to help me, kept life in us I cannot say. I had been an abstainer. Now I drank wine like water. All round her bed was an atmosphere as of a vault, though outside it was sunny June.

She raged like one possessed. "You are murdering, murdering me," she cried incessantly.

Dr. Byrne thought her mind wandering. I knew it centered with a monstrous, selfish sanity. He sent for one of the first London consultants. After a lengthy investigation the great man pronounced her suffering from some obscure nervous disease. "Nothing to be done," he said. "I give her three days: most interesting case. Hope you will succeed in getting a post-mortem."[1]

Once she fixed me with her baleful eyes, how baleful was seen now that their fine lustre and the bloom beneath them were gone.

"I have had ten years more of life and pleasure than my due," she chuckled in her shriveled throat—the throat now of an old, old woman.

1 Autopsy was rare and controversial at the time. It had only begun to be standardized in the early nineteenth century. Medical professionals needed permission to perform them even in cases of suspicious death.

Then she broke into dry-eyed crying. "I thought I could have lived another ten." She begged once for a mirror. I thank Heaven that with all my heat of indignation against her, I was not guilty of that cruelty.

Dr. Andrew called daily for my bulletin. Everything science afforded in the way of food and stimulant, he scrupulously got down from London.

"We must give her every chance," he said, "every justifiable chance, that is."

After a few days I was again single-handed. My nurse-colleague succumbed. I felt my powers failing. I could scarcely drag about. I prayed Providence for strength to last so long as she should. Even in the moment of dissolution, such was her frenzied greed of life, that I believed should some non-resistant person take my place, she would struggle back to health.

Once when I arranged her pillows, she seized my hand, and before I could withdraw it she had carried it to her mouth and bitten into it. I felt her suck the blood voraciously. She cried out and struck at me as I wrenched it away.

She died in the third week of her isolation. I saw the death change come into her shriveled face. Then in the moment wherein life left her she made one supremest effort.

It seemed as though my heart stopped. My head took on my chest, my hands dropped at my side. Then I swayed and fell headlong across her bed. They found me later lying on her corpse. I am convinced that had she been a moment earlier, had she nerved her powers the instant before, rather than on the instant life was leaving her, she would be alive to this day, and I—As it was, I did not leave my bed for a month.

"If I were to write that story in the *Lancet*,"[1] Dr. Andrew said, "I should be the laughing-stock of the profession. Yet it is the very keynote of human health and human disease, this interchange of vital force which goes on continually between individuals. Such rapacity and greed as the Deverish's are, fortunately, rare; but there are a score such vampires in this very town, vampires in lesser degree. When A. talks with me ten minutes I feel ten years older. It takes me an hour to bring my nerve-power up to par again. People call him a bore. In reality he is a rapacious egotist hungrily absorbing the life-force of anyone with whom he comes into relation—in other words, a human vampire."

1 Famous medical journal.

## Philip K. Dick

(1928–1982)

An acclaimed science-fiction writer, Philip Dick won the 1962 Hugo Award for his novel *The Man in the High Castle.* His visionary work, blurring the boundaries between fiction and an intensely skewed reality, is informed by his own psychological journey, which involved a period of drug addiction, and his anti-authoritarianism that was fueled by the political climate of the 1950s and 1960s. Many of his works have been adapted for film, most notably Ridley Scott's 1982 film *Blade Runner*, an adaptation of Dick's 1968 novel *Do Androids Dream of Electric Sheep?* The 1990 film *Total Recall* was influenced by his short story "We Can Remember It for You Wholesale" (1966). Dick is recognized for the eerily prophetic view of the future that characterizes his work. "The Cookie Lady" was first published in *Fantasy Fiction* in 1953.

# "The Cookie Lady"

(1953)

"Where you going, Bubber?" Ernie Mill shouted from across the street, fixing papers for his route.

"No place," Bubber Surle said.

"You going to see your lady friend?" Ernie laughed and laughed. "What do you go visit that old lady for? Let us in on it!"

Bubber went on. He turned the corner and went down Elm Street. Already, he could see the house, at the end of the street, set back a little on the lot. The front of the house was overgrown with weeds, old dry weeds that rustled and chattered in the wind. The house itself was a little gray box, shabby and unpainted, the porch steps sagging. There was an old weather-beaten rocking chair on the porch with a torn piece of cloth hanging over it.

Bubber went up the walk. As he started up the rickety steps he took a deep breath. He could smell it, the wonderful warm smell, and his mouth began to water. His heart thudding with anticipation, Bubber turned the handle of the bell. The bell grated rustily on the other side of the door. There was silence for a time, then the sounds of someone stirring.

Mrs. Drew opened the door. She was old, very old, a little dried-up old lady, like the weeds that grew along the front of the house. She smiled down at Bubber, holding the door wide for him to come in.

"You're just in time," she said. "Come on inside, Bernard. You're just in time—they're just now ready."

Bubber went to the kitchen door and looked in. He could see them, resting on a big blue plate on top of the stove. Cookies, a plate of warm, fresh cookies right out of the oven. Cookies with nuts and raisins in them.

"How do they look?" Mrs. Drew said. She rustled past him, into the kitchen. "And maybe some cold milk, too. You like cold milk with them." She got the milk pitcher from the window box on the back porch. Then she poured a glass of milk for him and set some of the cookies on a small plate. "Let's go into the living room," she said.

Bubber nodded. Mrs. Drew carried the milk and the cookies in and set them on the arm of the couch. Then she sat down in her own chair, watching Bubber plop himself down by the plate and begin to help himself.

Bubber ate greedily, as usual, intent on the cookies, silent except for chewing sounds. Mrs. Drew waited patiently, until the boy had finished, and his already ample sides bulged that much more. When Bubber was done with the plate he glanced toward the kitchen again, at the rest of the cookies on the stove.

"Wouldn't you like to wait until later for the rest?" Mrs. Drew said.

"All right," Bubber agreed.

"How were they?"

"Fine."

"That's good." She leaned back in her chair. "Well, what did you do in school today? How did it go?"

"All right."

The little old lady watched the boy look restlessly around the room. "Bernard," she said presently, "won't you stay and talk to me for a while?" He had some books on his lap, some school books. "Why don't you read to me from your books? You know, I don't see too well any more and it's a comfort to me to be read to."

"Can I have the rest of the cookies after?"

"Of course."

Bubber opened the big blue book at random. PERU. "Peru is bounded on the north by Ecuador and Colombia, on the south by Chile, and on the east by Brazil and Bolivia. Peru is divided into three main sections. These are, first—"

The little old lady watched him read, his fat cheeks wobbling as he read, holding his finger next to the line. She was silent, watching him, studying the boy intently as he read, drinking in each frown of concentration, every motion of his arms and hands. She relaxed, letting herself sink back in her chair. He was very close to her, only a little way off. There was only the table and lamp between them. How nice it was to have him come; he had been coming for over a month, now, ever since the day she had been sitting on her porch and seen him go by and thought to call to him, pointing to the cookies by her rocker.

Why had she done it? She did not know. She had been alone so long that she found herself saying strange things and doing strange things. She saw so few people, only when she went down to the store, or the mailman came with her pension check. Or the garbage men.

The boy's voice droned on. She was comfortable, peaceful and relaxed. The little old lady closed her eyes and folded her hands in her lap. And as she sat, dozing and listening, something began to happen. The little old lady was beginning to change, her gray wrinkles and lines dimming away. As she sat in the chair she was growing younger, the thin fragile body filling out with youth again. The gray hair thickened and darkened, color coming to the wispy strands. Her arms filled, too, the mottled flesh turning a rich hue as it had been once, many years before.

Mrs. Drew breathed deeply, not opening her eyes. She could feel *something* happening; but she did not know just what. *Something* was going on; she could feel it, and it was odd. But what it was she did not exactly know. It had happened before, almost every time the boy came and sat by her. Especially of late, since she had moved her chair nearer to the couch. She took a deep breath. How good it felt, the warm fullness, a breath of warmth inside her cold body for the first time in years!

In her chair the little old lady had become a dark-haired matron of perhaps thirty, a woman with full cheeks and plump arms and legs. Her lips were red again, her neck even a little too fleshy, as it had been once in the long forgotten past.

Suddenly the reading stopped. Bubber put down his book and stood up. "I have to go," he said. "Can I take the rest of the cookies with me?"

She blinked, rousing herself. The boy was in the kitchen, filling his pockets with cookies. She nodded, dazed, still under the spell. The boy took the last cookies. He went across the living room to the door. Mrs. Drew stood up. All at once the warmth left her. She looked down at her hands. Wrinkled, thin.

"Oh!" she murmured. Tears blurred her eyes. It was gone, gone again as soon as he moved away. She tottered to the mirror above the mantel and looked at herself. Old faded eyes stared back, eyes deep-set in a withered face. Gone, all gone, as soon as the boy had left her side.

"I'll see you later," Bubber said.

"Please," she whispered. "Please come back again. Will you come back?"

"Sure," Bubber said listlessly. He pushed the door open. "Good-bye." He went down the steps. In a moment she heard his shoes against the sidewalk. He was gone.

"Bubber, you come in here!" May Surle stood angrily on the porch. "You get in here and sit down at the table."

"All right." Bubber came slowly up on the porch, pushing inside the house.

"What's the matter with you?" She caught his arm. "Where have you been? Are you sick?"

"I'm tired." Bubber rubbed his forehead.

His father came through the living room with the newspapers, in his undershirt. "What's the matter?" he said.

"Look at him," May Surle said. "All worn out. What you been doing, Bubber?"

"He's been visiting that old lady," Ralf Surle said. "Can't you tell? He's always washed out after he's been visiting her. What do you go there for, Bub? What goes on?"

"She gives him cookies," May said. "You know how he is about things to eat. He'd do anything for a plate of cookies."

"Bub," his father said, "listen to me. I don't want you hanging around that crazy old lady any more. Do you hear me? I don't care how many cookies she gives you. You come home too tired! No more of that. You hear me?"

Bubber looked down at the floor, leaning against the door. His heart beat heavily, labored. "I told her I'd come back," he muttered.

"You can go once more," May said, going into the dining room, "but only once more. Tell her you won't be able to come back again, though. You make sure you tell her nice. Now go upstairs and get washed up."

"After dinner better have him lie down," Ralf said, looking up the stairs, watching Bubber climb slowly, his hand on the banister. He shook his head. "I don't like it," he murmured. "I don't want him going there any more. There's something strange about that old lady."

"Well, it'll be the last time," May said.

Wednesday was warm and sunny. Bubber strode along, his hands in his pockets. He stopped in front of McVane's drug store for a minute, looking speculatively at the comic books. At the soda fountain, a woman was drinking a big chocolate soda. The sight of it made Bubber's mouth water. That settled it. He turned and continued on his way, even increasing his pace a little.

A few minutes later he came up on the gray sagging porch and rang the bell. Below him the weeds blew and rustled with the wind. It was almost four o'clock; he could not stay too long. But then, it was the last time anyhow.

The door opened, Mrs. Drew's wrinkled face broke into smiles. "Come in, Bernard. It's good to see you standing there. It made me feel so young again to have you come visit."

He went inside, looking around.

"I'll start the cookies. I didn't know if you were coming." She padded into the kitchen. "I'll get them started right away. You sit down on the couch."

Bubber went over and sat down. He noticed that the table and lamp were gone; the chair was right up next to the couch. He was looking at the chair in perplexity when Mrs. Drew came rustling back into the room.

"They're in the oven. I had the batter all ready. Now." She sat down in the chair with a sigh. "Well, how did it go today? How was school?"

"Fine."

She nodded. How plump he was, the little boy, sitting just a little distance from her, his cheeks red and full! She could touch him, he was so close. Her aged heart thumped. Ah, to be young again. Youth was so much. It was everything. What did the world mean to the old? *When all the world is old, lad ...*[1]

"Do you want to read to me, Bernard?" she asked presently.

"I didn't bring any books."

"Oh." She nodded. "Well, I have some books," she said quickly. "I'll get them."

She got up, crossing to the bookcase. As she opened the doors, Bubber said, "Mrs. Drew, my father says I can't come here any more. He says this is the last time. I thought I'd tell you."

She stopped, standing rigid. Everything seemed to leap around her, the room twisting furiously. She took a harsh, frightened breath. "Bernard, you're—you're not coming back?"

"No, my father says not to."

There was silence. The old lady took a book at random and came slowly back to her chair. After a while she passed the book to him, her hands trembling. The boy took it without expression, looking at its cover.

"Please read, Bernard. Please."

"All right." He opened the book. "Where'll I start?"

"Anywhere. Anywhere, Bernard."

He began to read. It was something by Trollope;[2] she only half heard the words. She put her hand to her forehead, the dry skin, brittle and thin, like old paper. She trembled with anguish. The last time?

Bubber read on, slowly, monotonously. Against the window a fly buzzed. Outside the sun began to set, the air turning cool. A few clouds came up, and the wind in the trees rushed furiously.

The old lady sat, close by the boy, closer than ever, hearing him read, the sound of his voice, sensing him close by. Was this really the last time? Terror rose up in her and she pushed it back. The last time! She gazed at him, the boy sitting so close to her. After a time she reached out her thin, dry hand. She took a deep breath. He would never be back. There would be no more times, no more. This was the last time he would sit there.

---

1 Line from the poem "The Old Song" (1904) by Charles Kingsley.

2 Anthony Trollope was a Victorian novelist.

She touched his arm.

Bubber looked up. "What is it?" he murmured.

"You don't mind if I touch your arm, do you?"

"No, I guess not." He went on reading. The old lady could feel the youngness of him, flowing between her fingers through her arm. A pulsating, vibrating youngness, so close to her. It had never been that close, where she could actually touch it. The feel of life made her dizzy, unsteady.

And presently it began to happen, as before. She closed her eyes, letting it move over her, filling her up, carried into her by the sound of the voice and the feel of the arm. The change, the glow, was coming over her, the warm, rising feeling. She was blooming again, filling with life, swelling into richness, as she had been, once, long ago.

She looked down at her arms. Rounded, they were, and the nails clear. Her hair. Black again, heavy and black against her neck. She touched her cheek. The wrinkles had gone, the skin pliant and soft.

Joy filled her, a growing, bursting joy. She stared around her, at the room. She smiled, feeling her firm teeth and gums, red lips, strong white teeth. Suddenly she got to her feet, her body secure and confident. She turned a little, lithe, quick circle.

Bubber stopped reading. "Are the cookies ready?" he said.

"I'll see." Her voice was alive, deep with a quality that had dried out many years before. Now it was there again, *her* voice, throaty and sensual. She walked quickly to the kitchen and opened the oven. She took out the cookies and put them on top of the stove.

"All ready," she called gaily. "Come and get them."

Bubber came past her, his gaze fastened on the sight of the cookies. He did not even notice the woman by the door.

Mrs. Drew hurried from the kitchen. She went into the bedroom, closing the door after her. Then she turned, gazing into the full-length mirror on the door. Young—she was young again, filled out with the sap of vigorous youth. She took a deep breath, her steady bosom swelling. Her eyes flashed, and she smiled. She spun, her skirts flying. Young and lovely.

And this time it had not gone away.

She opened the door. Bubber had filled his mouth and his pockets. He was standing in the center of the living room, his face fat and dull, a dead white.

"What's the matter?" Mrs. Drew said.

"I'm going."

"All right, Bernard. And thanks for coming to read to me." She laid her hand on his shoulder. "Perhaps I'll see you again some time."

"My father—"

"I know." She laughed gaily, opening the door for him. "Good-bye, Bernard. Good-bye."

She watched him go slowly down the steps, one at a time. Then she closed the door and skipped back into the bedroom. She unfastened her dress and stepped out of it, the worn gray fabric suddenly distasteful to her. For a brief second she gazed at her full, rounded body, her hands on her hips.

She laughed with excitement, turning a little, her eyes bright. What a wonderful body, bursting with life. A swelling breast—she touched herself. The flesh was firm. There was so much, so many things to do! She gazed about her, breathing quickly. So many things! She started the water running in the bathtub and then went to tie her hair up.

The wind blew around him as he trudged home. It was late, the sun had set and the sky overhead was dark and cloudy. The wind that blew and nudged against him was cold, and it penetrated through his clothing, chilling him. The boy felt tired, his head ached, and he stopped every few minutes, rubbing his forehead and resting, his heart laboring. He left Elm Street and went up Pine Street. The wind screeched around him, pushing him from side to side. He shook his head, trying to clear it. How weary he was, how tired his arms and legs were. He felt the wind hammering at him, pushing and plucking at him.

He took a breath and went on, his head down. At the corner he stopped, holding on to a lamppost. The sky was quite dark, the street lights were beginning to come on. At last he went on, walking as best he could.

"Where is that boy?" May Surle said, going out on the porch for the tenth time. Ralf flicked on the light and they stood together. "What an awful wind."

The wind whistled and lashed at the porch. The two of them looked up and down the dark street, but they could see nothing but a few newspapers and trash being blown along.

"Let's go inside," Ralf said. "He sure is going to get a licking when he gets home."

They sat down at the dinner table. Presently May put down her fork. "Listen! Do you hear something?"

Ralf listened.

Outside, against the front door, there was a faint sound, a tapping sound. He stood up. The wind howled outside, blowing the shades in the room upstairs. "I'll go see what it is," he said.

He went to the door and opened it. Something gray, something gray and dry was blowing up against the porch, carried by the wind. He stared at it, but he could not make it out. A bundle of weeds, weeds and rags blown by the wind, perhaps.

The bundle bounced against his legs. He watched it drift past him, against the wall of the house. Then he closed the door again slowly.

"What is it?" May called.

"Just the wind," Ralf Surle said.

# VAMPIRES AND RACE

Uriah Derick D'Arcy, from "The Black Vampyre: A Legend of Saint Domingo" (1819)

Florence Marryat, from *The Blood of the Vampire* (1897)

James Weldon Johnson, "The White Witch" (1922)

William Crain, from *Blacula* (1972)

Ngũgĩ wa Thiong'o, from *Devil on the Cross* (1980)

Jewelle Gomez, from "Rosebud, Missouri: 1921," *The Gilda Stories* (1991)

Ibi Aanu Zoboi, "Old Flesh Song" (2004)

Octavia E. Butler, from *Fledgling* (2005)

Although in the vast majority of popular depictions the vampire is associated with whiteness, almost since the beginnings of the literary vampire tradition authors have used the figure of the vampire to explore the theme of race. By 1972, when the cult classic *Blacula* injected the issue of race into vampire cinema, the link between monstrosity and slavery already had a long history (see Illustrations, p. 521). The vampires in this chapter are often outsiders—invaders who embody the author's xenophobic cultural fears—but they are not always the villain of the story. Nor are the texts here exclusively works by writers of color; rather, what we have included are those stories that make the theme of race central to the horror that they depict. These texts use horror to explore cultural fears and preoccupations about race; however, as Sarah Kent observes, "the black vampire evades ideological stability." These monsters represent "complex linkages between vampirism, blackness, and histories of racialized violence."[1] Whether it is slavery, colonialism, or institutionalized racism, the texts in this chapter use vampirism to explore the monstrousness of racist power structures. As we saw in our opening chapter, power is a major theme in vampire literature; therefore, "envisioning vampirism's bloody transactions in relation to slavery is semiotically logical."[2] The past resonates strongly in these texts, elucidating the interplay of race and vampirism from a number of perspectives.

The specter of racist violence haunts vampire literature. In the first two texts, Uriah Derick D'Arcy's "The Black Vampyre" and Florence Marryat's *The Blood of the Vampire*, the white authors position the Caribbean as the origin of the monsters that threaten to infect white society, much as Stoker's *Dracula* explores the threat of monsters invading from the East. As Stephen Arata persuasively argues in "The Occidental Tourist: *Dracula* and the Anxiety of Reverse Colonialism," stories reflecting fears that the colonized would become the colonizer appeared often at the end of the nineteenth century.[3] Colonialism and slavery are prominent topics in any exploration of race and vampires. We open the chapter with Uriah Derick D'Arcy's "The Black Vampyre," published in 1819 shortly after Polidori's seminal *The Vampyre*. Darcy's tale is notable for its anti-slavery sentiment; however, its portrayal of race is extremely problematic. As Abby Good asks, "What are the racial politics of a text that depicts a slave rebellion but returns to the status quo of enslavement, leaving the master unscathed, un-aged?"[4] Notably, D'Arcy's vampire figure is both an African prince and a formerly enslaved person. He is powerful, wicked, and monstrous, yet he is also funny. D'Arcy is clearly aiming at humor, not horror, through much of the story and humor in a text about slavery can make engagement with the text challenging. The momentary disruption of the racist status quo represented by this vampire can be seen as both a satirical critique of racial ideology and a reinforcement of that very ideology.

This simultaneous challenge and retrenchment can also be seen in Florence Marryat's 1897 novel, *The Blood of the Vampire*. Like D'Arcy, Marryat is a white author using the figure of the vampire to interrogate the racism of her time. The excerpt we have included focuses on the plight of the mixed-race heiress, Harriet Brandt. As with D'Arcy's story, the character of the vampire as both victim and aggressor is problematic. Harriet's attitudes are imbued with the same nineteenth-century racism of which she is a victim. Ultimately, Harriet is a sympathetic figure playing into many "tragic mulatto" tropes,[5] but this text moves beyond the typical ill-fated romance of so many of these plots. Not

1 Kent, "'The Bloody Transaction'" 739.
2 Kent, "'The Bloody Transaction'" 739.
3 Arata, "The Occidental Tourist" 623.
4 Good, "'Teaching the Unfamiliar.'"
5 The "tragic mulatto" was a stock character from American literature during the nineteenth and early twentieth centuries. Mulatto was a term used to refer to a person of mixed race and is now considered offensive. The "tragic mulatto" narratives generally revolved around the depression of the central figure because they cannot fit into the white world.

only does Harriet initially not realize she is of mixed race, she also begins the novel unaware of the fact that she is a vampire—a monster who steals the life of those closest to her.

In James Weldon Johnson's poem "The White Witch" we move from white authors exploring race to the work of Black authors. While pre-colonial Africa did not have monsters immediately recognizable as vampires, many critics interpret the witches of African folklore as vampiric figures.[1] While witches are very different from the vampire created by Polidori in the early nineteenth century, they share certain key traits. Witches in these cultures may not drink blood, but they can summon spirits and possess seemingly vampiric powers to drain life. In 1922, during the Harlem Renaissance, this folklore is reflected in "The White Witch," a cautionary warning about the racist ideology underpinning the myth of white womanhood and negative stereotypes of Black masculinity (see Illustrations, "The Vampire That Hovers Over North Carolina," p. 518). In the poem, pre-colonial African folklore about witches is fused with connotations associated with the Western vampiric figure.

In most of the texts in this chapter, vampire stories are created to allow the authors to explore social oppression and exploitation. Toward the end of the twentieth century, as the vampire motif circulates in popular culture, the figure emerges once again as an African prince turned vampire in the 1972 Blaxploitation film *Blacula.* Just as in D'Arcy's "The Black Vampyre," the prince, Mamuwalde, makes a failed attempt to abolish the slave trade. In the pre-credits opening scene set in 1780, Mamuwalde and his wife have been lured to Transylvania by Dracula's promise to fund the fight to end slavery. Instead, Dracula attacks, transforming Mamuwalde and cursing him to "a living hell."

After Europeans brought the idea of the vampire to Africa, it was taken up as a metaphor for the evils of colonialism. This is certainly the case in the work of both Ngũgĩ wa Thiong'o and Ibi Aanu Zoboi. In *Devil on the Cross* (1980), Ngũgĩ incorporates both the African folklore of the witch and the Western idea of the vampire into his scathing indictment of postcolonial corruption in Kenya. In contrast, Zoboi sets her short story "Old Flesh Song" (2004) in twenty-first-century New York. Zoboi uses her soucouyant[2] to explore the enduring legacy of colonialism in the deep racial and economic inequalities of twenty-first-century culture. Like the work of earlier writers, Zoboi's tale fuses Caribbean folklore with American ideas of "bloodsuckers" to explore very real forms of oppression.

---

1 While such assertions may not specifically distinguish between diverse African nations, many critics of the supernatural in the African diaspora repeat them. See the work of critics such as J. Gordon Melton and Samuel Lumwe. Lumwe states: "as I review works of scholars who have examined African Traditional Religions and philosophy like Mbiti, Ayisi, Kirwen, Harries, and others, I constantly hear them state that witchcraft in the African traditional context is largely a worldview phenomenon" (2).

2 As previously noted, in Caribbean folklore, a soucouyant is a woman who can peel off her skin and fly around as a ball of fire. Soucouyants were believed to suck the life out of infants.

Not all of the vampires in this chapter are villains. Both Jewelle Gomez and Octavia Butler create narratives that feature vampires as heroic protagonists. In *The Gilda Stories* (1991), Gomez's portrayal of the vampire figure allows her to trace more than a century of the fight for racial equality and the victimization experienced during this era. The portion we have included evokes this fight, tying it to the earlier works but offering a new perspective on the theme. The ways in which such authors use the vampire to explore social concerns are perhaps "more obvious to those who lack the privileges of whiteness."[1] Gomez's vampires are opponents of oppression. They are outsiders, but their power enables them to aid the oppressed. For Gomez, it is the human beings who become the real monsters.

Finally, we end this chapter with a very different black vampire—Octavia Butler's Afrofuturist take on the genre in *Fledgling* (2005). This novel explores race and racism through its depiction of the Ina, a vampiric species that exists on Earth in a symbiotic relationship with humans. Butler's protagonist, Shori, is the result of a genetic experiment fusing African DNA with the Ina. The racism within the Ina community that fuels the plot of the novel forms the heart of the section we have anthologized. Once again, a writer of color uses the speculative fiction of a vampire novel to explore the very real racist ideologies of our own culture. In the end, Shori triumphs and the racists, both human and Ina, are shown to be the true monsters.

Throughout this chapter, the violence of racism and racist oppression interact with the horror of vampire fiction in evocative ways. Some of the texts here may disturb readers—often, they are intended to do so. These texts confront the monstrousness of racism, using the tropes of vampire literature to intensify, challenge, and deepen the emotional impact of the texts. As Melissa Anyiwo points out, the vampire has long represented "a core metaphor for the constructions of race, and the ways in which we identify, manufacture, and commodify marginalized groups." Just as in *Blacula*, when Dracula asserts "slavery has merit," the villains in this chapter are often those aligned with racism and colonialism. It is no accident that the historic horror of slavery features in so many of the texts in this unit. In pointing out the "ideological instability" of the Black vampire, the texts reveal the monstrousness of humanity.

1 Anyiwo, "Introduction" 2

## Uriah Derick D'Arcy

(1799-1832)

The authorship of "The Black Vampyre: A Legend of Saint Domingo" (1819) is shrouded in uncertainty. Some critics argue the short story was authored by Uriah Derick D'Arcy under the pseudonym Robert C. Sands, while others reverse that—claiming D'Arcy to be the pen name. Recent scholarship now points to Richard Varick Dey as the author.[1] Despite this ambiguity, the work is considered a transatlantic response to John Polidori's *The Vampyre* (1819) and a commentary on nineteenth-century politics, notable for its anti-slavery sentiment, including the theme of emancipation. As Andrew Barger notes in the introduction to his edition of the story, the narrative is "the first black vampire story, the first comedic vampire story, the first story to include a mulatto vampire, the first vampire story by an American author, and perhaps the first anti-slavery short story." Obeah ritual, or the ability to make the living appear dead through "secret" narcotic potions, is integral to vampiric power here. In the densely illusive text, D'Arcy mentions many of the social, artistic, political, and economic events of the day. The following text comes from the first edition of the story.

# from "The Black Vampyre: A Legend of Saint Domingo"

(1819)

"But first on earth, as Vampyre sent,
Thy corse shall from its tomb be rent;
Then ghastly haunt the native place,
And suck the blood of all thy race;

1 For example, White and Faherty explore this in "The Black Vampyre," note 5.

There from thy *daughter, sister, wife,*
At midnight drain the stream of life;
*Yet loathe the banquet which perforce*
Must feed thy livid living corse.

Thy victims, ere they yet expire,
Shall know the demon for their sire;
As cursing thee, thou cursing them,
Thy flowers are withered on the stem.
But one that for *thy crime* must fall,
The youngest, best beloved of all,
Shall bless thee with *A father's* name—
That word shall wrap thy heart in flame!

Yet thou must end thy task and mark
Her cheek's last tinge—her eye's last spark,
And the last glassy glance must view
Which freezes o'er its lifeless blue;
Then with unhallowed hand shall tear
The tresses of her yellow hair,
Of which, in life a lock when shorn
Affection's fondest pledge was worn—
But now is borne away by thee
Memorial of thine agony!

Yet with thine own best blood shall drip;
Thy gnashing tooth, and haggard lip;
Then stalking to thy sullen grave,
Go—and with Gouls and Afrits[1] rave,
Till these in horror shrink away
From spectre more accursed than they."

BYRON[2]

* * * * *

MR. ANTHONY GIBBONS was a gentleman of African extraction. His ancestors emigrated from the eastern coast of GUINEA, in a French ship, and were

1 A Ghoul is a legendary creature that robs graves and feeds on corpses. An Afrit is a powerful djinn or demon from Arabian mythology.

2 Polidori's *The Vampyre* quotes the same lines from Byron's "The Giaour." Slight word changes in lines 14 and 27 suggest that D'Arcy's source is Polidori's quote rather than Byron's original.

sold in ST. DOMINGO[1] remarkably cheap, as they were reduced to mere skeletons by the yaws[2] on the passage; and all died shortly after their arrival, except one small negro, of a very slender constitution, and fit for no work whatever. The gentleman who purchased *him*, charitably knocked out his brains; and the body was thrown into the ocean. The tide returning in the night, it was washed upon the sands; and the moon then shining bright, the gentleman was taking a walk to enjoy the coolness of the evening; judge of his surprise, when the little corpse got up, and complaining of a pain in its bowels, begged for some bread and butter!

The PLANTER, supposing his business to have been but half done, kicked him back into the water. The element seemed very familiar to him; and he swam back with much grace and agility; parting the sparkling waves with his jet black members, polished like ebony, but reflecting no single beam of light. His complexion was a dead black; his eyes a pure white; the iris was flame color; and the pupils of a clear, moonshiny lustre; but so peculiarly constructed, that, though prominent, they seemed to look into his own head. His hair was neither curled nor straight; but feathery, like the plumage of a crow. Having paddled again on shore, he came crawling, crab-fashion, to the feet of MR. PERSONNE. The latter gentleman, in considerable alarm, (not knowing whether it was Satan, Obi,[3] or some other worthy, with whom he had to deal,) mustered up sufficient resolution to tie a large stone round the boy's middle: then, with a main exertion of strength, he hurled him into the sparking ocean. He fell where the reflection of the moon was brightest, and sunk like lead; but immediately rose again like a cork, perpendicularly, with the stone under his arm; while the radiant lustre of the planet retreated from his dark figure, exhibiting in its most striking contrast its utter blackness!

In this predicament, he came buoyant to land; surrounded, as he seemed, by a sphere of magic lustre. He now walked up to the Frenchman, with his arms akimbo, and looking remarkably fierce. MR. PERSONNE'S particular hairs stood up on end,

______________ Tunc perculit horror
Membra ducis, riguere comæ, grossumque coercens
Languor in extrema tenuit vestigial ripa. LVC[4]

but being ashamed that a little negro boy of ten years old should put him in bodily fear, he knocked him down. The Guineaman rose again, without bending

1 The name was changed to Hayti in 1804, but it continued to be called St. Domingo in the US. It is now the Republic of Haiti.

2 A tropical disease.

3 Obi (also spelled Obeah, Obeya, or Obia) was a spiritual tradition among enslaved West Africans in the West Indies. D'Arcy seems to be suggesting that the spiritual system has a single god.

4 Quote from *The Civil War* by Marcus Annaeus Lucanus or "Lucan" (39–65 CE). LVC is the Italian truncation of Lucanus. J.D. Duff's translation: "Then trembling smote the leader's limbs, his hair on end, a faintness stopped his motion and fettered his feet on the edge of the river-bank."

a joint; as fast as MR. PERSONNE could upset him, he recovered his attitude; just like one of those small toys, fabricated from pith tipped with lead, called witches and hobgoblins by the rising generation. The planter, in utter amazement and despair, took hold of the child by both his extremities, and pressing him to the earth, sat down upon him! Then, hallooing for his attendants, he ordered a tremendous fire to be kindled on the sand. This was accordingly done. The GAUL[1] congratulated himself on his perseverance and sagacity; and as he had never heard of ignaqueous[2] animals, was confident that though the water-fiend was so expert in his own element, he could not stand the fiery ordeal. The boy, meanwhile, lay perfectly passive, as if he had been a mere log; but presently, when the pile was all in a light blaze, with a sudden expansion, like that of a compressed India-rubber, he popped MR. PERSONNE up into the air many yards, and he alighted head-foremost into the fire, where he had intended to have dedicated the sable brat, with his nine lives, to Moloch![3]

Whatever the negro was, it is notorious that MR. PERSONNE was no salamander. He was rescued from the pyre, which like Hercules he had (though unwittingly) erected for himself;[4] looking like a squizzed cat, and having apparently no life left in his body. The attention of the domestics was drawn entirely to their master; who soon betrayed signs of animation, though he exhibited a most awful spectacle, being one continual sore and blister. "His whole body was one wound," as Virgil or some other poet[5] has hyperbolically expressed himself.

MR. PERSONNE, when he had perfectly recovered his senses, found himself in his own bed, wrapped in greasy sheets, and smarting as if in a Cayenne bath.[6] He called for a glass of brandy, his dear wife EUPHEMIA, and his infant son, who had not yet been christened. His lady, with streaming eyes, presented herself before him, (with a voice interrupted with sobs and hiccups,) that when she went in the morning to see her baby, whom she had left in the cradle, there was nothing to be seen, but the *skin*, *hair*, and *nails*! She declared that there never was such another object; except, indeed, the exsiccation in Scudder's Museum![7]

On the receipt of this horrid intelligence, MR. PERSONNE was seized with a violent spasmodic affection; and shortly after expired, muttering something about *sacre*,[8] and the Guinea-negro.[9]

The amiable but unfortunate EUPHEMIA was thrown into several hysteri-

1 Ancient region of Europe encompassing today's France; i.e., a Frenchman.
2 "Able to live in fire and in water" (White and Faherty, "The Black Vampyre" 18).
3 Fallen angel associated with child sacrifice.
4 In Greek mythology, Hercules built a huge pyre and burned away his mortal parts leaving only the immortal.
5 Quote from Marcus Annaeus Lucanus ("Lucan"), not Virgil.
6 Hot pepper mixture used on the enslaved after harsh treatment (Karol Kovalovich Weaver, qtd. in White and Faherty, "The Black Vampyre" 18).
7 Reference to John Scudder's American Museum, which displayed exsiccated or dehydrated body parts in the early nineteenth century.
8 French: "sanctity" or "holiness."
9 Enslaved African from the Guinea coast.

cal convulsions; as well she might be, poor woman, when her husband had been made a holocaust, and served up like a broiled and peppered chicken, to feed the grim maw of death; and her interesting infant, the first pledge of her pure and perfect love, had been precociously sucked, like an unripe orange, and nothing left but its beautiful and tender skin. The disconsolate widow caused her husband to be embalmed; and he was buried amid the lamentations and tears of all the funeral; much regretted by all who had the honor of his acquaintance, particularly by his negroes; who could not soon forget him; as he had left too many sincere marks of his regard upon their backs, to be ever obliterated from their recollections.

Time, as all the Greek tragedians, Solomon, and others have remarked, is a benevolent deity. MRS. PERSONNE'S grief yielded to the soothing hand of the consoling power; and her bloom and spirits returned with more lustre and elasticity than they had before exhibited: as the rose, that had drooped in the fury of the passing storm, erects its blushing honors, and shows more beautiful and vivid tints when the squall is over!

Many years after these occurrences took place, while EUPHEMIA was in second mourning for her third husband, she was indulging in the luxury of solitary grief; and reading Burton's Anatomy of Melancholy, and The Melancholy Poems of Dr. Farmer,[1] in an orangerie.[2] The refreshing breezes from the ocean, which now tempered the sultry heats of the declining day; the soft perfume of the opening blossoms; and the mellow tints of the evening sky, shedding that holy light, so dear to sensitive hearts, diffused a calm over her soul, wrapped in the contemplation of departed days. While lost in this pensive reverie, she perceived two strangers approaching her, in the extremity of the long vista of the grove.

One of them was a colored gentleman, of remarkable height, and deep jetty blackness; a perfect model of the CONGO Apollo.[3] He was dressed in the rich garb of a Moorish Prince; and led by the hand a pale European boy, in an Asiatic dress, whose languid countenance, slender form, and tristful[4] gait were strongly contrasted with the portly appearance and majestic step of his conductor.

They both saluted the lovely widow, and after an interchange of compliments, accepted her polite invitation to sit down, and take tea with her in the bower. She learned from the elder stranger that he had brought out a cargo of slaves, whom his subjects had lately taken prisoners in war; and whom he had resolved to dispose of himself; as he was desirous of seeing the world. His page, he said, was an orphan, left by a slave-merchant in Africa.

The manners and conversation of the PRINCE had an irresistible charm. The

1 Seventeenth- and eighteenth-century texts on melancholy.

2 An orange grove.

3 A Black man with an ideal form. The Apollo Belvedere is a famous marble statue that was viewed as representing the ideal masculine form (White and Faherty, "The Black Vampyre" 20).

4 Full of sadness.

regal port was manifest in his gigantic and well-proportioned frame; and majesty was conspicuous on his brow, without its diadem. The turban and crescent had never graced a nobler front; but the winning condescension of his tones and language, while they could not banish the feeling of the presence of royalty, removed every restraint incident to that consciousness. He criticized the works which EUPHEMIA had been perusing, with masterly precision, and displayed more knowledge than even the accomplished ideologist of Lady Morgan;[1] with infinitely more discretion and good sense.

It is remarked by the Abbe Reynal,[2] that there is a peculiar elegance and beauty in the complexion of the Africans, (when the eyes and nose are accustomed to their hue and odor). This truth was realized by EUPHEMIA, as she gazed on the open visage of her illustrious guest. She thought surely that in him Nature might stand up and say "This was a man!" And certainly it is only the weakness and imperfection of our human senses, which, penetrating no farther than the surface is forever deceived by superficial shadows. The empyrean[3] is always blue, whatever vapors may float in our contracted atmosphere. And if we gaze on the rows of skulls which festoon and garnish Surgeon's Hall,[4] we can apply no standard to determine their relative beauty. They are all equally ugly; and the block of Helen might be mistaken for that of Medusa.[5] Shakespeare, true to nature, has also remarked, "Black men are pearls in beauteous ladies' eyes."[6]

The beauty then, the royalty, gentility, and various accomplishments of the BAMBUCK[7] monarch, made captive the too sensible heart of the French widow. She forgot her ogles, graces, and even her loquacity; rooted to her seat, and fixed in immovable contemplation of the AFRICAN'S face. What peculiar feature or lineament attracted her attention, she knew not: his eyes, though bright, did not sparkle; and the iris, though of a more vivid red than the roseate line in the rainbow, emitted no scintillations. In fact, his whole countenance seemed to look and to perambulate her own.

The conversation gradually assumed a more empassioned and amorous complexion; and the little page, (who, though meagre and emaciated, evidently showed that he was no gump for his years,) taking certain broad hints, cast a mournful and intelligent look on the widow, said he would fetch a short walk in the plantation, and left the orangerie.

---

1 Popular Anglo-Irish novelist (1776–1859).

2 Abbé Guillaume-Thomas Raynal (1713–96) was an anti-slavery author (see Barger, *The Best Vampire Stories* 154).

3 Highest extent of heaven.

4 Museum of the Royal College of Surgeons of Edinburgh where anatomist John Barclay (1758–1826) donated a collection of over 2,500 human remains (Barger, *The Best Vampire Stories* 155).

5 From Greek mythology, Helen of Troy was the most beautiful woman in the world, while Medusa was so hideous that her gaze turned men to stone.

6 From *Two Gentlemen of Verona* (1589–93), but also an old proverb: "A black man is a jewel in a fair woman's eyes."

7 A territory in eastern Senegal and western Mali. Also a reference to a work by Abbé Renal (White and Faherty, "The Black Vampyre" 22).

The PRINCE then spreading his glittering sash upon the grass, went down on his knees upon it, and broke out into the most ardent exclamations of love and admiration, and professions of constant attachment. He said that the flat-nosed beauties of Zara; the scarred, squab figures of the golden coast; the well-proportioned Zilias, Calypsos, and Zamas on the banks of the Niger; and even the great Hottentot Venus herself, had never for a moment made the least impression on his heart.[1] His passion was a mystery to himself; its origin secret as the source of the Nile; but full and impetuous as its ample channel, when replenished from the celestial fountains of Abyssinia;[2] while if MRS. DUBOIS would shine upon its waves, its enlivened currents would fertilize his vast dominions in the luxuriant realms of central Africa; making them to fructify yet more abundantly, with burning gold and radiant diamonds!

What female heart could resist such pleadings, and the compliment implied in such a preference? When ZEMBO (the page) returned, the parties had agreed to be privately united on the same evening. The ceremony was accordingly performed, on the spot, by the family chaplain of MRS. DUBOIS: not without many remonstrances on his part, as to the impropriety of marrying a negro. The PRINCE did not seem to resent the affront; which, by the by, he had no right to do, as the priest got nothing for the job. ZEMBO too was extremely restless, till MRS. DUBOIS gave him some sweet-meats, which seemed to quiet his conscience; after which he took some stiff punch, and fell asleep!

About midnight, the PRINCE came to him; and shaking him by the ears, bade him rise and follow him. His bride was hanging on his arm, in an enchanting dishabille;[3] and did not seem to be in perfect possession of her right senses. ZEMBO mournfully followed the new married pair.

They went silently out of the back door, with cautious steps, and proceeded through the orangerie. No breath of wind was stirring. The moon was in the zenith, surrounded by a pale halo of ghostly lustre. When they had crossed the plantation, they came to a place of sepulture;[4] where the dark cypresses and lugubrious mahogany admitted but sparse and glimmering streaks of funereal light; which, falling on the rank foliage, the white monuments and broken ground beneath, presented a thousand dusky shapes, flitting in the dim uncertainty, dear to superstition.

Vague terrors seized on the mind of the bride; and she began very naturally to inquire, what was the use of getting out of a comfortable bed, and trailing through the heavy dew, in her undress, to such an unusual spot for midnight recreation.

---

1 The places listed are all in Africa. The term Hottentot is now considered to be offensive. The Hottentot Venus was the name given to Saarjite Baartman in 1810 when she was brought from Cape Town to London and put on display. Also a reference to a work by Abbé Renal (White and Faherty, "The Black Vampyre" 22).

2 Ethiopian Empire known for underground water fountains (Barger, *The Best Vampire Stories* 166).

3 State of undress; her night clothes.

4 Burial or interment.

They now stood near the spot where her three husbands, several children, and the *skin*, *hair* and *nails* of her first baby, were deposited in a row. At the foot of a tamarind lay her third son, whose Christian name was SPOONER, and who died, according to the tomb-stone, in a fit of intoxication, aged seven years and six months. On him she had bestowed a greater share of tenderness than on any of her other offspring; and his loss had caused her most affliction.[1] The African, making observations on the grave, began to strip himself very expeditiously, assisted by ZEMBO, who seemed to recover from his blues; and by his activity and eagerness, manifested his expectation of soon seeing some fine sport.

Presently the two genii, or gentlemen, or whatever they were, turned towards the East, and performed certain antic prostrations; throwing handfuls of earth three times over their heads. Then returning to the tomb, they tore up the sods with ravenous fury; and soon drew out the last-mentioned son of the Lady, and threw him on the grass, beside the grave. ZEMBO fell as fiercely upon the corpse, as a hungry dog upon his dinner; but was arrested by the AFRICAN, who lent him a severe box on the ear, which sent him blubbering to a corner of the cemetery.

What added both to the mother's horrors and admiration, was, that the body of her child was perfectly fresh, and the olfactory nerves experienced no unsavoury sensation from its proximity; while its cheeks were diffused with so deep a tinge of scarlet, that they shone like ruddy fireballs in the darkness of the spot.[2]

Her husband drew a golden goblet from beneath a large stone; then, bending over the corse; he scooped out the heart, with his long and polished nails; and, having pressed the blood into the chalice, mingled with it some dark particles, gathered from the newly turned up earth. From the pure and scanty lymph,[3] which gushed nearby and flickered like a streak of quicksilvery-light in the moonbeam, he added a third ingredient of the potion.

Then seizing his passive and trembling spouse by the throat, and presenting the unnatural mixture to her lips; he cried in a hollow voice, whose every inflection thrilled through each fibre of its victim,—"Swear, or if that is against your principles, affirm, by this dirty blood,—and bloody water;—that you will never disclose in any manner, aught of what you have seen and shall see this night. Call them all to witness your wish, that in the moment when you even conceive the thought of perjury, your bowels may burst out, and your bones rot! Swear and drink!"[4]

1 "[T]his Spooner Dubois having never been heard of since, it is probable that he has been roaming about the world; and it is possible, that he may be the same Lord Ruthven, whose adventures have recently been related." [Author's note]

2 "The universal belief is, that a person sucked by a Vampyre becomes a Vampyre himself, and sucks in his turn." [Author's note]

3 Pure water; a stream.

4 "Among their other superstitions also, must not be omitted their mode of administering an oath of secrecy or purgation. Human blood, and earth taken from the grave of some near relation, are mixed with water, and given to the party to be sworn, who is compelled to drink the mixture, with an imprecation, that it may cause the belly to burst, and the bones to rot, if the truth be not spoken." [Author's note]

The affrighted woman murmured, (as articulately as the iron gripe of the monster would suffer her,) that she was not thirsty; and had not breath enough to aspirate such a terrible conjuration.

"No trifling"; roared the fiend, "you have not a moment to deliberate."

But his bellowing and threats were in vain; and he found to his mortification that he had gotten the wrong sow by the ear, or rather by the throat. She stuttered out, in the most pitiful accents, which would have softened any heart, (but a Vampyre has none,) that though she was by no means partial to the delectable confectionary of the pharmacopeia, calomel and jalap, ipecacuanha, rhubarb, and tartar-emetic,[1] she would rather take them all, collectively and individually, than the unchristian decoction he held against her teeth.

Foaming with madness, til the white slaver[2] flowed down his sable limbs, the African hurled MRS. PERSONNE, DUBOIS, &c. &c. on the grave of her first husband, and stamping violently on the earth, it seemed to heave as with the throes of an earthquake. Immediately the tumuli[3] yawned! The ponderous stones and slabs were shaken from their ancient sockets; and the ghastly dead, in uncouth attitudes, crawled from their nooks; with their hair curling in tortuous and serpent twinings; and their eyeballs of fire bursting from their heads; while, as they extended their withered arms, and tapering fingers, furnished with blood-hound claws, their gory shrouds fell in wild drapery around them, transiently revealing their forms, bloated as if to bursting, and often incarnadined with clotted blood, yet warm and dripping!!!

The Lady, (as those who have been in similar predicaments may suppose,) soon lost her recollection; not, however, before she had seen ZEMBO busily employed in tearing up the grave of her first husband; she saw herself surrounded by the specters, and lost all consciousness.

When reason and sense returned, she found herself in the same place; and it was also the midnight hour. She was laying by the grave of MR. PERSONNE, and her breast was stained with blood. A wide wound appeared to have been inflicted there, but was cicatrized. Imagine, if you can, her surprise; when, by a certain carnivorous craving in her maw, and by putting this and that together, she found she was a—vampire!!! And gathered from her indistinct reminiscences, of the preceding night, that she had been their sucked; and that it was now her turn to eject the peaceful tenants of the grave!

*[The tale continues with the vampiric resurrection of all three of Euphemia's husbands. They fight over her, and ultimately the prince sends Eupehmia and her first husband Mr. Personne away, revealing to them that Zembo is their son. The group finds themselves in a cave witnessing a vampire ball attended by both vampire*

1 All these are purgatives, expectorants, or laxatives.

2 Saliva.

3 Ancient burial mound.

*monarchs and armed military. The vampire monarchs call for the enslaved people to commence the fight for emancipation. Before any action ensues, the proposition is averted by the arrival of the French military, who, along with the Personne family slay the vampires, including the prince. Mr. and Mrs. Personne return to the plantation and are able to reverse their vampiric state with a potion Zembo stole from the prince. Euphemia, as it turns out, is pregnant with the prince's son who subsequently remains a vampire as there is no potion left for a cure.*]

The intelligent reader, (if any such there be,) will remember that this narrative commenced with the name of MR. ANTHONY GIBBONS, of whom nothing has since been said; and whose adventures (to use a FORUM trope) "must remain buried in the bowels of futurity," until a more convenient opportunity. He is a lineal descendant from the last-mentioned mulatto; and the manuscript, which is now given to the public, was transmitted to him from his ancestors.

He is a resident in Essex county, New Jersey; and candour requires us to state, that he is no relation to his celebrated namesake at ELIZABETH-TOWN[1] as it is notorious to all who have had the pleasure of witnessing the size of the later gentleman's waist, that he has too much bowels for so diabolical a profession; and it is to be hoped in charity, that though he is such a delicate morsel, when he is laid in the sepulcher of his fathers, he may not prove a titbit, to GLUT THE THIRST OF A VAMPYRE!!![2]

1 Thomas Gibbons (1757–1826) steamboat company owner with a summer home in Elizabethtown, New Jersey. Defendant in United States Supreme Court case, *Gibbons v. Ogden*, 22 U.S. 1 (1824) over the steamboat rights between New Jersey and New York.

2 Parodies the ending of vampire tales like Polidori's.

# Florence Marryat

(1833–1899)

Florence Marryat was the daughter of the British author Captain Frederick Marryat, but became famous in her own right as an actress and an author of more than sixty novels. Best known for her sensation fiction, Marryat's life at times took on the qualities of a novel. Her parents separated when she was small and she was educated at home. She married Thomas Ross Church, an army officer, in 1854, and the couple traveled to India where they lived for seven years. In 1860, Marryat returned to England with her children. Her husband only visited her and their eight children occasionally after her return home. Marryat began writing in the mid-1860s, eventually becoming an internationally known author. Church eventually sued for divorce in 1878 citing his wife's adultery, and Marryat married Colonel Francis Lean with whom she had been living. This marriage was short-lived, and the couple divorced a year later. Marryat supported herself and her children with writing and acting. In 1899, Marryat died from complications of diabetes and pneumonia. Published in the final years of her life, *The Blood of the Vampire* (1897) exhibits classic elements of both horror and sensation fiction. Featuring a protagonist of mixed race, it reveals many of the racist attitudes and assumptions prevalent in the late Victorian period. While Marryat's novel borrows much from both the sensation fiction and the "tragic mulatto" tropes popular in nineteenth-century fiction, the addition of vampirism and the sympathetic qualities of the vampire make the depiction of race and racism complex. It provides insight into racial dynamics at the end of the nineteenth century, although some readers may be understandably disturbed at the racist stereotypes, eugenic heredity arguments, and racist sentiments voiced by some of the characters.

# from *The Blood of the Vampire*

(1897)

[*The first passage takes place in the seaside resort of Heyst. Margaret Pullen, her infant daughter, and her future sister-in-law, Elinor Leyton, are visiting while they wait for Colonel Pullen to return from India. Margaret and her daughter have befriended Harriet Brandt, a wealthy young heiress from Jamaica. This passage opens with Margaret's friend, Dr. Phillips, arriving and expressing concern over her intimacy with Harriet. The racism expressed by Dr. Phillips and others is part of the novel's exploration of monstrosity. At this point in the novel, the vampire, Harriet, is unaware of her background.*]

## CHAPTER VII.

[...] "It is about that Miss Brandt! You seem pretty intimate with her! You must stop it at once. You must have nothing more to do with her."

Margaret's eyes opened wide with distress.

"But Doctor Phillips, for what reason? I don't see how we could give her up now, unless we leave the place."

"Then leave the place! You mustn't know her, neither must Miss Leyton. She comes of a terrible parentage. No good can ever ensue of association with her."

"You must tell me more than this, Doctor, if you wish me to follow your advice!"

"I will tell you all I know myself! Some twelve or thirteen years ago I was quartered in medical charge of the Thirteenth Lances,[1] and stationed in Jamaica, where I knew of, rather than knew, the father of this girl, Henry Brandt. You called him a doctor—he was not worthy of the name. He was a scientist perhaps—a murderer certainly!"

"How horrible! Do you really mean it?"

"Listen to me! This man Brandt matriculated in the Swiss hospitals, whence he was expelled for having caused the death of more than one patient by trying his scientific experiments upon them. The Swiss laboratories are renowned for being the foremost in Vivisection[2] and other branches of science that gratify the curiosity and harden the heart of man more than they confer any lasting benefit on humanity. Even there, Henry Brandt's barbarity was considered to render him unfit for association with civilized practitioners, and he was expelled

1 British military unit.

2 Vivisection was the scientific practice of dissecting animals while alive to study the operations of various organ systems. As it caused extreme suffering to the animal, the practice was controversial and spawned a significant anti-vivisection movement.

with ignominy. Having a private fortune he settled in Jamaica, and set up his laboratory there, and I would not shock your ears by detailing one hundredth part of the atrocities that were said to take place under his supervision, and in company of this man Trawler, who the girl calls her trustee, and who is one of the greatest brutes unhung."

"Are you not a little prejudiced, dear Doctor?"

"Not at all! If when you have heard all, you still say so, you are not the woman I have taken you for. Brandt did not confine his scientific investigations to the poor dumb creation. He was known to have decoyed natives into his Pandemonium,[1] who were never heard of again, which raised, at last, the public feeling so much against him, that I am glad to say that his negroes revolted, and after having murdered him with appropriate atrocity, set fire to his house and burned it and all his property to the ground. Don't look so shocked! I repeat that I am *glad* to say it, for he richly deserved his fate, and no torture could be too severe for one who spent his worthless life in torturing God's helpless animals!"

"And his wife—" commenced Margaret.

"He had no wife! He was never married!"

"Never married! But this girl Harriet Brandt—"

"Has no more right to the name than you have! Henry Brandt was not the man to regard the laws, either of God or man. There was no reason why he should not have married—for that very cause, I suppose, he preferred to live in concubinage."

"Poor Harriet! Poor child! And her mother, did you know her?"

"Don't speak to me of her mother. She was not a woman, she was a fiend, a fitting match for Henry Brandt! To my mind she was a revolting creature. A fat, flabby half-caste,[2] who hardly ever moved out of her chair but sat eating all day long, until the power to move had almost left her! I can see her now, with her sensual mouth, her greedy eyes, her low forehead and half-formed brain, and her lust for blood. It was said that the only thing which made her laugh, was to watch the dying agonies of the poor creatures her brutal protector slaughtered. But she thirsted for blood, she loved the sight and smell of it, she would taste it on the tip of her finger when it came her way. Her servants had some story amongst themselves to account for this lust. They declared that when her slave mother was pregnant with her, she was bitten by a Vampire bat, which are formidable creatures in the West Indies, and are said to fan their victims to sleep with their enormous wings, whilst they suck their blood. Anyway the slave woman did not survive her delivery, and her fellows prophesied that the child would grow up to be a murderess. Which doubtless she was in heart, if not in deed!"

"What an awful description! And what became of her?"

1 Pandæmonium is the capital of Hell in John Milton's epic poem *Paradise Lost*.

2 Derogatory term applied to people of mixed race, generally associated with the British occupation of India, but here applied to a woman whose father enslaved her mother in the Caribbean.

"She was killed at the same time as Brandt, indeed the natives would have killed her in preference to him, had they been obliged to choose, for they attributed all the atrocities that went on in the laboratory to her influence. They said she was 'Obeah'[1] which means diabolical witchcraft in their language. And doubtless their unfortunate child would have been slaughtered also, had not the overseer of the plantation carried her off to his cabin, and afterwards, when the disturbance was quelled, to the Convent, where, you say, she has been educated."

"But terrible as all this is, dear Doctor, it is not the poor girl's fault. Why should we give up her acquaintance for that?"

"My dear Margaret, are you so ignorant as not to see that a child born under such conditions cannot turn out well? The bastard of a man like Henry Brandt, cruel, dastardly, Godless, and a woman like her terrible mother, a sensual, self-loving, crafty and bloodthirsty half-caste—what do you expect their daughter to become? She may seem harmless enough at present, so does the tiger cub as it suckles its dam, but that which is bred in her will come out sooner or later, and curse those with whom she may be associated. I beg and pray of you, Margaret, not to let that girl come near you, or your child, any more. There is a curse upon her, and it will affect all within her influence!" [...]

[*The second passage is from the novel's final chapter. After the death of Margaret Pullen's child, Harriet stays with the baroness (also known as Madame Gobelli) and her family. While there, Harriet falls in love with a worthy man, Anthony Pennell, but tragedy strikes. The baroness's son, who was fond of Harriet, dies. The baroness then tells Harriet of her parentage. Harriet flees the house in despair and seeks the counsel of Dr. Phillips, who provides Harriet with background information about her ancestry. When Anthony proposes to her, she shares this information with him. He insists on marrying her anyway, arguing that her parents, sins are not her own. After considerable resistance, she finally agrees to marry him.*]

## CHAPTER XVIII.

A fortnight[2] afterwards, the married couple found themselves at Nice. Much as has been said and sung of the *lune di miel*,[3] none ever surpassed, if it ever reached, this one in happiness. Harriet passed the time in silent ecstasy of delight. Her cup of bliss was filled to overflowing; her satisfaction was too deep for words. To this girl, for whom the world had been seen as yet only through the barred windows of a convent—who had never enjoyed the society of an intel-

1 A term for spiritual practices in Jamaica and the Caribbean.

2 Two weeks.

3 Honeymoon.

lectual companion before; who had viewed no scenery but that of the Island; seen no records of the past; and visited no foreign capital—the first weeks of her married life were a panorama of novelties, her days one long astonishment and delight. [...]

And Pennell, on the other hand, though he had been much sought after and flattered by the fair sex for the sake of the fame he had acquired and the money he made, had never lost his heart to any woman as he had done to his little unknown wife. He had never met anyone like Hally before. She combined the intelligence of the Englishwoman with the *espièglerie*[1] of the French—the devotion of the Creole with the fiery passion of the Spanish or Italian. He could conceive her quite capable of dying silently and uncomplainingly for him, or anyone she loved; or on the other hand stabbing her lover without remorse if roused by jealousy or insult.

He was hourly discovering new traits in her character which delighted him, because they were so utterly unlike any possessed by the women of the world, with whom he had hitherto associated. He felt as though he had captured some beautiful wild creature and was taming it for his own pleasure.

Harriet would sit for hours at a time in profound silence, contemplating his features or watching his actions—crouched on the floor at his feet, until he was fain to lay down his book or writing, and take to fondling her instead. She was an ever-constant joy to him; he felt it would be impossible to do anything to displease her so long as he loved her—that like the patient Griselda[2] she would submit to any injustice and meekly call it justice if from *his* hand. And yet he knew all the while that the savage in her was *not* tamed—that at any moment, like the domesticated lion or tiger, her nature might assert itself and become furious, wild and intractable. It was the very uncertainty that pleased him; men love the women of whom they are not quite certain, all the more. [...]

"Don't you feel well, Tony?" asked Harriet, anxiously.

"Never better in my life, Dear! I am afraid you will not make an interesting invalid out of me. I am as fit as a fiddle." [...]

He left the room, as she thought rather hurriedly, but as he gained the hotel corridor he lightly staggered and leaned against the wall. He had told his wife that he was quite well, but he knew it was not the truth. He had felt weak and enervated ever since coming to Mentone,[3] but he ascribed it to the soft mild atmosphere.

"Confound this dizziness!" he said inwardly, as the corridor swam before his eyes, "I think my liver must be out of order, and yet I have been taking plenty

1 Playfulness.

2 Character from European folklore of extreme patience and devotion. A peasant who wins the love of a prince, her husband tests her love repeatedly even to the point of making her give up her children and make way for him to take a new wife. It is all his plot to make her prove her love. In the end, she is rewarded by the return of her children and position as wife.

3 Town in the French Riviera. They are traveling through France and Italy on their honeymoon.

of exercise. It must be this mild moist air. Heat never did agree with me. I shall be glad to get on. We shall find Florence cold by comparison." [...]

By mutual agreement they never spoke of Heyst, or the Red House, or anything which was associated with what Pennell called his wife's infatuation regarding herself. [...]

They "did" Florence very thoroughly during the first week of their stay there, and were both completely tired.

"I must really stay at home to-morrow," cried Hally one afternoon on returning to dinner, "Tony, I am regularly fagged[1] out! I feel as if I had a corn upon every toe!"

"So do I," replied her husband, "and I cannot have my darling knocked up[2] by fatigue! We will be lazy to-morrow, Hally, and lie on two sofas and read our books all day! I have been thinking for the last few days that we have been going a little too fast! Let me see, child!—how long have we been married?"

"Six weeks to-morrow," she answered glibly.

"Bless my soul! [...] and have you been happy, Hally?"

The tears of excitement rushed into her dark eyes.

"*Happy!* That is no word for what I have been, Tony; I have been in Heaven—in Heaven all the while!"

"And so have I," rejoined her husband.

"I met some nuns whilst I was out this morning," continued Hally, "the sisters of the Annunciation, and they stopped and spoke to me, and were so pleased to hear that I had been brought up in a convent. 'And have you no vocation, my child?' asked one of them. 'Yes! Sister,' I replied, 'I have—a big, strong, handsome vocation called my husband.' They looked quite shocked, poor dears, at first, but I gave them a subscription for their orphan schools—one hundred francs[3]—and they were so pleased. They said if I was sick whilst in Florence, I must send for one of them, and she would come and nurse me! I gave it as a thanksgiving, Tony—a thanksgiving offering because I am so very happy. I am not a good woman like Margaret Pullen, I know that, but I love you—*I love you!*"

"Who said that you were not a good woman?" asked Pennell, as he drew her fondly to his side, and kissed away the tears that hung on her dark lashes. [...]

"Ah! Neither of us could do without the other, Tony!" [...]

"Then come here and sit down on the sofa beside me, and let us talk!"

She did as he desired, but Pennell was too sleepy to talk. In five minutes he had fallen fast asleep, and it was with difficulty she could persuade him to abandon the couch and drag his weary limbs up to bed, where he threw himself down in a profound slumber. Harriet was also tired. Her husband was breathing

1 British slang for tired.
2 Meaning "laid up," not the American colloquialism for pregnancy.
3 It is unclear if she means French or Swiss francs (and they are in Italy, so perhaps she really means lira). In any case, this is a large sum. Many people would not earn this much in a year.

heavily as she slipped into her place beside him. His arm was thrown out over her pillow, as though he feared she might go to sleep without remembering to wish him good-night! She bent over him and kissed him passionately on the lips.

"Good-night, my beloved," she whispered, "sleep well, and wake in happiness!"

She kissed the big hand too that lay upon her pillow and composed herself to sleep while it still encircled her.

The dawn is early in Florence, but it had broken for some time before she roused herself again. The sun was streaming brightly into the long, narrow, uncurtained windows, and everything it lighted on was touched with a molten glory. Harriet started up in bed. Her husband's arm was still beneath her body.

"Oh! my poor darling!" she exclaimed, as though the fault were her own, "how cramped he must be! How soundly we must have slept not to have once moved through the night!"

She raised Tony's arm and commenced to chafe it. How strangely heavy and cold it felt. Why! he was cold all over! She drew up the bedclothes and tucked them in around his chin. Then, for the first time, she looked at his face. His eyes were open.

"Tony, Tony!" she exclaimed, "are you making fun of me? Have you been awake all the time?"

She bent over his face laughingly, and pressed a kiss upon his cheek.

How stiff it felt! My God! what was the matter? Could he have fainted? She leapt from the bed, and running to her husband's side, pulled down the bedclothes again and placed her hand upon his heart. The body was cold—cold and still all over! His eyes were glazed and dull. His mouth was slightly open. In one awful moment she knew the truth. Tony was—*dead!*

She stood for some moments—some hours—some months—she could not have reckoned the time, silent and motionless, trying to realise what had occurred. Then—as it came upon her, like a resistless flood which she could not stem, nor escape, Harriet gave one fearful shriek which brought the servants hurrying upstairs to know what could be the matter. [...]

The old palazzo became like a disturbed ant-hill. The servants ran hither and thither, unknowing how to act, whilst the mistress sat by the bedside with staring, tearless eyes, holding the hand of her dead husband. But there were a dozen things to be done—half a hundred orders to be issued. Death in Florence is quickly followed by burial. The law does not permit a mourner to lament his Dead for more than four-and-twenty hours.

But the signora would give no orders for the funeral nor answer any questions put to her! She had no friends in Florence—for ought they knew, she had no money—what were they to do? At last one of them thought of the neighbouring Convent of the Annunciation and ran to implore one of the good sisters to come to their mistress in her extremity. [...]

The little sister stood by her and held her hand, as the professional assistants entered the death chamber and arranged and straightened the body for the grave, finally placing it in a coffin and carrying it away. [...] Harriet made no resistance to the ceremony and no sign. She did not even say "Good-bye" as Tony was carried from her sight for ever! Sister Angelica talked to her of the glorious Heaven where they must hope that her dear husband would be translated, of the peace and happiness he would enjoy, of the reunion which awaited them when her term of life was also past.

She pressed her to make the Convent her refuge until the first agony of her loss was overcome. [...]

Harriet listened dully and at last in order to get rid of her well-intentioned but rather wearisome consoler, she promised to do all that she wished. [...] So the good little sister went away rejoicing that she had succeeded in her errand of mercy. [...]

When she had gone and the old palazzo was quiet and empty, the bewildered girl rose to her feet and tried to steady her shaking limbs sufficiently, to write what seemed to be a letter but was in reality a will.

"I leave all that I possess," so it ran, "to Margaret Pullen, wife of Colonel Arthur Pullen, the best woman Tony said that he had ever met, and I beg her to accept it in return for the kindness she showed to me when I went to Heyst, a stranger. Signed, HARRIET PENNELL."

She put the paper into an envelope, and as soon as the morning had dawned, she asked her servant Lorenzo to show her the way to the nearest notary in whose presence she signed the document and directed him to whom it should be sent in case of her own death.

And after another visit to a pharmacien,[1] she returned to the Palazzo and took up her watch again in the now deserted bedchamber.

Her servants brought her refreshments and pressed her to eat, without effect. All she desired, she told them, was to be left alone, until the sister came for her in the afternoon.

Sister Angelica arrived true to her appointment, and went at once to the bedchamber. To her surprise she found Harriet lying on the bed, just where the corpse of Anthony Pennell had lain, and apparently asleep.

"*Pauvre enfant!*"[2] thought the kind-hearted nun, "grief has exhausted her! I should not have attended to her request, but have watched with her through the night! "*Eh, donc! Ma pauvre,*"[3] she continued, gently touching the girl on the shoulder, "*levez-vous! Je suis la.*"[4]

1 Pharmacist or chemist.
2 "Poor child." It is not clear why an Italian nun is speaking French.
3 "So, poor thing."
4 "Get up! I am here."

But there was no awakening on this earth for Harriet Pennell. She had taken an overdose of chloral[1] and joined her husband.

When Margaret Pullen received the will which Harriet had left behind her, she found these words with it, scribbled in a very trembling hand upon a scrap of paper.

"Do not think more unkindly of me than you can help. My parents have made me unfit to live. Let me go to a world where the curse of heredity which they laid upon me may be mercifully wiped out."

THE END

1 Chloral hydrate, a once widely used sedative.

## James Weldon Johnson

(1871–1938)

James Weldon Johnson, a prominent figure in the Harlem Renaissance movement, was born in Florida. His maternal ancestors fled the 1802 Saint-Dominigue (now Haiti) Revolution, settling in the Bahamas; his parents eventually immigrated to the United States. Influenced by his mother, an educator, he studied English literature and music. Johnson collaborated with his brother, a composer, on the spiritual "Lift Ev'ry Voice and Sing," now known as the Black National Anthem. His background in law was influential in his pioneering of the NAACP movement. He was a fervent civil rights activist in his roles as educator of formerly enslaved students, lobbyist for anti-lynching legislation, and organizer of the protests against racial discrimination and violence post-World War I. Many of his works, such as *The Autobiography of an Ex-Colored Man* (1912), explore the personal and cultural conflict over racial identity and passing for white. Johnson was known for his diversified collection of folklore texts and would have been aware of the figure of the witch in African folklore.

# "The White Witch"

(1922)

O brothers mine, take care! Take care!
The great white witch rides out to-night.
Trust not your prowess nor your strength,
Your only safety lies in flight;
For in her glance there is a snare,
And in her smile there is a blight.

The great white witch you have not seen?
Then, younger brothers mine, forsooth,

Like nursery children you have looked
For ancient hag and snaggle-tooth;
But no, not so; the witch appears
In all the glowing charms of youth.

Her lips are like carnations, red,
Her face like new-born lilies, fair,
Her eyes like ocean waters, blue,
She moves with subtle grace and air,
And all about her head there floats
The golden glory of her hair.

But though she always thus appears
In form of youth and mood of mirth,
Unnumbered centuries are hers,
The infant planets saw her birth;
The child of throbbing Life is she,
Twin sister to the greedy earth.

And back behind those smiling lips,
And down within those laughing eyes,
And underneath the soft caress
Of hand and voice and purring sighs,
The shadow of the panther lurks,
The spirit of the vampire lies.

For I have seen the great white witch,
And she has led me to her lair,
And I have kissed her red, red lips
And cruel face so white and fair;
Around me she has twined her arms,
And bound me with her yellow hair.

I felt those red lips burn and sear
My body like a living coal;
Obeyed the power of those eyes
As the needle trembles to the pole;
And did not care although I felt
The strength go ebbing from my soul.

Oh! she has seen your strong young limbs,
And heard your laughter loud and gay,

And in your voices she has caught
The echo of a far-off day,
When man was closer to the earth;
And she has marked you for her prey.

She feels the old Antaean[1] strength
In you, the great dynamic beat
Of primal passions, and she sees
In you the last besieged retreat
Of love relentless, lusty, fierce,
Love pain-ecstatic, cruel-sweet.

O, brothers mine, take care! Take care!
The great white witch rides out to-night.
O, younger brothers mine, beware!
Look not upon her beauty bright;
For in her glance there is a snare,
And in her smile there is a blight.

1 Superhuman Antaeus was a half-giant slain by Hercules.

## William Crain

(B. 1949)

Now a cult classic, the Blaxploitation film *Blacula* was not originally well received by critics. It was directed by William Crain. Crain graduated from the University of California and was one of the first black filmmakers to achieve commercial success. In addition to the *Blacula* films, Crain directed a number of films and television shows throughout the later twentieth and early twenty-first century. He was featured in a 2019 documentary called *Horror Noire: A History of Black Horror*. *Blacula* tells the story of an African prince, Mamuwalde, who is transformed into a vampire by Count Dracula. This excerpt comes from the film's pre-credits opening scene. While the rest of the film is set in the late twentieth-century US, this opening moment connects the film's depiction of a Black vampire to earlier texts. In exploring Blacula's origins, it emphasizes the link between slavery, racial oppression, and vampires.

# from *Blacula*

(1972)

Cast:

Mamuwalde, an African Prince .............. William Marshall
Luva, his wife .................................. Vonetta McGee
Count Dracula ................................. Charles Macaulay
Dracula's Henchmen and Brides.............. uncredited

*Scene:* Thunder crashes revealing a gothic edifice.

Transylvania, 1780
Castle Dracula

Interior. A dining hall. The table is set with candles and a decanter of red wine.

*Count Dracula escorts Luva followed by Mamuwalde.*

DRACULA: I've never before had the opportunity of entertaining personages from the… "dark continent." (*Dracula holds Luva's chair as they all sit at the table.*) I hope the reception was not boring for you and your lovely wife.

MAMUWALDE: Quite the contrary, Count Dracula. The evening has been a splendid one, and we've found your guests to be most impressive.

DRACULA: (*chuckles*)

MAMUWALDE: I liked in particular your Dr Duvalier.

DRACULA: It was you who impressed him.

LUVA: Mamuwalde is the crystallization of our people's pride.

MAMUWALDE: My Luva… she does me too much credit.

*Dracula pours the wine.*

MAMUWALDE: But notwithstanding, my people are eager to bring our ancient culture into the community of nations.

DRACULA: That may take a good deal of time.

MAMUWALDE: It will at least be time well spent, as opposed to an exchange of banalities with pseudo-intellectuals and dilettantes.

DRACULA: Charming.

MAMUWALDE: What with dignitaries of your stature lending the weight of your statesmanship to the fulfillment of our objectives, I believe we will succeed. Luva?

*Luva unfolds a document and passes it to Dracula.*
*Dracula stands and reads it.*

DRACULA: To totally cease the slave trade? That is unrealistic. Slavery has merit, I believe.

MAMUWALDE: Merit? You find merit in barbarity?

DRACULA: Barbarous from the standpoint of the slave, perhaps. (*he leers at Luva*) Intriguing and delightful from mine. I would pay for so beautiful an addition to my household as your delicious wife.

MAMUWALDE: Sir, are you ill?

DRACULA: Oh…I meant no insult, prince (*he returns to his seat at the head of the table*). It is a compliment for a man of my station to look with desire on one of your color.

MAMUWALDE: Sir, I suddenly find your cognac as…(*rises from his seat*) distasteful as your manner.

*Dracula rises as well. They lock eyes.*

You're behaving like some animal.

DRACULA: Really?

MAMUWALDE: Really.

DRACULA: Let us not forget, sir, it is you who comes from the jungle.

MAMUWALDE: Our evening is finished.

*Mamuwalde and Luva move to leave.*

I bid you arouse your coachman. We are leaving.

DRACULA: I do not think so.

*Dracula snaps his fingers calling henchmen.*

MAMUWALDE: How dare you!

*Mamuwalde fights the henchmen.*
*Dracula seizes Luva, revealing his fangs.*

LUVA: Let me go!

*Mamuwalde wrestles with the henchman.*
*Mamuwalde grabs a torch from the wall and faces off with a henchman armed with a sword.*
*They fight, and Mamuwalde disarms him.*
*Dracula leaves the room.*

LUVA: Look out!

*Three henchmen tackle Mamuwalde.*

No!

*Mamuwalde is overpowered and knocked unconscious. Luva screams.*
*Dracula returns with five female vampires.*
*The female vampires surround Luva and drag her off.*
*Dracula bites the unconscious Mamuwalde. Luva screams.*

*Scene:* A stone-walled crypt with a large coffin.

DRACULA: (*laughing*) You shall pay, black prince. I shall place a curse of suffering on you that will doom you to a living hell.

*Mamuwalde appears unconscious in a coffin.*

A hunger, a wild, gnawing, animal hunger will grow in you, a hunger for human blood.

*Luva looks on, held by the female vampires.*

Here you will starve for an eternity, torn by an unquenchable lust. I curse you with my name. You shall be... Blacula!

*A bell tolls. Mamuwalde stirs.*

A vampire like myself, a living fiend, you will be doomed never to know that sweet blood which will become your only... desire.

*Dracula slams the lid of the coffin and locks it.*

LUVA: (*sobbing*) No!

DRACULA: (*to Luva*) You will watch, helpless and dying, until the black flesh rots from your bones. Listen... for his cries. They will comfort you until your death (*he laughs*).

*Dracula and his minions leave.*
*The stone door shuts, leaving Luva alone with the coffin.*

LUVA: No! Let me out!

*She pounds on the door.*

Help. Oh, help.

*She collapses sobbing on his coffin.*

Mamuwalde.

# Ngũgĩ wa Thiong'o

(B. 1938)

Considered to be one of Africa's greatest living writers, Ngũgĩ, a self-described "language warrior," is a powerful voice whose literary career spans six decades. Born in Kenya, and coming of age during the lengthiest and most violent rebellion against British domination in the region, Ngũgĩ is a fierce Kenyan devotee on a mission to inscribe the original Bantu language of Kenya's Gikuyu people in his works. This inscription is a symbol of Ngũgĩ's resistance to colonialism, an inscription by which he attempts to decolonize the mind because, as he asserts, "The lasting effect of the master's tongue is part of the master's logic." Although written in English, his novel *Devil on the Cross* exemplifies Ngũgĩ's harsh critique of Western exploitation and corruption. Perceived as a political dissident by the Kenyan government because of his writings, Ngũgĩ was imprisoned without trial for a year (1977–78), during which time he wrote the novel on toilet paper. The novel tells the story of Wariinga (translated as "woman in chains") and her odyssey from abuse and exploitation by the patriarchy to a self-sufficient spokeswoman for the nation. The pivotal point in the novel is the Devil's Feast, a competition among the most cunning thieves and robbers, a gathering of Kenyan elite for the purpose of giving boastful speeches about their capitalist endeavors and corrupt exploits. Ngũgĩ holds a dual professorship in comparative literature and English at the University of California, Irvine. He has been awarded 12 honorary PhDs from universities all over the world and has received several nominations for the Nobel Prize in Literature.

## from *Devil on the Cross*

(1980)

"A long, long time ago there lived an old man called Nding'ũri. Nding'ũri did not own much property. But he had a soul that was richly endowed. He was much respected because of his courage whenever enemies attacked his village, and because of the wisdom of his heart and tongue. He preserved the culture of his nation and observed all the proper rituals. Many a time he would sacrifice a goat and pour a little beer on to the ground for the good spirits, asking them to deliver him from evils that might have been caused by his own failings or brought into the homestead through the ill-will of wicked spirits. He was not a lazy man, and he was able to provide enough food to eat and clothes to wear for himself and his family. What he did not suffer from was greedy desire for other people's herds or land belonging to his clan or to other clans. His lack of greed, added to his famed generosity, prevented him from amassing the kind of wealth that made some elders wear rings on their fingers and leave the tilling of the fields and the grazing of herds to slaves, servants, laborers, peasants and their wives and children, while they themselves feasted daily off honey beer. Hands make a man; this was what Nding'ũri believed.

"But one day, a strange pestilence attacked the village. The pestilence destroyed all Nding'ũri's possessions and struck at his goat in its special pen. What could Nding'ũri do now? He asked himself: Why, when I have always sacrificed goats to the good spirits and brewed beer for them, have they now turned against me? Never again will I sacrifice to them.

"Early one morning, before dawn broke, Nding'ũri went to a certain cave where the evil spirits dwelled. At the entrance to the cave he was met by a spirit in the shape of an ogre. He had long hair, the color of moleskin, and the hair fell on to his shoulders like a girl's. He had two mouths, one on his forehead and the other at the back of his head. The one at the back of his head was covered by his long hair, and it was visible only when the wind blew the hair aside. The bad spirit asked him: 'Why have you come to my cave with empty hands? Does a man take an empty basket to market if he is planning to barter his wares? Have you been abandoned by the spirits to whom you have always sacrificed? Do you think that we ourselves don't like sacrifices and some beer to wash down the meat?' Nding'ũri replied that it was poverty that had brought him there. The generosity of a poor man remains locked in the heart. The bad spirit laughed slyly and said: 'But have I not heard that you possess a rich soul? Nothing good is ever born of perfect conditions. I will give you riches. But you must give me your soul, and you must never again sacrifice to the good spirits, for good and evil have never been friends.' Nding'ũri asked himself: What is a soul? Just a whispering voice. He told the bad spirit: 'Take my soul.' The bad spirit said to him: 'I have taken possession of it. Go away now. Go home and observe these conditions. First, never tell anybody that you are a man without a soul. Second, when you reach home, seize the child you love most, pierce one of the veins in his neck, drink up all his blood until his body is completely dry, cook the body, eat the flesh. Nding'ũri, I have turned you into an eater of human flesh and a drinker of human blood.' Nding'ũri said: 'What! How can that be? Am I to destroy the beauty of my own children?' The bad spirit told him: 'Have you already forgotten that you no longer have a soul? That you have sold it for property? Listen: from today onwards you'll never be able to see the beauty of children, or of women, or of any other human being. You'll be able to see only the beauty of property. Go now, go home. Devour other people's shadows. That's the task I have given you until the day I come to fetch you!'

"From that day on, Nding'ũri began to fart property, to shit property, to sneeze property, to scratch property, to laugh property, to think property, to dream property, to talk property, to sweat property, to piss property. Property would fly from other people's hands to land in Nding'ũri's palms. People started wondering: How is it that our property slips through our fingers in to the hand of Nding'ũri? Furthermore, he was now wearing iron rings on his fingers, which prevented him from working himself.

"Nding'ũri's character and behavior altered. He became mean. He became cruel. He was always involved in lawsuits as he grabbed other people's land, extending the boundaries of his own property further and further. He had no friends. His meanness protruded like the shoots of a sweet potato. When people were dying from famine, that was when Nding'ũri was happiest because at such times people would dispose of their property as readily as they would give away broken pots.

"People in his village started asking themselves: Where has his kindly tongue gone? What is that thing he eats alone in the middle of the night, like a witch? When he sees another man's property, his mouth waters: when he acquires his own, his mouth quickly dries up. See now how his shadow grows bigger and bigger, while ours become smaller and smaller. Could it be that his shadow is swallowing our shadows, making us fall dead, one by one?

"A delegation of elders, Nding'ũri's age-mates, was sent to him to remind him that no one digs a deep hole in the yard of the village, for his own children might fall into it. They told him: 'Nding'ũri, son of Kahahami, listen to the voice of the people. You have no wax in your ears—or if you have, take a splinter of wood and remove it.

"'The voice of the village is the voice of the Ridge, and it is the voice of the country, and it is the voice of the nation, and it is the voice of the people. Nding'ũri, the voice of the people is the voice of God. We come to bring you this message: avoid the ways of the witches and murderers. Allow yourself to be dazzled by the splendor of property, and you will be dazzled only by the splendor of the evil spirit. But in the glory of your nation you'll see the face of God. Happy is the man who willingly defends the shadow of his nation, for he will never die; his name shall live forever in the hearts of the people. But he who sells the shadow of his nation is damned, for his name shall forever be cursed by generations to come, and when he dies he will become an evil spirit.'

"Nding'ũri just laughed, and he asked them: 'What's a village? What's a nation? What's a people? Go away and tell all this to someone else. Why are you unable to take care of yourselves and your shadows? Why are you so lazy that you can't even bend down to remove a jigger[1] from your legs? Go on talking until it rains or the heavens fall—your words will only be carried away by the wind. See, now, all my affairs are in perfect order. My fart never smells. Why? Let me tell you. Because property is the great creator and the great judge. Property turns disobedience into obedience, evil into good, ugliness into beauty, hate into love, cowardice into bravery, vice into virtue. Property changes bow legs into legs that are fought over by the beauties of the land. Property sweetens evil smells, banishes rot. The wound of a rich man never produces pus. The fart of a rich man never smells. Go back to your homes. Go back to your shacks, which you have the audacity to call farms. If you are unable to do that, come back here and work as wage laborers in my many fields. There is nothing you can do to me, Nding'ũri, son of Kahahami, because I have no soul!'

"When they heard that, the elders of the village were greatly alarmed, and they looked askance at one another: "So we have been harboring a witch in our village? We have been sheltering a louse in our bodies? This one will drink up all the blood of all the people until there is no more blood left in the land." And then and there they seized him, and wrapped him up with dry banana leaves, and burned him and his house."

1 A tropical flea that burrows under the skin.

# Jewelle Gomez

(B. 1948)

Descended from African American and Native American ancestry, Jewelle Gomez is an esteemed forerunner in Afrofuturism, the Black science fiction movement, and is important to the Indigenous Futurism movement that focuses on the speculative fiction of Native peoples. As a founding member of GLAAD (Gay and Lesbian Alliance Against Defamation), she is renowned for the activism that is integral to her work. Gomez asserts, "Everyone is writing from some political perspective whether knowingly or not... I write as a lesbian feminist of color always." This political perspective is evident in *The Gilda Stories*, featuring Gilda, a woman who escapes from slavery and becomes a vampire . The disparate chapters of this novel represent a coming-of-age story spanning 200 years. In the narrative, Gomez departs from the stereotypical image of the predatory vampire; in the process of her awakening, Gilda experiences life as a queer Black woman with the privileges of vampire powers. However, she operates with a heightened awareness, a kind of moral compass, realizing that mortals do not have this same power. Gomez won two Lambda awards for *The Gilda Stories*. She is the recipient of numerous commissions and fellowships including the National Endowment for the Arts, and has presented lectures at many distinguished universities. In addition to writing fiction, Gomez is a poet and playwright; her trilogy *Words and Music* is a collection of plays about African American artists in the first half of the twentieth century. In this excerpt from *The Gilda Stories*, the racists who confront Gilda use offensive language that may be disturbing for readers.

# from "Rosebud, Missouri: 1921," *The Gilda Stories*

(1991)

Gilda drove back through the town onto the road leading southwest to her farmhouse. Tonight the car made her impatient. She longed to be free of the dress and stockings, to wear her dark, men's trousers and woolen shirt. She always looked forward to night when she'd race through the wooded area between Rosebud and St. Louis hunting for the blood. The feel of wind whipping around her swept away the long past and with it her loneliness for the company of Sorel and Anthony.[1] When she moved through the night with the wind she forgot she was still awaiting some message from Bird.[2]

The light from the full moon and her acute vision made a lamp unnecessary inside her house. Gilda walked slowly through the sitting room and narrow hallway to her sleeping room with its double-locked door. Entering its draped darkness, she slipped into her more familiar clothes. She went through the hall again, back to her desk, and sat down before her open journal. It had been some time since her last entry. She passed her hands over the dried ink and looked out the window to the empty road winding away from her front porch to the east and west. Three years here, she thought. What a ridiculously short time. What a horribly long time. It had been fifty years since she last saw Bird and almost as long since she left Woodard's.[3] Yet the loss of them lay heavily on her, a weight that would not relent until she finally spoke with Bird and peace was made.

Gilda flipped the journal pages backward to a passage near the book's beginning. When Gilda and Bird were alone, running Woodard's together, Bird had passed on the wisdom and cunning of the woman who had given both of them life. Looking down at the flat words, she found that despite their sparseness, they evoked a memory as sharply defined as a daguerreotype. She could see the full brow and stern mouth as Bird taught her the ways of the hunt. Her low

1 These are characters introduced in previous chapters. Sorel is a vampire who runs a gambling parlor in Yerba Buena in 1890. Anthony is his partner of more than 100 years. They mentor Gilda and offer an example of found family as she struggles to carve out an identity for herself.

2 A Lakota vampire, Bird becomes a complicated mother figure for Gilda. Bird was the original Gilda's partner when she took in "the Girl" who had escaped from slavery in Louisiana of 1850. This girl would grow into a young woman with Bird and the original Gilda. Then, the original Gilda turns the Girl into a vampire. The Girl agrees to take the name of Gilda, a name she will carry throughout the rest of the novel. The original Gilda ends her long life by swimming out into the Gulf as the sun rises.

3 Woodard's is the brothel run by Bird and the original Gilda where the Girl who will become the central character of *The Gilda Stories* takes refuge.

and level voice hummed in Gilda's head with instructions about survival in the sun's rays, about avoiding suspicion and keeping the secret of their lives.

Bird had given her the first journal, a fine-lined green ledger.

"You may want to save your thoughts here. To remember the feelings, the turn of events. It's best to write in one of the other languages in the event someone should stumble upon the book. I sometimes even wrote as though it were fiction," Bird had said, smiling at the memory.

Gilda began by writing questions she had about their life, the many answers Bird gave her, and the many she did not.

"Why do you say others may kill and we must not?"

"Some are said to live through the energy of fear. That is their sustenance more than the sharing. The truth is we hunger for connection to life, but it needn't be through horror or destruction. Those are just the easiest links to evoke. Once learned, this lesson mustn't be forgotten. To ignore it, to wallow in death as the white man has done, can only bring bitterness."

"And what of our bodies? Do they really never grow old?"

"Only the mind grows old. You are already tighter, more solid than you were as a child. There will be no grey hair, no aching limbs, no wound that does not heal."

"And the sun?"

"A danger. It can weaken you, even take you to the true death. But it needn't do that unless you give yourself up to it or are already ill. The soil of your birthplace will protect you. All new garments can be constructed to discreetly contain pockets of it. Other things—your cloak, your shoes, all laced with your earth—will serve you. You needn't fear small doses of the sun unless you're unprotected. It may even become your ally when you wish to let go of life."

As always, when Bird spoke of something that reminded her of the past she ended the discussion and turned abruptly to some other task. Gilda longed to ask Bird why the other had left them, but anytime she started to voice the question, Bird withdrew. So Gilda contented herself with lessons in the new ways of life and new languages. She had just begun to grow used to the altered rhythm of her life, to the speed and strength of her limbs, to her vision which pierced mortal duplicity, and to the reality of their isolation, when Bird announced her departure.

Gilda bitterly regretted never having confronted Bird, never demanding to know why Bird blamed her for the other's death. Instead she'd waved good-bye stolidly from her upstairs window as Bird rode away. When Gilda still found herself, after some time, listening for Bird's voice among those of the others, when she could no longer endure the earth and lavender scent of Bird's room without collapsing in dry sobs, she deeded Woodard's to Bernice's[1] youngest daughter and started northward.

---

1 In the first chapter of *The Gilda Stories*, "Louisiana: 1850," Bernice is Woodard's cook.

On her third night of leisurely travel Gilda built a fire in a dark clearing beside the road. She took in the warmth as she gazed at the flames but was more absorbed by the portentous shapes and shadows. In that circle of heat and light the dark, chilling shape of her life found Gilda. Panic settled on her shoulders, obliterating the past and the future. Without Bird she was floating out of control on a dangerous sea. Once again she needed to give shape to a world that was beyond her comprehension, much as she had been forced to do when her mother died.[1] She sat before the roadside fire trying to gain a focus, some sense of anticipation, but she found no grounding for them. The wind and flame were too free. It was then she pulled out a map and began to plot her journey—marking places where she should hide caches of her soil, choosing things she wanted to see. The plains of Texas, the towering trees of California, the many communities of freed blacks. Including her stay with Sorel and Anthony, she had spent almost half a century on the road before arriving in Rosebud.

Gilda closed her journal and looked around the room, her eyes picking out the few things she'd saved from Woodard's: a colorful quilt, the small desk at which she now sat, the rows of books that lined the wall. Her trunk still held the metal cross her mother had given her and the leather-encased knife from Bird. These possessions were the legacy of a few short years and more lifetimes than most others would ever know. She shut the door of her sleeping room and the front door of the house, then walked east, slowly trying to reconstruct the time that had passed.

The years with Sorel—learning as much as there was time to absorb, from financial investing to Eastern philosophy—were as pristinely clear as her language lessons with Bird. She could feel the damp air on her skin from the evening walks with Anthony on fog-enshrouded piers. The vision of Eleanor,[2] her scarlet hair dimming the lamplight, still took away her breath.

But many of the years were simply a broad strip of darkness into which she peered, out of which she could draw little. Whenever she wanted to remember them she read through her journal as she had just done, but still they held little meaning for her. Most decades were dazed watercolor views sketched from a distance. They provided a precise narrative of journeys but few sensations.

Tonight the full moon illuminated the road, making it feel like dusk, so Gilda moved cautiously off to the side into the thickets. On the road, or in the anonymity of St. Louis, she would take her share of the blood and then return to her books and papers to examine her memories. Her dark skin remained unlined, just as Bird had said it would. Her thick black hair, which she now

1 Her mother's death in slavery is what prompts the Girl (later known as Gilda) to escape, thus bringing her to the vampires who make her part of their family.

2 Eleanor is a vampire Gilda knew in Yerba Buena. She is a daughter figure to Sorel and, briefly, Gilda's romantic interest. While very beautiful, Eleanor's cold and twisted personality ultimately drive Gilda away.

wore pulled tightly back and tied in a bun at the nape of her neck, was still as dark as brushed velvet.

She moved speedily through the night, unafraid of animals or the nightriders who prowled looking for blacks whose lives were their sport. She slowed and lifted her face toward the moon. Her eyes closed. She was an eerie worshipper, part of the secret lore of ha'nts[1] and spirits that lived with African people, even in Missouri. In the half light Gilda felt the moon's warmth as she had once felt the scorch of the sun on her back in the fields. But here the warmth was a fascination. Once taken for granted, the moon was now the center of her orbit.

She resisted the impulse to reach out for Bird, to try to touch her consciousness wherever she might be. Too often since their separation Gilda had come to a dead-end road trying to scan the miles.

She had almost agreed with Sorel when she left California that her task now was simply to live. As she did so, among the free blacks on farms and in small towns, she came closer to knowing, through them, who she was. Her preternatural life made her an outsider, but still she enjoyed their evocation of the secrets of the past and their unequivocal faith in the future. Gilda was chagrined by her concept of *they* and how her life separated her from them. Still she took comfort in the familiar smells and sounds and the rare sense of unity that sometimes crept into her.

Gilda moved away from these thoughts by opening her eyes and beginning her sprint toward the city. Before she could quite pull away, another sensation washed over her. A restlessness, much like the angry flower that had grown inside of Bird. Gilda didn't know its root, but the need to move on, to look elsewhere for something still undefined, was like a hard wind at her back. The faint stirrings of the anxious hunger inside her turned her mind toward the blood that would replenish her life. Unconsciously, however, she planned what direction she'd follow next, not considering how she would force herself to part from Aurelia.[2]

She had already stepped back onto the road intent on fulfilling the stirring inside her when she saw two men on horseback approaching from the west. They were moving at a good pace, as if racing, but they slowed when they noticed her and pulled up short a few feet away. One swung down from the saddle immediately. He stood before her with an angry glare that quickly turned into a leer when he realized she was not a man.

"This here's a niggah gal, we got here. What you doin' out on the road this hour?"

Gilda didn't respond but let herself breathe in the smell of the horses and sense their anxiety and dissatisfaction with their masters. There was an idle

1 A ha'nt or "haint" is a type of evil ghost in African American vernacular. The mythology came from Africa with enslaved people and can simply mean a ghost or more specifically refer to a more witch-like creature.

2 Aurelia is an activist in Rosebud. A close friend, Gilda tells her the secret of her vampire identity.

communication between them and her that went unnoticed by the riders. Gilda felt reassured by the horses' solid presence, their lack of malevolence, and their easy response to comforting messages she sent them. The other horseman dismounted holding a glistening whip coiled at his hip.

"Maybe we teach one more niggah a lesson tonight, hey Cook?" Gilda peered at the braided leather, dark with blood she could smell. She wondered who had been their most recent pupil.

"Yeah, Zach, I think there's a lesson here for sure."

Gilda still didn't move or speak. She stood as if frozen, but her mind flooded with the words Bird had given her. She was not afraid as she had been that night long ago in the root cellar.[1] She tasted the acid of hatred inside her mouth and wanted to be full of it, to teach the lesson these two needed to learn.

"She must be mute, Zach. Don't seem to talk, do she?"

The taller man moved close to Gilda and yanked her hair, pulling her face up toward his. The moonlight glistened on her dark skin. Before he could press his advantage, Gilda grabbed his wrist, the crack of bone audible in the night. She pulled his hand from her head and twisted it behind his back, raising it so high the pain cut his voice before he could scream. She gave a sharp twist and let go only when she felt his muscles quaking with pain. He whipped around toward her again, and she smashed the side of his face with her fist. The snap of his neck broke through the night as his body crumpled into the ditch beside the road.

His fellow rider backed away, reaching behind him for the reins of his horse, but his mount deliberately twisted out of his reach and Gilda was upon him before he realized his position. She caught his whip in her left hand and pulled him backward. He fell to the ground, then scurried back off the road to the brush with Gilda bounding behind him. She cracked the whip once over his head, then lay a stroke across his back. That she hit him with his own whip seemed to startle him more than the pain. At the second lash he turned to face Gilda, his eyes filled with rage. He gasped when he saw the swirling amber of her eyes and the sinewy strength of her body, thinking that they'd been wrong, that it was a man. An Indian he thought, confused by the moonlight and his own fear. She cracked the whip this time across his chest, then his cheek, opening the flesh almost to the bone.

Gilda threw the whip down and leapt upon him, twisting his head to expose the pulsing vein in his neck. He was already faint with shock, yet Gilda sensed his disbelieving terror build. She scraped his flesh roughly with her nails and watched the blood pulse from his neck, searching for what he felt when he lay open the flesh of men. Her chest swelled with anticipation as she understood the terrible joy he experienced at demanding terror and death. She drew his blood into her quickly and then let him slip to the ground. She watched the

1 The novel opens with the Girl, who has just escaped from slavery, having to kill a white man who attempts to rape her.

blood continue to stream from his neck, soaking into the muddy ditch. She could feel life ebbing from him and was shocked at the excitement it aroused. One death was enough. It had been so long since she'd been caught unawares like this. She knelt beside him, holding her hands to the wounds on his neck and cheek until the bleeding stopped.

She left him nothing in exchange except a simple recollection of falling instead of the horror of the real memory. His breath was shallow, but he was no longer in danger.

Gilda was sickened by her anger and the thrill the confrontation had given her. It was the nightmarish pleasure she had seen in Eleanor's eyes and the one she feared could become hers. She climbed back up to the road and stared down at the face of the one who was dead, frozen in the moonlight. She took in his features as she'd been taught and tried to absorb some sense of his true spirit. This was only the second one. His image now took its place beside the other in a corner inside herself that Gilda seldom visited. The first one had been taken on a road not unlike this one, in the dark when mortals seemed to feel that what was done was not seen. She had not talked with anyone about that time, not even Sorel or Anthony. Just as she wouldn't speak of this death until she could talk of it with Bird.

She turned back toward her farm. Instead of her usual swift pace, Gilda took each step with deliberation. She was leaden with exhaustion. Anger had flared and burned out leaving the taste of ashes. One death. She was grateful it had not been two. When she finally arrived home she eagerly sponged the blood from her hands and face. The memory of her rage and the death made her tremble, so she avoided her desk and its temptation to record her anguish. Instead she sank into the earth-filled comforter, flying into the arms of dreamless sleep.

## Ibi Aanu Zoboi

Ibi Zoboi was born in Port-au-Prince, Haiti, and at the age of four immigrated to New York with her mother. Zoboi's chosen name is "Ibi," which is Yoruba for rebirth, a name that applies to her literary mission, a renaissance whereby people of color will reclaim the mythologies severed from them by the diaspora. Zoboi laments that "The dearth of people of color writing fantasy literature is directly related to our collective proximity to what was stolen from us; pried out of our hands, hearts, and minds; or stomped out and beat out of us—our gods." In "Old Flesh Song," published in the award-winning collection of African American speculative fiction *Dark Matter: Reading the Bones*, Zoboi embarks on this reclamation with the soucouyant, a shape-shifting figure from Caribbean folklore who appears in the guise of an old woman by day, but sheds her skin at night and as a ball of fire jettisons across the sky in search of victims. Her narrative focuses on the conflict between two soucouyants that signify, historically, the exploitation of women of color: a stereotypical dark "mammy" figure and a light-skinned Latina figure, both of whom care for the children of their white owners/employers. In her works, Zoboi is answering her own call to "uphold our respective mythologies and preserve them within published pages so that we can immortalize our truths for all of eternity," a directive that her teacher the late Octavia Butler would applaud! Zoboi holds an MFA from Vermont College of Fine Arts; her novel *American Street*, destined to become a classic in the young adult genre, was a National Book Award finalist.

# "Old Flesh Song"

(2004)

mati pa a wélé—
mati pa a wélé wélé
wélé wélé kojo polo polo
wélé kojo pa a polo—
kojo pa a polo.[1]

1 Zoboi provides the translation to this verse later in the text. Essentially, Old Flesh's song calls children to her to feed her flesh.

She did not sing for money. Nor did anyone want to get close enough to drop a coin in her basket. She reeked of death—the odor of the underworld, the nether life, where the aroma of things sustaining growth and change is halted. Her life cycle was stagnant, circulating in its own juice—like cells forming blood clots. She lived in death and emanated its essence—stale, old flesh. Nothing sweet and joyous would come from this. So she sang a melancholy song, with no audience and no requests for charity.

Of all the sidewalks, subways, and street corners in the callous city, she decided to settle in front of the Willoughby & Company Toy and Gift Shop on Seventy-seventh and Lexington. There were no others of her kind around. She was an isolated sore oozing bitterness onto the lively, cosmopolitan Upper East Side of Manhattan. She sat there on the cold concrete wrapped in African mud cloth, the tapestry of her native home. It was neither dirty nor clean; mud cloth has the semblance of filth even in its purest state—like her face, blue-black, hard, old, yet innocent. Her hair was matted into seven coils extending from her head with lives of their own like serpents. Around her sat three bags: one of the same mud cloth, a woven backpack basket embroidered with cowry shells, and a pastel-colored baby bag. All three filled with life, contrary to the odor, stuffed with odd things she's picked up from here and there and claimed as her own. They've held her and fed her to this point—kept her grounded and connected to this material world—treasured things of no value. She carried the three bags with her, never let them out of her sight, and held on to them, just as they held her, for dear death.

She would sing her sad song whenever a stroller passed her, usually being pushed through the sliding doors of Willoughby & Company. Always in a stroller, never in a slingy or carried in enveloping arms. And only certain babies—babies that were not pushed by their own relatives, but by temporary, rented parents. She would see the baby nestled in blankets cooing and waving pinkish hands and feet at her. They never winced or turned up *their* tiny noses at her. She would watch the guardians send a quick cold glance—their faces contrasting the pale, transparent hue of the fresh young blood—some blue-black like hers and others in various shades of brown.

*Baby's parents are gone for the day. So Ms. Nanny will take care of precious Baby. Keep Baby in a stroller so there's no confusion. Here's a list. Ms. Nanny can take Baby for a walk over to Willoughby & Company for some toys. And here's a little extra for Ms. Nanny if she wants to get herself something nice. Watch out for Lady Bag, though. She likes babies.*

Old Flesh was hungry. Not for food. Nothing grown or processed in this decaying world would sustain her. She yearned for something fresh and abundant with life. It would keep her here in this sprawling city, watching everything else decay around her, and she remaining on the brink of death itself, never entering its gateway.

It was mid-May, and nannies were to take the babies out of their luxuriant condos for some spring air. Always with the list for Willoughby & Company. *Not that they don't trust Ms. Nanny's taste, but they know just what Baby needs. A ceramic oriental-painted rattle for Baby. Stay away from Lady Bag. They understand that those people need a little help... well, some more than others. Ms. Nanny may want to help, but she shouldn't get too close with the baby and all.*

Old Flesh had noticed them crossing the busy intersection. A three-wheeled carriage, something she's been seeing more of lately. Maybe not called a stroller, but a jogger, since she'd watched parents pushing the baby along while they went for early morning or late afternoon jogs through Central Park. Of course Ms. Nanny wouldn't be the one jogging. But this one was pushing the jogger toward the corner nonetheless. Young Blood had no socks; plump legs and tiny feet were exposed. Old Flesh licked her lips. And sang her invocation:

*"mati pa a wélé—*
*mati pa a wélé wélé*
*wélé wélé kojo polo polo*
*wélé kojo pa a polo—*
*kojo pa a polo."*

Her focus shifted toward this Ms. Nanny. She was young, her skin a smooth caramel brown, high cheekbones, thick lips, and broad nose—raw features from native soil. Starting out too early. Lured to leave home with the promise of food, shelter, and if lucky education, to be at the beck and call of nice folks—good families that take care of you, if you take care of them.

*Put you out your misery, girl,* Old Flesh thought. She grunted, wiped her salivating mouth with the back of her hand, and continued her commanding chant.

Young Blood noticed her immediately. They always did. Bright blue eyes glared at her from the shadow of the hood. Ms. Nanny swerved the jogger toward the edge of the sidewalk away from Old Flesh, nearly bumping a pedestrian. Old Flesh wrapped the mud cloth around her shoulders and large bosom and began to move from her comfortable spot. She pushed the basket aside and pushed herself up to her feet. Ms. Nanny and Young Blood were making their way into Willoughby's, of course. Old Flesh sang louder—sound vibrations luring them back to her. Her muscles ached as she moved closer to the sliding-door entrance. She did not walk placing one foot in front of the other, but wobbled—her rotund hips moving from side to side, adding an invisible drumbeat rhythm to her chant. Her stench followed her like a ghost, deterring pedestrians from her presumed path. She waited. They would soon come out. Young Blood first, then Ms. Nanny pushing behind. Old Flesh's song came to a stop. Its spell had reached.

The doors slid open; the first wheel was visible. White bottom of Young Blood's feet greeted her. Ms. Nanny was looking around as if searching. Old Flesh nodded to herself in approval of the traveling words of her song. Young Blood had heard and obeyed. So had Ms. Nanny, but not in the same way. Old

Flesh knew she would recognize the broken cadence—not as a pleasant spell, but as a bold command. Old Flesh watched Ms. Nanny search for the spell caster. Their eyes met. Ms. Nanny's face twisted in confusion. The grating sound resonated from Old Flesh, but her lips merely drizzled salvia like a feasting predator. Ms. Nanny looked elsewhere. Her attention was diverted, the stench was concealed from her, and she focused on her mission to search for the lips sending incantations into the noisy city wind.

Then and there Old Flesh seized her opportunity to quench her hunger. Quick as the tongue, a fatty charcoal hand pulls the pink/white tiny feet, its body came with it, wiggling, squirming, but not resisting. A mere fifteen pounds, feather-light to Old Flesh. It was routine for her, scooping babies with one large hand. A Ms. Nanny's skill—baby in one hand, and dusting, cooking, or perhaps twin in the other. This Ms. Nanny was too young and unseasoned. *Keep one eye on Baby and the other on everyone else.* Old Flesh pulled Young Blood toward her and underneath her mud-cloth wrap—like stealing a porcelain baby doll from Willoughby's.

Young Blood didn't cry, of course, lulled by the remnants of the command/ spell. Old Flesh didn't move just yet. She saw Ms. Nanny's face disappointed, looking every which way for the witch's lips. The incantation withered into an echo, far into the distance, away from its victim's ear. Ms. Nanny was now conscious of the odor. She took a quick glance at Old Flesh. Old Flesh returned a toothless grin. A perfectly still Young Blood bulged from beneath the mud-cloth wrap. Ms. Nanny was oblivious; she turned the empty stroller toward the other direction, away from Lady Bag. Old Flesh watched her. She wouldn't look into the stroller for a while, still mesmerized by the chant now only echoing in her memory.

Old Flesh smiled, then giggled, then laughed—deep and hard, throwing her head back in amusement at herself and the stupidity of herself. She remembered being just as oblivious at one point in her life/death. She had succeeded. First of the three Young Bloods she needed to feed on to keep alive in death. These Young Bloods would be different since they were not in her immediate possession like the ones before. Two more attempts like this and she was done.

Young Blood began to squirm. Its instinct told it to search for food just the same. Old Flesh felt its head move around her right breast. Of course she had no milk. But it was the sensation she longed for—the quenching of her thirst/ hunger. She went back to her spot, and eased down onto the concrete with Young Blood wrapped in the mud cloth and her thick arms. She leaned against the brick wall and sighed to herself, smiling in pleasure. She pulled the three bags securely around her and Young Blood: protection. Old Flesh uncovered Young Blood's face. White with the semblance of purity, cheeks pink for love needed, eyes blue reflecting Old Flesh's matron Yemaya,[1] goddess of deep ocean waters—motherhood. She pulled out a sagging left breast and placed a shriveled

1 Originally from a Yoruba religion in what is today Nigeria, Yemaya was brought to the Americas by enslaved Africans. She is often considered the ultimate female power in this religion.

black nipple in Young Blood's mouth. Young Blood was eager, deprived of its natural joy, since probably weaned at a too-young age. *They know what's best for baby. But a baby need milk like mother breast need sucking. But IT AIN'T YOURS! IT AIN'T... But it mine if I care for it. It mine if I feed it with my own.*

Old Flesh gasped at the sensation of Young Blood's tiny, warm mouth wrapped around her nipple. Young Blood sucked and pulled, making snapping sounds at the back of its throat. It began to writhe in frustration. No milk. Young Blood was not the one hungry, Old Flesh was. But she fed it emptiness/death nonetheless—feeding herself in the process. Young Blood pulled, Old Flesh pulled harder—her desiccated breast suctioned for life, for blood. Young Blood's plump cheeks stiffened in the pull, Old Flesh's breast inflated. Not giving milk, but receiving fresh young blood for her old flesh. She leaned her head back, ecstatic from the sensation. *Ms. Nanny, Baby hungry now. Can't eat until Baby is fed. Can't go home until Baby sleep.*

*wélé kojo pa a polo*, Old Flesh whispered to herself.

Young Blood lay limp in her arms. Skin pale, no more pink cheeks, frozen eyes a deathly gray. Old Flesh, her soul now one-third vitalized, bent her head to place a chapped-lip kiss on its forehead. Not a young blood anymore, but a lifeless thing—flesh, not old but young, useless just the same. She pulled its mouth away from her now perky nipple. She looked up to watch passersby afraid to look in her direction wondering what she was up to, diverting from her shielding stink. Old flesh discreetly took young flesh from the warmth of the mud cloth, opened the pastel-colored baby bag, and gently placed the body inside. There was room for two more.

Old Flesh zipped the baby bag, and gently tapped the young flesh inside. She readjusted the mud cloth around her and caressed her left breast. She felt the blood travel from what was once the food source for young bloods, penetrate warrior cells, travel through her veins and into her pumping heart. Decayed body ached for more if only to slow its putrefying process. Old Flesh breathed in, gathering all else for it in her body—blood and flesh was sufficient. She held her breath, grabbed the mud cloth bag, opened it, and released Young Blood's life force into it, along with the others. The distant cries of young blood souls emerged—like smoke from a burning inferno. She quickly closed the bag so no one else heard.

Rest. Only two more.

Old Flesh was awoken by another young blood's cry penetrating the afternoon city noise. She wiped her eyes, licked her lips, and smiled. The sound came from the fruit stand in the middle of the block. The carriage faced her. A large one, enough for two. Twins. Old Flesh kissed her fingertips and raised them up to the sky, thanking her matron Yemaya. With the same hand, knocked on the concrete beneath her three times for the nameless gods/ancestors of the underworld. She took another look at the twin young bloods—plump hands and feet moving in unison. She licked her lips, cleared her throat, and pulled the magic sound vibration from her soulless body:

*"mati pa a wélé..."*

The song traveled past irrelevant bystanders to reach its subjects. She craned her neck to see the Twin Young Bloods. One, just as pale as she liked, wispy blond hair with blue baby suit. The other a contrast to its sibling with lush dark hair, large fisted hands, and pink baby suit. Blond Twin Young Blood moved about in its section of the carriage. It had reached. To Old Flesh's surprise, Fisted Young Blood began to whimper, defiant to the command/spell. Louder. *mati pa a wélé*... Old Flesh saw the back of a large woman turn in her direction. Thicker, stronger than her. She did not look around, but gazed right at her. This Ms. Nanny was old and conditioned. Old Flesh's challenge.

*You been in this for a long time, woman. Put you out your misery too. Be easy if only you know you miserable*, Old Flesh thought, while stirring the entrancing words into the city noise.

Ms. Nanny's high-yellow face twisted—not in confusion, but in resentment. She was beautiful. Long dark hair braided above her shoulders. Eyes deep and suspicious. *Keep one eye on baby and the other on everyone else*. She watched Old Flesh. Old Flesh continued her command/spell. Louder. *wélé wélé kojo polo polo*...

Ms. Nanny picked the crying Fisted Twin Young Blood from its section of the carriage. She held it against her bosom, rocking back and forth. Fisted Twin Young Blood continued to cry. Old Flesh could not stop until both young bloods obeyed. The echo of the command/spell was to be left for Ms. Nanny.

It did not reach. Old Flesh's eyes traveled down to Blond Twin Young Blood. His tiny head was moving from side to side as if annoyed by the grating sound. He was most vulnerable. Louder. *wélé kojo pa a polo*... If not the other, then definitely this one. But one of them had to be out of Ms. Nanny's protective glare. Ms. Nanny tried to hush Fisted Twin Young Blood, and began to push the stroller with her free hand—a Ms. Nanny skill. *Shit! She ain't 'posed to come to me*. Ms. Nanny's jaws were clenched, eyes fierce, ready for confrontation. Old Flesh reduced the chant to a whisper, strengthening its power to her defiant subjects. She could hear Ms. Nanny as she approached.

"Shh, *mija. No tengas miedo.*[1] Don't be scared, my daughter." She wrinkled her nose as she approached Old Flesh's stink shield.

Old Flesh merely stared up at her. Softly. *mati pa a wélé* ...

"What are you doing, old lady?" Her Spanish accent was thick, her voice was commanding—typical of a seasoned Ms. Nanny.

Old Flesh could not stop the command/spell. They were too close. She was still hungry. Two more to go. She had at least one young blood within her reach.

1 The nanny speaks first in Spanish then gives the English translation.

She could not let it slip. She whispered one last strong verse to herself, watching Blond Twin Young Blood, hoping its eyes would meet hers for confirmation:

*"mati pa a wélé—*
*mati pa a wélé wélé*
*wélé wélé kojo polo polo*
*wélé kojo pa a polo—*
*kojo pa a polo."*

(come to me young blood—/come to me fresh young blood/fresh young blood feeds stale old flesh/young blood feed my old flesh—/feed my old flesh.)

"No!" Ms. Nanny yelled, holding Fisted Twin Young Blood away from Lady Bag.

Old Flesh's whispered spell/command had not reached. Fisted Twin Young Blood's cry permeated its power. She glared at them, curious of their shield.

"*Qué haces?*"[1] Ms. Nanny repeated. She heard the words. Merely words to her that she had deciphered.

"Exactly what I just said. You heard me, ain't you?" Old Flesh's voice raspy, strong, and commanding just the same.

"You can't have them!"

"I *can* if you give 'em to me," Old Flesh toyed with her. "I won't hurt you. Just need a little something to sustain me, that's all."

Ms. Nanny chuckled—a knowing, confident laugh. Old Flesh joined her. She had already been defeated with the spell/command song. Now she would charm her way to one of the young bloods.

"Come on. Won't you give 'em to me. They ain't yours."

"*Peneja loca!* Crazy bitch! I know what you've been doing. *Chupasangre! Soucouyant!* Bloodsucker!"[2] Ms. Nanny's eyes glowed red, ready to aim at Old Flesh. Fisted Twin Young Blood stared just the same.

Old Flesh smiled, giggled, then laughed. "You can see me? You know what I want? I know what you want. Let's make a deal." Old Flesh reached over to open the backpack basket in front of her, releasing more of the deathly aroma—her last resort.

Ms. Nanny watched her and quickly placed her hand over her mouth, releasing her firm clutch on the stroller.

Old Flesh saw her mistake from the corner of her locked stare. "Them babies ain't yours. Why care for them so? Give 'em to me and you can go back to your own children."

1 "What are you doing?"

2 Once again, she provides the translation immediately after the original statement. As discussed in the introduction, a soucouyant is a shapeshifter from Caribbean folklore who appears as an old woman by day and then transforms into a ball of fire to suck the life out of infants at night.

Ms. Nanny tightened her hold on Fisted Twin Young Blood and reached into her bag for …

Old Flesh seized her moment. Quick as the tongue, she grabbed the foot of blond Twin Young Blood; its body came with it, wiggling, squirming, but not resisting. This one was heavier—one quick pull toward her bosom and beneath her mud-cloth wrap.

Ms. Nanny leaped forward. *"No, mijo! Dame mi hijo, chupasangre!"*[1]

"Somebody call the cops! Police, over here. Emergency!" A faceless voice yelled from the now encircling crowd. Not too close; Old Flesh's stink shield kept them far enough away not to interfere.

Ms. Nanny froze when the baby in her arms began to cry again. *"Por favor, Señora.*[2] Don't hurt my baby," she pleaded, choking on tears. "Is fresh blood you want? I can give to you, please."

*"My? My baby?* Now you know damn well they ain't your babies. I'm trying to help *you* out, Ms. Nanny. Get you back to your own children." Old Flesh's mouth watered, her heart raced. The young blood against her bosom increased her hunger.

Ms. Nanny straightened herself, hoisted the baby onto her hip, and sniffed back her tears. "My name no Ms. Nanny. You know who I am. *Dame lo.*[3] Give me the baby, Lorraine." Her eyes glowed red again.

"Don't make a difference what your name is." Old Flesh caressed Blond Twin Young Blood's face. "It's all the same work. Other people's babies suck the life out of you. Ain't even have time to watch your own seed die. Just taking back what's owed to me, that's all." She slowly began to uncover her left breast. "And I ain't nobody's Lorraine, you hear. Lorraine is gone. Gone!"

"You no want to keep doing this, Lorraine," Ms. Nanny responded.

Old Flesh's stink shield began to take form as the crowd began to grow. It became a thin, pale green resistant wall of smoke surrounding her and her prey. The city noise was muffled. The cops had already surrounded it, punching and shooting unsuccessfully at the stink shield.

"Oh yes I do. Fed, cleaned, healed them little sickly things 'til my breasts fell flat. Never had enough for my own. My own …" Old Flesh looked down at Blond Twin Young Blood. Its drooling mouth was instinctively searching for food from her breast. She would fulfill its desire.

*"mati pa a wélé …"*

Old Flesh looked up. The command/spell did not come from her. Blond Twin Young Blood looked around in curiosity, its attention diverted from the breast.

---

1 "No, my son! Give me my son, bloodsucker!"

2 "Please, ma'am."

3 "Give it to me."

Ms. Nanny sang the words. Sweet and tender. Deadly and entrancing, nonetheless.

"You not too smart, Lorraine. You no let them suck up dry like that. You come first. Feed you first."

"You *soucouyant* woman too, eh? Who you?"

"Celia. I clean up your mess, Lorraine. You eating all those babies. You put yourself out of work, you want to put us out of work, too? Have those good people going crazy looking for missing babies? No one wants to hire us. I serve Yemaya." She kissed her fingertips up to the sky. "This is my life's work. I will cook you in your own stolen blood before I let you take what's mine!" Celia hissed, eyes enflamed.

"How dare you blaspheme her name!" Old Flesh leaned toward Celia. "Yemaya don't take, she give. I mothered them babies like they my own. But they wasn't. Was supposed to be taking care of mine. Let them die instead. She cursed me. Can't go nowhere but here, in between. Can't live, can't die. I need young blood."

Celia laughs. Baby fully alert in her arms. "*Pobrecita.*[1] You got it all wrong. That's why you here. Yemaya, the great mother, she no curse. She love and cares. You, *mija,* hurt yourself. You don't know there's enough love in those *tetás*[2] to feed the whole world. Heh, Lady Bag?"

"Ain't enough love for me! Ain't enough love for me!" Old Flesh pounded her free hand on her chest, tapping into the vacant body. If a soul were there, she would've been crying by now.

"Yes there is, *mija.*"[3] Celia placed out a warm hand. "You serve good, and you will get what you want."

Old Flesh, confused by the sudden warmth and kindness, didn't know if she should reach for Fisted Twin Young Blood or Celia.

"No! You can't fool me!"

"Give me the young blood, Lorraine," Celia's commanding voice returned. She stepped closer into the stink shield and knocked over the mud-cloth bag with her foot. Surprisingly light, it fell over and opened. Smoke from the burning inferno of young-blood souls escaped from the opening.

"No!" Old Flesh screamed, unable to grab the bag from her sitting position. Blond Twin Young Blood, startled by the sound, began to cry. A melody of baby cries joined with it. The weeping souls escaped from the bag, permeating the stink shield, lingering above Old Flesh in search of their blood and bodies.

"*mati pa a wélé—*" Celia began to sing the command/spell, sweetly, luring the weeping souls out of the bag. Both babies cried along with the weeping souls, moving their heads about as if watching the souls fly around.

"You can't have 'em." Old Flesh needed the souls; they sustained her just as well.

1 "Poor dear."
2 "Breasts."
3 "Darling."

*"mati pa a wélé wélé—"* Celia continued, with a chorus of crying babies, adding harmony.

The weeping young-blood souls formed a halo of smoke above Old Flesh's head. Old Flesh was getting weaker. She needed young blood to continue. She could no longer hold Blond Twin Young Blood in her arm. She quickly grabbed the pastel-colored baby bag to place its squirming body into it.

Celia smiled at her mistake. The baby was no longer in her possession. *"wélé wélé kojo polo polo,"* she continued, commanding the bodiless young bloods.

The halo of weeping souls encircled Old Flesh. Baby cries became shrieks, piercing Old Flesh's ears. She placed both hands over her ears and began her grating version: *"mati pa a wélé,"* contrasting Celia's melody, impenetrable to the screams.

Old Flesh's command/spell could not reach. She felt her body become weaker as the strength of the previous young blood began to diminish. The halo descended. Screaming. *Old Flesh feed my young blood. Feed my young blood.* The smoke of weeping souls surrounded her body. Her blue-black skin began to sag, and fade. The smoke of weeping souls spiraled her breast, pulling life, just as they were supposed to.

"No!" Old Flesh screamed, feeling her death pulled from the life source.

The smoke of weeping souls grew larger, high-pitched sounds muting the encompassing noise. Old Flesh's body became a deflated prune, slowly decaying, releasing her life/death into the stolen souls. The halo grew larger. Old Flesh dissipated into the sea of screams, becoming one with the halo. No more Old Flesh. Old soul merged with young blood. The baby screams diminished into the noise. A slight echo of the whispered broken command/spell trailed off into the wind: *"wélé kojo pa a polo—kojo pa a polo."* (young blood feed my old flesh—feed my old flesh)

The twin babies stopped crying just as the halo of smoke disappeared.

"I put you out your misery, Lady Bag," Celia said. She looked at the three bags, then noticed the perplexed crowd around her. The frightened cops didn't know which way to point their guns. The stink shield dissipated with the spring breeze. She placed the dark-haired baby girl in her section of the stroller. She reached down into the pastel-colored baby bag and removed the blond baby boy and placed him next to his sister. She grabbed the body-filled bag and licked her lips.

There were enough bodies to feed her for a while.

She turned the stroller away from the stench and the other two bags and made her way through the crowd.

"'Scuse me, *por favor.*" She pushed the stroller over to Willoughby & Company and reached down into her pocket for her list.

# Octavia E. Butler

(1947–2006)

Renowned as the first Black female science fiction writer to receive national acclaim, Octavia Butler received numerous prestigious awards including the first MacArthur "Genius" fellowship granted to a science fiction writer. Butler recounts that her decision to become a science fiction writer was made at the age of nine after watching the 1954 B movie *Devil Girl from Mars* and deciding she could write a better story. As an only child, diagnosed with dyslexia, she found solace in books and the playground of her imagination. She is the author of 12 novels, including *Kindred*, considered a classic and widely taught in high schools and colleges. In *Kindred*, a feminist narrative, Butler fuses the neo-slave narrative genre and the science fiction genre, a type of fusion that often characterizes her work. We see this same fusion in *Fledgling*, her last novel, in which she conceptualizes a sci-fi vampire narrative. The Ina are not predatory monstrous blood-sucking creatures; rather they are a separate species who have a symbiotic relationship with humans. In much of her work, Butler employs biological hybridity as a vehicle to examine constructions of race. In this coming-of-age tale, Shori, an amnesiac 53-year-old member of the Ina species, who appears to be a 10-year-old girl, embarks on a journey of survival in this interdependent community. Considered the godmother of Afrofuturism, Butler is the forerunner of an ongoing literary tradition, which also includes such writers as Nalo Hopkinson and Tananarive Due. Indeed, her influence is far reaching; the socio-political themes in her work are an inspiration for social justice activism, evidenced by the 2015 publication of *Octavia's Brood: Science Fiction Stories from Social Justice Movements*.

# from *Fledgling*

(2005)

[*The excerpts we have chosen reveal the vampire mythology that Butler has created and vividly display her interrogation of racism. The first excerpt details Shori's meeting with her father when she learns that she is the product of a genetic experiment to incorporate DNA from an African American woman into the Ina genome.*]

## FROM "CHAPTER SEVEN"

[...] "I woke up weeks ago in a cave not far from here. I have no memory of anything that happened before then. And I don't know you."

He reached out to me, but I stepped back out of his reach.

"I don't know you," I repeated.

Off to one side, I saw Wright[1] come to attention. He didn't point the rifle at the stranger, he pointed it downward. He held it across his body in both hands, his right forefinger near the trigger, so that aiming it at the man would only be a matter of moving it slightly.

The man dropped his hand to his side. He glanced at Wright, then seemed to dismiss him. "My name is Iosif Petrescu," he said. "I'm your father."

I stood staring at him, feeling nothing for him. I didn't know him. And yet he might be telling the truth. How could I know? Would he lie about such a thing? Why?

"And I'm... Shori?"

"The name your human mother gave you is Shori. Your surname is Matthews. Your Ina mothers were distant relatives of mine named Mateescu, but in the 1950s, when there was a great deal of suspicion about foreign-sounding names, they decided to Anglicize the name to Matthews."

"My mothers ...?"

He looked around at the rubble. "Listen," he said. "We don't have to talk here in the midst of all this. Come to my home."

"I lived... here?"

"You did, yes. You were born here. Doesn't this setting stir any memories?"

"No memories. Only a feeling that I'm somehow connected to this place. I

1 Wright is the human who found Shori after the attack on her mothers' compound. At this point in the novel, neither of them know what has happened. Shori has amnesia and does not even know her own name. Although Shori does not yet know who or what she is, she and Wright have initiated a symbiotic relationship characteristic of the Ina and their human companions.

came here when I was able to leave the cave where I woke up, but I didn't know why. It was as though my feet just brought me here."

"Home," he said. "For you, this was home."

I nodded. "But you don't live here?"

He looked surprised. "No. We don't live males and females together as humans do."

I swallowed, then asked the question I had to ask: "What are we?"

"Vampires, of course—not that we call ourselves by that name." He smiled, showing his very human-looking teeth, except for the canines, which looked a little longer and sharper than the other people's, as my own did. If his teeth were like mine, they were all sharper than other people's. They had to be. He said, "We have very little in common with the vampire creatures Bram Stoker described in *Dracula*, but we are long-lived blood drinkers." He looked at Wright. "You knew what she was, didn't you?"

Wright nodded. "I knew she needed blood to live."

Iosif sighed, then spoke wearily as though he were saying something he had to say too many times before. "We live alongside, yet apart from, human beings, except for those humans who become our symbionts. We have much longer lives than humans. Most of us must sleep during the day and, yes, we need blood to live. Human blood is most satisfying to us, and fortunately, we don't have to injure the humans we take it from. But we are born as we are. We can't magically convert humans into our kind. We do keep those who join with us healthier, stronger, and harder to kill than they would be without us. In that way, we lengthen their lives by several decades."

That got Wright's attention. "How long?" he asked.

"How long will you live?"

"Yes."

Iosif took a deep breath, then said, "Barring accident or homicide, chances are you'll live to be between 170 and 200 years old."

"Two hundred... I will? Healthy years?"

"Yes. Your immune system will be greatly strengthened by Shori's venom, and it will be less likely to turn on you and give you one of humanity's many autoimmune diseases. And her venom will help keep your heart and circulatory system healthy. Your health is important to her."

"Sounds too good to be true."

"It is mutualistic symbiosis."

[...]

"Who did this?" I asked, gesturing at the ruin. "Who set the fire? Did anyone else survive?"

"I wasn't here," Iosif said. "I don't know who did it. And I haven't found... any other survivors. I've arranged for the other people who live in this area to keep their eyes open."

That got my attention. "You were careless. Raleigh Curtis wasn't just keeping his eyes open. He was going to shoot Wright. He did shoot me."

"Accident. He didn't know you were one of us. If he'd seen you clearly, he wouldn't have fired."

"Why would he want to shoot Wright?"

"He didn't know Wright was with you."

"Iosif, why shoot anyone over this rubble? Only the people who did this should be punished."

He stared at me. "Someone burned your mothers and your sisters as well as all of the human members of your family to death here. They shot the ones who tried to get out, shot them and threw most of them back into the fire. How you escaped, I have no idea, but we found the others, burned, broken... My people and I found them. We were coming for a visit, and we actually arrived before the firemen, which meant we were able to get control of them and see to it that they recalled this place as abandoned. When the fire was out, we cleaned up and covered up because we didn't want the remains examined by the coroner. We searched the area for several nights, hunting for survivors and questioning the local humans, finding out what they knew and seeing to it that they only remembered things that wouldn't expose or damage us. In fact, the neighbors didn't know anything. So we didn't catch the killers. We thought, though, that some of them might come back to enjoy remembering what they'd done. Criminals have done that in the past."

"To enjoy the memory of killing... How many people?" I demanded.

"Seventy-eight. Everyone except you."

[...]

"I'm sorry," I repeated, my voice not much more than a whisper.

He stared at me, first with anger and grief, then, it seemed, only with sorrow. "You are, aren't you? I'm glad of that. You've forgotten who and what you are, but you still have at least some of the morality you were taught."

After a while, Wright asked, "Why did you think she had a better chance of surviving?"

"Her dark skin," Iosif said. "The sun wouldn't disable her at once. She's a faster runner than most of us, in spite of her small size. And she would have come awake faster when everything started. She's a light sleeper, compared to most of us, and she doesn't absolutely have to sleep during the day."

"She said she thought she was an experiment of some kind," Wright said.

"Yes. Some of us have tried for centuries to find ways to be less vulnerable during the day. Shori is our latest and most successful effort in that direction. She's also, through genetic engineering, part human. We were experimenting with genetic engineering well before humanity learned to do it—before they even learned that it was possible."

"We, who?" I asked.

"Our kind. We are Ina. We are probably responsible for much of the world's vampire mythology, but among ourselves, we are Ina."

The name meant no more to me than his face did. It was so hard to know nothing—absolutely nothing all the time. "I hate this," I said. "You tell me things, and I still don't feel as though I know them. They aren't real to me. What are we? Why are we different from human beings? Are we just another race?"

"No. We're not another race, we're another species. We can't interbreed with them. We've never been able to do that. Sex, but no children."

"Are we related to them? Where do we come from?"

"I think we must be related to them," he said. "We're too genetically similar to them for any other explanation to be likely. Not all of us believe that, though. We have our own traditions—our own folklore, our own religions. You can read my books if you want to."

I nodded. "I'll read them. I wonder if they'll mean anything to me."

"You've probably suffered a severe head injury," Iosif said. "I've heard of this happening to us before. Our tissue regenerates, even our brain tissue. But memories ... well, sometimes they return."

"And sometimes they don't."

"Yes."

"I know I had a head wound—more than one. The bones of my skull were broken, but they healed. How can we survive such things?"

He smiled. "There's a recently developed belief among some of our younger people that the Ina landed here from another world thousands of years ago. I think it's nonsense, but who knows. I suppose that idea's no worse than one of our oldest legends. It says we were placed here by a great mother goddess who created us and gave us Earth to live on until we became wise enough to come home to live in paradise with her. Actually, I think we evolved right here on Earth alongside humanity as a cousin species like the chimpanzee. Perhaps we're the more gifted cousin."

I didn't know what to think—or say—about any of that. "All right," I said.
[...]

[*After her father and brothers are killed by the same mysterious group who targeted her maternal relatives, Shori and her new symbionts make their way to distant Ina connections, the Gordons, and begin their quest to solve the mystery and seek justice.*]

## FROM "CHAPTER FOURTEEN"

Wright thought for a moment, frowning a little. Then he said, "Chances are, this is all happening for one of three reasons. It's happening because some human group has spotted your kind and decided you're all dangerous, evil vampires. Or it's happening because some Ina group or Ina individual is jealous of the success Shori's family had with blending human and Ina DNA and having children who can stay awake through the day and not burn so easily in the sun. Or it's happening because Shori is black, and racists—probably Ina racists—don't like the idea that a good part of the answer to your daytime problems is melanin. Those are the most obvious possibilities. I wondered at first whether it could be someone or some family who just hated Shori's family—an old fashioned Hatfields and McCoys family feud—but Iosif and his sons would have known about anyone who hated them that much."

Philip Gordon, younger than Daniel, older than William, said, "You're assuming that if Ina did it, they used humans as their daytime weapons."

"I am assuming that," Wright said.

"We don't do that!" Preston said, his mouth turned down with disgust.

"I'm glad to hear it," Wright told him. "Of course I didn't think that anyone Iosif would introduce to his female family would do that. But there are other Ina. And your species seems to be as much made up of individuals as mine is. Some people are ethical, some aren't."

I watched the Gordons as he spoke. The younger ones listened, indifferent, but the older ones didn't much like what he was saying. It seemed to make them uncomfortable, embarrassed. I wondered why. At least no one tried to shut Wright up. That was important. I wouldn't have wanted to stay in a community that was contemptuous of my symbionts.

I also liked the fact that Wright wasn't afraid to say what he thought.

The Gordons talked among themselves about the possibilities Wright had offered, and they didn't seem to like any of them, but I suspected that their objections came more from wounded pride than from logic. Ina didn't use humans as daytime weapons against other Ina. They hadn't done anything like that for centuries.

And Ina were careful, both Preston and Hayden insisted. No Ina would leave evidence of vampiric behavior for humans to find. And according to Daniel, Ina families all over the world were happy about my family's success with genetic engineering. They hoped to use the same methods to enable their own future generations to function during the day.

And the Ina weren't racists, Wells insisted. Human racism meant nothing to the Ina because human races meant nothing to them. They looked for congenial human symbionts wherever they happened to be, without regard for anything but personal appeal.

And of course, there was no feud. According to Preston, nothing of that kind had happened for more than a thousand years. Nothing of the kind could happen without a great many people knowing about it. Iosif certainly would have known, and he and his mates would have been on guard.

[...]

[*After the Gordons' compound is attacked, Shori and the symbionts capture some of the humans being used as weapons. It is revealed that an Ina family, the Silks, are indeed responsible and that their principle motive is racism. The next excerpt comes from the Council of Judgement, which is initiated to prosecute the Silks for the murder of Shori's families and their symbionts.*]

## FROM "CHAPTER TWENTY-TWO"

Preston introduced them all, then introduced me and welcomed me. Finally, he asked me to stand and tell my story.

I stood, holding my microphone the way Milo[1] had. I began my story with my first memory of awakening in the cave, confused, in pain, without my memory, and racked with intense hunger. I told them about [...] the ruin that I had not recognized as my home, about Wright and my father and the destruction of my father's community—the whole story up to and including the raid on the Gordons and the capturing and questioning of Victor and his two friends.[2] The telling took more than an hour.

At last, I finished and sat down. There were several seconds of absolute silence. Then Milo Silk stood up. "Does this child have an advocate?" he demanded. He spoke the word "child" as though he wanted to say a much nastier word but restrained himself.

Before I could say that I didn't yet have an advocate, Vladimir Leontyev spoke up.

"I am one of the fathers of Shori Matthew's mothers," he said. "I believe I'm her nearest living relative on the Council. My brothers and I may be her nearest living relatives period. If Shori wishes it, I will be her advocate."

I leaned forward so that I could see him and said, "I must ask questions because of my memory loss. I mean no offense, Vladimir, but if you become my advocate, will it be a problem that you and I don't really know each other anymore?"

"It won't be a problem," he said. "Family is what matters here. You are of great importance to me because you are one of my descendants."

[...]

Preston Gordon said "Milo, in our negotiations with your family, one of your sons mentioned that a member of the Dahlman family might be persuaded to be your advocate."

"When have you known me to need someone to speak for me?" he demanded.

Preston looked at him, looked down at his own spidery hands resting on the table, then faced Milo again. "Let me advise you, just this once. Your family

1 Milo Silk, the 541-year-old patriarch of the Silk clan.

2 The humans who had been mesmerized to attack the Gordon community.

needs more protection than you can give it. Don't let your pride destroy your family."

Milo looked away from him, kept quiet for several seconds. After a while, he said, "Katharine Dahlman is the oldest daughter of my sisters," Milo said. "I ask that she be my advocate."

Katharine Dahlman managed, by sitting very straight, to look not only important, but a little taller. She lowered her head in a slow nod. "Of course," she said in a deep, quiet contralto—a female version of Milo's voice. It was the voice of a larger woman, somehow. "Will you question the child, Milo, or shall I?"

Milo looked down at the table, and I remembered that he had been writing while I spoke. Perhaps he had not trusted the two video cameras that were being used to record the session. Perhaps he had made notes of the questions he wanted to ask me. Or perhaps he had his own memory problems. I faced him across the arc, ready to be questioned, but he turned his body and tried to face Preston.

"I have my doubts, Preston, whether this child should even be here," he said. "She has suffered terrible losses, and she admits that she hasn't recovered from her injuries."

I resisted an impulse to say that I had recovered, or had recovered as much as I was likely to. Instead, I waited to see what Preston would say. He looked at me, then at Vladimir.

Vladimir said, "Shori, have you recovered from your injuries?"

"I am recovered," I said. "My memory may or may not return. I'm beginning to relearn what I've lost, and I remember clearly all that has happened to me since I awoke in the cave." I looked across at Milo and decided that he would speak directly to me in a minute or two. He didn't want to, but he would.

"Has the child been examined by a physician?" Milo asked. "I understand there is a human physician among the symbionts here. If not, one of my family's symbionts is a physician."

That was too much. I had been at Punta Nublada[1] long enough to recognize that Milo was being openly insulting. He was saying that my body was not Ina enough to heal itself, that the human part of me had somehow crippled me.

"Milo!" I said, not loudly, but sharply. He looked at me before he could stop himself and then looked away smoothly, as though he had only glanced at me by accident. I leaned forward, facing him across the arc. "I am Ina, Milo."

He stared a time, then turned again to Preston. "For the child's own sake, I request that she be examined by a physician."

I said, "What are those notes you're making there, Milo? No one else is taking notes. Are you having difficulties with your memory, too?"

He glared at me. Katharine Dahlman glared at me.

"I am Ina, Milo, and if the doctor must examine me, then for your own sake, I request that she also examine you."

---

1 The name of the Gordons' community.

"You're not Ina!" he shouted. He slammed his palm down on the table, making a sound like a gunshot. "You're not! And you have no more business at the Council than would a clever dog!"

[…]

[*The Council of Judgement proceeds. Milo's son Russell is the first to take the stand.*]

FROM "CHAPTER TWENTY-THREE"

Russell Silk had no story to tell. He denied all involvement in the death of my families and the attacks on the Arlington house and on the Gordons. He denied that his family was involved in any of it. He suggested that I was confused or mistaken or that the humans who had been used as weapons had been given false information intended to incriminate the Silk family—which happened to be the only male Ina family in Los Angeles County.[1] Who would create such a fiction? He did not know. He and his family were victims…just as I was.

That was a sickening enough lie to make me wonder if I would have been able to keep my temper had I not lost my memory. If I could remember my mothers, my sisters, and my symbionts, if I could recall my father and my brothers as anything more than kindly strangers, I might not have been able to bear it. I thought Russell might have said it hoping to make me angry, hoping to pay me back for what I said to Milo.

Vladimir Leotyev spoke up. "Russell, are you saying that you know as a matter of fact that neither your father, your brothers, your sons, or their sons were involved in collecting a group of human males, making them your tools, and then sending them to kill the Petrescu, Matthews, and Gordon families?"

Russell looked offended. "I don't believe any member of my family would do such a thing," he said.

Vladimir shook his head. "That isn't what I asked. Do you know for a fact that no member of your family did this?"

"I haven't investigated my family," he said. "I'm not a human police detective."

"So you don't know for certain whether or not members of your family did this?"

"I don't believe they did!" He paused and looked away from Vladimir. "But I don't know with absolute certainty."

I didn't believe him. […] By his silence or by his active participation, he had helped to murder my families.

[…]

No speeches were permitted, no arguments except through questions, no interrupting each other. Preston Gordon could and did cut us off, though,

1 All the captured humans were from Los Angeles.

whenever he heard us stray from these guidelines. He did this with a fairness that infuriated both Russell and me, and he paid no attention when we glared at him.

The Council members could ask us questions and question our answers. The purpose of accused and accuser questioning one another was to give the Council the opportunity to make use of their formidable senses. They watched, listened, and breathed the air as we spoke. Together, they had thousands of years of experience reading body language.

[...]

[*On a break between sessions, one of Shori's new symbionts, an older woman named Theodora Harden, is murdered. The evidence reveals Katharine Dahlman's guilt, forcing a confrontation with the Silks' advocate.*]

## FROM "CHAPTER TWENTY-SIX"

I looked along the arc at the other Council members. "I request that she be removed from this Council."

"You request!" Katharine seemed to choke on the words. "I request that you be removed from this room! You're a child, clearly too young to know how to behave. And I challenge your right to represent the interests of families who are unfortunately dead. You are their descendent, but because of their error, because of their great error, you are not Ina! No one can be certain of the truth of anything you say because you are neither Ina nor human. Your scent, your reactions, your facial expressions, your body language—none of it is right. [...] We are Ina. You are nothing!"

There was a swell of voices from the audience—much denial, but some agreement. All the visiting and local Ina were present in the audience or on the Council. The rest of the seats were filled by symbionts who also had opinions about me. Not surprisingly, the symbionts who spoke were on my side. It was the Ina who were divided.

Preston stood up. "Listen to me!" he roared in a voice Milo Silk would have been proud of, and the room went utterly silent. After a few seconds, he repeated more quietly, "Listen to me. Shori Matthews is as Ina as the rest of us. In addition, she carries the potentially life-saving human DNA that has darkened her skin and given her something we've sought for generations: the ability to walk in sunlight, to stay awake and alert during the day." He paused, then raised his voice again. "Her mothers, her sisters, her father, and her brothers were Ina, and they have been murdered along with all but two of their symbionts. All of Shori's own first symbionts have been murdered. This Council has met to determine who's responsible for those murders, and now it must also consider the murder of Theodora Harden, one of Shori's new symbionts. We are here to discover the guilt or innocence of those accused of these murders and, if they are found guilty, to decide what is to be done with the murderers. Based on what we've heard so far, I don't believe Katharine Dahlman should be a member of this Council."

Katharine Dahlman sat very straight and stared angrily at Preston. "You want your sons to mate with this person. You want them to get black, human children from her. Here in the United States, even most humans will look down on them. When I came to this country, such people were kept as property, as slaves. You are biased in Shori's favor and not a voting member of this Council. I won't give up my place because you say so."

Preston stared at her, expressionless, still. "Council members, count yourselves for or against Katharine remaining one of you."

[...]

[*One by one, the Council votes. The results are close, but ultimately, against Katharine.*]

Katharine seemed surprised that the vote went against her. She had truly expected to benefit from what she had done. She had gotten her symbiont out of my reach so that I couldn't track him and kill him before she awoke. In fact, I wouldn't have killed him. His life did not interest me. Hers did. But she didn't know me, and she wasn't willing to take chances... She had imagined that her fellow Council members—all Ina, all around her age—would accept what she had done, even if they didn't like it. She believed I would either lose control and disgrace myself before the Council—possibly by attacking her—or if I didn't, she could use my apparent lack of feeling to point out how un-Ina I was. She won either way. What did the life of my Theodora matter?

Katharine left the table, glaring at me as though I had somehow done her an injury. I hadn't. But I would. I surely would. [...]

## FROM "CHAPTER TWENTY-EIGHT"

There were no parties on the night of the third Council session. The hall was so full that there was not enough seating for everyone. People stood or brought chairs from the houses. No one seemed to want to sit on the concrete floor. Seats had been roped off for my symbionts in front, as had seats on the opposite side of the hall for the Silks and their symbionts.

The members of the Council seated themselves as usual, in the same order, and when they were all settled, Preston stood up. This was everyone's signal to be quiet and pay attention. Preston waited until silence had worked its way from the front to the back of the room. Then he said, "Russell Silk, do you have anything further to say or any more questions to ask of Shori Matthews or of anyone that you or she has asked to speak to this Council?"

This was Russell's last chance to speak, to defend his family, and to make me look bad. Of course, anyone he called, I could question, too.

Russell stood up. "I have no one else to call," he said, holding his microphone, looking out toward the audience. Then he turned and faced the Council. "I suppose in a sense, I call on all of you to remember that my family has maintained good and honorable friendships with many of you. Remember that the Silk family helped some of you immigrate to this country in times of war or political chaos in your former homes. Remember that in all the time you've known us, we have not lied to you or cheated you.

"What matters most to us, to every member of the Silk family, is the welfare of the Ina people. We Ina are vastly outnumbered by the human beings of this world. And how many of us have been butchered in their wars? They destroy one another by the millions, and it makes no difference to their numbers. They breed and breed and breed, while we live long and breed slowly. Their lives are brief and, without us, riddled with disease and violence. And yet, we need them. We take them into our families, and with our help, they are able to live longer, stay free of disease, and get along with one another. We could not live without them.

"But we are not them!

"We are not them!"

He shook with the intensity of his feeling. He had to take several breaths before he could continue. "We are not them," he whispered. "Nor should we try to be them. Ever. Not for any reason. Not even to gain the day; the cost is too great."

He stood for a second longer in silence, then sat down and put his microphone back on its stand. The room had gone completely silent.

Once he sat down, Preston broke the silence. "Shori, is there anyone you would like to question or anything you would like to say?"

"I have questions," I said, standing up with my microphone. I had thought of something as Russell spoke—something prompted by what he had said. [...] It seemed to me that Russell had just admitted that his family had killed my families. He wanted us to believe that he had done it for a good reason. I said to Preston, "I want to ask you a few questions, if that's all right."

Preston looked surprised. "All right. Russell questioned me so I do qualify as someone you can question now."

I nodded. "I ask this because of my limited knowledge of Ina law. Preston, is there a legal, nonlethal way of questioning someone's behavior? I mean, if I believed that you were doing something that could be harmful to other Ina, would I be able to bring it to the attention of a council of some kind or some other group?"

Preston did not smile, did not change expression at all, but I got the impression he was pleased with me. "There is," he said. "If you believed I were doing something to the detriment of the Ina, something that was not exactly against law, but that you seriously believed was harmful, you could ask for a Council of the Goddess."

Russell snatched up his microphone and protested. "Council of the... That hasn't been done for at least twenty-five hundred years."

"You are aware of it, then?" I asked him.

"It wouldn't have been taken seriously. No one's done it for two thousand—"

"Did you try?"

"Your families made no secret of the fact that they didn't even believe in the Goddess!"

From the hypothetical to the real. Careless of him. "Would that have mattered?" I asked. "Could my family have ignored a call to take part in a Council of the Goddess?"

Russell said nothing. Perhaps he had remembered where he was and exactly what was being argued.

"Preston, would it have mattered?"

"The rule of seven[1] would apply," Preston answered. "If the rule of seven is satisfied and the accused family refuses to attend, the Council would be carried on regardless of its absence. The family would be bound by any vote of the Council, as though it had been present. If the family were ordered to stop whatever they were doing, and they refused to stop, they would be punished."

I stared across at Russell. "Preston, has the Silk family ever tried to assemble a Council of the Goddess to discuss or warn against the genetic work of my eldermothers?"

"Not to my knowledge," Preston said. "Russell?"

Again, Russell said nothing. It didn't matter. Surely he had already said enough. I sat down and put my microphone back in its place.

"Does any Council member have questions?" Preston asked.

No one spoke.

"All right," he said. "Council members, I ask you now to count yourselves. Is the Silk family guilty of having made human beings their tools and sent those human tools to kill the Petrescu and Matthews families? Are the Silks also guilty of sending their tools to burn the Petrescu guest house where Shori Matthews and her symbionts were staying? Are the Silks guilty of sending their tools to attack the Gordon family here at Punta Nublada? And also, was Katharine Dahlman, the Silks' first advocate, guilty of sending one of her symbionts, Jack Roan, to kill one of Shori Matthews's symbionts, Theodora Harden?" He paused, then said, "Zoë Fotopoulos?"

1 This is an important part of Ina culture explained earlier in the novel. For trials or councils to be held, seven Ina families connected by a common ancestor within seven generations have to agree to send representatives. This is what set up the Council of Judgement currently taking place and would also be employed in the event of a Council of the Goddess being called.

I had decided that Zoë was the most beautiful Ina I had ever seen. Her age—over three hundred—didn't seem to matter. She was tall, lean, and blond like most Ina but was a striking, memorable woman. [...]

"Shori Matthews has told us the truth," Zoë said. "I have not once caught her in a lie. Either she has been very careful or she is exactly what she seems to be. My impression is that she is exactly what she appears to be—a child, deeply wronged by both the Silk family and Katharine Dahlman. Members of the Silk family, on the other hand, have lied again and again. And Katharine Dahlman has lied. It seems that all this killing was done because Shori's families were experimenting with ways of using human DNA to enable us to walk in daylight. And it seems that no legal methods of questioning or stopping the experiments were even attempted." She took a deep breath. "I stand with Shori against both the Silks and Katharine Dahlman."

"Joan Braithwaite?" Preston said.

"Shori told the truth, and Katharine and the Silks lied," Joan said. "That's all that matters. I must stand with Shori against both."

"Alexander Svoboda?"

"I stand with Shori against Katharine Dahlman," he said. "But I must stand with the Silks against Shori. Shori has told the truth, as far as she knows, as far as she is able to understand with her damaged memory, but I can't condemn the Silks as a family because of what one child, one seriously impaired child, believes."

And yet, every Silk who had spoken to the Council had lied about what he had done, about what he knew, or both. How could Katharine Dahlman be punished for killing one symbiont and the Silks let off for killing twelve Ina and nearly a hundred symbionts? But that was Alexander's less than courageous decision.

"Peter Marcu?" Preston said.

"I stand with Shori," Peter Marcu said. "I don't want to. My family has been friends with the Silks for four generations. There was even a time when we got along well with the Dahlmans. But Shori has been telling the truth all along, and the others have been lying. Whatever their reasons are for what they've done, they did do it, and for the sake of the rest of our people and all our symbionts, we cannot allow this to go unpunished."

"Ana Morariu?"

"I stand with the Silks and with Katharine Dahlman," Ana said. "Shori Matthews is much too impaired to be permitted to speak against other Ina. How can we destroy people's lives, even kill them on the word of a child whose mind has been all but destroyed and who, even if she were healthy, is barely Ina at all? It is a tragedy that the Petrescu and Matthews families are dead. We shouldn't deepen the tragedy by killing or disrupting other families."

She was the one who had said Katharine Dahlman might be telling the truth. Now she seemed to be saying that my families had simply been unlucky and had, for some unknown reason, died, and that it would be wrong to punish anyone for that. Nothing wrong, she seemed to think, with letting your friends get away with mass murder.

"Alice Rappaport?"

"I stand with Shori," Alice said. "Katharine and the Silks are liars, people who use murder but never think to use the law. They know better than anyone here that we can't let them go unpunished. And what about the rest of you? Do you want to return to a world of lawless family feuds and mass killing?"

"Harold Westfall?"

"I stand with Shori," Harold said. "To let this go would be to endanger us all in the long run. Both the Silks and Katharine must be punished for what we all know they've done."

He glanced at me unhappily. I got the impression he didn't want to be here. He didn't want to stand with me. I suspected he didn't even like me much. But he was doing his duty and trying to do it as honestly as he could. I respected that and was grateful for it.

"Kira Nicolau."

"I stand with Shori as far as Katharine is concerned," Kira said. "What Katharine did was completely wrong, and I have no doubt that she did it. I don't believe she even meant to convince us otherwise; it just didn't seem very important to her. But as to the other problem, I must stand with the Silks. I don't believe Shori's memories and accusations should be trusted. I'm not convinced that Shori understands the situation as well as she believes she does. She believes what she says, that's clear. In that sense, she is telling the truth. But like Alexander, I'm not willing to disrupt or destroy the Silk family on the word of someone as disabled as Shori Matthews clearly is."

Nothing about the lies the Silks had told. Nothing about my dead families. And yet, Kira herself was telling the truth as far as I could see. She really seemed to believe that I was so impaired that I didn't know what I was talking about. She had somehow convinced herself of that.

"Ion Andrei?"

There was a moment of silence. Finally, Ion said, "I stand with the Silks and with Katharine Dahlman. I don't want to. I believe the Silks may have murdered Shori's families. It's certainly possible. And Katharine may have sent her symbiont after Shori's symbiont. But, like Kira, I cannot in good conscience base such a judgement on the words of someone as disabled as Shori is."

It was painful to listen to them. I wanted to scream at them. How could they blind all their senses so selectively? And how could they see me as so impaired? Maybe they needed to see me that way. Maybe it helped them deal with their conscience.

"Walter Nagy?"

"I stand with Shori," Walter said. "And I would stand with her even if she were out of her mind because it is so painfully obvious that the Silks and Katharine Dahlman were lying almost every time they answered a question. They have committed murder and, in the case of the Silks, mass murder. If we excuse that in those we like, we open a door that we tried to lock tight centuries ago. Make no mistake. If we ignore these murders, we invite people to settle disputes themselves, and we risk exposure in the human world. We are, every one of us, vulnerable to the fires that consumed Shori's families."

There was a moment of silence. Finally, Preston said, "Elizabeth Akhmatova?"

"I stand with Shori," Elizabeth said. "For all the reasons Walter's just given, I stand with her. And I stand with her because I've watched her. She *is* impaired. I can't imagine what it would be like to lose the memory of nearly all of the years of one's life. Her memory was stolen from her. But her ability to reason wasn't stolen. The questions she's asked—questions that were answered again and again with lies and misdirection—were good, sensible questions. The questions she answered, she answered honestly. The murderers who killed her families and her symbiont, the thieves who stole her past from her—should these people be rewarded because they did such a savagely thorough job? No, of course not. Shori, on the other hand, should be rewarded for using her intellect to protect herself and to find the murderers."

## FROM "CHAPTER TWENTY-NINE"

And that was that.

There was a moment of silence, then Preston stood up. "The decision is made," he said.

"A majority of seven members of this eleven-member Council of Judgement have stood with Shori Matthews and against both Katharine Dahlman and the Silk family. Therefore, Katharine Dahlman and the Silk family must be punished for the wrongs they have done. But because the decision was not unanimous, their punishment must be other than death."

# VAMPIRES AND SEXUALITY

Henrich August Ossenfelder, "Der Vampir" (1748)

Johann Wolfgang von Goethe, "The Bride of Corinth" (1797)

Sheridan Le Fanu, *Carmilla* (1872)

Eric Stenbock, "The True Story of a Vampire" (1894)

Poppy Z. Brite/Billy Martin, from *Lost Souls* (1992)

One of the most potent images in Tod Browning's 1931 film *Dracula* is the recurring close-up of Bela Lugosi's eyes (see Illustrations, p. 520). Dracula's gaze freezes women. It woos them. It terrifies them. From the humble flower seller to the seductive Lucy with her platinum bob and plunging neckline, no one seems immune to his gaze. Even demure and innocent Mina succumbs to the intensity of Dracula's eyes, but in this film, as in so many vampire texts, sex equals death. Dracula leans over Lucy's bed and the scene abruptly shifts to her autopsy. To today's audience, Bela Lugosi's stare is almost comical, but at the time, he was an object of desire for the viewer, as well as the characters on screen. This film, like so many other vampire narratives, appears to draw direct links between sexuality, desire, and death.

When most readers think about vampires and sexuality, desire is at the forefront of their minds. Today's popular presses churn out paranormal romances depicting erotic vampire–human relationships. For older generations of readers, vampire literature (and film) became one of the first places where LGBTQ+ youth saw their sexualities depicted. But when all of these texts are considered on a deeper level, the sexual aspects of vampire literature take on a far darker and less liberating aspect. While Nick Groom suggests that "[i]t is all too easy to over-sexualize"[1] these stories, there is no denying that both sexual desire and sexual violence remain quintessential aspects of vampire literature. In this chapter, we explore the theme of sexuality from a variety of perspectives including desire, violence, and consent. In fact, in these texts such topics are often in tension with each other. In these tales, sexuality may stand in for any number of anxieties, but it is hard to escape the fact that these tales are generally read as just what they seem—sexual.

Vampire literature again and again links the vampire's attack with sexual violence. As we saw in "Vampires and Power," the vampire's attack can easily be read as analogous to rape. Since Polidori first published in 1819, vampires have often been depicted as "sexually voracious"[2] and, as Nina Auerbach observes, Dracula himself is "fundamentally a rapist."[3] This trope is certainly evident in texts earlier in this anthology, like Rymer and Prest's *Varney the Vampire*, but the texts in this chapter introduce additional complexity to the depiction of desire in the tales. They implicate the reader by eroticizing the victim and inviting us to voyeuristically relish the disturbingly violent and sexual depiction of the vampire's attack. The two poems with which we begin this chapter, Ossenfelder's "Der Vampir" (1748) and Goethe's "The Bride of Corinth" (1797), explicitly depict the victims' desire as part of the vampires' attack.

In contrast to the violence of the attacks in Polidori, Rymer and Prest, and Stoker, the vampires in this chapter also disturb us with their very desirability (see Illustrations: Munch, *Love and Pain/The Vampire*, p. 513; Burne-Jones, *The Vampire*, p. 516; and Ernst *The Vampire's Kiss*, p. 517). Their allure and the helplessness of their victims is part of the horror elicited by the tales. Physically, these vampires have little of the monster about them. Many appear fragile and vulnerable before revealing their fangs. There are obvious Freudian implications of a vampire's attack regardless of the genders or sexualities involved. Whatever the monster's apparent gender, the very phallic shape of the vampire's fang lends itself to a psychoanalytic reading.

In many ways, Sheridan Le Fanu's 1872 novella *Carmilla* represents a shift in how we link the terms sexuality and vampire (see Illustrations, p. 510). One of the major inspirations for *Dracula*, Le Fanu's novella goes further into challenging the restrictions of Victorian sexuality than Stoker dared. Carmilla's end is as brutal and blood drenched as that of Stoker's Lucy: "intense, sensually imagined, ferocious in its detail."[4] The brutal punishments meted out to these female vampires show the fear of the sexually aggressive female who would penetrate rather than be passively receptive. The sexuality for which Carmilla

1 Groom, *The Vampire* 161.
2 Senf, *The Vampire* 161.
3 Auerbach, *Our Vampires* 114.
4 Craft, "'Kiss me with Those Red Lips:' Gender and Inversion in Bram Stoker's *Dracula*" 122.

is punished is, however, quite different from Stoker's *femme fatales*. In "Tracking the Vampire," Sue-Ellen Case uses vampiric seduction as a metaphor for lesbian desire,[1] but the implications of identifying LGBTQ+ representation with the monstrous are complex and potentially problematic today. Narratives like *Carmilla* appear rife with a desire that mingles feeding with feeling. There are clear emotional and sexual components of these tales that give them a unique brand of horror.

The move from vampire as rapist to vampire as lover complicates the depiction of sexuality in vampire literature. Nineteenth-century male vampires like Lord Ruthven are clearly more rapist than seducer, but by the twentieth century, the seductive aspect of vampire tales becomes infused with romance. While vampires pervaded popular culture in the early twentieth century, by mid-century censorship meant that vampire texts with strong sexual themes became more difficult to publish. Vampires haunted movie theaters, not the pages of literature. Their triumphant return to literature in the later decades of the twentieth century introduced a new genre: vampire romance. Vampires began to be depicted not as the brutal rapists of the Romantic era or the vile seducers of the first half of the twentieth century, but as desirable romantic figures. This genre remains common today, yet despite the popularity of these romances, the issue of power inequality can raise questions. What does consent mean with a vampire?

The fantasy vampire lover of so many late twentieth- and early twenty-first-century texts is still a creature in possession of far superior experience, wisdom, and power than their victims. In virtually all vampire literature, vampires are significantly older than their victims, with supernatural strength and the ability to influence thoughts and emotions. A deeper consideration of even the most romantic of vampire literature reveals the problem of consent. From Anne Rice's beguiling Lestat to Stephanie Meyer's tortured Edward, vampires may pay lip service to consent, but they give their partners little genuine opportunity to comprehend what is being offered. Today's popular and highly sexual vampire romances are read with pleasure by millions who rarely stop to consider the implications of the texts' strange combination of desire, manipulation, and violence. As Groom observes, "vampires have tended to be lustful, depraved and super-sexy: models of transgression, avatars of forbidden fantasies and fallen angels of the death drive."[2] Even in literature that depicts a seductive fantasy relationship, the genre's history of violence and hunger lingers, raising disturbing questions.

The darker side to the sexuality of vampire stories became even more ominous in the last decades of the twentieth century in the midst of the AIDS

1 Case, "Tracking the Vampire" 2.
2 Groom, *The Vampire* 184.

epidemic. Many critics have read novels like Stoker's *Dracula* through the lens of venereal disease, but there is a clear division in narratives between a vampire as vector of infection and a vampire as fatal plague. Nonetheless, in both, we see a reflection of the epidemics of our time. Later Victorian writers such as Eric Stenbock follow Le Fanu's pattern of vampires pursuing same-sex victims, but it wasn't until later twentieth-century writers such as Anne Rice and Poppy Z. Brite[1] that the shift to gay male desire came to dominate vampire narratives. At the same time, the cultural association of gay men with the deathly sexuality of vampires becomes particularly problematic: as Auerbach observes, "Once the etiology of AIDS became clear, blood could no longer be the life."[2] The history of vampire literature may offer some unprecedented portrayals of same-sex desire, but it is a desire that infects and kills. Rarely is it depicted as an equal alternative to the heteronormative human relationships in the story.

Power, rape, seduction, compulsion, disease, and desire—all stain vampire narratives as indelibly as blood. Desirable as they may be, the fact remains that for the vampire, every victim is ultimately food: "The sexual nature of the vampire's desire—the embrace, the kiss to the neck, the longing glances—are all as symptomatic of sexual desire as they are of bloodlust."[3] With so much longing and desire lurking in these texts, it is important to question the deeper message being sent to the reader by the depiction of sexuality. Bela Lugosi's intense stare that rendered female victims helpless in his arms seems simplistic and naïve compared to the complex history of sexuality in vampire literature.

1 While Martin has transitioned, he has requested that his work continue to be published under the name of Poppy Z. Brite.

2 Auerbach, *Our Vampires* 175.

3 Gomez, "Recasting the Mythology" 85.

# Henrich August Ossenfelder

(1725–1801)

The German poet Henrich Ossenfelder penned the first known poem about vampires, "Der Vampir," which was published in the scientific journal *Der Naturforsher* (1748). The publication of a poem about vampires in a scientific journal is curious, yet indicative of the cultural climate of the time. Discussions about vampires were topical during the mid-eighteenth century; vampire sightings were recorded throughout Europe and vampires were the subject of serious scientific research. In Ossenfelder's erotically charged poem, the vampire is a scorned lover, seeking revenge through the seduction of an innocent maiden. This theme, adopted by Bram Stoker in *Dracula*, becomes archetypal in vampire lore.

## "Der Vampir"[1]

(1748)

My dear young maiden believeth
Unbending, fast and firm
In all the furnished teachings
Of her ever pious mother;
As people along the Tisza
Believe staunchly and heyduck[2]-like
In vampires that bring death.
Just wait now, dear Christiane,
You do not wish to love me;
On you I take revenge.

1 This translation is taken from Heidi Crawford's "The Cultural-Historical Origins of the Literary Vampire in Germany" and is based on that of J. Gordon Melton, with corrections by Crawford.

2 A Hungarian word meaning lightly armed foot soldier. In Germany, it is used for a servant—Ossenfelder associates her superstition with the working class.

And in Tockay[1] today
Will drink you into a vampire.
And when softly you are sleeping
From your rosy cheeks
Will I the color suck.
Then will you be startled
When I kiss you thus
And as a vampire kiss:
When you then start to tremble
And weakly, like one dying,
Sink down into my arms
Then to you I pose my question,
Are not my teachings better
Than those of your good mother?

1 Hungarian wine popular in eighteenth-century Germany.

# Johann Wolfgang von Goethe

(1749–1832)

In addition to a varied career in science, law, humanities, and art, German writer Johann Wolfgang von Goethe had a tremendous literary output. He penned the most popular eighteenth-century novel, *The Sorrows of Young Werther* (1774), and the epic drama *Faust* (1832). His writing career spanned the genres of poetry, drama, and fiction. During his lifetime, he was one of Germany's most famous celebrities. In 1782, he was granted permission to add the "von" to his name—a sign of nobility. In 1786, he traveled to Italy and returned 18 months later, a changed man. Goethe's 1797 ballad "The Bride of Corinth" was written after this life-altering trip. The poem's depiction of the erotic reflects his growing hostility to the prudishness of conventional Christian morality as taught by the church of his day. Opposed to the church, he refused to have a formal wedding and instead had a common-law marriage with a lower-middle-class woman, Christiane Vulpius. Although Vulpius bore him a son, Goethe did not legally marry her until 1806 when Napoleon's army attacked the city in which they were living. Goethe continued writing throughout his life—he was still editing the second part of *Faust* in the weeks before his death.

## "The Bride of Corinth"[1]

(1797)

I.

There once descended a youth from Athens
Unto a sleepy Corinthian town;
Eager to meet his new family, friends
And bride in waiting of great renown.

1 Translated by David B. Gosselin.

They had recently
Both been dearly
Paired, soon by the heavens to be bound.

II.

But will this warm and graceful welcome last
If one so dearly has to pay?
He is still among a heathen race classed,
She already walks the Christian way.
With a new creed born,
With Love and truth torn,
The dark night quickly consumes each day.

III.

The house already silently sleeps,
Father, daughter, only mother wakes;
Wishing him goodnight she quickly retreats—
Alone in his room now sleep awaits:
Food and wine are laid,
Lavishly displayed,
But he retires to his silken drapes.

IV.

He cared neither for hunger nor for thirst,
He had no thought of sense's pleasures;
All was forgotten by his weary body—
Into bed he fell still sporting trousers;
Almost slumbering,
A guest comes creeping
By his door—enters his sleeping quarters.

V.

By his shimmering night lamp, he beholds
A maiden wearing her veil and robe,
Appearing with angel's graces and silken folds,
And sporting a band of black and gold;
But as she sees him,
By a light so dim
She unveils a pallid hand so cold.

VI.

"Am I so forgotten in this household,
That no word of guests was sent to me?
Oh! How they in this prison chamber hold
Me, and in this deep shame keep me.
These dreams must now cease,
I must leave in peace,
And fade before anyone can see."

VII.

"Wait! Beautiful maiden" the young boy pleads,
Rising from his bed so quickly:
"Let us enjoy the gifts of Bacchus[1] and Ceres[2]
And welcome blushing Cupid[3] warmly.
Why now look so pale
Why not sweetly hail
These gifts, which Gods offer graciously."

VIII.

"Stay away oh young soul! stay far away,
Joy's grape no longer greets my pallet,
I know no bliss, night consumes each day;
For my mother with her devout fears
Has taken her oath
And pledged my troth
To heaven, along with all my youthful years."

IX.

"The ancient throng of Gods have taken flight,
Our home has been emptied of their lore.
For unseen there lies in the heavens' light
A son who once mercifully bore
Man's every sin
To save our kin—
So we pledge our woe forevermore."

---

1 Bacchus: Ancient Roman god of wine.
2 Ceres: Ancient Roman goddess of agriculture.
3 Cupid: Ancient Roman god of love.

X.

He listens, weighing every word she speaks,
Not one of them escaping his mind:
"I cannot fathom in such a quiet place
Such a dream I could have never feigned.
Oh but be mine now!
For our father's vow
Has been by the heavens so ordained."

XI.

"Though my hand you cannot have faithful soul
My fair sister will be your delight;
Yet when I am weeping in my dark cell
Think on me as you hold her at night.
I think but of you,
I dream but of you
Soon to hide my face where there is no light."

XII.

"No wait! By the sacred flame I already swore
That you would be kept on Hymen's[1] throne;
But let us not leave all forsaken,
Come with me to my father's home.
What should we afear
When there is so much cheer
And a wonderful feast before us shown!"

XIII.

Tokens of their faith were swiftly exchanged:
She hands him a glittering chain of gold,
And he offers her an exquisite chalice
Of shining silver and beauty untold:
"This I cannot take,
But please for my sake,
Give me just one lock of your dark hair."

1 Hymen: Ancient Greek god of marriage.

XIV.

The unhallowed midnight hour knell rang—
Suddenly the maiden came alive:
With a parching thirst, she quickly drank
The dark and purple tinctured wine,
But of the wheat bread
Upon which he fed,
She refused to take the slightest bite.

XV.

She handed her same cup to the youth
And he, like she, quickly drank each drop.
He implored the maid for her true ruth.
Alas! Love had been lit in his heart.
But as he persists,
She only resists
Until, weeping he sinks into bed.

XVI.

The maiden pitifully leans over him
"Oh! How it pains me to see you so,
But were you to feel these limbs
You would shudder, knowing what they conceal.
A snow-white maiden,
Whose blood is frozen—
Such is the love that these limbs reveal."

XVII.

The ardent youth wraps his arms around her
With the strength young love inspires:
"Were you risen directly from your grave
My love would set your every limb on fire."
Kissing and caressing,
Love overflowing,
"Don't you feel it, the burning desire?"

XVIII.

Holding each other closely, neither contain
Their tears falling with the sweetest ardor,
His hot breath surges through her frame,
Each thinks of nothing but the other.
So a fiery flood
Warms her frozen blood
But alas! No heart beats in her breast.

XIX.

Meanwhile the devout mother makes her way
Through the halls. As she tends to her chores,
She hears a murmur and wonders what might lay
On the other side of one of those doors:
Wailing and crying,
Sobbing and sighing,
Who can allay Love's frenzied pangs?

XX.

She halts in front of the door, listening,
Hoping to convince herself that what she heard
Was nothing real—then she hears lamenting
Entreaties and passionate parting words:
"Quick! The cock now crows,
But come tomorrow,
Won't you return?" and then kiss on kiss.

XXI.

Without hesitation, she quickly opens
The door, anger swelling across her face:
"Have such shameless scandals and unbridled sins
Made their home in my own hearth?" she screams.
Looking through the door,
A sight to abhor,
Her daughter in a heathen's embrace.

XXII.

Terrified, the youth seeks to cover her,
Draping a white sheet over her head,
Yet she slyly slips from her lover's
Embraces, and she reveals herself:
With ghostly mien,
She begins rising
Like a wraith from the depths of the tomb.

XXIII.

"Mother! Mother! Give me one good reason why
I was born for loveless nights alone,
Ripped from Love's warm embraces—
Left here only to pitifully moan.
You bereft my heart
Of both life and art,
And left it cold and sullen like a headstone.

XXIV.

"Alas in this frigid and dark cave,
I will end my wretched sleeplessness;
Your priests and their holy hymns can't save
Me—nor holy prayers from above.
Salt and water cools,
But the heart of fools;
Yet the frigid grave cannot cool Love!

XXV.

"My vows had already been pledged to this boy
When Aphrodite's[1] temple still stood.
Mother, have you chosen to destroy
Sacred vows that you once understood.
No God lends his ear
To mothers who dare
Forsake one of their own innocent brood.

1 Aphrodite: Ancient Greek goddess of love, beauty, and sexuality.

XXVI.

"Driven nightly from my grave, forsaken,
I walk this land in hopes of quenching
My desire for the one who'd been given
My hand—to draw the blood from his being.
His life is now mine,
But there's more to find—
Many helpless souls are still in waiting.

XXVII.

"Oh beautiful boy! Your heart has run its course:
This dark chamber will soon be your grave.
While my neck chain is wrapped around your neck
This lock of your hair I'll gladly save—
Though now it is dark,
Soon it will be grey,
As its sable luster flees the grave.

XXVIII.

"Dear mother, this life has taken its toll:
Lay out a funeral pyre on this ground,
And let me grant succor to my wretched soul—
At last, the peace I've always longed for!
When glistening flames flow,
When the ashes glow,
To the ancient Gods aloft we'll soar."

# Sheridan Le Fanu

(1814–1873)

Joseph Thomas Sheridan Le Fanu grew up in Ireland and was a member of an old Anglo-Irish family. He often published under the name Sheridan Le Fanu to emphasize his famous maternal ancestor, Richard Brinsley Sheridan (1751–1816). One of the most popular horror writers of the nineteenth century, Le Fanu helped develop the Victorian genre of the ghost story. While he graduated with honors from Trinity College, Dublin, and was called to the bar, he never practiced law. Le Fanu began his career in journalism. When his beloved wife died in 1858, he became a recluse, writing late into the night producing the gothic tales that would make him famous. His famous gothic horror text, *Carmilla* (1872) offers one of the most vivid depictions of a female vampire. It has become the inspiration for many other tales and films, including Bram Stoker's *Dracula* (1897). Le Fanu died of a heart attack at the age of 58—he had suffered for years from nightmares and legend has it that the great horror writer actually died of fright. This story, however, probably has more to do with Le Fanu's reputation than it does with medical fact.

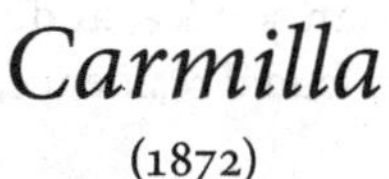

# *Carmilla*

(1872)

## PROLOGUE

*Upon a paper attached to the Narrative which follows, Doctor Hesselius*[1] *has written a rather elaborate note, which he accompanies with a reference to his Essay on the strange subject which the M.S. illuminates.*

1 One of literature's first occult investigators. This character reoccurs in several of Le Fanu's works, most notably in the short story "Green Tea." This novella purports to come from his case notes.

*This mysterious subject he treats, in that Essay, with his usual learning and acumen, and with remarkable directness and condensation. It will form but one volume of the series of that extraordinary man's collected papers.*

*As I publish the case, in this volume, simply to interest the "laity," I shall forestall the intelligent lady, who relates it, in nothing; and after due consideration, I have determined, therefore, to abstain from presenting any précis of the learned Doctor's reasoning, or extract from his statement on a subject which he describes as "involving, not improbably, some of the profoundest arcana of our dual existence, and its intermediates."*

*I was anxious on discovering this paper, to reopen the correspondence commenced by Doctor Hesselius, so many years before, with a person so clever and careful as his informant seems to have been. Much to my regret, however, I found that she had died in the interval.*

*She, probably, could have added little to the Narrative which she communicates in the following pages, with, so far as I can pronounce, such conscientious particularity.*

## I

## AN EARLY FRIGHT

In Styria,[1] we, though by no means magnificent people, inhabit a castle, or schloss.[2] A small income, in that part of the world, goes a great way. Eight or nine hundred a year[3] does wonders. Scantily enough ours would have answered among wealthy people at home. My father is English, and I bear an English name, although I never saw England. But here, in this lonely and primitive place, where everything is so marvelously cheap, I really don't see how ever so much more money would at all materially add to our comforts, or even luxuries.

My father was in the Austrian service, and retired upon a pension and his patrimony, and purchased this feudal residence, and the small estate on which it stands, a bargain.

Nothing can be more picturesque or solitary. It stands on a slight eminence in a forest. The road, very old and narrow, passes in front of its drawbridge, never raised in my time, and its moat, stocked with perch, and sailed over by many swans, and floating on its surface white fleets of water lilies.

Over all this the schloss shows its many-windowed front; its towers, and its Gothic chapel.

The forest opens in an irregular and very picturesque glade before its gate, and at the right a steep Gothic bridge carries the road over a stream that winds

1 State in southeast Austria on the border with Hungary.

2 German word for castle or manor house.

3 While calculating inflation can be notoriously misleading, this would be approximately £105,000–£120,000 today.

in deep shadow through the wood. I have said that this is a very lonely place. Judge whether I say truth. Looking from the hall door towards the road, the forest in which our castle stands extends fifteen miles to the right, and twelve to the left. The nearest inhabited village is about seven of your English miles to the left. The nearest inhabited schloss of any historic associations, is that of old General Spielsdorf, nearly twenty miles away to the right.

I have said "the nearest *inhabited* village," because there is, only three miles westward, that is to say in the direction of General Spielsdorf's schloss, a ruined village, with its quaint little church, now roofless, in the aisle of which are the moldering tombs of the proud family of Karnstein, now extinct, who once owned the equally desolate chateau which, in the thick of the forest, overlooks the silent ruins of the town.

Respecting the cause of the desertion of this striking and melancholy spot, there is a legend which I shall relate to you another time.

I must tell you now, how very small is the party who constitute the inhabitants of our castle. I don't include servants, or those dependents who occupy rooms in the buildings attached to the schloss. Listen, and wonder! My father, who is the kindest man on earth, but growing old; and I, at the date of my story, only nineteen. Eight years have passed since then.

I and my father constituted the family at the schloss. My mother, a Styrian lady, died in my infancy, but I had a good-natured governess, who had been with me from, I might almost say, my infancy. I could not remember the time when her fat, benignant face was not a familiar picture in my memory.

This was Madame Perrodon, a native of Berne, whose care and good nature now in part supplied to me the loss of my mother, whom I do not even remember, so early I lost her. She made a third at our little dinner party. There was a fourth, Mademoiselle De Lafontaine, a lady such as you term, I believe, a "finishing governess." She spoke French and German, Madame Perrodon French and broken English, to which my father and I added English, which, partly to prevent its becoming a lost language among us, and partly from patriotic motives, we spoke every day. The consequence was a Babel, at which strangers used to laugh, and which I shall make no attempt to reproduce in this narrative. And there were two or three young lady friends besides, pretty nearly of my own age, who were occasional visitors, for longer or shorter terms; and these visits I sometimes returned.

These were our regular social resources; but of course there were chance visits from "neighbors" of only five or six leagues distance.[1] My life was, notwithstanding, rather a solitary one, I can assure you.

My gouvernantes[2] had just so much control over me as you might conjecture

1 A league is a measure of distance. Five to six leagues would be approximately 15–18 miles or 24–28 kilometers.

2 French for governesses.

such sage persons would have in the case of a rather spoiled girl, whose only parent allowed her pretty nearly her own way in everything.

The first occurrence in my existence, which produced a terrible impression upon my mind, which, in fact, never has been effaced, was one of the very earliest incidents of my life which I can recollect. Some people will think it so trifling that it should not be recorded here. You will see, however, by-and-by, why I mention it. The nursery, as it was called, though I had it all to myself, was a large room in the upper story of the castle, with a steep oak roof. I can't have been more than six years old, when one night I awoke, and looking round the room from my bed, failed to see the nursery maid. Neither was my nurse there; and I thought myself alone. I was not frightened, for I was one of those happy children who are studiously kept in ignorance of ghost stories, of fairy tales, and of all such lore as makes us cover up our heads when the door cracks suddenly, or the flicker of an expiring candle makes the shadow of a bedpost dance upon the wall, nearer to our faces. I was vexed and insulted at finding myself, as I conceived, neglected, and I began to whimper, preparatory to a hearty bout of roaring; when to my surprise, I saw a solemn, but very pretty face looking at me from the side of the bed. It was that of a young lady who was kneeling, with her hands under the coverlet. I looked at her with a kind of pleased wonder, and ceased whimpering. She caressed me with her hands, and lay down beside me on the bed, and drew me towards her, smiling; I felt immediately delightfully soothed, and fell asleep again. I was wakened by a sensation as if two needles ran into my breast very deep at the same moment, and I cried loudly. The lady started back, with her eyes fixed on me, and then slipped down upon the floor, and, as I thought, hid herself under the bed.

I was now for the first time frightened, and I yelled with all my might and main. Nurse, nursery maid, housekeeper, all came running in, and hearing my story, they made light of it, soothing me all they could meanwhile. But, child as I was, I could perceive that their faces were pale with an unwonted look of anxiety, and I saw them look under the bed, and about the room, and peep under tables and pluck open cupboards; and the housekeeper whispered to the nurse: "Lay your hand along that hollow in the bed; someone *did* lie there, so sure as you did not; the place is still warm."

I remember the nursery maid petting me, and all three examining my chest, where I told them I felt the puncture, and pronouncing that there was no sign visible that any such thing had happened to me.

The housekeeper and the two other servants who were in charge of the nursery, remained sitting up all night; and from that time a servant always sat up in the nursery until I was about fourteen.

I was very nervous for a long time after this. A doctor was called in, he was pallid and elderly. How well I remember his long saturnine[1] face, slightly pitted

1 Dark and gloomy.

with smallpox, and his chestnut wig. For a good while, every second day, he came and gave me medicine, which of course I hated.

The morning after I saw this apparition I was in a state of terror, and could not bear to be left alone, daylight though it was, for a moment.

I remember my father coming up and standing at the bedside, and talking cheerfully, and asking the nurse a number of questions, and laughing very heartily at one of the answers; and patting me on the shoulder, and kissing me, and telling me not to be frightened, that it was nothing but a dream and could not hurt me.

But I was not comforted, for I knew the visit of the strange woman was *not* a dream; and I was *awfully* frightened.

I was a little consoled by the nursery maid's assuring me that it was she who had come and looked at me, and lain down beside me in the bed, and that I must have been half-dreaming not to have known her face. But this, though supported by the nurse, did not quite satisfy me.

I remembered, in the course of that day, a venerable old man, in a black cassock, coming into the room with the nurse and housekeeper, and talking a little to them, and very kindly to me; his face was very sweet and gentle, and he told me they were going to pray, and joined my hands together, and desired me to say, softly, while they were praying, "Lord hear all good prayers for us, for Jesus' sake." I think these were the very words, for I often repeated them to myself, and my nurse used for years to make me say them in my prayers.

I remembered so well the thoughtful sweet face of that white-haired old man, in his black cassock, as he stood in that rude, lofty, brown room, with the clumsy furniture of a fashion three hundred years old about him, and the scanty light entering its shadowy atmosphere through the small lattice. He kneeled, and the three women with him, and he prayed aloud with an earnest quavering voice for, what appeared to me, a long time. I forget all my life preceding that event, and for some time after it is all obscure also, but the scenes I have just described stand out vivid as the isolated pictures of the phantasmagoria[1] surrounded by darkness.

## II

## A GUEST

I am now going to tell you something so strange that it will require all your faith in my veracity to believe my story. It is not only true, nevertheless, but truth of which I have been an eyewitness.

1 Unsettling dream-like images. Also, an exhibition of optical special effects popular in the nineteenth century.

It was a sweet summer evening, and my father asked me, as he sometimes did, to take a little ramble with him along that beautiful forest vista which I have mentioned as lying in front of the schloss.

"General Spielsdorf cannot come to us so soon as I had hoped," said my father, as we pursued our walk.

He was to have paid us a visit of some weeks, and we had expected his arrival next day. He was to have brought with him a young lady, his niece and ward, Mademoiselle Rheinfeldt, whom I had never seen, but whom I had heard described as a very charming girl, and in whose society I had promised myself many happy days. I was more disappointed than a young lady living in a town, or a bustling neighborhood can possibly imagine. This visit, and the new acquaintance it promised, had furnished my day dream for many weeks.

"And how soon does he come?" I asked.

"Not till autumn. Not for two months, I dare say," he answered. "And I am very glad now, dear, that you never knew Mademoiselle Rheinfeldt."

"And why?" I asked, both mortified and curious.

"Because the poor young lady is dead," he replied. "I quite forgot I had not told you, but you were not in the room when I received the General's letter this evening."

I was very much shocked. General Spielsdorf had mentioned in his first letter, six or seven weeks before, that she was not so well as he would wish her, but there was nothing to suggest the remotest suspicion of danger.

"Here is the General's letter," he said, handing it to me. "I am afraid he is in great affliction; the letter appears to me to have been written very nearly in distraction."

We sat down on a rude bench, under a group of magnificent lime trees. The sun was setting with all its melancholy splendor behind the sylvan horizon, and the stream that flows beside our home, and passes under the steep old bridge I have mentioned, wound through many a group of noble trees, almost at our feet, reflecting in its current the fading crimson of the sky. General Spielsdorf's letter was so extraordinary, so vehement, and in some places so self-contradictory, that I read it twice over—the second time aloud to my father—and was still unable to account for it, except by supposing that grief had unsettled his mind.

It said "I have lost my darling daughter, for as such I loved her. During the last days of dear Bertha's illness I was not able to write to you. Before then I had no idea of her danger. I have lost her, and now learn *all*, too late. She died in the peace of innocence, and in the glorious hope of a blessed futurity. The fiend who betrayed our infatuated hospitality has done it all. I thought I was receiving into my house innocence, gaiety, a charming companion for my lost Bertha. Heavens! what a fool have I been! I thank God my child died without a suspicion of the cause of her sufferings. She is gone without so much as conjecturing the nature of her illness, and the accursed passion of the agent of all this misery. I devote my remaining days to tracking and extinguishing a monster. I am told I may hope to accomplish my righteous and merciful purpose. At present there is scarcely a gleam of light to guide me. I curse my conceited incredulity, my despicable affectation of superiority, my blindness, my obstinacy—all—too late. I cannot write or talk collectedly now. I am distracted. So soon as I shall have a little recovered, I mean to devote myself for a time to enquiry, which may possibly lead me as far as Vienna. Some time in the autumn, two months hence, or earlier if I live, I will see you—that is, if you permit me; I will then tell you all that I scarce dare put upon paper now. Farewell. Pray for me, dear friend."

In these terms ended this strange letter. Though I had never seen Bertha Rheinfeldt my eyes filled with tears at the sudden intelligence; I was startled, as well as profoundly disappointed.

The sun had now set, and it was twilight by the time I had returned the General's letter to my father.

It was a soft clear evening, and we loitered, speculating upon the possible meanings of the violent and incoherent sentences which I had just been reading. We had nearly a mile to walk before reaching the road that passes the schloss in front, and by that time the moon was shining brilliantly. At the drawbridge we met Madame Perrodon and Mademoiselle De Lafontaine, who had come out, without their bonnets, to enjoy the exquisite moonlight.

We heard their voices gabbling in animated dialogue as we approached. We joined them at the drawbridge, and turned about to admire with them the beautiful scene.

The glade through which we had just walked lay before us. At our left the narrow road wound away under clumps of lordly trees, and was lost to sight amid the thickening forest. At the right the same road crosses the steep and picturesque bridge, near which stands a ruined tower which once guarded that pass; and beyond the bridge an abrupt eminence rises, covered with trees, and showing in the shadows some grey ivy-clustered rocks.

Over the sward and low grounds a thin film of mist was stealing like smoke, marking the distances with a transparent veil; and here and there we could see the river faintly flashing in the moonlight.

No softer, sweeter scene could be imagined. The news I had just heard made it melancholy; but nothing could disturb its character of profound serenity, and the enchanted glory and vagueness of the prospect.

My father, who enjoyed the picturesque, and I, stood looking in silence over the expanse beneath us. The two good governesses, standing a little way behind us, discoursed upon the scene, and were eloquent upon the moon.

Madame Perrodon was fat, middle-aged, and romantic, and talked and sighed poetically. Mademoiselle De Lafontaine—in right of her father who was a German, assumed to be psychological, metaphysical, and something of a mystic—now declared that when the moon shone with a light so intense it was well known that it indicated a special spiritual activity. The effect of the full moon in such a state of brilliancy was manifold. It acted on dreams, it acted on lunacy, it acted on nervous people, it had marvelous physical influences connected with life. Mademoiselle related that her cousin, who was mate of a merchant ship, having taken a nap on deck on such a night, lying on his back, with his face full in the light of the moon, had wakened, after a dream of an old woman clawing him by the cheek, with his features horribly drawn to one side; and his countenance had never quite recovered its equilibrium.

"The moon, this night," she said, "is full of idyllic and magnetic influence[1]—and see, when you look behind you at the front of the schloss how all its windows flash and twinkle with that silvery splendor, as if unseen hands had lighted up the rooms to receive fairy guests."

There are indolent styles of the spirits in which, indisposed to talk ourselves, the talk of others is pleasant to our listless ears; and I gazed on, pleased with the tinkle of the ladies' conversation.

"I have got into one of my moping moods tonight," said my father, after a silence, and quoting Shakespeare, whom, by way of keeping up our English, he used to read aloud, he said:

"In truth I know not why I am so sad.
It wearies me: you say it wearies you;
But how I got it—came by it."[2]

I forget the rest. But I feel as if some great misfortune were hanging over us. I suppose the poor General's afflicted letter has had something to do with it."

At this moment the unwonted sound of carriage wheels and many hoofs upon the road, arrested our attention.

They seemed to be approaching from the high ground overlooking the bridge, and very soon the equipage emerged from that point. Two horsemen first crossed the bridge, then came a carriage drawn by four horses, and two men rode behind.

It seemed to be the traveling carriage of a person of rank; and we were all immediately absorbed in watching that very unusual spectacle. It became, in a few moments, greatly more interesting, for just as the carriage had passed the summit of the steep bridge, one of the leaders,[3] taking fright, communicated his panic to the rest, and after a plunge or two, the whole team broke into a wild gallop together, and dashing between the horsemen who rode in front, came thundering along the road towards us with the speed of a hurricane.

1 Pseudoscientist Baron Carl von Reichenbach (1788–1869) argued for the existence of an odic force related to electromagnetism and producing auras that some could see, which could produce a hypnotic effect.

2 Opening lines of Shakespeare's *The Merchant of Venice*.

3 One of the front pair of a team of horses pulling the carriage.

The excitement of the scene was made more painful by the clear, long-drawn screams of a female voice from the carriage window.

We all advanced in curiosity and horror; me rather in silence, the rest with various ejaculations of terror.

Our suspense did not last long. Just before you reach the castle drawbridge, on the route they were coming, there stands by the roadside a magnificent lime tree,[1] on the other stands an ancient stone cross, at sight of which the horses, now going at a pace that was perfectly frightful, swerved so as to bring the wheel over the projecting roots of the tree.

I knew what was coming. I covered my eyes, unable to see it out, and turned my head away; at the same moment I heard a cry from my lady friends, who had gone on a little.

Curiosity opened my eyes, and I saw a scene of utter confusion. Two of the horses were on the ground, the carriage lay upon its side with two wheels in the air; the men were busy removing the traces, and a lady with a commanding air and figure had got out, and stood with clasped hands, raising the handkerchief that was in them every now and then to her eyes.

Through the carriage door was now lifted a young lady, who appeared to be lifeless. My dear old father was already beside the elder lady, with his hat in his hand, evidently tendering his aid and the resources of his schloss. The lady did not appear to hear him, or to have eyes for anything but the slender girl who was being placed against the slope of the bank.

I approached; the young lady was apparently stunned, but she was certainly not dead. My father, who piqued himself on being something of a physician, had just had his fingers on her wrist and assured the lady, who declared herself her mother, that her pulse, though faint and irregular, was undoubtedly still distinguishable. The lady clasped her hands and looked upward, as if in a momentary transport of gratitude; but immediately she broke out again in that theatrical way which is, I believe, natural to some people.

She was what is called a fine-looking woman for her time of life, and must have been handsome; she was tall, but not thin, and dressed in black velvet, and looked rather pale, but with a proud and commanding countenance, though now agitated strangely.

"Who was ever being so born to calamity?" I heard her say, with clasped hands, as I came up. "Here am I, on a journey of life and death, in prosecuting which to lose an hour is possibly to lose all. My child will not have recovered sufficiently to resume her route for who can say how long. I must leave her: I cannot, dare not, delay. How far on, sir, can you tell, is the nearest village? I must leave her there; and shall not see my darling, or even hear of her till my return, three months hence."

1 Linden or Tilia (not the citrus fruit). A large deciduous tree typically reaching up to 40 meters (130 feet) tall.

I plucked my father by the coat, and whispered earnestly in his ear: "Oh! papa, pray ask her to let her stay with us—it would be so delightful. Do, pray."

"If Madame will entrust her child to the care of my daughter, and of her good gouvernante, Madame Perrodon, and permit her to remain as our guest, under my charge, until her return, it will confer a distinction and an obligation upon us, and we shall treat her with all the care and devotion which so sacred a trust deserves."

"I cannot do that, sir, it would be to task your kindness and chivalry too cruelly," said the lady, distractedly.

"It would, on the contrary, be to confer on us a very great kindness at the moment when we most need it. My daughter has just been disappointed by a cruel misfortune, in a visit from which she had long anticipated a great deal of happiness. If you confide this young lady to our care it will be her best consolation. The nearest village on your route is distant, and affords no such inn as you could think of placing your daughter at; you cannot allow her to continue her journey for any considerable distance without danger. If, as you say, you cannot suspend your journey, you must part with her tonight, and nowhere could you do so with more honest assurances of care and tenderness than here."

There was something in this lady's air and appearance so distinguished and even imposing, and in her manner so engaging, as to impress one, quite apart from the dignity of her equipage, with a conviction that she was a person of consequence.

By this time the carriage was replaced in its upright position, and the horses, quite tractable, in the traces again.

The lady threw on her daughter a glance which I fancied was not quite so affectionate as one might have anticipated from the beginning of the scene; then she beckoned slightly to my father, and withdrew two or three steps with him out of hearing; and talked to him with a fixed and stern countenance, not at all like that with which she had hitherto spoken.

I was filled with wonder that my father did not seem to perceive the change, and also unspeakably curious to learn what it could be that she was speaking, almost in his ear, with so much earnestness and rapidity.

Two or three minutes at most I think she remained thus employed, then she turned, and a few steps brought her to where her daughter lay, supported by Madame Perrodon. She kneeled beside her for a moment and whispered, as Madame supposed, a little benediction in her ear; then hastily kissing her she stepped into her carriage, the door was closed, the footmen in stately liveries[1] jumped up behind, the outriders spurred on, the postilions cracked their whips, the horses plunged and broke suddenly into a furious canter that threatened soon again to become a gallop, and the carriage whirled away, followed at the same rapid pace by the two horsemen in the rear.

1 Special uniform worn by servants in a wealthy household.

## III

## WE COMPARE NOTES

We followed the *cortege*[1] with our eyes until it was swiftly lost to sight in the misty wood; and the very sound of the hoofs and the wheels died away in the silent night air.

Nothing remained to assure us that the adventure had not been an illusion of a moment but the young lady, who just at that moment opened her eyes. I could not see, for her face was turned from me, but she raised her head, evidently looking about her, and I heard a very sweet voice ask complainingly, "Where is mamma?"

Our good Madame Perrodon answered tenderly, and added some comfortable assurances.

I then heard her ask:

"Where am I? What is this place?" and after that she said, "I don't see the carriage; and Matska, where is she?"

Madame answered all her questions in so far as she understood them; and gradually the young lady remembered how the misadventure came about, and was glad to hear that no one in, or in attendance on, the carriage was hurt; and on learning that her mamma had left her here, till her return in about three months, she wept.

I was going to add my consolations to those of Madame Perrodon when Mademoiselle De Lafontaine placed her hand upon my arm, saying:

"Don't approach, one at a time is as much as she can at present converse with; a very little excitement would possibly overpower her now."

As soon as she is comfortably in bed, I thought, I will run up to her room and see her.

My father in the meantime had sent a servant on horseback for the physician, who lived about two leagues away; and a bedroom was being prepared for the young lady's reception.

The stranger now rose, and leaning on Madame's arm, walked slowly over the drawbridge and into the castle gate.

In the hall, servants waited to receive her, and she was conducted forthwith to her room. The room we usually sat in as our drawing room is long, having four windows, that looked over the moat and drawbridge, upon the forest scene I have just described.

It is furnished in old carved oak, with large carved cabinets, and the chairs are cushioned with crimson Utrecht velvet.[2] The walls are covered with tapestry, and surrounded with great gold frames, the figures being as large as life, in

1 An entourage or retinue. Often used in association with a formal procession, as for a funeral.

2 A cotton and mohair velvet used in upholstery.

ancient and very curious costume, and the subjects represented are hunting, hawking, and generally festive. It is not too stately to be extremely comfortable; and here we had our tea, for with his usual patriotic leanings he insisted that the national beverage should make its appearance regularly with our coffee and chocolate.

We sat here this night, and with candles lighted, were talking over the adventure of the evening.

Madame Perrodon and Mademoiselle De Lafontaine were both of our party. The young stranger had hardly lain down in her bed when she sank into a deep sleep; and those ladies had left her in the care of a servant.

"How do you like our guest?" I asked, as soon as Madame entered. "Tell me all about her?"

"I like her extremely," answered Madame, "she is, I almost think, the prettiest creature I ever saw; about your age, and so gentle and nice."

"She is absolutely beautiful," threw in Mademoiselle, who had peeped for a moment into the stranger's room.

"And such a sweet voice!" added Madame Perrodon.

"Did you remark a woman in the carriage, after it was set up again, who did not get out," inquired Mademoiselle, "but only looked from the window?"

"No, we had not seen her."

Then she described a hideous black woman,[1] with a sort of colored turban on her head, and who was gazing all the time from the carriage window, nodding and grinning derisively towards the ladies, with gleaming eyes and large white eyeballs, and her teeth set as if in fury.

"Did you remark what an ill-looking pack of men the servants were?" asked Madame.

"Yes," said my father, who had just come in, "ugly, hang-dog looking fellows as ever I beheld in my life. I hope they mayn't rob the poor lady in the forest. They are clever rogues, however; they got everything to rights in a minute."

"I dare say they are worn out with too long traveling," said Madame.

"Besides looking wicked, their faces were so strangely lean, and dark, and sullen. I am very curious, I own; but I dare say the young lady will tell you all about it tomorrow, if she is sufficiently recovered."

"I don't think she will," said my father, with a mysterious smile, and a little nod of his head, as if he knew more about it than he cared to tell us.

This made us all the more inquisitive as to what had passed between him and the lady in the black velvet, in the brief but earnest interview that had immediately preceded her departure.

We were scarcely alone, when I entreated him to tell me. He did not need much pressing.

1 The casual racism of this statement is made even more appalling by the fact that Le Fanu drops this character from the rest of the story.

"There is no particular reason why I should not tell you. She expressed a reluctance to trouble us with the care of her daughter, saying she was in delicate health, and nervous, but not subject to any kind of seizure—she volunteered that—nor to any illusion; being, in fact, perfectly sane."

"How very odd to say all that!" I interpolated. "It was so unnecessary."

"At all events it *was* said," he laughed, "and as you wish to know all that passed, which was indeed very little, I tell you. She then said, 'I am making a long journey of *vital* importance—she emphasized the word—rapid and secret; I shall return for my child in three months; in the meantime, she will be silent as to who we are, whence we come, and whither we are traveling.' That is all she said. She spoke very pure French. When she said the word 'secret,' she paused for a few seconds, looking sternly, her eyes fixed on mine. I fancy she makes a great point of that. You saw how quickly she was gone. I hope I have not done a very foolish thing, in taking charge of the young lady."

For my part, I was delighted. I was longing to see and talk to her; and only waiting till the doctor should give me leave. You, who live in towns, can have no idea how great an event the introduction of a new friend is, in such a solitude as surrounded us.

The doctor did not arrive till nearly one o'clock; but I could no more have gone to my bed and slept, than I could have overtaken, on foot, the carriage in which the princess in black velvet had driven away.

When the physician came down to the drawing room, it was to report very favorably upon his patient. She was now sitting up, her pulse quite regular, apparently perfectly well. She had sustained no injury, and the little shock to her nerves had passed away quite harmlessly. There could be no harm certainly in my seeing her, if we both wished it; and, with this permission I sent, forthwith, to know whether she would allow me to visit her for a few minutes in her room.

The servant returned immediately to say that she desired nothing more.

You may be sure I was not long in availing myself of this permission.

Our visitor lay in one of the handsomest rooms in the schloss. It was, perhaps, a little stately. There was a somber piece of tapestry opposite the foot of the bed, representing Cleopatra with the asps to her bosom;[1] and other solemn classic scenes were displayed, a little faded, upon the other walls. But there was gold carving, and rich and varied color enough in the other decorations of the room, to more than redeem the gloom of the old tapestry.

There were candles at the bedside. She was sitting up; her slender pretty figure enveloped in the soft silk dressing gown, embroidered with flowers, and lined with thick quilted silk, which her mother had thrown over her feet as she lay upon the ground.

What was it that, as I reached the bedside and had just begun my little

1 Given the fact that Le Fanu's vampire attacks her prey by biting the breast, this classical tapestry serves as foreshadowing.

greeting, struck me dumb in a moment, and made me recoil a step or two from before her? I will tell you.

I saw the very face which had visited me in my childhood at night, which remained so fixed in my memory, and on which I had for so many years so often ruminated with horror, when no one suspected of what I was thinking.

It was pretty, even beautiful; and when I first beheld it, wore the same melancholy expression.

But this almost instantly lighted into a strange fixed smile of recognition.

There was a silence of fully a minute, and then at length she spoke; I could not.

"How wonderful!" she exclaimed. "Twelve years ago, I saw your face in a dream, and it has haunted me ever since."

"Wonderful indeed!" I repeated, overcoming with an effort the horror that had for a time suspended my utterances. "Twelve years ago, in vision or reality, I certainly saw you. I could not forget your face. It has remained before my eyes ever since."

Her smile had softened. Whatever I had fancied strange in it, was gone, and it and her dimpling cheeks were now delightfully pretty and intelligent.

I felt reassured, and continued more in the vein which hospitality indicated, to bid her welcome, and to tell her how much pleasure her accidental arrival had given us all, and especially what a happiness it was to me.

I took her hand as I spoke. I was a little shy, as lonely people are, but the situation made me eloquent, and even bold. She pressed my hand, she laid hers upon it, and her eyes glowed, as, looking hastily into mine, she smiled again, and blushed.

She answered my welcome very prettily. I sat down beside her, still wondering; and she said:

"I must tell you my vision about you; it is so very strange that you and I should have had, each of the other so vivid a dream, that each should have seen, I you and you me, looking as we do now, when of course we both were mere children. I was a child, about six years old, and I awoke from a confused and troubled dream, and found myself in a room, unlike my nursery, wainscoted clumsily in some dark wood, and with cupboards and bedsteads, and chairs, and benches placed about it. The beds were, I thought, all empty, and the room itself without anyone but myself in it; and I, after looking about me for some time, and admiring especially an iron candlestick with two branches, which I should certainly know again, crept under one of the beds to reach the window; but as I got from under the bed, I heard someone crying; and looking up, while I was still upon my knees, I saw you—most assuredly you—as I see you now; a beautiful young lady, with golden hair and large blue eyes, and lips—your lips—you as you are here. Your looks won me; I climbed on the bed and put my arms about you, and I think we both fell asleep. I was aroused by a scream; you were sitting up screaming. I was frightened, and slipped down upon the ground, and, it seemed to me, lost consciousness for a moment; and when I came to myself, I was again in my nursery at home. Your face I have never forgotten since. I could not be misled by mere resemblance. You are the lady whom I saw then."

It was now my turn to relate my corresponding vision, which I did, to the undisguised wonder of my new acquaintance.

"I don't know which should be most afraid of the other," she said, again smiling—"If you were less pretty I think I should be very much afraid of you, but being as you are, and you and I both so young, I feel only that I have made your acquaintance twelve years ago, and have already a right to your intimacy; at all events it does seem as if we were destined, from our earliest childhood, to be friends. I wonder whether you feel as strangely[1] drawn towards me as I do to you; I have never had a friend—shall I find one now?" She sighed, and her fine dark eyes gazed passionately on me.

Now the truth is, I felt rather unaccountably towards the beautiful stranger. I did feel, as she said, "drawn towards her," but there was also something of repulsion. In this ambiguous feeling, however, the sense of attraction immensely prevailed. She interested and won me; she was so beautiful and so indescribably engaging.

I perceived now something of languor and exhaustion stealing over her, and hastened to bid her good night.

"The doctor thinks," I added, "that you ought to have a maid to sit up with you tonight; one of ours is waiting, and you will find her a very useful and quiet creature."

"How kind of you, but I could not sleep, I never could with an attendant in the room. I shan't require any assistance—and, shall I confess my weakness, I am haunted with a terror of robbers. Our house was robbed once, and two servants murdered, so I always lock my door. It has become a habit—and you look so kind I know you will forgive me. I see there is a key in the lock."

She held me close in her pretty arms for a moment and whispered in my ear, "Good night, darling, it is very hard to part with you, but good night; tomorrow, but not early, I shall see you again."

She sank back on the pillow with a sigh, and her fine eyes followed me with a fond and melancholy gaze, and she murmured again "Good night, dear friend."

Young people like, and even love, on impulse. I was flattered by the evident, though as yet undeserved, fondness she showed me. I liked the confidence with which she at once received me. She was determined that we should be very near friends.

Next day came and we met again. I was delighted with my companion; that is to say, in many respects.

1 Critics such as Nina Auerbach have noted that Le Fanu's repeated use of the word "strange" to describe the feelings between vampire and victim connects to the Victorian code for same-sex desire.

Her looks lost nothing in daylight—she was certainly the most beautiful creature I had ever seen, and the unpleasant remembrance of the face presented in my early dream, had lost the effect of the first unexpected recognition.

She confessed that she had experienced a similar shock on seeing me, and precisely the same faint antipathy that had mingled with my admiration of her. We now laughed together over our momentary horrors.

## IV

## HER HABITS—A SAUNTER

I told you that I was charmed with her in most particulars.

There were some that did not please me so well.

She was above the middle height of women. I shall begin by describing her.

She was slender, and wonderfully graceful. Except that her movements were languid—very languid—indeed, there was nothing in her appearance to indicate an invalid. Her complexion was rich and brilliant; her features were small and beautifully formed; her eyes large, dark, and lustrous; her hair was quite wonderful, I never saw hair so magnificently thick and long when it was down about her shoulders; I have often placed my hands under it, and laughed with wonder at its weight. It was exquisitely fine and soft, and in color a rich very dark brown, with something of gold. I loved to let it down, tumbling with its own weight, as, in her room, she lay back in her chair talking in her sweet low voice, I used to fold and braid it, and spread it out and play with it. Heavens! If I had but known all!

I said there were particulars which did not please me. I have told you that her confidence won me the first night I saw her; but I found that she exercised with respect to herself, her mother, her history, everything in fact connected with her life, plans, and people, an ever wakeful reserve. I dare say I was unreasonable, perhaps I was wrong; I dare say I ought to have respected the solemn injunction laid upon my father by the stately lady in black velvet. But curiosity is a restless and unscrupulous passion, and no one girl can endure, with patience, that hers should be baffled by another. What harm could it do anyone to tell me what I so ardently desired to know? Had she no trust in my good sense or honor? Why would she not believe me when I assured her, so solemnly, that I would not divulge one syllable of what she told me to any mortal breathing.

There was a coldness, it seemed to me, beyond her years, in her smiling melancholy persistent refusal to afford me the least ray of light.

I cannot say we quarreled upon this point, for she would not quarrel upon any. It was, of course, very unfair of me to press her, very ill-bred, but I really could not help it; and I might just as well have let it alone.

What she did tell me amounted, in my unconscionable estimation—to nothing.

It was all summed up in three very vague disclosures:

First—Her name was Carmilla.

Second—Her family was very ancient and noble.

Third—Her home lay in the direction of the west.

She would not tell me the name of her family, nor their armorial bearings,[1] nor the name of their estate, nor even that of the country they lived in.

You are not to suppose that I worried her incessantly on these subjects. I watched opportunity, and rather insinuated than urged my inquiries. Once or twice, indeed, I did attack her more directly. But no matter what my tactics, utter failure was invariably the result. Reproaches and caresses were all lost upon her. But I must add this, that her evasion was conducted with so pretty a melancholy and deprecation, with so many, and even passionate declarations of her liking for me, and trust in my honor, and with so many promises that I should at last know all, that I could not find it in my heart long to be offended with her.

She used to place her pretty arms about my neck, draw me to her, and laying her cheek to mine, murmur with her lips near my ear, "Dearest, your little heart is wounded; think me not cruel because I obey the irresistible law of my strength and weakness; if your dear heart is wounded, my wild heart bleeds with yours. In the rapture of my enormous humiliation I live in your warm life, and you shall die—die, sweetly die—into mine.[2] I cannot help it; as I draw near to you, you, in your turn, will draw near to others, and learn the rapture of that cruelty, which yet is love; so, for a while, seek to know no more of me and mine, but trust me with all your loving spirit."

And when she had spoken such a rhapsody, she would press me more closely in her trembling embrace, and her lips in soft kisses gently glow upon my cheek.

Her agitations and her language were unintelligible to me.

From these foolish embraces, which were not of very frequent occurrence, I must allow, I used to wish to extricate myself; but my energies seemed to fail me. Her murmured words sounded like a lullaby in my ear, and soothed my resistance into a trance, from which I only seemed to recover myself when she withdrew her arms.

In these mysterious moods I did not like her. I experienced a strange tumultuous excitement that was pleasurable, ever and anon, mingled with a vague sense of fear and disgust. I had no distinct thoughts about her while such scenes lasted, but I was conscious of a love growing into adoration, and also of abhorrence. This I know is paradox, but I can make no other attempt to explain the feeling.

1 Heraldry; symbol for a noble family displayed on shields, etc.

2 Here, Carmilla's words echo the double entendre of so much Renaissance poetry where "to die" is to achieve orgasm.

I now write, after an interval of more than ten years, with a trembling hand, with a confused and horrible recollection of certain occurrences and situations, in the ordeal through which I was unconsciously passing; though with a vivid and very sharp remembrance of the main current of my story.

But, I suspect, in all lives there are certain emotional scenes, those in which our passions have been most wildly and terribly roused, that are of all others the most vaguely and dimly remembered.

Sometimes after an hour of apathy, my strange and beautiful companion would take my hand and hold it with a fond pressure, renewed again and again; blushing softly, gazing in my face with languid and burning eyes, and breathing so fast that her dress rose and fell with the tumultuous respiration. It was like the ardor of a lover; it embarrassed me; it was hateful and yet over-powering; and with gloating eyes she drew me to her, and her hot lips traveled along my cheek in kisses;[1] and she would whisper, almost in sobs, "You are mine, you *shall* be mine, you and I are one for ever." Then she had thrown herself back in her chair, with her small hands over her eyes, leaving me trembling.

"Are we related," I used to ask; "what can you mean by all this? I remind you perhaps of someone whom you love; but you must not, I hate it; I don't know you—I don't know myself when you look so and talk so."

She used to sigh at my vehemence, then turn away and drop my hand.

Respecting these very extraordinary manifestations I strove in vain to form any satisfactory theory—I could not refer them to affectation or trick. It was unmistakably the momentary breaking out of suppressed instinct and emotion. Was she, notwithstanding her mother's volunteered denial, subject to brief visitations of insanity; or was there here a disguise and a romance? I had read in old storybooks of such things. What if a boyish lover had found his way into the house, and sought to prosecute his suit in masquerade, with the assistance of a clever old adventuress.[2] But there were many things against this hypothesis, highly interesting as it was to my vanity.

I could boast of no little attentions such as masculine gallantry delights to offer. Between these passionate moments there were long intervals of commonplace, of gaiety, of brooding melancholy, during which, except that I detected her eyes so full of melancholy fire, following me, at times I might have been as nothing to her. Except in these brief periods of mysterious excitement her ways were girlish; and there was always a languor about her, quite incompatible with a masculine system in a state of health.

In some respects her habits were odd. Perhaps not so singular in the opinion of a town lady like you, as they appeared to us rustic people. She used to

1 Physical affection between female friends was far more common in the nineteenth century than it is in most Western countries today. Holding hands, embracing, kissing, and even sharing a bed were not necessarily indicators of a sexual relationship. Still, Le Fanu's descriptions in scenes such as this one seem to cross a line and have often been interpreted by critics as evidence of the sexual overtones of Carmilla and Laura's relationship.

2 A common trope in Romance literature dating back to the Renaissance and beyond.

come down very late, generally not till one o'clock, she would then take a cup of chocolate, but eat nothing; we then went out for a walk, which was a mere saunter, and she seemed, almost immediately, exhausted, and either returned to the schloss or sat on one of the benches that were placed, here and there, among the trees. This was a bodily languor in which her mind did not sympathize. She was always an animated talker, and very intelligent.

She sometimes alluded for a moment to her own home, or mentioned an adventure or situation, or an early recollection, which indicated a people of strange manners, and described customs of which we knew nothing. I gathered from these chance hints that her native country was much more remote than I had at first fancied.

As we sat thus one afternoon under the trees a funeral passed us by. It was that of a pretty young girl, whom I had often seen, the daughter of one of the rangers of the forest. The poor man was walking behind the coffin of his darling; she was his only child, and he looked quite heartbroken.

Peasants walking two-and-two came behind, they were singing a funeral hymn.

I rose to mark my respect as they passed, and joined in the hymn they were very sweetly singing.

My companion shook me a little roughly, and I turned surprised.

She said brusquely, "Don't you perceive how discordant that is?"

"I think it very sweet, on the contrary," I answered, vexed at the interruption, and very uncomfortable, lest the people who composed the little procession should observe and resent what was passing.

I resumed, therefore, instantly, and was again interrupted. "You pierce my ears," said Carmilla, almost angrily, and stopping her ears with her tiny fingers. "Besides, how can you tell that your religion and mine are the same; your forms wound me, and I hate funerals. What a fuss! Why you must die—*everyone* must die; and all are happier when they do. Come home."

"My father has gone on with the clergyman to the churchyard. I thought you knew she was to be buried today."

"She? I don't trouble my head about peasants. I don't know who she is," answered Carmilla, with a flash from her fine eyes.

"She is the poor girl who fancied she saw a ghost a fortnight[1] ago, and has been dying ever since, till yesterday, when she expired."

"Tell me nothing about ghosts. I shan't sleep tonight if you do."

"I hope there is no plague or fever coming; all this looks very like it," I continued. "The swineherd's young wife died only a week ago, and she thought something seized her by the throat as she lay in her bed, and nearly strangled her. Papa says such horrible fancies do accompany some forms of fever. She was quite well the day before. She sank afterwards, and died before a week."

1 Two weeks.

"Well, *her* funeral is over, I hope, and *her* hymn sung; and our ears shan't be tortured with that discord and jargon. It has made me nervous. Sit down here, beside me; sit close; hold my hand; press it hard-hard-harder."

We had moved a little back, and had come to another seat.

She sat down. Her face underwent a change that alarmed and even terrified me for a moment. It darkened, and became horribly livid; her teeth and hands were clenched, and she frowned and compressed her lips, while she stared down upon the ground at her feet, and trembled all over with a continued shudder as irrepressible as ague. All her energies seemed strained to suppress a fit, with which she was then breathlessly tugging; and at length a low convulsive cry of suffering broke from her, and gradually the hysteria subsided. "There! That comes of strangling people with hymns!" she said at last. "Hold me, hold me still. It is passing away."

And so gradually it did; and perhaps to dissipate the somber impression which the spectacle had left upon me, she became unusually animated and chatty; and so we got home.

This was the first time I had seen her exhibit any definable symptoms of that delicacy of health which her mother had spoken of. It was the first time, also, I had seen her exhibit anything like temper.

Both passed away like a summer cloud; and never but once afterwards did I witness on her part a momentary sign of anger. I will tell you how it happened.

She and I were looking out of one of the long drawing room windows, when there entered the courtyard, over the drawbridge, a figure of a wanderer whom I knew very well. He used to visit the schloss generally twice a year.

It was the figure of a hunchback, with the sharp lean features that generally accompany deformity. He wore a pointed black beard, and he was smiling from ear to ear, showing his white fangs. He was dressed in buff, black, and scarlet, and crossed with more straps and belts than I could count, from which hung all manner of things. Behind, he carried a magic lantern, and two boxes, which I well knew, in one of which was a salamander, and in the other a mandrake.[1] These monsters used to make my father laugh. They were compounded of parts of monkeys, parrots, squirrels, fish, and hedgehogs, dried and stitched together with great neatness and startling effect. He had a fiddle, a box of conjuring apparatus, a pair of foils and masks attached to his belt, several other mysterious cases dangling about him, and a black staff with copper ferrules in his hand. His companion was a rough spare dog, that followed at his heels, but stopped short, suspiciously at the drawbridge, and in a little while began to howl dismally.

In the meantime, the mountebank,[2] standing in the midst of the courtyard,

1 Mythical creatures. A salamander could endure fire without harm, while a mandrake was a plant whose roots were said to contain a demon that would kill anyone who attempted to uproot it. The roots of a mandrake often resemble a human form.

2 A con man or charlatan. Someone who deceives for money.

raised his grotesque hat, and made us a very ceremonious bow, paying his compliments very volubly in execrable French, and German not much better.

Then, disengaging his fiddle, he began to scrape a lively air to which he sang with a merry discord, dancing with ludicrous airs and activity, that made me laugh, in spite of the dog's howling.

Then he advanced to the window with many smiles and salutations, and his hat in his left hand, his fiddle under his arm, and with a fluency that never took breath, he gabbled a long advertisement of all his accomplishments, and the resources of the various arts which he placed at our service, and the curiosities and entertainments which it was in his power, at our bidding, to display.

"Will your ladyships be pleased to buy an amulet against the oupire,[1] which is going like the wolf, I hear, through these woods," he said dropping his hat on the pavement. "They are dying of it right and left and here is a charm that never fails; only pinned to the pillow, and you may laugh in his face."

These charms consisted of oblong slips of vellum, with cabalistic ciphers[2] and diagrams upon them.

Carmilla instantly purchased one, and so did I.

He was looking up, and we were smiling down upon him, amused; at least, I can answer for myself. His piercing black eye, as he looked up in our faces, seemed to detect something that fixed for a moment his curiosity.

In an instant he unrolled a leather case, full of all manner of odd little steel instruments.

"See here, my lady," he said, displaying it, and addressing me, "I profess, among other things less useful, the art of dentistry. Plague take the dog!" he interpolated. "Silence, beast! He howls so that your ladyships can scarcely hear a word. Your noble friend, the young lady at your right, has the sharpest tooth,—long, thin, pointed, like an awl, like a needle; ha, ha! With my sharp and long sight, as I look up, I have seen it distinctly; now if it happens to hurt the young lady, and I think it must, here am I, here are my file, my punch, my nippers; I will make it round and blunt, if her ladyship pleases; no longer the tooth of a fish, but of a beautiful young lady as she is. Hey? Is the young lady displeased? Have I been too bold? Have I offended her?"

The young lady, indeed, looked very angry as she drew back from the window.

"How dares that mountebank insult us so? Where is your father? I shall demand redress from him. My father would have had the wretch tied up to the pump, and flogged with a cart whip, and burnt to the bones with the cattle brand!"

She retired from the window a step or two, and sat down, and had hardly lost sight of the offender, when her wrath subsided as suddenly as it had risen,

1 Polish word for vampire.

2 Symbols with a secret occult meaning; a code.

and she gradually recovered her usual tone, and seemed to forget the little hunchback and his follies.

My father was out of spirits that evening. On coming in he told us that there had been another case very similar to the two fatal ones which had lately occurred. The sister of a young peasant on his estate, only a mile away, was very ill, had been, as she described it, attacked very nearly in the same way, and was now slowly but steadily sinking.

"All this," said my father, "is strictly referable to natural causes. These poor people infect one another with their superstitions, and so repeat in imagination the images of terror that have infested their neighbors."

"But that very circumstance frightens one horribly," said Carmilla.

"How so?" inquired my father.

"I am so afraid of fancying I see such things; I think it would be as bad as reality."

"We are in God's hands: nothing can happen without his permission, and all will end well for those who love him. He is our faithful creator; He has made us all, and will take care of us."

"Creator! *Nature!*" said the young lady in answer to my gentle father. "And this disease that invades the country is natural. Nature. All things proceed from Nature—don't they? All things in the heaven, in the earth, and under the earth, act and live as Nature ordains? I think so."

"The doctor said he would come here today," said my father, after a silence. "I want to know what he thinks about it, and what he thinks we had better do."

"Doctors never did me any good," said Carmilla.

"Then you have been ill?" I asked.

"More ill than ever you were," she answered.

"Long ago?"

"Yes, a long time. I suffered from this very illness; but I forget all but my pain and weakness, and they were not so bad as are suffered in other diseases."

"You were very young then?"

"I dare say, let us talk no more of it. You would not wound a friend?"

She looked languidly in my eyes, and passed her arm round my waist lovingly, and led me out of the room. My father was busy over some papers near the window.

"Why does your papa like to frighten us?" said the pretty girl with a sigh and a little shudder.

"He doesn't, dear Carmilla, it is the very furthest thing from his mind."

"Are you afraid, dearest?"

"I should be very much if I fancied there was any real danger of my being attacked as those poor people were."

"You are afraid to die?"

"Yes, every one is."

"But to die as lovers may—to die together, so that they may live together. Girls are caterpillars while they live in the world, to be finally butterflies when the summer comes; but in the meantime there are grubs and larvae, don't you see—each with their peculiar propensities, necessities and structure. So says Monsieur Buffon, in his big book, in the next room."

Later in the day the doctor came, and was closeted with papa for some time.

He was a skillful man, of sixty and upwards, he wore powder, and shaved his pale face as smooth as a pumpkin. He and papa emerged from the room together, and I heard papa laugh, and say as they came out:

"Well, I do wonder at a wise man like you. What do you say to hippogriffs[1] and dragons?"

The doctor was smiling, and made answer, shaking his head—

"Nevertheless life and death are mysterious states, and we know little of the resources of either."

And so they walked on, and I heard no more. I did not then know what the doctor had been broaching, but I think I guess it now.

## V

## A WONDERFUL LIKENESS

This evening there arrived from Gratz[2] the grave, dark-faced son of the picture cleaner, with a horse and cart laden with two large packing cases, having many pictures in each. It was a journey of ten leagues, and whenever a messenger arrived at the schloss from our little capital of Gratz, we used to crowd about him in the hall, to hear the news.

This arrival created in our secluded quarters quite a sensation. The cases remained in the hall, and the messenger was taken charge of by the servants till he had eaten his supper. Then with assistants, and armed with hammer, ripping chisel, and turnscrew, he met us in the hall, where we had assembled to witness the unpacking of the cases.

Carmilla sat looking listlessly on, while one after the other the old pictures, nearly all portraits, which had undergone the process of renovation, were brought to light. My mother was of an old Hungarian family, and most of these pictures, which were about to be restored to their places, had come to us through her.

My father had a list in his hand, from which he read, as the artist rummaged out the corresponding numbers. I don't know that the pictures were very good, but they were, undoubtedly, very old, and some of them very curious also. They

1 Mythical creature with the front half of an eagle and the hind quarters of a horse.

2 Capital of Styria.

had, for the most part, the merit of being now seen by me, I may say, for the first time; for the smoke and dust of time had all but obliterated them.

"There is a picture that I have not seen yet," said my father. "In one corner, at the top of it, is the name, as well as I could read, 'Marcia Karnstein,' and the date '1698'; and I am curious to see how it has turned out."

I remembered it; it was a small picture, about a foot and a half high, and nearly square, without a frame; but it was so blackened by age that I could not make it out.

The artist now produced it, with evident pride. It was quite beautiful; it was startling; it seemed to live. It was the effigy of Carmilla!

"Carmilla, dear, here is an absolute miracle. Here you are, living, smiling, ready to speak, in this picture. Isn't it beautiful, Papa? And see, even the little mole on her throat."

My father laughed, and said "Certainly it is a wonderful likeness," but he looked away, and to my surprise seemed but little struck by it, and went on talking to the picture cleaner, who was also something of an artist, and discoursed with intelligence about the portraits or other works, which his art had just brought into light and color, while I was more and more lost in wonder the more I looked at the picture.

"Will you let me hang this picture in my room, papa?" I asked.

"Certainly, dear," said he, smiling, "I'm very glad you think it so like. It must be prettier even than I thought it, if it is."

The young lady did not acknowledge this pretty speech, did not seem to hear it. She was leaning back in her seat, her fine eyes under their long lashes gazing on me in contemplation, and she smiled in a kind of rapture.

"And now you can read quite plainly the name that is written in the corner. It is not Marcia; it looks as if it was done in gold. The name is Mircalla, Countess Karnstein, and this is a little coronet over and underneath A.D. 1698. I am descended from the Karnsteins; that is, mamma was."

"Ah!" said the lady, languidly, "so am I, I think, a very long descent, very ancient. Are there any Karnsteins living now?"

"None who bear the name, I believe. The family were ruined, I believe, in some civil wars, long ago, but the ruins of the castle are only about three miles away."

"How interesting!" she said, languidly. "But see what beautiful moonlight!" She glanced through the hall door, which stood a little open. "Suppose you take a little ramble round the court, and look down at the road and river."

"It is so like the night you came to us," I said.

She sighed; smiling.

She rose, and each with her arm about the other's waist, we walked out upon the pavement.

In silence, slowly we walked down to the drawbridge, where the beautiful landscape opened before us.

"And so you were thinking of the night I came here?" she almost whispered. "Are you glad I came?" "Delighted, dear Carmilla," I answered.

"And you asked for the picture you think like me, to hang in your room," she murmured with a sigh, as she drew her arm closer about my waist, and let her pretty head sink upon my shoulder. "How romantic you are, Carmilla," I said. "Whenever you tell me your story, it will be made up chiefly of some one great romance."

She kissed me silently.

"I am sure, Carmilla, you have been in love; that there is, at this moment, an affair of the heart going on."

"I have been in love with no one, and never shall," she whispered, "unless it should be with you."

How beautiful she looked in the moonlight!

Shy and strange was the look with which she quickly hid her face in my neck and hair, with tumultuous sighs, that seemed almost to sob, and pressed in mine a hand that trembled.

Her soft cheek was glowing against mine. "Darling, darling," she murmured, "I live in you; and you would die for me, I love you so."

I started from her.

She was gazing on me with eyes from which all fire, all meaning had flown, and a face colorless and apathetic.

"Is there a chill in the air, dear?" she said drowsily. "I almost shiver; have I been dreaming? Let us come in. Come; come; come in."

"You look ill, Carmilla; a little faint. You certainly must take some wine," I said.

"Yes. I will. I'm better now. I shall be quite well in a few minutes. Yes, do give me a little wine," answered Carmilla, as we approached the door.

"Let us look again for a moment; it is the last time, perhaps, I shall see the moonlight with you."

"How do you feel now, dear Carmilla? Are you really better?" I asked.

I was beginning to take alarm, lest she should have been stricken with the strange epidemic that they said had invaded the country about us.

"Papa would be grieved beyond measure," I added, "if he thought you were ever so little ill, without immediately letting us know. We have a very skillful doctor near us, the physician who was with papa today."

"I'm sure he is. I know how kind you all are; but, dear child, I am quite well again. There is nothing ever wrong with me, but a little weakness. People say I am languid; I am incapable of exertion; I can scarcely walk as far as a child of three years old: and every now and then the little strength I have falters, and I become as you have just seen me. But after all I am very easily set up again; in a moment I am perfectly myself. See how I have recovered."

So, indeed, she had; and she and I talked a great deal, and very animated she was; and the remainder of that evening passed without any recurrence of what

I called her infatuations. I mean her crazy talk and looks, which embarrassed, and even frightened me.

But there occurred that night an event which gave my thoughts quite a new turn, and seemed to startle even Carmilla's languid nature into momentary energy.

## VI

## A VERY STRANGE AGONY

When we got into the drawing room, and had sat down to our coffee and chocolate, although Carmilla did not take any, she seemed quite herself again, and Madame, and Mademoiselle De Lafontaine, joined us, and made a little card party, in the course of which papa came in for what he called his "dish of tea."[1]

When the game was over he sat down beside Carmilla on the sofa, and asked her, a little anxiously, whether she had heard from her mother since her arrival.

She answered "No."

He then asked whether she knew where a letter would reach her at present.

"I cannot tell," she answered ambiguously, "but I have been thinking of leaving you; you have been already too hospitable and too kind to me. I have given you an infinity of trouble, and I should wish to take a carriage tomorrow, and post in pursuit of her; I know where I shall ultimately find her, although I dare not yet tell you."

"But you must not dream of any such thing," exclaimed my father, to my great relief. "We can't afford to lose you so, and I won't consent to your leaving us, except under the care of your mother, who was so good as to consent to your remaining with us till she should herself return. I should be quite happy if I knew that you heard from her: but this evening the accounts of the progress of the mysterious disease that has invaded our neighborhood, grow even more alarming; and my beautiful guest, I do feel the responsibility, unaided by advice from your mother, very much. But I shall do my best; and one thing is certain, that you must not think of leaving us without her distinct direction to that effect. We should suffer too much in parting from you to consent to it easily."

"Thank you, sir, a thousand times for your hospitality," she answered, smiling bashfully. "You have all been too kind to me; I have seldom been so happy in all my life before, as in your beautiful chateau,[2] under your care, and in the society of your dear daughter."

So he gallantly, in his old-fashioned way, kissed her hand, smiling and pleased at her little speech.

1 Victorian expression harkening back to when tea was served in a bowl-like cup without a handle. This is further evidence of Laura's father's attempts to preserve the family's Englishness.

2 French for a large country house or castle.

I accompanied Carmilla as usual to her room, and sat and chatted with her while she was preparing for bed.

"Do you think," I said at length, "that you will ever confide fully in me?"

She turned round smiling, but made no answer, only continued to smile on me.

"You won't answer that?" I said. "You can't answer pleasantly; I ought not to have asked you."

"You were quite right to ask me that, or anything. You do not know how dear you are to me, or you could not think any confidence too great to look for. But I am under vows, no nun half so awfully, and I dare not tell my story yet, even to you. The time is very near when you shall know everything. You will think me cruel, very selfish, but love is always selfish; the more ardent the more selfish. How jealous I am you cannot know. You must come with me, loving me, to death; or else hate me and still come with me, and *hating* me through death and after. There is no such word as indifference in my apathetic nature."

"Now, Carmilla, you are going to talk your wild nonsense again," I said hastily.

"Not I, silly little fool as I am, and full of whims and fancies; for your sake I'll talk like a sage. Were you ever at a ball?"

"No; how you do run on. What is it like? How charming it must be."

"I almost forget, it is years ago."

I laughed.

"You are not so old. Your first ball can hardly be forgotten yet."

"I remember everything about it—with an effort. I see it all, as divers see what is going on above them, through a medium, dense, rippling, but transparent. There occurred that night what has confused the picture, and made its colors faint. I was all but assassinated in my bed, wounded here," she touched her breast, "and never was the same since."

"Were you near dying?"

"Yes, very—a cruel love—strange love, that would have taken my life. Love will have its sacrifices. No sacrifice without blood. Let us go to sleep now; I feel so lazy. How can I get up just now and lock my door?"

She was lying with her tiny hands buried in her rich wavy hair, under her cheek, her little head upon the pillow, and her glittering eyes followed me wherever I moved, with a kind of shy smile that I could not decipher.

I bid her good night, and crept from the room with an uncomfortable sensation.

I often wondered whether our pretty guest ever said her prayers. I certainly had never seen her upon her knees. In the morning she never came down until long after our family prayers were over, and at night she never left the drawing room to attend our brief evening prayers in the hall.

If it had not been that it had casually come out in one of our careless talks that she had been baptised, I should have doubted her being a Christian. Religion was a subject on which I had never heard her speak a word. If I had known the world better, this particular neglect or antipathy would not have so much surprised me.

The precautions of nervous people are infectious, and persons of a like temperament are pretty sure, after a time, to imitate them. I had adopted Carmilla's habit of locking her bedroom door, having taken into my head all her whimsical alarms about midnight invaders and prowling assassins. I had also adopted her precaution of making a brief search through her room, to satisfy herself that no lurking assassin or robber was "ensconced."

These wise measures taken, I got into my bed and fell asleep. A light was burning in my room. This was an old habit, of very early date, and which nothing could have tempted me to dispense with.

Thus fortified I might take my rest in peace. But dreams come through stone walls, light up dark rooms, or darken light ones, and their persons make their exits and their entrances as they please, and laugh at locksmiths.

I had a dream that night that was the beginning of a very strange agony.

I cannot call it a nightmare, for I was quite conscious of being asleep.

But I was equally conscious of being in my room, and lying in bed, precisely as I actually was. I saw, or fancied I saw, the room and its furniture just as I had seen it last, except that it was very dark, and I saw something moving round the foot of the bed, which at first I could not accurately distinguish. But I soon saw that it was a sooty-black animal that resembled a monstrous cat. It appeared to me about four or five feet long for it measured fully the length of the hearthrug as it passed over it; and it continued to-ing and fro-ing with the lithe, sinister restlessness of a beast in a cage. I could not cry out, although as you may suppose, I was terrified. Its pace was growing faster, and the room rapidly darker and darker, and at length so dark that I could no longer see anything of it but its eyes. I felt it spring lightly on the bed. The two broad eyes approached my face, and suddenly I felt a stinging pain as if two large needles darted, an inch or two apart, deep into my breast.[1] I waked with a scream. The room was lighted by the candle that burnt there all through the night, and I saw a female figure standing at the foot of the bed, a little at the right side. It was in a dark loose dress, and its hair was down and covered its shoulders. A block of stone could not have been more still. There was not the slightest stir of respiration. As I stared at it, the figure appeared to have changed its place, and was now nearer the door; then, close to it, the door opened, and it passed out.

I was now relieved, and able to breathe and move. My first thought was that Carmilla had been playing me a trick, and that I had forgotten to secure my door. I hastened to it, and found it locked as usual on the inside. I was afraid to

1 According to Groom, in Eastern European folklore, the vampire attacks the breast not the throat (*The Vampire* 13).

open it—I was horrified. I sprang into my bed and covered my head up in the bedclothes and lay there more dead than alive till morning.

## VII

## DESCENDING

It would be vain my attempting to tell you the horror with which, even now, I recall the occurrence of that night. It was no such transitory terror as a dream leaves behind it. It seemed to deepen by time, and communicated itself to the room and the very furniture that had encompassed the apparition.

I could not bear next day to be alone for a moment. I should have told papa, but for two opposite reasons. At one time I thought he would laugh at my story, and I could not bear its being treated as a jest; and at another I thought he might fancy that I had been attacked by the mysterious complaint which had invaded our neighborhood. I had myself no misgiving of the kind, and as he had been rather an invalid for some time, I was afraid of alarming him.

I was comfortable enough with my good-natured companions, Madame Perrodon, and the vivacious Mademoiselle De Lafontaine. They both perceived that I was out of spirits and nervous, and at length I told them what lay so heavy at my heart.

Mademoiselle laughed, but I fancied that Madame Perrodon looked anxious.

"By-the-by," said Mademoiselle, laughing, "the long lime tree walk, behind Carmilla's bedroom window, is haunted!"

"Nonsense!" exclaimed Madame, who probably thought the theme rather inopportune, "and who tells that story, my dear?"

"Martin says that he came up twice, when the old yard gate was being repaired, before sunrise, and twice saw the same female figure walking down the lime tree avenue."

"So he well might, as long as there are cows to milk in the river fields," said Madame.

"I daresay; but Martin chooses to be frightened, and never did I see fool more frightened."

"You must not say a word about it to Carmilla, because she can see down that walk from her room window," I interposed, "and she is, if possible, a greater coward than I."

Carmilla came down rather later than usual that day.

"I was so frightened last night," she said, so soon as were together, "and I am sure I should have seen something dreadful if it had not been for that charm I bought from the poor little hunchback whom I called such hard names. I had a dream of something black coming round my bed, and I awoke in a perfect horror, and I really thought, for some seconds, I saw a dark figure near the chimneypiece, but I felt under my pillow for my charm, and the moment my fingers touched it, the figure disappeared, and I felt quite certain, only that I had it by me, that something frightful would have made its appearance, and, perhaps, throttled me, as it did those poor people we heard of."

"Well, listen to me," I began, and recounted my adventure, at the recital of which she appeared horrified.

"And had you the charm near you?" she asked, earnestly.

"No, I had dropped it into a china vase in the drawing room, but I shall certainly take it with me tonight, as you have so much faith in it."

At this distance of time I cannot tell you, or even understand, how I overcame my horror so effectually as to lie alone in my room that night. I remember distinctly that I pinned the charm to my pillow. I fell asleep almost immediately, and slept even more soundly than usual all night.

Next night I passed as well. My sleep was delightfully deep and dreamless.

But I wakened with a sense of lassitude and melancholy, which, however, did not exceed a degree that was almost luxurious.

"Well, I told you so," said Carmilla, when I described my quiet sleep, "I had such delightful sleep myself last night; I pinned the charm to the breast of my nightdress. It was too far away the night before. I am quite sure it was all fancy, except the dreams. I used to think that evil spirits made dreams, but our doctor told me it is no such thing. Only a fever passing by, or some other malady, as they often do, he said, knocks at the door, and not being able to get in, passes on, with that alarm."

"And what do you think the charm is?" said I.

"It has been fumigated or immersed in some drug, and is an antidote against the malaria," she answered.

"Then it acts only on the body?"

"Certainly; you don't suppose that evil spirits are frightened by bits of ribbon, or the perfumes of a druggist's shop? No, these complaints, wandering in the air, begin by trying the nerves, and so infect the brain, but before they can seize upon you, the antidote repels them. That I am sure is what the charm has done for us. It is nothing magical, it is simply natural."

I should have been happier if I could have quite agreed with Carmilla, but I did my best, and the impression was a little losing its force.

For some nights I slept profoundly; but still every morning I felt the same lassitude, and a languor weighed upon me all day. I felt myself a changed girl. A strange melancholy was stealing over me, a melancholy that I would not have interrupted. Dim thoughts of death began to open, and an idea that I was slowly sinking took gentle, and, somehow, not unwelcome, possession of me. If it was sad, the tone of mind which this induced was also sweet.

Whatever it might be, my soul acquiesced in it.

I would not admit that I was ill, I would not consent to tell my papa, or to have the doctor sent for.

Carmilla became more devoted to me than ever, and her strange paroxysms of languid adoration more frequent. She used to gloat on me with increasing ardor the more my strength and spirits waned. This always shocked me like a momentary glare of insanity.

Without knowing it, I was now in a pretty advanced stage of the strangest illness under which mortal ever suffered. There was an unaccountable fascination in its earlier symptoms that more than reconciled me to the incapacitating effect of that stage of the malady. This fascination increased for a time, until it reached a certain point, when gradually a sense of the horrible mingled itself with it, deepening, as you shall hear, until it discolored and perverted the whole state of my life.

The first change I experienced was rather agreeable. It was very near the turning point from which began the descent of Avernus.[1]

Certain vague and strange sensations visited me in my sleep. The prevailing one was of that pleasant, peculiar cold thrill which we feel in bathing, when we move against the current of a river. This was soon accompanied by dreams that seemed interminable, and were so vague that I could never recollect their scenery and persons, or any one connected portion of their action. But they left an awful impression, and a sense of exhaustion, as if I had passed through a long period of great mental exertion and danger.

After all these dreams there remained on waking a remembrance of having been in a place very nearly dark, and of having spoken to people whom I could not see; and especially of one clear voice, of a female's, very deep, that spoke as if at a distance, slowly, and producing always the same sensation of indescribable solemnity and fear. Sometimes there came a sensation as if a hand was drawn softly along my cheek and neck. Sometimes it was as if warm lips kissed me, and longer and longer and more lovingly as they reached my throat, but there the caress fixed itself. My heart beat faster, my breathing rose and fell rapidly and full drawn; a sobbing, that rose into a sense of strangulation, supervened, and turned into a dreadful convulsion, in which my senses left me and I became unconscious.

It was now three weeks since the commencement of this unaccountable state.

My sufferings had, during the last week, told upon my appearance. I had grown pale, my eyes were dilated and darkened underneath, and the languor which I had long felt began to display itself in my countenance.

My father asked me often whether I was ill; but, with an obstinacy which now seems to me unaccountable, I persisted in assuring him that I was quite well.

In a sense this was true. I had no pain, I could complain of no bodily derangement. My complaint seemed to be one of the imagination, or the nerves, and,

1 In Greek mythology, the entrance to the underworld, Hades.

horrible as my sufferings were, I kept them, with a morbid reserve, very nearly to myself.

It could not be that terrible complaint which the peasants called the oupire, for I had now been suffering for three weeks, and they were seldom ill for much more than three days, when death put an end to their miseries.

Carmilla complained of dreams and feverish sensations, but by no means of so alarming a kind as mine. I say that mine were extremely alarming. Had I been capable of comprehending my condition, I would have invoked aid and advice on my knees. The narcotic of an unsuspected influence was acting upon me, and my perceptions were benumbed.

I am going to tell you now of a dream that led immediately to an odd discovery.

One night, instead of the voice I was accustomed to hear in the dark, I heard one, sweet and tender, and at the same time terrible, which said, "Your mother warns you to beware of the assassin." At the same time a light unexpectedly sprang up, and I saw Carmilla, standing, near the foot of my bed, in her white nightdress, bathed, from her chin to her feet, in one great stain of blood.

I wakened with a shriek, possessed with the one idea that Carmilla was being murdered. I remember springing from my bed, and my next recollection is that of standing on the lobby, crying for help.

Madame and Mademoiselle came scurrying out of their rooms in alarm; a lamp burned always on the lobby, and seeing me, they soon learned the cause of my terror.

I insisted on our knocking at Carmilla's door. Our knocking was unanswered.

It soon became a pounding and an uproar. We shrieked her name, but all was vain.

We all grew frightened, for the door was locked. We hurried back, in panic, to my room. There we rang the bell long and furiously. If my father's room had been at that side of the house, we would have called him up at once to our aid. But, alas! he was quite out of hearing, and to reach him involved an excursion for which we none of us had courage.

Servants, however, soon came running up the stairs; I had got on my dressing gown and slippers meanwhile, and my companions were already similarly furnished. Recognizing the voices of the servants on the lobby, we sallied out together; and having renewed, as fruitlessly, our summons at Carmilla's door, I ordered the men to force the lock. They did so, and we stood, holding our lights aloft, in the doorway, and so stared into the room.

We called her by name; but there was still no reply. We looked round the room. Everything was undisturbed. It was exactly in the state in which I had left it on bidding her good night. But Carmilla was gone.

## VIII

## SEARCH

At sight of the room, perfectly undisturbed except for our violent entrance, we began to cool a little, and soon recovered our senses sufficiently to dismiss the men. It had struck Mademoiselle that possibly Carmilla had been wakened by the uproar at her door, and in her first panic had jumped from her bed, and hid herself in a press, or behind a curtain, from which she could not, of course, emerge until the majordomo and his myrmidons[1] had withdrawn. We now recommenced our search, and began to call her name again.

It was all to no purpose. Our perplexity and agitation increased. We examined the windows, but they were secured. I implored of Carmilla, if she had concealed herself, to play this cruel trick no longer—to come out and to end our anxieties. It was all useless. I was by this time convinced that she was not in the room, nor in the dressing room, the door of which was still locked on this side. She could not have passed it. I was utterly puzzled. Had Carmilla discovered one of those secret passages which the old housekeeper said were known to exist in the schloss, although the tradition of their exact situation had been lost? A little time would, no doubt, explain all—utterly perplexed as, for the present, we were.

It was past four o'clock, and I preferred passing the remaining hours of darkness in Madame's room. Daylight brought no solution of the difficulty.

The whole household, with my father at its head, was in a state of agitation next morning. Every part of the chateau was searched. The grounds were explored. No trace of the missing lady could be discovered. The stream was about to be dragged; my father was in distraction; what a tale to have to tell the poor girl's mother on her return. I, too, was almost beside myself, though my grief was quite of a different kind.

The morning was passed in alarm and excitement. It was now one o'clock, and still no tidings. I ran up to Carmilla's room, and found her standing at her dressing table. I was astounded. I could not believe my eyes. She beckoned me to her with her pretty finger, in silence. Her face expressed extreme fear.

I ran to her in an ecstasy of joy; I kissed and embraced her again and again. I ran to the bell and rang it vehemently, to bring others to the spot who might at once relieve my father's anxiety.

"Dear Carmilla, what has become of you all this time? We have been in agonies of anxiety about you," I exclaimed. "Where have you been? How did you come back?"

1 A majordomo is the head steward of a large household, while the myrmidons are the lower servants. Here, Laura switches from the more straightforward terminology used in the previous chapter.

"Last night has been a night of wonders," she said.

"For mercy's sake, explain all you can."

"It was past two last night," she said, "when I went to sleep as usual in my bed, with my doors locked, that of the dressing room, and that opening upon the gallery. My sleep was uninterrupted, and, so far as I know, dreamless; but I woke just now on the sofa in the dressing room there, and I found the door between the rooms open, and the other door forced. How could all this have happened without my being wakened? It must have been accompanied with a great deal of noise, and I am particularly easily wakened; and how could I have been carried out of my bed without my sleep having been interrupted, I whom the slightest stir startles?"

By this time, Madame, Mademoiselle, my father, and a number of the servants were in the room. Carmilla was, of course, overwhelmed with inquiries, congratulations, and welcomes. She had but one story to tell, and seemed the least able of all the party to suggest any way of accounting for what had happened.

My father took a turn up and down the room, thinking. I saw Carmilla's eye follow him for a moment with a sly, dark glance.

When my father had sent the servants away, Mademoiselle having gone in search of a little bottle of valerian and salvolatile,[1] and there being no one now in the room with Carmilla, except my father, Madame, and myself, he came to her thoughtfully, took her hand very kindly, led her to the sofa, and sat down beside her.

"Will you forgive me, my dear, if I risk a conjecture, and ask a question?"

"Who can have a better right?" she said. "Ask what you please, and I will tell you everything. But my story is simply one of bewilderment and darkness. I know absolutely nothing. Put any question you please, but you know, of course, the limitations mamma has placed me under."

"Perfectly, my dear child. I need not approach the topics on which she desires our silence. Now, the marvel of last night consists in your having been removed from your bed and your room, without being wakened, and this removal having occurred apparently while the windows were still secured, and the two doors locked upon the inside. I will tell you my theory and ask you a question."

Carmilla was leaning on her hand dejectedly; Madame and I were listening breathlessly.

"Now, my question is this. Have you ever been suspected of walking in your sleep?"

"Never, since I was very young indeed."

"But you did walk in your sleep when you were young?"

"Yes; I know I did. I have been told so often by my old nurse."

---

1 Valerian is a root commonly used for sleep disorders. Salvolatile is an ammonia solution used as smelling salts to help patients recover from fainting.

My father smiled and nodded.

"Well, what has happened is this. You got up in your sleep, unlocked the door, not leaving the key, as usual, in the lock, but taking it out and locking it on the outside; you again took the key out, and carried it away with you to some one of the five-and-twenty rooms on this floor, or perhaps upstairs or downstairs. There are so many rooms and closets, so much heavy furniture, and such accumulations of lumber, that it would require a week to search this old house thoroughly. Do you see, now, what I mean?"

"I do, but not all," she answered.

"And how, papa, do you account for her finding herself on the sofa in the dressing room, which we had searched so carefully?"

"She came there after you had searched it, still in her sleep, and at last awoke spontaneously, and was as much surprised to find herself where she was as any one else. I wish all mysteries were as easily and innocently explained as yours, Carmilla," he said, laughing. "And so we may congratulate ourselves on the certainty that the most natural explanation of the occurrence is one that involves no drugging, no tampering with locks, no burglars, or poisoners, or witches—nothing that need alarm Carmilla, or anyone else, for our safety."

Carmilla was looking charmingly. Nothing could be more beautiful than her tints. Her beauty was, I think, enhanced by that graceful languor that was peculiar to her. I think my father was silently contrasting her looks with mine, for he said:

"I wish my poor Laura was looking more like herself," and he sighed.

So our alarms were happily ended, and Carmilla restored to her friends.

## IX

## THE DOCTOR

As Carmilla would not hear of an attendant sleeping in her room, my father arranged that a servant should sleep outside her door, so that she would not attempt to make another such excursion without being arrested at her own door.

That night passed quietly; and next morning early, the doctor, whom my father had sent for without telling me a word about it, arrived to see me.

Madame accompanied me to the library; and there the grave little doctor, with white hair and spectacles, whom I mentioned before, was waiting to receive me.

I told him my story, and as I proceeded he grew graver and graver.

We were standing, he and I, in the recess of one of the windows, facing one another. When my statement was over, he leaned with his shoulders against the wall, and with his eyes fixed on me earnestly, with an interest in which was a dash of horror.

After a minute's reflection, he asked Madame if he could see my father.

He was sent for accordingly, and as he entered, smiling, he said:

"I dare say, doctor, you are going to tell me that I am an old fool for having brought you here; I hope I am."

But his smile faded into shadow as the doctor, with a very grave face, beckoned him to him.

He and the doctor talked for some time in the same recess where I had just conferred with the physician. It seemed an earnest and argumentative conversation. The room is very large, and I and Madame stood together, burning with curiosity, at the farther end. Not a word could we hear, however, for they spoke in a very low tone, and the deep recess of the window quite concealed the doctor from view, and very nearly my father, whose foot, arm, and shoulder only could we see; and the voices were, I suppose, all the less audible for the sort of closet which the thick wall and window formed.

After a time my father's face looked into the room; it was pale, thoughtful, and, I fancied, agitated.

"Laura, dear, come here for a moment. Madame, we shan't trouble you, the doctor says, at present."

Accordingly I approached, for the first time a little alarmed; for, although I felt very weak, I did not feel ill; and strength, one always fancies, is a thing that may be picked up when we please.

My father held out his hand to me, as I drew near, but he was looking at the doctor, and he said:

"It certainly is very odd; I don't understand it quite. Laura, come here, dear; now attend to Doctor Spielsberg, and recollect yourself."

"You mentioned a sensation like that of two needles piercing the skin, somewhere about your neck, on the night when you experienced your first horrible dream. Is there still any soreness?"

"None at all," I answered.

"Can you indicate with your finger about the point at which you think this occurred?"

"Very little below my throat—here," I answered.

I wore a morning dress, which covered the place I pointed to.

"Now you can satisfy yourself," said the doctor. "You won't mind your papa's lowering your dress a very little. It is necessary, to detect a symptom of the complaint under which you have been suffering."

I acquiesced. It was only an inch or two below the edge of my collar.

"God bless me!—so it is," exclaimed my father, growing pale.

"You see it now with your own eyes," said the doctor, with a gloomy triumph.

"What is it?" I exclaimed, beginning to be frightened.

"Nothing, my dear young lady, but a small blue spot, about the size of the tip of your little finger; and now," he continued, turning to papa, "the question is what is best to be done?"

"Is there any danger?" I urged, in great trepidation.

"I trust not, my dear," answered the doctor. "I don't see why you should not recover. I don't see why you should not begin immediately to get better. That is the point at which the sense of strangulation begins?"

"Yes," I answered.

"And—recollect as well as you can—the same point was a kind of center of that thrill which you described just now, like the current of a cold stream running against you?"

"It may have been; I think it was."

"Ay, you see?" he added, turning to my father. "Shall I say a word to Madame?"

"Certainly," said my father.

He called Madame to him, and said:

"I find my young friend here far from well. It won't be of any great consequence, I hope; but it will be necessary that some steps be taken, which I will explain by-and-by; but in the meantime, Madame, you will be so good as not to let Miss Laura be alone for one moment. That is the only direction I need give for the present. It is indispensable."

"We may rely upon your kindness, Madame, I know," added my father.

Madame satisfied him eagerly.

"And you, dear Laura, I know you will observe the doctor's direction."

"I shall have to ask your opinion upon another patient, whose symptoms slightly resemble those of my daughter, that have just been detailed to you—very much milder in degree, but I believe quite of the same sort. She is a young lady—our guest; but as you say you will be passing this way again this evening, you can't do better than take your supper here, and you can then see her. She does not come down till the afternoon."

"I thank you," said the doctor. "I shall be with you, then, at about seven this evening."

And then they repeated their directions to me and to Madame, and with this parting charge my father left us, and walked out with the doctor; and I saw them pacing together up and down between the road and the moat, on the grassy platform in front of the castle, evidently absorbed in earnest conversation.

The doctor did not return. I saw him mount his horse there, take his leave, and ride away eastward through the forest.

Nearly at the same time I saw the man arrive from Dranfield[1] with the letters, and dismount and hand the bag to my father.

In the meantime, Madame and I were both busy, lost in conjecture as to the reasons of the singular and earnest direction which the doctor and my father had concurred in imposing. Madame, as she afterwards told me, was afraid the

1 In "Jane Ann Cranstoun, Countess Purgstall: A Possible Inspiration for Le Fanu's 'Carmilla,'" Matthew Gibson suggests that Dranfield is Le Fanu's reworking of the town Hainfeld from Captain Basil Hall's 1836 travel book, *Schloss Hainfeld; Or, a Winter in Lower Styria*. Gibson argues that this book was Le Fanu's main source of information on the area.

doctor apprehended a sudden seizure, and that, without prompt assistance, I might either lose my life in a fit, or at least be seriously hurt.

The interpretation did not strike me; and I fancied, perhaps luckily for my nerves, that the arrangement was prescribed simply to secure a companion, who would prevent my taking too much exercise, or eating unripe fruit, or doing any of the fifty foolish things to which young people are supposed to be prone.

About half an hour after my father came in—he had a letter in his hand—and said:

"This letter had been delayed; it is from General Spielsdorf. He might have been here yesterday, he may not come till tomorrow or he may be here today."

He put the open letter into my hand; but he did not look pleased, as he used when a guest, especially one so much loved as the General, was coming.

On the contrary, he looked as if he wished him at the bottom of the Red Sea. There was plainly something on his mind which he did not choose to divulge.

"Papa, darling, will you tell me this?" said I, suddenly laying my hand on his arm, and looking, I am sure, imploringly in his face.

"Perhaps," he answered, smoothing my hair caressingly over my eyes.

"Does the doctor think me very ill?"

"No, dear; he thinks, if right steps are taken, you will be quite well again, at least, on the high road to a complete recovery, in a day or two," he answered, a little dryly. "I wish our good friend, the General, had chosen any other time; that is, I wish you had been perfectly well to receive him."

"But do tell me, papa," I insisted, "what does he think is the matter with me?"

"Nothing; you must not plague me with questions," he answered, with more irritation than I ever remember him to have displayed before; and seeing that I looked wounded, I suppose, he kissed me, and added, "You shall know all about it in a day or two; that is, all that I know. In the meantime you are not to trouble your head about it."

He turned and left the room, but came back before I had done wondering and puzzling over the oddity of all this; it was merely to say that he was going to Karnstein, and had ordered the carriage to be ready at twelve, and that I and Madame should accompany him; he was going to see the priest who lived near those picturesque grounds, upon business, and as Carmilla had never seen them, she could follow, when she came down, with Mademoiselle, who would bring materials for what you call a picnic, which might be laid for us in the ruined castle.

At twelve o'clock, accordingly, I was ready, and not long after, my father, Madame and I set out upon our projected drive.

Passing the drawbridge we turn to the right, and follow the road over the steep Gothic bridge, westward, to reach the deserted village and ruined castle of Karnstein.

No sylvan drive can be fancied prettier. The ground breaks into gentle hills and hollows, all clothed with beautiful wood, totally destitute of the comparative formality which artificial planting and early culture and pruning impart. The irregularities of the ground often lead the road out of its course, and cause it to wind beautifully round the sides of broken hollows and the steeper sides of the hills, among varieties of ground almost inexhaustible.

Turning one of these points, we suddenly encountered our old friend, the General, riding towards us, attended by a mounted servant. His portmanteaus[1] were following in a hired wagon, such as we term a cart.

The General dismounted as we pulled up, and, after the usual greetings, was easily persuaded to accept the vacant seat in the carriage and send his horse on with his servant to the schloss.

## X

## BEREAVED

It was about ten months since we had last seen him: but that time had sufficed to make an alteration of years in his appearance. He had grown thinner; something of gloom and anxiety had taken the place of that cordial serenity which used to characterize his features. His dark blue eyes, always penetrating, now gleamed with a sterner light from under his shaggy grey eyebrows. It was not such a change as grief alone usually induces, and angrier passions seemed to have had their share in bringing it about.

We had not long resumed our drive, when the General began to talk, with his usual soldierly directness, of the bereavement, as he termed it, which he had sustained in the death of his beloved niece and ward; and he then broke out in a tone of intense bitterness and fury, inveighing against the "hellish arts" to which she had fallen a victim, and expressing, with more exasperation than piety, his wonder that Heaven should tolerate so monstrous an indulgence of the lusts and malignity of hell.

My father, who saw at once that something very extraordinary had befallen, asked him, if not too painful to him, to detail the circumstances which he thought justified the strong terms in which he expressed himself.

"I should tell you all with pleasure," said the General, "but you would not believe me."

"Why should I not?" he asked.

"Because," he answered testily, "you believe in nothing but what consists with your own prejudices and illusions. I remember when I was like you, but I have learned better."

1 Large trunks or cases; luggage.

"Try me," said my father; "I am not such a dogmatist[1] as you suppose. Besides which, I very well know that you generally require proof for what you believe, and am, therefore, very strongly predisposed to respect your conclusions."

"You are right in supposing that I have not been led lightly into a belief in the marvelous—for what I have experienced is marvelous—and I have been forced by extraordinary evidence to credit that which ran counter, diametrically, to all my theories. I have been made the dupe of a preternatural conspiracy."

Notwithstanding his professions of confidence in the General's penetration, I saw my father, at this point, glance at the General, with, as I thought, a marked suspicion of his sanity.

The General did not see it, luckily. He was looking gloomily and curiously into the glades and vistas of the woods that were opening before us.

"You are going to the Ruins of Karnstein?" he said. "Yes, it is a lucky coincidence; do you know I was going to ask you to bring me there to inspect them. I have a special object in exploring. There is a ruined chapel, ain't there, with a great many tombs of that extinct family?"

"So there are—highly interesting," said my father. "I hope you are thinking of claiming the title and estates?"

My father said this gaily, but the General did not recollect the laugh, or even the smile, which courtesy exacts for a friend's joke; on the contrary, he looked grave and even fierce, ruminating on a matter that stirred his anger and horror.

"Something very different," he said, gruffly. "I mean to unearth some of those fine people. I hope, by God's blessing, to accomplish a pious sacrilege here, which will relieve our earth of certain monsters, and enable honest people to sleep in their beds without being assailed by murderers. I have strange things to tell you, my dear friend, such as I myself would have scouted as incredible a few months since."

My father looked at him again, but this time not with a glance of suspicion—with an eye, rather, of keen intelligence and alarm.

"The house of Karnstein," he said, "has been long extinct: a hundred years at least. My dear wife was maternally descended from the Karnsteins. But the name and title have long ceased to exist. The castle is a ruin; the very village is deserted; it is fifty years since the smoke of a chimney was seen there; not a roof left."

"Quite true. I have heard a great deal about that since I last saw you; a great deal that will astonish you. But I had better relate everything in the order in which it occurred," said the General. "You saw my dear ward—my child, I may call her. No creature could have been more beautiful, and only three months ago none more blooming."

"Yes, poor thing! when I saw her last she certainly was quite lovely," said my

1 One who expresses opinions, especially of religious nature, very strongly or as if they were facts.

father. "I was grieved and shocked more than I can tell you, my dear friend; I knew what a blow it was to you."

He took the General's hand, and they exchanged a kind pressure. Tears gathered in the old soldier's eyes. He did not seek to conceal them. He said:

"We have been very old friends; I knew you would feel for me, childless as I am. She had become an object of very near interest to me, and repaid my care by an affection that cheered my home and made my life happy. That is all gone. The years that remain to me on earth may not be very long; but by God's mercy I hope to accomplish a service to mankind before I die, and to subserve[1] the vengeance of Heaven upon the fiends who have murdered my poor child in the spring of her hopes and beauty!"

"You said, just now, that you intended relating everything as it occurred," said my father. "Pray do; I assure you that it is not mere curiosity that prompts me."

By this time we had reached the point at which the Drunstall[2] road, by which the General had come, diverges from the road which we were traveling to Karnstein.

"How far is it to the ruins?" inquired the General, looking anxiously forward.

"About half a league," answered my father. "Pray let us hear the story you were so good as to promise."

## XI

## THE STORY

"With all my heart," said the General, with an effort; and after a short pause in which to arrange his subject, he commenced one of the strangest narratives I ever heard.

"My dear child was looking forward with great pleasure to the visit you had been so good as to arrange for her to your charming daughter." Here he made me a gallant but melancholy bow. "In the meantime we had an invitation to my old friend the Count Carlsfeld, whose schloss is about six leagues to the other side of Karnstein. It was to attend the series of fetes[3] which, you remember, were given by him in honor of his illustrious visitor, the Grand Duke Charles."[4]

"Yes; and very splendid, I believe, they were," said my father.

"Princely! But then his hospitalities are quite regal. He has Aladdin's lamp.[5]

1 Assist.
2 Gibson also suggests that Drunstall is Le Fanu's reworking of Purgstall, a place in Hall's travel book (14).
3 A celebration or festival.
4 Charles, Grand Duke of Baden (1786–1818).
5 I.e., he can grant any wish. A reference to *The Arabian Nights*.

The night from which my sorrow dates was devoted to a magnificent masquerade.[1] The grounds were thrown open, the trees hung with colored lamps. There was such a display of fireworks as Paris itself had never witnessed. And such music—music, you know, is my weakness—such ravishing music! The finest instrumental band, perhaps, in the world, and the finest singers who could be collected from all the great operas in Europe. As you wandered through these fantastically illuminated grounds, the moon-lighted chateau throwing a rosy light from its long rows of windows, you would suddenly hear these ravishing voices stealing from the silence of some grove, or rising from boats upon the lake. I felt myself, as I looked and listened, carried back into the romance and poetry of my early youth.

"When the fireworks were ended, and the ball beginning, we returned to the noble suite of rooms that were thrown open to the dancers. A masked ball, you know, is a beautiful sight; but so brilliant a spectacle of the kind I never saw before.

"It was a very aristocratic assembly. I was myself almost the only 'nobody' present.

"My dear child was looking quite beautiful. She wore no mask. Her excitement and delight added an unspeakable charm to her features, always lovely. I remarked a young lady, dressed magnificently, but wearing a mask, who appeared to me to be observing my ward with extraordinary interest. I had seen her, earlier in the evening, in the great hall, and again, for a few minutes, walking near us, on the terrace under the castle windows, similarly employed. A lady, also masked, richly and gravely dressed, and with a stately air, like a person of rank, accompanied her as a chaperon. Had the young lady not worn a mask, I could, of course, have been much more certain upon the question whether she was really watching my poor darling. I am now well assured that she was.

"We were now in one of the salons. My poor dear child had been dancing, and was resting a little in one of the chairs near the door; I was standing near. The two ladies I have mentioned had approached and the younger took the chair next my ward; while her companion stood beside me, and for a little time addressed herself, in a low tone, to her charge.

"Availing herself of the privilege of her mask, she turned to me, and in the tone of an old friend, and calling me by my name, opened a conversation with me, which piqued my curiosity a good deal. She referred to many scenes where she had met me—at Court, and at distinguished houses. She alluded to little incidents which I had long ceased to think of, but which, I found, had only lain in abeyance in my memory, for they instantly started into life at her touch.

"I became more and more curious to ascertain who she was, every moment. She parried my attempts to discover very adroitly and pleasantly. The knowledge she showed of many passages in my life seemed to me all but unaccountable;

1 Masked costume party.

and she appeared to take a not unnatural pleasure in foiling my curiosity, and in seeing me flounder in my eager perplexity, from one conjecture to another.

"In the meantime the young lady, whom her mother called by the odd name of Millarca, when she once or twice addressed her, had, with the same ease and grace, got into conversation with my ward.

"She introduced herself by saying that her mother was a very old acquaintance of mine. She spoke of the agreeable audacity which a mask rendered practicable; she talked like a friend; she admired her dress, and insinuated very prettily her admiration of her beauty. She amused her with laughing criticisms upon the people who crowded the ballroom, and laughed at my poor child's fun. She was very witty and lively when she pleased, and after a time they had grown very good friends, and the young stranger lowered her mask, displaying a remarkably beautiful face. I had never seen it before, neither had my dear child. But though it was new to us, the features were so engaging, as well as lovely, that it was impossible not to feel the attraction powerfully. My poor girl did so. I never saw anyone more taken with another at first sight, unless, indeed, it was the stranger herself, who seemed quite to have lost her heart to her.

"In the meantime, availing myself of the license of a masquerade, I put not a few questions to the elder lady.

"'You have puzzled me utterly,' I said, laughing. 'Is that not enough? Won't you, now, consent to stand on equal terms, and do me the kindness to remove your mask?'

"'Can any request be more unreasonable?' she replied. 'Ask a lady to yield an advantage! Beside, how do you know you should recognize me? Years make changes.'

"'As you see,' I said, with a bow, and, I suppose, a rather melancholy little laugh.

"'As philosophers tell us,' she said; 'and how do you know that a sight of my face would help you?'

"'I should take chance for that,' I answered. 'It is vain trying to make yourself out an old woman; your figure betrays you.'

"'Years, nevertheless, have passed since I saw you, rather since you saw me, for that is what I am considering. Millarca, there, is my daughter; I cannot then be young, even in the opinion of people whom time has taught to be indulgent, and I may not like to be compared with what you remember me. You have no mask to remove. You can offer me nothing in exchange.'

"'My petition is to your pity, to remove it.'

"'And mine to yours, to let it stay where it is,' she replied.

"'Well, then, at least you will tell me whether you are French or German; you speak both languages so perfectly.'

"'I don't think I shall tell you that, General; you intend a surprise, and are meditating the particular point of attack.'

"'At all events, you won't deny this,' I said, 'that being honored by your permission to converse, I ought to know how to address you. Shall I say Madame la Comtesse?'

"She laughed, and she would, no doubt, have met me with another evasion—if, indeed, I can treat any occurrence in an interview every circumstance of which was prearranged, as I now believe, with the profoundest cunning, as liable to be modified by accident.

"'As to that,' she began; but she was interrupted, almost as she opened her lips, by a gentleman, dressed in black, who looked particularly elegant and distinguished, with this drawback, that his face was the most deadly pale I ever saw, except in death. He was in no masquerade—in the plain evening dress of a gentleman; and he said, without a smile, but with a courtly and unusually low bow:—

"'Will Madame la Comtesse permit me to say a very few words which may interest her?'

"The lady turned quickly to him, and touched her lip in token of silence; she then said to me, 'Keep my place for me, General; I shall return when I have said a few words.'

"And with this injunction, playfully given, she walked a little aside with the gentleman in black, and talked for some minutes, apparently very earnestly. They then walked away slowly together in the crowd, and I lost them for some minutes.

"I spent the interval in cudgeling my brains for a conjecture as to the identity of the lady who seemed to remember me so kindly, and I was thinking of turning about and joining in the conversation between my pretty ward and the Countess's daughter, and trying whether, by the time she returned, I might not have a surprise in store for her, by having her name, title, chateau, and estates at my fingers' ends. But at this moment she returned, accompanied by the pale man in black, who said:

"'I shall return and inform Madame la Comtesse when her carriage is at the door.'

"He withdrew with a bow."

## XII

## A PETITION

"'Then we are to lose Madame la Comtesse, but I hope only for a few hours,' I said, with a low bow.

"'It may be that only, or it may be a few weeks. It was very unlucky his speaking to me just now as he did. Do you now know me?'

"I assured her I did not.

"'You shall know me,' she said, 'but not at present. We are older and better friends than, perhaps, you suspect. I cannot yet declare myself. I shall in three weeks pass your beautiful schloss, about which I have been making enquiries. I shall then look in upon you for an hour or two, and renew a friendship which I never think of without a thousand pleasant recollections. This moment a piece of news has reached me like a thunderbolt. I must set out now, and travel by a devious route, nearly a hundred miles, with all the dispatch I can possibly make. My perplexities multiply. I am only deterred by the compulsory reserve I practice as to my name from making a very singular request of you. My poor child has not quite recovered her strength. Her horse fell with her, at a hunt which she had ridden out to witness, her nerves have not yet recovered the shock, and our physician says that she must on no account exert herself for some time to come. We came here, in consequence, by very easy stages—hardly six leagues a day. I must now travel day and night, on a mission of life and death—a mission the critical and momentous nature of which I shall be able to explain to you when we meet, as I hope we shall, in a few weeks, without the necessity of any concealment.'

"She went on to make her petition, and it was in the tone of a person from whom such a request amounted to conferring, rather than seeking a favor. This was only in manner, and, as it seemed, quite unconsciously. Than the terms in which it was expressed, nothing could be more deprecatory. It was simply that I would consent to take charge of her daughter during her absence.

"This was, all things considered, a strange, not to say, an audacious request. She in some sort disarmed me, by stating and admitting everything that could be urged against it, and throwing herself entirely upon my chivalry. At the same moment, by a fatality that seems to have predetermined all that happened, my poor child came to my side, and, in an undertone, besought me to invite her new friend, Millarca, to pay us a visit. She had just been sounding her, and thought, if her mamma would allow her, she would like it extremely.

"At another time I should have told her to wait a little, until, at least, we knew who they were. But I had not a moment to think in. The two ladies assailed me together, and I must confess the refined and beautiful face of the young lady, about which there was something extremely engaging, as well as the elegance and fire of high birth, determined me; and, quite overpowered, I submitted, and undertook, too easily, the care of the young lady, whom her mother called Millarca.

"The Countess beckoned to her daughter, who listened with grave attention while she told her, in general terms, how suddenly and peremptorily she had been summoned, and also of the arrangement she had made for her under my care, adding that I was one of her earliest and most valued friends.

"I made, of course, such speeches as the case seemed to call for, and found myself, on reflection, in a position which I did not half like.

"The gentleman in black returned, and very ceremoniously conducted the lady from the room.

"The demeanor of this gentleman was such as to impress me with the conviction that the Countess was a lady of very much more importance than her modest title alone might have led me to assume.

"Her last charge to me was that no attempt was to be made to learn more about her than I might have already guessed, until her return. Our distinguished host, whose guest she was, knew her reasons.

"'But here,' she said, 'neither I nor my daughter could safely remain for more than a day. I removed my mask imprudently for a moment, about an hour ago, and, too late, I fancied you saw me. So I resolved to seek an opportunity of talking a little to you. Had I found that you had seen me, I would have thrown myself on your high sense of honor to keep my secret some weeks. As it is, I am satisfied that you did not see me; but if you now suspect, or, on reflection, should suspect, who I am, I commit myself, in like manner, entirely to your honor. My daughter will observe the same secrecy, and I well know that you will, from time to time, remind her, lest she should thoughtlessly disclose it.'

"She whispered a few words to her daughter, kissed her hurriedly twice, and went away, accompanied by the pale gentleman in black, and disappeared in the crowd.

"'In the next room,' said Millarca, 'there is a window that looks upon the hall door. I should like to see the last of mamma, and to kiss my hand to her.'

"We assented, of course, and accompanied her to the window. We looked out, and saw a handsome old-fashioned carriage, with a troop of couriers and footmen. We saw the slim figure of the pale gentleman in black, as he held a thick velvet cloak, and placed it about her shoulders and threw the hood over her head. She nodded to him, and just touched his hand with hers. He bowed low repeatedly as the door closed, and the carriage began to move.

"'She is gone,' said Millarca, with a sigh.

"'She is gone,' I repeated to myself, for the first time—in the hurried moments that had elapsed since my consent—reflecting upon the folly of my act.

"'She did not look up,' said the young lady, plaintively.

"'The Countess had taken off her mask, perhaps, and did not care to show her face,' I said; 'and she could not know that you were in the window.'

"She sighed, and looked in my face. She was so beautiful that I relented. I was sorry I had for a moment repented of my hospitality, and I determined to make her amends for the unavowed churlishness of my reception.

"The young lady, replacing her mask, joined my ward in persuading me to return to the grounds, where the concert was soon to be renewed. We did so, and walked up and down the terrace that lies under the castle windows.

Millarca became very intimate with us, and amused us with lively descriptions and stories of most of the great people whom we saw upon the terrace. I liked her more and more every minute. Her gossip without being ill-natured, was extremely diverting to me, who had been so long out of the great world. I thought what life she would give to our sometimes lonely evenings at home.

"This ball was not over until the morning sun had almost reached the horizon. It pleased the Grand Duke to dance till then, so loyal people could not go away, or think of bed.

"We had just got through a crowded saloon,[1] when my ward asked me what had become of Millarca. I thought she had been by her side, and she fancied she was by mine. The fact was, we had lost her.

"All my efforts to find her were vain. I feared that she had mistaken, in the confusion of a momentary separation from us, other people for her new friends, and had, possibly, pursued and lost them in the extensive grounds which were thrown open to us.

"Now, in its full force, I recognized a new folly in my having undertaken the charge of a young lady without so much as knowing her name; and fettered as I was by promises, of the reasons for imposing which I knew nothing, I could not even point my inquiries by saying that the missing young lady was the daughter of the Countess who had taken her departure a few hours before.

"Morning broke. It was clear daylight before I gave up my search. It was not till near two o'clock next day that we heard anything of my missing charge.

"At about that time a servant knocked at my niece's door, to say that he had been earnestly requested by a young lady, who appeared to be in great distress, to make out where she could find the General Baron Spielsdorf and the young lady his daughter, in whose charge she had been left by her mother.

"There could be no doubt, notwithstanding the slight inaccuracy, that our young friend had turned up; and so she had. Would to heaven we had lost her!

"She told my poor child a story to account for her having failed to recover us for so long. Very late, she said, she had got to the housekeeper's bedroom in despair of finding us, and had then fallen into a deep sleep which, long as it was, had hardly sufficed to recruit her strength after the fatigues of the ball.

"That day Millarca came home with us. I was only too happy, after all, to have secured so charming a companion for my dear girl."

## XIII

## THE WOODMAN

"There soon, however, appeared some drawbacks. In the first place, Millarca complained of extreme languor—the weakness that remained after her late illness—and she never emerged from her room till the afternoon was pretty far

1 Saloon or salon: a large room to entertain guests.

advanced. In the next place, it was accidentally discovered, although she always locked her door on the inside, and never disturbed the key from its place till she admitted the maid to assist at her toilet, that she was undoubtedly sometimes absent from her room in the very early morning, and at various times later in the day, before she wished it to be understood that she was stirring. She was repeatedly seen from the windows of the schloss, in the first faint grey of the morning, walking through the trees, in an easterly direction, and looking like a person in a trance. This convinced me that she walked in her sleep. But this hypothesis did not solve the puzzle. How did she pass out from her room, leaving the door locked on the inside? How did she escape from the house without unbarring door or window?

"In the midst of my perplexities, an anxiety of a far more urgent kind presented itself.

"My dear child began to lose her looks and health, and that in a manner so mysterious, and even horrible, that I became thoroughly frightened.

"She was at first visited by appalling dreams; then, as she fancied, by a specter, sometimes resembling Millarca, sometimes in the shape of a beast, indistinctly seen, walking round the foot of her bed, from side to side. Lastly came sensations. One, not unpleasant, but very peculiar, she said, resembled the flow of an icy stream against her breast. At a later time, she felt something like a pair of large needles pierce her, a little below the throat, with a very sharp pain. A few nights after, followed a gradual and convulsive sense of strangulation; then came unconsciousness."

I could hear distinctly every word the kind old General was saying, because by this time we were driving upon the short grass that spreads on either side of the road as you approach the roofless village which had not shown the smoke of a chimney for more than half a century.

You may guess how strangely I felt as I heard my own symptoms so exactly described in those which had been experienced by the poor girl who, but for the catastrophe which followed, would have been at that moment a visitor at my father's chateau. You may suppose, also, how I felt as I heard him detail habits and mysterious peculiarities which were, in fact, those of our beautiful guest, Carmilla!

A vista opened in the forest; we were on a sudden under the chimneys and gables of the ruined village, and the towers and battlements of the dismantled castle, round which gigantic trees are grouped, overhung us from a slight eminence.

In a frightened dream I got down from the carriage, and in silence, for we had each abundant matter for thinking; we soon mounted the ascent, and were among the spacious chambers, winding stairs, and dark corridors of the castle.

"And this was once the palatial residence of the Karnsteins!" said the old General at length, as from a great window he looked out across the village, and saw the wide, undulating expanse of forest. "It was a bad family, and here its bloodstained annals were written," he continued. "It is hard that they should, after death, continue to plague the human race with their atrocious lusts. That is the chapel of the Karnsteins, down there."

He pointed down to the grey walls of the Gothic building partly visible through the foliage, a little way down the steep. "And I hear the axe of a woodman," he added, "busy among the trees that surround it; he possibly may give us the information of which I am in search, and point out the grave of Mircalla, Countess of Karnstein. These rustics preserve the local traditions of great families, whose stories die out among the rich and titled so soon as the families themselves become extinct."

"We have a portrait, at home, of Mircalla, the Countess Karnstein; should you like to see it?" asked my father.

"Time enough, dear friend," replied the General. "I believe that I have seen the original; and one motive which has led me to you earlier than I at first intended, was to explore the chapel which we are now approaching."

"What! see the Countess Mircalla," exclaimed my father; "why, she has been dead more than a century!"

"Not so dead as you fancy, I am told," answered the General.

"I confess, General, you puzzle me utterly," replied my father, looking at him, I fancied, for a moment with a return of the suspicion I detected before. But although there was anger and detestation, at times, in the old General's manner, there was nothing flighty.

"There remains to me," he said, as we passed under the heavy arch of the Gothic church—for its dimensions would have justified its being so styled—"but one object which can interest me during the few years that remain to me on earth, and that is to wreak on her the vengeance which, I thank God, may still be accomplished by a mortal arm."

"What vengeance can you mean?" asked my father, in increasing amazement.

"I mean, to decapitate the monster," he answered, with a fierce flush, and a stamp that echoed mournfully through the hollow ruin, and his clenched hand was at the same moment raised, as if it grasped the handle of an axe, while he shook it ferociously in the air.

"What?" exclaimed my father, more than ever bewildered.

"To strike her head off."

"Cut her head off!"

"Aye, with a hatchet, with a spade, or with anything that can cleave through her murderous throat. You shall hear," he answered, trembling with rage. And hurrying forward he said:

"That beam will answer for a seat; your dear child is fatigued; let her be seated, and I will, in a few sentences, close my dreadful story."

The squared block of wood, which lay on the grass-grown pavement of the chapel, formed a bench on which I was very glad to seat myself, and in the meantime the General called to the woodman, who had been removing some boughs which leaned upon the old walls; and, axe in hand, the hardy old fellow stood before us.

He could not tell us anything of these monuments; but there was an old man, he said, a ranger of this forest, at present sojourning in the house of the priest, about two miles away, who could point out every monument of the old Karnstein family; and, for a trifle, he undertook to bring him back with him, if we would lend him one of our horses, in little more than half an hour.

"Have you been long employed about this forest?" asked my father of the old man.

"I have been a woodman here," he answered in his patois,[1] "under the forester, all my days; so has my father before me, and so on, as many generations as I can count up. I could show you the very house in the village here, in which my ancestors lived."

"How came the village to be deserted?" asked the General.

"It was troubled by revenants,[2] sir; several were tracked to their graves, there detected by the usual tests, and extinguished in the usual way, by decapitation, by the stake, and by burning; but not until many of the villagers were killed.

"But after all these proceedings according to law," he continued—"so many graves opened, and so many vampires deprived of their horrible animation—the village was not relieved. But a Moravian[3] nobleman, who happened to be traveling this way, heard how matters were, and being skilled—as many people are in his country—in such affairs, he offered to deliver the village from its tormentor. He did so thus: There being a bright moon that night, he ascended, shortly after sunset, the towers of the chapel here, from whence he could distinctly see the churchyard beneath him; you can see it from that window. From this point he watched until he saw the vampire come out of his grave, and place near it the linen clothes in which he had been folded, and then glide away towards the village to plague its inhabitants.

"The stranger, having seen all this, came down from the steeple, took the linen wrappings of the vampire, and carried them up to the top of the tower, which he again mounted. When the vampire returned from his prowlings and missed his clothes, he cried furiously to the Moravian, whom he saw at the summit of the tower, and who, in reply, beckoned him to ascend and take them. Whereupon the vampire, accepting his invitation, began to climb the steeple, and so soon as he had reached the battlements, the Moravian, with a stroke of his sword, clove his skull in twain, hurling him down to the churchyard, whither, descending by the winding stairs, the stranger followed and cut

1 Common dialect of a region.

2 Folklore term for an animated corpse, and sometimes used to refer to vampires.

3 From the region of Moravia, now in the Czech Republic.

his head off, and next day delivered it and the body to the villagers, who duly impaled and burnt them.

"This Moravian nobleman had authority from the then head of the family to remove the tomb of Mircalla, Countess Karnstein, which he did effectually, so that in a little while its site was quite forgotten."

"Can you point out where it stood?" asked the General, eagerly.

The forester shook his head, and smiled.

"Not a soul living could tell you that now," he said; "besides, they say her body was removed; but no one is sure of that either."

Having thus spoken, as time pressed, he dropped his axe and departed, leaving us to hear the remainder of the General's strange story.

## XIV

## THE MEETING

"My beloved child," he resumed, "was now growing rapidly worse. The physician who attended her had failed to produce the slightest impression on her disease, for such I then supposed it to be. He saw my alarm, and suggested a consultation. I called in an abler physician, from Gratz. Several days elapsed before he arrived. He was a good and pious, as well as a learned man. Having seen my poor ward together, they withdrew to my library to confer and discuss. I, from the adjoining room, where I awaited their summons, heard these two gentlemen's voices raised in something sharper than a strictly philosophical discussion. I knocked at the door and entered. I found the old physician from Gratz maintaining his theory. His rival was combating it with undisguised ridicule, accompanied with bursts of laughter. This unseemly manifestation subsided and the altercation ended on my entrance.

"'Sir,' said my first physician, 'my learned brother seems to think that you want a conjuror, and not a doctor.'

"'Pardon me,' said the old physician from Gratz, looking displeased, 'I shall state my own view of the case in my own way another time. I grieve, Monsieur le General, that by my skill and science I can be of no use. Before I go I shall do myself the honor to suggest something to you.'

"He seemed thoughtful, and sat down at a table and began to write. Profoundly disappointed, I made my bow, and as I turned to go, the other doctor pointed over his shoulder to his companion who was writing, and then, with a shrug, significantly touched his forehead.

"This consultation, then, left me precisely where I was. I walked out into the grounds, all but distracted. The doctor from Gratz, in ten or fifteen minutes, overtook me. He apologized for having followed me, but said that he could not conscientiously take his leave without a few words more. He told me that he could not be mistaken; no natural disease exhibited the same symptoms; and that death was already very near. There remained, however, a day, or possibly two, of life. If the fatal seizure were at once arrested, with great care and skill her strength might possibly return. But all hung now upon the confines of the irrevocable. One more assault might extinguish the last spark of vitality which is, every moment, ready to die.

"'And what is the nature of the seizure you speak of?' I entreated.

"'I have stated all fully in this note, which I place in your hands upon the distinct condition that you send for the nearest clergyman, and open my letter in his presence, and on no account read it till he is with you; you would despise it else, and it is a matter of life and death. Should the priest fail you, then, indeed, you may read it.'

"He asked me, before taking his leave finally, whether I would wish to see a man curiously learned upon the very subject, which, after I had read his letter, would probably interest me above all others, and he urged me earnestly to invite him to visit him there; and so took his leave.

"The ecclesiastic was absent, and I read the letter by myself. At another time, or in another case, it might have excited my ridicule. But into what quackeries will not people rush for a last chance, where all accustomed means have failed, and the life of a beloved object is at stake?

"Nothing, you will say, could be more absurd than the learned man's letter. It was monstrous enough to have consigned him to a madhouse. He said that the patient was suffering from the visits of a vampire! The punctures which she described as having occurred near the throat, were, he insisted, the insertion of those two long, thin, and sharp teeth which, it is well known, are peculiar to vampires; and there could be no doubt, he added, as to the well-defined presence of the small livid mark which all concurred in describing as that induced by the demon's lips, and every symptom described by the sufferer was in exact conformity with those recorded in every case of a similar visitation.

"Being myself wholly skeptical as to the existence of any such portent as the vampire, the supernatural theory of the good doctor furnished, in my opinion, but another instance of learning and intelligence oddly associated with some one hallucination. I was so miserable, however, that, rather than try nothing, I acted upon the instructions of the letter.

"I concealed myself in the dark dressing room, that opened upon the poor patient's room, in which a candle was burning, and watched there till she was fast asleep. I stood at the door, peeping through the small crevice, my sword laid on the table beside me, as my directions prescribed, until, a little after one, I saw a large black object, very ill-defined, crawl, as it seemed to me, over the foot of the bed, and swiftly spread itself up to the poor girl's throat, where it swelled, in a moment, into a great, palpitating mass.

"For a few moments I had stood petrified. I now sprang forward, with my sword in my hand. The black creature suddenly contracted towards the foot of the bed, glided over it, and, standing on the floor about a yard below the foot of the bed, with a glare of skulking ferocity and horror fixed on me, I saw Millarca. Speculating I know not what, I struck at her instantly with my sword; but I saw her standing near the door, unscathed. Horrified, I pursued, and struck again. She was gone; and my sword flew to shivers against the door.

"I can't describe to you all that passed on that horrible night. The whole house was up and stirring. The specter Millarca was gone. But her victim was sinking fast, and before the morning dawned, she died."

The old General was agitated. We did not speak to him. My father walked to some little distance, and began reading the inscriptions on the tombstones; and thus occupied, he strolled into the door of a side chapel to prosecute his researches. The General leaned against the wall, dried his eyes, and sighed heavily. I was relieved on hearing the voices of Carmilla and Madame, who were at that moment approaching. The voices died away.

In this solitude, having just listened to so strange a story, connected, as it was, with the great and titled dead, whose monuments were moldering among the dust and ivy round us, and every incident of which bore so awfully upon my own mysterious case—in this haunted spot, darkened by the towering foliage that rose on every side, dense and high above its noiseless walls—a horror began to steal over me, and my heart sank as I thought that my friends were, after all, not about to enter and disturb this triste[1] and ominous scene.

The old General's eyes were fixed on the ground, as he leaned with his hand upon the basement of a shattered monument.

Under a narrow, arched doorway, surmounted by one of those demoniacal grotesques in which the cynical and ghastly fancy of old Gothic carving delights, I saw very gladly the beautiful face and figure of Carmilla enter the shadowy chapel.

I was just about to rise and speak, and nodded smiling, in answer to her peculiarly engaging smile; when with a cry, the old man by my side caught up the woodman's hatchet, and started forward. On seeing him a brutalized change came over her features. It was an instantaneous and horrible transformation, as she made a crouching step backwards. Before I could utter a scream, he struck at her with all his force, but she dived under his blow, and unscathed, caught him in her tiny grasp by the wrist. He struggled for a moment to release his arm, but his hand opened, the axe fell to the ground, and the girl was gone.

He staggered against the wall. His grey hair stood upon his head, and a moisture shone over his face, as if he were at the point of death.

The frightful scene had passed in a moment. The first thing I recollect after, is Madame standing before me, and impatiently repeating again and again, the question, "Where is Mademoiselle Carmilla?"

---

1 Sad.

I answered at length, "I don't know—I can't tell—she went there," and I pointed to the door through which Madame had just entered; "only a minute or two since."

"But I have been standing there, in the passage, ever since Mademoiselle Carmilla entered; and she did not return."

She then began to call "Carmilla," through every door and passage and from the windows, but no answer came.

"She called herself Carmilla?" asked the General, still agitated.

"Carmilla, yes," I answered.

"Aye," he said; "that is Millarca. That is the same person who long ago was called Mircalla, Countess Karnstein. Depart from this accursed ground, my poor child, as quickly as you can. Drive to the clergyman's house, and stay there till we come. Begone! May you never behold Carmilla more; you will not find her here."

## XV

## ORDEAL AND EXECUTION

As he spoke one of the strangest looking men I ever beheld entered the chapel at the door through which Carmilla had made her entrance and her exit. He was tall, narrow-chested, stooping, with high shoulders, and dressed in black. His face was brown and dried in with deep furrows; he wore an oddly-shaped hat with a broad leaf. His hair, long and grizzled, hung on his shoulders. He wore a pair of gold spectacles, and walked slowly, with an odd shambling gait, with his face sometimes turned up to the sky, and sometimes bowed down towards the ground, seemed to wear a perpetual smile; his long thin arms were swinging, and his lank hands, in old black gloves ever so much too wide for them, waving and gesticulating in utter abstraction.

"The very man!" exclaimed the General, advancing with manifest delight. "My dear Baron, how happy I am to see you, I had no hope of meeting you so soon." He signed to my father, who had by this time returned, and leading the fantastic old gentleman, whom he called the Baron to meet him. He introduced him formally, and they at once entered into earnest conversation. The stranger took a roll of paper from his pocket, and spread it on the worn surface of a tomb that stood by. He had a pencil case in his fingers, with which he traced imaginary lines from point to point on the paper, which from their often glancing from it, together, at certain points of the building, I concluded to be a plan of the chapel. He accompanied, what I may term, his lecture, with occasional readings from a dirty little book, whose yellow leaves were closely written over.

They sauntered together down the side aisle, opposite to the spot where I was standing, conversing as they went; then they began measuring distances by paces, and finally they all stood together, facing a piece of the sidewall, which they began to examine with great minuteness; pulling off the ivy that clung over it, and rapping the plaster with the ends of their sticks, scraping here, and knocking there. At length they ascertained the existence of a broad marble tablet, with letters carved in relief upon it.

With the assistance of the woodman, who soon returned, a monumental inscription, and carved escutcheon, were disclosed. They proved to be those of the long lost monument of Mircalla, Countess Karnstein.

The old General, though not I fear given to the praying mood, raised his hands and eyes to heaven, in mute thanksgiving for some moments.

"Tomorrow," I heard him say; "the commissioner will be here, and the Inquisition will be held according to law."

Then turning to the old man with the gold spectacles, whom I have described, he shook him warmly by both hands and said:

"Baron, how can I thank you? How can we all thank you? You will have delivered this region from a plague that has scourged its inhabitants for more than a century. The horrible enemy, thank God, is at last tracked."

My father led the stranger aside, and the General followed. I know that he had led them out of hearing, that he might relate my case, and I saw them glance often quickly at me, as the discussion proceeded.

My father came to me, kissed me again and again, and leading me from the chapel, said:

"It is time to return, but before we go home, we must add to our party the good priest, who lives but a little way from this; and persuade him to accompany us to the schloss."

In this quest we were successful: and I was glad, being unspeakably fatigued when we reached home. But my satisfaction was changed to dismay, on discovering that there were no tidings of Carmilla. Of the scene that had occurred in the ruined chapel, no explanation was offered to me, and it was clear that it was a secret which my father for the present determined to keep from me.

The sinister absence of Carmilla made the remembrance of the scene more horrible to me. The arrangements for the night were singular. Two servants, and Madame were to sit up in my room that night; and the ecclesiastic with my father kept watch in the adjoining dressing room.

The priest had performed certain solemn rites that night, the purport of which I did not understand any more than I comprehended the reason of this extraordinary precaution taken for my safety during sleep.

I saw all clearly a few days later.

The disappearance of Carmilla was followed by the discontinuance of my nightly sufferings.

You have heard, no doubt, of the appalling superstition that prevails in

Upper and Lower Styria, in Moravia, Silesia, in Turkish Serbia, in Poland, even in Russia;[1] the superstition, so we must call it, of the Vampire.

If human testimony, taken with every care and solemnity, judicially, before commissions innumerable, each consisting of many members, all chosen for integrity and intelligence, and constituting reports more voluminous perhaps than exist upon any one other class of cases, is worth anything, it is difficult to deny, or even to doubt the existence of such a phenomenon as the Vampire.

For my part I have heard no theory by which to explain what I myself have witnessed and experienced, other than that supplied by the ancient and well-attested belief of the country.

The next day the formal proceedings took place in the Chapel of Karnstein.

The grave of the Countess Mircalla was opened; and the General and my father recognized each his perfidious and beautiful guest, in the face now disclosed to view. The features, though a hundred and fifty years had passed since her funeral, were tinted with the warmth of life. Her eyes were open; no cadaverous smell exhaled from the coffin. The two medical men, one officially present, the other on the part of the promoter of the inquiry, attested the marvelous fact that there was a faint but appreciable respiration, and a corresponding action of the heart. The limbs were perfectly flexible, the flesh elastic; and the leaden coffin floated with blood, in which to a depth of seven inches, the body lay immersed.

Here then, were all the admitted signs and proofs of vampirism. The body, therefore, in accordance with the ancient practice, was raised, and a sharp stake driven through the heart of the vampire, who uttered a piercing shriek at the moment, in all respects such as might escape from a living person in the last agony. Then the head was struck off, and a torrent of blood flowed from the severed neck. The body and head were next placed on a pile of wood, and reduced to ashes, which were thrown upon the river and borne away, and that territory has never since been plagued by the visits of a vampire.

My father has a copy of the report of the Imperial Commission, with the signatures of all who were present at these proceedings, attached in verification of the statement. It is from this official paper that I have summarized my account of this last shocking scene.

## XVI

## CONCLUSION

I write all this you suppose with composure. But far from it; I cannot think of it without agitation. Nothing but your earnest desire so repeatedly expressed, could have induced me to sit down to a task that has unstrung my nerves for months to come, and reinduced a shadow of the unspeakable horror which

1 These are all historic names for places in Eastern Europe with folklore traditions of vampires.

years after my deliverance continued to make my days and nights dreadful, and solitude insupportably terrific.

Let me add a word or two about that quaint Baron Vordenburg, to whose curious lore we were indebted for the discovery of the Countess Mircalla's grave.

He had taken up his abode in Gratz, where, living upon a mere pittance, which was all that remained to him of the once princely estates of his family, in Upper Styria, he devoted himself to the minute and laborious investigation of the marvelously authenticated tradition of Vampirism. He had at his fingers' ends all the great and little works upon the subject.

"Magia Posthuma," "Phlegon de Mirabilibus," "Augustinus de cura pro Mortuis," "Philosophicae et Christianae Cogitationes de Vampiris,"[1] by John Christofer Herenberg; and a thousand others, among which I remember only a few of those which he lent to my father. He had a voluminous digest of all the judicial cases, from which he had extracted a system of principles that appear to govern—some always, and others occasionally only—the condition of the vampire. I may mention, in passing, that the deadly pallor attributed to that sort of revenants, is a mere melodramatic fiction. They present, in the grave, and when they show themselves in human society, the appearance of healthy life. When disclosed to light in their coffins, they exhibit all the symptoms that are enumerated as those which proved the vampire-life of the long-dead Countess Karnstein.

How they escape from their graves and return to them for certain hours every day, without displacing the clay or leaving any trace of disturbance in the state of the coffin or the cerements, has always been admitted to be utterly inexplicable. The amphibious existence of the vampire is sustained by daily renewed slumber in the grave. Its horrible lust for living blood supplies the vigor of its waking existence. The vampire is prone to be fascinated with an engrossing vehemence, resembling the passion of love, by particular persons. In pursuit of these it will exercise inexhaustible patience and stratagem, for access to a particular object may be obstructed in a hundred ways. It will never desist until it has satiated its passion, and drained the very life of its coveted victim. But it will, in these cases, husband and protract its murderous enjoyment with the refinement of an epicure, and heighten it by the gradual approaches of an artful courtship. In these cases it seems to yearn for something like sympathy and consent. In ordinary ones it goes direct to its object, overpowers with violence, and strangles and exhausts often at a single feast.

The vampire is, apparently, subject, in certain situations, to special conditions. In the particular instance of which I have given you a relation, Mircalla seemed to be limited to a name which, if not her real one, should at least reproduce, without the omission or addition of a single letter, those, as we say, anagrammatically, which compose it.

---

1 Well-known works on vampires originally published in German in 1733.

Carmilla did this; so did Millarca.

My father related to the Baron Vordenburg, who remained with us for two or three weeks after the expulsion of Carmilla, the story about the Moravian nobleman and the vampire at Karnstein churchyard, and then he asked the Baron how he had discovered the exact position of the long-concealed tomb of the Countess Mircalla? The Baron's grotesque features puckered up into a mysterious smile; he looked down, still smiling on his worn spectacle case and fumbled with it. Then looking up, he said:

"I have many journals, and other papers, written by that remarkable man; the most curious among them is one treating of the visit of which you speak, to Karnstein. The tradition, of course, discolors and distorts a little. He might have been termed a Moravian nobleman, for he had changed his abode to that territory, and was, beside, a noble. But he was, in truth, a native of Upper Styria. It is enough to say that in very early youth he had been a passionate and favored lover of the beautiful Mircalla, Countess Karnstein. Her early death plunged him into inconsolable grief. It is the nature of vampires to increase and multiply, but according to an ascertained and ghostly law.

"Assume, at starting, a territory perfectly free from that pest. How does it begin, and how does it multiply itself? I will tell you. A person, more or less wicked, puts an end to himself. A suicide, under certain circumstances, becomes a vampire. That specter visits living people in their slumbers; they die, and almost invariably, in the grave, develop into vampires. This happened in the case of the beautiful Mircalla, who was haunted by one of those demons. My ancestor, Vordenburg, whose title I still bear, soon discovered this, and in the course of the studies to which he devoted himself, learned a great deal more.

"Among other things, he concluded that suspicion of vampirism would probably fall, sooner or later, upon the dead Countess, who in life had been his idol. He conceived a horror, be she what she might, of her remains being profaned by the outrage of a posthumous execution. He has left a curious paper to prove that the vampire, on its expulsion from its amphibious existence, is projected into a far more horrible life; and he resolved to save his once beloved Mircalla from this.

"He adopted the stratagem of a journey here, a pretended removal of her remains, and a real obliteration of her monument. When age had stolen upon him, and from the vale of years, he looked back on the scenes he was leaving, he considered, in a different spirit, what he had done, and a horror took possession of him. He made the tracings and notes which have guided me to the very spot, and drew up a confession of the deception that he had practiced. If he had intended any further action in this matter, death prevented him; and the hand of a remote descendant has, too late for many, directed the pursuit to the lair of the beast."

We talked a little more, and among other things he said was this:

"One sign of the vampire is the power of the hand. The slender hand of Mircalla closed like a vice of steel on the General's wrist when he raised the hatchet to strike. But its power is not confined to its grasp; it leaves a numbness in the limb it seizes, which is slowly, if ever, recovered from."

The following Spring my father took me a tour through Italy. We remained away for more than a year. It was long before the terror of recent events subsided; and to this hour the image of Carmilla returns to memory with ambiguous alternations—sometimes the playful, languid, beautiful girl; sometimes the writhing fiend I saw in the ruined church; and often from a reverie I have started, fancying I heard the light step of Carmilla at the drawing room door.

THE END

# Eric Stenbock

(1860–1895)

Son of a Swedish aristocrat and a wealthy heiress of a Manchester cotton manufacturer, Count Eric Stenbock grew up privileged. His father died when he was only one and his maternal grandfather when he was six, leaving him their estates. He attended Oxford but never completed his studies. He was strongly influenced by the Pre-Raphaelites, the aesthetes, and the decadents. In 1885, he inherited his title from his paternal grandfather and came into possession of family estates in Estonia. Throughout his adult life, Stenbock struggled with alcoholism and drug addiction. A noted eccentric, he kept a zoo in his garden and traveled with a dog, a monkey, and a life-sized doll. His tale "The True Story of a Vampire" is an obvious reworking of Le Fanu's *Carmilla*, but it also shows a response to the late nineteenth-century fears of degeneration.

# "The True Story of a Vampire"

(1894)

Vampire stories are generally located in Styria;[1] mine is also. Styria is by no means the romantic kind of place described by those who have certainly never been there. It is a flat, uninteresting country, only celebrated for its turkeys, its capons, and the stupidity of its inhabitants. Vampires generally arrive at night, in carriages drawn by two black horses.

Our Vampire arrived by the commonplace means of the railway train, and in the afternoon.

You must think I am joking, or perhaps that by the word "Vampire" I mean a financial vampire.

No, I am quite serious. The Vampire of whom I am speaking, who laid waste our hearth and home, was a real vampire.

1 Like Le Fanu, Stenbock sets his tale in this state in southeast Austria on the border with Hungary.

Vampires are generally described as dark, sinister-looking, and singularly handsome. Our Vampire was, on the contrary, rather fair, and certainly was not at first sight sinister-looking, and though decidedly attractive in appearance, not what one would call singularly handsome.

Yes, he desolated our home, killed my brother—the one object of my adoration—also my dear father. Yet, at the same time, I must say that I myself came under the spell of his fascination, and, in spite of all, have no ill-will towards him now.

Doubtless you have read in the papers passim[1] of "the Baroness and her beasts." It is to tell how I came to spend most of my useless wealth on an asylum for stray animals that I am writing this.

I am old now; what happened then was when I was a little girl of about thirteen. I will begin by describing our household. We were Poles: our name was Wronski: we lived in Styria, where we had a castle. Our household was very limited. It consisted, with the exclusion of domestics, of only my father, our governess—a worthy Belgian named Mademoiselle Vonnaert—my brother, and myself. Let me begin with my father: he was old and both my brother and I were children of his old age. Of my mother I remember nothing: she died in giving birth to my brother, who was only one year, or not as much, younger than my self. Our father was studious, continually occupied in reading books, chiefly on recondite subjects and in all kinds of unknown languages.

He had a long white beard, and wore habitually a black velvet skull-cap.

How kind he was to us! It was more than I could tell. Still it was not I who was the favourite.

His whole heart went out to Gabriel—Gabryel as we spelt it in Polish. He was always called by the Russian abbreviation Gavril—I mean, of course, my brother, who had a resemblance to the only portrait of my mother, a slight chalk sketch which hung in my father's study. But I was by no means jealous: my brother was and has been the only love of my life. It is for his sake that I am now keeping in Westbourne Park a home for stray cats and dogs.

I was at that time, as I said before, a little girl; my name was Carmela. My long tangled hair was always all over the place, and never would be combed straight. I was not pretty—at least, looking at a photograph of me at that time. I do not think I could describe myself as such. Yet at the same time, when I look at the photograph, I think my expression may have been pleasing to some people: irregular features, large mouth, and large wild eyes.

I was by way of being naughty—not so naughty as Gabriel in the opinion of Mlle Vonnaert. Mlle Vonnaert, I may intercalate,[2] was a wholly excellent person, middle-aged, who really did speak good French, although she was a Belgian, and could also make herself understood in German, which, as you may or may not know, is the current language of Styria.

1 Allusions or references in a published work.

2 To insert something, usually in reference to a calendar.

I find it difficult to describe my brother Gabriel; there was something about him strange and superhuman, or perhaps I should rather say praeterhuman, something between the animal and the divine. Perhaps the Greek idea of the Faun might illustrate what I mean: but that will not do either. He had large, wild, gazelle-like eyes: his hair, like mine, was in a perpetual tangle—that point he had in common with me, and indeed, as I afterwards heard, our mother having been of gipsy[1] race, it will account for much of the innate wildness there was in our natures. I was wild enough, but Gabriel was much wilder. Nothing would induce him to put on shoes and stockings, except on Sundays—when he also allowed his hair to be combed, but only by me. How shall I describe the grace of that lovely mouth, shaped verily "en arc d'amour."[2] I always think of the text in the Psalm, "Grace is shed forth on thy lips, therefore has God blessed thee eternally"[3]—lips that seemed to exhale the very breath of life. Then that beautiful, lithe, living, elastic form!

He could run faster than any deer: spring like a squirrel to the topmost branch of a tree: he might have stood for the sign and symbol of vitality itself. But seldom could he be induced by Mlle Vonnaert to learn lessons; but when he did so, he learnt with extraordinary quickness. He would play upon every conceivable instrument, holding a violin here, there, and everywhere except the right place: manufacturing instruments for himself out of reeds—even sticks. Mlle Vonnaert made futile efforts to induce him to learn to play the piano. I suppose he was what was called spoilt, though merely in the superficial sense of the word. Our father allowed him to indulge in every caprice.

One of his peculiarities, when quite a little child, was horror at the sight of meat. Nothing on earth would induce him to taste it. Another thing which was particularly remarkable about him was his extraordinary power over animals. Everything seemed to come tame to his hand. Birds would sit on his shoulder. Then sometimes Mlle Vonnaert and I would lose him in the woods—he would suddenly dart away. Then we would find him singing softly or whistling to himself, with all manner of woodland creatures around him—hedgehogs, little foxes, wild rabbits, marmots, squirrels, and such like. He would frequently bring these things home with him and insist on keeping them. This strange menagerie was the terror of poor Mlle Vonnaert's heart. He chose to live in a little room at the top of a turret; but which, instead of going upstairs, he chose to reach by means of a very tall chestnut-tree, through the window. But in contradiction of all this, it was his custom to serve every Sunday Mass in the parish church, with hair nicely combed and with white surplice and red cassock. He looked as demure and tamed as possible. Then came the element of the divine. What an expression of ecstasy there was in those glorious eyes!

1 Now considered a racist and derogatory term, in the nineteenth century, the word "gypsy" was commonly used in reference to the Romany.

2 Literally, "arc of love." Gabriel has a cupid's bow–shaped mouth.

3 Psalm 45:2. The verse should read "Grace has anointed your lips, therefore God has blessed you forever."

Thus far I have not been speaking about the Vampire. However, let me begin with my narrative at last. One day my father had to go to the neighbouring town—as he frequently had. This time he returned accompanied by a guest. The gentleman, he said, had missed his train, through the late arrival of another at our station, which was a junction, and he would therefore, as trains were not frequent in our parts, have had to wait there all night. He had joined in conversation with my father in the too-late-arriving train from the town: and had consequently accepted my father's invitation to stay the night at our house. But of course, you know, in those out-of-the-way parts we are almost patriarchal in our hospitality.

He was announced under the name of Count Vardalek—the name being Hungarian. But he spoke German well enough: not with the monotonous accentuation of Hungarians, but rather, if anything, with a slight Slavonic intonation. His voice was peculiarly soft and insinuating. We soon afterwards found that he could talk Polish, and Mlle Vonnaert vouched for his good French.

Indeed he seemed to know all languages. But let me give my first impressions. He was rather tall with fair wavy hair, rather long, which accentuated a certain effeminacy about his smooth face.

His figure had something—I cannot say what—serpentine about it. The features were refined; and he had long, slender, subtle, magnetic-looking hands, a somewhat long sinuous nose, a graceful mouth, and an attractive smile, which belied the intense sadness of the expression of the eyes. When he arrived his eyes were half closed—indeed they were habitually so—so that I could not decide their color. He looked worn and wearied. I could not possibly guess his age.

Suddenly Gabriel burst into the room: a yellow butterfly was clinging to his hair. He was carrying in his arms a little squirrel. Of course he was barelegged as usual. The stranger looked up at his approach; then I noticed his eyes. They were green: they seemed to dilate and grow larger. Gabriel stood stock-still, with a startled look, like that of a bird fascinated by a serpent.

But nevertheless he held out his hand to the newcomer Vardalek, taking his hand—I don't know why I noticed this trivial thing—pressed the pulse with his forefinger. Suddenly Gabriel darted from the room and rushed upstairs, going to his turret-room this time by the staircase instead of the tree. I was in terror what the Count might think of him. Great was my relief when he came down in his velvet Sunday suit, and shoes and stockings. I combed his hair, and set him generally right.

When the stranger came down to dinner his appearance had somewhat altered; he looked much younger. There was an elasticity of the skin, combined with a delicate complexion, rarely to be found in a man. Before, he had struck me as being very pale.

Well, at dinner we were all charmed with him, especially my father. He seemed to be thoroughly acquainted with all my father's particular hobbies.

Once, when my father was relating some of his military experiences, he said something about a drummer-boy who was wounded in battle. His eyes opened completely again and dilated: this time with a particularly disagreeable expression, dull and dead, yet at the same time animated by some horrible excitement. But this was only momentary.

The chief subject of his conversation with my father was about certain curious mystical books which my father had just lately picked up, and which he could not make out, but Vardalek seemed completely to understand. At dessert-time my father asked him if he were in a great hurry to reach his destination: if not, would he not stay with us a little while: though our place was out of the way, he would find much that would interest him in his library.

He answered, "I am in no hurry. I have no particular reason for going to that place at all, and if I can be of service to you in deciphering these books, I shall be only too glad." He added with a smile which was bitter, very very bitter: "You see I am a cosmopolitan, a wanderer on the face of the earth."

After dinner my father asked him if he played the piano. He said, "Yes, I can a little," and he sat down at the piano. Then he played a Hungarian csardas[1]—wild, rhapsodic, wonderful.

That is the music which makes men mad. He went on in the same strain.

Gabriel stood stock-still by the piano, his eyes dilated and fixed, his form quivering. At last he said very slowly, at one particular motive—for want of a better word you may call it the relâche[2] of a csardas, by which I mean that point where the original quasi-slow movement begins again—"Yes, I think I could play that."

Then he quickly fetched his fiddle and self-made xylophone, and did, actually alternating the instruments, render the same very well indeed.

Vardalek looked at him, and said in a very sad voice, "Poor child! you have the soul of music within you."

I could not understand why he should seem to commiserate instead of congratulate Gabriel on what certainly showed an extraordinary talent.

Gabriel was shy even as the wild animals who were tame to him. Never before had he taken to a stranger. Indeed, as a rule, if any stranger came to the house by any chance, he would hide himself, and I had to bring him up his food to the turret chamber. You may imagine what was my surprise when I saw him walking about hand in hand with Vardalek the next morning, in the garden, talking lively with him, and showing his collection of pet animals, which he had gathered from the woods, and for which we had had to fit up a regular zoological gardens. He seemed utterly under the domination of Vardalek. What surprised us was (for otherwise we liked the stranger, especially for being kind to him) that he seemed, though not noticeably at first—except perhaps to me,

1 Traditional Hungarian folk dance.

2 Rest or break.

who noticed everything with regard to him—to be gradually losing his general health and vitality. He did not become pale as yet; but there was a certain languor about his movements which certainly there was by no means before.

My father got more and more devoted to Count Vardalek. He helped him in his studies: and my father would hardly allow him to go away, which he did sometimes—to Trieste,[1] he said: he always came back, bringing us presents of strange Oriental jewelry or textures.

I knew all kinds of people came to Trieste, Orientals[2] included. Still, there was a strangeness and magnificence about these things which I was sure even then could not possibly have come from such a place as Trieste, memorable to me chiefly for its necktie shops.

When Vardalek was away, Gabriel was continually asking for him and talking about him. Then at the same time he seemed to regain his old vitality and spirits. Vardalek always returned looking much older, wan, and weary. Gabriel would rush to meet him, and kiss him on the mouth. Then he gave a slight shiver: and after a little while began to look quite young again.

Things continued like this for some time. My father would not hear of Vardalek's going away permanently. He came to be an inmate of our house. I indeed, and Mlle Vonnaert also, could not help noticing what a difference there was altogether about Gabriel. But my father seemed totally blind to it.

One night I had gone downstairs to fetch something which I had left in the drawing-room. As I was going up again I passed Vardalek's room. He was playing on a piano, which had been specially put there for him, one of Chopin's nocturnes,[3] very beautifully: I stopped, leaning on the banisters to listen.

Something white appeared on the dark staircase. We believed in ghosts in our part. I was transfixed with terror, and clung to the ballisters. What was my astonishment to see Gabriel walking slowly down the staircase, his eyes fixed as though in a trance! This terrified me even more than a ghost would. Could I believe my senses? Could that be Gabriel?

I simply could not move. Gabriel, clad in his long white night-shirt, came downstairs and opened the door. He left it open. Vardalek still continued playing, but talked as he played.

He said—this time speaking in Polish—Nie umiem wyrazic jak ciechi kocham—"My darling, I fain would spare thee: but thy life is my life, and I must live, I who would rather die. Will God not have any mercy on me? Oh! Oh! life; oh, the torture of life!" Here he struck one agonized and strange chord, then continued playing softly, "O, Gabriel, my beloved! my life, yes life—oh, why life? I am sure this is but a little that I demand of thee. Sorely thy superabundance

1 City in northeastern Italy.

2 Currently considered to be an offensive term, in the nineteenth century, Oriental referred to countries spanning the regions from Asia to the Middle East.

3 Famous solo piano pieces written between 1827 and 1846. Nocturnes generally feature a melancholy mood.

of life can spare little to one who is already dead. No, stay," he said now almost harshly, "what must be, must be!"

Gabriel stood there quite still, with the same fixed vacant expression, in the room. He was evidently walking in his sleep. Vardalek played on: then said, "Ah!" with a sign of terrible agony. Then very gently, "Go now, Gabriel; it is enough." And Gabriel went out of the room and ascended the staircase at the same slow pace, with the same unconscious stare. Vardalek struck the piano, and although he did not play loudly, it seemed as though the strings would break. You never heard music so strange and so heart-rending!

I only know I was found by Mlle Vonnaert in the morning, in an unconscious state, at the foot of the stairs. Was it a dream after all? I am sure now that it was not. I thought then it might be, and said nothing to anyone about it. Indeed, what could I say?

Well, to let me cut a long story short, Gabriel, who had never known a moment's sickness in his life, grew ill: and we had to send to Gratz[1] for a doctor, who could give no explanation of Gabriel's strange illness. Gradual wasting away, he said: absolutely no organic complaint. What could this mean?

My father at last became conscious of the fact that Gabriel was ill. His anxiety was fearful. The last trace of grey faded from his hair, and it became quite white. We sent to Vienna for doctors.

But all with the same result.

Gabriel was generally unconscious, and when conscious, only seemed to recognize Vardalek, who sat continually by his bedside, nursing him with the utmost tenderness.

One day I was alone in the room: and Vardalek cried suddenly, almost fiercely, "Send for a priest at once, at once," he repeated. "It is now almost too late!"

Gabriel stretched out his arms spasmodically, and put them round Vardalek's neck. This was the only movement he had made, for some time. Vardalek bent down and kissed him on the lips.

I rushed downstairs: and the priest was sent for. When I came back Vardalek was not there. The priest administered extreme unction. I think Gabriel was already dead, although we did not think so at the time.

Vardalek had utterly disappeared; and when we looked for him he was nowhere to be found; nor have I seen or heard of him since.

My father died very soon afterwards: suddenly aged, and bent down with grief. And so the whole of the Wronski property came into my sole possession. And here I am, an old woman, generally laughed at for keeping, in memory of Gabriel, an asylum for stray animals—and—people do not, as a rule, believe in Vampires!

1 Gratz is the capital of Styria.

# Poppy Z. Brite/Billy Martin[1]

(B. 1967)

Since Anne Rice's *Interview with a Vampire* (1976), New Orleans has been indelibly associated with the undead, a trend that continued with the 1992 novel *Lost Souls*. Prior to his transition, Billy Martin published under the name of Poppy Z. Brite. Born in Kentucky, Martin moved to New Orleans in 1993. Much of his work is set in New Orleans and features openly gay or bisexual characters. Martin grew up with gender dysphoria and has written about his transition extensively. He has said that he always considered himself a gay man. He began his transition in 2010. This excerpt connects to the themes of sexuality and consent addressed in the texts throughout this chapter.

## from *Lost Souls*

(1992)

Christian still wore a cloak, long and black and lined with silk, whenever he went out. Old habits died hard, if they ever died at all. The night had cooled. A black iron railing under Christian's hand was warm, still saturated with the heat of the day, but a dark-smelling breeze wound its way up from the river, brushing Christian's face, reviving him. Now he had nearly forgotten the burning in his stomach and the vomiting that had made his throat bloody and raw.[2]

His step quickened. His boot heels clocked along the sidewalk. He fell to wondering how many times he had walked along these ways, how infinitesimally his steps had worn down the sidewalks of these old streets, these exotically named, haunted streets—Ursulines, Bienville, Decatur.[3] He wondered how

1 While the author has transitioned, he still wishes to be published under the name of Poppy Z. Brite.

2 Christian had tried to drink Chartreuse liqueur like the younger vampires, but it made him ill. He can only consume blood.

3 Central streets in the French Quarter of New Orleans.

much of his substance he had left here, how much of his substance was made up of the dust of these streets.

There had always been New Orleans. Christian had lived in other places, far away across sunless seas, places older and darker and just as strange, with ghosts aplenty. But where else did slave spirits still lament in the Royal Street house of sadistic Madame Lalaurie,[1] where else could one still smell the lingering sweat of a slave woman chained to a stove all the years of her life? Where else did crows flap over the crumbling ruins of St. Louis Cemetery[2] and settle, inky and baleful of eye, on a tomb slashed with hundreds of red *X*'s—*X*'s in faded crimson chalk, *X*'s to invoke the wrath of Marie Laveau, the voodoo queen who had stayed young forever?[3]

Christian passed a dark doorway. Inside, pale shapes moved through dull blue light. He remembered when this hole-in-the-wall had been a jazz club, when bright brassy music floated out late at night and spiraled up to the sky, when smoky skinned women with ripe lips and red dresses stood outside smiling dark smiles at passersby. Once he had seen Louis Armstrong[4] standing there on the sidewalk with his shirtsleeves rolled up, talking to a crowd of friends.

Christian remembered the slow laughter, the white eyes that shone out of faces blue-black with sweat, the flasks of illicit liquor raw enough to burn a hole in the guts of even Molochai, Twig, or Zillah.[5] Now the figures that waited uneasily on the sidewalk were as white as white could be, with eyes smudged black and ripped black clothes, little ghosts, like photonegatives of the dusky dancers who had once swirled all night to bright jazz. Now the music that drifted out of the doorway and up toward the moon was sparse and dark and strange, the anthem of all the lost children who began their lives at night, when the bars opened and the music began to play.

Right now it was sainted Bauhaus, the pale long-boned gods of this crowd, doing "Bela Lugosi's Dead."[6] The eyeliner eyes glazed and the black lipstick lips moved in time with the words, and the children danced slowly, for their blood was thin, and they were under the spell of the DJ and the music and the night.

Christian went in. As he passed the bar, he heard a girl say, "God, how tall *is* that guy?" He turned but could not search out her eyes. He rose like a narrow, pale beacon above most of the children in the club, and he could look down on leather-clad, studded shoulders, on earlobes hung heavy with chains and

1 Madame Lalaurie is infamous for torturing and murdering enslaved people in her Royal Street mansion. The house is still reputed to be haunted by the spirits of her victims.

2 Famous cemetery on the edge of the French Quarter said to contain the grave of Marie Laveau, a famous voodoo priestess.

3 The Xs on Marie Laveau's grave are part of New Orleans folklore. According to legend, if you draw an X on her grave and complete a ritual, she will grant your wish.

4 A famous jazz trumpeter (1901–71), Armstrong was born and raised in New Orleans.

5 The younger vampires Christian encountered earlier in the novel.

6 "Bela Lugosi's Dead" is one of the best-known songs by Bauhaus, a Goth band popular in the late 1980s–1990s.

crucifixes and tiny silver skulls, on heads of hair dyed every unnatural color possible—blue-black, orange, red, white. The club smelled of sweat and melting hair mousse and hot leather, all underlaid with the sweet, spicy smell of clove cigarettes. A veil of smoke twisted gently around Christian's shoulders.

He stood against the back wall, not smoking, not drinking, just watching the children move, watching their faces lift and their hands flicker in the blue light. A boy came up to him and said, "Will you watch my leather?" When Christian nodded, the boy dumped the jacket on a chair near Christian and danced back into the crowd, lithe and T-shirted, his thin arms raised above his head. These children trusted one another; the adult world was obtuse and threatening, but in one another they had absolute faith. Still, a leather jacket was nothing to be left unattended. Each one was an individual masterpiece marked by its owner with intricate arrangements of studs and safety pins, arcane band logos, patches and chains.

Bela Lugosi was still dead. The singer's voice was low and smooth and insidious as throat cancer. Christian imagined him gaunt and bone-white, writhing onstage. When the song was over, the boy danced back and slung his jacket over his shoulders. He offered Christian a cigarette and lit it for him. Christian inhaled once: a clove, tasting of the Orient and ash, its paper sugared. Then he held it between two long fingers and let it burn, raising it to his lips occasionally, pretending to smoke. The taste nauseated him; all tastes nauseated him save one. And now he was so hungry, so thirsty.

When the boy cupped his hand around his mouth and went on tiptoe to shout something in Christian's ear—his name, perhaps, though Christian never caught it—Christian laid his hand flat against the small of the boy's back. Through the T-shirt damp with sweat, the boy's skin was hot, alive. Christian felt the little ridges of the spine through the thin cloth. The boy looked at Christian for a moment, his eyes darker than before. Then he smiled and moved so that his hip was touching Christian's. Their hipbones met and spoke to each other in a secret bone language. The boy's smile was heartbreakingly sweet.

"Mind-eraser," the boy shouted when they were at the bar. Christian paid for the concoction. It was the drink of a child alcoholic, a sweet fizz with a deadly bite. "Share with me," the boy offered, holding up the cup. There were two straws in it.

"No," Christian said, remembering the nausea, imagining how Molochai, Twig, and Zillah would howl. "You have it."

For a moment he thought he heard them laughing raucously behind him, thought he saw them from the corner of his eye: three clumps of hair, three smudged faces. When he turned, there were only three girls in leather dresses giggling and staring at him. Christian turned back to the bar, but the boy was sharing his mind-eraser with the girl on his left. The girl's teased red hair ticked the boy's face, and Christian saw him laugh and brush strands of it away.

But when the drink was gone, the girl went off on the arm of a skinhead, and the boy turned to Christian. "Do you want to go somewhere?"

The air outside was amazingly cool and fresh after the haze of smoke and liquor in the club, and the boy stood still for a few seconds, gazing up at the stars, breathing deeply. He smiled at Christian. "It's nice. Let's go down to the river."

As they wandered down to the river's edge, Christian watched the boy, saw the ripe shine of his eyes and mouth in the dark, the softness of the blond hair that was cut short at the sides and tumbled in a pale cascade down the boy's back, the grace of the boy's drunken hands and the unconcerned, achingly lithe motion of his hips, the soft place under his jaw where his pulse beat. He smelled the leather and the clean sweat and soap and skin of the boy, and he smelled the French Quarter around them, the spice and the garbage, the grainy golden smell of beer, the deep brown fish smell of the river.

The water shone dark and still tonight. Near its edge, the boy spread his jacket and pulled Christian down with him. Their tongues melted together. The boy's spit was as sour and sweet as wine. Christian sucked at the boy's mouth, let the spit flow down his throat, warming him, awakening his hunger even more.

The boy twisted and stretched under him, hugging him close to bony childish chest and soft thin skin, and then the boy sat up and pulled his T-shirt over his head. The moonlight made him a creature of white and silver, striped dark with jutting ribs. He slipped back into his leather. "I like to feel it against my skin," he explained shyly.

Christian held the boy close, cradled him, kissed his throat. The boy moaned very softly when he felt the first touch of the long needle-sharp teeth that curved over Christian's lips now, drawn out by the night and the smell of the river and the delicious beauty of the boy in his arms.

The boy twisted his head to look at Christian. His eyes were big in his thin face, and very dark. "What are you?" he asked.

Christian was silent. But his teeth had pricked the boy's skin, and the first faint scent of blood reached him.

"Are you a vampire?"

Christian stroked the boy's hair back from his forehead, kissed the side of the boy's face tenderly, flicking the tip of his tongue across the smooth skin.

"Make me into one too," said the boy. "Please? I want to be one. I want to walk at night with you and fall in love and drink blood. Kill me. Make me into a vampire too. Bite me. Take me with you."

Christian nipped the boy's throat gently, not breaking the skin this time. He ran his hands along the length of the boy's body under the jacket, caressed his smooth bare chest, slipped one hand beneath the belt of the boy's jeans and found molten trembling heat there. The boy's back arched; he made a low gasping sound. Christian's tongue found the tender spot under the jaw, and he sank his teeth in. The boy whimpered and went rigid in his arms. The raw yolky taste of life spilled into Christian's mouth, bubbling out of the boy fresh and strong.

Christian eased the boy's body to the ground, held him, and sucked. The taste was all he remembered, all he dreamed about, all he would ever need. The boy pressed himself up against Christian. His hands found the long black hair that spilled down over Christian's shoulders and tore at it in a passion born of pain.

Then suddenly Christian's vision blossomed red, black, red again, great gauzy flowers of light and darkness that blotted out the French Quarter, the river, the boy's face. He clasped the boy more tightly, and their bodies locked together in a final wash of ecstasy, Christian's belly warming and filling, the boy beginning to die. The boy's sperm flooded warm over Christian's fingers. Christian brought his hand up to his lips and sucked at that too. The two tastes mingling in his mouth, creamy and delicate and bitter and salty, raw as life, were almost too exquisite to bear.

When the boy's veins ran dry and his hair and hands trailed limply on the wet ground, Christian picked him up and held him like a baby, gazing into the face gone paler than before, the rapturous half-closed eyes. For several minutes he held the boy, and then he turned his cold eyes to the cold moon, and something passed between them, between Christian and the moon, something as ancient and implacable as the tides, as the distances between the stars.

And had the moon been able to look into Christian's eyes, it would have seen that Christian did not love what he had done, but now he was no longer hungry. He was no longer sick and cold. The drinking of a life left him a little less alone than he had been before, and if the boy had died thinking he would rise again as one with Christian, that could not be helped. It was kinder to let the children die believing as they did. He could not turn the boy into one of his kind any more than the boy could have bitten him and turned him human. They were of separate races, races that were close enough to mate but still as far away from each other as dusk and dawn. But the dead slept, and did not know.

Christian kissed the white forehead and eased the empty little body into the river. The weight of the leather dragged it down, and for a moment Christian saw it hanging beneath the surface, limp and cold as a dream. Then it was gone.

# VAMPIRE HUNGER

C.L. Moore, "Shambleau" (1933)

Fritz Leiber, "The Girl with the Hungry Eyes" (1949)

Angela Carter, "The Lady of the House of Love" (1979)

Karen Russell, "The Vampires in the Lemon Grove" (2013)

From the insatiable need of *Salem's Lot* to the orgiastic feasting of *From Dusk till Dawn*, hunger is a defining feature of vampire narratives. Vampires consume life. In most Western vampire literature, that life is consumed through blood. As Stoker's Renfield repeatedly asserts, "the blood is the life."[1] Unlike other monsters, such as zombies, windigos, werewolves, or even witches, vampires typically do not consume flesh. Their victims are left pristine, virtually unmarked by the attack. It is human life the vampire craves, not flesh. There is a long history of associating blood with life: "Bloodsucking demons have haunted civilized society since at least biblical times."[2] From the bloody violence of Lord Ruthven's attacks in Polidori to Le Fanu's depiction of Carmilla floating in her blood-filled coffin, hunger for blood has characterized most popular depictions of vampirism; however, it is not just blood, but this greedy conspicuous consumption of life that marks the vampire as monstrous.

This blood imagery illustrates how pervasively vampires are defined by their appetites. Oral greed signifies part of the horror of vampirism, a fixation that lends itself to a Freudian reading of these tales. In *The Psychology of Vampires*,

1 Renfield presumably quotes Deuteronomy 12:23–24: "But be sure you do not eat the blood, because the blood is the life, and you must not eat the life with the meat."

2 Groom, *The Vampire* 6.

David Cohen suggests that for Freud this oral greed "represented the wildest primitive instincts" and infants who are denied during the oral phase can grow into adults with "highly manipulative" personalities.[1] The traits of a psychologically dependent, highly manipulative adult align with many characterizations of vampires. Yet, despite the Freudian overtones, fundamentally, it is life that is stolen in vampire lore. Bodily fluids are simply one of the vehicles for this theft.

Taboos about blood are particularly interesting to examine in texts with female vampires. Critics like Sue-Ellen Case have linked women's menstrual cycle to myths about vampires.[2] One famous example is seventeenth-century Hungarian noblewoman Elizabeth Bathory, who died in 1614. The myths surrounding her report that she was wont to "bathe in the blood of young girls in order to retain her youthful beauty."[3] In addition, women are more prone to anemia, leading to a shift in the typical appearance of vampires from "the ruddy and replete beings of Eastern European cases to the pale and cadaverous features of the corpse-like *femmes fatales*."[4] Despite these links between women and blood, the late nineteenth- and twentieth-century tales included in this unit are surprisingly bloodless.

But is the blood compulsory? Many vampire tales show no trace of the bodily fluid; in fact, the first two stories in this chapter, C.L. Moore's "Shambleau" (1933) and Fritz Leiber's "The Girl with the Hungry Eyes" (1949), feature no biting at all. The lack of physical penetration does not appear to lessen the threat of these vampires' ravenous appetites. As Bernadino in Silvia Moreno-Garcia's 2016 novel, *Certain Dark Things*, asserts, vampires "are a diverse lot. So many differences. Yet we are united by one simple unavoidable fact: we *are* our hunger."[5] Prior to the twentieth century, blood was a common sight; medical care took place in the home as did the slaughtering and preparation of meat. As these aspects of life moved outside the domestic sphere, blood became more and more invisible and taboo.[6] Throughout the history of vampire literature, these monsters hunger for human life, and blood is just one of a variety of vehicles for its consumption.

In addition to the diminished presence of blood in daily life, other cultural shifts may have contributed to changes in the depiction of vampire hunger. The growing interest in mesmerism and psychic research that captivated the public for much of the late nineteenth and early twentieth centuries is another factor in the evolving depictions of vampire hunger. This surfaces prominently in the chilling ability of Stoker's *Dracula* to invade minds. Psychic vampires like Kenealy's Lady Deverish or Leiber's Girl hunger for life energy just as intensely as those in other texts hunger for blood. They share the same manipulative ploys,

1 Cohen, *The Psychology of Vampires* 29.
2 Case, "Tracking the Vampire" 7.
3 Groom, *The Vampire* 10.
4 Groom, *The Vampire* 149.
5 Moreno-Garcia, *Certain Dark Things* 172, emphasis added.
6 Groom, *The Vampire* 10.

insatiable needs, and narcissistic selfishness as their more violent predecessors.

Whether it is blood, energy, life force, experiences, emotion, or youth, vampires are defined by their need to prey on humans to survive. In this predatory dynamic, even the vampires with the most sympathetic characteristics are necessarily self-centered and highly manipulative. With the exception of Angela Carter's more traditional Nosferatu, the vampires in this chapter all take something other than blood from their victims. As we have seen earlier in the anthology, vampires whose appetite is for the less sanguine aspects of life have surfaced again and again in the history of the literary vampire from Marryat's *The Blood of the Vampire* to Dick's "The Cookie Lady" (see also the chapters "Vampires and Immortality" and "Vampires and Race").

While their survival depends upon killing, for some of the monsters in this chapter the victim's death is not something they seek but rather an inevitable consequence. Just as in Marryat's novel, Angela Carter's Nosferatu becomes the focus of the reader's sympathy. Like Marryat's Harriet, Carter's vampire is born to her condition, but unlike Harriet, she is fully aware that she must kill to survive. Whereas other vampires' greed and selfishness mark them as beyond the readers' sympathies, Carter depicts her Nosferatu as a pathetic, self-hating damsel in distress longing to love the prey she must kill.

In the texts in this chapter, hunger and desire are inextricably linked, particularly when the fulfillment of this hunger is contingent upon sexuality and seduction. In many vampire narratives, hunger for sustenance is conflated with hunger for sex (see Illustrations, Burne-Jones *The Vampire* [1897] p. 516). As we saw in the last chapter, the depiction of female vampires' sexual appetite parallels the control often placed on female consumption in patriarchal cultures. The female vampires in this chapter are monstrous at least in part because they are women who desire.

In depictions of female vampires, hunger can become monstrous in and of itself. Emma Domínguez-Rué observes that in Bram Stoker's *Dracula*, the gluttonous female vampires whose voluptuous forms personify their hunger threaten the Victorian construct of ideal femininity. For the Victorians, the woman was often "angelic, bodiless and passionless."[1] Domínguez-Rué notes that the ideal Victorian woman was defined by an aesthetic of renunciation that verged on anorexia. Interestingly, despite their beauty, female vampires like Leiber's Girl and Carter's Nosferatu are painfully thin. This thinness emphasizes a continuation of this aesthetic of renunciation; "[t]his, physical emaciation, however, is misleading, as this apparently virtuous refusal of food hides a much more dangerous hunger."[2] Female desire and hunger are both dangerous in these texts where the female ideal is one of renunciation. Greed, whether for sustenance or sex, makes these women monstrous.

1 Domínguez-Rué, "Sins of the Flesh" 298.
2 Domínguez-Rué, "Sins of the Flesh" 300.

The uncontrollable appetite of the vampire is a defining characteristic throughout much of its literary history, and while certainly not exclusive to depictions of female monsters, the depiction of hunger in male vampires is inherently different. As Jess Zimmerman suggests in her 2016 essay "Hunger Makes Me": "A man's appetite can be hearty, but a woman with an appetite is always voracious: her hunger always overreaches, because it is not supposed to exist."[1] Hunger is often very gendered. Karen Russell plays on this in her 2013 short story, "The Vampires in the Lemon Grove." Her vampire protagonist, Clyde, has searched the world for an alternative to blood—something other than humans to satisfy his hunger. Reduced to broken-down old age and eclipsed by his still vibrant vampire wife, he spends his time sitting on a bench in a lemon grove patronized as "a kindly Italian grandfather, a *nonno*" (see p. 368). The weight of eternity hangs heavily on him as the lemons no longer quell his cravings. Such incessant hunger is inherently horrifying, yet Clyde's final attack seems motivated more by impotence than appetite.

Tied as it is to power and sexuality, hunger pervades vampire literature. Gluttony may be one of the seven deadly sins, but in most cultures, murder is considered a much greater threat. Vampires are, of course, guilty of both. When eating is overtly linked to both sustenance and sexual gratification, the temptation is exponentially increased. In other texts in the anthology, vampire heroes like Gomez's Gilda or Butler's Shori do not need to kill to satisfy their hunger, but in the texts included here, satisfying vampiric hunger means killing. Thus, it becomes not just about gratification but about survival as well. No longer simply a matter of oral greed, a vampire's hunger is inherently monstrous.

1 Zimmerman, "Hunger Makes Me."

## C.L. Moore

(1911–1987)

Catherine Lucille Moore was a science fiction and fantasy writer. She was one of the first American women to write in the genre, and paved the way for many other female writers in speculative fiction. Moore is from Indiana. She was born in 1911 and as a child she was frequently ill and read fantasy literature during her convalescence. She began to study at Indiana University but her education was interrupted by the Great Depression. Moore worked as a secretary to support herself while writing. Her early stories were published in *Weird Tales.* This popular pulp fiction magazine often features horror and supernatural short stories like "Shambleau." This story represents an unusal combination of the genres of science fiction and vampire literature. Moore died in 1987 at her home in Hollywood, California, after a long battle with Alzheimer's.

# "Shambleau"

(1933)

"Shambleau! Ha…Shambleau!" The wild hysteria of the mob rocketed from wall to wall of Lakkdarol's narrow streets and the storming of heavy boots over the slag-red pavement made an ominous undernote to that swelling bay, "Shambleau! Shambleau!"

Northwest Smith heard it coming and stepped into the nearest doorway, laying a wary hand on his heat-gun's grip, and his colorless eyes narrowed. Strange sounds were common enough in the streets of Earth's latest colony on Mars—a raw, red little town where anything might happen, and very often did. But Northwest Smith, whose name is known and respected in every dive and wild outpost on a dozen wild planets, was a cautious man, despite his reputation. He set his back against the wall and gripped his pistol, and heard the rising shout come nearer and nearer.

Then into his range of vision flashed a red running figure, dodging like a hunted hare from shelter to shelter in the narrow street. It was a girl—a berry-brown girl in a single tattered garment whose scarlet burnt the eyes with its brilliance. She ran wearily, and he could hear her gasping breath from where he stood. As she came into view he saw her hesitate and lean one hand against the wall for support, and glance wildly around for shelter. She must not have seen him in the depths of the doorway, for as the bay of the mob grew louder and the pounding of feet sounded almost at the corner she gave a despairing little moan and dodged into the recess at his very side.

When she saw him standing there, tall and leather-brown, hand on his heat-gun, she sobbed once, inarticulately, and collapsed at his feet, a huddle of burning scarlet and bare, brown limbs.

Smith had not seen her face, but she was a girl, and sweetly made and in danger; and though he had not the reputation of a chivalrous man, something in her hopeless huddle at his feet touched that chord of sympathy for the underdog that stirs in every Earthman, and he pushed her gently into the corner behind him and jerked out his gun, just as the first of the running mob rounded the corner.

It was a motley crowd, Earthmen and Martians and a sprinkling of Venusian swampmen and strange, nameless denizens of unnamed planets—a typical Lakkdarol mob. When the first of them turned the corner and saw the empty street before them there was a faltering in the rush and the foremost spread out and began to search the doorways on both sides of the street.

"Looking for something?" Smith's sardonic call sounded clear above the clamor of the mob.

They turned. The shouting died for a moment as they took in the scene before them—tall Earthman in the space-explorer's leathern garb, all one color from the burning of savage suns save for the sinister pallor of his no-colored eyes in a scarred and resolute face, gun in his steady hand and the scarlet girl crouched behind him, panting.

The foremost of the crowd—a burly Earthman in tattered leather from which the Patrol insignia had been ripped away—stared for a moment with a strange expression of incredulity on his face overspreading the savage exultation of the chase. Then he let loose a deep-throated bellow, "Shambleau!" and lunged forward. Behind him the mob took up the cry again. "Shambleau! Shambleau! Shambleau!" and surged after.

Smith, lounging negligently against the wall, arms folded and gun-hand draped over his left forearm, looked incapable of swift motion, but at the leader's first forward step the pistol swept in a practiced half-circle and the dazzle of blue-white heat leaping from its muzzle seared an arc in the slag pavement at his feet. It was an old gesture, and not a man in the crowd but understood it. The foremost recoiled swiftly against the surge of those in the rear, and for a moment there was confusion as the two tides met and struggled. Smith's mouth curled into a grim curve as he watched. The man in the mutilated Patrol uniform lifted a threatening fist and stepped to the very edge of the deadline, while the crowd rocked to and fro behind him.

"Are you crossing that line?" queried Smith in an ominously gentle voice.

"We want that girl!"

"Come and get her!" Recklessly Smith grinned into his face. He saw danger there, but his defiance was not the foolhardy gesture it seemed. An expert psychologist of mobs from long experience, he sensed no murder here. Not a gun had appeared in any hand in the crowd. They desired the girl with an inexplicable bloodthirstiness he was at a loss to understand, but toward himself he sensed no such fury. A mauling he might expect, but his life was in no danger. Guns would have appeared before now if they were coming out at all. So he grinned in the man's angry face and leaned lazily against the wall.

Behind their self-appointed leader the crowd milled impatiently, and threatening voices began to rise again. Smith heard the girl moan at his feet.

"What do you want with her?" he demanded.

"She's Shambleau! Shambleau, you fool! Kick her out of there—we'll take care of her!"

"I'm taking care of her," drawled Smith.

"She's Shambleau, I tell you! Damn your hide, man, we never let those things live! Kick her out here!"

The repeated name had no meaning to him, but Smith's innate stubbornness rose defiantly as the crowd surged forward to the very edge of the arc, their clamor growing louder. "Shambleau! Kick her out here! Give us Shambleau! Shambleau!"

Smith dropped his indolent pose like a cloak and planted both feet wide, swinging up his gun threatening. "Keep back!" he yelled. "She's mine! Keep back!"

He had no intention of using that heat-beam. He knew by now that they would not kill him unless he started the gunplay himself, and he did not mean to give up his life for any girl alive. But a severe mauling he expected, and he braced himself instinctively as the mob heaved within itself.

To his astonishment a thing happened then that he had never known to happen before. At his shouted defiance the foremost of the mob—those who had heard him clearly—drew back a little, not in alarm but evidently surprised. The ex-Patrolman said, "Yours! She's *yours?*" in a voice from which puzzlement crowded out the anger.

Smith spread his booted legs wide before the crouching figure and flourished his gun.

"Yes," he said. "And I'm keeping her! Stand back there!"

The man stared at him wordlessly, and horror and disgust and incredulity mingled on his weather-beaten face. The incredulity triumphed for a moment and he said again,

"Yours!"

Smith nodded defiance.

The man stepped back suddenly, unutterable contempt in his very pose. He waved an arm to the crowd and said loudly, "It's—his!" and the press melted away, gone silent, too, and the look of contempt spread from face to face.

The ex-Patrolman spat on the slag-paved street and turned his back indifferently. "Keep her, then," he advised briefly over one shoulder. "But don't let her out again in this town!"

† † †

Smith stared in perplexity almost open-mouthed as the suddenly scornful mob began to break up. His mind was in a whirl. That such bloodthirsty animosity should vanish in a breath he could not believe. And the curious mingling of contempt and disgust on the faces he saw baffled him even more. Lakkdarol was anything but a puritan town—it did not enter his head for a moment that his claiming the brown girl as his own had caused that strangely shocked revulsion to spread through the crowd. No, it was something deeper-rooted than that. Instinctive, instant disgust had been in the faces he saw—they would have looked less so if he had admitted cannibalism or *Pharol*-worship.

And they were leaving his vicinity as swiftly as if whatever unknowing sin he had committed were contagious. The street was emptying as rapidly as it had filled. He saw a sleek Venusian glance back over his shoulder as he turned the corner and sneer, "Shambleau!" and the word awoke a new line of speculation in Smith's mind. Shambleau! Vaguely of French origin, it must be. And strange enough to hear it from the lips of Venusian and Martian drylanders, but it was their use of it that puzzled him more. "We never let those things live," the ex-Patrolman had said. It reminded him dimly of something... an ancient line from some writing in his own tongue... "Thou shalt not suffer a witch to live." He smiled to himself at the similarity, and simultaneously was aware of the girl at his elbow.

She had risen soundlessly. He turned to face her, sheathing his gun and stared at first with curiosity and then in the entirely frank openness with which men regard that which is not wholly human. For she was not. He knew it at a glance, though the brown, sweet body was shaped like a woman's and she wore the garment of scarlet—he saw it was leather—with an ease that few unhuman beings achieve toward clothing. He knew it from the moment he looked into her eyes, and a shiver of unrest went over him as he met them. They were frankly green as young grass, with slit-like, feline pupils that pulsed unceasingly, and there was a look of dark, animal wisdom in their depths—that look of the beast which sees more than man.

There was no hair upon her face—neither brows nor lashes, and he would have sworn that the tight scarlet turban bound around her head covered baldness. She had three fingers and a thumb, and her feet had four digits apiece too, and all sixteen of them were tipped with round claws that sheathed back into the flesh like a cat's. She ran her tongue over her lips—a thin, pink, flat tongue as feline as her eyes—and spoke with difficulty. He felt that that throat and tongue had never been shaped for human speech.

"Not—afraid now," she said softly, and her little teeth were white and polished as a kitten's.

"What did they want you for?" he asked her curiously. "What have you done? Shambleau ... is that your name?"

"I—not talk your—speech," she demurred hesitantly.

"Well, try to—I want to know. Why were they chasing you? Will you be safe on the street now, or hadn't you better get indoors somewhere? They looked dangerous."

"I—go with you." She brought it out with difficulty.

"Say you!" Smith grinned. "What are you, anyhow? You look like a kitten to me."

"Shambleau." She said it somberly.

"Where d'you live? Are you a Martian?"

"I come from—from far—from long ago—far country—"

"Wait!" laughed Smith. "You're getting your wires crossed. You're not a Martian?"

She drew herself up very straight beside him, lifting the turbaned head, and there was something queenly in the pose of her.

"Martian?" she said scornfully. "My people—are—are—you have no word. Your speech—hard for me."

"What's yours? I might know it—try me."

She lifted her head and met his eyes squarely, and there was in hers a subtle amusement—he could have sworn it.

"Someday I—speak to you in—my own language," she promised, and the pink tongue flicked out over her lips, swiftly, hungrily.

Approaching footsteps on the red pavement interrupted Smith's reply. A dryland Martian came past, reeling a little and exuding an aroma of *segir*-whisky, the Venusian brand. When he caught the red flash of the girl's tatters he turned his head sharply, and as his *segir*-steeped brain took in the fact of her presence he lurched toward the recess unsteadily, bawling, "Shambleau, by *Pharol!* Shambleau!" and reached out a clutching hand.

Smith struck it aside contemptuously.

"On your way, drylander," he advised.

The man drew back and stared, bleary-eyed.

"Yours, eh?" he croaked. "*Zut!* You're welcome to it!" And like the ex-Patrolman before him he spat on the pavement and turned away, muttering harshly in the blasphemous tongue of the drylands.

Smith watched him shuffle off, and there was a crease between his colorless eyes, a nameless unease rising within him.

"Come on," he said abruptly to the girl. "If this sort of thing is going to happen we'd better get indoors. Where shall I take you?"

"With—you," she murmured.

He stared down into the flat green eyes. Those ceaselessly pulsing pupils disturbed him, but it seemed to him, vaguely, that behind the animal shallows of her gaze was a shutter—a closed barrier that might at any moment open to reveal the very deeps of that dark knowledge he sensed there.

Roughly he said again, "Come on, then," and stepped down into the street.

She pattered along a pace or two behind him, making no effort to keep up with his long strides, and though Smith—as men know from Venus to Jupiter's moons—walks as softly as a cat, even in spacemen's boots, the girl at his heels slid like a shadow over the rough pavement, making so little sound that even the lightness of his footsteps was loud in the empty street.

Smith chose the less frequented ways of Lakkdarol, and somewhat shamefacedly thanked his nameless gods that his lodgings were not far away, for the few pedestrians he met turned and stared after the two with that by now familiar mingling of horror and contempt which he was as far as ever from understanding.

The room he had engaged was a single cubicle in a lodging-house on the edge of the city. Lakkdarol, raw camptown that it was in those days, could have furnished little better anywhere within its limits, and Smith's errand there was not one he wished to advertise. He had slept in worse places than this before, and knew that he would do so again.

There was no one in sight when he entered, and the girl slipped up the stairs at his heels and vanished through the door, shadowy, unseen by anyone in the house. Smith closed the door and leaned his broad shoulders against the panels, regarding her speculatively.

She took in what little the room had to offer in a glance—frowsy bed, rickety table, mirror hanging unevenly and cracked against the wall, unpainted chairs—a typical camptown room in an Earth settlement abroad. She accepted its poverty in that single glance, dismissed it, then crossed to the window and leaned out for a moment, gazing across the low roof-tops toward the barren countryside beyond, red slag under the late afternoon sun.

"You can stay here," said Smith abruptly, "until I leave town. I'm waiting here for a friend to come in from Venus. Have you eaten?"

"Yes," said the girl quickly. "I shall—need no—food for—a while."

"Well—" Smith glanced around the room. "I'll be in sometime tonight. You can go or stay just as you please. Better lock the door behind me."

With no more formality than that he left her. The door closed and he heard the key turn, and smiled to himself. He did not expect, then, ever to see her again.

He went down the steps and out into the late-slanting sunlight with a mind so full of other matters that the brown girl receded very quickly into the background. Smith's errand in Lakkdarol, like most of his errands, is better not spoken of. Man lives as he must, and Smith's living was a perilous affair outside the law and ruled by the ray-gun only. It is enough to say that the shipping-port and its cargoes outbound interested him deeply just now, and that the friend he awaited was Yarol the Venusian, in that swift little Edsel ship the *Maid* that can flash from world to world with a derisive speed that laughs at Patrol boats and leaves pursuers floundering in the ether far behind. Smith and Yarol and the *Maid* were a trinity that had caused Patrol leaders much worry and many gray hairs in the past, and the future looked very bright to Smith himself that evening as he left his lodging-house.

† † †

Lakkdarol roars by night, as Earthmen's camptowns have a way of doing on every planet where Earth's outposts are, and it was beginning lustily as Smith went down among the awakening lights toward the center of town. His business there does not concern us. He mingled with the crowd where the lights were brightest, and there was the click of ivory counters and the jingle of silver, and red *segir* gurgled invitingly from black Venusian bottles, and much later Smith strolled homeward under the moving moons of Mars, and if the street wavered a little under his feet now and then—why, that is only understandable. Not even Smith could drink red *segir* at every bar from the *Martian Lamb* to the *New Chicago* and remain entirely steady on his feet. But he found his way back with very little difficulty—considering—and spent a good five minutes hunting for his key before he remembered he had left it in the inner lock for the girl.

He knocked then, and there was no sound of footsteps from within, but in a few moments the latch clicked and the door swung open. She retreated soundlessly before him as he entered, and took up her favorite place against the window, leaning back on the sill and outlined against the starry sky beyond. The room was in darkness.

Smith flipped the switch by the door and then leaned back against the panels, steadying himself. The cool night air had sobered him a little and his head was clear enough—liquor went to Smith's feet, not his head, or he would never have come this far along the lawless way he had chosen. He lounged against the door now and regarded the girl in the sudden glare of the bulbs, blinking a little as much at the scarlet of her clothing as at the light.

"So you stayed," he said.

"I—waited," she answered softly, leaning farther back against the sill and clasping the rough wood with slim, three-fingered hands, pale brown against the darkness.

"Why?"

She did not answer that, but her mouth curved into a slow smile. On a woman it would have been reply enough—provocative, daring. On Shambleau there was something pitiful and horrible in it—so human on the face of one half-animal. And yet... that sweet brown body curving so softly from the tatters of scarlet leather—the velvety texture of that brownness—the white-flashing smile... Smith was aware of a stirring excitement within him. After all—time would be hanging heavy now until Yarol came... Speculatively he allowed the steel-pale eyes to wander over her, with a slow regard that missed nothing. And when he spoke he was aware that his voice had deepened a little....

"Come here," he said.

She came forward slowly, on bare clawed feet that made no sound on the floor, and stood before him with downcast eyes and mouth trembling in that pitifully human smile. He took her by the shoulders—velvety soft shoulders, of a creamy smoothness that was not the texture of human flesh. A little tremor went over her, perceptibly, at the contact of his hands. Northwest Smith caught his breath suddenly and dragged her to him... sweet yielding brownness in the circle of his arms... heard her own breath catch and quicken as her velvety arms closed about his neck. And then he was looking down into her face, very near, and the green animal eyes met his with the pulsing pupils and the flicker of—something—deep behind their shallows—and through the rising clamor of his blood, even as he stooped his lips to hers, Smith felt something deep within him shudder away—inexplicable, instinctive, revolted. What it might be he had no words to tell, but the very touch of her was suddenly loathsome—so soft and velvet and unhuman—and it might have been an animal's face that lifted itself to his mouth—the dark knowledge looked hungrily from the darkness of those slit pupils—and for a mad instant he knew that same wild, feverish revulsion he had seen in the faces of the mob....

"God!" he gasped, a far more ancient invocation against evil than he realized, then or ever, and he ripped her arms from his neck, swung her away with such a force that she reeled half across the room. Smith fell back against the door, breathing heavily, and stared at her while the wild revolt died slowly within him.

She had fallen to the floor beneath the window, and as she lay there against the wall with bent head he saw, curiously, that her turban had slipped—the turban that he had been so sure covered baldness—and a lock of scarlet hair fell below the binding leather, hair as scarlet as her garment, as unhumanly red as her eyes were unhumanly green. He stared, and shook his head dizzily and stared again, for it seemed to him that the thick lock of crimson had moved, *squirmed* of itself against her cheek.

At the contact of it her hands flew up and she tucked it away with a very human gesture and then dropped her head again into her hands. And from the deep shadow of her fingers he thought she was staring up at him covertly.

Smith drew a deep breath and passed a hand across his forehead. The inexplicable moment had gone as quickly as it came—too swiftly for him to understand or analyze it. "Got to lay off the *segir*," he told himself unsteadily. Had he imagined that scarlet hair? After all, she was no more than a pretty brown girl-creature from one of the many half-human races peopling the planets. No more than that, after all. A pretty little thing, but animal.... He laughed, a little shakily.

"No more of that," he said. "God knows I'm no angel, but there's got to be a limit somewhere. Here." He crossed to the bed and sorted out a pair of blankets from the untidy heap, tossing them to the far corner of the room. "You can sleep there."

Wordlessly she rose from the floor and began to rearrange the blankets, the uncomprehending resignation of the animal eloquent in every line of her.

† † †

Smith had a strange dream that night. He thought he had awakened to a room full of darkness and moonlight and moving shadows, for the nearer moon of Mars was racing through the sky and everything on the planet below her was endued with a restless life in the dark. And something... some nameless, unthinkable *thing*... was coiled about his throat... something like a soft snake, wet and warm. It lay loose and light about his neck... and it was moving gently, very gently, with a soft, caressive pressure that sent little thrills of delight through every nerve and fiber of him, a perilous delight—beyond physical pleasure, deeper than joy of the mind. That warm softness was caressing the very roots of his soul and with a terrible intimacy. The ecstasy of it left him weak, and yet he knew—in a flash of knowledge born of this impossible dream—that the soul should not be handled... And with that knowledge a horror broke upon him, turning the pleasure into a rapture of revulsion, hateful, horrible—but still most foully sweet. He tried to lift his hands and tear the dream-monstrosity from his throat—tired but half-heartedly; for though his soul was revolted to its very deeps, yet the delight of his body was so great that his hands all but refused the attempt. But when at last he tried to lift his arms a cold shock went over him and he found that he could not stir... his body lay stony as marble beneath the blankets, a living marble that shuddered with a dreadful delight through every rigid vein.

The revulsion grew strong upon him as he struggled against the paralyzing dream—a struggle of soul against sluggish body—titanically, until the moving dark was streaked with blankness that clouded and closed about him at last and he sank back into the oblivion from which he had awakened.

Next morning, when the bright sunlight shining through Mars' clear thin air awakened him, Smith lay for a while trying to remember. The dream had been more vivid than reality, but he could not now quite recall... only that it had been more sweet and horrible than anything else in life. He lay puzzling for a while, until a soft sound from the corner aroused him from his thoughts and he sat up to see the girl lying in a cat-like coil on her blankets, watching him with round, grave eyes. He regarded her somewhat ruefully.

"Morning," he said. "I've just had the devil of a dream.... Well, hungry?"

She shook her head silently, and he could have sworn there was a covert gleam of strange amusement in her eyes.

He stretched and yawned, dismissing the nightmare temporarily from his mind.

"What am I going to do with you?" he inquired, turning to more immediate matters. "I'm leaving here in a day or two and I can't take you along, you know. Where'd you come from in the first place?"

Again she shook her head.

"Not telling? Well, it's your business. You can stay here until I give up the room. From then on you'll have to do your own worrying."

He swung his feet to the floor and reached for his clothes.

Ten minutes later, slipping the heat-gun into its holster at his thigh, Smith turned to the girl. "There's food-concentrate in that box on the table. It ought to hold you until I get back. And you'd better lock the door again after I've gone."

Her wide, unwavering stare was his only answer, and he was not sure she had understood, but at any rate the lock clicked after him as before, and he went down the steps with a faint grin on his lips.

The memory of last night's extraordinary dream was slipping from him, as such memories do, and by the time he had reached the street the girl and the dream and all of yesterday's happenings were blotted out by the sharp necessities of the present.

Again the intricate business that had brought him here claimed his attention. He went about it to the exclusion of all else, and there was a good reason behind everything he did from the moment he stepped out into the street until the time when he turned back again at evening; though had one chosen to follow him during the day his apparently aimless rambling through Lakkdarol would have seemed very pointless.

He must have spent two hours at the least idling by the space-port, watching with sleepy, colorless eyes the ships that came and went, the passengers, the vessels lying at wait, the cargoes—particularly the cargoes. He made the rounds of the town's saloons once more, consuming many glasses of varied liquors in the course of the day and engaging in idle conversation with men of all races and worlds, usually in their own languages, for Smith was a linguist of repute among his contemporaries. He heard the gossip of the spaceways, news from a dozen planets of a thousand different events. He heard the latest joke about the Venusian Emperor and the latest report on the Chino-Aryan war and the latest song hot from the lips of Rose Robertson, whom every man on the civilized planets adored as "the Georgia Rose." He passed the day quite profitably, for his own purposes, which do not concern us now, and it was not until late evening, when he turned homeward again, that the thought of the brown girl in his room took definite shape in his mind, though it had been lurking there, formless and submerged, all day.

He had no idea what comprised her usual diet, but he bought a can of New York roast beef and one of Venusian frog-broth and a dozen fresh canal-apples and two pounds of that Earth lettuce that grows so vigorously in the fertile canal-soil of Mars. He felt that she must surely find something to her liking in this broad variety of edibles, and—for his day had been very satisfactory—he hummed "The Green Hills of Earth" to himself in a surprisingly good baritone as he climbed the stairs.

† † †

The door was locked, as before, and he was reduced to kicking the lower panels gently with his boot, for his arms were full. She opened the door with that softness that was characteristic of her and stood regarding him in the semidarkness as he stumbled to the table with his load. The room was unlit again.

"Why don't you turn on the lights?" he demanded irritably after he had barked his shin on the chair by the table in an effort to deposit his burden there.

"Light and—dark—they are alike—to me," she murmured.

"Cat eyes, eh? Well, you look the part. Here, I've brought you some dinner. Take your choice. Fond of roast beef? Or how about a little frog-broth?"

She shook her head and backed away a step.

"No," she said. "I cannot—eat your food."

Smith's brows wrinkled. "Didn't you have any of the food-tablets?"

Again the red turban shook negatively.

"Then you haven't had anything for—why, more than twenty-four hours! You must be starved."

"Not hungry," she denied.

"What can I find for you to eat, then? There's time yet if I hurry. You've got to eat, child."

"I shall—eat," she said softly. "Before long—I shall—feed. Have no—worry."

She turned away then and stood at the window, looking out over the moonlit landscape as if to end the conversation. Smith cast her a puzzled glance as he opened the can of roast beef. There had been an odd undernote in that assurance that, undefinably, he did not like. And the girl had teeth and tongue and presumably a fairly human digestive system, to judge from her human form. It was nonsense for her to pretend that he could find nothing that she could eat. She must have had some of the food concentrate after all, he decided, prying up the thermos lid of the inner container to release the long-sealed savor of the hot meat inside.

"Well, if you won't eat you won't," he observed philosophically as he poured hot broth and diced beef into the dish-like lid of the thermos can and extracted the spoon from its hiding-place between the inner and outer receptacles. She turned a little to watch him as he pulled up a rickety chair and sat down to the food, and after a while the realization that her green gaze was fixed so unwinkingly upon him made the man nervous, and he said between bites of creamy canal-apple, "Why don't you try a little of this? It's good."

"The food—I eat is—better," her soft voice told him in its hesitant murmur, and again he felt rather than heard a faint undernote of unpleasantness in the words. A sudden suspicion struck him as he pondered on that last remark—some vague memory of horror-tales told about campfires in the past—and he swung round in the chair to look at her, a tiny, creeping fear unaccountably arising. There had been that in her words—in her unspoken words, that menaced....

She stood up beneath his gaze demurely, wide green eyes with their pulsing pupils meeting his without a falter. But her mouth was scarlet and her teeth were sharp...

"What food do you eat?" he demanded. And then, after a pause, very softly, "Blood?"

She stared at him for a moment, uncomprehending; then something like amusement curled her lips and she said scornfully, "You think me—vampire, eh? No—I am Shambleau!"

Unmistakably there were scorn and amusement in her voice at the suggestion, but as unmistakably she knew what he meant—accepted it as a logical suspicion—vampire! Fairy-tales—but fairy-tales this unhuman, outland creature was most familiar with. Smith was not a credulous man, nor a superstitious one, but he had seen too many strange things himself to doubt that the wildest legend might have a basis of fact. And there was something namelessly strange about her....

He puzzled over it for a while between deep bites of the canal-apple. And though he wanted to question her about a great many things, he did not, for he knew how futile it would be.

He said nothing more until the meat was finished and another canal-apple had followed the first, and he had cleared away the meal by the simple expedient of tossing the empty can out of the window. Then he lay back in the chair and surveyed her from half-closed eyes, colorless in a face tanned like saddle-leather. And again he was conscious of the brown, soft curves of her, velvety—subtle arcs and planes of smooth flesh under the tatters of scarlet leather. Vampire she might be, unhuman she certainly was, but desirable beyond words as she sat submissive beneath his low regard, her red-turbaned head bent, her clawed fingers lying in her lap. They sat very still for a while, and the silence throbbed between them.

She was so like a woman—an Earth woman—sweet and submissive and demure, and softer than soft fur, if he could forget the three-fingered claws and the pulsing eyes—and that deeper strangeness beyond words.... (Had he dreamed that red lock of hair that moved? Had it been *segir* that woke the wild revulsion he knew when he held her in his arms? Why had the mob so thirsted for her?) He sat and stared, and despite the mystery of her and the half-suspicions that thronged his mind—for she was so beautifully soft and curved under those revealing tatters—he slowly realized that his pulses were mounting, became aware of a kindling within... brown girl-creature with downcast eyes... and then the lids lifted and the green flatness of a cat's gaze met his, and last night's revulsion woke swiftly again, like a warning bell that clanged as their eyes met—animal, after all, too sleek and soft for humanity, and that inner strangeness....

Smith shrugged and sat up. His failings were legion, but the weakness of the flesh was not among the major ones. He motioned the girl to her pallet of blankets in the corner and turned to his own bed.

† † †

From deeps of sound sleep he awoke much later. He awoke suddenly and completely, and with that inner excitement that presages something momentous. He awoke to brilliant moonlight, turning the room so bright that he could see the scarlet of the girl's rags as she sat up on her pallet. She was awake, she was sitting with her shoulder half turned to him and her head bent, and some warning instinct crawled coldly up his spine as he watched what she was doing. And yet it was a very ordinary thing for a girl to do—any girl, anywhere. She was unbinding her turban....

He watched, not breathing, a presentiment of something horrible stirring in his brain, inexplicably.... The red folds loosened, and—he knew then that he had not dreamed—again a scarlet lock swung down against her cheek... a hair, was it? a lock of hair?... thick as a thick worm it fell, plumply, against that smooth cheek... more scarlet than blood and thick as a crawling worm... and like a worm it crawled.

Smith rose on an elbow, not realizing the motion, and fixed an unwinking stare, with a sort of sick, fascinated incredulity, on that—that lock of hair. He had not dreamed. Until now he had taken it for granted that it was the *segir* which had made it seem to move on that evening before. But now... it was lengthening, stretching, moving of itself. It must be hair, but it *crawled*; with a sickening life of its own it squirmed down against her cheek, caressingly, revoltingly, impossibly.... Wet, it was, and round and thick and shining....

She unfastened the last fold and whipped the turban off. From what he saw then Smith would have turned his eyes away—and he had looked on dreadful things before, without flinching—but he could not stir. He could only lie there on elbow staring at the mass of scarlet, squirming—worms, hairs, what?—that writhed over her head in a dreadful mockery of ringlets. And it was lengthening, falling, somehow growing before his eyes, down over her shoulders in a spilling cascade, a mass that even at the beginning could never have been hidden under the skull-tight turban she had worn. He was beyond wondering, but he realized that. And still it squirmed and lengthened and fell, and she shook it out in a horrible travesty of a woman shaking out her unbound hair—until the unspeakable tangle of it—twisting, writhing, obscenely scarlet—hung to her waist and beyond, and still lengthened, an endless mass of crawling horror that until now, somehow, impossibly, had been hidden under the tight-bound turban. It was like a nest of blind, restless red worms... it was—it was like naked entrails endowed with an unnatural aliveness, terrible beyond words.

Smith lay in the shadows, frozen without and within in a sick numbness that came of utter shock and revulsion.

She shook out the obscene, unspeakable tangle over her shoulders, and somehow he knew that she was going to turn in a moment and that he must meet her eyes. The thought of that meeting stopped his heart with dread, more awfully than anything else in this nightmare horror; for nightmare it must be, surely. But he knew without trying that he could not wrench his eyes away—the sickened fascination of that sight held him motionless, and somehow there was a certain beauty....

Her head was turning. The crawling awfulness rippled and squirmed at the motion, writhing thick and wet and shining over the soft brown shoulders about which they fell now in obscene cascades that all but hid her body. Her head was turning. Smith lay numb. And very slowly he saw the round of her cheek foreshorten and her profile come into view, all the scarlet horrors twisting ominously, and the profile shortened in turn and her full face came slowly round toward the bed—moonlight shining brilliantly as day on the pretty girl-face, demure and sweet, framed in tangled obscenity that crawled....

The green eyes met his. He felt a perceptible shock, and a shudder rippled down his paralyzed spine, leaving an icy numbness in its wake. He felt the goose-flesh rising. But that numbness and cold horror he scarcely realized, for the green eyes were locked with his in a long, long look that somehow presaged nameless things—not altogether unpleasant things—the voiceless voice of her mind assailing him with little murmurous promises....

For a moment he went down into a blind abyss of submission; and then somehow the very sight of that obscenity in eyes that did not then realize they saw it, was dreadful enough to draw him out of the seductive darkness... the sight of her crawling and alive with unnamable horror.

She rose, and down about her in a cascade fell the squirming scarlet of—of what grew upon her head. It fell in a long, alive cloak to her bare feet on the floor, hiding her in a wave of dreadful, wet, writhing life. She put up her hands and like a swimmer she parted the waterfall of it, tossing the masses back over her shoulders to reveal her own brown body, sweetly curved. She smiled exquisitely, and in starting waves back from her forehead and down about her in a hideous background writhed the snaky wetness of her living tresses. And Smith knew that he looked upon Medusa.[1]

The knowledge of that—the realization of vast backgrounds reaching into misted history—shook him out of his frozen horror for a moment, and in that moment he met her eyes again, smiling, green as glass in the moonlight, half hooded under drooping lids. Through the twisting scarlet she held out her arms. And there was something soul-shakingly desirable about her, so that all the blood surged to his head suddenly and he stumbled to his feet like a sleeper in a dream as she swayed toward him, infinitely graceful, infinitely sweet in her cloak of living horror.

And somehow there was beauty in it, the wet scarlet writhings with moonlight sliding and shining along the thick, worm-round tresses and losing itself in the masses only to glint again and move silvery along writhing tendrils—an awful, shuddering beauty more dreadful than any ugliness could be.

But all this, again, he but half realized, for the insidious murmur was coiling again through his brain, promising, caressing, alluring, sweeter than honey; and the green eyes that held his were clear and burning like the depths of a jewel, and behind the pulsing slits of darkness he was staring into a greater dark that held all things.... He had known—dimly he had known when he first gazed into those flat animal shallows that behind them lay this—all beauty and terror, all horror and delight, in the infinite darkness upon which her eyes opened like windows, paned with emerald glass.

Her lips moved, and in a murmur that blended indistinguishably with the silence and the sway of her body and the dreadful sway of her—her hair—she whispered—very softly, very passionately, "I shall—speak to you now—in my own tongue—oh, beloved!"

And in her living cloak she swayed to him, the murmur swelling seductive and caressing in his innermost brain—promising, compelling, sweeter than sweet. His flesh crawled to the horror of her, but it was a perverted revulsion that clasped what it loathed. His arms slid round her under the sliding cloak, wet, wet and warm and hideously alive—and the sweet velvet body was clinging to his, her arms locked about his neck—and with a whisper and a rush the unspeakable horror closed about them both.

In nightmares until he died he remembered that moment when the living

1 One of three monstrous gorgons in Greek mythology. Medusa had snakes for hair and her gaze turned men into stone.

tresses of Shambleau first folded him in their embrace. A nauseous, smothering odor as the wetness shut around him—thick, pulsing worms clasping every inch of his body, sliding, writhing, their wetness and warmth striking through his garments as if he stood naked to their embrace.

All this in a graven instant—and after that a tangled flash of conflicting sensation before oblivion closed over him for he remembered the dream—and knew it for nightmare reality now, and the sliding, gently moving caresses of those wet, warm worms upon his flesh was an ecstasy above words—that deeper ecstasy that strikes beyond the body and beyond the mind and tickles the very roots of soul with unnatural delight. So he stood, rigid as marble, as helplessly stony as any of Medusa's victims in ancient legends were, while the terrible pleasure of Shambleau thrilled and shuddered through every fiber of him; through every atom of his body and the intangible atoms of what men call the soul, through all that was Smith the dreadful pleasure ran. And it was truly dreadful. Dimly he knew it, even as his body answered to the root-deep ecstasy, a foul and dreadful wooing from which his very soul shuddered away—and yet in the innermost depths of that soul some grinning traitor shivered with delight. But deeply, behind all this, he knew horror and revulsion and despair beyond telling, while the intimate caresses crawled obscenely in the secret places of his soul—knew that the soul should not be handled—and shook with the perilous pleasure through it all.

And this conflict and knowledge, this mingling of rapture and revulsion all took place in the flashing of a moment while the scarlet worms coiled and crawled upon him, sending deep, obscene tremors of that infinite pleasure into every atom that made up Smith. And he could not stir in that slimy, ecstatic embrace—and a weakness was flooding that grew deeper after each succeeding wave of intense delight, and the traitor in his soul strengthened and drowned out the revulsion—and something within him ceased to struggle as he sank wholly into a blazing darkness that was oblivion to all else but that devouring rapture....

† † †

The young Venusian climbing the stairs to his friend's lodging-room pulled out his key absent-mindedly, a pucker forming between his fine brows. He was slim, as all Venusians are, as fair and sleek as any of them, and as with most of his countrymen the look of cherubic innocence on his face was wholly deceptive. He had the face of a fallen angel, without Lucifer's majesty to redeem it; for a black devil grinned in his eyes and there were faint lines of ruthlessness and dissipation about his mouth to tell of the long years behind him that had run the gamut of experiences and made his name, next to Smith's, the most hated and the most respected in the records of the Patrol.

He mounted the stairs now with a puzzled frown between his eyes. He had come into Lakkdarol on the noon liner—the *Maid* in her hold very skillfully disguised with paint and otherwise—to find in lamentable disorder the affairs he had expected to be settled. And cautious inquiry elicited the information that Smith had not been seen for three days. That was not like his friend—he had never failed before, and the two stood to lose not only a large sum of money but also their personal safety by the inexplicable lapse on the part of Smith. Yarol could think of one solution only: fate had at last caught up with his friend. Nothing but physical disability could explain it.

Still puzzling, he fitted his key in the lock and swung the door open.

In that first moment, as the door opened, he sensed something very wrong.... The room was darkened, and for a while he could see nothing, but at the first breath he scented a strange, unnamable odor, half sickening, half sweet. And deep stirrings of ancestral memory awoke within him—ancient swamp-born memories from Venusian ancestors far away and long ago....

Yarol laid his hand on his gun, lightly, and opened the door wider. In the dimness all he could see at first was a curious mound in the far corner.... Then his eyes grew accustomed to the dark, and he saw it more clearly, a mound that somehow heaved and stirred within itself.... A mound of—he caught his breath sharply—a mound like a mass of entrails, living, moving, writhing with an unspeakable aliveness. Then a hot Venusian oath broke from his lips and he cleared the door-sill in a swift stride, slammed the door and set his back against it, gun ready in his hand, although his flesh crawled—for he *knew*....

"Smith!" he said softly, in a voice thick with horror.

The moving mass stirred—shuddered—sank back into crawling quiescence again.

"Smith! Smith!" The Venusian's voice was gentle and insistent, and it quivered a little with terror.

An impatient ripple went over the whole mass of aliveness in the corner. It stirred again, reluctantly, and then tendril by writhing tendril it began to part itself and fall aside, and very slowly the brown of a spaceman's leather appeared beneath it, all slimed and shining.

"Smith! Northwest!" Yarol's persistent whisper came again, urgently, and with a dream-like slowness the leather garments moved... a man sat up in the midst of the writhing worms, a man who once, long ago, might have been Northwest Smith. From head to foot he was slimy from the embrace of the crawling horror about him. His face was that of some creature beyond humanity—dead-alive, fixed in a gray stare, and the look of terrible ecstasy that overspread it seemed to come from somewhere far within, a faint reflection from immeasurable distances beyond the flesh. And as there is mystery and magic in the moonlight which is after all but a reflection of the everyday sun, so in that gray face turned to the door was a terror unnamable and sweet, a reflection of ecstasy beyond the understanding of any who had known only earthly ecstasy themselves. And as he sat there turning a blank, eyeless face to Yarol the red worms writhed ceaselessly about him, very gently, with a soft, caressive motion that never slacked.

"Smith... come here! Smith... get up... Smith, Smith!" Yarol's whisper hissed in the silence, commanding, urgent—but he made no move to leave the door.

And with a dreadful slowness, like a dead man rising, Smith stood up in the nest of slimy scarlet. He swayed drunkenly on his feet, and two or three crimson tendrils came writhing up his legs to the knees and wound themselves there, supportingly, moving with a ceaseless caress that seemed to give him some hidden strength, for he said then, without inflection.

"Go away. Go away. Leave me alone." And the dead ecstatic face never changed.

"Smith!" Yarol's voice was desperate. "Smith, listen! Smith, can't you hear me?"

"Go away," the monotonous voice said. "Go away. Go away. Go—"

"Not unless you come too. Can't you hear? Smith! Smith! I'll—"

He hushed in mid-phrase, and once more the ancestral prickle of race-memory shivered down his back, for the scarlet mass was moving again, violently, rising....

Yarol pressed back against the door and gripped his gun, and the name of a god he had forgotten years ago rose to his lips unbidden. For he knew what was coming next, and the knowledge was more dreadful than any ignorance could have been.

The red, writhing mass rose higher, and the tendrils parted and a human face looked out—no, half human, with green cat-eyes that shone in that dimness like lighted jewels, compellingly....

Yarol breathed "Shar!" again, and flung up an arm across his face, and the tingle of meeting that green gaze for even an instant went thrilling through him perilously.

"Smith!" he called in despair. "Smith, can't you hear me?"

"Go away," said that voice that was not Smith's. "Go away."

And somehow, although he dared not look, Yarol knew that the—the other—had parted those worm-thick tresses and stood there in all the human sweetness of the brown, curved woman's body, cloaked in living horror. And he felt the eyes upon him, and something was crying insistently in his brain to lower that shielding arm.... He was lost—he knew it, and the knowledge gave him that courage which comes from despair. The voice in his brain was growing, swelling, deafening him with a roaring command that all but swept him before it—command to lower that arm—to meet the eyes that opened upon darkness—to submit—and a promise, murmurous and sweet and evil beyond words, of pleasure to come....

But somehow he kept his head—somehow, dizzily, he was gripping his gun in his upflung hand—somehow, incredibly, crossing the narrow room with averted face, groping for Smith's shoulder. There was a moment of blind fumbling in emptiness, and then he found it, and gripped the leather that was slimy and dreadful and wet—and simultaneously he felt something loop gently about his ankle and a shock of repulsive pleasure went through him, and then another coil, and another, wound about his feet....

Yarol set his teeth and gripped the shoulder hard, and his hand shuddered of itself, for the feel of that leather was slimy as the worms about his ankles, and a faint tingle of obscene delight went through him from the contact.

That caressive pressure on his legs was all he could feel, and the voice in his brain drowned out all other sounds, and his body obeyed him reluctantly—but somehow he gave one heave of tremendous effort and swung Smith, stumbling, out of that nest of horror. The twining tendrils ripped loose with a little sucking sound, and the whole mass quivered and reached after, and then Yarol forgot his friend utterly and turned his whole being to the hopeless task of freeing himself. For only a part of him was fighting, now—only a part of him struggled against the twining obscenities, and in his innermost brain the sweet, seductive murmur sounded, and his body clamored to surrender....

"*Shar! Shar y'danis... Shar mor'la-rol—*" prayed Yarol, gasping and half unconscious that he spoke, boy's prayers that he had forgotten years ago, and with his back half turned to the central mass he kicked desperately with his heavy boots at the red, writhing worms about him. They gave back before him, quivering and curling themselves out of reach, and though he knew that more were reaching for his throat from behind, at least he could go on struggling until he was forced to meet those eyes....

He stamped and kicked and stamped again, and for one instant he was free of the slimy grip as the bruised worms curled back from his heavy feet, and he lurched away dizzily, sick with revulsion and despair as he fought off the coils, and then he lifted his eyes and saw the cracked mirror on the wall. Dimly in its reflection he could see the writhing scarlet horror behind him, cat face peering out with its demure girl-smile, dreadfully human, and all the red tendrils reaching after him. And remembrance of something he had read long ago swept incongruously over him, and the gasp of relief and hope that he gave shook for a moment the grip of the command in his brain.

Without pausing for a breath he swung the gun over his shoulder, the reflected barrel in line with the reflected horror in the mirror, and flicked the catch.

In the mirror he saw its blue flame leap in a dazzling spate across the dimness, full into the midst of that squirming, reaching mass behind him. There was a hiss and a blaze and a high, thin scream of inhuman malice and despair—the flame cut a wide arc and went out as the gun fell from his hand, and Yarol pitched forward to the floor.

† † †

Northwest Smith opened his eyes to Martian sunlight streaming thinly through the dingy window. Something wet and cold was slapping his face, and the familiar fiery sting of *segir*-whiskey burnt his throat.

"Smith!" Yarol's voice was saying from far away. "N.W.! Wake up, damn you! Wake up!"

"I'm—awake," Smith managed to articulate thickly. "Wha's matter?"

Then a cup-rim was thrust against his teeth and Yarol said irritably, "Drink it, you fool!"

Smith swallowed obediently and more of the fire-hot *segir* flowed down his grateful throat. It spread a warmth through his body that awakened him from the numbness that had gripped him until now, and helped a little toward driving out the all-devouring weakness he was becoming aware of slowly. He lay still for a few minutes while the warmth of the whisky went through him, and memory sluggishly began to permeate his brain with the spread of the *segir*. Nightmare memories... sweet and terrible... memories of—

"God!" gasped Smith suddenly, and tried to sit up. Weakness smote him like a blow, and for an instant the room wheeled as he fell back against something firm and warm—Yarol's shoulder. The Venusian's arm supported him while the room steadied, and after a while he twisted a little and stared into the other's black gaze.

Yarol was holding him with one arm and finishing the mug of *segir* himself, and the black eyes met his over the rim and crinkled into sudden laughter, half hysterical after that terror that was passed.

"By *Pharol!*" gasped Yarol, choking into his mug. "By *Pharol*, N.W.! I'm never gonna let you forget this! Next time you have to drag me out of a mess I'll say—"

"Let it go," said Smith. "What's been going on? How—"

"Shambleau," Yarol's laughter died. "Shambleau! What were you doing with a thing like that?"

"What was it?" Smith asked soberly.

"Mean to say you didn't know? But where'd you find it? How—"

"Suppose you tell me first what you know," said Smith firmly. "And another swig of that *segir*, too. I need it."

"Can you hold the mug now? Feel better?"

"Yeah—some. I can hold it—thanks. Now go on."

"Well—I don't know just where to start. They call them Shambleau—"

"Good God, is there more than one?"

"It's a—a sort of race, I think, one of the very oldest. Where they come from nobody knows. The name sounds a little French, doesn't it? But it goes back beyond the start of history. There have always been Shambleau."

"I never heard of 'em."

"Not many people have. And those who know don't care to talk about it much."

"Well, half this town knows. I hadn't any idea what they were talking about, then. And I still don't understand—"

"Yes, it happens like this, sometimes. They'll appear, and the news will spread and the town will get together and hunt them down, and after that—well, the story doesn't get around very far. It's too—too unbelievable."

"But—my God, Yarol!—what was it? Where'd it come from? How—"

"Nobody knows just where they come from. Another planet—maybe some undiscovered one. Some say Venus—I know there are some rather awful legends of them handed down in our family—that's how I've heard about it. And the minute I opened that door, awhile back—I—I think I knew that smell...."

"But—what *are* they?"

"God knows. Not human, though they have the human form. Or that may be only an illusion... or maybe I'm crazy. I don't know. They're a species of the vampire—or maybe the vampire is a species of—of them. Their normal form must be that—that mass, and in that form they draw nourishment from the—I suppose the life-forces of men. And they take some form—usually a woman form, I think, and key you up to the highest pitch of emotion before they—begin. That's to work the life-force up to intensity so it'll be easier.... And they give, always, that horrible, foul pleasure as they—feed. There are some men who, if they survive the first experience, take to it like a drug—can't give it up—keep the thing with them all their lives—which isn't long—feeding it for that ghastly satisfaction. Worse than smoking *ming* or—or 'praying to *Pharol*.'"

"Yes," said Smith. "I'm beginning to understand why that crowd was so surprised and—and disgusted when I said—well, never mind. Go on."

"Did you get to talk to—to it?" asked Yarol.

"I tried to. It couldn't speak very well. I asked it where it came from and it said—'from far away and long ago'—something like that."

"I wonder. Possibly some unknown planet—but I think not. You know there are so many wild stories with some basis of fact to start from, that I've sometimes wondered—mightn't there be a lot more of even worse and wilder superstitions we've never even heard of? Things like this, blasphemous and foul, that those who know have to keep still about? Awful, fantastic things running around loose that we never hear rumors of at all!

"These things—they've been in existence for countless ages. No one knows when or where they first appeared. Those who've seen them, as we saw this one, don't talk about it. It's just one of those vague, misty rumors you find half hinted at in old books sometimes.... I believe they are an older race than man, spawned from ancient seed in times before ours, perhaps on planets that have gone to dust, and so horrible to man that when they are discovered the discoverers keep still about it—forget them again as quickly as they can.

"And they go back to time immemorial. I suppose you recognized the legend of Medusa? There isn't any question that the ancient Greeks knew of them. Does it mean that there have been civilizations before yours that set out from Earth and explored other planets? Or did one of the Shambleau somehow make its way into Greece three thousand years ago? If you think about it long enough you'll go off your head! I wonder how many other legends are based on things like this—things we don't suspect, things we'll never know.

"The Gorgon, Medusa, a beautiful woman with—with snakes for hair, and a gaze that turned men to stone, and Perseus finally killed her—I remembered this just by accident, N.W., and it saved your life and mine—Perseus killed her by using a mirror as he fought to reflect what he dared not look at directly. I wonder what the old Greek who first started that legend would have thought if he'd known that three thousand years later his story would save the lives of two men on another planet. I wonder what that Greek's own story was, and how he met the thing, and what happened....

"Well, there's a lot we'll never know. Wouldn't the records of that race of—of *things*, whatever they are, be worth reading! Records of other planets and other ages and all the beginnings of mankind! But I don't suppose they've kept any records. I don't suppose they've even any place to keep them—from what little I know, or anyone knows about it, they're like the Wandering Jew,[1] just bobbing up here and there at long intervals, and where they stay in the meantime I'd give my eyes to know! But I don't believe that terribly hypnotic power they have indicates any superhuman intelligence. It's their means of getting food—just like a frog's long tongue or a carnivorous flower's odor. Those are physical because the frog and the flower eat physical food. The Shambleau uses a—a mental reach to get mental food. I don't quite know how to put it. And just as a beast that eats the bodies of other animals acquires with each meal greater power over the bodies of the rest, so the Shambleau, stoking itself up with the life-forces of men, increases its power over the minds and souls of other men. But I'm talking about things I can't define—things I'm not sure exist.

"I only know that when I felt—when those tentacles closed around my legs—I didn't want to pull loose, I felt sensations that—that—oh, I'm fouled and filthy to the very deepest part of me by that—pleasure—and yet—"

"I know," said Smith slowly. The effect of the *segir* was beginning to wear off, and weakness was washing back over him in waves, and when he spoke he was half meditating in a lower voice, scarcely realizing that Yarol listened. "I know it—much better than you do—and there's something so indescribably awful that the thing emanates, something so utterly at odds with everything human—there aren't any words to say it. For a while I was a part of it, literally, sharing its thoughts and memories and emotions and hungers, and—well, it's over now and I don't remember very clearly, but the only part left free was that part of me that was all but insane from the—the obscenity of the thing.

1 The Wandering Jew was a man who taunted Jesus on the way to the Crucifixion. In punishment, he was cursed to walk the earth until Jesus returned in the Second Coming.

And yet it was a pleasure so sweet—I think there must be some nucleus of utter evil in me—in everyone—that needs only the proper stimulus to get complete control; because even while I was sick all through from the touch of those—things—there was something in me that was—was simply gibbering with delight... Because of that I saw things—and knew things—horrible, wild things I can't quite remember—visited unbelievable places, looked backward through the memory of that—creature—I was one with, and saw—God, I wish I could remember!"

"You ought to thank your God you can't," said Yarol soberly.

† † †

His voice roused Smith from the half-trance he had fallen into, and he rose on his elbow, swaying a little from weakness. The room was wavering before him, and he closed his eyes, not to see it, but he asked, "You say they—they don't turn up again? No way of finding—another?"

Yarol did not answer for a moment. He laid his hands on the other man's shoulders and pressed him back, and then sat staring down into the dark, ravaged face with a new, strange, undefinable look upon it that he had never seen there before—whose meaning he knew, too well.

"Smith," he said finally, and his black eyes for once were steady and serious, and the little grinning devil had vanished from behind them, "Smith, I've never asked your word on anything before, but I've—I've earned the right to do it now, and I'm asking you to promise me one thing."

Smith's colorless eyes met the black gaze unsteadily. Irresolution was in them, and a little fear of what that promise might be. And for just a moment Yarol was looking, not into his friend's familiar eyes, but into a wide gray blankness that held all horror and delight—a pale sea with unspeakable pleasures sunk beneath it. Then the wide stare focused again and Smith's eyes met his squarely and Smith's voice said, "Go ahead. I'll promise."

"That if you ever should meet a Shambleau again—ever, anywhere—you'll draw your gun and burn it to hell the instant you realize what it is. Will you promise me that?"

There was a long silence. Yarol's somber black eyes bored relentlessly into the colorless ones of Smith, not wavering. And the veins stood out on Smith's tanned forehead. He never broke his word—he had given it perhaps half a dozen times in his life, but once he had given it, he was incapable of breaking it. And once more the gray seas flooded in a dim tide of memories, sweet and horrible beyond dreams. Once more Yarol was staring into blankness that hid nameless things. The room was very still.

The gray tide ebbed. Smith's eyes, pale and resolute as steel, met Yarol's levelly.

"I'll—try," he said. And his voice wavered.

# Fritz Leiber

(1910–1992)

Influential fantasy writer Fritz Leiber was instrumental in defining the "Sword and Sorcery" subgenre in the late 1930s. He coined this term to describe the fantasy adventure narratives of Robert Ervin Howard, the creator of the anti-hero Conan the Barbarian. In classic sword-and-sorcery narratives, a solitary hero or heroine embarks on a quest in a fantasy landscape inhabited by supernatural beings. Leiber was encouraged to pursue a literary career by the horror fiction writer H.P. Lovecraft. Much of his fiction has been referred to as modern urban horror, an apt description for the short story "The Girl with the Hungry Eyes" (1949), which is a critical response to post–World War II consumerism. The story was adapted for television and featured in Rod Serling's *Night Gallery* (1972).

## "The Girl with the Hungry Eyes"

(1949)

All right, I'll tell you why the Girl gives me the creeps. Why I can't stand to go downtown and see the mob slavering up at her on the tower, with that pop bottle or pack of cigarettes or whatever it is beside her. Why I hate to look at magazines any more because I know she'll turn up somewhere in a brassiere or a bubble bath. Why I don't like to think of millions of Americans drinking in that poisonous halfsmile.

It's quite a story—more story than you're expecting.

No, I haven't suddenly developed any long-haired indignation at the evils of advertising and the national glamour-girl complex. That'd be a laugh for a man in my racket, wouldn't it? Though I think you'll agree there's something a little perverted about trying to capitalize on sex that way. But it's okay with me. And I know we've had the Face and the Body and the Look and what not else, so why shouldn't someone come along who sums it all up so completely, that we have to call her the Girl and blazon her on all the billboards from Times Square to Telegraph Hill?

But the Girl isn't like any of the others. She's unnatural. She's morbid. She's unholy.

Oh it's 1948, is it, and the sort of thing I'm hinting at went out with witchcraft? But you see I'm not altogether sure myself what I'm hinting at, beyond a certain point. There are vampires and vampires, and not all of them suck blood.

And there were the murders, if they were murders. Besides, let me ask you this. Why, when America is obsessed with the Girl, don't we find out more about her? Why doesn't she rate a *Time* cover with a droll biography inside? Why hasn't there been a feature in *Life* or the *Post*? A profile in *The New Yorker*? Why hasn't *Charm* or *Mademoiselle* done her career saga? Not ready for it? Nuts!

Why haven't the movies snapped her up? Why hasn't she been on "Information, Please"? Why don't we see her kissing candidates at political rallies? Why isn't she chosen queen of some sort of junk or other at a convention?

Why don't we read about her tastes and hobbies, her views of the Russian situation? Why haven't the columnists interviewed her in a kimono on the top floor of the tallest hotel in Manhattan and told us who her boyfriends are?

Finally—and this is the real killer—why hasn't she ever been drawn or painted?

Oh, no she hasn't. If you knew anything about commercial art you'd know that. Every blessed one of those pictures was worked up from a photograph. Expertly? Of course. They've got the top artists on it.

But that's how it's done.

And now I'll tell you the why of all that. It's because from the top to the bottom of the whole world of advertising, news, and business, there isn't a solitary soul who knows where the Girl came from, where she lives, what she does, who she is, even what her name is.

You heard me. What's more, not a single solitary soul ever sees her—except one poor damned photographer, who's making more money off her than he ever hoped to in his life and who's scared and miserable as hell every minute of the day.

No, I haven't the faintest idea who he is or where he has his studio. But I know there has to be such a man and I'm morally certain he feels just like I said.

Yes, I might be able to find her, if I tried. I'm not sure though—by now she probably has other safeguards. Besides, I don't want to.

Oh, I'm off my rocker, am I? That sort of thing can't happen in this Era of the Atom 1948? People can't keep out of sight that way, not even Garbo?

Well I happen to know they can, because last year I was that poor damned photographer I was telling you about. Yes, last year, in 1947, when the Girl made her first poisonous splash right here in this big little city of ours.

Yes, I knew you weren't here last year and you don't know about it. Even the Girl had to start small. But if you hunted through the files of the local newspapers, you'd find some ads, and I might be able to locate you some of the old displays—I think Lovelybelt is still using one of them. I used to have a mountain of photos myself, until I burned them.

Yes, I made my cut off her. Nothing like what that other photographer must be making, but enough so it still bought this whisky. She was funny about money. I'll tell you about that.

But first picture me in 1947. I had a fourth-floor studio in that rathole the Hauser Building, catty-corner from Ardleigh Park.

I'd been working at the Marsh-Mason studios until I'd got my bellyful of it and decided to start in for myself. The Hauser Building was crummy—I'll never forget how the stairs creaked—but it was cheap and there was a skylight.

Business was lousy. I kept making the rounds of all the advertisers and agencies, and some of them didn't object to me too much personally, but my stuff never clicked. I was pretty near broke. I was behind on my rent. Hell, I didn't even have enough money to have a girl.

It was one of those dark gray afternoons. The building was awfully quiet—even with the shortage they can't half rent the Hauser. I'd just finished developing some pix I was doing on speculation for Lovelybelt Girdles and Buford's Pool and Playground—the last a faked-up beach scene. My model had left. A Miss Leon. She was a civics teacher at one of the high schools and modeled for me on the side, just lately on speculation too. After one look at the prints, I decided that Miss Leon probably wasn't just what Lovelybelt was looking for—or my photography either. I was about to call it a day.

And then the street door slammed four storeys down and there were steps on the stairs and she came in. She was wearing a cheap, shiny black dress. Black pumps. No stockings. And except that she had a gray cloth coat over one of them, those skinny arms of hers were bare. Her arms are pretty skinny, you know, or can you see things like that any more?

And then the thin neck, the slightly gaunt, almost prim face, the tumbling mass of dark hair, and looking out from under it the hungriest eyes in the world.

That's the real reason she's plastered all over the country today, you know—those eyes. Nothing vulgar, but just the same they're looking at you with a hunger that's all sex and something more than sex. That's what everybody's been looking for since the Year One—something a little more than sex.

Well, boys, there I was, along with the Girl, in an office that was getting shadowy, in a nearly empty building. A situation that a million male Americans have undoubtedly pictured to themselves with various lush details. How was I feeling? Scared.

I know sex can be frightening. That cold, heart-thumping when you're alone with a girl and feel you're going to touch her. But if it was sex this time, it was overlaid with something else.

At least I wasn't thinking about sex.

I remember that I took a backward step and that my hand jerked so that the photos I was looking at sailed to the floor.

There was the faintest dizzy feeling like something was being drawn out of me. Just a little bit.

That was all. Then she opened her mouth and everything was back to normal for a while.

"I see you're a photographer, mister," she said. "Could you use a model?"

Her voice wasn't very cultivated.

"I doubt it," I told her, picking up the pix. You see, I wasn't impressed. The commercial possibilities of her eyes hadn't registered on me yet, by a long shot. "What have you done?"

Well she gave me a vague sort of story and I began to check her knowledge of model agencies and studios and rates and what not and pretty soon I said to her, "Look here, you never modeled for a photographer in your life. You just walked in here cold."

Well, she admitted that was more or less so.

All along through our talk I got the idea she was feeling her way, like someone in a strange place. Not that she was uncertain of herself, or of me, but just of the general situation.

"And you think anyone can model?" I asked her pityingly.

"Sure," she said.

"Look," I said, "a photographer can waste a dozen negatives trying to get one halfway human photo of an average woman. How many do you think he'd have to waste before he got a real catchy, glamorous photo of her?"

"I think I could do it," she said.

Well, I should have kicked her out right then. Maybe I admired the cool way she stuck to her dumb little guns. Maybe I was touched by her underfed look. More likely I was feeling mean on account of the way my pix had been snubbed by everybody and I wanted to take it out on her by showing her up.

"Okay, I'm going to put you on the spot," I told her. "I'm going to try a couple of shots of you. Understand, it's strictly on spec. If somebody should ever want to use a photo of you, which is about one chance in two million, I'll pay you regular rates for your time. Not otherwise."

She gave me a smile. The first. "That's swell by me," she said.

Well, I took three or four shots, close-ups of her face since I didn't fancy her cheap dress, and at least she stood up to my sarcasm. Then I remembered I still had the Lovelybelt stuff and I guess the meanness was still working in me because I handed her a girdle and told her to go behind the screen and get into it and she did, without getting flustered as I'd expected, and since we'd gone that far I figured we might as well shoot the beach scene to round it out, and that was that.

All this time I wasn't feeling anything particular in one way or the other except every once in a while I'd get one of those faint dizzy flashes and wonder if there was something wrong with my stomach or if I could have been a bit careless with my chemicals.

Still, you know, I think the uneasiness was in me all the while.

I tossed her a card and pencil. "Write your name and address and phone," I told her and made for the darkroom.

A little later she walked out. I didn't call any good-byes. I was irked because she hadn't fussed around or seemed anxious about her poses, or even thanked me, except for that one smile.

I finished developing the negatives, made some prints, glanced at them, decided they weren't a great deal worse than Miss Leon. On an impulse I slipped them in with the pix I was going to take on the rounds next morning.

By now I'd worked long enough so I was a bit fagged and nervous, but I didn't dare waste enough money on liquor to help that. I wasn't very hungry. I think I went to a cheap movie.

I didn't think of the Girl at all, except maybe to wonder faintly why in my present womanless state I hadn't made a pass at her. She had seemed to belong to a, well, distinctly more approachable social stratum than Miss Leon. But then of course there were all sorts of arguable reasons for my not doing that.

Next morning I made the rounds. My first step was Munsch's Brewery. They were looking for a "Munsch Girl." Papa Munsch had a sort of affection for me, though he razzed my photography. He had a good natural judgment about that, too. Fifty years ago he might have been one of the shoestring boys who made Hollywood.

Right now he was out in the plant pursuing his favorite occupation. He put down the beaded can, smacked his lips, gabbled something technical to someone about hops, wiped his fat hands on the big apron he was wearing, and grabbed my thin stack of pix.

He was about halfway through, making noises with his tongue and teeth, when he came to her. I kicked myself for even having stuck her in.

"That's her," he said. "The photography's not so hot, but that's the girl."

It was all decided. I wondered now why Papa Munsch sensed what the girl had right away, while I didn't. I think it was because I saw her first in the flesh, if that's the right word.

At the time I just felt faint.

"Who is she?" he asked.

"One of my new models." I tried to make it casual.

"Bring her out tomorrow morning," he told me. "And your stuff. We'll photograph her here. I want to show you.

"Here, don't look so sick," he added. "Have some beer."

Well I went away telling myself it was just a fluke, so that she'd probably blow it tomorrow with her inexperience, and so on.

Just the same, when I reverently laid my next stack of pix on Mr. Fitch, of Lovelybelt's rose-colored blotter, I had hers on top.

Mr. Fitch went through the motions of being an art critic. He leaned over backward, squinted his eyes, waved his long fingers, and said, "Hmmm. What do you think, Miss Willow? Here, in this light. Of course the photograph doesn't show the bias cut. And perhaps we should use the Lovelybelt Imp instead of the Angel. Still, the girl... Come over here, Binns." More finger-waving. "I want a married man's reaction."

He couldn't hide the fact that he was hooked.

Exactly the same thing happened at Buford's Pool and Playground, except that Da Costa didn't need a married man's say-so.

"Hot stuff," he said, sucking his lips. "Oh, boy, you photographers!"

I hot-footed it back to the office and grabbed up the card I'd given to her to put down her name and address. It was blank.

I don't mind telling you that the next five days were about the worst I ever went through, in an ordinary way. When next morning rolled around and I still hadn't got hold of her, I had to start stalling.

"She's sick," I told Papa Munsch over the phone.

"She at a hospital?" he asked me.

"Nothing that serious." I told him.

"Get her out here then. What's a little headache?"

"Sorry, I can't."

Papa Munsch got suspicious. "You really got this girl?"

"Of course I have."

"Well, I don't know. I'd think it was some New York model, except I recognized your lousy photography."

I laughed.

"Well look, you get her here tomorrow morning, you hear?"

"I'll try."

"Try nothing. You get her out here."

He didn't know half of what I tried. I went around to all the model and employment agencies. I did some slick detective work at the photographic and art studios. I used up some of my last dimes putting advertisements in all three papers. I looked at high school yearbooks and at employee photos in local house organs. I went to restaurants and drugstores, looking for waitresses, and to dime stores and department stores, looking at clerks. I watched the crowds coming out of movie theatres. I roamed the streets.

Evenings I spent quite a bit of time along Pick-up Row. Somehow that seemed the right place.

The fifth afternoon I knew I was licked. Papa Munsch's deadline—he'd given me several, but this was it—was due to run out at six o'clock. Mr. Fitch had already canceled.

I was at the studio window, looking out at Ardleigh Park.

She walked in.

I'd gone over this moment so often in my mind that I had no trouble putting on my act. Even the faint dizzy feeling didn't throw me off.

"Hello," I said, hardly looking at her.

"Hello," she said.

"Not discouraged yet?"

"No." It didn't sound uneasy or defiant. It was just a statement.

I snapped a look at my watch, got up and said curtly, "Look here, I'm going to give you a chance. There's a client of mine looking for a girl your general type. If you do a real good job you may break into the modeling business.

"We can see him this afternoon if we hurry." I said. I picked up my stuff. "Come on. And next time, if you expect favors, don't forget to leave your phone number."

"Uh, uh," she said, not moving.

"What do you mean?" I said.

"I'm not going to see any client of yours."

"The hell you aren't," I said. "You little nut, I'm giving you a break."

She shook her head slowly. "You're not fooling me, baby, you're not fooling me at all. They want me."

And she gave me the second smile.

At the time I thought she must have seen my newspaper ad. Now I'm not so sure.

"And now I'll tell you how we're going to work," she went on. "You aren't going to have my name or address or phone number. Nobody is. And we're going to do all the pictures right here. Just you and me."

You can imagine the roar I raised at that. I was everything—angry, sarcastic, patiently explanatory, off my nut, threatening, pleading.

I would have slapped her face off, except it was photographic capital.

In the end all I could do was phone Papa Munsch and tell him her conditions. I know I didn't have a chance, but I had to take it.

He gave me a really angry bawling out, said "no" several times and hung up.

It didn't faze her. "We'll start shooting at ten o'clock tomorrow," she said.

It was just like her, using that corny line from the movie magazines.

About midnight Papa Munsch called me up.

"I don't know what insane asylum you're renting this girl from," he said, "but I'll take her. Come around tomorrow morning and I'll try to get it through your head just how I want the pictures. And I'm glad I got you out of bed!"

After that it was a breeze. Even Mr. Fitch reconsidered and after taking two days to tell me it was quite impossible, he accepted the conditions too.

Of course you're all under the spell of the Girl, so you can't understand how much self-sacrifice it represented on Mr. Fitch's part when he agreed to forego supervising the photography of my model in the Lovelybelt Imp or Vixen or whatever it was we finally used.

Next morning she turned up on time according to her schedule, and we went to work. I'll say one thing for her, she never got tired and she never kicked at the way I fussed over shots. I got along okay except I still had the feeling of something being shoved away gently. Maybe you've felt it just a little, looking at her picture.

When we finished I found out there were still more rules. It was about the middle of the afternoon. I started down with her to get a sandwich and coffee.

"Uh uh," she said, "I'm going down alone. And look, baby, if you ever try to follow me, if you ever so much as stick your head out that window when I go, you can hire yourself another model."

You can imagine how all this crazy stuff strained my temper—and my imagination. I remember opening the window after she was gone—I waited a few minutes first—and standing there getting some fresh air and trying to figure out what could be behind it, whether she was hiding from the police, or was somebody's ruined daughter, or maybe had got the idea it was smart to be temperamental, or more likely Papa Munsch was right and she was partly nuts.

But I had my pix to finish up.

Looking back it's amazing to think how fast her magic began to take hold of the city after that. Remembering what came after, I'm frightened of what's happening to the whole country—and maybe the world. Yesterday I read something in *Time* about the Girl's picture turning up on billboards in Egypt.

The rest of my story will help show you why I'm frightened in that big general way. But I have a theory, too, that helps explain, though it's one of those things that's beyond that "certain point." It's about the Girl. I'll give it to you in a few words.

You know how modern advertising gets everybody's mind set in the same direction, wanting the same things, imagining the same things. And you know the psychologists aren't so sceptical of telepathy as they used to be.

Add up the two ideas. Suppose the identical desires of millions of people focused on one telepathic person. Say a girl. Shaped her in their image.

Imagine her knowing the hiddenmost hungers of millions of men. Imagine her seeing deeper into those hungers than the people that had them, seeing the hatred and the wish for death behind the lust. Imagine her shaping herself in that complete image, keeping herself as aloof as marble. Yet imagine the hunger she might feel in answer to their hunger.

But that's getting a long way from the facts of my story. And some of those facts are darn solid. Like money. We made money.

That was the funny thing I was going to tell you. I was afraid the Girl was going to hold me up. She really had me over a barrel, you know.

But she didn't ask for anything but the regular rates. Later on I insisted on pushing more money at her, a whole lot. But she always took it with that same contemptuous look, as if she were going to toss it down the first drain when she got outside.

Maybe she did.

At any rate, I had money. For the first time in months I had money enough to get drunk, buy new clothes, take taxicabs. I could make a play for any girl I wanted to. I only had to pick.

And so of course I had to go and pick—

But first let me tell you about Papa Munsch.

Papa Munsch wasn't the first of the boys to try to meet my model but I think he was the first to really go soft on her. I could watch the change in his eyes as he looked at her pictures. They began to get sentimental, reverent. Mama Munsch had been dead for two years.

He was smart about the way he planned it. He got me to drop some information which told him when she came to work, and then one morning he came pounding up the stairs a few minutes before.

"I've got to see her, Dave," he told me.

I argued with him, I kidded him. I explained he didn't know just how serious she was about her crazy ideas. I pointed out he was cutting both our throats. I even amazed myself by bawling him out.

He didn't take any of it in his usual way. He just kept repeating, "But, Dave, I've got to see her."

The street door slammed.

"That's her," I said, lowering my voice. "You've got to get out."

He wouldn't, so I shoved him in the darkroom. "And keep quiet," I whispered. "I'll tell her I can't work today."

I knew he'd try to look at her and probably come busting in, but there wasn't anything else I could do.

The footsteps came to the fourth floor. But she never showed at the door. I got uneasy.

"Get that bum out of there!" she yelled suddenly from beyond the door. Not very loud, but in her commonest voice.

"I'm going up to the next landing," she said, "And if that fat-bellied bum doesn't march straight down to the street, he'll never get another picture of me except spitting in his lousy beer."

Papa Munsch came out of the darkroom. He was white. He didn't look at me as he went out. He never looked at her pictures in front of me again.

That was Papa Munsch. Now it's me I'm telling about. I talked about the subject with her, I hinted, eventually I made my pass.

She lifted my hand off her as if it were a damp rag.

"Nix, baby," she said. "This is working time."

"But afterward..." I pressed.

"The rules still hold." And I got what I think was the fifth smile.

It's hard to believe, but she never budged an inch from that crazy line. I mustn't make a pass at her in the office, because our work was very important and she loved it and there mustn't be any distractions. And I couldn't see her anywhere else, because if I tried to, I'd never snap another picture of her—and all this with more money coming in all the time and me never so stupid as to think my photography had anything to do with it.

Of course I wouldn't have been human if I hadn't made more passes. But they always got the wet-rag treatment and there weren't any more smiles.

I changed. I went sort of crazy and light-headed—only sometimes I felt my head was going to burst.

And I started to talk to her all the time. About myself.

It was like being in a constant delirium that never interfered with business. I didn't pay attention to the dizzy feeling. It seemed natural.

I'd walk around and for a moment the reflector would look like a sheet of white-hot steel, or the shadows would seem like armies of moths, or the camera would be a big black coal car. But the next instant they'd come all right again.

I think sometimes I was scared to death of her. She'd seem the strangest, horriblest person in the world.

But other times...

And I talked. It didn't matter what I was doing—lighting her, posing her, fussing with props, snapping my pix—or where she was—on the platform, behind the screen, relaxing with a magazine—I kept up a steady gab.

I told her everything I knew about myself. I told her about my first girl. I told her about my brother Bob's bicycle. I told her about running away on a freight and the licking Pa gave me when I came home.

I told her about shipping to South America and the blue sky at night. I told her about Betty. I told her about my mother dying of cancer. I told her about being beaten up in a fight in an alley behind a bar. I told her about Mildred. I told her about the first picture I ever sold. I told her how Chicago looked from a sailboat. I told her about the longest drunk I was ever on. I told her about Marsh-Mason. I told her about Gwen. I told her about how I met Papa Munsch. I told her about hunting her. I told her about how I felt now.

She never paid the slightest attention to what I said. I couldn't even tell if she heard me.

It was when we were getting our first nibble from national advertisers that I decided to follow her when she went home.

Wait, I can place it better than that. Something you'll remember from the out-of-town papers—those maybe-murders I mentioned. I think there were six.

I say "maybe" because the police could never be sure they weren't heart attacks. But there's bound to be suspicion when heart attacks happen to people whose hearts have been okay, and always at night when they're alone and away from home and there's a question of what they were doing.

The six deaths created one of those "mystery poisoner" scares. And afterward there was a feeling that they hadn't really stopped, but were being continued in a less suspicious way.

That's one of the things that scares me now.

But at that time my only feeling was relief that I'd decided to follow her.

I made her work until dark one afternoon. I didn't need any excuses, we were snowed under with orders.

I waited until the street door slammed, then I ran down. I was wearing rubber-soled shoes. I'd slipped on a dark coat she'd never seen me in, and a dark hat.

I stood in the doorway until I spotted her. She was walking by Ardleigh Park toward the heart of town. It was one of those warm fall nights. I followed her on the other side of the street. My idea for tonight was just to find out where she lived. That would give me a hold on her.

She stopped in front of a display window of Everly's department store, standing back from the glow.

She stood there looking in.

I remembered we'd done a big photograph of her for Everly's, to make a flat model for a lingerie display. That was what she was looking at.

At the time it seemed all right to me that she should adore herself, if that was what she was doing.

When people passed she'd turn away a little or drift back farther into the shadows.

Then a man came by alone. I couldn't see his face very well, but he looked middle-aged. He stopped and stood looking in the window.

She came out of the shadows and stepped up beside him.

How would you boys feel if you were looking at a poster of the Girl and suddenly she was there beside you, her arm linked with yours?

This fellow's reaction showed plain as day. A crazy dream had come to life for him.

They talked for a moment. Then he waved a taxi to the curb. They got in and drove off.

I got drunk that night. It was almost as if she'd known I was following her and had picked that way to hurt me. Maybe she had. Maybe this was the finish.

But the next morning she turned up at the usual time and I was back in the delirium, only now with some new angles added.

That night when I followed her she picked a spot under a street lamp, opposite one of the Munsch Girl billboards.

Now it frightens me to think of her lurking that way.

After about twenty minutes a convertible slowed down going past her, backed up, swung in to the curb.

I was closer this time. I got a good look at the fellow's face. He was a little younger, about my age.

Next morning the same face looked up at me from the front page of the paper. The convertible had been found parked on a side street. He had been in it. As in the other maybe-murders, the cause of death was uncertain.

All kinds of thoughts were spinning in my head that day, but there were only two things I knew for sure.

That I'd got the first real offer from a national advertiser, and that I was going to take the Girl's arm and walk down the stairs with her when we quit work.

She didn't seem surprised. "You know what you're doing?" she said.

"I know."

She smiled. "I was wondering when you'd get around to it."

I began to feel good. I was kissing everything good-bye, but I had my arm around hers.

It was another of those warm fall evenings. We cut across into Ardleigh Park. It was dark there, but all around the sky was a sallow pink from the advertising signs.

We walked for a long time in the park. She didn't say anything and she didn't look at me, but I could see her lips twitching and after a while her hand tightened on my arm.

We stopped. We'd been walking across the grass. She dropped down and pulled me after her. She put her hands on my shoulders. I was looking down at her face. It was the faintest sallow pink from the glow in the sky. The hungry eyes were dark smudges.

I was fumbling with her blouse. She took my hand away, not like she had in the studio. "I don't want that," she said.

First I'll tell you what I did afterward. Then I'll tell you why I did it. Then I'll tell you what she said.

What I did was run away. I don't remember all of that because I was dizzy, and the pink sky was swinging against the dark trees. But after a while I staggered into the lights of the street. The next day I closed up the studio. The telephone was ringing when I locked the door and there were unopened letters on the floor. I never saw the Girl again in the flesh, if that's the right word.

I did it because I didn't want to die. I didn't want the life drawn out of me. There are vampires and vampires, and the ones that suck blood aren't the worst. If it hadn't been for the warning of those dizzy flashes, and Papa Munsch and the face in the morning paper, I'd have gone the way the others did. But I realized what I was up against while there was still time to tear myself away. I realized that wherever she came from, whatever shaped her, she's the quintessence of the horror behind the bright billboard. She's the smile that tricks you into throwing away your money and your life. She's the eyes that lead you on and on, and then show you death. She's the creature you give everything for and never really get. She's the being that takes everything you've got and gives nothing in return.

When you yearn toward her face on the billboards, remember that. She's the lure. She's the bait. She's the Girl.

And this is what she said, "I want you. I want your high spots. I want everything that's made you happy and everything that's hurt you bad. I want your first girl. I want that shiny bicycle. I want that licking. I want that pinhole camera. I want Betty's legs. I want the blue sky filled with stars. I want your mother's death. I want your blood on the cobblestones. I want Mildred's mouth. I want the first picture you sold. I want the lights of Chicago. I want the gin. I want Gwen's hands. I want your wanting me. I want your life. Feed me, baby, feed me."

# Angela Carter

(1940–1992)

Angela Carter is widely known as one of the most unique and powerful writers of the twentieth century. Her postmodern work weaves together a wide range of influences from fairy tales to Shakespeare to gothic horror. Often graphic, her work offers a subversive feminist exploration of literature and society. Born in Eastbourne in East Sussex, Carter spent much of her childhood with her grandmother in Yorkshire, where she had been sent to escape the Blitz. This story was published in *The Bloody Chamber*, one of Carter's most successful books. It weaves together traditional tropes from vampire literature and fairy tale to tease out and subversively challenge the sexual undercurrents in both genres. Carter died in 1992 of lung cancer.

## "The Lady of the House of Love"

(1979)

At last the revenants became so troublesome the peasants abandoned the village and it fell solely into the possession of subtle and vindictive inhabitants who manifest their presences by shadows that fall almost imperceptibly awry, too many shadows, even at midday, shadows that have no source in anything visible; by the sound, sometimes, of sobbing in a derelict bedroom where a cracked mirror suspended from a wall does not reflect a presence; by a sense of unease that will afflict the traveller unwise enough to pause to drink from the fountain in the square that still gushes spring water from a faucet stuck in a stone lion's mouth. A cat prowls in a weedy garden; he grins and spits, arches his back, bounces away from an intangible on four fear-stiffened legs. Now all shun the village below the chateau in which the beautiful somnambulist helplessly perpetuates her ancestral crimes.

Wearing an antique bridal gown, the beautiful queen of the vampires sits all alone in her dark, high house under the eyes of the portraits of her demented and atrocious ancestors, each one of whom, through her, projects a baleful posthumous existence; she counts out the Tarot cards,[1] ceaselessly construing a constellation of possibilities as if the random fall of the cards on the red plush tablecloth before her could precipitate her from her chill, shuttered room into a country of perpetual summer and obliterate the perennial sadness of a girl who is both death and the maiden.

Her voice is filled with distant sonorities, like reverberations in a cave: now you are at the place of annihilation, now you are at the place of annihilation. And she is herself a cave full of echoes, she is a system of repetitions, she is a closed circuit. 'Can a bird sing only the song it knows or can it learn a new song?' She draws her long, sharp fingernail across the bars of the cage in which her pet lark sings, striking a plangent twang like that of the plucked heartstrings of a woman of metal. Her hair falls down like tears.

The castle is mostly given over to ghostly occupants but she herself has her own suite of drawing room and bedroom. Closely barred shutters and heavy velvet curtains keep out every leak of natural light. There is a round table on a single leg covered with a red plush cloth on which she lays out her inevitable Tarot; this room is never more than faintly illuminated by a heavily shaded lamp on the mantelpiece and the dark red figured wallpaper is obscurely, distressingly patterned by the rain that drives in through the neglected roof and leaves behind it random areas of staining, ominous marks like those left on the sheets by dead lovers. Depredations of rot and fungus everywhere. The unlit chandelier is so heavy with dust the individual prisms no longer show any shapes; industrious spiders have woven canopies in the corners of this ornate and rotting place, have trapped the porcelain vases on the mantelpiece in soft grey nets. But the mistress of all this disintegration notices nothing.

She sits in a chair covered in moth-ravaged burgundy velvet at the low, round table and distributes the cards; sometimes the lark sings, but more often remains a sullen mound of drab feathers. Sometimes the Countess will wake it for a brief cadenza by strumming the bars of its cage; she likes to hear it announce how it cannot escape.

She rises when the sun sets and goes immediately to her table where she plays her game of patience until she grows hungry, until she becomes ravenous. She is so beautiful she is unnatural; her beauty is an abnormality, a deformity, for none of her features exhibit any of those touching imperfections that reconcile us to the imperfection of the human condition. Her beauty is a symptom of her disorder, of her soullessness.

The white hands of the tenebrous belle deal the hand of destiny. Her fingernails are longer than those of the mandarins of ancient China[2] and each is pared

1 Since the fifteenth century, these cards have been used in divination. The cards take on archetypal meanings that Carter uses throughout the story.

2 Long fingernails, sometimes curling around the hand, were a symbol of wealth and beauty in Ancient China. Grown so long as to impede the use of the hand, these fingernails were a sign that the individual did not need to work.

to a fine point. These and teeth as fine and white as spikes of spun sugar are the visible signs of the destiny she wistfully attempts to evade via the arcana; her claws and teeth have been sharpened on centuries of corpses, she is the last bud of the poison tree that sprang from the loins of Vlad the Impaler[1] who picnicked on corpses in the forests of Transylvania.

The walls of her bedroom are hung with black satin, embroidered with tears of pearl. At the room's four corners are funerary urns and bowls which emit slumbrous, pungent fumes of incense. In the centre is an elaborate catafalque,[2] in ebony, surrounded by long candles in enormous silver candlesticks. In a white lace négligé stained a little with blood, the Countess climbs up on her catafalque at dawn each morning and lies down in an open coffin.

A chignoned priest of the Orthodox faith staked out her wicked father at a Carpathian crossroad before her milk teeth grew. Just as they staked him out, the fatal Count cried: 'Nosferatu is dead; long live Nosferatu!' Now she possesses all the haunted forests and mysterious habitations of his vast domain; she is the hereditary commandant of the army of shadows who camp in the village below her chateau, who penetrate the woods in the form of owls, bats and foxes, who make the milk curdle and the butter refuse to come, who ride the horses all night on a wild hunt so they are sacks of skin and bone in the morning, who milk the cows dry and, especially, torment pubescent girls with fainting fits, disorders of the blood, diseases of the imagination.

But the Countess herself is indifferent to her own weird authority, as if she were dreaming it. In her dream, she would like to be human; but she does not know if that is possible. The Tarot always shows the same configuration: always she turns up La Papesse, La Mort, La Tour Abolie, wisdom, death, dissolution.[3]

On moonless nights, her keeper lets her out into the garden. This garden, an exceedingly sombre place, bears a strong resemblance to a burial ground and all the roses her dead mother planted have grown up into a huge, spiked wall that incarcerates her in the castle of her inheritance. When the back door opens, the Countess will sniff the air and howl. She drops, now, on all fours. Crouching, quivering, she catches the scent of her prey. Delicious crunch of the fragile bones of rabbits and small, furry things she pursues with fleet, four-footed speed; she will creep home, whimpering, with blood smeared on her cheeks. She pours water from the ewer in her bedroom into the bowl, she washes her face with the wincing, fastidious gestures of a cat.

---

1 Vlad Dracula (1431–76) is considered one of the most important rulers in Wallachian history and a national hero of Romania. Famously, he was also one of Bram Stoker's inspirations for Dracula.

2 The decorated wooden framework that supports a coffin while an important person lies in state.

3 More commonly referred to in English as The Hierophant, Death, and the Tower, all three are in the Major Arcana of the Tarot often seen as representing life lessons. The Hierophant is associated with conformity to traditions and institutions. Apart from its obvious associations, Death is often read as representing change and transformations. The Tower indicates upheaval and chaos, as well as revelation or awakening.

The voracious margin of huntress's nights in the gloomy garden, crouch and pounce, surrounds her habitual tormented somnambulism, her life or imitation of life. The eyes of this nocturnal creature enlarge and glow. All claws and teeth, she strikes, she gorges; but nothing can console her for the ghastliness of her condition, nothing. She resorts to the magic comfort of the Tarot pack and shuffles the cards, lays them out, reads them, gathers them up with a sigh, shuffles them again, constantly constructing hypotheses about a future which is irreversible.

An old mute looks after her, to make sure she never sees the sun, that all day she stays in her coffin, to keep mirrors and all reflective surfaces away from her—in short, to perform all the functions of the servants of vampires. Everything about this beautiful and ghastly lady is as it should be, queen of night, queen of terror—except her horrible reluctance for the role.

Nevertheless, if an unwise adventurer pauses in the square of the deserted village to refresh himself at the fountain, a crone in a black dress and white apron presently emerges from a house. She will invite you with smiles and gestures; you will follow her. The Countess wants fresh meat. When she was a little girl, she was like a fox and contented herself entirely with baby rabbits that squeaked piteously as she bit into their necks with a nauseated voluptuousness, with voles and field-mice that palpitated for a bare moment between her embroidress's fingers. But now she is a woman, she must have men. If you stop too long beside the giggling fountain, you will be led by the hand to the Countess's larder.

All day, she lies in her coffin in her négligé of blood-stained lace. When the sun drops behind the mountain, she yawns and stirs and puts on the only dress she has, her mother's wedding dress, to sit and read her cards until she grows hungry. She loathes the food she eats; she would have liked to take the rabbits home with her, feed them on lettuce, pet them and make them a nest in her red-and-black chinoiserie escritoire,[1] but hunger always overcomes her. She sinks her teeth into the neck where an artery throbs with fear; she will drop the deflated skin from which she has extracted all the nourishment with a small cry of both pain and disgust. And it is the same with the shepherd boys and gipsy[2] lads who, ignorant or foolhardy, come to wash the dust from their feet in the water of the fountain; the Countess's governess brings them into the drawing room where the cards on the table always show the Grim Reaper.[3] The Countess herself will serve them coffee in tiny cracked, precious cups, and little sugar cakes. The hobbledehoys[4] sit with a spilling cup in one hand and a biscuit in the other, gaping at the Countess in her satin finery as she pours from a silver

1 Cabinet with a fold-out writing desk painted with figures.
2 This term for the Romany people was common at the time Carter wrote, but it is now considered derogatory.
3 The Death card.
4 Clumsy or awkward youths.

pot and chatters distractedly to put them at their fatal ease. A certain desolate stillness of her eyes indicates she is inconsolable. She would like to caress their lean brown cheeks and stroke their ragged hair. When she takes them by the hand and leads them to her bedroom, they can scarcely believe their luck.

Afterwards, her governess will tidy the remains into a neat pile and wrap it in its own discarded clothes. This mortal parcel she then discreetly buries in the garden. The blood on the Countess's cheeks will be mixed with tears; her keeper probes her fingernails for her with a little silver toothpick, to get rid of the fragments of skin and bone that have lodged there.

Fee fie fo film
I smell the blood of an Englishman.[1]

One hot, ripe summer in the pubescent years of the present century,[2] a young officer in the British army, blond, blue-eyed, heavy-muscled, visiting friends in Vienna, decided to spend the remainder of his furlough exploring the little-known uplands of Romania. When he quixotically decided to travel the rutted cart-tracks by bicycle, he saw all the humour of it: 'on two wheels in the land of the vampires.' So, laughing, he sets out on his adventure.

He has the special quality of virginity, most and least ambiguous of states: ignorance, yet at the same time, power in potentia, and, furthermore, unknowingness, which is not the same as ignorance. He is more than he knows—and has about him, besides, the special glamour of that generation for whom history has already prepared a special, exemplary fate in the trenches of France. This being, rooted in change and time, is about to collide with the timeless Gothic eternity of the vampires, for whom all is as it has always been and will be, whose cards always fall in the same pattern.

Although so young, he is also rational. He has chosen the most rational mode of transport in the world for his trip round the Carpathians. To ride a bicycle is in itself some protection against superstitious fears, since the bicycle is the product of pure reason applied to motion. Geometry at the service of man! Give me two spheres and a straight line and I will show you how far I can take them. Voltaire himself might have invented the bicycle, since it contributes so much to man's welfare and nothing at all to his bane. Beneficial to the health, it emits no harmful fumes and permits only the most decorous speeds. How can a bicycle ever be an implement of harm?

A single kiss woke up the Sleeping Beauty in the Wood.[3]

The waxen fingers of the Countess, fingers of a holy image, turn up the card

1 Famous line spoken by the giant in popular versions of "Jack and the Beanstalk."

2 This story is set on the eve of World War I.

3 Throughout the story, Carter directly evokes both "Jack and the Beanstalk" and "Sleeping Beauty." The collection in which this story was originally published, *The Bloody Chamber*, features many feminist and postmodern reworkings of fairy tales.

called Les Amoureux.[1] Never, never before... never before has the Countess cast herself a fate involving love. She shakes, she trembles, her great eyes close beneath her finely veined, nervously fluttering eyelids; the lovely cartomancer[2] has, this time, the first time, dealt herself a hand of love and death.

Be he alive or be he dead
I'll grind his bones to make my bread.

At the mauvish beginnings of evening, the English m'sieu[3] toils up the hill to the village he glimpsed from a great way off; he must dismount and push his bicycle before him, the path too steep to ride. He hopes to find a friendly inn to rest the night; he's hot, hungry, thirsty, weary, dusty... At first, such disappointment, to discover the roofs of all the cottages caved in and tall weeds thrusting through the piles of fallen tiles, shutters hanging disconsolately from their hinges, an entirely uninhabited place. And the rank vegetation whispers, as if foul secrets, here, where, if one were sufficiently imaginative, one could almost imagine twisted faces appearing momentarily beneath the crumbling eaves... but the adventure of it all, and the consolation of the poignant brightness of the hollyhocks still bravely blooming in the shaggy gardens, and the beauty of the flaming sunset, all these considerations soon overcame his disappointment, even assuaged the faint unease he'd felt. And the fountain where the village women used to wash their clothes still gushed out bright, clear water; he gratefully washed his feet and hands, applied his mouth to the faucet, then let the icy stream run over his face.

When he raised his dripping, gratified head from the lion's mouth, he saw, silently arrived beside him in the square, an old woman who smiled eagerly, almost conciliatorily at him. She wore a black dress and a white apron, with a housekeeper's key ring at the waist; her grey hair was neatly coiled in a chignon beneath the white linen headdress worn by elderly women of that region. She bobbed a curtsy at the young man and beckoned him to follow her. When he hesitated, she pointed towards the great bulk of the mansion above them, whose façade loured over the village, rubbed her stomach, pointed to her mouth, rubbed her stomach again, clearly miming an invitation to supper. Then she beckoned him again, this time turning determinedly upon her heel as though she would brook no opposition.

A great, intoxicated surge of the heavy scent of red roses blew into his face as soon as they left the village, inducing a sensuous vertigo; a blast of rich, faintly corrupt sweetness strong enough almost, to fell him. Too many roses. Too many roses bloomed on enormous thickets that lined the path, thickets

1 The Lovers. This Tarot card can symbolize love and relationships.

2 Tarot card reader.

3 Abbreviated version of the French "Monsieur."

bristling with thorns, and the flowers themselves were almost too luxuriant, their huge congregations of plush petals somehow obscene in their excess, their whorled, tightly budded cores outrageous in their implications. The mansion emerged grudgingly out of this jungle.

In the subtle and haunting light of the setting sun, that golden light rich with nostalgia for the day that is just past, the sombre visage of the place, part manor house, part fortified farmhouse, immense, rambling, a dilapidated eagle's nest atop the crag down which its attendant village meandered, reminded him of childhood tales on winter evenings, when he and his brothers and sisters scared themselves half out of their wits with ghost stories set in just such places and then had to have candles to light them up newly terrifying stairs to bed. He could almost have regretted accepting the crone's unspoken invitation; but now, standing before the door of time-eroded oak while she selected a huge iron key from the clanking ringful at her waist, he knew it was too late to turn back and brusquely reminded himself he was no child, now, to be frightened of his own fancies.

The old lady unlocked the door, which swung back on melodramatically creaking hinges, and fussily took charge of his bicycle, in spite of his protests. He felt a certain involuntary sinking of the heart to see his beautiful two-wheeled symbol of rationality vanish into the dark entrails of the mansion, to, no doubt, some damp outhouse where they would not oil it or check its tyres. But, in for a penny, in for a pound—in his youth and strength and blond beauty, in the invisible, even unacknowledged pentacle[1] of his virginity, the young man stepped over the threshold of Nosferatu's castle and did not shiver in the blast of cold air, as from the mouth of a grave, that emanated from the lightless, cavernous interior.

The crone took him to a little chamber where there was a black oak table spread with a clean white cloth and this cloth was carefully laid with heavy silverware, a little tarnished, as if someone with foul breath had breathed on it, but laid with one place only. Curiouser and curiouser; invited to the castle for dinner, now he must dine alone. All the same, he sat down as she had bid him. Although it was not yet dark outside, the curtains were closely drawn and only the sparing light trickling from a single oil lamp showed him how dismal his surroundings were. The crone bustled about to get him a bottle of wine and a glass from an ancient cabinet of wormy oak; while he bemusedly drank his wine, she disappeared but soon returned bearing a steaming platter of the local spiced meat stew with dumplings, and a shank of black bread. He was hungry after his long day's ride, he ate heartily and polished his plate with the crust, but this coarse food was hardly the entertainment he'd expected from the gentry and he was puzzled by the assessing glint in the dumb woman's eyes as she watched him eating.

---

1 Talisman or magical object that is generally depicted as a five-pointed star in a circle. Also one of the four suits in the Tarot.

But she darted off to get him a second helping as soon as he'd finished the first one and she seemed so friendly and helpful, besides, that he knew he could count on a bed for the night in the castle, as well as his supper, so he sharply reprimanded himself for his own childish lack of enthusiasm for the eerie silence, the clammy chill of the place.

When he'd put away the second plateful, the old woman came and gestured he should leave the table and follow her once again. She made a pantomime of drinking; he deduced he was now invited to take after-dinner coffee in another room with some more elevated member of the household who had not wished to dine with him but, all the same, wanted to make his acquaintance. An honour, no doubt; in deference to his host's opinion of himself, he straightened his tie, brushed the crumbs from his tweed jacket.

He was surprised to find how ruinous the interior of the house was—cobwebs, worm-eaten beams, crumbling plaster; but the mute crone resolutely wound him on the reel of her lantern down endless corridors, up winding staircases, through the galleries where the painted eyes of family portraits briefly flickered as they passed, eyes that belonged, he noticed, to faces, one and all, of a quite memorable beastliness. At last she paused and, behind the door where they'd halted, he heard a faint, metallic twang as of, perhaps, a chord struck on a harpsichord. And then, wonderfully, the liquid cascade of the song of a lark, bringing to him, in the heart—had he but known it—of Juliet's tomb,[1] all the freshness of morning.

The crone rapped with her knuckles on the panels; the most seductively caressing voice he had ever heard in his life softly called out, in heavily accented French, the adopted language of the Romanian aristocracy: 'Entrez.'[2]

First of all, he saw only a shape, a shape imbued with a faint luminosity since it caught and reflected in its yellowed surfaces what little light there was in the ill-lit room; this shape resolved itself into that of, of all things, a hoop-skirted dress of white satin draped here and there with lace, a dress fifty or sixty years out of fashion but once, obviously, intended for a wedding. And then he saw the girl who wore the dress, a girl with the fragility of the skeleton of a moth, so thin, so frail that her dress seemed to him to hang suspended, as if untenanted in the dank air, a fabulous lending, a self-articulated garment in which she lived like a ghost in a machine. All the light in the room came from a low-burning lamp with a thick greenish shade on a distant mantelpiece; the crone who accompanied him shielded her lantern with her hand, as if to protect her mistress from too suddenly seeing, or their guest from too suddenly seeing her.

So that it was little by little, as his eyes grew accustomed to the half-dark, that he saw how beautiful and how very young the bedizened scarecrow was,

1 Reference to William Shakespeare's *Romeo and Juliet.* The tomb is the site of the suicides of both Romeo and Juliet.

2 French: "Come in."

and he thought of a child dressing up in her mother's clothes, perhaps a child putting on the clothes of a dead mother in order to bring her, however briefly, to life again.

The Countess stood behind a low table, beside a pretty, silly, gilt-and-wire birdcage, hands outstretched in a distracted attitude that was almost one of flight; she looked as startled by their entry as if she had not requested it. With her stark white face, her lovely death's head surrounded by long dark hair that fell down as straight as if it were soaking wet, she looked like a shipwrecked bride. Her huge dark eyes almost broke his heart with their waiflike, lost look; yet he was disturbed, almost repelled, by her extraordinarily fleshy mouth, a mouth with wide, full, prominent lips of a vibrant purplish-crimson, a morbid mouth. Even—but he put the thought away from him immediately—a whore's mouth.[1] She shivered all the time, a starveling chill, a malarial agitation of the bones. He thought she must be only sixteen or seventeen years old, no more, with the hectic, unhealthy beauty of a consumptive.[2] She was the chatelaine[3] of all this decay.

With many tender precautions, the crone now raised the light she held to show his hostess her guest's face. At that, the Countess let out a faint, mewing cry and made a blind, appalled gesture with her hands, as if pushing him away, so that she knocked against the table and a butterfly dazzle of painted cards fell to the floor. Her mouth formed a round 'o' of woe, she swayed a little and then sank into her chair, where she lay as if now scarcely capable of moving. A bewildering reception. Tsk'ing under her breath, the crone busily poked about on the table until she found an enormous pair of dark green glasses, such as blind beggars wear, and perched them on the Countess's nose.

He went forward to pick up her cards for her from a carpet that, he saw to his surprise, was part rotted away, partly encroached upon by all kinds of virulent-looking fungi. He retrieved the cards and shuffled them carelessly together, for they meant nothing to him, though they seemed strange playthings for a young girl. What a grisly picture of a capering skeleton! He covered it up with a happier one—of two young lovers, smiling at one another, and put her toys back into a hand so slender you could almost see the frail net of bone beneath the translucent skin, a hand with fingernails as long, as finely pointed, as banjo picks.

At his touch, she seemed to revive a little and almost smiled, raising herself upright.

'Coffee,' she said. 'You must have coffee.' And scooped up her cards into a pile so that the crone could set before her a silver spirit kettle, a silver coffee pot,

1 In her description of the Countess, Carter is referencing the racist nineteenth-century ideas of physiognomy. This pseudoscience was used in character descriptions in many nineteenth-century works, such as Bram Stoker's *Dracula*.

2 Someone suffering from tuberculosis.

3 Woman in charge of a large house.

cream jug, sugar basin, cups ready on a silver tray, a strange touch of elegance, even if discoloured, in this devastated interior whose mistress ethereally shone as if with her own blighted, submarine radiance.

The crone found him a chair and, tittering noiselessly, departed, leaving the room a little darker.

While the young lady attended to the coffee-making, he had time to contemplate with some distaste a further series of family portraits which decorated the stained and peeling walls of the room; these livid faces all seemed contorted with a febrile madness and the blubber lips, the huge, demented eyes that all had in common bore a disquieting resemblance to those of the hapless victim of inbreeding now patiently filtering her fragrant brew, even if some rare grace has so finely transformed those features when it came to her case. The lark, its chorus done, had long ago fallen silent; no sound but the chink of silver on china. Soon, she held out to him a tiny cup of rose-painted china.

'Welcome,' she said in her voice with the rushing sonorities of the ocean in it, a voice that seemed to come elsewhere than from her white, still throat. 'Welcome to my chateau. I rarely receive visitors and that's a misfortune since nothing animates me half as much as the presence of a stranger... This place is so lonely, now the village is deserted, and my one companion, alas, she cannot speak. Often I am so silent that I think I, too, will soon forget how to do so and nobody here will ever talk any more.'

She offered him a sugar biscuit from a Limoges plate;[1] her fingernails struck carillons from the antique china. Her voice, issuing from those red lips like the obese roses in her garden, lips that do not move—her voice is curiously disembodied; she is like a doll, he thought, a ventriloquist's doll, or, more, like a great, ingenious piece of clockwork. For she seemed inadequately powered by some slow energy of which she was not in control; as if she had been wound up years ago, when she was born, and now the mechanism was inexorably running down and would leave her lifeless. This idea that she might be an automaton,[2] made of white velvet and black fur, that could not move of its own accord, never quite deserted him; indeed, it deeply moved his heart. The carnival air of her white dress emphasized her unreality, like a sad Columbine[3] who lost her way in the wood a long time ago and never reached the fair.

'And the light. I must apologize for the lack of light... a hereditary affliction of the eyes ...'

Her blind spectacles gave him his handsome face back to himself twice over; if he presented himself to her naked face, he would dazzle her like the sun she is forbidden to look at because it would shrivel her up at once, poor night bird, poor butcher bird.

---

1 Famous decorated French porcelain.

2 Wind-up doll.

3 Character in British Harlequinade, a popular comic pantomime theater genre. Columbine is a beautiful young woman beloved by Harlequin.

Vous serez ma proie.[1]

You have such a fine throat, m'sieu, like a column of marble. When you came through the door retaining about you all the golden light of the summer's day of which I know nothing, nothing, the card called 'Les Amoureux' had just emerged from the tumbling chaos of imagery before me; it seemed to me you had stepped off the card into my darkness and, for a moment, I thought, perhaps, you might irradiate it.

I do not mean to hurt you. I shall wait for you in my bride's dress in the dark.

The bridegroom is come, he will go into the chamber which has been prepared for him.

I am condemned to solitude and dark; I do not mean to hurt you.

I will be very gentle.

(And could love free me from the shadows? Can a bird sing only the song it knows, or can it learn a new song?)

See, how I'm ready for you. I've always been ready for you; I've been waiting for you in my wedding dress, why have you delayed for so long ... it will all be over very quickly.

You will feel no pain, my darling.

She herself is a haunted house. She does not possess herself; her ancestors sometimes come and peer out of the windows of her eyes and that is very frightening. She has the mysterious solitude of ambiguous states; she hovers in a no-man's land between life and death, sleeping and waking, behind the hedge of spiked flowers, Nosferatu's sanguinary rosebud. The beastly forebears on the walls condemn her to a perpetual repetition of their passions.

(One kiss, however, and only one, woke up the Sleeping Beauty in the Wood.)

Nervously, to conceal her inner voices, she keeps up a front of inconsequential chatter in French while her ancestors leer and grimace on the walls; however hard she tries to think of any other, she only knows of one kind of consummation.

He was struck, once again, by the birdlike, predatory claws which tipped her marvelous hands; the sense of strangeness that had been growing on him since he buried his head under the streaming water in the village, since he entered the dark portals of the fatal castle, now fully overcame him. Had he been a cat, he would have bounced backwards from her hands on four fear-stiffened legs, but he is not a cat: he is a hero.

A fundamental disbelief in what he sees before him sustains him, even in the boudoir of Countess Nosferatu herself; he would have said, perhaps, that there are some things which, even if they *are* true, we should not believe possible. He might have said: it is folly to believe one's eyes. Not so much that he does not believe in her; he can see her, she is real. If she takes off her dark glasses, from her eyes will stream all the images that populate this vampire-haunted land,

1 French: "You will be my prey."

but, since he himself is immune to shadow, due to his virginity—he does not yet know what there is to be afraid of—and due to his heroism, which makes him like the sun, he sees before him, first and foremost, an inbred, highly strung girl child, fatherless, motherless, kept in the dark too long and pale as a plant that never sees the light, half-blinded by some hereditary condition of the eyes. And though he feels unease, he cannot feel terror; so he is like the boy in the fairy tale, who does not know how to shudder, and not spooks, ghouls, beasties, the Devil himself and all his retinue could do the trick.

This lack of imagination gives his heroism to the hero.

He will learn to shudder in the trenches. But this girl cannot make him shudder.

Now it is dark. Bats swoop and squeak outside the tightly shuttered windows. The coffee is all drunk, the sugar biscuits eaten. Her chatter comes trickling and diminishing to a stop; she twists her fingers together, picks at the lace of her dress, shifts nervously in her chair. Owls shriek; the impedimenta of her condition squeak and gibber all around us. Now you are at the place of annihilation, now you are at the place of annihilation. She turns her head away from the blue beams of his eyes; she knows no other consummation than the only one she can offer him. She has not eaten for three days. It is dinner-time. It is bedtime.

Suivez-moi.
Je vous attendais.
Vous serez ma proie.[1]

The raven caws on the accursed roof. 'Dinnertime, dinnertime,' clang the portraits on the walls. A ghastly hunger gnaws her entrails; she has waited for him all her life without knowing it.

The handsome bicyclist, scarcely believing his luck, will follow her into her bedroom; the candles around her sacrificial altar burn with a low, clear flame, light catches on the silver tears stitched to the wall. She will assure him, in the very voice of temptation: 'My clothes have but to fall and you will see before you a succession of mysteries.'

She has no mouth with which to kiss, no hands with which to caress, only the fangs and talons of a beast of prey. To touch the mineral sheen of the flesh revealed in the cool candle gleam is to invite her fatal embrace; in her low, sweet voice, she will croon the lullaby of the House of Nosferatu.

Embraces, kisses; your golden head, of a lion, although I have never seen a lion, only imagined one, of the sun, even if I've only seen the picture of the sun on the Tarot card,[2] your golden head of the lover whom I dreamed would

1 French: "Follow me. I was waiting for you. You will be my prey."
2 The sun represents positivity, warmth, success, and vitality. It is an appropriate card to associate with this young soldier.

one day free me, this head will fall back, its eyes roll upwards in a spasm you will mistake for that of love and not of death. The bridegroom bleeds on my inverted marriage bed. Stark and dead, poor bicyclist; he has paid the price of a night with the Countess and some think it too high a fee while some do not.

Tomorrow, her keeper will bury his bones under her roses. The food her roses feed on gives them their rich colour, their swooning odour, that breathes lasciviously of forbidden pleasures.

Suivez-moi.

'Suivez-moi!'[1]

The handsome bicyclist, fearful for his hostess's health, her sanity, gingerly follows her hysterical imperiousness into the other room; he would like to take her into his arms and protect her from the ancestors who leer down from the walls.

What a macabre bedroom!

His colonel, an old goat with jaded appetites, had given him the visiting card of a brothel in Paris where, the satyr[2] assured him, ten louis would buy just such a lugubrious bedroom, with a naked girl upon a coffin; offstage, the brothel pianist played the *Dies Irae*[3] on a harmonium and, amidst all the perfumes of the embalming parlour, the customer took his necrophiliac pleasure of a pretended corpse. He had good-naturedly refused the old man's offer of such an initiation; how can he now take criminal advantage of the disordered girl with fever-hot, bone-dry, taloned hands and eyes that deny all the erotic promises of her body with their terror, their sadness, their dreadful, balked tenderness?

So delicate and damned, poor thing. Quite damned.

Yet I do believe she scarcely knows what she is doing.

She is shaking as if her limbs were not efficiently joined together, as if she might shake into pieces. She raises her hands to unfasten the neck of her dress and her eyes well with tears, they trickle down beneath the rim of her dark glasses. She can't take off her mother's wedding dress unless she takes off her dark glasses; she has fumbled the ritual, it is no longer inexorable. The mechanism within her fails her, now, when she needs it most. When she takes off the dark glasses, they slip from her fingers and smash to pieces on the tiled floor. There is no room in her drama for improvisation; and this unexpected, mundane noise of breaking glass breaks the wicked spell in the room, entirely. She gapes blindly down at the splinters and ineffectively smears the tears across her face with her fist. What is she to do now?

1 French: "Follow me. Follow me."

2 Lustful drunken woodland god in Greek mythology.

3 Literally: "Day of Wrath." Medieval Latin poem set to music in Gregorian chant and used in Requiems or the Funeral Mass.

When she kneels to try to gather the fragments of glass together, a sharp sliver pierces deeply into the pad of her thumb; she cries out, sharp, real. She kneels among the broken glass and watches the bright bead of blood form a drop. She has never seen her own blood before, not her *own* blood. It exercises upon her an awed fascination.

Into this vile and murderous room, the handsome bicyclist brings the innocent remedies of the nursery; in himself, by his presence, he is an exorcism. He gently takes her hand away from her and dabs the blood with his own handkerchief, but still it spurts out. And so he puts his mouth to the wound. He will kiss it better for her, as her mother, had she lived, would have done.

All the silver tears fall from the wall with a flimsy tinkle. Her painted ancestors turn away their eyes and grind their fangs.

How can she bear the pain of becoming human?

The end of exile is the end of being.

He was awakened by larksong. The shutters, the curtains, even the long-sealed windows of the horrid bedroom were all opened up and light and air streamed in; now you could see how tawdry it all was, how thin and cheap the satin, the catafalque not ebony at all but black-painted paper stretched on struts of wood, as in the theatre. The wind had blown droves of petals from the roses outside into the room and this crimson residue swirled fragrantly about the floor. The candles had burnt out and she must have set her pet lark free because it perched on the edge of the silly coffin to sing him its ecstatic morning song. His bones were stiff and aching, he'd slept on the floor with his bundled-up jacket for a pillow, after he'd put her to bed.

But now there was no trace of her to be seen, except, lightly tossed across the crumpled black satin bedcover, a lace négligée lightly soiled with blood, as it might be from a woman's menses, and a rose that must have come from the fierce bushes nodding through the window. The air was heavy with incense and roses and made him cough. The Countess must have got up early to enjoy the sunshine, slipped outside to gather him a rose. He got to his feet, coaxed the lark on to his wrist and took it to the window. At first, it exhibited the reluctance for the sky of a long-caged thing, but, when he tossed it up on to the currents of the air, it spread its wings and was up and away into the clear blue bowl of the heavens; he watched its trajectory with a lift of joy in his heart.

Then he padded into the boudoir, his mind busy with plans. We shall take her to Zurich,[1] to a clinic; she will be treated for nervous hysteria.[2] Then to an eye specialist, for her photophobia, and to a dentist to put her teeth into better shape. Any competent manicurist will deal with her claws. We shall turn her into the lovely girl she is; I shall cure her of all these nightmares.

1 Largest city in Switzerland. It was known for health clinics and spas.

2 Any number of symptoms could be associated with hysteria—from frigidity to sexual desire, from nervousness to lethargy. Because of the term's association with the uterus (hyster), it was essentially used to pathologize women.

The heavy curtains are pulled back, to let in brilliant fusillades of early morning light; in the desolation of the boudoir, she sits at her round table in her white dress, with the cards laid out before her. She has dropped off to sleep over the cards of destiny that are so fingered, so soiled, so worn by constant shuffling that you can no longer make the image out on any single one of them.

She is not sleeping.

In death, she looked far older, less beautiful and so, for the first time, fully human.

I will vanish in the morning light; I was only an invention of darkness.

And I leave you as a souvenir the dark, fanged rose I plucked from between my thighs, like a flower laid on a grave. On a grave.

My keeper will attend to everything.

Nosferatu always attends his own obsequies;[1] she will not go to the graveyard unattended. And now the crone materialized, weeping, and roughly gestured him to begone. After a search in some foul-smelling outhouses, he discovered his bicycle and, abandoning his holiday, rode directly to Bucharest[2] where, at the poste restante,[3] he found a telegram summoning him to rejoin his regiment at once. Much later, when he changed back into uniform in his quarters, he discovered he still had the Countess's rose, he must have tucked it into the breast pocket of his cycling jacket after he had found her body. Curiously enough, although he had brought it so far away from Romania, the flower did not seem to be quite dead and, on impulse, because the girl had been so lovely and her death so unexpected and pathetic, he decided to try and resurrect her rose. He filled his tooth glass with water from the carafe on his locker and popped the rose into it, so that its withered head floated on the surface.

When he returned from the mess that evening, the heavy fragrance of Count Nosferatu's roses drifted down the stone corridor of the barracks to greet him, and his spartan quarters brimmed with the reeling odour of a glowing, velvet, monstrous flower whose petals had regained all their former bloom and elasticity, their corrupt, brilliant, baleful splendour.

Next day, his regiment embarked for France.

1 Funeral rites.

2 Capital city of Romania.

3 Post office that holds mail until it can be collected by the recipient.

# Karen Russell

(b. 1981)

A self-described writer of "magical thinking," Karen Russell credits the Florida swamps where she grew up as the inspiration for many of her speculative fiction short stories. Her highly imaginative narratives blend fantasy and psychological realism with comic overtones, resulting in a distinct and unique style. She is the recipient of numerous honors and awards including the Bard Fiction Prize in 2011 for her first short story collection, *St. Lucy's Home for Girls Raised by Wolves*, and a 2013 MacArthur Foundation "Genius Grant."

## "The Vampires in the Lemon Grove"

(2013)

In October, the men and women of Sorrento harvest the *primofiore*, or "first flowering fruit," the most succulent lemons; in March, the yellow bianchetti ripen, followed in June by the green *verdelli*. In every season you can find me sitting at my bench, watching them fall. Only one or two lemons tumble from the branches each hour, but I've been sitting here so long their falls seem contiguous, close as raindrops. My wife has no patience for this sort of meditation. "Jesus Christ, Clyde," she says. "You need a hobby."

Most people mistake me for a small, kindly Italian grandfather, a *nonno*. I have an old *nonno*'s coloring, the dark walnut stain peculiar to southern Italians, a tan that won't fade until I die (which I never will). I wear a neat periwinkle shirt, a canvas sunhat, black suspenders that sag at my chest. My loafers are battered but always polished. The few visitors to the lemon grove who notice me smile blankly into my raisin face and catch the whiff of some sort of tragedy; they whisper that I am a widower, or an old man who has survived his children. They never guess that I am a vampire.

Santa Francesca's Lemon Grove, where I spend my days and nights, was part of a Jesuit convent in the 1800s. Today it's privately owned by the Alberti family, the prices are excessive, and the locals know to buy their lemons elsewhere. In summers a teenage girl named Fila mans a wooden stall at the back of the grove. She's painfully thin, with heavy black bangs. I can tell by the careful way she saves the best lemons for me, slyly kicking them under my bench, that she knows I am a monster. Sometimes she'll smile vacantly in my direction, but she never gives me any trouble. And because of her benevolent indifference to me, I feel a swell of love for the girl.

Fila makes the lemonade and monitors the hot dog machine, watching the meat rotate on wire spigots. I'm fascinated by this machine. The Italian name for it translates as "carousel of beef." Who would have guessed at such a device two hundred years ago? Back then we were all preoccupied with visions of apocalypse; Santa Francesca, the foundress of this very grove, gouged out her eyes while dictating premonitions of fire. What a shame, I often think, that she foresaw only the end times, never hot dogs. A sign posted just outside the grove reads:

CIGERETTE PIE
HEAT DOGS
GRANITE DRINKS
*Santa Francesca's Limonata—*
THE MOST REFRISHING DRANK ON THE PLENET!!

Every day, tourists from Wales and Germany and America are ferried over from cruise ships to the base of these cliffs. They ride the funicular[1] up here to visit the grove, to eat "heat dogs" with speckly brown mustard and sip lemon ices. They snap photographs of the Alberti brothers, Benny and Luciano, teenage twins who cling to the trees' wooden supports and make a grudging show of harvesting lemons, who spear each other with trowels and refer to the tourist women as "vaginas" in Italian slang. "*Buona sera*, vaginas!" they cry from the trees. I think the tourists are getting stupider. None of them speak Italian anymore, and these new women seem deaf to aggression. Often I fantasize about flashing my fangs at the brothers, just to keep them in line.

As I said, the tourists usually ignore me; perhaps it's the dominoes. A few years back, I bought a battered red set from Benny, a prop piece, and this makes me invisible, sufficiently banal to be hidden in plain sight. I have no real interest in the game; I mostly stack the pieces into little houses and corrals.

At sunset, the tourists all around begin to shout. "Look! Up there!" It's time for the path of *I Pipistrelli Impazziti*—the descent of the bats.

They flow from cliffs that glow like pale chalk, expelled from caves in the seeming billions. Their drop is steep and vertical, a black hail. Sometimes a change in weather sucks a bat beyond the lemon trees and into the turquoise sea. It's three hundred feet to the lemon grove, six hundred feet to the churning

1 A cable-driven transportation system for ascending and descending steep terrain.

foam of the Tyrrhenian.[1] At the precipice, they soar upward and crash around the green tops of the trees.

"Oh!" the tourists shriek, delighted, ducking their heads.

Up close, the bats' spread wings are alien membranes—fragile, like something internal flipped out. The waning sun washes their bodies a dusky red. They have wrinkled black faces, these bats, tiny, like gargoyles or angry grandfathers. They have teeth like mine.

Tonight, one of the tourists, a Texan lady with a big strawberry red updo, has successfully captured a bat in her hair, simultaneously crying real tears and howling: "TAKE THE GODDAMN PICTURE, Sarah!"

I stare ahead at a fixed point above the trees and light a cigarette. My bent spine goes rigid. Mortal terror always trips some old wire that leaves me sad and irritable. It will be whole minutes now before everybody stops screaming.

The moon is a muted shade of orange. Twin disks of light burn in the sky and the sea. I scan the darker indents in the skyline, the cloudless spots that I know to be caves. I check my watch again. It's eight o'clock, and all the bats have disappeared into the interior branches. Where is Magreb? My fangs are throbbing, but I won't start without her.

I once pictured time as a black magnifying glass and myself as a microscopic flightless insect trapped in that circle of night. But then Magreb came along, and eternity ceased to frighten me. Suddenly each moment followed its antecedent in a neat chain, moments we filled with each other.

I watch a single bat falling from the cliffs, dropping like a stone: headfirst, motionless, dizzying to witness.

*Pull up.*

I close my eyes. I press my palms flat against the picnic table and tense the muscles of my neck.

*Pull UP.* I tense until my temples pulse, until little black-and-red stars flutter behind my eyelids.

"You can look now."

Magreb is sitting on the bench, blinking her bright pumpkin eyes. "You weren't even *watching.* If you saw me coming down, you'd know you have nothing to worry about." I try to smile at her and find I can't. My own eyes feel like ice cubes.

"It's stupid to go so fast." I don't look at her. "That easterly could knock you over the rocks."

"Don't be ridiculous. I'm an excellent flier."

She's right. Magreb can shape-shift midair, much more smoothly than I ever could. Even back in the 1850s, when I used to transmute into a bat two, three times a night, my metamorphosis was a shy, halting process.

"Look!" she says, triumphant, mocking. "You're still trembling!"

1 Part of the Mediterranean Sea, the Tyrrhenian Sea is located off the western coast of Italy.

I look down at my hands, angry to realize it's true.

Magreb roots through the tall, black blades of grass. "It's late, Clyde; where's my lemon?"

I pluck a soft, round lemon from the grass, a summer moon, and hand it to her. The *verdelli* I have chosen is perfect, flawless. She looks at it with distaste and makes a big show of brushing off a marching ribbon of ants.

"A toast!" I say.

"A toast," Magreb replies, with the rote enthusiasm of a Christian saying grace. We lift the lemons and swing them to our faces. We plunge our fangs, piercing the skin, and emit a long, united hiss: "*Aaah!*"

Over the years, Magreb and I have tried everything—fangs in apples, fangs in rubber balls. We have lived everywhere: Tunis, Laos, Cincinnati, Salamanca. We spent our honeymoon hopping continents, hunting liquid chimeras: mint tea in Fez, coconut slurries in Oahu, jet-black coffee in Bogotá, jackal's milk in Dakar, Cherry Coke floats in rural Alabama, a thousand beverages purported to have magical quenching properties. We went thirsty in every region of the globe before finding our oasis here, in the blue boot of Italy, at this dead nun's lemonade stand. It's only these lemons that give us any relief.

When we first landed in Sorrento I was skeptical. The pitcher of lemonade we ordered looked cloudy and adulterated. Sugar clumped at the bottom. I took a gulp, and a whole small lemon lodged in my mouth; there is no word sufficiently lovely for the first taste, the first feeling of my fangs in that lemon. It was bracingly sour, with a delicate hint of ocean salt. After an initial prickling—a sort of chemical effervescence along my gums—a soothing blankness traveled from the tip of each fang to my fevered brain. These lemons are a vampire's analgesic. If you have been thirsty for a long time, if you have been suffering, then the absence of those two feelings—however brief—becomes a kind of heaven. I breathed deeply through my nostrils. My throbbing fangs were still.

By daybreak, the numbness had begun to wear off. The lemons relieve our thirst without ending it, like a drink we can hold in our mouths but never swallow. Eventually the original hunger returns. I have tried to be very good, very correct and conscientious about not confusing this original hunger with the thing I feel for Magreb.

I can't joke about my early years on the blood, can't even think about them without guilt and acidic embarrassment. Unlike Magreb, who has never had a sip of the stuff, I listened to the village gossips and believed every rumor, internalized every report of corrupted bodies and boiled blood. Vampires were the favorite undead of the Enlightenment, and as a young boy I aped the diction and mannerisms I read about in books: Vlad the Impaler, Count Heinrich the Despoiler, Goethe's bloodsucking bride of Corinth.[1] I eavesdropped on the

1 Famous historic and literary vampires.

terrified prayers of an old woman in a cemetery, begging God to protect her from... me. I felt a dislocation then, a spreading numbness, as if I were invisible or already dead. After that, I did only what the stories suggested, beginning with that old woman's blood. I slept in coffins, in black cedar boxes, and woke every night with a fierce headache. I was famished, perennially dizzy. I had unspeakable dreams about the sun.

In practice I was no suave viscount, just a teenager in a red velvet cape, awkward and voracious. I wanted to touch the edges of my life—the same instinct, I think, that inspires young mortals to flip tractors and enlist in foreign wars. One night I skulked into a late Mass with some vague plan to defeat eternity. At the back of the nave, I tossed my mousy curls, rolled my eyes heavenward, and then plunged my entire arm into the bronze pail of holy water. Death would be painful, probably, but I didn't care about pain. I wanted to overturn my sentence. It was working; I could feel the burn beginning to spread. Actually, it was more like an itch, but I was sure the burning would start any second. I slid into a pew, snug in my misery, and waited for my body to turn to ash.

By sunrise, I'd developed a rash between my eyebrows, a little late-flowering acne, but was otherwise fine, and I understood I truly was immortal. At that moment I yielded all discrimination; I bit anyone kind or slow enough to let me get close: men, women, even some older boys and girls. The littlest children I left alone, very proud at the time of this one scruple. I'd read stories about Hungarian *vampirs* who drank the blood of orphan girls, and mentioned this to Magreb early on, hoping to impress her with my decency. Not *children*! she wept.

She wept for a day and a half.

Our first date was in Cementerio de Colón,[1] if I can call a chance meeting between headstones a date. I had been stalking her, following her swishing hips as she took a shortcut through the cemetery grass. She wore her hair in a low, snaky braid that was coming unraveled. When I was near enough to touch her trailing ribbon she whipped around. "Are you following me?" she asked, annoyed, not scared. She regarded my face with the contempt of a woman confronting the town drunk. "Oh," she said, "your teeth..."

And then she grinned. Magreb was the first and only other vampire I'd ever met. We bared our fangs over a tombstone and recognized each other. There is a loneliness that must be particular to monsters, I think, the feeling that each is the only child of a species. And now that loneliness was over.

Our first date lasted all night. Magreb's talk seemed to lunge forward like a train without a conductor; I suspect even she didn't know what she was saying. I certainly wasn't paying attention, staring dopily at her fangs, and then I heard her ask: "So, when did you figure out that the blood does nothing?"

At the time of this conversation, I was edging on 130. I had never gone a day since early childhood without drinking several pints of blood. *The blood does nothing?* My forehead burned and burned.

1 Cemetery in Havana, Cuba, founded in 1876.

"Didn't you think it suspicious that you had a heartbeat?" she asked me. "That you had a reflection in water?"

When I didn't answer, Magreb went on, "Every time I saw my own face in a mirror, I knew I wasn't any of those ridiculous things, a bloodsucker, a *sanguina*. You know?"

"Sure," I said, nodding. For me, mirrors had the opposite effect: I saw a mouth ringed in black blood. I saw the pale son of the villagers' fears.

Those initial days with Magreb nearly undid me. At first my euphoria was sharp and blinding, all my thoughts spooling into a single blue thread of relief—*The blood does nothing! I don't have to drink the blood!*—but when that subsided, I found I had nothing left. If we didn't have to drink the blood, then what on earth were these fangs for?

Sometimes I think she preferred me then: I was like her own child, raw and amazed. We smashed my coffin with an ax and spent the night at a hotel. I lay there wide-eyed in the big bed, my heart thudding like a fish tail against the floor of a boat.

"You're really sure?" I whispered to her. "I don't have to sleep in a coffin? I don't have to sleep through the day?" She had already drifted off.

A few months later, she suggested a picnic.

"But the sun."

Magreb shook her head. "You poor thing, believing all that garbage."

By this time we'd found a dirt cellar in which to live in Western Australia, where the sun burned through the clouds like dining lace. That sun ate lakes, rising out of dead volcanoes at dawn, triple the size of a harvest moon and skull-white, a grass-scorcher. Go ahead, try to walk into that sun when you've been told your bones are tinder.

I stared at the warped planks of the trapdoor above us, the copper ladder that led rung by rung to the bright world beyond. Time fell away from me and I was a child again, afraid, afraid. Magreb rested her hand on the small of my back. "You can do it," she said, nudging me gently. I took a deep breath and hunched my shoulders, my scalp grazing the cellar door, my hair soaked through with sweat. I focused my thoughts to still the tremors, lest my fangs slice the inside of my mouth, and turned my face away from Magreb.

"Go on."

I pushed up and felt the wood give way. Light exploded through the cellar. My pupils shrank to dots.

Outside, the whole world was on fire. Mute explosions rocked the scrubby forest, motes of light burning like silent rockets. The sun fell through the eucalyptus and Australian pines in bright red bars. I pulled myself out onto my belly, balled up in the soil, and screamed for mercy until I'd exhausted myself. Then I opened one watery eye and took a long look around. The sun wasn't fatal! It was just uncomfortable, making my eyes itch and water and inducing a sneezing attack.

After that, and for the whole of our next thirty years together, I watched the auroral colors and waited to feel anything but terror. Fingers of light spread across the gray sea toward me, and I couldn't see these colors as beautiful. The sky I lived under was a hideous, lethal mix of orange and pink, a physical deformity. By the 1950s we were living in a Cincinnati suburb; and as the day's first light hit the kitchen windows, I'd press my face against the linoleum and gibber my terror into the cracks.

"Sooo," Magreb would say, "I can tell you're not a morning person." Then she'd sit on the porch swing and rock with me, patting my hand.

"What's wrong, Clyde?"

I shook my head. This was a new sadness, difficult to express. My bloodlust was undiminished but now the blood wouldn't fix it.

"It never fixed it," Magreb reminded me, and I wished she would please stop talking.

That cluster of years was a very confusing period. Mostly I felt grateful, aboveground feelings. I was in love. For a vampire, my life was very normal. Instead of stalking prostitutes, I went on long bicycle rides with Magreb. We visited botanical gardens and rowed in boats. In a short time, my face had gone from lithium white to the color of milky coffee. Yet sometimes, especially at high noon, I'd study Magreb's face with a hot, illogical hatred, each pore opening up to swallow me. *You've ruined my life*, I'd think. To correct for her power over my mind I tried to fantasize about mortal women, their wild eyes and bare swan necks; I couldn't do it, not anymore—an eternity of vague female smiles eclipsed by Magreb's tiny razor fangs. Two gray tabs against her lower lip.

But like I said, I was mostly happy. I was making a kind of progress.

One night, children wearing necklaces of garlic bulbs arrived giggling at our door. It was Halloween; they were vampire hunters. The smell of garlic blasted through the mail slot, along with their voices: "Trick or treat!" In the old days, I would have cowered from these children. I would have run downstairs to barricade myself in my coffin. But that night, I pulled on an undershirt and opened the door. I stood in a square of green light in my boxer shorts hefting a bag of Tootsie Pops, a small victory over the old fear.

"Mister, you okay?"

I blinked down at a little blond child and then saw that my two hands were shaking violently, soundlessly, like old friends wishing not to burden me with their troubles. I dropped the candies into the children's bags, thinking: *You small mortals don't realize the power of your stories.*

We were downing strawberry velvet cocktails on the Seine when something inside me changed. Thirty years. Eleven thousand dawns. That's how long it took for me to believe the sun wouldn't kill me.

"Want to go see a museum or something? We're in Paris, after all."

"Okay."

We walked over a busy pedestrian bridge in a flood of light, and my heart was in my throat. Without any discussion, I understood that Magreb was my wife.

Because I love her, my hunger pangs have gradually mellowed into a comfortable despair. Sometimes I think of us as two holes cleaved together, two twin hungers. Our bellies growl at each other like companionable dogs. I love the sound, assuring me we're equals in our thirst. We bump our fangs and feel like we're coming up against the same hard truth.

Human marriages amuse me: the brevity of the commitment and all the ceremony that surrounds it, the calla lilies, the veiled mother-in-laws like lilac spiders, the tears and earnest toasts. Till death do us part! Easy. These mortal couples need only keep each other in sight for fifty, sixty years.

Often I wonder to what extent a mortal's love grows from the bedrock of his or her foreknowledge of death, love coiling like a green stem out of that blankness in a way I'll never quite understand. And lately I've been having a terrible thought: *Our love affair will end before the world does.*

One day, without any preamble, Magreb flew up to the caves. She called over her furry, muscled shoulder that she just wanted to sleep for a while.

"What? Wait! What's wrong?"

I'd caught her mid-shift, halfway between a wife and a bat.

"Don't be so sensitive, Clyde! I'm just tired of this century, so very tired, maybe it's the heat? I think I need a little rest..."

I assumed this was an experiment, like my cape, an old habit to which she was returning, and from the clumsy, ambivalent way she crashed around on the wind I understood I was supposed to follow her. Well, too bad. Magreb likes to say she freed me, disabused me of the old stories, but I gave up more than I intended: I can't shudder myself out of this old man's body. I can't fly anymore.

Fila and I are alone. I press my dry lips together and shove dominoes around the table; they buckle like the cars of a tiny train.

"More lemonade, *nonno*?" She smiles. She leans from her waist and boldly touches my right fang, a thin string of hanging drool. "Looks like you're thirsty."

"Please," I gesture at the bench. "Have a seat."

Fila is seventeen now and has known about me for some time. She's toying with the idea of telling her boss, weighing the sentence within her like a bullet in a gun: *There is a vampire in our grove.*

"You don't believe me, Signore Alberti?" she'll say, before taking him by the wrist and leading him to this bench, and I'll choose that moment to rise up and bite him in his hog-thick neck. "Right through his stupid tie!" she says with a grin.

But this is just idle fantasy, she assures me. Fila is content to let me alone. "You remind me of my *nonno*," she says approvingly, "you look very Italian."

In fact, she wants to help me hide here. It gives her a warm feeling to do so, like helping her own fierce *nonno* do up the small buttons of his trousers, now too intricate a maneuver for his palsied hands. She worries about me, too. And she should: lately I've gotten sloppy, incontinent about my secrets. I've stopped polishing my shoes; I let the tip of one fang hang over my pink lip. "You must be more careful," she reprimands. "There are tourists *everywhere*."

I study her neck as she says this, her head rolling with the natural expressiveness of a girl. She checks to see if I am watching her collarbone, and I let her see that I am. I feel like a threat again.

Last night I went on a rampage. On my seventh lemon I found with a sort of drowsy despair that I couldn't stop. I crawled around on all fours looking for the last *bianchettis* in the dewy grass: soft with rot, mildewed, sun-shriveled, blackened. Lemon skin bulging with tiny cellophane-green worms. Dirt smells, rain smells, all swirled through with the tart sting of decay.

In the morning, Magreb steps around the wreckage and doesn't say a word.

"I came up with a new name," I say, hoping to distract her. "*Brandolino.* What do you think?"

I have spent the last several years trying to choose an Italian name, and every day that I remain Clyde feels like a defeat. Our names are relics of the places we've been. "Clyde" is a souvenir from the California Gold Rush. I was callow and blood-crazed back then, and I saw my echo in the freckly youths panning along the Sacramento River. I used the name as a kind of bait. "Clyde" sounded innocuous, like someone a boy might get a malt beer with or follow into the woods.

Magreb chose her name in the Atlas Mountains[1] for its etymology, the root word *ghuroob*, which means "to set" or "to be hidden." "That's what we're looking for," she tells me. "The setting place. Some final answer." She won't change her name until we find it.

She takes a lemon from her mouth, slides it down the length of her fangs, and places its shriveled core on the picnic table. When she finally speaks, her voice is so low the words are almost unintelligible.

"The lemons aren't working, Clyde."

But the lemons have never worked. At best, they give us eight hours of peace. We aren't talking about the lemons.

"How long?"

"Longer than I've let on. I'm sorry."

"Well, maybe it's this crop. Those Alberti boys haven't been fertilizing properly, maybe the *primofiore* will turn out better."

Magreb fixes me with one fish-bright eye. "Clyde, I think it's time for us to go."

Wind blows the leaves apart. Lemons wink like a firmament of yellow stars, slowly ripening, and I can see the other, truer night behind them.

"Go where?" Our marriage, as I conceive it, is a commitment to starve together. "We've been resting here for decades. I think it's time... what is that thing?"

1 A mountain range in North Africa, the Atlas Mountains separate the Sahara Desert from the Mediterranean Sea.

I have been preparing a present for Magreb, for our anniversary, a "cave" of scavenged materials—newspaper and bottle glass and wooden beams from the lemon tree supports—so that she can sleep down here with me. I've smashed dozens of bottles of fruity beer to make stalactites. Looking at it now, though, I see the cave is very small. It looks like an umbrella mauled by a dog.

"That thing?" I say. "That's nothing. I think it's part of the hot dog machine."

"Jesus. Did it catch on fire?"

"Yes. The girl threw it out yesterday."

"Clyde." Magreb shakes her head. "We never meant to stay here forever, did we? That was never the plan."

"I didn't know we had a plan," I snap. "What if we've outlived our food supply? What if there's nothing left for us to find?"

"You don't really believe that."

"Why can't you just be grateful? Why can't you be happy and admit defeat? Look at what we've found here!" I grab a lemon and wave it in her face.

"Good night, Clyde."

I watch my wife fly up into the watery dawn, and again I feel the awful tension. In the flats of my feet, in my knobbed spine. Love has infected me with a muscular superstition that one body can do the work of another.

I consider taking the funicular, the ultimate degradation—worse than the dominoes, worse than an eternity of sucking cut lemons. All day I watch the cars ascend, and I'm reminded of those American fools who accompany their wives to the beach but refuse to wear bathing suits. I've seen them by the harbor, sulking in their trousers, panting through menthol cigarettes and pacing the dock while the women sea-bathe. They pretend they don't mind when sweat darkens the armpits of their suits. When their wives swim out and leave them. When their wives are just a splash in the distance.

Tickets for the funicular are twenty lire.[1] I sit at the bench and count as the cars go by.

That evening, I take Magreb on a date. I haven't left the lemon grove in upward of two years, and blood roars in my ears as I stand and clutch at her like an old man. We're going to the Thursday night show at an antique theater in a castle in the center of town. I want her to see that I'm happy to travel with her, so long as our destination is within walking distance.

A teenage usher in a vintage red jacket with puffed sleeves escorts us to our seats, his biceps manacled in clouds, threads loosening from the badge on his chest. I am jealous of the name there: GUGLIELMO.

The movie's title is already scrolling across the black screen: SOMETHING CLANDESTINE IS HAPPENING IN THE CORN!

Magreb snorts. "That's a pretty lousy name for a horror movie. It sounds like a student film."

---

1 Italian unit of money before the Euro.

"Here's your ticket," I say. "I didn't make the title up."

It's a vampire movie set in the Dust Bowl. Magreb expects a comedy, but the Dracula actor fills me with the sadness of an old photo album. An Okie[1] has unwittingly fallen in love with the monster, whom she's mistaken for a rich European creditor eager to pay off the mortgage on her family's farm.

"That Okie," says Magreb, "is an idiot."

I turn my head miserably and there's Fila, sitting two rows in front of us with a greasy young man. Benny Alberti. Her white neck is bent to the left, Benny's lips affixed to it as she impassively sips a soda.

"Poor thing," Magreb whispers, indicating the pigtailed actress. "She thinks he's going to save her."

Dracula shows his fangs, and the Okie flees through a cornfield. Cornstalks smack her face. "Help!" she screams to a sky full of crows. "He's not actually from Europe!"

There is no music, only the girl's breath and the *fwap-fwap-fwap* of the off-screen fan blades. Dracula's mouth hangs wide as a sewer grate. His cape is curiously still.

The movie picture is frozen. The *fwap*ping is emanating from the projection booth; it rises to a grinding *r-r-r*, followed by lyrical Italian cussing and silence and finally a tidal sigh. Magreb shifts in her seat.

"Let's wait," I say, seized with empathy for these two still figures on the screen, mutely pleading for repair. "They'll fix it."

People begin to file out of the theater, first in twos and threes and then in droves. "I'm tired, Clyde."

"Don't you want to know what happens?" My voice is more frantic than I intend.

"I already know what happens."

"Don't you leave now, Magreb. I'm telling you, they're going to fix it. If you leave now, that's it for us, I'll never..."

Her voice is beautiful, like gravel underfoot: "I'm going to the caves."

I'm alone in the theater. When I turn to exit, the picture is still frozen, the Okie's blue dress floating over windless corn, Dracula's mouth a hole in his white greasepaint.

Outside I see Fila standing in a clot of her friends, lit by the marquee. These kids wear too much makeup and clothes that move like colored oils. They all look rained on. I scowl at them and they scowl back, and then Fila crosses to me.

"Hey, you," she says, grinning, breathless, so very close to my face. "Are you stalking somebody?"

My throat tightens.

"Guys!" Her eyes gleam. "Guys, come over and meet the *vampire*."

But the kids are gone.

---

1 Slang term for someone from Oklahoma.

"Well! Some friends," she says, then winks. "Leaving me alone, defenseless..."

"You want the old vampire to bite you, eh?" I hiss. "You want a story for your friends?"

Fila laughs. Her horror is a round, genuine thing, bouncing in both her black eyes. She smells like hard water and glycerin. The hum of her young life all around me makes it difficult to think. A bat filters my thoughts, opens its trembling lampshade wings.

*Magreb.* She'll want to hear about this. How ridiculous, at my age, to find myself down this alley with a young girl: Fila powdering her neck, doing her hair up with little temptress pins, yanking me behind this Dumpster. "Can you imagine"—Magreb will laugh—"a teenager goading you to attack her! You're still a menace, Clyde."

I stare vacantly at a pale mole above the girl's collarbone. *Magreb*, I think again, and I smile, and the smile feels like a muzzle stretched taut against my teeth. It seems my hand has tightened on the girl's wrist, and I realize with surprise, as if from a great distance, that she is twisting away.

"Hey, *nonno*, come on now, what are you—"

The girl's head lolls against my shoulder like a sleepy child's, then swings forward in a rag-doll circle. The starlight is white mercury compared to her blotted-out eyes. There's a dark stain on my periwinkle shirt, and one suspender has snapped. I sit Fila's body against the alley wall, watch it dim and stiffen. Spidery graffiti weaves over the brick behind her, and I scan for some answer contained there: GIOVANNA & FABIANO. VAFFANCULO! VAI IN CULO.[1]

A scabby-furred creature, our only witness, arches its orange back against the Dumpster. If not for the lock I would ease the girl inside. I would climb in with her and let the red stench fill my nostrils, let the flies crawl into the red corners of my eyes. I am a monster again.

I ransack Fila's pockets and find the key to the funicular office, careful not to look at her face. Then I'm walking, running for the lemon grove. I jimmy my way into the control room and turn the silver key, relieved to hear the engine roar to life. Locked, locked, every funicular car is locked, but then I find one with thick tape in Xs over a busted door. I dash after it and pull myself onto the cushion, quickly, because the cars are already moving. Even now, after what I've done, I am still unable to fly, still imprisoned in my wretched *nonno*'s body, reduced to using the mortals' machinery to carry me up to find my wife. The box jounces and trembles. The chain pulls me into the heavens link by link.

My lips are soon chapped; I stare through a crack in the glass window. The box swings wildly in the wind. The sky is a deep blue vacuum. I can still smell the girl in the folds of my clothes.

The cave system at the top of the cliffs is vaster than I expected; and with their grandfather faces tucked away, the bats are anonymous as stones.

1 First names followed by a string of Italian curse words.

I walk beneath a chandelier of furry bodies, heartbeats wrapped in wings the color of rose petals or corn silk. Breath ripples through each of them, a tiny life in its translucent envelope.

"Magreb?"

*Is she up here?*

*Has she left me?*

*(I will never find another vampire.)*

I double back to the moonlit entrance that leads to the open air of the cliffs, the funicular cars. When I find Magreb, I'll beg her to tell me what she dreams up here. I'll tell her my waking dreams in the lemon grove: The mortal men and women floating serenely by in balloons freighted with the ballast of their deaths. Millions of balloons ride over a wide ocean, lives darkening the sky. Death is a dense powder cinched inside tiny sandbags, and in the dream I am given to understand that instead of a sandbag I have Magreb.

I make the bats' descent in a cable car with no wings to spread, knocked around by the wind with a force that feels personal. I struggle to hold the door shut and look for the green speck of our grove.

The box is plunging now, far too quickly. It swings wide, and the igneous[1] surface of the mountain fills the left window. The tufa[2] shines like water, like a black, heat-bubbled river. For a dizzying instant I expect the rock to seep through the glass.

Each swing takes me higher than the last, a grinding pendulum that approaches a full revolution around the cable. I'm on my hands and knees on the car floor, seasick in the high air, pressing my face against the floor grate. I can see stars or boats burning there, and also a ribbon of white, a widening fissure. Air gushes through the cracks in the glass box. With a lurch of surprise, I realize that I could die.

What does Magreb see, if she is watching? Is she waking from a nightmare to see the line snap, the glass box plummet? From her inverted vantage, dangling from the roof of the cave, does the car seem to be sucked upward, rushing not toward the sea but into another sort of sky? To a black mouth open and foaming with stars?

I like to picture my wife like this: Magreb shuts her thin eyelids tighter. She digs her claws into the rock. Little clouds of dust plume around her toes as she swings upside down. She feels something growing inside her, a dreadful suspicion. It is solid, this new thing, it is the opposite of hunger. She's emerging from a dream of distant thunder, rumbling and loose. Something has happened tonight that she thought impossible. In the morning, she will want to tell me about it.

---

1 Rock formed from lava.

2 Porous rock; a variety of limestone.

# VAMPIRE FAMILIES

Aleksey Konstantinovich Tolstoy, "The Family of the Vourdalak" (1839)

Stephen King, "One for the Road" (1977)

Jane Yolen, "Mama Gone" (1991)

Toni Brown, "Immunity" (1996)

Nalo Hopkinson, "Greedy Choke Puppy" (2001)

Silvia Moreno-Garcia, "A Handful of Earth" (2011)

Kazuki Sakuraba, from *A Small Charred Face* (2014)

We close the anthology on a very different theme: family. The link between vampires and family may have its origins in Eastern European folklore, but it has continued to evolve, mirroring cultural anxieties about familial relationships. The iconic 1987 film *The Lost Boys* exemplifies the tensions in late twentieth-century families. The parents of the only intact nuclear family we see, the Frogs, are so stoned their children essentially parent themselves. In contrast, the community of teenaged vampires form a mutually supportive collective—a found family. The film relishes the glamor of their immortal adolescent rebellion. It is only in the film's conclusion that we learn that they are ruled by the classically patriarchal Max. Unlike other vampires, it is not power or sex that Max truly desires; rather, all he has ever wanted is "one big happy family."[1]

All the angst and teenage rebellion in *The Lost Boys* is ultimately nothing more than a Peter Pan-esqe search for a mother. As Latham suggests, *The Lost*

1 *The Lost Boys.*

*Boys* "cannot escape finally the power of the family to structure and command desire."[1] Family weaves its way through vampire mythology in many ways. From Eastern European folkloric vampires irresistibly drawn to feed on their own kin to the found families of the vampire literature created as the twentieth century drew to a close, family has been part of the horror and romance of vampire literature almost since it began.

The theme of family has shifted dramatically throughout the more than 200 years since Polidori drew on the monsters of folklore to create his Byronic vampire. The Western vampires of the Romantic and Victorian eras tend to be solitary predators. In contrast, the first story in this chapter, Aleksey Konstantinovich Tolstoy's "The Family of the Vourdalak" (1839), is one of the few nineteenth-century texts to harken back to the Eastern European folklore from which Polidori departs so dramatically. In Tolstoy's tale, the threat comes from familial bonds—the tension between desire to protect the vulnerable and the respect the Vourdalaks still feel for their lost father. The tension in Tolstoy's narrative feels dramatically different from other vampire texts of the nineteenth century like those by Polidori, Le Fanu, and Stoker. Over a century later, Stephen King traces a very similar tension in his 1977 short story, "One for the Road," set in the same town that features in his famous novel *Salem's Lot* (1975) and the films inspired by it. Familial love and fear of infection remain common social themes reflected in vampire literature.

Two short stories from the 1990s, Jane Yolen's "Mama Gone" (1991) and Toni Brown's "Immunity" (1996), present feminist revisions of this link between familial love and the horror of vampires. At first glance, "Mama Gone" appears to be a throwback to the same Eastern European folklore that inspired Tolstoy and King, yet Yolen's tale uses the familial love between the daughter and her vampire mother to bring about an ending that was not possible for either the Vourdalaks or Lumleys.

The intertwined concepts of infection and maternity are also central to Toni Brown's "Immunity." Brown shifts the origin of vampires from Eastern Europe to Africa. In "Immunity," vampires arose from a union of Greek lamias with African witches. Vampirism is not contagious, and Brown's vampire Celeste cannot pass her powers to her beloved adopted daughter, but she can give immunity from other monsters. This mother–daughter relationship displays a very different kind of family from those depicted in nineteenth-century vampire literature. For many nineteenth-century male writers, monstrous women are a key aspect of the titillating horror of their texts. As noted in our chapter "Vampire Hunger," in Stoker's *Dracula*, the female vampires are far more horrifying than the count, primarily because of the way they invert "a favorite Victorian maternal function"—the female vampires "feed upon" rather than feed the children.[2] Carol Senf suggests that female vampires like Lucy and Carmilla are

1 Latham, *Consuming Youth* 110

2 Craft, "'Kiss Me with Those Red Lips'" 120.

depicted as bad mothers[1]—greedy and desiring, they violate the selflessness of the Victorian ideal. In contrast, in the stories of Yolen, Brown, and the feminist writers who follow, the female vampires are capable of intense familial love.

It is no accident that the theme of family in vampire literature is often centered around the mother. The role of maternity and the ideal of maternal love are key to these depictions of vampires. Joan Gordon argues that for over 200 years, vampire literature can be seen to reflect much "about motherhood and family which dominant culture suppresses."[2] The icon of the mother, nurturing a child at her breast, is pervasive in Western culture and the vampire, in turn, can be read as a metaphor for conflicted desires surrounding the mother. Christopher Craft explores this idea at length in his examination of one of Dracula's attacks: "We are at the Count's breast, encouraged once again to substitute white for red, as blood becomes milk.... Such fluidity of substitution and displacement entails a confusion of Dracula's sexual identity, or an interfusion of masculine and feminine functions, as Dracula here becomes a lurid mother offering not a breast but an open and bleeding wound."[3] The male body of Dracula embodies the fear of the power of the mother, and his victims are simultaneously both his brides and his children. The link between vampire feeding, reproduction, and maternity is a powerful one. As we saw in earlier chapters, Le Fanu's Carmilla first bites Laura on the breast not the neck (see "Vampires and Sexuality"), and Zoboi's soucouyant uses her breast to drain the infants rather than feeding them (see "Vampires and Race"). Nineteenth- and early twentieth-century female vampires often steal the lives of those they should care for in an inversion of the cultural stereotypes of feminine self-sacrifice and nurture. We see this explored in Nalo Hopkinson's 2001 soucouyant tale, "Greedy Choke Puppy."

Many of the more contemporary tales in this chapter present the vampire's point of view. Since Anne Rice's *Interview with the Vampire* (1976), tales featuring a vampire as protagonist have become popular. In this chapter, the stories by Brown, Hopkinson, and Moreno-Garcia are all told from the perspective of the vampire with varying degrees of empathy. As Joan Gordon and Veronica Hollinger point out in their introduction to *Blood Read: The Vampire as Metaphor in Contemporary Culture*, this empathy would have been unthinkable in earlier decades.[4] The focus in these texts is no longer on a vampire as a threat to the family, but on vampires in search of a family.

The idea of found families can be a particularly powerful one in vampire tales. Unlike other monsters, vampires are generative: their contagion spreads intentionally. The vampire chooses to share its gift/curse, to create another member of its family. From Anne Rice's *Interview with a Vampire* (1976) to

1 Senf, *The Vampire* 158.
2 Gordon, "Sharper Than a Serpent's Tooth" 54.
3 Craft, "'Kiss Me with Those Red Lips'" 125.
4 Gordon and Hollinger, "Introduction" 2.

Poppy Z. Brite's[1] *Lost Souls* (1992), we often see late twentieth-century vampires actively forming families. This raises questions: If vampirism is an infection, what does that make the relationships? Parenthood or infection vector? Are the resulting ties familial or sexual? Navigating the depictions of these relationships and their popularity in the vampire literature of the late twentieth and early twenty-first centuries can reveal much cultural anxiety surrounding the family.

The concept of found families is an important one in much fantasy literature of the late twentieth and early twenty-first centuries and has proven a vital part of the LGBTQ+ community. Certainly, the concept of shaping families as we choose rather than through law and biology no longer seems as radical as it may have in the 1980s and 1990s. The adoptive relationships depicted in tales such as Brown's "Immunity" and Moreno-Garcia's "A Handful of Earth" are loving despite the presence of monsters. We end the chapter with an excerpt from the opening of Kazuki Sakuraba's 2014 novel, *A Small Charred Face*. Here, the vampire rescues a child from the destruction that human gang violence has wrought on his family. The found family that forms between the vampires and the boy will become the heart of the rest of the novel.

In the end, most of the stories in this chapter depict broken families—whether they are broken by the vampires or by humanity. In his classic of psychoanalysis, *On the Nightmare* (1931), Ernest Jones links vampires to the love and hate embodied in the nuclear family. *The Lost Boys* presents the enduring power of the fantasy of the nuclear family, but this fantasy was already far from reality for the majority of its viewers even in the 1980s. In this film, as in the texts in this chapter, the vampire becomes a way of both revealing the tensions within the nuclear family and of challenging the importance of the families into which we are born.

1 As noted previously, Billy Martin published under the name of Poppy Z. Brite before he transitioned, but he has requested his works to be published under the name of Poppy Z. Brite.

## Aleksey Konstantinovich Tolstoy

(1817–1875)

A diplomat, poet, novelist, dramatist, and satirist, Aleksey Tolstoy was a childhood playmate of the future crown prince Alexander II and a member of a family of Russian authors. He was the second cousin of the more famous Count Lev Nikolayevich Tolstoy, author of *War and Peace* and *Anna Karenina*. While working in the diplomatic service in the late 1830s and early 1840s, Aleksey Tolstoy wrote several gothic stories. He ultimately left the diplomatic service to pursue his literary career full time. Originally published in French, a language often used by the Russian elite, this gothic novella begins among urbane European aristocrats but quickly moves into a flashback exploring a traditional Eastern European folklore version of a vampire attack. Tolstoy wrote it in 1839, but it was not published until 1884 (after his death in 1875 from a morphine overdose). The central themes of this text are family and contagion. Once turned, the vampire is irresistibly drawn to attack his or her own home and family in a monstrous reversal of the normative emotions evoked by both. In this, Tolstoy repeats the pattern of most Eastern European folklore. Familial love is in tension with duty. It is through the family bond that the vampire is able to attack even those who should know better. As is so often the case, a child is the first victim.

# "The Family of the Vourdalak"[1]

(1839)

Gathered in Vienna in the year 1815 was the cream of Europe's intellectuals, the elite of the international diplomatic set and all the towering social figures of the day. The congress[2] was coming to an end. Royalist émigrés were preparing to

1 Translated by Fedor Nikanov.

2 This congress was a meeting of representatives from various European countries to discuss borders.

return to their restored châteaux, and Russian fighters to their forsaken homes, while a number of discontented Poles were scheming to bring to Cracow their dreams of liberty and freedom, dubiously promised them by Prince Metternich, Prince Gartenberg and Count Nesselrode.[1]

The scene resembled the aftermath of an animated social ball. For, in those late hours, after the fanfare and revelry had subsided, there remained a small core of people who, still possessing a taste for amusement and the delightful company of the Austrian ladies, were delaying their departures. This congenial circle, of which I was a member, gathered twice weekly in the manor of the Dowager Princess Schwarzenberg,[2] several miles from the city on the outskirts of the tiny village, Gitzing. The aristocratic bearing of the mistress of the manor, her gracious amiability and her astute intellect held for her guests a magnetic attraction. On these blissful occasions, the mornings were devoted to promenades, and the afternoons to lunching in the manor or its environs. Evenings we spent luxuriating by the hearth, chatting—but never about politics, which was strictly forbidden. We surely had had our fill of that. Sometimes we related tales, either the superstitions and legends of our mother countries or our own experiences.

One evening, after a round of story-telling which left everyone in that strained condition relieved only by the enveloping semidarkness, the Marquis d'Urfé,[3] an elderly émigré who was loved for his youthful gaiety and penetrating wit, interrupted the ensuing silence.

"Your tales, gentlemen, are unusual of course, but each, it seems to me, lacks the critical ingredient of personal involvement. I don't know whether any of you has ever actually witnessed the supernatural phenomenon of which you speak or if you can back it up with your word of honor."

Since not one of us could comply, the old man continued, decorously straightening his jabot.

"As for myself, gentlemen, I know of only one case similar to yours, but so strange, horrible and, what is most essential, authentic is it that even the most incredulous man will be left horror-stricken. I unfortunately was both witness and actor, and though I rarely like to recall the experience, I will do so if our charming ladies will only grant me their permission."

General consent followed immediately. A few apprehensive faces glanced toward the moonlit squares on the parquet marble of the hall where we were assembled. Slowly our small circle drew closer together, silently awaiting the tale. The marquis took out his gold snuffbox, drew a pinch, languorously inhaled and thus began.

---

1 These are the names of diplomats from Austria, Prussia, and Russia. At the time, Austria, Prussia, and Russia were in control of the city-state of Krakow.

2 The house of Schwarzenberg was one of the most prominent European aristocratic families connected to both the Czech and German nobility.

3 There was a family of aristocrats of this name and title, but this particular character appears to be an invention of Tolstoy's.

"First of all, mesdames, I wish to ask your forgiveness if during my story I allude to my affairs of the heart more often than is agreeable for a man my age. But, as you will see, they are essential for the clarity of my story. And since it is excusable in old age to forget oneself, I hope none of you will mind if I imagine myself a young man again. It was in 1769 that I fell hopelessly in love with the exquisite Duchess de Gramont.[1] This passion, which at the time I considered deep indeed, left me no peace either day or night, and the duchess, like most beautiful women, prolonged my anguish. In a moment of extreme agitation, I requested and received a diplomatic mission to the Gospodar of Moldavia,[2] where negotiations were being held with Versailles on matters of great importance to France. Before my departure, I visited the duchess. She greeted me less mockingly than ever before; in fact, with genuine concern.

"'D'Urfé, you are acting like a madman. But I know you, and I know you will never change your mind. And so, I beg you only one thing. Please accept this small cross as a token of my friendship. Wear it until you return. It's a family relic which we value highly.'

"With a gallantry perhaps misplaced at that moment, I kissed not the family relic, but the delicate hand and I fastened the cross around my neck. I have never removed it since.

"I shan't bore you, mesdames, with the details of my trip, with my observations about the Hungarians and Serbs—those poor but brave and honest people, who in spite of Turkish enslavement, had forsaken neither their dignity nor their former independence. It's enough to tell you that having learned Polish during my extended stay in Warsaw, I also managed to acquire some Serbian. Thus, I was able to make myself understood when I finally came upon a particular village, the name of which does not matter. Upon arriving at my quarters, I found my hosts in a state of profound confusion. This seemed especially strange since it was Sunday, the day Serbs abandon themselves to such amusements as dancing, sharp-shooting, wrestling and the like. Ascribing their mood to some recent misfortune, I was about to depart when an imposing young man approached and took my hand.

"'Enter. Enter, foreigner,' he urged. 'Don't be upset by our sadness. You will understand when I explain its origin.'

"He told me that his elderly father, Gorcha, a restless and wild-tempered man, arose one morning and took a long Turkish rifle from the wall.

"'Children,' he said to his two sons, George and Peter, 'I'm going up in the mountains to join the brave ones who are chasing the scoundrel, Ali Beg.'

"Such was called the Turkish bandit who continued to harass the neighborhood.

"'Wait ten days for me, and if by then I do not return, have a priest say a funeral Mass, for it will mean that I have been killed. But,' added old Gorcha

1 A French salonnière and bibliophile.

2 Moldavia is a historical region and former principality in Central and Eastern Europe.

sternly, 'if, and may God save you, I should return after those ten days, then, for your own sakes, do not permit me to enter the house. I order you to pierce me with a stake made of ash, regardless of what I will say or do. Because then I will no longer be myself, but rather a cursed vourdalak come to suck your blood.'

"I must digress, mesdames, to explain that the vourdalaks, or vampires, are, according to local opinion in Slavic nations, dead bodies that rise from graves in order to suck blood from the living. Although their habits are similar to vampires of other countries, vourdalaks prefer to suck the blood of close relatives and friends, who die and become vampires also. In Estonia and Herzegovina entire villages may be composed of vourdalaks. Indeed, the Abbot Augustine Colliné,[1] in his curious book on ghosts indicates terrible examples of this phenomenon. Moreover, commissioners appointed by German emperors to investigate cases of vampirism have printed evidence of vourdalaks, who, being pierced through the heart with ash stakes, were buried in the village squares. Testimony offered by those officials who had been present at the piercings assure us that they heard the corpses moaning as the stakes struck their hearts. I might add that all such testimony was delivered under oath and backed by signatures and authoritative seals.

"Keeping this in mind, it should be easy, mesdames, for you to comprehend the effect of Gorcha's words upon his sons. Both threw themselves at his feet, pleading that he let them go to the mountains in his place. Gorcha didn't even reply. He simply turned his back on them and set forth, whistling an old ballad.

"The day I arrived in this village was the day appointed by Gorcha for his return, so it was not difficult for me to appreciate his family's alarm. Also, this was a fine family. George, the elder of the two sons, married and with two children, seemed to be the serious and firm one. His brother, Peter, a handsome eighteen-year-old youth, had a gentle manner. He was obviously a favorite of his younger sister, Zdenka, a true Slavic beauty. I was immediately struck by her resemblance to the Duchesse de Gramont, particularly with respect to one characteristic, a delicate line on her forehead. To this day, I have never seen it on anyone other than those two. This faint line, which did not seem appealing at first, became irresistible once you had noticed it a few times.

"Perhaps I was too impressionable then, or maybe this characteristic resemblance combined with Zdenka's charming naïveté was, in fact, irresistible. Having spoken to her briefly, I felt an affection that was destined to become even more tender.

"I remember we were all sitting at the table that was set with farmer's cheese and a jug of milk. Zdenka was weaving; her sister-in-law was preparing supper for the children who were playing in the sand at her feet. Peter was lightheartedly whistling as he cleaned his *jitagan*, a long Turkish dagger. George, who

1 More commonly called Abbot Augustine Calmet, he wrote an eighteenth-century treatise on vampires.

was leaning his elbows on the table with his chin in his hands, could not take his eyes off the main road. He sat there brooding.

"I, also confused by the melancholy atmosphere, stared at the evening clouds and at the monastery rising above the pines of a nearby forest. This monastery, as I later discovered, had been famous at one time for its miraculous icon of the Holy Virgin which, according to legend, was brought by the angels and hung on the branches of an oak tree. During the preceding century the invading Turks had slaughtered the monks and destroyed this cloister. Now there remained only the walls and a shrine where a mysterious hermit served Mass. He also guided travelers through the ruins and sheltered pilgrims who, journeying from shrine to shrine, preferred to stop at Our Lady under the Oak. Of course, I learned all of this later, since that evening my thoughts were hardly on the archeology of Serbia. As often happens when one gives free rein to thought, I became engrossed with memories of earlier days, with the enchanting period of my childhood and with friends whom I had left for this remote and uncivilized country. And I was dreaming about the Duchesse de Gramont, and—but what is the use of hiding my sinful thoughts?—I mused, mesdames, about several other contemporaries of your grandmothers', whose beauty, in spite of my will, reminded me, each in turn, of the charming duchess. Thus obsessed, I was soon oblivious to my hosts and their anxiety.

"Suddenly, George broke the silence to ask his wife about the exact time the old man had left.

"'At eight o'clock,' she replied. 'I remember hearing the monastery bell strike then.'

"'Well, now it must be no later than half past seven,' he said, becoming pensive and gazing again at the long road leading into the forest.

"I failed to mention, mesdames, that when the Serbs suspect someone of vampirism, they avoid referring to him directly. Otherwise they would call him forth from his grave. Consequently, George alluded to his father as the 'old man.'

"Several minutes of silence lasted until one of the boys pulled Zdenka by the apron, asking, 'Auntie, when is Grandfather coming home?'

"George responded to this question with a violent slap. The child began to cry, whereupon his younger brother asked, surprised and frightened, 'Why do you forbid us, Father, to speak of Grandfather?' Another slap silenced him instantly. Then both began to howl as the rest of the family made a sign of the cross. At that very moment, the monastery clock struck the first chime of eight and a human figure emerged from the forest.

"'It's he, thank God!' exclaimed Zdenka, Peter and their sister-in-law all at once.

"'God protect us!' George cried. 'And how are we to tell if the ten days appointed by him have passed or not?'

"Everyone gazed at him in horror. Meanwhile, the human figure was approaching closer, closer, closer. A tall old man with a gray mustache and a pale and stern face dragged himself with the aid of a stick. The closer he drew, the gloomier George became.

"Finally, the newcomer stopped and circled his family with a look that seemed oblivious, so glazed and distant were his eyes.

"'Well' he said in a timbreless voice, 'why does no one meet me? What does this silence mean? Don't you see I'm wounded?'

"Then we all noticed that the old man's left side was drenched with blood.

"'Hold your father up,' I motioned to George. 'And you Zdenka, give him something to strengthen him; otherwise, he will collapse.'

"'Father,' said George approaching Gorcha, 'show me your wound. I know about wounds and I'll bandage it for you.' But as soon as the son attempted to take off his coat, the old man pushed him away viciously, clasping his side with both hands.

"'Let go, clumsy one. You are hurting me.'

"'That means you're wounded in the heart!' George exclaimed, his face blanching. 'Take off your coat! Take it off, do you hear! It's crucial, do you hear me!'

"The old man rose to his full height. 'Watch out!' he warned, in the same flat voice. 'If you touch me, I shall curse you.'

"Peter placed himself between George and his father. 'Let him be. You must see he's suffering.'

"'Don't go against his will,' his wife advised. 'You know he'll never tolerate such a thing.'

"At that moment we saw the herd heading toward the house in a cloud of dust. It was not certain whether the dog escorting them did not recognize her old master or if something else influenced her, for as soon as she spied Gorcha, she halted. Her fur bristled. She growled, shivering in her tracks as if she were seeing something extraordinary.

"'What's the matter with the dog?' the old man asked, his frown deepening. 'Have I become a stranger to my own family? Did the ten days in the mountain change me so much that my own dog does not recognize me?'

"'Do you hear?' George nudged his wife.

"'What, George?'

"'He said himself that ten days have passed.'

"'Oh, no! And did he not come at the appointed hour?'

"'Yes, yes. It's clear what has to be done.'

"'The accursed dog is still howling. Shoot her!' Gorcha commanded. 'Do you hear me?'

"George didn't move. But Peter, with tears in his eyes, arose, lifted his father's rifle and shot the dog which whimpered, rolling in the dust. 'This one was my favorite,' he said huskily. 'I don't know why my father had to have her killed.'

"'Because that's all she was worth,' Gorcha snapped. 'But it has grown cool. I want to be under the roof.'

"While all this took place, Zdenka prepared a drink of vodka with pears, honey and raisins for the old man, which he pushed away with disgust. He displayed the same loathing for the lamb and rice that George placed before him. Then he went to sit in a corner, muttering unintelligibly.

"The pine logs were flaming in the fireplace, their flicker illuminating the old man's gaunt and pallid face. Were it not for the fire's glow, he could have been taken for a dead man. Zdenka sat down beside him.

"'Father, you do not eat or rest. But do tell us about your adventures in the mountain.'

"By saying this, the girl knew she was striking the most sensitive cord in the old man's heart. He loved to recount his battles and exploits against the Turks. A faint smile crossed his livid lips, though his eyes remained unexpressive. He responded by stroking his daughter's lovely blond hair.

"'Zdenka,' he said, 'I will tell you what I saw in the mountain, but not now, not today. I am tired after all. I can tell you one thing. Ali Beg is dead. He perished by your father's stroke. If anyone doubts it, here is the proof!' He pulled open the bag which was slung across his shoulder, removing a bloody head, not much less cadaverous than his own. We all turned away with a shudder. Gorcha, handing it to Peter, said, 'Hang it over the door of our house so that all those who pass may know that Ali Beg is dead, that the roads are free of villains—unless one counts the Yanychars of the Sultan!'[1]

"Peter obeyed, though with obvious aversion. 'Now everything's clear to me,' he reflected. 'The poor dog was growling because she smelled dead flesh.'

"'Yes, she smelled dead flesh ...' George mumbled, after having returned unobtrusively with something in his hand which he rested in a nearby corner. It looked like a sharply pointed pole.

"'George,' whispered his wife, 'you don't mean you intend to ...'

"'Brother,' murmured Zdenka, 'what do you have in mind? No, no, no. You're not going to do this! It's inconceivable!'

"Meanwhile, night had fallen and the family wandered off to sleep in that part of the house which was separated from my own room by a thin partition. I must confess that everything I had observed affected me strangely. I snuffed out the candle. The moon shone through my window, casting bluish reflections on the floor—similar to those, mesdames, you see before your very own eyes. I felt sleepy, but, needless to say, I could not fall asleep. Attributing it to the moonlight, I searched for something to drape across the window. But I couldn't find anything. I was startled by voices coming from the other side of the partition and strained to hear what they were saying.

1 An elite unit of Turkish soldiers. They served as bodyguards to the sultan until they were abolished in 1826.

"'Lie down, wife,' George said soothingly. 'You, Peter, and you, Zdenka, don't worry about anything. I'll stand watch.'

"'No, George,' answered his wife. 'It's I who should not be sleeping. You worked all last night; you're exhausted. Besides, I have to attend our elder son who's been ill since yesterday. Don't worry. Lie down. I'll watch for you.'

"'Brother,' Zdenka said in her caressing voice, 'it seems that nobody has to watch for anything. See how peacefully Father sleeps.'

"'Not my wife, nor you, nor anyone seems to have much sense,' George replied in a voice that left no room for contradiction. 'Now I've told you to go to sleep. I'll be the guard!'

"Complete silence followed. Soon, my eyelids grew heavy, and I too fell asleep. The slow creaking of my door awakened me. The old man, Gorcha was entering. I could feel his presence through the pitch darkness. He seemed to be observing me through his vacant eyes. He lifted one foot after another, stealthily, until he was by my side. Consumed with terror, I nevertheless managed to remain still. The old man bent over me, his livid face so close to mine that I could feel his corpselike breath. Then, exerting superhuman effort, I discovered myself sitting up in bed, perspiring profusely. No one was in the room. But through the window I detected Gorcha, his face pressed against the pane, his uncanny eyes riveted upon me. I didn't have the strength to cry out, only enough composure to remain in bed and pretend I saw nothing. The old man was evidently reassuring himself that I was asleep, for, having stared at me thus, he slowly moved away from the window. George was snoring so loudly that the walls rattled. Then I heard Gorcha's voice in the next room. The sick child coughed.

"'You're not asleep, my little boy?' Gorcha asked.

"'No, Grandfather, and I'd like very much to talk to you.'

"'Ah, you want to talk with me. And what will it be about?'

"'I'd like you to tell me how you fought the Turks because I also want to fight them.'

"'I thought you would, my dear child. Tomorrow, I will give you the small dagger I've been saving.'

"'Oh, Grandfather, please give it to me now.'

"'Well, my little one, why didn't you talk with me earlier today?'

"'Because... because Father wouldn't let me.'

"'Your father is very cautious. But you want the dagger very much ...'

"'Yes, I want it *very* much. Only not here because Father might wake up.'

"'Where, then?'

"'Well, let's go outside quietly, Grandfather, so no one can hear us.'

"Gorcha seemed to laugh as the boy got out of bed. I didn't believe in vampires. But my nerves had been so shattered by my nightmare that I got up and slammed my fist against the partition lest I reproach myself later. No one woke, though my blow sounded loud enough to waken the seven sleepers in the Arabian fairy tale.[1] Determined to save the child, I hurled myself against the door, but it was locked from the outside. To intensify my frustration, the old man was already passing the window with the child in his arms.

"'Get up! Get up!, I screamed with all my might, shaking the partition vehemently. Only then did George awaken.

"'Hurry,' I cried. 'He's carrying your child away.' With one swift kick, George broke down the door and darted toward the forest. With some trouble I wakened Peter, then his sister-in-law and Zdenka. Huddled in front of the house, we saw George a few minutes later returning with the boy in his arms. The child had already fainted when George stumbled upon him on the main highway. We revived him, though he appeared no sicker than before. To our anxious interrogation, he explained that Grandfather had done him no harm, that they had strolled together, quietly chatting; that once they were in the fresh air, he had fainted, though he couldn't remember how or why.

"Gorcha was nowhere to be found, so the remainder of the night was spent in hushed consultation.

"The next morning I learned that ice was floating in the river, preventing anyone from crossing to the mainland for several days. Even if it were possible for me to leave, however, I could not have done so. The more I saw Zdenka, the more I craved her. And, mesdames, I am not, mind you, one of those who believe in sudden, uncontrollable passion, the kind exalted in novels. Yet I do believe that love can sometimes develop more quickly than is usual. In Zdenka's remarkable beauty I encountered the Duchesse de Gramont, the duchess transformed by pastoral garb and melodious foreign speech. The characteristic line both had on their foreheads was the *coup de grâce*. Yet perhaps it really was the incredible situation in which I had become an actor that ignited my intense passion.

"During that day I overheard Zdenka speaking with her younger brother. 'What do you think about Father, Peter?' she asked. 'I can't believe you suspect him.'

"'I dare not suspect him, especially since the boy assured us that Father didn't harm him. As for his sudden disappearance, well, you know he has done this before and never explained his activities and departures.'

"'I know,' Zdenka agreed. 'But you know that George is—'

"'Yes, I know. I know. It's useless talking to him. I'm afraid we'll have to hide the stake. He won't be able to get another one. There are no ash trees on this side of the mountain.'

"Yes, let's hide it. But don't tell the children, for they'll surely tell George.'

"'We must be cautious,' Peter urged, and they separated.

1 I.e., loud enough to wake someone in a magical slumber. In "The Seven Sleepers," youths fleeing persecution hide in a cave to escape. They fall into an enchanted sleep and awake one hundred and eighty years later.

"Night came, and still not a trace of the old man, Gorcha. Like the previous night, I was in bed, distracted by the moonbeams that illuminated my room. Sleep was beginning to distort my thoughts when I instinctively felt the presence of the old man. Opening my eyes, I saw his deathlike face pressed against the pane. This time I tried to get up, but my limbs were paralyzed. I heard the old man go around the house and knock on George's window. The child tossed and moaned in his sleep. For a while, silence prevailed. Then there was a knock at the child's window. He moaned again and woke up.

"'Is that you, Grandfather?'

"'It's me,' he answered solemnly. 'I brought you the little dagger.'

"'I don't dare come out. Father has forbidden it.'

"'But you don't have to. Just open the window and kiss me.'

"As the window was being opened, I summoned all my nerve, jumped off the bed and began knocking on the partition. George was immediately up. I heard him cursing and his wife screaming. A minute later the entire household clustered around the fainted child. As before, Gorcha had vanished. We revived the child, though he was weak and could barely breathe. The poor little thing didn't understand why he had fainted. His mother and Zdenka ascribed it to the child's fear of being caught in a forbidden conversation with his grandfather. I said nothing. When the boy grew quiet, everyone but George went to sleep. At dawn, I heard him awaken his wife. They were whispering. Zdenka joined them. The women were crying.

"The child died. I shall not elaborate on the family's despair, except to mention that, peculiarly enough, nobody attributed his death to Gorcha. At least not publicly.

"George remained reticent, his gloomy expression menacing. For two days the old man did not reappear. The third night, on the day of the little one's burial, I sensed that somebody was roaming through the house murmuring the name of the child who was still alive. It even seemed to me, momentarily, that Gorcha glanced into my window. I couldn't be sure, since the moon was obscured by clouds. Nevertheless, I reported this to George. He questioned the child, who acknowledged that he had heard his grandfather calling him and had seen him at the window outside his room. George commanded his son to awaken him the next time the old man appeared.

"These events curiously intensified my tenderness for Zdenka. I existed in constant agitation. During the day it was impossible to speak with her alone. At night, I was tormented by the prospect of my imminent departure.

"Zdenka's room was separated from mine by a hall which led on one side to the street, on the other to the yard. On my way for a walk before sleeping, I passed through the hall and noticed her door slightly ajar. In spite of myself, I stood behind it, listening. The familiar rustle of her dress made my heart pound. She was singing a song about a Serbian knight saying farewell to his girl.

'Oh, my young poplar,' the old king said, 'I am off to the wars and you will forget me. The trees that grow at the foot of the mountain are slender and easily bent, but your young body is even more slender and even more easily bent. Bittersweet berries are red. They are effortlessly blown by the wind. But your lips are redder than the berries. And I am like the old oak without leaves; my beard whiter than the Danube's foam. You will forget me, little heart, and I will perish from longing, for the enemy will not dare to kill the old king.'

Then the beautiful girl answered. 'I swear to remain faithful to you, never to forget you. If I break my oath, then return after death to suck my heart's blood.' To which the old king replied, 'Amen.' He went off to war and the beautiful girl forgot him.[1]

"Here Zdenka stopped as if afraid to finish the song. I could no longer contain myself. Her soft eloquence was an echo of the Duchesse de Gramont. Disregarding the consequences, I flung open the door. My intrusion made her blush, for she had just removed her outer garment and was wearing only a gold-embroidered red silk blouse and a richly colored petticoat. The outline of her supple limbs was visible, her abundant blond hair unbraided. In this state of half-undress, she looked more ravishing than ever. 'Zdenka, my life, please do not fear me,' I implored. 'Everybody is asleep. Only the crickets in the grass and the dragonfly in the air can hear what I'm going to tell you.'

"'Go away, go away, my dearest. If my brother sees us, I'm lost.'

"'Zdenka, I will not leave until you promise to love me as the lovely maiden in your song promised to love the king. Zdenka, I soon will have to depart. Who knows whether we shall ever see each other again. I love you more than my own soul, more than my salvation. My life and my blood are yours. Won't you give me but an hour?'

"'Too much can happen in an hour,' Zdenka said softly, leaving her hand in mine. 'You don't know my brother. I have a premonition that he will see us.'

"'Don't worry, Zdenka, my darling Zdenka. Your brother is exhausted by these sleepless nights. He is lulled by the wind rustling through the trees. His slumber is deep. Our night is long, and I beg you for only one hour, whereas, the farewell may last forever.'

"'No, no. Not forever!'

"'Perhaps, Zdenka. Yet I see only you, hear only you. I am no longer master over my own fate. It's as if I were compelled by a superior power. Forgive me!' and like a madman I pressed her to my heart.

"'You're not a friend to me, no, no, no,' she gasped, breaking away from my arms and hiding in a corner.

"I don't recall what I replied to her at that moment, for my sudden boldness

1 This song is probably invented by Tolstoy.

alarmed me, though not because I was inhibited in the past, but because, in spite of my passion, I deeply respected Zdenka's purity. Thus, my gallant manner, so successful with the beautiful maidens of the time, shamed me. I realized that the young girl, in all her simplicity, had not fathomed the intent of my artful words, though, mesdames, judging from your smiles, I can see it is readily apparent to you. I stood before her bewildered, when unexpectedly she pointed toward the window, shivering. There was Gorcha peering at us. A heavy arm grabbed my shoulder. I turned around. It was George.

"'What are you doing here?' he scowled.

"Embarrassed by this turn of events, I directed his attention toward his father, who was still standing at the window but who vanished once George saw him.

"'I heard the old man and came to warn your sister,' I explained. George stared as if to penetrate my innermost thoughts. Taking my arm, he walked me to my room and left without a word.

"The next day the family was gathered in front of the house at a table set with dairy foods.

"'Where is the boy?' asked George.

"'In the yard,' his wife answered. 'He's playing his favorite game, imagining that he's fighting against the Turks.'

"No sooner had she said this than to our great surprise we detected the hulking form of old Gorcha lumbering toward us from the forest, in a manner reminiscent of his initial arrival.

"'You are most welcome, Father,' said his daughter-in-law in a low tone.

"'We are happy to see you, Father,' chorused Zdenka and Peter.

"'Father,' George said, 'we were expecting you. Will you say grace?'

"The old man turned away, frowning.

"'Say grace this very minute,' urged George, 'and make the sign of the cross. Or, I swear by St. George ...'

"Zdenka and her sister-in-law begged the old man to say grace.

"'No,' insisted Gorcha. 'He doesn't dare give me orders. If he tries to force me, I will curse him.'

"George darted into the house, returning in a fury. 'Where is the stake?' he cried. 'Where did you put the stake?'

"Zdenka and Peter glanced at each other furtively.

"'You corpse!' George shouted at his father. 'What have you done with my elder son? Give me my son, you dead man!'

"Speaking this way, he turned more and more pale as rage burned in his eyes. The old man stood motionless, an evil sneer on his lips.

"'Where in heaven's name is the stake? Where is that stake?' George continued. 'Let misery befall those who have hidden it, all the misery possible in one lifetime.'

"Then the most terrible thing occurred. Riding toward us on an enormous stake was the younger son, his blood-curdling laughter resounding in our ears. As he neared us, he screeched the Serbian battle cry.

"George flushed, grabbing the stake away from the child. The youngster threw himself on his father who let forth a howl, and then darted away in the direction of the forest with a speed that seemed supernatural. George chased him across the field and also faded out of sight. The sun had already set when George, pale as death, his hair on end, came back. As he sat by the fire, his teeth seemed to be chattering. Nobody dared question him. As bedtime approached, he regained his self-control and, calling me to his side, spoke in a casual manner.

"'My dear guest, I just saw that the river is cleared of ice. Nothing detains you any longer. No need to say good-bye to my family,' he added, glancing at Zdenka. 'She wishes you well and hopes you remember us kindly. At dawn, you will find your horse saddled and a guide to direct you out of the village. Farewell, and forgive your hosts for the difficult times you spent with them.'

"George seemed almost friendly as he accompanied me to my room and shook my hand for the last time. Then he shuddered and his teeth chattered as if from the cold.

"Once alone, I thought of the despair I had suffered over former love affairs, the tenderness, jealousy and rage. Yet never until that moment, not even during encounters with the Duchesse de Gramont, had I experienced such despondence. I changed into my traveling clothes before the sun had risen, hoping to see Zdenka before my departure. But George was already awaiting me in the hall.

"I spurred my horse on, promising myself that I would stop at the village when returning from Yassa.[1] Although this was a long time off, the prospect relieved my sadness. I was already contemplating a pleasurable return, and my imagination was working out the sweet details, when my horse bolted, almost hurling me from the saddle. She stopped, stretched out her forelegs and snorted as if in danger. I looked about in every direction until I noticed a wolf about a hundred steps ahead of us, digging in the ground. Seeing us, it raced away. I rode over and found a freshly dug hole, with a stake sticking out a few inches above the ground. Yet I couldn't be sure of this, since I rode by swiftly."

At this point, the marquis stopped talking and took a pinch of snuff.

"Is that all?" the ladies asked.

"Oh, no, not at all," assured d'Urfé. "It's very painful for me to recall what I am about to relate. Gladly would I forfeit worldly pleasures to free my mind forever of these memories.

"It took me about half a year to conclude my affairs in Yassa, much longer than anticipated. How can I tell you what I experienced through that stretch

1 Also known as Iaşi or Jassy, this is the second largest city in Romania in the historic region of Moldavia. It was known for academics and the arts.

of time? It's the sad truth that stable emotions do not exist in this world. The success of my negotiations regarding the revolting politics which have recently caused so much trouble brought me strong praise from Versailles. But my tormenting memories of Zdenka were intensified. Even the ladies, particularly the wife of the Seigneur of Moldavia—a beauty who spoke our language to perfection and who singled me out from all the other young foreigners in Yassa—could not relieve my pain. Yet, reared according to French gallantry and ruled by the Gallic blood in my veins, I, of course, could not refuse this lady's flattering approaches. Moreover, considering that I was the French representative at the court of her husband, I regarded it as my singular duty to satisfy the desires of the seigneur's noble wife. As you can see, mesdames, I always put the interests of my country above all else...

"Upon my return home, I journeyed by the same road I had taken to Yassa. By then I had forgotten Zdenka and her family and was reminded of them while riding through a field where I heard a bell ring eight times. Its ring was familiar. My guide informed me that it came from a nearby shrine, the Monastery of Our Lady under the Oak. With this, I headed for the guest house which was swarming with pilgrims. A monk assured me I could find lodging practically anywhere, that, due to 'damned Gorcha,' there were many empty houses.

"'Do you mean,' I gasped, 'that the old man is still alive?'

"'No. Apparently, he is lying quietly in the earth with a stake through his heart. He sucked the blood of his grandson, the younger child of George. One night, the little boy knocked at the house begging to be admitted, crying that he was cold. His foolish mother, though she herself had buried him that very day, was unable to summon the courage to send her son back to his grave. No sooner had she let him in than he threw himself upon her, sucking her life's blood. After she was buried, she in turn came for the blood of her husband and her brother-in-law. They all shared the same fate.'

"'And Zdenka? What happened to her?' I asked, trembling.

"'Well, as for her, the poor thing went mad from sorrow. It's really better we don't speak of her.'

"The monk's comments were puzzling, but I had no heart to pursue them further.

"'Still,' he continued, 'vampirism is contagious. Many families in the village suffer from it. If you accept my advice, you'll remain in the monastery for the night. Out there, whether the vourdalaks get you or not, you'll undergo such terror that your hair will turn snow white before I ring for early Mass. Of course, I'm only a poor monk, yet the generosity of the travelers enables me to care for their needs. I can offer you such excellent farmer's cheese and currants that your mouth will water at the sight of them. There are a few bottles of Tokay wine which are as fine as those served at the table of His Holiness.'

"I seemed to be speaking with an innkeeper rather than a monk, and his purpose in relating these horror stories appeared bent upon coercing me into imitating the generosity of the other travelers who provided the holy man with the means of gratifying their needs. Aside from this, the word 'terror' never fails to affect me like a trumpet affects a war horse. How ashamed I would have been had I not proceeded instantly to investigate the rumors!

"My shivering guide begged permission, which I granted, to remain at the monastery. I thus arrived alone at the deserted village. No lights were on; no songs sung. Through the eerie silence, I passed those familiar houses until I reached George's. Whether I was influenced by a romantic whim or simply by youthful boldness, I resolved to spend the night, though no one answered my knock at the gates. Pushing, I managed to get them open. I tied my saddled horse to the shed and crept up to the house. Not a single door was locked, yet the house seemed abandoned. Zdenka's room appeared to have been forsaken that very day. Several dresses lay across the bed. A few pieces of jewelry, gifts from me, were scattered on the bureau. A small enamel cross, which I had purchased in Budapest, sparkled in the moonlight.

"My heart pounded at a dreadful speed. Regardless of my waning love, I sighed, wrapped myself in my cape, stretched out on the bed and slept. I can't recall the precise details, but I do remember envisioning Zdenka as a charming, ingenuous, devoted creature shamed by my fickleness. How, I agonized, could I have forgotten the sweet maiden who had loved me so very much? The vision of her became intertwined with my memories of the Duchesse de Gramont, and, in those two silhouettes, I saw one and the same person. Kneeling at Zdenka's feet, I prayed for her forgiveness. My entire being, my very soul, became infused with both sadness and happiness. Thus, I continued to dream until gently wakened by wheat stalks waving in the wind. I heard the distant chirping of birds, the rushing of a waterfall and the brushing of leaves, when it seemed that all those sounds could actually have emanated from the rustling of a lady's dress. With this notion, I opened my eyes and beheld Zdenka by my bedside. So bright was the moon that I could distinguish every feature, each more enchanting than I remembered. She was dressed in the garb she had worn on the eve of our farewell: her silk peasant blouse embroidered in gold and dirndl[1] skirt gathered tightly around her slim waist.

"'Zdenka,' I cried, rising quickly from the bed. 'Is it you?'

"'Yes, it is me,' she responded in a small, pathetic voice. 'Yes, it is your forgotten Zdenka. Why didn't you return sooner? Now everything is ended and you must leave at once. A moment's delay and you are lost. Farewell, my friend. Farewell forever.'

"'Zdenka. Zdenka, you have been through so much sorrow. Please speak with me at least. It will relieve your anxiety.'

1 A dirndl is a traditional folk costume in German speaking countries. It features a fitted low-cut bodice over a full skirt.

"'My friend, do not believe all you hear about us. But do go. Go quickly, or else you will die without reprieve.'

"'But Zdenka, what is there to fear? Is it possible you will not grant me an hour?' She shuddered and for a second seemed almost imperceptibly transformed.

"'All right. An hour—just one. Is it not the same request you made the night you overheard me singing about the old king? So be it again. I'll permit you this hour... But no, no,' she screamed, as if coming to her senses. 'Go. Run. Run far away. I'm telling you to hurry while you still have the chance.'

"A wild frenzy distorted her features. I couldn't understand what forced her to speak this way. I only knew how lovely she was and decided to remain in spite of her wishes. Finally, complying with my request, she sat beside me and confessed that she had loved me at first sight. As she spoke, the change in her became gradually more and more distinct. Her eyes glinted boldly. Her movements challenged me provocatively. Indeed, she was emerging as someone quite unmaidenly, even wicked, completely different from the reserved young virgin of my memories.

"Is it possible, I asked myself, that Zdenka was never the chaste girl she appeared to be six months ago? Is it possible that being afraid of her brother, she had assumed a convenient disguise? Had I been tricked by a modest façade? But then, I countered, why did she urge me to leave? Was this simply a coy move? I imagined for the moment that I saw the former Zdenka... But no, she was still transfigured... If Zdenka is not the Diana[1] I thought she was, could she not be compared to another goddess at least as charming? Anyway, I prefer the fate of Adonis to that of Acteon.[2] If this classical reference seems out of place, mesdames, please remember that I am relating events of 1769. At that time, mythology was à la mode, and I made the pretense of being avant-garde. Since then, times have changed, for the revolution has eclipsed both paganism and Christianity. The new religion, reason, is erected in their place. I never favored this cult, reason, especially in the company of women. As my story was transpiring, I was particularly unwilling to worship this deity. Quite naturally, I abandoned myself to Zdenka, responding pleasurably to her irresistible advances. Some time passed in sweet forgetfulness. Zdenka amused me by trying on one piece of jewelry after another, until it occurred to me to place the enamel cross around her swanlike neck. Anticipating my intention, Zdenka withdrew with a shudder.

1 Roman name for the Virgin goddess of the moon and the hunt.

2 The Greek goddess of love, Aphrodite, became enchanted with the beautiful youth Adonis. His name would come to signify male beauty. Acteon in contrast, was a hunter who accidentally saw the virgin goddess Diana/Artemis bathing. In punishment, she turned him into a stag and he was killed by his own hounds. In making these classical allusions, the narrator is suggesting that Zdenka is not quite the innocent she seemed to be on his last visit.

"'Enough of this foolishness, my love,' she smiled, regaining her composure. 'Let us leave all these trinkets and discuss you and your intentions.'

"In spite of my feelings, Zdenka's odd behavior forced me to study her more closely. Unlike the past, she did not have on the holy medals and relics which Serbians commonly wear from childhood to death. I questioned her about this.

"'I lost them,' she answered, impatient to change the subject.

"A sense of foreboding came over me. I decided to leave, but Zdenka stood in my way.

"'What's the meaning of this?' she scowled. 'You begged me for an hour of my time, and now you're leaving so abruptly.'

"'Zdenka, you were right in convincing me to leave. I just heard a noise. I'm afraid we will be discovered together,' I said, attempting to conciliate her.

"'Don't worry, my friend. Everyone around us is asleep. Only the cricket in the grass and the dragon fly in the air can hear what we say.'

"'No, no, Zdenka, this won't do. I must go.'

"'Please wait,' she implored. 'I love you more than my own soul, more than my salvation. You once told me that your life and blood were mine.'

"'But your brother! I have the feeling he is about to arrive.'

"'Be still, my heart. My brother is asleep, too, lulled by the wind that is rustling in the trees. His sleep is deep and the night is long. I am requesting but a moment longer.'

"As she said this, Zdenka looked so beautiful that the anxiety that had gripped me vanished with my desire to remain by her side. A strange mixture of fright and rapture filled me. Slowly, as my will weakened, Zdenka became increasingly tender. I resolved to give in to her while I maintained my guard. But alas! I was only half sensible, as usual. Noticing my reserve, she offered me a few drafts of wine to warm myself, saying that she had purchased it from the good monk. My compliance elicited a smile, and the wine surely produced its intended effect. After the second glass, my reservations over the little cross and holy medals were completely erased from my consciousness. Zdenka, in her informal attire, her blond hair unbraided, her bracelets gleaming in the moonlight, was hopelessly enticing. I could not restrain myself and impulsively embraced her.

"Then, mesdames, then one of those inexplicable signs appeared. I have never been able to explain it to myself. In fact, at that time I was inclined not to believe in it at all. Nevertheless, when I pressed Zdenka's body to my own, one of the points of the cross, which the Duchesse de Gramont had given me, stuck into my chest. That momentary pain served as a bolt from heaven. Glancing at Zdenka, I saw that her features, though beautiful, were imprinted with death, that her eyes were glazed and that her smile was convulsed with the agony of a condemned prisoner. Simultaneously, I sensed in the room a putrid odor like some half-opened tomb. The loathsome truth stunned me. Only too late did I recall the monk's warning. What a desperate situation I was in! Everything depended upon boldness and cunning. Not wanting her to notice my doubt, I turned away. My gaze passed for a second across the window where Gorcha was leaning on a bloody stake, peering at me with the eyes of a hyena. In the other window stood George, looking exactly like his father. They were both following my movements closely. Undoubtedly they would descend upon me at my slightest effort to escape. So I pretended not to have seen them but continued, with all my will, to caress Zdenka as if nothing unusual were happening. My mind raced through plans of escape. The wailing of women and children floated in from the yard, piercing the silence like the howling of wild cats.

"It is time to escape, I said to myself, and the sooner the better. Turning to Zdenka, I spoke loudly enough for her ghastly relatives to hear. 'I am tired, my dearest, and must lie down for a while. Yet, first, my horse should be fed. I beg you not to leave. Wait for me,' I said, kissing her cold mouth. Outside, my horse was covered with foam, trying vainly to gallop out of the shed. Her neighing made me wary lest she give me away. But the vourdalaks who overheard my conversation with Zdenka did not move. Certain that the gates were ajar, I jumped onto the saddle and spurred my horse on. Having passed swiftly through the gates, I barely noticed the crowd gathered round the house, gaping through the windows. My sudden departure must have startled them. Yet for those first few moments I only concentrated on the rhythmic clatter of my horse's hoofs as they resounded in the unearthly silence.

"On the verge of congratulating myself on a safe escape, I was interrupted by a noise that resembled a hurricane. Voices moaned, howled and argued with one another. Silence. Then a resounding beat as if a corps of infantrymen were in hot pursuit, I spurred on until my horse spurted blood and my veins almost burst from the fire within. A voice was calling me.

"'Wait, wait, my dear. I love you more than my soul, more than my salvation. Wait, wait. Your blood is mine.'

"A cold breath touched my ears as Zdenka leaped upon my horse from behind.

"'My heart, my soul,' she whispered to me. 'I see only you. I want only you. I have no power over myself. I obey a superior force. Forgive me, my dear one, forgive me.' Placing her arms around me, she bit my neck and tried to throw me from my horse.

"A terrible struggle ensued between us. Mustering all my energy, I managed to grab Zdenka with one arm around her waist, the other hand on her braids. Lifting myself in the stirrups, I hurled her to the ground. My strength drained, I became delirious. Gruesome images menaced me. First George, then Peter, was running along the road's edge trying to veer me off course. Neither one succeeded. I was rejoicing over this victory when, turning back, I saw old man Gorcha leaning on his stake, making incredible leaps with it as the Tyroleans[1] do when they jump over crevices. But even he remained behind. His daughter-in-

1 Inhabitants of a region in the eastern Alps.

law, who was dragging the two children, threw one of them to him. He caught it on the sharp point, then, operating the stake like a sling-shot, hurled the child at me. I avoided the blow, but the child, like a fierce bulldog, set his teeth in the neck of my horse. With some effort, I tore him away. Gorcha discharged the other one at me, but he was crushed under my horse's hoofs. I don't know what happened next. When I regained consciousness, it was already daylight, and I was sprawled at the edge of the road, my horse dying nearby.

"And so, mesdames, ended the love affair which, it would seem, should have numbed all my subsequent desires to search for others among your grandmothers. Those who still survive will testify that I did become far more sensible.

"The events I have related to you this evening are strange indeed. To this very day I shiver at the thought that I had fallen into the power of my enemies. I might have become a vampire in turn. But Providence did not permit this, and I, mesdames, am not thirsty for your blood. And, though an old man, I am prepared to defend you till the last drop of blood courses from my veins."

# Stephen King

(B. 1947)

Stephen King, known as the King of Horror, is the most prolific and popular contemporary writer of supernatural, science fiction, fantasy, and crime narratives. King blends conventional gothic elements with modern psychological terror in his portrayal of ordinary people in everyday scenarios who are confronted unexpectedly by evil. This startling juxtaposition between the normal and the abnormal in present-day settings is the reason that many of his works, particularly those adapted into films, such as *Carrie* (1973), *The Shining* (1977), and *Misery* (1987), have made an indelible impression on late twentieth-century culture. King has authored several comics and graphic novels including *American Vampire Vol. 1* (2014). He is an avid music fan, particularly of rock and roll, and has contributed spoken word segments for several musical groups, including the Foo Fighters. His numerous awards include Bram Stoker Awards, World Fantasy Awards, and the 2007 Grand Master Award from the Mystery Writers of America.

## "One for the Road"

(1977)

It was quarter past ten and Herb Tooklander was thinking of closing for the night when the man in the fancy overcoat and the white, staring face burst into Tookey's Bar, which lies in the northern part of Falmouth. It was the tenth of January, just about the time most folks are learning to live comfortably with all the New Year's resolutions they broke, and there was one hell of a northeaster blowing outside. Six inches had come down before dark and it had been going hard and heavy since then. Twice we had seen Billy Larribee go by high in the cab of the town plow, and the second time Tookey ran him out a beer—an act of pure charity my mother would have called it, and my God knows she put down enough of Tookey's beer in her time. Billy told him they were keeping ahead of it on the main road, but the side ones were closed and apt to stay that way until next morning. The radio in Portland was forecasting another foot and a forty-mile-an-hour wind to pile up the drifts.

There was just Tookey and me in the bar, listening to the wind howl around the eaves and watching it dance the fire around on the hearth. "Have one for the road, Booth," Tookey says, "I'm gonna shut her down."

He poured me one and himself one and that's when the door cracked open and this stranger staggered in, snow up to his shoulders and in his hair, like he had rolled around in confectioner's sugar. The wind billowed a sand-fine sheet of snow in after him.

"Close the door!" Tookey roars at him. "Was you born in a barn?"

I've never seen a man who looked that scared. He was like a horse that's spent an afternoon eating fire nettles. His eyes rolled toward Tookey and he said, "My wife—my daughter—" and he collapsed on the floor in a dead faint.

"Holy Joe," Tookey says. "Close the door, Booth, would you?"

I went and shut it, and pushing it against the wind was something of a chore. Tookey was down on one knee holding the fellow's head up and patting his cheeks. I got over to him and saw right off that it was nasty. His face was fiery red, but there were gray blotches here and there, and when you've lived through winters in Maine since the time Woodrow Wilson was President, as I have, you know those gray blotches mean frostbite.

"Fainted," Tookey said. "Get the brandy off the backbar, will you?"

I got it and came back. Tookey had opened the fellow's coat. He had come around a little; his eyes were half open and he was muttering something too low to catch.

"Pour a capful," Tookey says.

"Just a cap?" I asks him.

"That stuff's dynamite," Tookey says. "No sense overloading his carb."

I poured out a capful and looked at Tookey. He nodded. "Straight down the hatch."

I poured it down. It was a remarkable thing to watch. The man trembled all over and began to cough. His face got redder. His eyelids, which had been at half-mast, flew up like window shades. I was a bit alarmed, but Tookey only sat him up like a big baby and clapped him on the back.

The man started to retch, and Tookey clapped him again.

"Hold onto it," he says, "that brandy comes dear."

The man coughed some more, but it was diminishing now. I got my first good look at him. City fellow, all right, and from somewhere south of Boston, at a guess. He was wearing kid gloves, expensive but thin. There were probably some more of those grayish-white patches on his hands, and he would be lucky not to lose a finger or two. His coat was fancy, all right; a three-hundred-dollar job if ever I'd seen one. He was wearing tiny little boots that hardly came up over his ankles, and I began to wonder about his toes.

"Better," he said.

"All right," Tookey said. "Can you come over to the fire?"

"My wife and my daughter," he said. "They're out there ... in the storm."

"From the way you came in, I didn't figure they were at home watching the TV," Tookey said. "You can tell us by the fire as easy as here on the floor. Hook on, Booth."

He got to his feet, but a little groan came out of him and his mouth twisted down in pain. I wondered about his toes again, and I wondered why God felt he had to make fools from New York City who would try driving around in southern Maine at the height of a northeast blizzard. And I wondered if his wife and his little girl were dressed any warmer than him.

We hiked him across to the fireplace and got him sat down in a rocker that used to be Missus Tookey's favorite until she passed on in '74. It was Missus Tookey that was responsible for most of the place, which had been written up in *Down East* and the *Sunday Telegram* and even once in the Sunday supplement of the Boston *Globe*. It's really more of a public house than a bar, with its big wooden floor, pegged together rather than nailed, the maple bar, the old barn-raftered ceiling, and the monstrous big fieldstone hearth. Missus Tookey started to get some ideas in her head after the Down East article came out, wanted to start calling the place Tookey's Inn or Tookey's Rest, and I admit it has sort of a Colonial ring to it, but I prefer plain old Tookey's Bar. It's one thing to get uppish in the summer, when the state's full of tourists, another thing altogether in the winter, when you and your neighbors have to trade together. And there had been plenty of winter nights, like this one, that Tookey and I had spent all alone together, drinking scotch and water or just a few beers. My own Victoria passed on in '73, and Tookey's was a place to go where there were enough voices to mute the steady ticking of the deathwatch beetle—even if there was just Tookey and me, it was enough. I wouldn't have felt the same about it if the place had been Tookey's Rest. It's crazy but it's true.

We got this fellow in front of the fire and he got the shakes harder than ever. He hugged onto his knees and his teeth clattered together and a few drops of clear mucus spilled off the end of his nose. I think he was starting to realize that another fifteen minutes out there might have been enough to kill him. It's not the snow, it's the wind-chill factor. It steals your heat.

"Where did you go off the road?" Tookey asked him.

"S-six miles s-s-south of h-here," he said.

Tookey and I stared at each other, and all of a sudden I felt cold. Cold all over.

"You sure?" Tookey demanded. "You came six miles through the snow?"

He nodded. "I checked the odometer when we came through t-town. I was following directions ... going to see my wife's s-sister ... in Cumberland ... never been there before ... we're from New Jersey ..."

New Jersey. If there's anyone more purely foolish than a New Yorker it's a fellow from New Jersey.

"Six miles, you're sure?" Tookey demanded.

"Pretty sure, yeah. I found the turnoff but it was drifted in... it was..."

Tookey grabbed him. In the shifting glow of the fire his face looked pale and strained, older than his sixty-six years by ten. "You made a right turn?"

"Right turn, yeah. My wife—"

"Did you see a sign?"

"Sign?" He looked up at Tookey blankly and wiped the end of his nose. "Of course I did. It was on my instructions. Take Jointner Avenue through Jerusalem's Lot to the 295 entrance ramp." He looked from Tookey to me and back to Tookey again. Outside, the wind whistled and howled and moaned through the eaves. "Wasn't that right, mister?"

"The Lot," Tookey said, almost too soft to hear. "Oh my God."

"What's wrong?" the man said. His voice was rising. "Wasn't that right? I mean, the road looked drifted in, but I thought... if there's a town there, the plows will be out and... and then I..."

He just sort of tailed off.

"Booth," Tookey said to me, low. "Get on the phone. Call the sheriff."

"Sure," this fool from New Jersey says, "that's right. What's wrong with you guys, anyway? You look like you saw a ghost."

Tookey said, "No ghosts in the Lot, mister. Did you tell them to stay in the car?"

"Sure I did," he said, sounding injured. "I'm not crazy."

Well, you couldn't have proved it by me.

"What's your name?" I asked him. "For the sheriff."

"Lumley," he says. "Gerard Lumley."

He started in with Tookey again, and I went across to the telephone. I picked it up and heard nothing but dead silence. I hit the cutoff buttons a couple of times. Still nothing.

I came back. Tookey had poured Gerard Lumley another tot of brandy, and this one was going down him a lot smoother.

"Was he out?" Tookey asked.

"Phone's dead."

"Hot damn," Tookey says, and we look at each other. Outside the wind gusted up, throwing snow against the windows.

Lumley looked from Tookey to me and back again.

"Well, haven't either of you got a car?" he asked. The anxiety was back in his voice. "They've got to run the engine to run the heater. I only had about a quarter of a tank of gas, and it took me an hour and a half to... Look, will you answer me?" He stood up and grabbed Tookey's shirt.

"Mister," Tookey says, "I think your hand just ran away from your brains, there."

Lumley looked at his hand, at Tookey, then dropped it. "Maine," he hissed. He made it sound like a dirty word about somebody's mother. "All right," he said. "Where's the nearest gas station? They must have a tow truck—"

"Nearest gas station is in Falmouth Center," I said. "That's three miles down the road from here."

"Thanks," he said, a bit sarcastic, and headed for the door, buttoning his coat.

"Won't be open, though," I added.

He turned back slowly and looked at us.

"What are you talking about, old man?"

"He's trying to tell you that the station in the Center belongs to Billy Larribee and Billy's out driving the plow, you damn fool," Tookey says patiently. "Now why don't you come back here and sit down, before you bust a gut?"

He came back, looking dazed and frightened. "Are you telling me you can't ... that there isn't ...?"

"I ain't telling you nothing," Tookey says. "You're doing all the telling, and if you stopped for a minute, we could think this over."

"What's this town, Jerusalem's Lot?" he asked. "Why was the road drifted in? And no lights on anywhere?"

I said, "Jerusalem's Lot burned out two years back."

"And they never rebuilt?" He looked like he didn't believe it.

"It appears that way," I said, and looked at Tookey. "What are we going to do about this?"

"Can't leave them out there," he said.

I got closer to him. Lumley had wandered away to look out the window into the snowy night.

"What if they've been got at?" I asked.

"That may be," he said. "But we don't know it for sure. I've got my Bible on the shelf. You still wear your Pope's medal?"

I pulled the crucifix out of my shirt and showed him. I was born and raised Congregational, but most folks who live around the Lot wear something—crucifix, St. Christopher's medal, rosary, something. Because two years ago, in the span of one dark October month, the Lot went bad. Sometimes, late at night, when there were just a few regulars drawn up around Tookey's fire, people would talk it over. Talk around it is more like the truth. You see, people in the Lot started to disappear. First a few, then a few more, than a whole slew. The schools closed. The town stood empty for most of a year. Oh, a few people moved in—mostly damn fools from out of state like this fine specimen here—drawn by the low property values, I suppose. But they didn't last. A lot of them moved out a month or two after they'd moved in. The others ... well, they disappeared. Then the town burned flat. It was at the end of a long dry fall. They figure it started up by the Marsten House on the hill that overlooked Jointner Avenue, but no one knows how it started, not to this day. It burned out of control for three days. After that, for a time, things were better. And then they started again.

I only heard the word "vampires" mentioned once. A crazy pulp truck driver named Richie Messina from over Freeport way was in Tookey's that night, pretty well liquored up. "Jesus Christ," this stampeder roars, standing up about nine feet tall in his wool pants and his plaid shirt and his leather-topped boots. "Are you all so damn afraid to say it out? Vampires! That's what you're all thinking, ain't it? Jesus-jumped-up-Christ in a chariot-driven sidecar! Just like a bunch of kids scared of the movies! You know what there is down there in 'Salem's Lot? Want me to tell you? Want me to tell you?"

"Do tell, Richie," Tookey says. It had got real quiet in the bar. You could hear the fire popping, and outside the soft drift of November rain coming down in the dark. "You got the floor."

"What you got over there is your basic wild dog pack," Richie Messina tells us. "That's what you got. That and a lot of old women who love a good spook story. Why, for eighty bucks I'd go up there and spend the night in what's left of that haunted house you're all so worried about. Well, what about it? Anyone want to put it up?"

But nobody would. Richie was a loudmouth and a mean drunk and no one was going to shed any tears at his wake, but none of us were willing to see him go into 'Salem's Lot after dark.

"Be screwed to the bunch of you," Richie says. "I got my four-ten in the trunk of my Chevy, and that'll stop anything in Falmouth, Cumberland, or Jerusalem's Lot. And that's where I'm goin'."

He slammed out of the bar and no one said a word for a while. Then Lamont Henry says, real quiet, "That's the last time anyone's gonna see Richie Messina. Holy God." And Lamont, raised to be a Methodist from his mother's knee, crossed himself.

"He'll sober off and change his mind," Tookey said, but he sounded uneasy. "He'll be back by closin' time, makin' out it was all a joke."

But Lamont had the right of that one, because no one ever saw Richie again. His wife told the state cops she thought he'd gone to Florida to beat a collection agency, but you could see the truth of the thing in her eyes—sick, scared eyes. Not long after, she moved away to Rhode Island. Maybe she thought Richie was going to come after her some dark night. And I'm not the man to say he might not have done.

Now Tookey was looking at me and I was looking at Tookey as I stuffed my crucifix back into my shirt. I never felt so old or so scared in my life.

Tookey said again, "We can't just leave them out there, Booth."

"Yeah. I know."

We looked at each other for a moment longer, and then he reached out and gripped my shoulder. "You're a good man, Booth." That was enough to buck me up some. It seems like when you pass seventy, people start forgetting that you are a man, or that you ever were.

Tookey walked over to Lumley and said, "I've got a four-wheel-drive Scout. I'll get it out."

"For God's sake, man, why didn't you say so before?" He had whirled around from the window and was staring angrily at Tookey. "Why'd you have to spend ten minutes beating around the bush?"

Tookey said, very softly, "Mister, you shut your jaw. And if you get the urge to open it, you remember who made that turn onto an unplowed road in the middle of a goddamned blizzard."

He started to say something, and then shut his mouth. Thick color had risen up in his cheeks. Tookey went out to get his Scout out of the garage. I felt around under the bar for his chrome flask and filled it full of brandy. Figured we might need it before this night was over.

Maine blizzard—ever been out in one?

The snow comes flying so thick and fine that it looks like sand and sounds like that, beating on the sides of your car or pickup. You don't want to use your high beams because they reflect off the snow and you can't see ten feet in front of you. With the low beams on, you can see maybe fifteen feet. But I can live with the snow. It's the wind I don't like, when it picks up and begins to howl, driving the snow into a hundred weird flying shapes and sounding like all the hate and pain and fear in the world. There's death in the throat of a snowstorm wind, white death—and maybe something beyond death. That's no sound to hear when you're tucked up all cozy in your own bed with the shutters bolted and the doors locked. It's that much worse if you're driving. And we were driving smack into Salem's Lot.

"Hurry up a little, can't you?" Lumley asked.

I said, "For a man who came in half frozen, you're in one hell of a hurry to end up walking again."

He gave me a resentful, baffled look and didn't say anything else. We were moving up the highway at a steady twenty-five miles an hour. It was hard to believe that Billy Larribee had just plowed this stretch an hour ago; another two inches had covered it, and it was drifting in. The strongest gusts of wind rocked the Scout on her springs. The headlights showed a swirling white nothing up ahead of us. We hadn't met a single car.

About ten minutes later Lumley gasps: "Hey! What's that?"

He was pointing out my side of the car; I'd been looking dead ahead. I turned, but was a shade too late. I thought I could see some sort of slumped form fading back from the car, back into the snow, but that could have been imagination.

"What was it? A deer?" I asked.

"I guess so," he says, sounding shaky. "But its eyes—they looked red." He looked at me. "Is that how a deer's eyes look at night?" He sounded almost as if he were pleading.

"They can look like anything," I says, thinking that might be true, but I've seen a lot of deer at night from a lot of cars, and never saw any set of eyes reflect back red.

Tookey didn't say anything.

About fifteen minutes later, we came to a place where the snowbank on the right of the road wasn't so high because the plows are supposed to raise their blades a little when they go through an intersection.

"This looks like where we turned," Lumley said, not sounding too sure about it. "I don't see the sign—"

"This is it," Tookey answered. He didn't sound like himself at all. "You can just see the top of the signpost."

"Oh. Sure." Lumley sounded relieved. "Listen, Mr. Tooklander, I'm sorry about being so short back there. I was cold and worried and calling myself two hundred kinds of fool. And I want to thank you both—"

"Don't thank Booth and me until we've got them in this car," Tookey said. He put the Scout in four-wheel drive and slammed his way through the snowbank and onto Jointner Avenue, which goes through the Lot and out to 295. Snow flew up from the mudguards. The rear end tried to break a little bit, but Tookey's been driving through snow since Hector was a pup. He jockeyed it a bit, talked to it, and on we went. The headlights picked out the bare indication of other tire tracks from time to time, the ones made by Lumley's car, and then they would disappear again. Lumley was leaning forward, looking for his car. And all at once Tookey said, "Mr. Lumley."

"What?" He looked around at Tookey.

"People around these parts are kind of superstitious about 'Salem's Lot," Tookey says, sounding easy enough—but I could see the deep lines of strain around his mouth, and the way his eyes kept moving from side to side. "If your people are in the car, why, that's fine. We'll pack them up, go back to my place, and tomorrow, when the storm's over, Billy will be glad to yank your car out of the snowbank. But if they're not in the car—"

"Not in the car?" Lumley broke in sharply. "Why wouldn't they be in the car?"

"If they're not in the car," Tookey goes on, not answering, "we're going to turn around and drive back to Falmouth Center and whistle for the sheriff. Makes no sense to go wallowing around at night in a snowstorm anyway, does it?"

"They'll be in the car. Where else would they be?"

I said, "One other thing, Mr. Lumley. If we should see anybody, we're not going to talk to them. Not even if they talk to us. You understand that?"

Very slow, Lumley says, "Just what are these superstitions?"

Before I could say anything—God alone knows what I would have said—Tookey broke in. "We're there."

We were coming up on the back end of a big Mercedes. The whole hood of the thing was buried in a snowdrift, and another drift had socked in the whole left side of the car. But the taillights were on and we could see exhaust drifting out of the tailpipe.

"They didn't run out of gas, anyway," Lumley said.

Tookey pulled up and pulled on the Scout's emergency brake. "You remember what Booth told you, Lumley."

"Sure, sure." But he wasn't thinking of anything but his wife and daughter. I don't see how anybody could blame him, either.

"Ready, Booth?" Tookey asked me. His eyes held on mine, grim and gray in the dashboard lights.

"I guess I am," I said.

We all got out and the wind grabbed us, throwing snow in our faces. Lumley was first, bending into the wind, his fancy topcoat billowing out behind him like a sail. He cast two shadows, one from Tookey's headlights, the other from his own taillights. I was behind him, and Tookey was a step behind me. When I got to the trunk of the Mercedes, Tookey grabbed me.

"Let him go," he said.

"Janey! Francie!" Lumley yelled. "Everything okay?" He pulled open the driver's-side door and leaned in. "Everything—"

He froze to a dead stop. The wind ripped the heavy door right out of his hand and pushed it all the way open.

"Holy God, Booth," Tookey said, just below the scream of the wind. "I think it's happened again."

Lumley turned back toward us. His face was scared and bewildered, his eyes wide. All of a sudden he lunged toward us through the snow, slipping and almost falling. He brushed me away like I was nothing and grabbed Tookey.

"How did you know?" he roared. "Where are they? What the hell is going on here?"

Tookey broke his grip and shoved past him. He and I looked into the Mercedes together. Warm as toast it was, but it wasn't going to be for much longer. The little amber low-fuel light was glowing. The big car was empty. There was a child's Barbie doll on the passenger's floormat. And a child's ski parka was crumpled over the seatback.

Tookey put his hands over his face…and then he was gone. Lumley had grabbed him and shoved him right back into the snowbank. His face was pale and wild. His mouth was working as if he had chewed down on some bitter stuff he couldn't yet unpucker enough to spit out. He reached in and grabbed the parka.

"Francie's coat?" he kind of whispered. And then loud, bellowing:

"Francie's coat!" He turned around, holding it in front of him by the little fur-trimmed hood. He looked at me, blank and unbelieving. "She can't be out without her coat on, Mr. Booth. Why…why…she'll freeze to death."

"Mr. Lumley—"

He blundered past me, still holding the parka, shouting:

"Francie! Janey! Where are you? Where are youuu?"

I gave Tookey my hand and pulled him onto his feet. "Are you all—"

"Never mind me," he says. "We've got to get hold of him, Booth."

We went after him as fast as we could, which wasn't very fast with the snow hip-deep in some places. But then he stopped and we caught up to him.

"Mr. Lumley—" Tookey started, laying a hand on his shoulder.

"This way," Lumley said. "This is the way they went. Look!"

We looked down. We were in a kind of dip here, and most of the wind went right over our heads. And you could see two sets of tracks, one large and one small, just filling up with snow. If we had been five minutes later, they would have been gone.

He started to walk away, his head down, and Tookey grabbed him back. "No! No, Lumley!"

Lumley turned his wild face up to Tookey's and made a fist. He drew it back...but something in Tookey's face made him falter. He looked from Tookey to me and then back again.

"She'll freeze," he said, as if we were a couple of stupid kids. "Don't you get it? She doesn't have her jacket on and she's only seven years old—"

"They could be anywhere," Tookey said. "You can't follow those tracks. They'll be gone in the next drift."

"What do you suggest?" Lumley yells, his voice high and hysterical. "If we go back to get the police, she'll freeze to death! Francie and my wife!"

"They may be frozen already," Tookey said. His eyes caught Lumley's. "Frozen, or something worse."

"What do you mean?" Lumley whispered. "Get it straight, goddamn it! Tell me!"

"Mr. Lumley," Tookey says, "there's something in the Lot—"

But I was the one who came out with it finally, said the word I never expected to say. "Vampires, Mr. Lumley. Jerusalem's Lot is full of vampires. I expect that's hard for you to swallow—"

He was staring at me as if I'd gone green. "Loonies," he whispers. "You're a couple of loonies." Then he turned away, cupped his hands around his mouth, and bellowed,

"FRANCIE! JANEY!" He started floundering off again. The snow was up to the hem of his fancy coat.

I looked at Tookey. "What do we do now?"

"Follow him," Tookey says. His hair was plastered with snow, and he did look a little bit loony. "I can't just leave him out here. Booth. Can you?"

"No," I says. "Guess not."

So we started to wade through the snow after Lumley as best we could. But he kept getting further and further ahead. He had his youth to spend, you see. He was breaking the trail, going through that snow like a bull. My arthritis began to bother me something terrible, and I started to look down at my legs, telling myself: A little further, just a little further, keep goin', damn it, keep goin'...

I piled right into Tookey, who was standing spread-legged in a drift. His head was hanging and both of his hands were pressed to his chest.

"Tookey," I says, "you okay?"

"I'm all right," he said, taking his hands away. "We'll stick with him, Booth, and when he fags out[1] he'll see reason."

We topped a rise and there was Lumley at the bottom, looking desperately for more tracks. Poor man, there wasn't a chance he was going to find them. The wind blew straight across down there where he was, and any tracks would have been rubbed out three minutes after they was made, let alone a couple of hours.

He raised his head and screamed into the night:

"FRANCIE! JANEY! FOR GOD'S SAKE!" And you could hear the desperation in his voice, the terror, and pity him for it. The only answer he got was the freight-train wail of the wind. It almost seemed to be laughin' at him, saying: I took them Mister New Jersey with your fancy car and camel's-hair topcoat. I took them and I rubbed out their tracks and by morning I'll have them just as neat and frozen as two strawberries in a deepfreeze...

"Lumley!" Tookey bawled over the wind. "Listen, you never mind vampires or boogies or nothing like that, but you mind this! You're just making it worse for them! We got to get the—"

And then there was an answer, a voice coming out of the dark like little tinkling silver bells, and my heart turned cold as ice in a cistern.

"Jerry... Jerry, is that you?"

Lumley wheeled at the sound. And then she came, drifting out of the dark shadows of a little copse of trees like a ghost.

She was a city woman, all right, and right then she seemed like the most beautiful woman I had ever seen. I felt like I wanted to go to her and tell her how glad I was she was safe after all. She was wearing a heavy green pullover sort of thing, a poncho, I believe they're called. It floated all around her, and her dark hair streamed out in the wild wind like water in a December creek, just before the winter freeze stills it and locks it in.

Maybe I did take a step toward her, because I felt Tookey's hand on my shoulder, rough and warm. And still—how can I say it?—I yearned after her, so dark and beautiful with that green poncho floating around her neck and shoulders, as exotic and strange as to make you think of some beautiful woman from a Walter de la Mare[2] poem.

"Janey!" Lumley cried.

"Janey!" He began to struggle through the snow toward her, his arms outstretched.

---

1 In American vernacular in the 1970s, the expression "fags out" meant to become exhausted.

2 Walter de la Mare (1873–1956) was an English poet, short-story writer, and novelist known for exploring the romantic imagination.

"No!" Tookey cried.

"No, Lumley!"

He never even looked... but she did. She looked up at us and grinned. And when she did, I felt my longing, my yearning turn to horror as cold as the grave, as white and silent as bones in a shroud. Even from the rise we could see the sullen red glare in those eyes. They were less human than a wolf's eyes. And when she grinned you could see how long her teeth had become. She wasn't human anymore. She was a dead thing somehow come back to life in this black howling storm.

Tookey made the sign of the cross at her. She flinched back... and then grinned at us again. We were too far away, and maybe too scared.

"Stop it!" I whispered. "Can't we stop it?"

"Too late, Booth!" Tookey says grimly.

Lumley had reached her. He looked like a ghost himself, coated in snow like he was. He reached for her... and then he began to scream. I'll hear that sound in my dreams, that man screaming like a child in a nightmare. He tried to back away from her, but her arms, long and bare and as white as the snow, snaked out and pulled him to her. I could see her cock her head and then thrust it forward—

"Booth!" Tookey said hoarsely. "We've got to get out of here!"

And so we ran. Ran like rats, I suppose some would say, but those who would weren't there that night. We fled back down along our own backtrail, falling down, getting up again, slipping and sliding. I kept looking back over my shoulder to see if that woman was coming after us, grinning that grin and watching us with those red eyes.

We got back to the Scout and Tookey doubled over, holding his chest. "Tookey!" I said, badly scared. "What—"

"Ticker," he said. "Been bad for five years or more. Get me around in the shotgun seat, Booth, and then get us the hell out of here."

I hooked an arm under his coat and dragged him around and somehow boosted him up and in. He leaned his head back and shut his eyes. His skin was waxy-looking and yellow.

I went back around the hood of the truck at a trot, and I damned near ran into the little girl. She was just standing there beside the driver's-side door, her hair in pigtails, wearing nothing but a little bit of a yellow dress.

"Mister," she said in a high, clear voice, as sweet as morning mist, "won't you help me find my mother? She's gone and I'm so cold—"

"Honey," I said, "honey, you better get in the truck. Your mother's—"

I broke off, and if there was ever a time in my life I was close to swooning, that was the moment. She was standing there, you see, but she was standing on top of the snow and there were no tracks, not in any direction.

She looked up at me then, Lumley's daughter Francie. She was no more than seven years old, and she was going to be seven for an eternity of nights. Her little face was a ghastly corpse white, her eyes a red and silver that you could fall into. And below her jaw I could see two small punctures like pinpricks, their edges horribly mangled.

She held out her arms at me and smiled. "Pick me up, mister," she said softly. "I want to give you a kiss. Then you can take me to my mommy."

I didn't want to, but there was nothing I could do. I was leaning forward, my arms outstretched. I could see her mouth opening, I could see the little fangs inside the pink ring of her lips. Something slipped down her chin, bright and silvery, and with a dim, distant, faraway horror, I realized she was drooling.

Her small hands clasped themselves around my neck and I was thinking: Well, maybe it won't be so bad, not so bad, maybe it won't be so awful after a while—when something black flew out of the Scout and struck her on the chest. There was a puff of strange-smelling smoke, a flashing glow that was gone an instant later, and then she was backing away, hissing. Her face was twisted into a vulpine[1] mask of rage, hate, and pain. She turned sideways and then ... and then she was gone. One moment she was there, and the next there was a twisting knot of snow that looked a little bit like a human shape. Then the wind tattered it away across the fields.

"Booth!" Tookey whispered. "Be quick, now!" And I was. But not so quick that I didn't have time to pick up what he had thrown at that little girl from hell. His mother's Douay Bible.[2]

That was some time ago. I'm a sight older now, and I was no chicken then. Herb Tooklander passed on two years ago. He went peaceful, in the night. The bar is still there, some man and his wife from Waterville bought it, nice people, and they've kept it pretty much the same. But I don't go by much. It's different somehow with Tookey gone.

Things in the Lot go on pretty much as they always have. The sheriff found that fellow Lumley's car the next day, out of gas, the battery dead. Neither Tookey nor I said anything about it. What would have been the point? And every now and then a hitchhiker or a camper will disappear around there someplace, up on Schoolyard Hill or out near the Harmony Hill cemetery. They'll turn up the fellow's packsack or a paperback book all swollen and bleached out by the rain or snow, or some such. But never the people.

I still have bad dreams about that stormy night we went out there. Not about the woman so much as the little girl, and the way she smiled when she held her arms up so I could pick her up. So she could give me a kiss. But I'm an old man and the time comes soon when dreams are done.

You may have an occasion to be traveling in southern Maine yourself one of these days. Pretty part of the countryside. You may even stop by Tookey's Bar

1 To be related to a fox; crafty or cunning.

2 Also known as the Douay-Rheims Bible. A Catholic translation of the Bible made in France in the sixteenth century.

for a drink. Nice place. They kept the name just the same. So have your drink, and then my advice to you is to keep right on moving north. Whatever you do, don't go up that road to Jerusalem's Lot.

Especially not after dark.

There's a little girl somewhere out there. And I think she's still waiting for her good-night kiss.

# Jane Yolen

(B. 1939)

Jane Yolen is a popular author of young adult and children's books and is noted for her mastery of folklore, fantasy, and myth. For Yolen, folklore is an archetype for the human condition: "a perfect second skin. From under its hide, we can see all the shimmering, shadowy uncertainties of the world." She was raised in a predominately non-religious household and says that she did not truly embrace her Jewish identity until she wrote her series of Holocaust novels, *Briar Rose* (1992), *Devil's Arithmetic* (1998), and *Mapping the Bones* (2018)—all winners of prestigious literature awards. "Of all the novels I've written," Yolen remarks, "the Holocaust novels are maybe the ones I'm most proud of." In much of her fiction, Yolen combines myth and folklore. This approach is apparent in "Mama Gone" where she weaves the refrains of a Southern lullaby and Eastern European vampire lore into the story of a daughter's love.

# "Mama Gone"

(1991)

Mama died four nights ago, giving birth to my sister Ann. Bubba cried and cried, "Mama gone," in his little-boy voice, but I never let out a single tear.

There was blood as red as sunset all over the bed from that birthing, and when Papa saw it he rubbed his head against the cabin wall over and over and over and made little animal sounds. Sukey washed Mama down and placed the baby on her breast for a moment. "Remember," she whispered.

"Mama gone," Bubba wailed again.

But I never cried.

By all rights we should have buried her with garlic in her mouth and her hands and feet cut off, what with her being vampire kin and all. But Papa absolutely refused.

"Your Mama couldn't stand garlic," he said when the sounds stopped rushing out of his mouth and his eyes had cleared. "It made her come all over with rashes. She had the sweetest mouth and hands."

And that was that. Not a one of us could make him change his mind, not even Granddad Stokes or Pop Wilbur or any other of the men who come to pay their last respects. And as Papa is a preacher, and a brimstone man, they let it be. The onliest thing he would allow was for us to tie red ribbons round her ankles and wrists, a kind of sign like a line of blood. Everybody hoped that would do.

But on the next day, she rose from out her grave and commenced to prey upon the good folks of Taunton.

Of course she came to our house first, that being the dearest place she knew. I saw her outside my window, gray as a gravestone, her dark eyes like holes in a shroud. When she stared in, she didn't know me, though I had always been her favorite.

"Mama, be gone," I said and waved my little cross at her, the one she had given me the very day I'd been born. "Avaunt." The old bible word sat heavy in my mouth.

She put her hand up on the window frame, and as I watched, the gray fingers turned splotchy pink from all the garlic I had rubbed into the wood.

Black tears dropped from her black eyes, then. But I never cried.

She tried each window in turn and not a person awake in the house but me. But I had done my work well and the garlic held her out. She even tried the door, but it was no use. By the time she left, I was so sleepy, I dropped right down by the door. Papa found me there at cockcrow. He never did ask what I was doing, and if he ever guessed, he never said.

Little Joshua Greenough was found dead in his crib. The doctor took two days to come over the mountains to pronounce it. By then the garlic around his little bed to keep him from waking, too, had mixed with the death smells. Everybody knew. Even the doctor, and him a city man. It hurt his mama and papa sore to do the cutting. But it had to be done.

The men came to our house that very noon to talk about what had to be. Papa kept shaking his head all through their talking. But even his being preacher didn't stop them. Once a vampire walks these mountain hollars, there's nary a house or barn that's safe. Nighttime is lost time. And no one can afford to lose much stock.

So they made their sharp sticks out of green wood, the curling shavings littering our cabin floor. Bubba played in them, not understanding. Sukey was busy with the baby, nursing it with a bottle and a sugar teat. It was my job to sweep up the wood curls. They felt slick on one side, bumpy on the other. Like my heart.

Papa said, "I was the one to let her turn into a night walker. It's my business to stake her out."

No one argued. Specially not the Greenoughs, their eyes still red from weeping.

"Just take my children," Papa said. "And if anything goes wrong, cut off my hands and feet and bury me at Mill's cross, under the stone. There's garlic hanging in the pantry. Mandy Jane will string me some."

So Sukey took the baby and Bubba off to the Greenough's house, that seeming the right thing to do, and I stayed the rest of the afternoon with Papa, stringing garlic and pressing more into windows. But the strand over the door he took down.

"I have to let her in somewhere," he said. "And this is where I'll make my stand." He touched me on the cheek, the first time ever. Papa has never been much for show.

"Now you run along to the Greenoughs', Mandy Jane," he said. "And remember how much your mama loved you. This isn't her, child. Mama's gone. Something else has come to take her place. I should have remembered that the Good Book says, 'The living know that they shall die; but the dead know not anything.'"

I wanted to ask him how the vampire knew to come first to our house, then, but I was silent, for Papa had been asleep and hadn't seen her.

I left without giving him a daughter's kiss, for his mind was well set on the night's doing. But I didn't go down the lane to the Greenoughs' at all. Wearing my triple strands of garlic, with my cross about my neck, I went to the burying ground, to Mama's grave.

It looked so raw against the greening hillside. The dirt was red clay, but all it looked like to me was blood. There was no cross on it yet, no stone. That would come in a year. Just a humping, a heaping of red dirt over her coffin, the plain pinewood box hastily made.

I lay facedown in the dirt, my arms opened wide. "Oh, Mama," I said, "the Good Book says you are not dead but sleepeth. Sleep quietly, Mama, sleep well." And I sang to her the lullaby she had always sung to me and then to Bubba and would have sung to baby Ann had she lived to hold her.

*"Blacks and bays,*
*Dapples and grays,*
*All the pretty little horses."*[1]

And as I sang I remembered Papa thundering at prayer meeting once, "Behold, a pale white horse: and his name that sat on him was Death." The rest of the song just stuck in my throat then, so I turned over on the grave and stared up at the setting sun.

1 "All the Pretty Little Horses" is a traditional lullaby from the United States.

It had been a long and wearying day, and I fell asleep right there in the burying ground. Any other time fear might have overcome sleep. But I just closed my eyes and slept.

When I woke, it was dead night. The moon was full and sitting between the horns of two hills. There was a sprinkling of stars overhead. And Mama began to move the ground beneath me, trying to rise.

The garlic strands must have worried her, for she did not come out of the earth all at once. It was the scrambling of her long nails at my back that woke me. I leaped off that grave and was wide awake.

Standing aside the grave, I watched as first her long gray arms reached out of the earth. Then her head, its hair that was once so gold now gray and streaked with black and its shroud eyes, emerged. And then her body in its winding sheet, stained with dirt and torn from walking to and fro upon the land. Then her bare feet with blackened nails, though alive Mama used to paint those nails, her one vanity and Papa allowed it seeing she was so pretty and otherwise not vain.

She turned toward me as a hummingbird toward a flower, and she raised her face up and it was gray and bony. Her mouth peeled back from her teeth and I saw that they were pointed and her tongue was barbed.

"Mama, gone," I whispered in Bubba's voice, but so low I could hardly hear it myself.

She stepped toward me off that grave, lurching down the hump of dirt. But when she got close, the garlic strands and the cross stayed her.

"Mama."

She turned her head back and forth. It was clear she could not see with those black shroud eyes. She only sensed me there, something warm, something alive, something with the blood running like satisfying streams through the blue veins.

"Mama," I said again. "Try and remember."

That searching awful face turned toward me again, and the pointy teeth were bared once more. Her hands reached out to grab me, then pulled back.

"Remember how Bubba always sucks his thumb with that funny little noise you always said was like a little chuck in its hole. And how Sukey hums through her nose when she's baking bread. And how I listened to your belly to hear the baby. And how Papa always starts each meal with the blessing on things that grow fresh in the field."

The gray face turned for a moment toward the hills, and I wasn't even sure she could hear me. But I had to keep trying.

"And remember when we picked the blueberries and Bubba fell down the hill, tumbling head-end over. And we laughed until we heard him, and he was saying the same six things over and over till long past bed."

The gray face turned back toward me and I thought I saw a bit of light in the eyes. But it was just reflected moonlight.

"And the day Papa came home with the new ewe lamb and we fed her on a sugar teat. You stayed up all night and I slept in the straw by your side."

It was as if the stars were twinkling in those dead eyes. I couldn't stop staring, but I didn't dare stop talking either.

"And remember the day the bluebird stunned itself on the kitchen window and you held it in your hands. You warmed it to life, you said. To life, Mama."

Those stars began to run down the gray cheeks.

"There's living, Mama, and there's dead. You've given so much life. Don't be bringing death to these hills now." I could see that the stars were gone from the sky over her head; the moon was setting.

"Papa loved you too much to cut off your hands and feet. You gotta return that love, Mama. You gotta."

Veins of red ran down the hills, outlining the rocks. As the sun began to rise, I took off one strand of garlic. Then the second. Then the last. I opened my arms. "Have you come back, Mama, or are you gone?"

The gray woman leaned over and clasped me tight in her arms. Her head bent down towards mine, her mouth on my forehead, my neck, the outline of my little gold cross burning across her lips.

She whispered, "Here and gone, child, here and gone," in a voice like wind in the coppice, like the shaking of willow leaves. I felt her kiss on my cheek, a brand.

Then the sun came between the hills and hit her full in the face, burning her red as the earth. She smiled at me and then there was only dust motes in the air, dancing. When I looked down at my feet, the grave dirt was hardly disturbed but Mama's gold wedding band gleamed atop it.

I knelt down and picked it up, and unhooked the chain holding my cross. I slid the ring onto the chain, and the two nestled together right in the hollow of my throat. I sang:

*"Blacks and bays,*
*Dapples and grays…"*

And from the earth itself, the final words sang out,

*"All the pretty little horses."*

That was when I cried, long and loud, a sound I never hope to make again as long as I live.

Then I went back down the hill and home, where Papa still waited by an open door.

# Toni Brown

(1952–2008)

Toni Brown grew up in Boston and spent most of her adult life in Philadelphia. Coming of age as a lesbian feminist in the Northampton lesbian community in the 1970s, her lesbianism and African-American heritage were important to her identity as a writer. This sensibility is apparent in her vampire stories, many published in *Out for Blood: Tales of Mystery and Suspense by Women* (1995), *Night Bites: Vampire Stories by Women* (1996), and *Night Shade: Gothic Tales by Women* (1999). Later in her journey as a writer, she began to focus exclusively on poetry. As a college writing teacher and mentor to at-risk young girls in the position of director of education, training, and outreach for Girls Inc., Brown was invested in community service. She was a distinguished poetry fellow in the annual Cave Canem summer workshop, a retreat designed in 1996 as a "safe haven" for black poets.

## "Immunity"

(1996)

"Wait, Mom! Look at my mosquito bite. I think it's bleeding!"

Celeste leaned into the doorway of her six-year-old daughter's room and clicked on the light. Out of the darkness appeared four lavender walls decorated with pictures made with crayon and water paints. There were wooden shelves, on which books leaned and stuffed animals haphazardly slumped. From the ceiling, a balsa wood pterodactyl hung on fishing line. The bed's ebony headboard was trimmed with a border of speckled cowrie shells. Carved into the center of the headboard was a yellowing ivory mask from the Nigerian province of Benin.

Nia, round faced and the color of dark plums, sat up in bed. She had kicked the covers aside and was closely examining her right wrist. She wore white pajama bottoms and a T-shirt that barely covered her baby-fat stomach or the thumb-tip belly button that protruded from it. Printed on the shirt in red block letters was the word *Monster!*

"I could bleed to death," she said plaintively. "It's over a vein, you know."

Her mother smiled slightly as she crossed the room to the edge of the bed. She seemed to float over the floor, making no sound. She looked at the bump on her daughter's wrist, rubbed it gently, then kissed it.

"It's not bleeding, sweetie." Celeste knew the small raised bump was not a mosquito bite. She pulled the covers up, making a tent, into which Nia automatically lay down.

"It's time for sleep now, Nia." Celeste tucked in the covers and then kissed her daughter's warm cheek. Nia seemed comforted. She hoped Nia would quiet down and that this would be her last trip into her daughter's room tonight.

"Mom?" Celeste crossed the room, headed for the door.

"Mom, can I have another glass of juice?" Celeste's hand reached for the light switch. Nia lifted her head from the pillow expectantly. Her mother turned off the light.

"Good night, Nia." Celeste used her tired, final voice as she closed the door.

"I'm really thirsty, Mom!" Nia's voice pleaded, slightly muffled.

"Good night, Nia." Celeste walked along the dimly lit hall and slowly descended the stairs.

Each night the ritual was the same. Nia would try to engage her in last-minute bedtime conversation, and Celeste would respond by monotonously repeating good night until Nia finally gave up and went to sleep. Usually Nia got the message after two or three tries, but this was Celeste's fourth trip to her room and Nia still looked very much awake.

Nia had come home from school that afternoon talking about Dracula and vampires. "Could garlic really keep them away?" "Were they really afraid of crosses?" "Can't we have just *one* cross at our house?" This gave Celeste a bad feeling, stirring up anxieties she had tried to keep pushed to the back of her mind.

Celeste sat right down with Nia, and they talked about it. She thought she had convinced Nia that these were just stories made up to frighten and amuse, like at Halloween. Nia listened intently, taking it all in. She seemed fine until bedtime, until the lights were turned out. Celeste sucked her teeth in irritation and her stomach growled. Tonight was not the night for her to have problems with Nia falling asleep.

Celeste's dark fingers slid along the polished mahogany banister. Her knuckles, wrinkled and gnarled like ancient tree roots, belied her fortyish-appearing face. In the foyer, she passed an old, gilt-frame mirror. It reflected the ornate front door and nothing more. She passed through an arched doorway and into the living room, where she settled into a pale blue wing chair. The supports had given way long ago, so sitting down in this chair meant sitting nearly on the floor. Still, it was cozy and it faced the French doors and the courtyard. This was her favorite room, with its high ceiling and stone block floor. The walls were painted a neutral eggshell color, but sometimes when the light was right she could see a wallpaper pattern underneath. There was a large fireplace. Inside it, carved in the stone, were images of joyous women dancing with wolves and snakes and birds. When there was a fire blazing, the scenes seemed to come alive. Last year at this time she had needed a small fire to take the chill out of the room, but this October night there was no need, since it was unusually warm and raining gently. She wondered what the room had looked like when the Victorian mansion had all sixteen rooms intact, before being renovated into three spacious apartments.

They had come to this town when Nia was an infant. This house, on the outskirts of a large university campus, was just right for them, an older single woman and her child. The other apartments were always filled with busy, preoccupied students who moved in and out again with regularity and anonymity. Sometimes there would be someone willing to baby-sit for her during an infrequent evening out or someone willing to listen through the wall for the sound of Nia's voice. Generally she left her student neighbors alone though; things seemed to work better that way. And as Nia had grown older, Celeste had found it possible to leave Nia alone for short periods at night.

The rain softly pattered against the windows and the side of the house. She looked through sheer curtains at the full moon rising, reflecting silver on the surrounding clouds. There were many windows in this room; most were sparkling clean and bare. From early morning until late afternoon, the sun visited here, and while Nia was in school, Celeste would bask. Tonight she lit candles and let the room fill with moonlight. The French doors rattled against the intermittent wind.

She curled into the chair and relaxed, loosening the turban that was wound about her head. The day had been long, and she still had the night ahead of her.

She thought about Nia and this new fear. Celeste knew that this was only the first of many misrepresentations of people, distortions of history that Nia would learn. The vampire stories were just children spreading tales, but this was only the beginning. Anger flashed through her quickly, then dissipated as she sighed, resigned that despite her efforts Nia would learn about the world from those who knew the least about it. She wondered how long she would have before Nia began to question the difference between the world inside their home and the one outside.

The wind slapped a loose shutter against the house, distracting her. She heard a car drive past. Her breathing slowed. The blood began to drain from her face. She sank back in the wing chair until all that could be seen from the doorway were her dark hands gripping its thick blue arms. Her eyes closed. Her breathing became a rhythm that echoed the beating of her heart. The vision began.

She felt herself moving through a wooded patch of land. It was dark, and the last clear rays of sunlight seemed weak and cold. The ground was littered with pine needles. She could see the road in the distance. She was a snake from the belly down. Her head, shoulders and arms were bone and skin and hair, while the rest of her was rounded and thick and covered with glistening black scales. Ferns and stiff grasses grazed her sides. Her body rippled like the ocean meeting sand as she moved swiftly forward. In her mouth, the acrid taste of hunger. Saliva began to well beneath her tongue.

A short distance ahead was a disabled car, a man and woman standing by it. The woman, with her arms crossed over her chest and her back to the man, looked up the road.

The wind whispered, "Faster," and she plunged on, eyes focused on the figures ahead. She could smell them now.

First the man just glanced in her direction, then riveted his attention on the terrible apparition looming before him. He pressed himself against the car. He raised his arm as if to protect his face. He took in one sharp breath, and then she was upon him. She pinned his arms to his sides as she coiled her constricting body around him. He screamed, and the woman wrenched around—

"Mom! Mom!" Nia's bedroom door slammed. Celeste heard her daughter's footsteps as Nia ran toward the stairs. She blinked rapidly, trying to focus. She rubbed the goose flesh prickling her upper arms. Nia burst into the room and climbed into her lap.

"Mom, I heard something." She buried her face in her mother's chest and curled against her. Celeste hugged her. Nia was shivering. Celeste stroked her daughter's thick hair and then rubbed her back comfortingly. She began to rock Nia gently. Nia sat up and stopped her mother's rocking.

"I'm not a baby, you know."

"I know," Celeste sighed, and Nia rested her head against her shoulder again.

"It's all right, Nia," she patted her. "What's the matter?"

Nia looked down at her knees and picked at a scab, bumpy, beneath her cotton pajama pant. Celeste pulled her hand away.

"I heard something."

"Like what?"

"I don't know, something scary."

"Scary like a dog or thunder?"

"No, like a scratchy, growly sound. I don't know. It woke me up." Her voice had become an annoying whine.

"Nia, you have school tomorrow."

"I know, but I'm scared."

"Honey, there's nobody here but me. What is there to be afraid of?"

She already knew her daughter's answer, but waited patiently for Nia to whisper, "Vampires." She felt anger rise in her again like heat waves.

"Nia, listen. Those stories about dead men who walk the earth were made up to scare you. All that stuff about stakes through the heart"—she shuddered and wrinkled her nose at her daughter—"is just silly lies. The dead cannot walk, the dead cannot be killed. Once you are dead, you are dead. These tales made up by people who don't know anything about being dead, since they obviously are still alive themselves."

She smiled at her own joke, but Nia was not amused.

"You, my young pup, should be in bed. Don't you see that big, beautiful moon? Can't you her it calling you to sleep?" Her voice was soft and low, yet heavy. The weight of it was meant to pull her daughter's eyelids down. The rain dripped slowly off the edge of the roof.

"But where did all those stories come from? Why would anyone want to scare me?"

Celeste slid Nia off her lap and guided her out of the room.

"Nia," Celeste said, taking her hand and leading her slowly toward the stairs, "you have nothing to fear from vampires. Let me tell you a story. Long ago when our ancestors still lived in Africa, another people came to visit us. These people were from a place called Greece. They came to visit our tribe and brought us gifts and told us all kinds of strange and wonderful things. They called themselves Lamia.[1] The Lamia were a people similar in some ways to the ones they now call vampires. But they were not dead men. We danced with them and showed them our ways. We showed them our magic, and they were impressed. We decided to become as one tribe. We made an agreement with these Lamia." She paused as if trying to remember.

"To never hurt each other, to be as if sisters. All African people are protected by that agreement. That's why there are no stories about black people being bitten by vampires, Nia. Have you ever heard of any?" Celeste paused briefly.

"That agreement from so long ago keeps us safe. We have immunity. You are protected."

Celeste stopped. The story was over. They had reached the top of the stairs. Nia looked around as if confused.

"Honest?" Nia asked after a moment. She looked into her mother's eyes, searching for a lie. Celeste's eyes were dull black almonds. She turned her gaze away.

"Honest," she answered.

Nia was silent. Celeste led her into the darkened bedroom.

"Good night, Nia." She kissed her cheek. Nia scratched sleepily at the lump on her wrist.

"Mom," Nia yawned noisily, "what else did we get in the agreement we made?"

1 In Ancient Greek myth, the lamia was a child-eating monster with the head and torso of a beautiful woman and the tail of a serpent. It was also known to seduce men.

"That is a long story for another night, sweet. Sleep tight now. And Nia—don't get out of bed again." There was no fatigue in this final voice. She closed Nia's bedroom door.

As Celeste moved slowly down the stairs, she thought that in a very short time Nia would no longer be a child. When she had grown to be a young woman, maybe then Celeste could share the whole secret of her people.

Before the coming of the Lamia, in the villages south and far west of the Sudan, her kind were called *Awon Iya Wa Aje*[1]—our mothers, the witches. In the spring, when the rains came, the Yoruba people held festivals celebrating the season. Members of the Gelede cult[2] carved masks of dark wood and ivory. They danced to invite the witch mothers, or *Aje*, into the village. They courted good favor with music and prayed for the continued good health of the children already born. They left caches of cowrie shells and precious stones and gold hanging from the low branches of trees.

When the Lamia came, they told tales of their kin the great Medusa and her immortal Gorgon sisters. They sang songs about their great strength and the curse that left them with an appetite for human flesh. They spoke of Greek cities reduced to ashes, burned by humans provoked by the sight of a nest of snakes.

The Aje complained of the loneliness of immortality, the precariousness of a shifting noncorporeality. The Lamia and the Aje exchanged magic: from the Aje, the ability to change form from human to cat to jackal to bat to smoke. From the Lamia, a physically material body and the possibility of the blessed sleep of death. From the Aje, the secret of fecundity, the ability to bring about fruitfulness of soil and of women. From the Lamia, the terrible hunger for human flesh. Ironically, the very babies that the Aje had helped birth, the Lamia were devouring with delight.

Soon the seasonal dances of life were replaced by rituals of appeasement for the new spirits who made the children disappear. And it wasn't just the children who were eaten—anyone wandering the bush in the night or sleeping in an outlying hut could be taken. In time, the hunts became a rite of passage into manhood. Many of Celeste's ancestors were killed. Some escaped, disguised by shifting form.

For Celeste, Nia brought a focus to her eternity, a consanguinity. She remembered bringing the infant home. Home then was a battered old structure at the edge of a dying town. She rested in the shadows and held the wriggling stolen bundle at arm's length. The baby wailed, yet there was not a single tear on her dark face. Her little hands were balled into hard fists, which she waved uselessly in the night air. But as the child shook with fury, Celeste stared down at her hair. Her thick aureole of black curls seemed alive in the moon's bright light.

1 In Yoruba, "Awon Iya Wa" refers to mothers. Aje is a witch or other female magic-user.

2 A Yoruba group who perform publicly to honor and worship elderly women, female ancestors, and goddesses or "mothers."

The baby's hair looked like tiny, shiny snakes. Celeste had never been moved in this way. She felt a conflict between the instinct to eat the sweet, warm-blooded creature and the urge to somehow suckle it.

Celeste had not lied about Nia's protection. Nia was protected by her. She would not be harmed by the tiny sips of blood Celeste sometimes took from her wrist. As for the other people of African descent, Celeste could honestly say she had not feasted on their flesh since she left her native land.

Celeste was perhaps the only one of the joined beings, Lamia and Aje, still left. She had not seen one of her kind since she left her home in Africa. She had lived for centuries. She might live forever, but at least for a time in this foreign place, she would not be alone.

Deep in her chair again, she looked out at the swirling fog. She closed her eyes. Her breathing began its slow cadence. A rhythm that had become a rattling hiss echoed against the walls of the moonlit room. Her scalp began to tingle as her kinky, corded hair began to move, transformed into pencil-thin snakes that writhed sinuously. Her skin deepened to a shiny black. Her fingernails also blackened and grew long and pointed. She dug them into the arm of the chair. She opened her mouth to accommodate the sharp row of teeth that grew there. A cloudy thread of spittle spun slowly down her chin.

She looked past the flimsy glass door into the lights of the small town. Its sleeping people awaited her. The moon rose victoriously in the sky. The rain had stopped. Slithering out of the chair, she moved to and opened the French doors. The wind blew cool and sweet across her face. Her massive serpentine body glistened in the night's bright luminescence. She was hungry. She surged forward, undulating toward the low garden wall. Hair hissing in the damp autumn air, she stopped and listened. Had she heard a small voice call out from upstairs? No, it was only the wind. She murmured, "Good night, Nia," as she disappeared into the night.

# Nalo Hopkinson

(B. 1960)

Born in Kingston, Jamaica, Hopkinson spent her childhood in Trinidad and Guyana, eventually relocating to Canada in her teens. Her father, Muhammed Abdur-Rahman Slade Hopkinson, was a poet, playwright, and educator and her mother, Freda Hopkinson, was a librarian. With these parental influences it is not surprising that Hopkinson became an avid reader who, by the age of ten, had read Homer's *Iliad.* As a child she was drawn to fantastical literature, folklore, and science fiction. Hopkinson works primarily in the genre of speculative fiction with a focus on the Afro-diasporic Caribbean folkloric tradition, which is evident in the short story collection *Skin Folk* in which "Greedy Choke Puppy" was published. She has published numerous novels and short stories, including her award-winning novel *Brown Girl in the Ring* (1998). Hopkinson is a professor in the MFA program at University of California.

# "Greedy Choke Puppy"

(2001)

"I see a Lagahoo[1] last night. In the back of the house, behind the pigeon peas."[2]

"Yes, Granny." Sitting cross-legged on the floor, Jacky leaned back against her grandmother's knees and closed her eyes in bliss against the gentle tug of Granny's hands braiding her hair. Jacky still enjoyed this evening ritual, even though she was a big hard-back woman, thirty-two years next month.

The moon was shining in through the open jalousie[3] windows, bringing the sweet smell of Ladies-of-the-Night flowers[4] with it. The ceiling fan beat its soothing rhythm.

---

1 The Lagahoo is a shapeshifter in Caribbean folklore. Related to the French loup-garou and the German werewolf, Lagahoos can take on many forms including the donkey we see here.

2 *Cajanus cajan*; a staple of the diet in Asia, Africa, Latin America, and the Caribbean.

3 A louvre window made up of horizontal slats.

4 *Solanaceae*. Clusters of two-inch white flowers that are held on long slender tubes and release their fragrance at night.

"How you mean, 'Yes, Granny'? You even know what a Lagahoo is?"

"Don't you been frightening me with jumby[1] story from since I small? I putting a section on it in my thesis paper. Is a donkey with gold teeth, wearing a waistcoat with a pocket watch and two pair of tennis shoes on the hooves."

"Washekong,[2] you mean. I never teach you to say 'tennis shoes.'"

Jacky smiled. "Yes, Granny. So, what the Lagahoo was doing in the pigeon peas patch?"

"Just standing, looking at my window. Then he pull out he watch chain from out he waistcoat pocket, and he look at the time, and he put the watch back, and he bite off some pigeon peas from off one bush, and he walk away."

Jacky laughed, shaking so hard that her head pulled free of Granny's hands. "You mean to tell me that a Lagahoo come all the way to we little house in Diego Martin,[3] just to sample we so-so pigeon peas?" Still chuckling, she settled back against Granny's knees. Granny tugged at a hank of Jacky's hair, just a little harder than necessary.

Jacky could hear the smile in the old woman's voice. "Don't get fresh with me, young lady. You turn big woman now, Ph.D. student and thing, but is still your old nen-nen who does plait up your hair every evening, oui?"[4]

"Yes, Granny. You know I does live to make mako 'pon you, to tease you a little."

"This ain't no joke, child. My mammy used to say that a Lagahoo is God horse, and when you see one, somebody go dead. The last time I see one is just before your mother dead." The two women fell silent. The memory hung in the air between them, of the badly burned body retrieved from the wreckage of the car that had gone off the road. Jacky knew that her grandmother would soon change the subject. She blamed herself for the argument that had sent Jacky's mother raging from the house in the first place. And whatever Granny didn't want to think about, she certainly wasn't going to talk about.

Granny sighed. "Well, don't fret, doux-doux.[5] Just be careful when you go out so late at night. I couldn't stand to lose you, too."

"You self too, Granny. Always off to prayer meeting, sometimes 'fore day morning before you come home. I does worry about you, you know?"

Granny just grunted, "Mm-hmmm."

Jacky closed her eyes, dreamy in the gentle tugs on her hair, the cool stripes of oil that Granny laid down with a finger in the parts between each plait. "Granny, you want to hear how my thesis going?"

"Mm?"

"I write about La Diablesse already, the devil lady, how she pretty for so, but with sharpened teeth and one goat hoof, you did right about that part, Granny."

"I know."

1 Ghosts or demons in Caribbean folklore.
2 Flat canvas sneakers.
3 Diego Martin is a town in the Trinidad and Tobago region.
4 French: "yes."
5 Trinidad slang for darling.

"And you ever notice is only men she does appear to? I talk about how she represent masculine fears of female sexua—"

"Hold this plait here, Jacky. Yes, keep it out of the way."

"Yes, Granny. That Lagahoo, now, that we was just talking about? Well, it have a Jamaican equivalent. They call it the Rolling Calf—"

"All right, girl: I done." Granny finished off the last braid and gently stroked Jacky's head. "Go and wrap up your head in a scarf, so the plaits will stay nice while you sleeping."

"Thank you, Granny. What I would do without you to help me make myself pretty for the gentlemen, eh?"

Granny smiled, but with a worried look on her face.

"Never you mind all that. You just mind your studies. It have plenty of time to catch man."

Jacky stood and gave the old woman a kiss on one warm, soft cheek and headed towards her bedroom in search of a scarf. Behind her, she could hear Granny settling back into the faded wicker armchair, muttering distractedly to herself, "But why this Lagahoo come to bother me again, eh?"

*The first time, I ain't know what was happening to me. I was younger them times there, and sweet for so, you see? Sweet like Julie mango,*[1] *with two ripe tot-tot on the front of my body and two ripe maami-apple*[2] *behind. I only had was to walk down the street, twitching that maami-apple behind, and all the boys—them on the street corner would watch at me like them was starving, and I was food.*

*But I get to find out know how it is when the boys stop making sweet eye at you so much, and start watching after a next younger thing. I get to find out that when you pass you prime, and you ain't catch no man eye, nothing ain't left for you but to get old and dry-up like cane leaf in the fire. Is just so I was feeling that night. Like something wither-up. Like something that once used to drink in the feel of the sun on it skin, but now it dead and dry, and the sun only drying it out more. And the feeling make a burning in me belly, and the burning spread out to my skin, till I couldn't take it no more. I jump up from my little bed just so in the middle of the night, and snatch off my nightie. And when I do so, my skin come with it, and drop off on the floor. Inside my skin I was just one big ball of fire, and Lord, the night air feel nice and cool on the flame! I know then I was a soucouyant,*[3] *a hag-woman. I know what I had to do. When your youth start to leave you, you have to steal more from somebody who still have plenty. I fly out the window and start to search, search for a newborn baby.*

1 Also called "Saint Julian," a much sought-after variety of tropical fruit.

2 Fruit imagery for female breasts and buttocks.

3 In Eastern Caribbean folklore, a witch or vampire believed to shed her skin by night and suck the blood or life of her victims.

"Lagahoo? I know that word from somewhere, Jacky."

Jacky smiled at her friend Carmen, a librarian in the humanities section of the Library of the University of the West Indies. "You probably hear it from Granny. Is French creole for 'werewolf.' But as Trini people[1] tell it, is a donkey, not a wolf. Only we could come up with something so jokey as a were-donkey, oui?"

Carmen giggled, leaning back in her chair behind the information desk, legs sprawled under the bulge of her advanced pregnancy. "And that all going in your thesis paper, I suppose. You have a title for the paper yet?"

"'Magic in the Real: the Role of Folklore in Everyday Caribbean Life.'"

"'Magic in the Real': I like that." Carmen stretched, groaned. "Lord, girl, my back paining me for so, you see?"

"How much longer?" Jacky asked. A baby! To think Carmen would soon have a child.

"Two weeks. I could scarcely wait to get it out of me. I feel like I have a belly full of cement."

"Carmen!" Jacky was scandalized. "How you could talk so! I tell you, if it was me making baby, I would be happy, happy. I would be shining bright like the sun in the sky."

Carmen just chuckled. "From high school days you always been in such a hurry to turn big woman. Your turn to make baby will come, and then we will see how happy and shiny you talking by the time you due for labour."

Carmen was a little older than Jacky. They had known each other since they were girls together at Saint Alban's Primary School. Carmen was always very interested in Jacky's research.

"As far as I know, it doesn't change into a human being. Why does your granny think she saw a Lagahoo in the backyard?"

"You know Granny, Carmen. She sees all kinds of things, duppy and jumby and things like that. Remember the duppy[2] stories she used to tell us when we were small, so we would be scared and mind what she said?"

Carmen laughed. "And the soucouyant, don't forget that. My mother used to tell me that one too." She smiled a strange smile. "It didn't really frighten me, though. I always wondered what it would be like to take your skin off, leave your worries behind, and fly so free."

"Well, you sit there so and wonder. I have to keep researching this paper. The back issues come in yet?"

"Right here." Sighing with the effort of bending over, Carmen reached under the desk and pulled out a stack of slim bound volumes of *Huracan*, a Caribbean literary journal that was now out of print. A smell of wormwood and age rose from them. In the 1940s, *Huracan* had published a series of issues on folktales. Jacky hoped that these would provide her with more research material.

1 Slang for people from Trinidad and Tobago.
2 Word of African origin used in the Caribbean to refer to a ghost or spirit.

"Thanks, Carmen." She picked up the volumes and looked around for somewhere to sit. There was an empty private carrel, but there was also a free space at one of the large study tables. Terry was sitting there, head bent over a fat textbook. The navy blue of his shirt suited his skin, made it glow like a newly unwrapped chocolate. Jacky smiled. She went over to the desk, tapped Terry on the shoulder. "I could sit beside you, Terry?"

Startled, he looked up to see who had interrupted him. His handsome face brightened with welcome. "Uh, sure, no problem. Let me get…" He leapt to pull out the chair for her, overturning his own in the process. At the crash, everyone in the library looked up. "Shit." He bent over to pick up the chair. His glasses fell from his face. Pens and pencils rained from his shirt pocket.

Jacky giggled. She put her books down, retrieved Terry's glasses just before he would have stepped on them. "Here." She put the spectacles onto his face, let the warmth of her fingertips linger briefly at his temples.

Terry stepped back, sat quickly in the chair, even though it was still at an odd angle from the table. He crossed one leg over the other. "Sorry," he muttered bashfully. He bent over, reaching awkwardly for the scattered pens and pencils.

"Don't fret, Terry. You just collect yourself and come and sit back down next to me." Jacky glowed with the feeling of triumph. Half an hour of studying beside him, and she knew she'd have a date for lunch. She sat, opened a copy of *Huracan*, and read:

SOUCOUYANT/OL' HIGUE
(Trinidad/Guyana)

> Caribbean equivalent of the vampire myth. See also "Azeman." "Soucouyant," or "blood-sucker," derives from the French verb "sucer," to suck. "Ol' Higue" is the Guyanese creole expression for an old hag, or witch woman. The soucouyant is usually an old, evil-tempered woman who removes her skin at night, hides it, and then changes into a ball of fire. She flies through the air, searching for homes in which there are babies. She then enters the house through an open window or keyhole, goes into the child's room, and sucks the life from its body. She may visit one child's bedside a number of times, draining a little more life each time, as the frantic parents search for a cure, and the child gets progressively weaker and finally dies. Or she may kill all at once.

The smell of the soup Granny was cooking made Jacky's mouth water. She sat at Granny's wobbly old kitchen table, tracing her fingers along a familiar burn, the one shaped like a handprint. The wooden table had been Granny's as long as Jacky could remember. Grandpa had made the table for Granny long before Jacky was born. Diabetes had finally been the death of him. Granny had brought only the kitchen table and her clothing with her when she moved in with Jacky and her mother.

Granny looked up from the cornmeal and flower dough she was kneading. "Like you idle, doux-doux," she said. She slid the bowl of dough over to Jacky. "Make the dumplings then, nuh?"

Jacky took the bowl over to the stove, started pulling off pieces of dough and forming it into little cakes.

"Andrew make this table for me with he own two hand," Granny said.

"I know. You tell me already."

Granny ignored her. "Forty-two years we married, and every Sunday, I chop up the cabbage for the saltfish on this same table. Forty-two years we eat Sunday morning breakfast right here so. Saltfish and cabbage with a little small-leaf thyme from the back garden, and fry dumpling and cocoa-tea. I miss he too bad. You granddaddy did full up me life, make me feel young."

Jacky kept forming the dumplings for the soup. Granny came over to the stove and stirred the large pot with her wooden spoon. She blew on the spoon, cautiously tasted some of the liquid in it, and carefully floated a whole, ripe Scotch Bonnet pepper[1] on top of the bubbling mixture. "Jacky, when you put the dumpling-them in, don't break the pepper, all right? Otherwise this soup going to make we bawl tonight for pepper."

"Mm. Ain't Mummy used to help you make soup like this on a Saturday?"

"Yes, doux-doux. Just like this." Granny hobbled back to sit at the kitchen table. Tiny, graying braids were escaping the confinement of her stiff black wig. Her knobby legs looked frail in their too-beige stockings. Like so many of the old women that Jacky knew, Granny always wore stockings rolled down below the hems of her worn flower print shifts. "I thought you was going out tonight," Granny said. "With Terry."

"We break up," Jacky replied bitterly. "He say he not ready to settle down." She dipped the spoon into the soup, raised it to her mouth, spat it out when it burned her mouth. "Backside!"

Granny watched, frowning. "Greedy puppy does choke. You mother did always taste straight from the hot stove, too. I was forever telling she to take time. You come in just like she, always in a hurry. Your eyes bigger than your stomach."

Jacky sucked in an irritable breath. "Granny, Carmen have a baby boy last night. Eight pounds, four ounces. Carmen make she first baby already. I past thirty years old, and I ain't find nobody yet."

"You will find, Jacky. But you can't hurry people so. Is how long you and Terry did stepping out?"

1 One of the world's spiciest peppers. Popular in the Caribbean, most Scotch Bonnets have a heat rating of 100,000–350,000 Scoville units.

Jacky didn't respond.

"Eh, Jacky? How long?"

"Almost a month."

"Is scarcely two weeks, Jacky, don't lie to me. The boy barely learn where to find your house, and you was pestering he to settle down already. Me and your grandfather court for two years before we went to Parson to marry we."

When Granny started like this, she could go on for hours. Sullenly, Jacky began to drop the raw dumplings one by one into the fragrant, boiling soup.

"Child, you pretty, you have flirty ways, boys always coming and looking for you. You could pick and choose until you find the right one. Love will come. But take time. Love your studies, look out for your friends-them. Love your old Granny," she ended softly.

Hot tears rolled down Jacky's cheeks. She watched the dumplings bobbing back to the surface as they cooked; little warm, yellow suns.

"A new baby," Granny mused. "I must go and visit Carmen, take she some crab and callaloo to strengthen she blood. Hospital food does make you weak, oui."

*I need more time, more life. I need a baby breath. Must wait till people sleeping, though. Nobody awake to see a fireball flying up from the bedroom window.*

*The skin only confining me. I could feel it getting old, binding me up inside it. Sometimes I does just feel to take it off and never put it back on again, oui?*

*Three A.M. 'Fore day morning. Only me and the duppies going to be out this late. Up from out of the narrow bed, slip off the nightie, slip off the skin.*

*Oh God, I does be so free like this! Hide the skin under the bed, and fly out the jalousie window. The night air cool, and I flying so high. I know how many people it have in each house, and who sleeping. I could feel them, skin-bag people, breathing out their life, one-one breath. I know where it have a new one, too: down on Vanderpool Lane. Yes, over here. Feel it, the new one, the baby. So much life in that little body.*

*Fly down low now, right against the ground. Every door have a crack, no matter how small.*

*Right here. Slip into the house. Turn back into a woman. Is a nasty feeling, walking around with no skin, wet flesh dripping onto the floor, but I get used to it after so many years.*

*Here. The baby bedroom. Hear the young breath heating up in he lungs, blowing out, wasting away. He ain't know how to use it; I go take it.*

*Nice baby boy, so fat. Drink, soucouyant. Suck in he warm, warm life. God, it sweet. It sweet can't done. It sweet.*

*No more? I drink all already? But what a way this baby dead fast!*

Childbirth was once a risky thing for both mother and child. Even when they both survived the birth process, there were many unknown infectious diseases to which newborns were susceptible. Oliphant theorizes that the soucouyant lore was created in an attempt to explain infant deaths that would have seemed mysterious in more primitive times. Grieving parents could blame their loss on people who wished them ill. Women tend to have longer life spans than men, but in an even more superstitious age where life was hard and brief, old women in a community could seem sinister. It must have been easy to believe that the women were using sorcerous means to prolong their lives, and how better to do that than to steal the lifeblood of those who were very young?

Dozing, Jacky leaned against Granny's knees. Outside, the leaves of the Julie mango tree rustled and sighed in the evening breeze. Granny tapped on Jacky's shoulder, passed her a folded section of newspaper with a column circled. *Births/ Deaths*. Granny took a bitter pleasure in keeping track of whom she'd outlived each week. Sleepily, Jacky focused on the words on the page:

*Deceased: Raymond George Lewis, 5 days old, of natural causes. Son of Michael and Carmen, Diego Martin, Port of Spain. Funeral service 5:00 p.m., November 14, Church of the Holy Redeemer.*

"Jesus, Granny. Carmen's baby! But he was healthy, don't it?"

"I don't know, doux-doux. They say he just stop breathing in the night. Just so. What a sad thing. We must go to the funeral, pay we respects."

Sunlight is fatal to the soucouyant. She must be back in her skin before daylight. In fact, the tales say that the best way to discover a soucouyant is to find her skin, rub the raw side with hot pepper, and replace it in its hiding place. When she tries to put it back on, the pain of the burning pepper will cause the demon to cry out and reveal herself.

*Me fire belly full, oui. When a new breath fueling the fire, I does feel good, like I could never die. And then I does fly and fly, high like the moon. Time to go back home now, though.*

*Eh-eh! Why she leave the back door cotch open? Never mind; she does be preoccupied sometimes. Maybe she just forget to close the door. Just fly in the bedroom window. I go close the door after I put on my skin again.*

*Ai! What itching me so? Is what happen to me skin? Ai! Lord, Lord, it burning, it burning too bad. It scratching me all over, like it have fire ants inside there. I can't stand it!*

Hissing with pain, the soucouyant threw off her burning skin and stood flayed, dripping.

Calmly, Granny entered Jacky's room. Before Jacky could react Granny picked up the Jacky-skin. She held it close to her body, threatening the skin with the sharp, wicked kitchen knife she held in her other hand. Her look was sorrowful.

"I know it was you, doux-doux. When I see the Lagahoo, I know what I have to do."

Jacky cursed and flared to fireball form. She rushed at Granny, but backed off as Granny made a feint at the skin with her knife.

"You stay right there and listen to me, Jacky. The soucouyant blood in all of we, all the women in we family."

*You, too?*

"Even me. We blood hot: hot for life, hot for youth. Loving does cool we down. Making life does cool we down."

Jacky raged. The ceiling blackened, began to smoke.

"I know how it go, doux-doux. When we lives empty, the hunger does turn to blood hunger. But it have plenty other kinds of loving, Jacky. Ain't I been telling you so? Love your work. Love people close to you. Love your life."

The fireball surged towards Granny. "No. Stay right there, you hear? Or I go chop this skin for you."

Granny backed out through the living room. The hissing ball of fire followed close, drawn by the precious skin in the old woman's hands.

"You never had no patience. Doux-doux, you is my life, but you can't kill so. That little child you drink, you don't hear it spirit when night come, bawling for Carmen and Michael? I does weep to hear it. I try to tell you, like I try to tell you mother: Don't be greedy."

Granny had reached the back door. The open back door. The soucouyant made a desperate feint at Granny's knife arm, searing her right side from elbow to scalp. The smell of burnt flesh and hair filled the little kitchen but though the old lady cried out, she wouldn't drop the knife. The pain in her voice was more than physical.

"You devil!" She backed out the door into the cobalt light of early morning. Gritting her teeth, she slashed the Jacky-skin into two ragged halves and flung it into the pigeon peas patch. Jacky shrieked and turned back into her flayed self. Numbly, she picked up her skin, tried with oozing fingers to put the torn edges back together.

"You and me is the last two," Granny said. "Your mami woulda make three, but I had to kill she too, send my own flesh and blood into the sun. Is time, doux-doux. The Lagahoo calling you."

*My skin! Granny, how you could do me so? Oh God, morning coming already? Yes, I could feel it, the sun calling to the fire in me.*

Jacky threw the skin down again, leapt as a fireball into the brightening air. I going, I going, where I could burn clean, burn bright, and all you could go to the Devil, oui!

*Fireball flying high to the sun, and oh God, it burning, it burning, it burning!*

Granny hobbled to the pigeon peas patch, wincing as she cradled her burnt right side. Tears trickled down her wrinkled face. She sobbed, "Why all you must break my heart so?"

Painfully, she got down to her knees beside the ruined pieces of skin and placed one hand on them. She made her hand glow red hot, igniting her granddaughter's skin. It began to burn, crinkling and curling back on itself like bacon in a pan. Granny wrinkled her nose against the smell, but kept her hand on the smoking mass until there was nothing but ashes. Her hand faded back to its normal cocoa brown. Clambering to her feet again, she looked about her in the pigeon peas patch.

"I live to see the Lagahoo two time. Next time, God horse, you better be coming for me."

# Silvia Moreno-Garcia

(B. 1981)

Narco vampires, Mayan gods, and defiant gothic heroines are among the many intriguing characters that populate Moreno-Garcia's speculative fiction, narratives that are frequently set in various periods throughout Mexican history. Inspired by Mexican myth and folklore, her work also critiques prejudice in Mexican society, particularly colorism, which is the reason, she explains, that many of her main characters are dark-skinned. Born in Baja, Mexico, Moreno-Garcia attended Endicott College in Massachusetts, and eventually immigrated to Canada with her husband in 2004. Her parents were both journalists and after moving to Canada, Moreno-Garcia herself worked as a freelance journalist to support her young family. As a child she was drawn to the horror genre. She explains that the vampires and monsters in the stories were "always more welcoming and less intimidating than my real life growing up in Mexico City." Moreno-Garcia professes to have always liked vampires but regrets that the contemporary representations of the legendary creature focus on the romantic or erotic allure and have lost some of their predatory danger, danger that clearly lurks in "A Handful of Earth." She is an active participant in the #OwnVoices movement, which advocates for marginalized groups writing about their own experiences rather than the experience being authored by someone outside the particular cultural group. In addition to novels, she has published numerous short stories and essays, edited several anthologies, and co-edits the horror magazine *The Dark* with Sean Wallace. She is a columnist for *The Washington Post* and reviews books for NPR. Moreno-Garcia has an MA in science and technology studies from the University of British Columbia, and she is the recipient of numerous awards.

# "A Handful of Earth"

(2011)

He left, crates filled with earth, bound for England. Left us behind, promising to send for us. We believed him. But as the days went by, I realized he'd lied.

Live forever. Love forever.

Anca and Ioana looked to me for guidance, as they always did. Technically, they were older than me. I was the last one to be brought to the castle. Mentally, they were younger. Frozen in their teenage years, letting me mother them and lead. I'd had five sisters and watched over them. Authority came naturally.

My sisters and I had shared a single, cramped room. Some days, when I was tired of doing the washing and watching over the others—our mother died birthing the youngest child, our father was a strict man who filled my days with endless household tasks—I'd look out the window, towards the distant silhouette of the castle. It had no name. We simply called it "the castle." High upon a cliff, edging towards the sky, while we lived beneath its shadow. I pictured myself going up its hundreds of steps, rushing through the hallways and dancing in rooms decorated with rich tapestries.

When he swooped from the towers, a piece of night detaching from the sky, why would I resist?

I had five sisters, but disease took them from us. Tiny little graves marked their passing, though I did not recall their precise location afterwards.

My father and I sat alone at the table. He was quiet, staring at a distant point.

We were already half-dead. The air stank, everyone rotting and melting away. So why not live forever?

I stood in the highest tower of the castle and tried to pierce the night with my eyes, to see beyond the mountains and the forests and gaze upon the distant shores he'd escaped to. I wondered if he thought of us or if the memory had been ripped apart.

Anca and Ioana were not twins. But they might have been. So close in looks and mannerisms, with the same glossy black hair and knowing eyes. Something about them always made me think of birds of prey. They flew easily, bodies light and bone-thin, their laughter streaming from the rafters.

Flight did not come naturally to me. My other shape was of a massive white wolf. Smaller than his own wolf body had been, but still a sight to see.

Anca and Ioana feared the outside; they spoke of arrows raining over a castle. There had been a great battle, though they could not recall if it had taken place in this fortress or another one. Either way, they would not venture with me.

I rushed through the forest, seeing all manner of things in the dark as I hunted for us.

He had kept us in our rooms, like the women in a Turkish harem I spied in the etchings of books, before the books were ravaged by moths and time. There we were to patiently wait for him, never stepping outside the walls of the castle.

There is death outside, he'd warned us.

Yet he'd gone out, beyond the safe limits of our home and aboard a ship.

I'd been right. He had never loved. He never loves.[1]

Not that it mattered now.

There were Anca and Ioana to look after.

I ran through the forest, sometimes naked in my woman-shape, sometimes in the wolf's pelt. I chanced upon a traveler or sneaked into a small house, creeping through the windows. Then I'd drink upon a sleeper, compel him to follow me through the night, and back to the castle. I'd let him ride upon my back, my wolf legs taking us swiftly through the darkness. Up, up. Towards Anca and Ioana.

In the daytime we slept in the old chapel, inside carved sarcophagi much more ornate than the graves my sisters had been given. Ioana once told me the castle was built upon an older castle and I thought this might be true, for the sarcophagi seemed of a style that did not entirely correspond to the ruined chapel, images of women holding garlands of flowers upon the lids. But even Ioana could not say how long ago the previous castle had stood, or who had been its master.

Not that it mattered. Now we were its mistresses, laughing as we swirled inside the empty chambers, decked in clothes of ladies who had long turned to dust, ravaged by worms.

He had not liked our liquid laughter, the way it bounced against the ancient walls. Hating it as though it might peel the bricks away revealing an older layer of stones. He was gone, and we laughed.

I braided tiny flowers into Anca's hair while Ioana told us fairy tales from her childhood. Sometimes, she forgot the endings and we invented our own.

I was careful with my looks and attire. I'd compel Anca and Ioana to bathe with me under the cold rain. Or to pull water from an old well and fill a great copper tub. Anca always said I was the vainest of us all. Ioana said I was the fairest.

I knew I'd been his favorite and the constant ablutions, the ribbons in the hair and the heavy, old pieces of gold against my skin had been meant all for him. His absence had not altered my routine. I was still prim and careful with my clothes, my hair. Through the years, I had noticed that Anca and Ioana sometimes ignored such niceties, nails caked with dirt and blood. As though they had forgotten, or did not care, to keep any semblance of life.

---

1 Throughout this story Moreno-Garcia references Stoker's *Dracula*, particularly the scene where Dracula prevents the three brides from consuming Jonathan Harker and the final battle between the crew of light and Dracula.

When they were in this state—and they sank into this miasma, deeply upon his departure—they might remain still for several days. Not a muscle twitching. Nothing. Just a deep silence interrupted by bouts of terrible ferocity. They sometimes gnawed at each other, not a pup's nipping, but a full-blown attack.

In those moments I did not know them and I wondered if this was a sign of their true age. Or simply the vast melancholy that clothed them.

Either way, I reeled them out of this state. Reeled them into little dances and the clapping of hands. The castle vibrated with our voices.

And whenever I'd catch myself thinking of him again, my hands running over the maps he had left behind, I'd seek their comfort and their smiles.

It happened as it was meant to happen. The spell shattering abruptly, as it must.

Ioana dreamt the castle crashed into the river far below. I held her in my arms as she wept, speaking of a terrible omen. I convinced Ioana and Anca to play hide-and-seek with me, like I'd done with my sisters when we were little. We rushed through long corridors, sneaking beneath archways and laying still, as lizards and slugs crawled beside us. Night creatures, the lot of us, out to play.

The wind and rain whipped the castle, lightning striking nearby, and we giggled.

I raced up to the tallest tower of the castle, wolves howling, wind screeching, and stopped in my tracks feeling a tug and a pull inside my skull.

I knew he was returning home.

Emboldened by his nearness, Ioana and Anca agreed to step out of the fortress some nights later. We looked for him in the coldness, in the dark, hoping we might encounter his carriage. Instead, we found the woman and the strange man. The woman bore his mark upon her, glowing like an ember. Another sister for our tribe.

The man was untainted. Strongly-built and blue-eyed. He reminded me vaguely of my stern and resolute father and I stared at him for a long time. I thought of the night I slipped out of my house, headed up to the old castle, and the distant cry of surprise I must have imagined—I must have—springing from my father's lips, escaping the desolate, little white house.

We can never look back or we will be turned into pillars of salt. I suppose that is why Anca and Ioana remembered very little of their youth. Perhaps that is why they forgot themselves some days, growing fierce and empty.

I stared at the man and he stared back at me while Anca and Ioana laughed.

I think my silence, my eyes upon him, were my salvation.

I do not know why he did not kill me. Though he tried. He did try. But the stake did not lodge firm against the heart. Distraction? Weariness? Perhaps my own power over mortal minds, woven in that long look, shielded me. Perhaps he felt pity.

Whatever it was, I woke to the icy knowledge of Anca and Ioana's death. I did not even have to look at their sarcophagi to know. But I did look. Empty. Not a bit of hair, not a speck of bone. Nothing but dust.

I knew he was dead too. I felt his absence. I had not been this alone in years upon years. Centuries even. The loneliness reverberated through my body.

My shift was stained with my own blood upon the breast, where a stake or a knife bit the flesh before he pulled away. I let my usual sense of cleanliness escape me and did not change my dress, eating millipedes and insects for three whole days.

I feared leaving the chapel. I thought his enemies might return. On the third day there was a great murmur through the fortress, a rumble that startled me and had me pressed against the wall in terror. When I ventured out of the chapel I realized a section of the castle had collapsed. The old bricks had finally given away, groaning and plunging into the river below.

The sight roused me. I no longer felt safe in the chapel.

I turned into a wolf and leapt beyond the castle walls, not knowing where I'd go. The icy night air cut my hands, my feet.

It was easy to find my sisters' graves. I had not forgotten the location. I had merely buried it away, and now dug through layers of memory until I arrived at the plot of earth that kept their bones. My father's remains might be there too, though I did not know for sure.

I curled upon the ground and crossed my arms upon my chest.

He had never loved. But I had. I'd loved Anca and Ioana. Their little smiles and their games. Their sweetness and their cruelty, and the way their black eyes shone in the darkness, as if burnished. It was all gone and I couldn't even muster the energy to crave revenge.

My fingers dug into the earth and I thought I might bury myself with my sisters. Rest my bones against their own. Cradle them once more. I would not be alone then, for their ghosts would keep me company.

I lay like this for a very long time and then, finally, I stood up and ripped my shift off. I fashioned a simple pouch out of it, scooping earth into it and tying it close. I thought of returning to the castle for some of the valuables there. Perhaps one of the maps. I discarded the idea.

Years later, I wonder if I shouldn't have returned and scooped a trinket, a map, after all. My memories of those days have grown dimmer and dimmer. I sometimes wake up with a vision of two dark-haired women, but their names escape me. I wonder if a memento might help pin the thoughts in place. Or perhaps it would not make a difference. Perhaps we are all meant to wander with nothing but a handful of earth in our hands, never looking over our shoulders.

# Kazuki Sakuraba

(B. 1971)

Kazuki Sakuraba is a distinguished Japanese author recognized for her young adult fiction. Set predominantly in Japan, *A Small Charred Face* explores the relationship between humans and the Bamboo, Sakuraba's unique version of vampires. This opening passage from Sakuraba's novel details the protagonist's first encounter with these vampires who smell like grass and elegantly explode into bloom at the end of their 120-year lives. The Bamboo have come to Japan from China after the Cultural Revolution, and this episode detailing the loss and violence sets up the themes of family and gender that Sakuraba explores in the rest of the novel. The Bamboo are truly distinctive in the vampire pantheon. Sakuraba cites Virginia Woolf's *Orlando*, where the main character undergoes a gender transformation and experiences centuries of English history, as her inspiration. Her novels have been adapted for both anime and live action films, and she is the winner of numerous awards, including the Mystery Writers of Japan Award and the Naoki Prize.

# from *A Small Charred Face*[1]

(2014)

## BAMBOO

The snow danced through the air. A dance of death. I alone was motionless, my fingers numb with cold. My hands, my feet.

My teeth began to chatter, pebbles clacking up against each other. If they had been flints, flames would have sprung to life in my mouth.

Was I going to die too?

† † †

1 Translated by Jocelyne Allen in 2017.

I could hear the warm blood flowing out of Mama's body from where she lay in the hallway, her long legs splayed. The slow oozing had been echoing in my ears like the trumpets of the apocalypse. My teeth were chattering in time with the music. My tears froze solid on my cheeks.

The glass doors leading out to the terrace had been left open; huge drifts of pure-white snow gusted in. The heavy velvet curtains flapped threateningly in the direction of the gilded Japanese-style floor desk under which I hid.

From the neighboring hall, I heard my older sister start to scream. I squeezed my eyes shut. My shaking started to take on a noticeable rhythm.

The men's feet on the hard floor reverberated throughout the house.

In between wailing sobs, my sister groaned, "Kill me, kill me."

"This is some house!" I heard one man say.

"Take a look at that! This fucking fancy piano," another commented. "The sofa. And these sculptures!"

"I can't take it. Kill—"

An irritated gunshot cut my sister off.

Instantly, my eyes flew open. The sky said evening. The blue-gray light of late winter, colored with despair, poured into the room. The snow grew heavier. I curled into a ball, clutched my knees, tried to make myself almost impossibly small.

I heard the echoes of rough footfalls.

"Said to kill everyone?"

"Yeah."

"We're done here then. The woman and the kids. Three servants. A cook, a cleaning woman, and a washerwoman. Five people."

"There's still the son. He's like ten or something. I've seen him before. No one's come across him, huh?"

"He's probably out somewhere. We'll wait downstairs. One shot through the door when he comes back and we're done."

"Ten, huh? If he's as cute as his mother and sister…"

"*Pft!* You do what you want."

The men's footfalls faded down the stairs. The curtains fluttered up again in the wind, a gust mixed with icy snow, the breath of the god of death.

They were getting drunk downstairs. The bodies of the servants were still there in the kitchen.

On the other side of the window, dusk was falling too slowly, taunting me. It felt like a hundred years had passed already.

This town was nothing but organization men and people under their thumbs. Even if I did manage to somehow make it out of the house, there was nowhere for me to run. Nowhere in the world. This was the end.

Night finally fell, painting the other side of the window a chilly ultramarine. Shivering, I crawled out from under the low writing desk. An unflinching farewell.

*Sister.*

The thought of trying to walk without making any noise set me to trembling so badly I couldn't stay on my feet. Crawling awkwardly on all fours, I went out into the hallway and slipped slowly past Mama into the hall beyond her. My sister's eyes were wide open and glassy; she was dead. Her hands were clenched into tight fists, and she wasn't wearing any clothes. Her prestigious junior high uniform, the dream of every girl, was currently spread out all over the room, strewn across the furniture.

I crawled over to her. With a shaking hand, I closed her eyelids. I touched a finger to the hole between her eyebrows. Her eyelids were cold already, but the wound opening still held a faint warmth.

*My sister…*

I heard a sound and quickly looked over my shoulder. It couldn't have been the men coming back up here. They were talking about something downstairs.

I strained my ears. The glass doors? Had someone come in through the open doors in the next room?

The chattering of my teeth stopped. I listened with my whole body, with every suspicious, wary nerve ending.

The faintest of footsteps. Feet shuffling. Feet dragging? Who?

Whoever it was cut across the room, stumbled upon the desk I had only recently been hiding under, and then came out into the hallway.

I drew closer to the hallway and peered out quietly. There was someone in the shadows. The light of the winter moon carved out the silhouette of a young man—not too tall, with broad shoulders. In the time it took me to blink, he crouched down soundlessly. Right where Mama had fallen.

I squinted harder into the darkness. Held my breath. And then…

*Slp, slp, slp.* I heard the sound of drinking. Blood.

In my mind's eye, I saw Mama half-naked, her gold blouse stained red, striped miniskirt ripped. The man pressed his mouth to her neck and slurped up her blood.

This… this wasn't someone from the organization. The clothes he wore, the way he looked were just too different. I mean, he wasn't even human.

I remembered a scary story my second papa had told me a long, long time ago about a race of monsters that came from deep in the mountains of China. They were called the Bamboo. And true to their name, they were monsters of those tall grasses, carnivorous plants that drank the lifeblood of humans and ate their still-living flesh. They were nearly human in appearance. But unable to stand under the light of the sun, they walked the night…

That's why you weren't supposed to go out walking alone after the sunset. The Bamboo would find you and eat you.

Mama had looked at me shaking in fear and laughed in her high-pitched voice. "Isn't that just a story to frighten children?"

And now Mama was dead, crumpled on the floor like a marionette with its strings cut, and something was eagerly lapping at her blood.

I heard a noise like a blade slicing through flesh. It was that... *thing* lifting his face. My whole body shook. My teeth started chattering like crazed castanets again.

The man seemed sincerely surprised to find a living creature before him. I couldn't see his face. Only the blood around his mouth was visible, glistening in the dark.

"You." Was he smiling? "You're seriously good at making yourself invisible, boyo!" Surprisingly, the voice fell somewhere between that of a boy and a young man. It was teasing and unexpectedly gentle.

"Who are you?"

"Bamboo."

"Do the Bamboo really exist?"

"What? You've heard of us?"

"You walk at night! Drink lifeblood! Eat flesh!"

"Dummy. We don't drink lifeblood. We have laws, y'know."

"Laws?"

The men downstairs stopped talking abruptly. The Bamboo held his index finger up to his lips. *Shh!* That finger also glistened with fresh blood.

I stared at him, bewitched. Strangely, I wasn't frightened, even though I had cried so hard when my second papa had told me the story. I mean, I was going to die either way.

Downstairs, the men started speaking again.

The Bamboo in front of me slowly began to move his mouth once more, and something—hair wet with blood—bobbed up and down. "The smell of blood called out to me. I mean, this town constantly *reeks* of blood, y'know? All the different organizations fighting all the time. They never get sick of it. But what's the big hubbub here?"

"My papa slept with the boss's woman, and they found out," I replied, my voice absurdly calm. "He took the woman and the money and the goods and ran off. So they killed Mama and my sister and me tonight, as a lesson."

"Huh, makes sense. But you're still alive, aren't you?"

I closed my mouth.

There was a group of hitmen downstairs now, happily drinking the night away. Probably everyone in town knew by now that the only one they hadn't taken out yet was the son. I could never trust a living human being again.

But if I could choose the method of my death in a last moment of selfishness... Please, God. I took one step, then another, walking toward the unearthly monster.

"Huh? What?"

I reached out both hands. I wanted to be released from my terror! I'd had more than enough of this tired human instinct to survive working on overdrive, ordering me to run away, to push back against destiny, to fight desperately to live right up until the last, all despite the fact that the end result would be the same, no matter what I did—I would lose the battle and die. The finish line was the same. But somehow, I was supposed to fight, to resist. Any god that would order me to do something like that was a thoughtless, spoiled brat.

I heard muffled laughter—*heh heh heh*—and opened my eyes.

He was looking down on me, his own eyes large and turned downward at the corners, his eyelashes thick and long. In the darkness, his eyes and the red blood around his mouth alone seemed transparent; they shone with an eerie clarity.

"Meat on a plate then! Blood that flies into the cup! First time I've seen that!"

"Don't... make fun of me," I protested, my voice trembling. *Don't laugh at my last hope.*

The Bamboo stopped his snickering. And then he crouched down and met my eyes. "Hey, you're shaking." He touched my shoulders lightly, playfully exasperated.

"Okay, boyo," he said, kindly. "Listen up. We Bamboo have rules. Y'know? We have our own—well, I guess it's something like a government. It's different from the country you human beings have made, but it's ours. And we have our own strict laws. Or maybe you'd call them precepts? I dunno how it was in China in the beginning. I dunno anything about way back then. But for the Bamboo living in Japan right now, it's a thing that you're only allowed to eat the dead. Like, we can only drink the blood of the dead." The Bamboo cocked his head to one side slowly. "But maybe this is all over your head?"

"What happens if you break the rule?"

"You get locked up for sixty years! They stuff you in a barrel and bury you in the ground!"

"You'd be an old man after that!"

"Huh? Would not. Why would I?" the Bamboo retorted, curiously.

Now that he mentioned it, my second papa had said that the Bamboo were young forever. They never aged. And he said that, just like bamboo, just once, when they're around 120 years old, they bloom, bursting into a spray of white flowers. Then they disappear into nothingness.

The one who had left this morning with the boss's woman and money and stuff was my fourth papa. He had come to Japan from somewhere in Latin America. He'd joined one of the organizations in this town, the one for people from the same place as him, and had moved up through the ranks. After my poor Japanese mama had latched on to him, life in our family had suddenly gotten a whole lot easier. But that had ended this morning.

The wind whirled and carved out a circle, winding through the room. In the blink of an eye, the Bamboo was sitting on the edge of the open window. He waved. "Later, kid!"

I cocked my head to one side and stared at him. The icy light of the moon illuminated his face for the first time. His large eyes were dry like desert sand.

His eyebrows were thick, and a beard covered the lower half of his face. His clothing was oddly neat. It wasn't expensive like the stuff Papa and Mama wore, but it was well cut, and he wore it with dignity. With his sharply defined features, he looked half-Latino and half-Japanese. The way the moonlight caught his dark skin made me think, *Aah, if only he didn't have that beard, he could be one of those beautiful boys the girls love.*

But if the Bamboo had a rule, I guess that was that. I smiled. *Goodbye, Bamboo.* So the story about the bloodsucking grass monsters was true, after all. I wouldn't tell anyone, though, just because I'd seen one. I mean, I had no tomorrow.

Perhaps the men had heard our footsteps; there was an intent silence coming from down below, like they were straining their ears, listening. This was followed by the sound of feet climbing the stairs. The rustling of guns being drawn.

The Bamboo twisted his face up.

The footsteps came closer.

My teeth chattered. My whole body shook again.

My sister's wide-open eyes. Her scattered uniform. Her trampled dignity. Would I also tell them I couldn't stand it and beg them to kill me? The warmth of the wound between her eyebrows. My sister. The footsteps reached the hallway. My terror made me a stone statue. I closed my eyes.

Do the weak not even get to choose the way we die? Preyed upon, tormented, we die.

"The rule's absolute," the Bamboo muttered, almost like he was making excuses. "I'd get more than the barrel underground for sixty years for this. I mean, punishment by fire's no joke, y'know? It's pretty much the most painful way for us to disappear from this world. So it's a no-go. Sorry, 'kay?" For some reason, the words that followed sounded like he was whispering right in my ear. "I don't owe you anything. Right? Yeah?"

What was he talking about?

The men approached from the hallway. They entered the room, moved to turn on the light and banish the pitch-black dark.

"Aah, dammit…Goddamit! Quit making that face at me!" The Bamboo clicked his tongue surprisingly loudly. "Quit crying!"

*Click.* The lights came on. I knew even with my eyes shut that they were painfully bright.

*Aah, they've finally found me. It's the end of today, of tomorrow, of yesterday, of forever.*

And then the wind was roaring in my ears.

# CRITICISM



As the introductory sections throughout the anthology make clear, there are many critical perspectives that lend insights into vampire literature. In selecting texts for this chapter, we endeavored to find material that would prove useful to a critical interpretation of the works in this anthology and of the larger genre of vampire studies. The excerpts here display a range of approaches and theories by critics are often cited by other scholars in the field. These excerpts should provide a useful starting point for class discussions and for student research.

We open the chapter with an excerpt from Sigmund Freud's famous early twentieth-century psychoanalytic work "The Uncanny" (1919). This text elucidates many principles of psychoanalysis that are relevant to a study of the works in this anthology. Indeed, as monsters who are both living and dead, vampires can be seen to exemplify Freud's theories of the unheimlich (uncanny).

In the decades leading up to the end of the twentieth century, vampire literature as a genre was, for the most part, overlooked by critics. However, the work done to examine Bram Stoker's iconic novel, *Dracula*, in the final decades of the twentieth century initiated new directions in vampire studies. From the 1980s, we include excerpts from Christopher Craft's gender and sexuality reading, "'Kiss Me with Those Red Lips'" (1984). The critical focus on *Dracula* continues into the 1990s with Stephen D. Arata's ground-breaking post-colonial interpretation, "The Occidental Tourist" (1990). While Stoker's novel is not included in the anthology, these often-cited critical works present concepts that apply to many of the texts featured here. These articles represent new directions of criticism on vampire literature and remain relevant to contemporary readings of both historic and modern vampire texts.

As the twentieth century drew to a close, critics began to examine the broader genre of vampire literature and film. In her seminal work of queer theory, "Tracking the Vampire" (1991), Sue-Ellen Case uses the vampire as both character and metaphor for LGBTQ+ representation. In her introduction to *Our Vampires, Ourselves* (1995), Nina Auerbach examines the interplay between vampire texts, politics, and culture, while in "Daughters of Lilith" (1999), Carol Senf offers a historic exploration of the figure of the female vampire in literature.

We close the chapter with an excerpt from a twenty-first-century work that shows one of the new directions of vampire criticism. In her introduction to *Black Female Vampires in African American Women's Novels, 1977–2011: She Bites Back* (2018), Kendra R. Parker presents an insightful examination of race and gender in African American women's vampire fiction.

The range of critical texts included here is intended as an introduction of major concepts rather than an exhaustive list. As such, it should be useful for reading the texts in this anthology and for a broader examination of the vampire in both literature and culture.

# Sigmund Freud

## from "The Uncanny"[1]

(1919)

The subject of the "uncanny"... undoubtedly belongs to all that is terrible—to all that arouses dread and creeping horror; it is equally certain, too, that the word is not always used in a clearly definable sense, so that it tends to coincide with whatever excites dread. Yet we may expect that it implies some intrinsic quality which justifies the use of a special name. One is curious to know what this peculiar quality is which allows us to distinguish as "uncanny" certain things within the boundaries of what is "fearful."

As good as nothing is to be found upon this subject in elaborate treatises on aesthetics, which in general prefer to concern themselves with what is beautiful, attractive and sublime, that is with feelings of a positive nature, with the circumstances and the objects that call them forth, rather than with the opposite feelings of unpleasantness and repulsion. I know of only one attempt in medico-psychological literature, a fertile but not exhaustive paper by E. Jentsch.[2] But I must confess that I have not made a very thorough examination of the bibliography, especially the foreign literature, relating to this present modest contribution of mine, for reasons which must be obvious at this time;[3] so that my paper is presented to the reader without any claim of priority.

In his study of the "uncanny," Jentsch quite rightly lays stress on the obstacle presented by the fact that people vary so very greatly in their sensitivity to this quality of feeling. The writer of the present contribution, indeed, must himself plead guilty to a special obtuseness in the matter, where extreme delicacy of perception would be more in place. It is long since he has experienced or heard of anything which has given him an uncanny impression, and he will be obliged to translate himself into that state of feeling, and to awaken in himself the possibility of it before he begins. Still, difficulties of this kind make themselves felt powerfully in many other branches of aesthetics; we need not on this account

1 Originally published in *Imago* in 1919, this text was originally translated by Alix Strachey.
2 "Zur Psychologie des Unheimlichen."
3 World War I was just ending.

despair of finding instances in which the quality in question will be recognized without hesitation by most people.

Two courses are open to us at the start. Either we can find out what meaning has come to be attached to the word "uncanny" in the course of its history; or we can collect all those properties of persons, things, sensations, experiences and situation which arouse in us the feeling of uncanniness, and then infer the unknown nature of the uncanny from what they all have in common. I will say at once that both courses lead to the same result: the "uncanny" is that class of the terrifying which leads back to something long known to us, once very familiar. How this is possible, in what circumstances the familiar can become uncanny and frightening, I shall show in what follows. Let me also add that my investigation was actually begun by collecting a number of individual cases, and only later received confirmation after I had examined what language could tell us. In this discussion, however, I shall follow the opposite course.

The German word *unheimlich*[1] is obviously the opposite of *Heimlich, heimisch*, meaning "familiar," "native," "belonging to the home"; and we are tempted to conclude that what is "uncanny" is frightening precisely because it is *not* known and familiar. Naturally not everything which is new and unfamiliar is frightening, however; the relation cannot be inverted. We can only say that what is novel can easily become frightening and uncanny; some new things are frightening but not by any means all. Something has to be added to what is novel and unfamiliar to make it uncanny.

On the whole, Jentsch did not get beyond this relation of the uncanny to the novel and unfamiliar. He ascribes the essential factor in the production of the feeling of uncanniness to intellectual uncertainty; so that the uncanny would always be that in which one does not know where one is, as it were. The better orientated in his environment a person is, the less readily will he get the impression of something uncanny in regard to the objects and events in it. It is not difficult to see that this definition is incomplete, and we will therefore try to proceed beyond the equation of *unheimlich* with unfamiliar.

[...]

This is the place now to put forward two considerations which, I think, contain the gist of this short study. In the first place, if psychoanalytic theory is correct in maintaining that every emotional affect, whatever its quality, is transformed by repression into morbid anxiety, then among such cases of anxiety there must be a class in which the anxiety can be shown to come from something repressed which *recurs*. This class of morbid anxiety would then be no other than what is uncanny, irrespective of whether it originally aroused dread or some other affect. In the second place, if this is indeed the secret nature of the uncanny, we can understand why the usage of speech has extended *das*

1 Throughout most of the essay, the English translation "uncanny" is used. A closer translation of unheimlich might be "unhomely."

*Heimliche* into its opposite *das Unheimliche*; for this uncanny is in reality nothing new or foreign, but something familiar and old—established in the mind that has been estranged only by the process of repression. This reference to the factor of repression enables us, furthermore, to understand Schelling's[1] definition of the uncanny as something which ought to have been kept concealed but which has nevertheless come to light.

It only remains for us to test our new hypothesis on one or two more examples of the uncanny.

Many people experience the feeling in the highest degree in relation to death and dead bodies, to the return of the dead, and to spirits and ghosts. As we have seen, many languages in use today can only render the German expression "an *unheimliches* house" by "a *haunted* house." We might indeed have begun our investigation with this example, perhaps the most striking of all, of something uncanny, but we refrained from doing so because the uncanny in it is too much mingled with and in part covered by what is purely gruesome. There is scarcely any other matter, however, upon which our thoughts and feelings have changed so little since the very earliest times, and in which discarded forms have been so completely preserved under a thin disguise, as that of our relation to death. Two things account for our conservatism: the strength of our original emotional reaction to it, and the insufficiency of our scientific knowledge about it. Biology has not yet been able to decide whether death is the inevitable fate of every living being or whether it is only a regular but yet perhaps avoidable event in life. It is true that the proposition "All men are mortal" is paraded in text-books of logic as an example of a generalization, but no human being really grasps it, and our unconscious has as little use now as ever for the idea of its own mortality. Religions continue to dispute the undeniable fact of the death of each one of us and to postulate a life after death; civil governments still believe that they cannot maintain moral order among the living if they do not uphold this prospect of a better life after death as a recompense for earthly existence. In our great cities, placards announce lectures which will tell us how to get into touch with the souls of the departed; and it cannot be denied that many of the most able and penetrating minds among our scientific men have come to the conclusion, especially towards the close of their lives, that a contact of this kind is not utterly impossible. Since practically all of us still think as savages do on this topic, it is no matter for surprise that the primitive fear of the dead is still so strong within us and always ready to come to the surface at any opportunity. Most likely our fear still contains the old belief that the deceased becomes the enemy of his survivor and wants to carry him off to share his new life with him. Considering our unchanged attitude towards death, we might rather inquire what has become of the repression, that necessary condition for enabling a primitive feeling to recur in the shape of an uncanny effect. But

1 German philosopher F.W.J. Schelling.

repression is there, too. All so-called educated people have ceased to believe, officially at any rate, that the dead can become visible as spirits, and have hedged round any such appearances with improbable and remote circumstances; their emotional attitude towards the dead, moreover, once a highly dubious and ambivalent one, has been toned down in the higher strata of the mind into a simple feeling of reverence.

We have now only a few more remarks to add, for animism, magic and witchcraft, the omnipotence of thoughts, man's attitude to death, involuntary repetition and the castration-complex comprise practically all the factors which turn something fearful into an uncanny thing.

We also call a living person uncanny, usually when we ascribe evil motives to him. But that is not all; we must not only credit him with bad intentions but must attribute to these intentions capacity to achieve their aim in virtue of certain special powers. [...]

The uncanny effect of epilepsy and of madness has the same origin. The ordinary person sees in them the workings of forces hitherto unsuspected in his fellow man but which at the same time he is dimly aware of in a remote corner of his own being. The Middle Ages quite consistently ascribed all such maladies to daemonic influences, and in this their psychology was not so far out. Indeed, I should not be surprised to hear that psychoanalysis, which concerned with laying bare these hidden forces, has itself become uncanny to many people for that very reason. [...]

Dismembered limbs, a severed head, a hand cut off at the wrist, feet which dance by themselves—all these have something peculiarly uncanny about them, especially when, as in the last instance, they prove able to move of themselves in addition. As we already know, this kind of uncanniness springs from its association with the castration-complex. To many people the idea of being buried alive while appearing to be dead is the most uncanny thing of all. And yet psychoanalysis has taught us that this terrifying phantasy is only a transformation of another phantasy which had originally nothing terrifying about it at all, but was filled with a certain lustful pleasure—the phantasy, I mean, of intra-uterine existence.[1] [...]

Catalepsy and the re-animation of the dead have been represented as most uncanny themes. But things of this sort again are very common in fairy-stories. Who would be so bold as to call it an uncanny moment, for instance, when Snow-White opens her eyes once more? And the resuscitation of the dead in miracles, as in the New Testament, elicits feelings quite unrelated to the uncanny. [...] Another consideration is this: whence come the uncanny influences of silence, darkness and solitude? Do not these factors point to the part played by danger in the aetiology[2] of what is uncanny, notwithstanding that they

1 Returning to the womb.

2 A term, mainly used in medicine, for the science that researches the cause or origin of a disease.

are also the most frequent accompaniment of the expression of fear in infancy? And are we in truth justified in entirely ignoring intellectual uncertainty as a factor, seeing that we have admitted its importance in relation to death?

It is evident that we must be prepared to admit that there are other elements besides those set down here determining the production of uncanny feelings. We might say that these preliminary results have satisfied psychoanalytic interest in the problem of the uncanny, and that what remains probably calls for an aesthetic valuation. But that would be to open the door to doubts about the exact value of our general contention that the uncanny proceeds from something familiar which has been repressed.

One thing we may observe which may help us to resolve these uncertainties: nearly all the instances which contradict our hypothesis are taken from the realm of fiction and literary productions. This may suggest a possible differentiation between the uncanny that is actually experienced, and the uncanny as we merely picture it or read about it. [...]

The uncanny as it is depicted in *literature*, in stories and imaginative productions, merits in truth a separate discussion. To begin with, it is a much more fertile province than the uncanny in real life, for it contains the whole of the later and something more besides, something that cannot be found in real life. The distinction between what has been repressed and what has been surmounted cannot be transposed on to the uncanny in fiction without profound modification; for the realm of phantasy depends for its very existence on the fact that its content is not submitted to the reality-testing faculty. The somewhat paradoxical result is that *in the first place a great deal that is not uncanny in fiction would be so if it happened in real life; and in the second place that there are many more means of creating uncanny effects in fiction than there are in real life.*

The story-teller has this license among many others, that he can select his world of representation so that it either coincides with the realities we are familiar with or departs from them in what particulars he pleases. We accept his ruling in every case. In fairy-tales, for instance, the world of reality is left behind from the very start, and the animistic system of beliefs[1] is frankly adopted. Wish-fulfillments, secret powers, omnipotence of thoughts, animation of lifeless objects, all the elements so common in fairy-stories, can exert no uncanny influence here; for, as we have learnt, that feeling cannot arise unless there is a conflict of judgement whether things which have been "surmounted" and are regarded as incredible are not, after all, possible; and this problem is excluded from the beginning by the setting of the story. And thus we see that such stories as have furnished us with most of the contradictions to our hypothesis of the uncanny confirm the first part of our proposition—that in the realm of fiction many things are not uncanny which would be so if they happened in real life. In the case of the fairy-story there are other contributory factors, which we

1 Animism held that things, places, and animals all had spirits. It is at the core of many mythologies.

shall briefly touch upon later.

The story-teller can also choose a setting which, though less imaginary than the world of fairy tales, does yet differ from the real world by admitting superior spiritual entities such as daemonic influences or departed spirits. So long as they remain within their setting of poetic reality their usual attribute of uncanniness fails to attach to such beings. The souls in Dante's *Inferno*, or the ghostly apparitions in *Hamlet*, *Macbeth* or *Julius Caesar*, may be gloomy and terrible enough, but they are no more really uncanny than is Homer's jovial world of gods. We order our judgement to the imaginary reality imposed on us by the writer, and regard souls, spirits and spectres as though their existence had the same validity in their world as our own has in the external world. And then in this case too we are spared all trace of the uncanny.

The situation is altered as soon as the writer pretends to move in the world of common reality. In this case he accepts all the conditions operating to produce uncanny feelings in real life; and everything that would have an uncanny effect in reality has it in his story. But in this case, too, he can increase his effect and multiply it far beyond what could happen in reality, by bringing about events which never or very rarely happen in fact. He takes advantage, as it were, of our supposedly surmounted superstitiousness; he deceives us into thinking that he is giving us the sober truth, and then after all oversteps the bounds of possibility. We react to his inventions as we should have reacted to real experiences; by the time we have seen through his trick it is already too late and the author has achieved his object; but it must be added that his success is not unalloyed. We retain a feeling of dissatisfaction, a kind of grudge against the attempted deceit. [...] The writer has then one more means he can use to escape our rising vexation and at the same time to improve his chances of success. It is this, that he should keep us in the dark for a long time about the precise nature of the conditions he has selected for the world he writes about, or that he should cunningly and ingeniously avoid any definite information on the point at all throughout the book. Speaking generally, however, we find a confirmation of the second part of our proposition—that fiction presents more opportunities for creating uncanny sensations than are possible in real life.

Strictly speaking, all these complications relate only to that class of the uncanny which proceeds from forms of thought that have been surmounted. The class which proceeds from repressed complexes is more irrefragable and remains as powerful in fiction as in real experience, except in one point. The uncanny belonging to the first class—that proceeding from forms of thought that have been surmounted—retains this quality in fiction as in experience so long as the setting is one of physical reality; but as soon as it is given an arbitrary and unrealistic setting in fiction, it is apt to lose its quality of the uncanny.

It is clear that we have not exhausted the possibilities of poetic license and the privileges enjoyed by story writers in evoking or in excluding an uncanny feeling. In the main we adopt an unvarying passive attitude towards experience and are acted upon by our physical environment. But the story-teller has a peculiarly directive influence over us; by means of the states of mind into which he can put us and the expectations he can rouse in us, he is able to guide the current of our emotions, dam it up in one direction and make it flow in another, and he often obtains a great variety of effects from the same material. All this is nothing new, and has doubtless long since been fully taken into account by professors of aesthetics. We have drifted into this field of research half involuntarily, through the temptation to explain certain instances which contradicted our theory of the causes of the uncanny.

## Christopher Craft

# from "'Kiss Me with Those Red Lips': Gender and Inversion in Bram Stoker's *Dracula*"[1]

(1984)

When Joseph Sheridan Le Fanu observed in *Carmilla* (1872) that "the vampire is prone to be fascinated with an engrossing vehemence resembling the passion of love" and that vampiric pleasure is heightened "by the gradual approaches of an artful courtship," he identified clearly the analogy between monstrosity and sexual desire that would prove, under a subsequent Freudian stimulus, paradigmatic for future readings of vampirism.[2] Modern critical accounts of *Dracula*, for instance, almost universally agree that vampirism both expresses and distorts an originally sexual energy. That distortion, the representation of desire under the defensive mask of monstrosity, betrays the fundamental psychological ambivalence identified by Franco Moretti when he writes that "vampirism is an excellent example of the identity of desire and fear."[3] This interfusion of sexual desire and the fear that the moment of erotic fulfillment may occasion the erasure of the conventional and integral self informs both the central action in *Dracula* and the surcharged emotion of the characters about to be kissed by "those red lips."[4] So powerful an ambivalence, generating both errant erotic impulses and compensatory anxieties, demands a strict, indeed an almost schematic formal management of narrative material. In *Dracula* Stoker borrows from Mary Shelley's *Frankenstein* and Robert Louis Stevenson's *Dr. Jekyll and Mr. Hyde* a narrative strategy characterized by a predictable, if variable, triple rhythm. Each of these texts first invites or admits the monster, then entertains and is entertained by monstrosity for some extended duration, until

1 Originally published in *Representations*, vol. 8, Fall 1984, pp. 107–33.

2 Joseph Sheridan Le Fanu, *Carmilla*, in *The Best Ghost Stories of J.S. Le Fanu* (New York, 1964): p. 337; this novella of lesbian vampirism, which appeared first in Le Fanu's *In a Glass Darkly* (1872), predates *Dracula* by twenty-five years. [Craft's note]

3 Franco Moretti, *Signs Taken for Wonders* (Thetford, 1983), p. 100. [Craft's note]

4 Bram Stoker, *Dracula* (New York, 1979): p. 51. [Craft's note]

in its closing pages it expels or repudiates the monster and all the disruption that he/she/it brings.

Obviously enough, the first element in this triple rhythm corresponds formally to the text's beginning or generative moment, to its need to produce the monster, while the third element corresponds to the text's terminal moment, to its need both to destroy the monster it has previously admitted and to end the narrative that houses the monster. Interposed between these antithetical gestures of admission and expulsion is the gothic novel's prolonged middle, during which the text affords its ambivalence a degree of play intended to produce a pleasurable, indeed a thrilling anxiety. Within its extended middle, the gothic novel entertains its resident demon—is, indeed, entertained by it—and the monster, now ascendant in its strength, seems for a time potent enough to invert the "natural" order and overwhelm the comforting closure of the text. That threat, of course, is contained and finally nullified by the narrative requirement that the monster be repudiated and the world of normal relations restored; thus, the gesture of expulsion, compensating for the original irruption of the monstrous, brings the play of monstrosity to its predictable close. This narrative rhythm, whose tripartite cycle of admission-entertainment-expulsion enacts sequentially an essentially simultaneous psychological equivocation, provides aesthetic management of the fundamental ambivalence that motivates these texts and our reading of them.

While such isomorphism of narrative method obviously implies affinities and similarities among these different texts, it does not argue identity of meaning. However similar *Frankenstein*, *Dr. Jekyll and Mr. Hyde*, and *Dracula* may be, differences nevertheless obtain, and these differences bear the impress of authorial, historical, and institutional pressures. This essay therefore offers not a reading of monstrosity in general, but rather an account of Bram Stoker's particular articulation of the vampire metaphor in *Dracula*, a book whose fundamental anxiety, an equivocation about the relationship between desire and gender, repeats, with a monstrous difference, a pivotal anxiety of late Victorian culture. Jonathan Harker, whose diary opens the novel, provides *Dracula*'s most precise articulation of this anxiety. About to be kissed by the "weird sisters,"[1] the incestuous vampiric daughters who share Castle Dracula with the Count, a supine Harker thrills to a double passion:

> All three had brilliant white teeth, that shone like pearls against the ruby of their voluptuous lips. There was something about them that made me uneasy, *some longing and at the same time some deadly fear.* I felt in my heart a wicked, burning desire that they would kiss me with those red lips.[2]

1 *Dracula* 64. [Craft's note]
2 *Dracula* 51. [Craft's note and emphasis]

Immobilized by the competing imperatives of "wicked desire" and "deadly fear," Harker awaits an erotic fulfillment that entails both the dissolution of the boundaries of the self and the thorough subversion of conventional Victorian gender codes, which constrained the mobility of sexual desire and varieties of genital behavior by according to the more active male the right and responsibility of vigorous appetite, while requiring the more passive female to "suffer and be still." John Ruskin, concisely formulating Victorian conventions of sexual difference, provides us with a useful synopsis: "The man's power is active, progressive, defensive. He is eminently the doer, the creator, the discoverer, the defender. His intellect is for speculation and invention; his energy for adventure, for war, and for conquest...." Woman, predictably enough, bears a different burden: "She must be enduringly, incorruptibly, good; instinctively, infallibly wise—wise, not for self-development, but for self-renunciation... wise, not with the narrowness of insolent and loveless pride, but with the passionate gentleness of an infinitely variable, because infinitely applicable, modesty of service—the true changefulness of woman."[1] Stoker, whose vampiric women exercise a far more dangerous "changefulness" than Ruskin imagines, anxiously inverts this conventional pattern, as virile Jonathan Harker enjoys a "feminine" passivity and awaits a delicious penetration from a woman whose demonism is figured as the power to penetrate. A swooning desire for an overwhelming penetration and an intense aversion to the demonic potency empowered to gratify that desire compose the fundamental motivating action and emotion in *Dracula*.

This ambivalence, always excited by the imminence of the vampiric kiss, finds its most sensational representation in the image of the Vampire Mouth, the central and recurring image of the novel: "there was a deliberate voluptuousness which was both thrilling and repulsive... I could see in the moonlight the moisture shining on the red tongue as it lapped the white sharp teeth."[2] That is Harker describing one of the three vampire women at Castle Dracula. Here is Dr. Seward's description of the Count: "His eyes flamed red with devilish passion: the great nostrils of the white aquiline nose opened wide and quivered at the edges; and the white sharp teeth, behind the full lips of the blood-dripping mouth, champed together like those of a wild beast."[3] As the primary site of erotic experience in *Dracula*, this mouth equivocates, giving the lie to the easy separation of the masculine and the feminine. Luring at first with an inviting orifice, a promise of red softness, but delivering instead a piercing bone, the vampire mouth fuses and confuses what Dracula's civilized nemesis, Van Helsing and his Crew of Light, works so hard to separate—the gender-based categories of the penetrating and the receptive, or, to use Van Helsing's language, the complementary categories of "brave men" and "good women." With

1 John Ruskin's *Sesame and Lilies* (New York, 1974): pp. 59–60. [Craft's note]

2 *Dracula* 52. [Craft's note]

3 *Dracula* 336. [Craft's note]

its soft flesh barred by hard bone, its red crossed by white, this mouth compels opposites and contrasts into a frightening unity, and it asks some disturbing questions. Are we male or are we female? Do we have penetrators or orifices? And if both, what does that mean? And what about our bodily fluids, the red and the white? What are the relations between blood and semen, milk and blood? Furthermore, this mouth, bespeaking the subversion of the stable and lucid distinctions of gender, is the mouth of all vampires, male and female.

Yet we must remember that the vampire mouth is first of all Dracula's mouth, and that all subsequent versions of it (in *Dracula* all vampires other than the Count are female) merely repeat as diminished simulacra the desire of the Great Original, that "father or furtherer of a new order of beings."[1] Dracula himself, calling his children "my jackals to do my bidding when I want to feed," identifies the systematic creation of female surrogates who exact his will and desire.[2] This should remind us that the novel's opening anxiety, its first articulation of the vampiric threat, derives from Dracula's hovering interest in Jonathan Harker; the sexual threat that this novel first evokes, manipulates, sustains, but never finally represents is that Dracula will seduce, penetrate, drain another male. The suspense and power of *Dracula*'s opening section, of that phase of the narrative which we have called the invitation to monstrosity, proceeds precisely from this unfulfilled sexual ambition. Dracula's desire to fuse with a male, most explicitly evoked when Harker cuts himself shaving, subtly and dangerously suffuses this text. Always postponed and never directly enacted, this desire finds evasive fulfillment in an important series of heterosexual displacements.

Dracula's ungratified desire to vamp Harker is fulfilled instead by his three vampiric daughters, whose anatomical femininity permits, because it masks, the silently interdicted homoerotic embrace between Harker and the Count. Here, in a displacement typical both of this text and the gender-anxious culture from which it arose, an implicitly homoerotic desire achieves representation as a monstrous heterosexuality, as a demonic inversion of normal gender relations. Dracula's daughters offer Harker a feminine form but a masculine penetration:

> Lower and lower went her head as the lips went below the range of my mouth and chin and seemed to fasten on my throat.... I could feel the soft, shivering touch of the lips on the supersensitive skin of my throat, and the hard dents of the two sharp teeth, just touching and pausing there. I closed my eyes in a langorous ecstasy and waited—waited with a beating heart.[3]

1 *Dracula* 360. [Craft's note]
2 *Dracula* 365. [Craft's note]
3 *Dracula* 52. [Craft's note]

This moment, constituting the text's most direct and explicit representation of a male's desire to be penetrated, is governed by a double deflection: first, the agent of penetration is nominally and anatomically (from the mouth down, anyway) female; and second, this dangerous moment, fusing the maximum of desire and the maximum of anxiety, is poised precisely at the brink of penetration. Here the "two sharp teeth," just "touching" and "pausing" there, stop short of the transgression which would unsex Harker and toward which this text constantly aspires and then retreats: the actual penetration of the male.

This moment is interrupted, this penetration denied. Harker's pause at the end of the paragraph ("waited—waited with a beating heart"), which seems to anticipate an imminent piercing, in fact anticipates not the completion but the interruption of the scene of penetration. Dracula himself breaks into the room, drives the women away from Harker, and admonishes them: "How dare you touch him, any of you? How dare you cast eyes on him when I had forbidden it? Back, I tell you all! This man belongs to me."[1] Dracula's intercession here has two obvious effects: by interrupting the scene of penetration, it suspends and disperses throughout the text the desire maximized at the brink of penetration, and it repeats the threat of a more direct libidinous embrace between Dracula and Harker. Dracula's taunt, "This man belongs to me," is suggestive enough, but at no point subsequent to this moment does Dracula kiss Harker, preferring instead to pump him for his knowledge of English law, custom, and language. Dracula, soon departing for England, leaves Harker to the weird sisters, whose final penetration of him, implied but never represented, occurs in the dark interspace to which Harker's journal gives no access.

Hereafter *Dracula* will never represent so directly a male's desire to be penetrated; once in England Dracula, observing a decorous heterosexuality, vamps only women, in particular Lucy Westenra and Mina Harker. The novel, nonetheless, does not dismiss homoerotic desire and threat; rather it simply continues to diffuse and displace it. Late in the text, the Count himself announces a deflected homoeroticism when he admonishes the Crew of Light thus: "My revenge is just begun! I spread it over the centuries, and time is on my side. Your girls that you all love are mine already; and *through them you and others shall yet be mine*."[2] Here Dracula specifies the process of substitution by which "the girls that you all love" mediate and displace a more direct communion among males. Van Helsing, who provides for Lucy transfusions designed to counteract the dangerous influence of the Count, confirms Dracula's declaration of surrogation; he knows that once the transfusions begin, Dracula drains from Lucy's veins not her blood, but rather blood transferred from the veins of the Crew of Light: "even we four who gave our strength to Lucy it also is all to him[*sic*]."[3]

1 *Dracula* 53. [Craft's note]
2 *Dracula* 365. [Craft's note and emphasis]
3 *Dracula* 244. [Craft's note]

Here, emphatically, is another instance of the heterosexual displacement of a desire mobile enough to elude the boundaries of gender. Everywhere in this text such desire seeks a strangely deflected heterosexual distribution; only through women may men touch.

# Stephen D. Arata

## from "The Occidental[1] Tourist: *Dracula* and the Anxiety of Reverse Colonization"[2]

(1990)

II

In many respects, Dracula represents a break from the Gothic tradition of vampires. It is easy, for instance, to forget that the "natural" association of vampires with Transylvania begins with, rather than predates, *Dracula*. The site of Castle Dracula was in fact not determined until well after Stoker had begun to write. As Joseph Bierman points out, Stoker originally signaled his debt to his countryman Le Fanu's *Carmilla* (1872) by locating the castle in "Styria," the scene of the earlier Gothic novella.[3] In rewriting the novel's opening chapters, however, Stoker moved *his* Gothic story to a place that, for readers in 1897, resonated in ways Styria did not. Transylvania was known primarily as part of the vexed "Eastern Question" that so obsessed British foreign policy in the 1880s and '90s. The region was first and foremost the site, not of superstition

1 Occidental: relating to countries of the West as opposed to a term like Oriental: relating to the East.

2 Originally published in *Victorian Studies*, vol. 33, no. 4, 1990, pp. 621–45.

3 Joseph Bierman, "The Genesis and Dating of *Dracula* from Bram Stoker's Working Notes," *Notes and Queries* 24 (1977), 39–41. For a brief description of Stoker's manuscripts and notes for *Dracula*, including a "List of Sources" that Stoker drew up, see Phyllis Roth, *Bram Stoker* (Boston: Twayne, 1982), pp. 145–146. Stoker gleaned his version of Carpathian history and culture entirely from travel narratives, guidebooks, and various works on Eastern European superstitions, legends, and folktales. Daniel Farson, one of Stoker's biographers, mentions his "genius for research" (*The Man Who Wrote Dracula: A Biography of Bram Stoker* [London: Michael Joseph, 1975], p. 148). Stoker's debt to Le Fanu is most immediately evident in a chapter deleted from *Dracula*, in which Harker, travelling to Castle Dracula, discovers the mausoleum of a "Countess Dolingen of Gratz in Styria." The chapter was later reprinted separately as "Dracula's Guest." See *The Bram Stoker Bedside Companion: Ten Stories by the Author of "Dracula,"* ed. Charles Osborne (New York: Taplinger, 1973). [Arata's note]

and Gothic romance, but of political turbulence and racial strife. Victorian readers knew the Carpathians largely for its endemic cultural upheaval and its fostering of a dizzying succession of empires. By moving Castle Dracula there, Stoker gives distinctly political overtones to his Gothic narrative. In Stoker's version of the myth, vampires are intimately linked to military conquest and to the rise and fall of empires. According to Dr. Van Helsing, the vampire is the unavoidable consequence of any invasion: "He have follow the wake of the berserker Icelander, the devil-begotten Hun, the Slav, the Saxon, the Magyar."[1]

Nowhere else in the Europe of 1897 could provide a more fertile breeding ground for the undead than the Count's homeland. The Western accounts of the region that Stoker consulted invariably stress the ceaseless clash of antagonistic cultures in the Carpathians.[2] The cycle of empire—rise, decay, collapse, displacement—was there displayed in a particularly compressed and vivid manner. "Greeks, Romans, Huns, Avars, Magyars, Turks, Slavs, French and Germans, all have come and seen and gone, seeking conquest one over the other," opens one late-century account.[3] The Count himself confirms that his homeland has been the scene of perpetual invasion: "there is hardly a foot of soil in all this region that has not been enriched by the blood of men, patriots or invaders," he tells Harker.[4] His subsequent question is thus largely rhetorical: "Is it a wonder that we were a conquering race?"[5]

The "race" in which Dracula claims membership is left ambiguous here. He refers at once to his Szekely warrior past and to his vampiric present. The ambiguity underscores the impossibility of untangling the two aspects of Dracula's essential nature, since his vampirism is interwoven with his status as a conqueror and invader. Here Stoker departs significantly from his literary predecessors. Unlike Polidori and Le Fanu, for instance, who depict their vampires as wan and enervated, Stoker makes Dracula vigorous and energetic. Polidori's Count Ruthven and Le Fanu's Carmilla represent the aristocrat as decadent aesthete; their vampirism is an extension of the traditional aristocratic vices of sensualism and conspicuous consumption. Dracula represents the nobleman

1 Bram Stoker, *Dracula* (1897; rpt. Harmondsworth: Penguin, 1984), p. 286. [Arata's note]

2 I have based my observations on the standard Victorian and Edwardian works in English on the region, which include John Paget, *Hungary and Transylvania* (London: Murray, 1855); James O. Noyes, *Roumania* (New York: Rudd & Carlton, 1857); Charles Boner, *Transylvania: Its Products and Its People* (London: Longmans, 1865); Andrew W. Crosse, *Round about the Carpathians* (Edinburgh and London: William Blackwood and Sons, 1878); C. Johnson, *On the Track of the Crescent* (London: Hurst & Blackett, 1885); M. Edith Durham, *The Burden of the Balkans* (London: Edward Arnold, 1905); Jean Victor Bates, *Our Allies and Enemies in the Near East* (New York: E.P. Dutton & Co., n.d.); and especially Emily Gerard, *The Land Beyond the Forest: Facts, Figures, and Fancies from Transylvania, 2 vols.* (Edinburgh and London: William Blackwood and Sons, 1888). [Arata's note]

3 Bates p. 3. [Arata's note]

4 P. 33. [Arata's note]

5 P. 41. [Arata's note]

as warrior.[1] His activities after death carry on his activities in life; in both cases he has successfully engaged in forms of conquest and domination.

*Racial* conquest and domination, we should immediately add. Stoker continues a Western tradition of seeing unrest in Eastern Europe primarily in terms of racial strife. For Stoker, the vampire "race" is simply the most virulent and threatening of the numerous warrior races—Berserker, Hun, Turk, Saxon, Slovak, Magyar, Szekely—inhabiting the area. Nineteenth-century accounts of the Carpathians repeatedly stress its polyracial character. The standard Victorian work on the region, Charles Boner's *Transylvania* (1865), begins by marveling at this spectacle of variety:

> The diversity of character which the various physiognomies present that meet you at every step, also tell of the many nations which are here brought together.... The slim lithe Hungarian... the more oriental Wallachian, with softer, sensuous air,—in her style of dress and even in her carriage unlike a dweller in the West; a Moldavian princess, wrapped in a Turkish shawl.... And now a Serb marches proudly past, his countenance calm as a Turk's; or a Constantinople merchant sweeps along in his loose robes and snowy turban. There are, too, Greeks, Dalmations, and Croats, all different in feature: there is no end to the variety.[2]

Transylvania is what Dracula calls the "whirlpool of European races" (p. 41), but within that whirlpool racial interaction usually involved conflict, not accommodation. Racial violence could in fact reach appalling proportions, as in the wholesale massacres, widely reported by the British press, of Armenians by Turks in 1894 and 1896, the years in which *Dracula* was being written. For Western writers and readers, these characteristics—racial heterogeneity combined with racial intolerance considered barbaric in its intensity—defined the area east and south of the Danube, with the Carpathians at the imaginative center of the turmoil.

1 Several critics have, correctly I think, placed Dracula in the tradition of aristocratic rakes like Richardson's Lovelace, who in turn have their roots in the medieval lord with his demands for the *droit de seigneur*. This view can obscure Stoker's emphasis on Dracula's military, rather than just his sexual, prowess. [...] It is also possible to read *Dracula* as a bourgeois fantasy of aristocratic power and privilege: like the hereditary nobleman, Dracula is associated most closely with land (he must stay in contact with his native soil to survive), wealth (which he literally digs out of the land on the night of Harker's arrival in Transylvania), family (his name is transmitted through generations without the line being interrupted), and of course blood (which in turn is connected with the other three; remember, for instance, that when Harker cuts Dracula with his knife, he "bleeds" a "stream of gold" coins [p. 364]). For the middle-class Victorian audience, the vision of aristocratic puissance embodied by Dracula would have been deeply attractive, especially given the ineffectuality of the novel's only English aristocrat, Lord Godalming. [Arata's note]

2 Pp. 1–2. [Arata's note]

By situating Dracula in the Carpathians, and by continually blurring the lines between the Count's vampiric and warrior activities, Stoker forges seemingly "natural" links among three of his principal concerns: racial strife, the collapse of empire, and vampirism. It is important too to note the sequence of events. As Van Helsing says, vampires follow "in [the] wake of" imperial decay.[1] Vampires are generated by racial enervation and the decline of empire, not vice versa. They are produced, in other words, by the very conditions characterizing late-Victorian Britain.

Stoker thus transforms the materials of the vampire myth, making them bear the weight of the culture's fears over its declining status. The appearance of vampires becomes the sign of profound trouble. With vampirism marking the intersection of racial strife, political upheaval, and the fall of empire, Dracula's move to London indicates that Great Britain, rather than the Carpathians, is now the scene of these connected struggles. The Count has penetrated to the heart of modern Europe's largest empire, and his very presence seems to presage its doom:

> This was the being I was helping to transfer to London [Harker writes in anguish] where, perhaps for centuries to come, he might, amongst its teeming millions, satiate his lust for blood, and create a new and ever widening circle of semi-demons to batten on the helpless. (p. 67)

The late-Victorian nightmare of reverse colonization is expressed succinctly here: Harker envisions semi-demons spreading through the realm, colonizing bodies and land indiscriminately. The Count's "lust for blood" points in both directions: to the vampire's need for its special food, and also to the warrior's desire for conquest. The Count endangers Britain's integrity as a nation at the same time that he imperils the personal integrity of individual citizens.

Harker's lament highlights the double thrust—political and biological—of Dracula's invasion, while at the same time conflating the two into a single threat. Dracula's twin status as vampire and Szekely warrior suggests that for Stoker the Count's aggressions against the body are also aggressions against the body politic. Indeed, the Count can threaten the integrity of the nation precisely because of the nature of his threat to personal integrity. Again unlike Polidori's Count Ruthven or Le Fanu's Carmilla (or even Thomas Prest's Sir Francis Varney), Dracula imperils not simply his victims' personal identities, but also their cultural, political, and racial selves. In *Dracula* vampirism designates a kind of colonization of the body. Horror arises not because Dracula destroys bodies, but because he appropriates and transforms them. Having yielded to his assault, one literally "goes native" by becoming a vampire oneself. As John Allen Stevenson argues, if "blood" is a sign of racial identity, then Dracula effectively deracinates

1 P. 286. [Arata's note]

his victims.[1] In turn, they receive a new racial identity, one that marks them as literally "Other." Miscegenation leads, not to the mixing of races, but to the biological and political annihilation of the weaker race by the stronger.

Through the vampire myth, Stoker gothicizes the political threats to Britain caused by the enervation of the Anglo-Saxon "race." These threats also operate independently of the Count's vampirism, however, for the vampire was not considered alone in its ability to deracinate. Stoker learned from Emily Gerard that the Roumanians were themselves notable for the way they could "dissolve" the identities of those they came in contact with:

> The Hungarian woman who weds a Roumanian husband will necessarily adopt the dress and manners of his people, and her children will be as good Roumanians as though they had no drop of Magyar blood in their veins; while the Magyar who takes a Roumanian girl for his wife will not only fail to convert her to his ideas, but himself, subdued by her influence, will imperceptibly begin to lose his nationality. This is a fact well know and much lamented by the Hungarians themselves, who live in anticipated apprehension of seeing their people ultimately dissolving into Roumanians.[2]

Gerard's account of the "imperceptible" but inevitable loss of identity—national, cultural, racial—sounds remarkably like the transformations that Lucy and Mina suffer under Dracula's "influence." In life Dracula was a Roumanian (Gerard designates the Szekelys as a branch of the Roumanian race); his ability to deracinate could thus derive as easily from his Roumanian as from his vampire nature.

The "anticipated apprehension" of deracination—of seeing Britons "ultimately dissolving into Roumanians" or vampires or savages—is at the heart of the reverse colonization narrative. For both Gerard and Stoker, the Roumanians' dominance can be traced to a kind of racial puissance that overwhelms its weaker victims. The racial context helps account for what critics routinely note about Dracula: that he is by his very nature vigorous, masterful, energetic, robust. Such attributes are conspicuously absent among the novel's British characters, particularly the men. All the novel's vampires are distinguished by their robust health and their equally robust fertility. The vampire serves, then, to highlight the alarming decline among the British, since the undead are, paradoxically, both "healthier" and more "fertile" than the living. Perversely, a vampiric attack can serve to invigorate its victim. "The adventure of the night does not seem to have harmed her," Mina notes after Lucy's first

1 P. 144. [Arata's note]

2 Gerard, I, 304–305. Scholars have long recognized Stoker's reliance on Gerard. See Roth, *Bram Stoker*, pp. 13–14, and Leonard Wolf, *The Annotated Dracula* (New York: Clarkson Potter, 1975), pp. xiii–xiv and references in his annotations throughout. [Arata's note]

encounter with Dracula; "on the contrary, it has benefited her, for she looks better this morning than she has done in weeks."[1] Indeed, after his attack, Lucy's body initially appears stronger, her eyes brighter, her cheeks rosier. The corresponding enervation that marks the British men is most clearly visible in Harker (he is "pale," "weak-looking," "exhausted," "nervous," "a wreck"), but it can be seen in the other male British characters as well. Harker and Dracula in fact switch places during the novel; Harker becomes tired and white-haired as the action proceeds, while Dracula, whose white hair grows progressively darker, becomes more vigorous.

The vampire's vigor is in turn closely connected with its virility, its ability to produce literally endless numbers of offspring. Van Helsing's concern that the earth in Dracula's boxes be "sterilized"[2] underlines the connection between the Count's threat and his fecundity. In marked contrast, the nonvampires in the novel seem unable to reproduce themselves. Fathers in particular are in short supply: most are either dead (Mr. Westenra, Mr. Harker, Mr. Murray, Mr. Canon), dying (Mr. Hawkins, Lord Godalming, Mr. Swales), or missing (Mr. Seward, Mr. Morris), while the younger men, being unmarried, cannot father legitimately. Even Harker, the novel's only married man, is prohibited from touching Mina after she has been made "unclean." In *Dracula*'s lexicon, uncleanliness is closely related to fertility, but it is the wrong kind of fertility; Mina, the men fear, is perfectly capable of producing "offspring," but not with Jonathan. The prohibition regarding Mina is linked to the fear of vampiric fecundity, a fecundity that threatens to overwhelm the far less prolific British men. Thus, as many critics have pointed out, the arrival of little Quincy Harker at the story's close signals the final triumph over Dracula, since the Harkers' ability to secure an heir—an heir whose racial credentials are seemingly impeccable—is the surest indication that the vampire's threat has been mastered. Even this triumph is precarious, however. Harker proudly notes that his son is named after each of the men in the novel, making them all figurative fathers,[3] yet Quincy's multiple parentage only underscores the original problem. How secure is any racial line when five fathers are needed to produce one son?

Such racial anxieties are clearest in the case of Lucy Westenra. If Dracula's kiss serves to deracinate Lucy, and by doing so to unleash what the male characters consider her incipiently monstrous sexual appetite, then the only way to counter this process is to "re-racinate" her by reinfusing her with the "proper" blood. But Stoker is careful to establish a strict hierarchy among the potential donors. The men give blood in this order: Holmwood, Seward, Van Helsing, Morris. Arthur Holmwood is first choice ostensibly because he is engaged to Lucy, but also, and perhaps more importantly, because his blood is, in Van

1 P. 115. [Arata's note]
2 Pp. 347–355. [Arata's note]
3 P. 449. [Arata's note]

Helsing's words, "more good than" Seward's.[1] As the only English aristocrat in the novel, Holmwood possesses a "blood so pure"[2] that it can restore Lucy's compromised racial identity. Dr. Seward, whose blood though bourgeois is English nonetheless, comes next in line, followed by the two foreigners, Van Helsing and Morris. We should note that Van Helsing's old, Teutonic blood is still preferred over Morris's young, American blood, for reasons I will take up in a moment. Even foreign blood is better than lower-class blood, however. After Lucy suffers what proves to be the fatal attack by Dracula, Van Helsing, looking for blood donors, rejects the four apparently healthy female servants as unsafe: "I fear to trust those women."[3]

More precisely, Van Helsing's distrust of "those women" marks a point of intersection between his usually covert class prejudices and his often overt misogyny.[4] That Dracula propagates his race solely through the bodies of women suggests an affinity, or even an identity, between vampiric sexuality and female sexuality. Both are represented as primitive and voracious, and both threaten patriarchal hegemony. In the novel's (and Victorian Britain's) sexual economy, female sexuality has only one legitimate function, propagation within the bonds of marriage. Once separated from that function, as Lucy's desire is, female sexuality becomes monstrous. The violence of Lucy's demise is grisly enough, but we should not miss the fact that her subjection and Mina's final fate parallel one another. They differ in degree, not kind. By the novel's close, Mina's sexual energy has been harnessed for purely domestic use. In the end, women serve identical purposes for both Dracula and the Western characters. If in this novel blood stands for race, then women quite literally become the vehicles of racial propagation. The struggle between the two camps is thus on one level a struggle over access to women's bodies, and Dracula's biological colonization of women becomes a horrific parody of the sanctioned exploitation practiced by the Western male characters.

By considering the parallel fates of Lucy and Mina, moreover, we can see how the fear and guilt characteristic of reverse colonization narratives begin to overlap. The fear generated by the Count's colonization of his victims' bodies—a colonization appropriately designated monstrous—modulates into guilt that his practices simply repeat those of the "good" characters. Dracula's invasion and appropriation of female bodies does not distinguish him from his Western antagonists as much as at first appears. Instead of being uncannily Other, the vampire is here revealed as disquietingly familiar. And since the colonizations of bodies and territory are closely linked, the same blurring and distinctions occur when we consider more closely the nature of the Count's invasion of

1 P. 149. [Arata's note]
2 P. 149. [Arata's note]
3 P. 180. [Arata's note]
4 A full discussion of the gender issues raised by *Dracula* is outside the scope of this essay. Many critics have discussed the thinly disguised fear of women evident in the novel. [...] [Arata's note]

Britain. Just as Dracula's vampirism mirrors the domestic practices of Victorian patriarchs, so his invasion of London in order to "batten on the helpless" natives there mirrors British imperial activities abroad.

As a transplanted Irishman, one whose national allegiances were conspicuously split, Stoker was particularly sensitive to the issues raised by British imperial conquest and domination. Britain's subjugation of Ireland was marked by a brutality often exceeding what occurred in the colonies, while the stereotype of the "primitive... dirty, vengeful, and violent" Irishman was in most respects identical to that of the most despised "savage."[1] The ill will characterizing Anglo-Irish relations in the late nineteenth century, exacerbated by the rise of Fenianism and the debate over Home Rule, far surpassed the tensions that arose as a result of British rule elsewhere. When that ill will erupted into violence, as it did in the 1882 Phoenix Park murders, Victorian readers could see, up close and in sharp focus, the potential consequences of imperial domination. For Stoker's audience, Dracula's invasion of Britain would conceivably have aroused seldom dormant fears of an Irish uprising.

The lack of autobiographical materials makes it difficult to determine the extent, if any, to which Stoker consciously felt himself in solidarity with his Irish brethren. On the one hand, his few published essays, particularly one advocating censorship, reveal a deeply conservative outlook in which "duty to the [British] state" outweighs all other considerations, even those of a dubious freedom or self-determination. On the other hand, through Stoker's very adherence to what he calls "forms of restraint" runs a deeply anarchic streak. The attraction of forbidden, outlawed, disruptive action is evident enough in *Dracula* as well as in Stoker's other fictions; the same tension between restraint and rebellion may have characterized his relation to the ruling state. It probably also characterized his professional life. Certainly his status as glorified manservant to the autocratic Henry Irving almost uncannily reenacted, on the personal level, the larger cultural pattern of English domination and Irish subservience. Stoker's lifelong passion for Irving had its dark underside: the rumors, persistent in Stoker's lifetime, that Count Dracula was modelled on Irving suggests the deep ambivalence with which the transplanted Irishman regarded his professional benefactor. Like Quincey Morris, Stoker seems finally to stand in alliance with his English companions without ever being entirely of their camp.

*Dracula* suggests two equations in relation to English–Irish politics: not just, Dracula is to England as Ireland is to England, but, Dracula is to England as England is to Ireland. In Count Dracula, Victorian readers could recognize their culture's imperial ideology mirrored back as a kind of monstrosity. Dracula's journey from Transylvania to England could be read as a reversal of Britain's imperial exploitations of "weaker" races, including the Irish. This

1 See L.P. Curtis, *Anglo-Saxons and Celts: A Study of Anti-Irish Prejudice in Victorian England* (Bridgeport, CT: Bridgeport University Press, 1968). [Arata's note]

mirroring extends not just to the imperial practices themselves, but to their epistemological underpinnings. Before Dracula successfully invades the spaces of his victims' bodies or land, he first invades the spaces of their knowledge. The Count operates in several distinct registers in the novel. He is both the warrior nobleman, whose prowess dwarfs that of the novel's enfeebled English aristocrat, Lord Godalming, and the primitive savage, whose bestiality, fecundity, and vigor alternately repel and attract. But he is also what we might call an incipient "Occidentalist" scholar. Dracula's physical mastery of his British victims begins with an intellectual appropriation of their culture, which allows him to delve the workings of the "native mind." As Harker discovers, the Count's expertise in "English life and customs and manners"[1] provides the groundwork for his exploitative invasion of Britain. Thus, in Dracula the British characters see their own ideology reflected back as a form of bad faith, since the Count's Occidentalism both mimics and reverses the more familiar Orientalism underwriting Western imperial practices.[2]

1 P. 30. [Arata's note]
2 See Edward Said, *Orientalism* (New York: Vintage, 1979). [Arata's note]

## Sue-Ellen Case

# from "Tracking the Vampire"[1]

(1991)

The dominant image of the vampire began to appear in Western Europe in the eighteenth century through tales and reports from small villages in the East. In literature, Mario Praz[2] observes in *The Romantic Agony*, the vampire appears in the nineteenth century as the Byronic hero who destroys not only himself but his lovers. Praz finds "the love crime" to be essential to the figure, who early in the century was a man, but in the second half—what Praz calls "the time of Decadence"[3]—was a woman. For the purposes of queer theory, the most important work in the dominant tradition is "Carmilla" by Sheridan Le Fanu, the first lesbian vampire story, in which the lesbian, desiring and desired by her victim, slowly brings her closer through the killing kiss of blood. In the dominant discourse, this kiss of blood is a weakening device that played into male myths of menstruation, where women's monthly loss of blood was associated with their pale, weak image.[4] [...]

I realize that this seems to be a move away from the material, historical condition of lesbians. Yet the entry point of this theory rests upon my entrance, as an adolescent, into the speaking and hearing, reading and writing about my sexuality. Insofar as I am queer, or lesbian, this identity is in consonance with the discursive strategies that those words represent historically: my desire and my sexual practice are inscribed in these words and, conversely, these words—the historical practice of a discourse—are inscribed in my sexual practice. Take, for instance, my years of furtive pleasure between the sheets, or my years of promiscuous tweeking and twaddling. Both eras were performances of the

1 Originally published in *Differences: A Journal of Feminist Cultural Studies*, vol. 3, no. 2, 1991, pp. 1–20.

2 An Italian art and literature critic, Praz is most known for his survey of decadent and erotic themes in eighteenth- and nineteenth-century European literature, *The Romantic Agony* (1933).

3 Pp. 75–7. [Case's note]

4 The prejudice was so convincing that a fashion arose among middle-class women to visit the slaughterhouse and drink the blood of an ox to strengthen themselves. See Dijkstra, "Metamorphoses of the Vampire: Dracula and His Daughters," in *Idols* [*of Perversity: Fantasies of Feminine Evil in Fin-de-Siècle Culture* (1986)], particularly 337–38. [Case's note]

double trope of the "she," either as the doubly inferior, marked by oppression, or as double pleasure, reveling in transgression. To ask "will the real lesbian please stand up," when she is em-bedded in the dominant discursive mandate to disappear, or in the subcultural subversion to flaunt her distance from the "real," is like asking the vampire to appear in the mirror. (She made me write that. For now is the time of her entrance on screen.) The double "she," in combination with the queer fanged creature, produces the vampire. The vampire is the queer in its lesbian mode.

## THE EN-TRANCED TAKE: THE LESBIAN AND THE VAMPIRE

So, finally, now, the vampire can make her appearance. But how does she appear? How can she appear, when the visible is not in the domain of the queer, when the apparatus of representation still belongs to the un-queer? This far, we've had the fun, fun, fun of imagining the liberating, creative powers of the queer in representation. Unfortunately, daddy always takes the T-bird away and the vampire, those two "she's" in the driver's seat, is left standing at the cross-roads of queer theory and dominant discourse. Although the "she" is not mimetic of gender, "she" is shaped, in part, by her pronominal history—that is, how "she" is constructed elsewhere and previously in language. Along the metaphorical axis, "she" is somehow the queer relative of the other girls. What this "she" vampire flaunts is the cross—the crossing out of her seductive pleasure, the plenitude of proximity and the break. Thus, the dominant gaze constructs a vampire that serves only as a proscription—is perceived only as a transgression: interpolated between the viewer and the vampire is the cross—the crossing out of her image. Dominant representation has made of the vampire a horror story.

But this site/sight of proscription lingers in the theoretical construction of the gaze in feminist theory as well—specifically in theories of the gaze proceeding from psychoanalytic presumptions. There, the vampire is subjected to the familiar mode of "seduced and abandoned," or "the recreational use of the lesbian," for while such heterosexist feminist discourse flirts with her, it ultimately double-crosses her with the hegemonic notion of "woman," reinscribing "her" in the generational model and making horrible what must not be seductive. The vampire as the site or sight of the undead leads such feminist discourse back to the mother's right to life, where fruition becomes the counter discourse of exclusion. [...]

Popular lore tells us that if we look at the vampire without the proscriptions that expel her, our gaze will be hypnotically locked into hers and we will become her victims. The feminist theorists, aware of the seductive quality of the vampire's look, excavate the proscription to discover the desire below. For example, Linda Williams's ground-breaking article "When the Woman Looks" constructs a certain dynamic of women looking at monsters. Williams notes that when the woman sees the monster, she falls into a trance-like fascination that "fails to maintain the distance between observer and observed so essential to the 'pleasure' of the voyeur." As the woman looks at the monster, her "look of horror paralyzes her in such a way that distance is overcome."[1] Hers is an en-tranced look, and the fascination in it could be read as a response to lesbian desire.

However, Williams's notion of proximity in the look proceeds from the hegemonic notion of "woman." As Mary Ann Doane phrases it, woman is "[t]oo close to herself, entangled in her own enigma, she could not step back, could not achieve the necessary distance of a second look."[2] Thus Williams's reading of woman's trance-like lock into the gaze with the monster is an extension of "woman's" condition in the gaze. How this "woman" is locked in the gaze, or what constitutes her pleasurable proximity, figures Williams, is her identification with the monster—a shared identification between monster and woman in representation: since they both share the status of object, they have a special empathy between them. In other words, this entranced seeing and proximity in the vision, consonant with psychoanalytic theory, rests upon the special status of "woman" as object of the viewer's scopophilia—and hence the shared identification of woman and monster. I want to come back to this premise later, but let us continue for a moment to see how Williams situates sexuality within this monstrous looking.

Within the horror genre, she observes, it is in the monster's body that the sexual interest resides, and not in the bland hero's. The monster's power is one of sexual difference from the normal male; thus, the monster functions like woman in representing the threat of castration. So, as Williams would have it, when the woman looks at the monster and when the cross is removed from before her gaze, they are totally proximate and contiguous, alike in sexual difference from the male and transfixed, outside of scopophilia, in the pleasures of shared sexual transgression. Desire is aroused in this gaze, but Williams quickly defers it to identification. In relegating the proximity and desire in the trance between woman and monster to (female) identification, Williams has securely locked any promise of lesbian sexuality into an Oedipal, heterosexual context.

This "woman," then, in Doane, Williams, and others, is really heterosexual woman. Though her desire is aroused vis-à-vis another woman (a monstrous occasion), and they are totally proximate, they identify with rather than desire one another. Their desire is still locked in the phallocratic order, and the same-sex taboo is still safely in place. What melds monster to woman is not lesbian

1 [Williams, Linda. "When the Woman Looks." *Re-vision: Essays in Feminist Film Criticism*. Ed. Mary Ann Doane, Patricia Mellencamp, and Linda Williams. University Publications of America, 1984. 83–99.] P. 86. [Case's note]

2 [Doane, Mary Ann. "Film and the Masquerade: Theorizing the Female Spectator." *Screen* 23, 3–4 (1982): 74–87.] P. 75–6. [Case's note]

desire—trance is not entranced—but finally daughter emulating mother in the Oedipal triangle with the absent male still at the apex. By inscribing in this configuration of looking a sexuality that is shared and not male, Williams both raises the possibility of the site of lesbian looking and simultaneously cancels it out. Like the image of the vampire in the currency of dominant discourse, this heterosexist configuration of the gaze seems to derive some power for its formulation by careening dangerously close to the abyss of same-sex desire, both invoking and revoking it. The critical pleasure resides in configuring the look by what it refuses to see. Thus, the revels of transgression enjoyed by the queer remain outside the boundaries of heterosexist proscription. You can hear the music, but you can't go to the party. Nevertheless, the site/sight of the monstrous is invoked and, though horrible, is sometimes negatively accurate and often quite seductive.

The hegemonic spread of the psychoanalytic does not allow for an imaginary queer. It simply reconfigures queer desire back into the heterosexual by deploying sexual difference through metaphors. [...]

In his work on the supernatural, Tzvetan Todorov maintains that the central diegetic force in these tales is their atmosphere—an atmosphere of proximity. Settings in fog and gloom connect the disparate elements of the structure through a palpable, atmospheric "touching." Judith Mayne, writing on *Nosferatu* (1922), agrees, describing the twilight as a "dangerous territory where opposing terms are not so easily distinguishable."[1] From the entranced look, through the mise en scène, to the narrative structure, proximity pervades the vampire lore. But why is this proximate potential represented as horror by the dominant culture? There is a supernatural tale that unlocks the code of the prohibition against this proximity—Freud's paper on the uncanny. Freud's entry, so to speak, into the uncanny is through the notion of the double and of doubling processes, such as the feeling that we have been somewhere before. Thus, the uncanny for Freud is a kind of haunting proximity. [...]

So this proscribed proximity, the very world of vampires and of the "entranced" women who view them, is the desire for what Freud calls intra-uterine existence. More than the fog, the gloom, the cobwebs, and the twilight, Freud's article serves as an exact description of the vampire's sleep in her coffin: toward the end of every night, she races back there, to her native soil, and enjoys the lustful pleasure of being buried alive and dead—her intra-uterine re-creation. However, while Freud unlocks one repressive code to liberate a certain pleasure, his notion of intra-uterine pleasure further defers the actual pleasure proscribed here. And the feminist psychoanalytic theorists carry on his tradition: his intra-uterine pleasure, this *jouissance*, can only be enjoyed as a pre-Oedipal *jouissance* with the mother.

1 Mayne, Judith. "Dracula in the Twilight: Murnau's *Nosferatu* (1922)." *German Film and Literature: Adaptations and Transformations*. Ed. Eric Rentscheler. New York: Methuen, 1986. 25–39. p. 27. [Case's note]

If, for Lacan, sexuality is dominated by the phallus in a trench coat, for Kristeva and her ilk, it is the masked mother. The feminist allocation of this lascivious pleasure of proximity with the mother is simply a bad hangover from too much Freud—it shares his anxieties and proclivities. When Freud imagined this lustful recreation, he imagined the mise en scène as dirty and musty, with the sense of an old vampire who's about to exhibit her true wrinkled self. That's Freud's sexist anxiety about the wrinkled, musty vagina displaced onto an ageist fantasy of the old mother. Moreover, the idea of this pre-Oedipal *jouissance* with the mother reinscribes Freud's patriarchal obsession with genealogy and sexuality as generative—part of the nineteenth-century proscription against homosexuality. Locating *jouissance* in a mother keeps heterosexuality at the center of the picture—the son can insert himself into the site of *jouissance*. [...]

On the brighter (or the darker) side of things, in tracking the vampire, we can here re-imagine her various strengths: celebrating the fact that she cannot see herself in the mirror and remains outside that door into the symbolic, her proximate vanishing appears as a political strategy; her bite pierces platonic metaphysics and subject/object positions; and her fanged kiss brings her the chosen one, trembling with ontological, orgasmic shifts, into the state of the undead. What the dominant discourse represents as an emptying out, a draining away, in contrast to the impregnating kiss of the heterosexual, becomes an activism in representation.

Now, if you watch some recent vampire films, it may seem that things are getting better. Surely, you offer, the confining nineteenth-century codes are liberalized in the late twentieth century. For example, if you watch some recent vampire films, you may note that the vampire is actually portrayed as a lesbian. But this move only reflects a kind of post-Watergate strategy of representation; that is, don't keep any secrets because they can be revealed, just reveal the repression and that will serve to confirm it. So the vampire is portrayed as lesbian, but costumed in all the same conventions, simply making the proscription literal. The strategic shift here is in revelation, not representation. Whether she is the upper-class, decadent, cruel Baroness in *Daughters of Darkness* (1971; played by the late Delphine Seyrig, who was marked in the subculture as a lesbian actor), whose coercive lesbian sex act is practiced behind closed doors and whose languorous body proscribes the lesbian as an oozing, French dessert cheese; or, whether she is the rough-trade, breast-biting Austrian lesbian vampire in *Vampire Lovers* (1970), or even the late-capitalist, media-assimilated lesbian vampire in the independent film *Because the Dawn* (1988), her attraction is (in) her proscription. Only the proscription of the lesbian is literally portrayed—the occult becomes cult in the repression.

While the lesbian has become literalized in contemporary vampire films, the proscription against same-sex desire has also been reconfigured in a trope more consonant with late twentieth century conditions. For one thing, nature isn't what it used to be, and likewise, the undead have altered with it. In the nineteenth century, the stable notion of nature as natural and of the natural as good made it possible to configure same-sex desire as unnatural—thus monster—thus vampire. Beginning with horror films in the fifties, the binarism of natural/unnatural gives way. Nature is contaminated—it is a site of the unnatural. Metaphors of Romantic organicism fail where technology has transformed. The agrarian dream gives way to the nuclear nightmare. The representation of nature, contaminated by nuclear testing in the desert, is a site for the production of monsters that transgress what was considered natural. Hollywood produced *Them* (1954), *Tarantula* (1955), *Crab Monsters* (1956), *Giant Grasshoppers* (1957), and *Killer Shrews* (1959). The urban replaces the agrarian as a haven. The humanist scientist, such as Van Helsing, warring against the perverse isolated vampire gives way to the military-industrial complex warring against its own creations. The giant tarantula created by nuclear reaction is destroyed by napalm; another monster is killed by a shift in the ozone layer.

After the 50s, the lone vampire, or the family of vampires that threatened the human community, is replaced by a proliferation of the undead. Romero's trilogy illustrates the progression: in *Night of the Living Dead* (1968), a score of the undead threatens a family-unit-type group in a house; in the second film, *Dawn of the Dead* (1977), thousands of undead threaten a smaller, less-affiliated group in a shopping mall, one of the few places remaining; and in *Day of the Dead* (1985), the undead have successfully taken over the continent, finally threatening what dwindles down to the basic heterosexual-couple-unit in a military-industrial complex. Successively, the undead have eliminated the family unit, claimed commodity reification for their own in the shopping mall, and defeated the military-industrial complex. One hope remains in a kind of Adam and Eve ending of the final film, although it seems unlikely. The undead overrun things, proliferate wildly, are like contamination, pollution, a virus, disease—AIDS. Not AIDS as just any disease, but AIDS as it is used socially as a metaphor for same-sex desire among men, AIDS as a construction that signifies the plague of their sexuality. But why is the taboo now lodged in proliferation? This is Freud's double gone wild, the square root of proximity. The continual displacements in the system have become like a cancer, spreading, devouring, and reproducing themselves. The oppressive politics of representation have cathected to displacement, settling their sites/sights there again and again and again. The taboo against same sex becomes like the Stepford wives when they break down, pouring coffee over and over and over again.

These neo-undead doubly configure away the lesbian position, since same-sex desire appears as gay male. The lesbian position is only the motor for multiple displacements. Where does this all leave the lesbian vampire, then? Outside of the mirror, collapsing subject/object relations into the proximate, double occupancy of the sign, abandoning the category of woman as heterosexist, and entering representation only in a guise that proscribes her. You still can only see her, in horror and fear, when you don't.

# Nina Auerbach

## "Introduction: Living with the Undead," *Our Vampires, Ourselves*[1]

(1995)

We all know Dracula, or think we do, but as this book will show, there are many Draculas—and still more vampires who refuse to be Dracula or to play him. An alien nocturnal species, sleeping in coffins, living in shadows, drinking our lives in secrecy, vampires are easy to stereotype, but it is their variety that makes them survivors. They may look marginal, feeding on human history from some limbo of their own, but for me, they have always been central: what vampires are in any given generation is a part of what I am and what my times have become. This book is a history of Anglo-American culture through its mutating vampires.

From the beginning of nineteenth-century England through the close of twentieth-century America, vampires have been popular confederates of mortals. As parasites, they stretch back through folklore to the beginnings of recorded history, but they began their significant literary life in 1816, with the self-creations of Byron. The Byronic Lord Ruthven has something in common with his American cousin today, Anne Rice's Lestat, who preys on 1980s and '90s America. Both are enchanting companions; both are media stars; but each feeds on his age distinctively because he embodies that age. Why, for instance, does Ruthven attach himself to mortals, while Lestat is enthralled only by his fellow vampires? The differences that keep vampires alive are my subject.

This book took shape between 1989 and 1992—the span of George Bush's presidency—when impalpable fears afflicted America. Nationally, we were assaulted by plenty of devils we knew, but the most potent may have been the devils we had lost: a designated enemy in the seemingly almighty Soviet Union, and a designated patriarch in Ronald Reagan, who during the eight years of his presidency consummately played America's father. Suddenly stripped of its heroes

1 University of Chicago Press, 1995.

and villains, shorn of a script for its national morality play, America (as the press orchestrated it at least) turned its fears on itself. Among the most popular targets of a mounting backlash against the social gains of the 1970s were women, especially feminists, and university professors, especially feminists. As all of the above, I found myself living in a climate of intensifying hostile mutterings. In that ugly time, I began to imagine a book about fear.

Initially I was going to call it *Fear Itself* in tribute to the lost patriarch who had cast a beloved aura over my childhood, President Franklin D. Roosevelt. The fact that FDR was already dead when I was born made him, for me, incorruptible. In the spirit of his wonderful exhortation, "The only thing we have to fear is fear itself," I began thinking about fear as a phenomenon that could be contained and understood from without. Encompassing and unwritable, *Fear Itself* was not yet focused on vampires, but on all terror, which I thought I could explain.

But as fear took on a local habitation, especially in Republican rhetoric, my book narrowed itself down as well. In his 1968 presidential campaign, Richard Nixon had already enlisted FDR's embracing counsel in the service of a less expansive America: "Freedom from fear is a basic right of every American. We must restore it."[1] This campaign promise pits "every American," or "us," against darkly unspecified but presumably non-native agents of terror, embodied in any "them" the quaking voter imagines. Nixon didn't free Americans from fear; he taught his political heirs to relish it. The late 1980s and early '90s was an era of manipulated hate that came to define our national life: to name was to demonize. By the 1992 presidential campaign, a political cartoonist mordantly imagined George Bush inverting FDR's stirring words: sitting in front of a placard reading "BASH CONGRESS, BASH LAWYERS, BASH HILLARY, BASH CULTURAL ELITE, BASH SINGLE MOTHERS, BASH GAYS, BASH LESBIANS, BASH FEMINISTS," and so on, Bush growls: "We have nothing to fear—but fear it sells."[2]

Vampires and American presidents began to converge in my imagination, not because I think all presidents are equally vampiric (though all do absorb power from the electorate), but because both are personifications of their age. In the spirit of a changing America, I became increasingly implicated in this book as I wrote it: in the American half especially, I saw myself not so much explaining as expressing. My final title, *Our Vampires, Ourselves*, makes fear an ongoing cultural and personal presence, one no rational, Rooseveltian goodwill can dispel. I am not saying that vampires can be reduced to their political component; they are too mutable to be allegories. But the nervous national climate in which I imagined this book taught me that no fear is *only* personal: it must steep itself in its political and ideological ambience, without which our solitary terrors have no contagious resonance.

1 Quoted in the *Philadelphia Inquirer* (May 7, 1991) p. A24. [Auerbach's note]
2 Matson cartoon in the *New York Observer* (September 7, 1992), p. 1. [Auerbach's note]

Since I loved vampires before I hated Republicans, this book also reflects my idiosyncrasies, not only as a citizen, but as a woman. As a teenager chafing against the 1950s, an elated student in the 1960s, an academic in the '70s and '80s, I thought of vampires as my confederates, but most women I know are less accepting: I was received with polite revulsion at a Women's Studies symposium when I gave a paper on undeath. The leaders of the group, stalwart fighters all, claimed they never read horror—because they found it either too frightening or, in comparison to "real" fears like abuse, not frightening enough. Jane Austen's *Northanger Abbey* reminds us that in the eighteenth century, horror was by definition a woman's genre, but today, many women disclaim it (or try to), finding its alternative world alien, almost insulting. Here as so often, though, women's supposed resistance may unwittingly obey a taboo that originates in male exclusivity.

The most sophisticated and best-known experts on American popular horror insist that it is and always has been a boy's game.[1] Twitchell, Skal, and Kendrick construct a compelling paradigm of adolescent boys chafing against the smug domestication of the 1950s, but this paradigm assumes by definition that girls were contented domesticators. What about those of us who weren't? When I was twelve or thirteen, some enterprising ghoul began to televise 1930s horror movies on Saturday nights. These shadowy monsters were a revelation to my best friend and me. Trying to make us popular, our worried parents forced us away from Transylvania to dances and parties, where we spent most of the evening making vampire faces at each other with horrible contortions. We weren't popular (that beatifying condition of the mid-1950s); the monster-loving boys now supposed to have been prevalent in those years never showed up at our parties; but we did feel we had found a secret talisman against a nice girl's life. Vampires were supposed to menace women, but to me at least, they promised protection against a destiny of girdles, spike heels, and approval. I am writing in part to reclaim them for a female tradition, one that has not always known its allies.

When I subverted those parties, or thought I did, it had not yet occurred to me that vampires also personified the fears within the supposed national bliss of those years—fears of communism, of McCarthyism, of nuclear war, of not

1 James Twitchell, for instance, acknowledges that adolescents of both genders go to horror movies, but he goes on to explain their appeal by a Freudian "Ur-myth of adolescence" that is clearly based on the fantasies of boys. See *Dreadful Pleasures: An Anatomy of Modern Horror* (New York and Oxford: Oxford University Press, 1985), pp. 99–100. David J. Skal is more assured in quarantining girls like myself from vicarious bloodlust: "In a suburbanized, plasticized America [of the 1950s], monster culture answered a need among *male* baby boomers for haunted houses instead of tract houses, an ancient, Europeanized structure of meaning." *Hollywood Gothic: The Tangled Web of* Dracula *from Novel to Stage to Screen* (New York and London: W.W. Norton, 1990), p. 190; my italics. Walter Kendrick barely qualifies the maleness of his "horror maven": "This character exists in various subspecies, though *he is most likely to be male*, to be between fifteen and forty-five years old, and American." Walter Kendrick, *The Thrill of Fear: 250 Years of Scary Entertainment* (New York: Grove Weidenfeld, 1991), p. 257; my italics. [Auerbach's note]

being certified sexually normal by paternalistic Freudian authorities—fears that fueled the ghastly compulsion to be liked. When I made vampire faces in wholesome settings, I thought I was rebelling against my milieu. I know now that I expressed it—a knowledge that inspired this book.

Vampires changed with my life and times. In the 1960s, like so much else that had been denied in the '50s, they burst out of the underground crypts that had confined Bela Lugosi into the light of brightly colored Hammer films. In the 1970s, like American women, they broke out of their preordained plot to create self-generated new stories. If we each have a halcyon decade, the 1970s was mine; it saw the burgeoning of the women's movement; the beginning of my career (and of the frightening, exhilarating moves around America this career made possible); the end of the war in Vietnam; the end (we thought) of corrupt old ways in the fall of Nixon's presidency. It also saw the assimilation of horror into mainstream culture.[1] My exhilarating memories of the '70s are entwined with its innovative and self-defining vampires; my depression, in the '80s, about Ronald Reagan's grinning descent over the American imagination colors my memory of vampires newly subdued. The alacrity with which vampires shape themselves to personal and national moods is an adaptive trait their apparent uniformity masks.

There is no such creature as "The Vampire"; there are only vampires. Walter Kendrick emphasizes the formulaic stasis of a horror genre that responds monotonously to a universal fear of death, a genre reducible to an "apparently endless recycling of a few scant materials, all assembled two hundred years ago."[2] But since vampires are immortal, they are free to change incessantly. Eternally alive, they embody not fear of death, but fear of life: their power and their curse is their undying vitality. From Varney to Dracula (particularly as Bela Lugosi intones him), from Chelsea Quinn Yarbro's disenchanted idealist, Count Saint-Germain, to Lestat and his friends, vampires long to die, at least in certain moods, infecting readers with fears of their own interminable lives. Kendrick's formula may hold for most monsters, but vampires are wily enough to evade it.

Because they are always changing, their appeal is dramatically generational. In 1991 and 1993, I taught large classes at the University of Pennsylvania on the evolution of vampires. In none of my other courses have age differences been so central. Aficionados all, the students acknowledged my favorite vampires more or less politely, but had to teach me to appreciate theirs. Moreover, the 1991 class searched with obsessive unanimity for the rules governing vampirism, rules that bored students in 1993, the anxieties of the Persian Gulf War gave way to

1 See Noël Carroll, *The Philosophy of Horror, or Paradoxes of the Heart* (New York and London: Routledge, 1990), p. 2: "But what seems to have happened in the first half of the seventies is that horror, so to speak, entered the mainstream. Its audience was no longer specialized, but widened, and horror novels became increasingly easy to come by." [Auerbach's note]

2 Walter Kendrick, p. 255. [Auerbach's note]

the looser, more amorphous climate of the Clinton administration. Whyever it happened, the vampires covered in these courses took life from generational debates: along with the differences between two groups of students, between myself and both groups, there were the distinctive perspectives of my teaching assistants, women in their twenties who were devoted to the vampires of the 1980s.

To the jaded eye, all vampires seem alike, but they are wonderful in their versatility. Some come to life in moonlight, others are killed by the sun; some pierce with their eyes, others with fangs; some are reactionary, others are rebels; but all are disturbingly close to the mortals they prey on. I can think of no other monsters who are so receptive. Vampires are neither inhuman nor nonhuman nor all-too-human; they are simply more alive than they should be.

Ghosts, werewolves, and manufactured monsters are relatively changeless, more aligned with eternity than with time; vampires blend into the changing cultures they inhabit. They inhere in our most intimate relationships; they are also hideous invaders of the normal. I am writing about vampires because they can be everything we are, while at the same time, they are fearful reminders of the infinite things we are not.

Vampires go where power is: when, in the nineteenth century, England dominated the West, British vampires ruled the popular imagination, but with the birth of film, they migrated to America in time for the American century. My book follows them, concentrating on nineteenth-century England in the first half and resettling in twentieth-century America in the second.

England did not lose its taste for vampires in the twentieth century, but monsters, like other imports, became subject to the dominant American market. For this reason, in the second half of the book, I view through an American prism the films that swarmed out of England's Hammer Studios in the 1960s, and the mordant "alternative history" that British horror writers have been producing in the 1980s and '90s. As author I became, like many vampires, a time traveler, attempting to reconstruct a nineteenth-century perspective in the first half of this book, relying in the second half on my own experience as that was colored by my country and time.

In England (at least until the coming of Dracula), vampires offered an intimacy that threatened the sanctioned distance of class relationships and the hallowed authority of husbands and fathers. Vampires before Dracula were dangerously close friends. When they became charismatic stage performers, theatrical technology suffused them with a spectral aura, and popular mythology bestowed on them mystic lunar affinities, safely dissipating the erotic implications of their intimacy. At the end of the century, Bram Stoker's Dracula—animal rather than phantom, mesmerist rather than intimate, tyrant rather than friend—safely quarantined vampires from their human prey, foreclosing friendship and opening the door to the power-hungry predators so congenial to the twentieth century.

Vampires in the American century embody seditious urbanity rather than dangerous intimacy. Unlike their insinuating British counterparts, they gravitate to leadership, aping the tyrants they parody. In the vacuum of authority that afflicted and energized the 1970s, they devised innovative exhibitions of undeath. When Ronald Reagan's powerful persona took control of the American imagination in the 1980s, vampires began to die. Intimidated by ideological reaction and the AIDS epidemic, they mutated, as a species, into unprecedented mortality, lacking the tenacity of the Victorian theatrical phantoms they resembled. The best of them took on the holy isolation of angels, inspiring awe in a humanity they could no longer govern.

Despite these differences, their stories have much in common. In both England and America, vampires oscillate between aristocracy and democracy, at times taking command with elitist aplomb, at times embodying the predatory desires of the populace at large. In both cultures, vampires turn to women to perform the extreme implications of their monstrosity—erotic friendship in England, social rebellion in America. In general with striking exceptions (particularly in the American 1970s), vampires are male creations; their stellar incarnations are male; but in their well-bred inhibitions, many need women to act out their natures for them. Even solitary luminaries like Dracula turn their demonic designs into female plots.

In nineteenth-century England and twentieth-century America, vampires end their story and their century in retraction and reaction, collaborating to restore the patriarchy they had menaced. Stoker's *Dracula* is a compendium of fin-de-siècle phobias. Dracula's lonely rigidity repudiates the homoerotic intimacy with which earlier vampires had insinuated themselves into mortality. In America, Reaganesqure vampires, increasingly ghettoized, wilt, dissipate, and even shed undeath when challenged by the paternal authorities they had mocked in the '60s and '70s. In fin-de-siècle conservative reversions, vampires prop up the ideologies and institutions they had undermined when they (and their centuries) were in their prime. Posing as revolutionaries, they are consummate turncoats, more formidable in their flexibility than in their love, their occult powers, or their lust for blood. It is impossible either to exorcise or to trust a species whose immortality has given them supreme adaptability. [...]

"The Vampire" is a popular is nonexistent abstraction, but many particular vampires are frustratingly difficult to find. While *Dracula* has never been out of print, some of his most interesting progeny exist only in specialized science fiction/horror publications, ephemeral paperback originals, and rarely seen films. [...]

Individual vampires may die; after almost a century, even Dracula may be feeling his mortality; but as a species, vampires have been our companions for so long that it is hard to imagine living without them. They promise escape from our dull lives and the pressure of our times, but they matter because when properly understood, they make us see that our lives are implicated in theirs and our times are inescapable.

# Carol A. Senf

## from "Daughters of Lilith: Women Vampires in Popular Literature"[1]

(1999)

Dracula has entered the popular imagination as the vampire *par excellence*—brooding, powerful *and* intensely masculine. However, a survey of literary vampires, from classic figures to modern ones, includes a significant number of females. Depth psychology is not necessary to see that the connection between women and vampires often stems from a general fear of the Other, in this case, a fear of powerful and predatory women. Less obvious, however, and therefore more interesting is the recurring manifestation of this strong and destructive female figure in literature during certain periods, most notably in the early Romantic period, the Victorian period through 1900, and the mid-twentieth century. This discussion will define the characteristics of female vampire, describe her cycles in literature, and offer reasons why she flourished when she did.

Almost no vampires exist in literature before the nineteenth century. Both Kittredge in *Witchcraft in Old and New England* and Summers in *The Vampire in Europe* refer to the twelfth-century accounts of William of Newburgh and William of Malmesbury as the only accounts of the vampire in England. An article in an 1855 issue of *Household Words* refers to a third example, an Anglo-Saxon poem about the Vampyre of the Fens; and Nicholas K. Kiessling uses linguistic evidence to argue that Beowulf's fiercest rival, Grendel's mother, is an English lamia.[2] Christopher Fraying discusses the sources of the Romantic vampire: "Some of the early Romantics, such as Bürger, Goethe, and Keats, based their vampire visions (loosely) on classical Greek and Roman manifestations. More often vampire tales and poems in the nineteenth century ... were derived

1 Originally published in Leonard G. Heldreth and Mary Pharr, editors. *The Blood Is the Life: Vampires in Literature*. Bowling Green State U Popular P, 1999, pp. 199–216.

2 Kiessling, "Demonic Dred," 30. [Senf's note]

from folktales and eye-witness accounts of 'posthumous magic' in peasant communities, which dated from the period 1680–1760."[1] In addition, Frayling notes that Dom Augustin may have contributed to the popularity of the vampire.[2]

Like these other literary vampires, the female vampire originates in the folklore of primitive cultures and the myths of the classical world. Anthony Masters, who catalogues the belief in vampires according to country of origin in *The Natural History of the Vampire*, suggests that, in folklore, men, women, and children can all become vampires.[3] While only one type is exclusively male—the *Bajang* of Malaysia which generally assumes the body of a polecat—Masters notes that several types of exclusively female vampires exist. For example, Jewish legends warn against Lilith, Adam's first wife, who refused to bow to male authority, uttered the forbidden name of God, and became a female demon who seduced young men and killed infants. Greek and Roman legends tell of the Lamia and Striges, who also seduced and destroyed young men and drank the blood of children. The folklores of various European countries, the Orient, and the Malay Peninsula also reveal several versions of this supernatural female: the Portuguese *Bruzsa* seduces travelers, and both it and the Malaysian *Langsuir*, a flying female demon, suck the blood of children. The Scottish *baobham sith* takes the form of groups of beautiful girls to drain victims of blood while the Danish *Mara* takes human form during the day and destroys those who fall in love with her. Although some of these folklore creatures differ so radically from the modern vampire that the connection between folklore and literature is not immediately recognizable, most exhibit at least one of the three characteristics associated with women vampires in literature: bloodsucking, rebellious behavior, and overt eroticism. Thus, they are indirect forerunners and sometimes models for the women vampires who have become an important part of the popular imagination—women who are aggressive, destructive, rebellious, and, at the same time, irresistibly sensual—in short, everything traditional women were not supposed to be.

The vampire in folklore, often little more than an inhuman bloodsucker, is characterized primarily by the need to drink blood to sustain its unnatural existence; and many of the earliest literary versions are as horrifying and inhuman as their counterparts in folklore. For example, in Tieck's "Wake Not the Dead" (1800), Brunhilda, who is reanimated when her grieving husband begs the assistance of a sorceress, must drink the blood of her children and her husband to maintain her existence. Likewise, Aurelia in Hoffmann's *The Serapion Brethern* (1820) drinks blood, including that of her husband. The vampire had apparently become so common in German literature by 1847 that Charlotte Brontë has Jane Eyre call the apparition in her bedroom, "the foul German

1 Frayling, *The Vampire* 14. [Senf's note]
2 Frayling, *The Vampire* 91. [Senf's note]
3 Masters, *The Natural History of the Vampire* 43–150. [Senf's note]

spectre—the Vampyre."[1] She also portrays Bertha Mason as a vampire who sucks her brother's blood (albeit in the Ann Radcliffe tradition of an apparently supernatural creature who is eventually revealed to be a human being).

Le Fanu's aristocratic Carmilla (1872) not only sucks blood but lies awash in a coffin filled with it, while Bram Stoker's female vampires literally reek of their victims' blood, an odor that Jonathan Harker finds strangely arousing: "I could feel the movement of her breath upon me. Sweet it was in one sense, honey-sweet... but with a bitter offensiveness, as one smells in blood."[2] By 1897, when *Dracula* was published, the horror at having one's blood sucked by a lovely vampire was mixed with something approaching titillation. In fact, four of the five vampires in *Dracula* are women, and the original first chapter of the novel, deleted before publication and later published by Stoker's widow as the short story, "Dracula's Guest," included one more demonic woman, the Countess Dolingen of Gratz, who returns from the grave to haunt Jonathan Harker on his journey to Dracula's castle.

Harker's mixed feelings in *Dracula* indicate a turning point, for female vampires in twentieth-century literature are usually more sympathetically portrayed than their nineteenth-century counterparts. At the same time, their human counterparts become more horrifying. For example, Hanns Heinz Ewers (1871–1943), who wrote "The Spider" (1908), a literal vampire story, also wrote *Vampir* (1921), a work in which the term is used metaphorically: Frank Braun, a young German patriot during World War I, drinks the blood of his Jewish mistress to become a better fund raiser for his country. Clarimonde, the beautiful vampire in "The Spider," is much less horrifying than Braun, even though she is directly responsible for the deaths of at least three men.

[...]

Similarly, Whitley Strieber makes his vampire appealing. In *The Hunger* (1981) Miriam, a millennium-old vampire, is the daughter of Lamia and, therefore, a member of an entirely different species. While her hunger for the lives of human victims is horrifying, Miriam may be the last of her kind, and her appalling loneliness and perpetual search for an equally immortal companion arouse sympathy. In "Immunity" (1996), Lesbian writer Toni Brown makes her lamia figure more sympathetic by having her explain her heritage to her six-year-old foster daughter,[3] an explanation that also reveals the vampire's strong moral code:[4]

> Celeste had not lied about Nia's protection. Nia was protected by her. She would not be harmed by the tiny sips of blood Celeste sometimes took from her wrist. As for the other people of African descent, Celeste

---

1 Brontë, *Jane Eyre* ch. 25, 250. [Senf's note]

2 Stoker, *The Annotated Dracula* 39. [Senf's note]

3 The following quote is Celeste's internal monologue. Nia does not know that her mother is a vampire.

4 "Immunity" appears in an anthology, *Night Bites: Vampire Stories by Women.* [Senf's note]

> could honestly say she had not feasted on their flesh since she left her native land.... She had not seen one of her kind since she left her home in Africa. She had lived for centuries. She might live forever, but at least for a time in this foreign place, she would not be alone.[1]

Creating even more sympathetic vampires are Jan Jennings and Terri de la Peña. Jennings entirely removes the threat of bloodsucking in *Vampyr* (1981). Valan, an extremely attractive woman vampyre (her preferred spelling), has never tasted human blood although she can take nourishment only in the form of fresh blood—usually from cattle or horses. Attempting to find a quiet sanctuary, she leads an equally civilized group of vampires in punishing the "rogues" who do drink human blood. Refugio, the centuries-old Chicana vampire in Peña's story of the same name (1996), works as a nurse and gets blood from the hospital's blood bank instead of from the necks of victims. Neither goes as far as George R.R. Martin, who in *Fevre Dream* (1982) describes vampires who seek a substitute for blood. The vampires created by Jennings, Martin, and Peña wish to live within the human culture rather than prey on it.

[...]

While some works eliminate the horror from the vampire's thirst for blood, others modify the original superstition in different ways. For example, both *Dracula* and M.E. Braddon's "Good Lady Ducayne" (1896) link the sucking of blood with blood transfusions. However, Braddon's title character is not a supernatural creature. She is merely an ancient woman whose loyal doctor transfuses her with the blood of her young traveling companions. Two of them die, but Lady Ducayne is apparently not a vampire in any literal sense. Nor is the unnamed subject of Fritz Leiber's "The Girl with the Hungry Eyes" (1949), even though Leiber uses the traditional vampire attributes of a parasite who destroys her victim. Although human, she symbolizes the false promises of modern advertising and, being less obvious than the traditional vampire, is therefore deadlier than the supernatural version: "There are vampires and vampires, and the ones that suck blood aren't the worst.... She's the smile that tricks you into throwing away your money and your life. She's the eyes that lead you on and on, and then show you death. She's the being that takes everything you've got and gives nothing in return."[2] In this context, the term *bloodsucker* is a metaphor rather than a literal belief.

In addition to being bloodsuckers, a number of vampires rebel against authority. For example, Bertha Mason savagely attacks both her brother and her husband, the man responsible for her incarceration, but she does not harm Jane Eyre. Unlike Bertha Mason, Emily Brontë's Catherine Earnshaw (*Wuthering Heights*, 1847) is never described as a vampire, but certain characteristics indicate that

1 Brown, "Immunity" 78. [Senf's note]

2 Leiber, "The Girl with the Hungry Eyes" 205. [Senf's note]

Emily Brontë was also familiar with the character. For example, Catherine is able to haunt Heathcliff only after Lockwood invites her into her childhood bedroom, where he has sought refuge for the night; and Heathcliff, upon opening her coffin, is able to embrace her body, which apparently has not decomposed. Furthermore, Catherine is clearly a rebel against authority, for she dies in childbirth rather than bow to the authority of her husband and the responsibilities of her social position; and she returns to haunt Heathcliff, the man who was too weak to help her escape from this authority. Only in death can the two lovers attain the freedom that had been denied to them in life.

[...]

Many women vampires in literature are portrayed as bloodsuckers, rebels, or both, but virtually all of them are characterized by overt eroticism. This trait, although often treated sympathetically in twentieth-century literature, is more often associated with absolute evil in earlier works.

One of the earliest women vampires, the courtesan Clarimonde in Gautier's *La Morte Amoureuse* (1835), destroys her lovers by overcoming their inhibitions. As a result of her enticements, Romuald, a young country priest, becomes dissolute and supercilious. The title emphasizes Gautier's belief that erotic love is equivalent to death. A similar attitude appears in both Tieck and Hoffmann, although the erotic appeal is secondary to the sheer bestiality of these women.

Later in the century, in "Carmilla," *Dracula*, and F.G. Loring's "The Tomb of Sarah" (1900), horror at women's sexuality is replaced by ambivalence. Laura, the naïve narrator of "Carmilla," confesses her awareness of "love growing into adoration, and also of abhorrence" because Carmilla's behavior was "like the ardor of a lover; it embarrassed me; it was hateful and yet overpowering."[1] Too innocent to recognize that she is sexually attracted to Carmilla, Laura dreams erotic images: "Sometimes it was as if warm lips kissed me, and longer and more lovingly as they reached my throat, but there the caress fixed itself. My heart beat faster, my breathing rose and fell.... A sobbing, that rose into a dreadful convulsion, in which my sense left me, and I became unconscious."[2] The women vampires in *Dracula* are more openly erotic and approach their victims boldly. Even before Lucy dies and becomes a true vampire, she adopts the sensual behavior that Stoker associates with the woman vampire: "In a sort of sleep-walking, vague, unconscious way she opened her eyes...and said in a soft, voluptuous voice, such as I had never heard from her lips:—'Arthur! Oh, my love, I am so glad you have come! Kiss me!'"[3] Stoker emphasizes the woman vampire's erotic nature with the word "voluptuous" almost every time one appears in the novel. Dracula, in contrast, is never described as an erotic threat despite the ominous quality of his presence in the novel.

[...]

1 Le Fanu, "Carmilla" ch. 4, 93. [Senf's note]
2 Le Fanu, "Carmilla" ch. 7, 113–114. [Senf's note]
3 Stoker, *The Annotated Dracula* ch. 12, 147. [Senf's note]

To the seductiveness of the female vampire in nineteenth-century literature, Ambrose Bierce adds incest in "The Death of Halpin Frayser" (1893). Like Lilith, the Lamia and Striges, Brunhilda, and the three women in Dracula's castle, Halpin Frayser's mother is a destroyer of children. However, Bierce combines this characteristic with a rather perverse erotic attachment between the mother and her teenage son: "In these romantic natures was manifest... the dominance of the sexual element in all the relations of life, strengthening, softening, and beautifying even those of consanguinity. The two were nearly inseparable, and by strangers observing their manners were not infrequently mistaken for lovers."[1] Although definitely incestuous, the strange relationship between mother and son is initially appealing. When the dead Catherine returns, however, she is monstrous instead of loving, her laugh "so unnatural, so inhuman, so devilish, that it filled those hardy man-hunters with a sense of dread unspeakable!"[2] Furthermore, because she kills her son rather than the man who murdered her, Bierce suggests, like Gautier, that perverse love results in death.

The horror exhibited by the typical nineteenth-century writer confronted with the superhuman eroticism of the woman vampire carries over to early twentieth-century literature in works such as "The Death of Ilalotha" by Clark Ashton Smith (1937). Here, Ilalotha, a reputed sorceress, destroys her faithless lover when he visits her tomb: "there remained nothing of Ilalotha except the white, voluptuous arms, and a vague outline of human breasts.... The thing seemed to heed him not but withdrew its fingers from his bosom... as if to claw the queen [who observes the death] or fondle her with its dribbling talons."[3] More gruesome than most of its predecessors, "The Death of Ilalotha" goes beyond overt female eroticism in its descriptions to include the cloying eroticism of a decadent civilization as it degenerates into complete bestial behavior.

A more recent work, Raymond Rudorff's *The Dracula Archives* (1972), contains a conventional description of unbridled female eroticism. When a small group of travelers opens the tomb of Elizabeth Bathory (the historical sixteenth-century Hungarian noblewoman who murdered young women and bathed in their blood to maintain her youth), her spirit takes over a young neighborhood woman with predictable results: "She extended her arms toward me.... I came ever closer, yearning for the kiss that she would give me, for the feel of her arms around my neck, and had nearly reached her when... Father Johannes interposed himself... brandishing a cross. With a fearful shriek and a visage contorted with hatred, she backed away, hissing furiously."[4] The father figure prevents the young hero from succumbing to the power of a sensuous woman as Dr. Van Helsing prevents Arthur from kissing Lucy in a similar scene in *Dracula*.

1 Bierce, "The Death of Halpin Frayser" 149. [Senf's note]
2 Bierce, "The Death of Halpin Frayser" 159. [Senf's note]
3 Smith, "The Death of Ilalotha" 90–91. [Senf's note]
4 Rudorff, *The Dracula Archives* 84. [Senf's note]

Although obviously aware of its literary predecessors, *The Dracula Archives* is not typical of recent vampire literature. In fact, most works written since the 1960s reflect relaxed sexual mores and present female eroticism as a positive—or at least neutral—characteristic. For example, both Miriam in *The Hunger* and Valan in *Vampyr* are sensuous and physically ardent, and both have taken numerous lovers of both sexes. Furthermore, while Miriam requires human blood to sustain her existence, her eroticism, like that of Valan, is divorced from the blood-taking and presented as desirable, not dangerous.

[...]

So far, this essay has focused on three characteristics of female vampires—bloodsucking, rebellion, and overt eroticism. Since the rise of the vampire as a literary figure, these traits have been shared by many male vampires as well. The most important distinction is that these traits were more feared in traditional women than in men, primarily because the traditional woman was expected to be a nurturer rather than a bloodsucker, a docile creature rather than a rebel, and a being who sublimated her eroticism to child-rearing and monogamous marriage. Because of her extreme deviation from the ideal, therefore, the female vampire was both more fear-inspiring and more desire-provoking than her male counterpart.[1]

Traditional women were, however, associated with beauty; and the fact that vampires have no mirror reflection reveals exactly how much vampires differ from human beings. Originally, the vampire's lack of a reflection symbolized its lack of soul; however, the mirror, identified by Dracula as "a foul bauble of man's vanity,"[2] relates specifically to a supposedly feminine trait—vanity about one's physical appearance. Jane Eyre, two days after seeing the hideous face of the supposed vampire in the mirror, looks at the same glass and sees a veiled figure, "almost the image of a stranger."[3] Brontë uses this image, which appears on the morning Jane expects to marry Rochester, to suggest that women's identities are lost in those of their husbands. In fact, the remainder of *Jane Eyre* demonstrates that Jane must acquire a separate social, economic, and spiritual identity before she can marry Rochester.

[...]

This brief survey of the character of the typical literary vampire shows her to be a reanimated corpse who sucks the blood of human victims and often turns them into creatures like herself. Thus she is a parasite (and many writers—including Charlotte Brontë, Le Fanu, and Stoker—suggest a subtle connection between literal parasitism and economic parasitism) and a destroyer—sometimes joyfully, sometimes reluctantly—of human beings. Her victims are usu-

1 "Kathleen L. Spencer argues that Victorian men perceived the New Woman's apparent denial of her biological womanhood as a challenge to 'the distinctions between women and men upon which the family—and therefore society—depended" ([Spencer, "Purity and Danger"] 206). [Senf's note]

2 Stoker, *The Annotated Dracula* ch. 2, 27. [Senf's note]

3 Brontë, *Jane Eyre* ch. 26, 252. [Senf's note]

ally children or young men, although Coleridge, Le Fanu, and a number of modern works have focused on the lesbian attachment between the woman vampire and her victim.[1] Thus the traditional woman vampire was both a temptress and a bad mother—a particularly heinous role during the Victorian period when women were expected to be the guardian angels of the home and hearth. In fact, it is only recently that women vampires have been permitted to be good mothers, a role clearly developed in both "Sustenance" by Susanna Sturgis and "Immunity" (1996) by Toni Brown (although Brown's Celeste is obviously a foster-mother rather than a biological one). Finally, as both an openly erotic creature and a rebel against authority, the female vampire has evolved greatly, especially in twentieth-century literature with its greater tolerance of both sexuality and assertiveness in women.

Describing the characteristics of the female vampire is considerably easier than charting its chronology in literature. As Frayling notes, Goethe in "The Bride of Corinth" (1797) was "the first to make the vampire respectable in literature."[2] Thus the woman vampire enters the literary domain roughly with the vampire *per se*, though women vampires do seem to be more popular at specific historical periods, as Frayling argues: "The Fatal Woman made tentative appearances in Germany and France during the early period of Romanticism, but came into her own during 1840–80, a period of fascination with the exotic, the aesthetic and the decadent."[3] England should be added to Frayling's list of countries, even though Coleridge's Geraldine and Keats's Lamia and Belle Dame may not be vampires in the most literal sense. Moreover, although Frayling correctly argues that the vampire appears at certain historical periods, his time frame should be expanded to include 1900, for some of the most famous literary works that feature women vampires were published during the 1890s: *Dracula*, "The Tomb of Sarah," "The Death of Halpin Frayser," "Good Lady Ducayne," and Hume Nesbit's "The Vampire Maid" (1900). The richness of the nineteenth century is followed by a virtual hiatus, for the early twentieth century is comparatively poor in women vampires. Notable exceptions are Christina, the young peasant woman in "For the Blood Is the Life" (1911) by F. Marion Crawford; the lovely Perle, the victim of her dissolute brother, in Carl Jacobi's "Revelations in Black" (1933); and Elva Gauber, supposedly the inspiration for Poe's "The Black Cat," in Manly Wade Wellman's "When It Was Moonlight" (1940). Then, in the 1960s the woman vampire is literally resurrected as a literary (and cinematic) figure, a resurrection that continues through the *fin de siècle*.

These periods of waxing and waning activity raise the most interesting question of all: Why is the female vampire popular at certain periods and not at others? This question actually encompasses four related questions. First, why

1 "For a thorough discussion of lesbian vampires, see Bonnie Zimmerman's article, "Daughters of Darkness: Lesbian Vampires." A more recent discussion of the lesbian vampire in both literature and film appears in Brownworth and Redding's Introduction to *Night Bites*. [Senf's note]

2 Frayling, *The Vampire* 44. [Senf's note]

3 Frayling, *The Vampire* 66. [Senf's note]

did the vampire as a literary figure (male or female) suddenly rise to popularity in the early nineteenth century? Second, since the male vampire has remained popular since its origin, why has the woman vampire been popular only in particular historical periods? Third, why has the vampire figure in general changed so radically during this period? And, finally, why has the female vampire changed even more radically than her male counterpart?

M.M. Carlson explains the sudden popularity of the vampire by linking its appearance with the rise of scientific rationalism in the nineteenth century that "forced him out of his folkloric environment and into the new image-carrying element in our culture: literature."[1] Furthermore, Carlson argues that the interest in the vampire is connected to the Romantic interest in primitive people and "facilitated by Herder's romantic nationalism and a renewed interest in the folklore heritage of the various European nations."[2]

Carlson correctly links the literary vampire's origins to the early Romantic movement, when writers began to explore irrational or nonrational subjects. Vampirism had been a virtual epidemic during the eighteenth century in remote areas of East Prussia, Hungary, Austrian Serbia, Silesia, and Wallachia,[3] and it attracted the attention of some Enlightenment thinkers, including the Marquis d'Agens, Voltaire, Rousseau, Van Swieten (Empress Maria Theresa's personal physician and adviser), and the Chevalier De Jaucourt (a prolific contributor to the great *Encyclopedie*).[4] However, with the exception of Voltaire's entry in his *Dictionary* and a brief reference in one of Pope's letters, Enlightenment writers considered the vampire an unsuitable subject for literature.[5] Most of them were interested only in the scientific and philosophic implications of posthumous magic. Voltaire, like Marx and Engels in the following century, used the vampire as a metaphor for economic exploitation and equated it with the clergy who bleed people dry.

The Romantics, however, with their interest in mysterious and rebellious figures, such as Prometheus and Faust, who defy either the natural or the social order, turned the vampire into a suitable subject for literature. Recently

---

1 Carlson, "What Stoker Saw" 31. [Senf's note]

2 Carlson, "What Stoker Saw" 31. [Senf's note]

3 Frayling, *The Vampire* 37. [Senf's note]

4 Frayling, *The Vampire* 31. [Senf's note]

5 Anne Williams examines the link between Gothic literature and Enlightenment thinking in *Art of Darkness: A Poetics of Gothic* (1995):

> Thus I posit that the similarities between the Freudian model of the psyche and the conventions of Gothic fiction are best understood as parallel expressions of an Enlightenment frame of mind, which is both the last phase of patriarchy and the first of something else not yet articulated. The very word 'Enlightenment' creates a necessity for darkness; to celebrate, even to recognize, the known implies that there must be mysteries. As Michel Foucault has repeatedly shown, Enlightenment thought characteristically ordered and organized by creating institutions to enforce distinctions between society and its other, whether it resides in madness, illness, criminality, or sexuality. Like the haunted Gothic castle, the Freudian discourse of the self *creates* the haunted, dark, mysterious space even as it attempts to organize or control it. (248, Williams's emphasis) [Senf's note]

explored by Nina Auerbach in *Our Vampires, Ourselves* (1995), the Romantic vampire can be either male or female, with Polidori's Lord Ruthven serving as the model for future male vampires, and Coleridge's Geraldine and Keats's Lamia the model for future females. While vampires in most contemporary popular literature can trace their ancestry back to these Romantic figures, at least one modern writer has capitalized directly on these literary origins. J.N. Williamson has written several novels—*Death-Coach* (1981), *Death-Angel* (1981), *Death-School* (1982), and *Death-Doctor* (1982)—that feature Lamia Zacharius, a three-thousand-year-old vampire. In addition, Williamson is obviously quite conscious of his Romantic predecessors, for he often quotes Keats and Shelley. Further, *Death-Angel* also features the characters Demogorgon and Aether, yet one more way to recreate the atmosphere surrounding the Romantic Vampire.

The nineteenth century's preoccupation with women vampires, however, stems as much from a concern with the changing roles of women—a concern rooted in the period's interest in children and spontaneous behavior—as it stems from the Romantic fascination with the unusual, the mysterious, the perverse. At the end of the eighteenth century, a few people, such as Mary Wollstonecraft in *A Vindication of the Rights of Women* (1792), began to insist on greater rights for all women. Certain sections of Mme. de Stael's *Lettres sur les ouvrages et le caractère de J.J. Rousseau* (1787–1788)[1] also raise important questions about the relations between the sexes, including the right of women to express passion. Such works were only the beginning. The "Woman Question"—including such diverse facets as the right of women to enter the universities and the professions, the repeal of the Contagious Disease Acts, and the right of women to vote and own property—occupied almost everyone's mind to some degree from the nineteenth century on. The "Woman Question," of course, elicited a number of different responses, ranging from passionate support to equally passionate opposition. This real social issue kept the concept of alternate roles for women before the public eye, and the now-permissible variations in women's identities led to a reshaping and altering of the female vampire's character, which became monstrous and aberrant *and* overwhelmingly sensual—in short, everything that women should *not* be.

Although the vampire begins as this negative image—passionate, cruel, and rebellious—of desirable human attributes, it is not necessarily an alter-ego that people secretly desired. Recent studies, of the Victorian Age in particular, suggest that people in the nineteenth century were not as repressed as previously thought. Nonetheless, Douglas Hill accurately emphasizes the sexual element in the vampire's character:

> But behind this blood urge, which is the most compelling and dominant element in the nature and habits of vampires, there lurks a darker truth

1 Mme. de Stael's *Letters on the Works and Character of J.J. Rousseau.* [Senf's note]

> of a sort that the nineteenth century could only hint at or introduce obliquely. The vampire legend is not simply an assortment of good, gory horror tales spawned by primitive superstitions about the dead. It is a blatantly *sexual* motif—riddled with eroticism, clogged with sadism and other perversions.[1]

Certainly this eroticism, an important part of the woman vampire's character since Greece and Rome, is the most outstanding aspect of her character. While her male counterpart can be ruthless, seductive, or merely brutal, she is almost always an erotic threat, her destructive potential hidden by her more desirable traits.

In the development of the vampire in literature, the evolution of its character is remarkable. Beginning in folklore as a figure that inspires fear, horror, and revulsion, both male vampires and female vampires have become much more attractive in the twentieth century. The merely bestial figure of folklore—the undead bloodsucker whose thirst is all—has become Frank Langella, the handsome and sensitive vampire in John Badham's production of *Dracula*, or Catherine Deneuve, the pensive and fragile-looking Miriam in the movie *The Hunger.* More recently, because of the efforts of Anne Rice, Jewelle Gomez, Ouida Crozier, and Poppy Z. Brite, vampires have become positively vulnerable, often more sinned against than sinning.[2]

Part of this altered view, according to Margaret L. Carter, may be due to the greater tolerance brought about by increased knowledge of psychology and sociology:

> Today we no longer feel qualified to judge any man—even a man not quite human—as a monster. Current emphasis on minority problems may cause even a monster to be an appealing character, because he suffers for being 'different.' Furthermore, moral ambiguity is more acceptable in this century than the last; we are less apt than Stoker to consign any creature to irrevocable damnation.[3]

Carter adds other reasons, such as the need to alter an overworked literary figure. These reasons, all plausible, suggest why the general literary image of the vampire has evolved in the past century and a half. The woman vampire, however, differs significantly from her male counterpart in that her character is linked to specific historical periods, and that the factors most responsible for altering her character are the same as those which altered the characters

1 Hill, *The History of Ghosts, Vampires, and Werewolves* 30. [Senf's note]

2 Rice's vampires are so familiar that they need no introduction though one might observe that they endow those with whom they come in contact with a quasi-angelic "vampire sight." Gomez's *The Gilda Stories* introduce[s] an African-American lesbian vampire with a feminist aversion to killing; Crozier's vampire science-fiction novel *Shadows After Dark* links lesbianism and AIDS; and Brite often creates vampires who are haunted and lonely. [Senf's note]

3 Carter, *Shadow of a Shade* 126. [Senf's note]

of women in general over the past two centuries. The overt eroticism of the female vampire is no longer frightening because sexuality in women is now an acceptable, even desirable, trait. In the case of Vampirella, that sexuality is normal, even fun. In the case of Saint-Germain and his women companions, that sexuality is beautiful and healthy, far healthier than the sadism and brutality of their human opponents. Furthermore, the rebellion against authority that has been part of the woman vampire's character since the beginning is now more generally accepted. Even the vampire's most nasty and destructive habit, sucking blood, is far less horrifying than the various methods of mass destruction invented by modern humans. A remnant of a simpler time, the woman vampire today represents the fear and the desire that human beings can confront on a personal level rather than the anonymous threats that now seem so insurmountable. Our dark angel, she is Lilith triumphant, woman at her strong and invincible best, passionate, rebellious, and assertive.

## WORKS CITED

[...]

Alexander, Karl. *Curse of the Vampire.* New York: Pinnacle Books, 1982.

Auerbach, Nina. *Our Vampires, Ourselves.* Chicago: U of Chicago P, 1995.

Bierce, Ambrose. "The Death of Halpin Frayser." Dickie 143–59.

Braddon, M.E. "Good Lady Ducayne." *The Dracula Book of Great Vampire Stoires.* Ed. Leslie Shepard. Secaucus, NJ: Citadel P, 1977. 125–50.

Brite, Poppy Z., ed. *Love in Vein: Twenty Original Tales of Vampiric Erotica.* New York: HarperPrism, 1994.

———. *Love in Vein II: Eighteen More Original Tales of Vampiric Erotic.* New York: Harper Prism, 1997.

Brontë, Charlotte. *Jane Eyre.* 1847. New York: Norton, 1971.

Brontë, Emily. *Wuthering Heights.* 1847. New York: Norton, 1963.

Brown, Toni. "Immunity." Brownworth 71–79.

Brownworth, Victoria A., ed. *Night Bites: Vampire Stories by Women.* Seattle, WA: Seal P, 1996.

———. "Twelfth Night." Brownworth 195–217.

Brownworth, Victoria A. and Judith M. Redding. Introduction. Brownworth ix-xvi.

[...]

Carlson, M.M. "What Stoker Saw: An Introduction to the Literary Vampire." *Folklore Forum* 10 (1977) 2: 26–32.

Carter, Margaret L. *Shadow of a Shade: A Survey of Vampirism in Literature.* New York: Gordon P, 1975.

[...]

Crawford, F. Marion. "For the Blood Is the Life." Dickie 42–59.
[...]
Dickie, James, ed. *The Undead*. New York: Pocket Books, 1976.
Frayling, Christopher. *The Vampire: Lord Ruthven to Count Dracula*. London: Victor Gollancz, 1978.
Hill, Douglas. *The History of Ghosts, Vampires, and Werewolves*. New York: Castlebooks, 1970.
Jacobi, Carl. "Revelations in Black." Dickie 105–29.
Jennings, Jan. *Vampyr*. New York: Tom Doherty Associates, 1981.
Kiessling, Nicholas K. "Demonic Dred: The Incubus Figure in British Literature." *The Gothic Imagination: Essays in Dark Romanticism*. Ed. G.R. Thompson. Pullman, WA: Washington State UP, 1974. 22–41.
Kittredge, George Lyman. *Witchcraft in Old and New England*. 1929. New York: Atheneum, 1972.
[...]
Le Fanu, Joseph Sheridan. "Carmilla." 1872. *A Clutch of Vampires*. Ed. Raymond T. McNally. Greenwich, CT: New York Graphic Society, 1974. 69–154.
Leiber, Fritz. "The Girl with the Hungry Eyes." *The Midnight People*. Ed. Peter Haining. New York: Popular Library, 1968. 191–205.
Loring, F.G. "The Tomb of Sarah." Dickie 91–105.
Martin, George R.R. *Fevre Dream*. New York: Pocket Books, 1982.
Masters, Anthony. *The Natural History of the Vampire*. New York: G.P. Putnam's Sons, 1972.
[...]
Peña, Terry de la. "Refugio." Brownworth 165–78.
Rudorff, Raymond. *The Dracula Archives*. New York: Pocket Books, 1972.
Smith, Clark Ashton. "The Death of Ilalotha." Dickie 79–91.
Spencer, Kathleen. "Purity and Danger: *Dracula*, the Urban Gothic, and the Late Victorian Degeneracy Crisis." *ELH* 59 (1992): 197–225.
Stoker, Bram. *The Annotated Dracula*. Ed. Leonard Wolf. New York: Clarkson N. Potter, 1975.
Strieber, Whitley. *The Hunger*. New York: Pocket Books, 1981.
Sturgis, Susanna J. "Sustenance." Brownworth 81–95.
Summers Montague. *The Vampire in Europe*. 1929. New Hyde Park, NY: University Books, 1968.
Wellman, Manly Wade. "When It Was Moonlight." Dickie 1977–92.
Williams, Anne. *Art of Darkness: A Poetics of Gothic*. Chicago: U of Chicago P, 1995.
[...]
Zimmerman, Bonnie. "Daughters of Darkness: Lesbian Vampires." *Jump Cut* 24–25 (1981): 23–24.

# Kendra R. Parker

# from "Introduction: The First Bite," *Black Female Vampires in African American Women's Novels, 1977–2011: She Bites Back*[1]

(2018)

[…] From Dracula to Edward Cullen, from Stefan and Damon Salvatore to the Mikaelson family patriarchs, the archetypal vampire is a tall, slender, seductive, and economically privileged white male who blends in with society until humans expose his vampire origins. But what happens when the vampire is female *and* black? What happens when African American women writers reshape vampires in their own image? As Donna J. Haraway observes: "Defined by their categorical ambiguity and troubling mobility, vampires do not rest easy (or easily) in the boxes labeled good and bad. Always transported and shifting, the vampire's native soil is more nutritious and more unheimlich [uncanny], than that."[2] *She Bites Back* asks what it means to represent African American womanhood through the lens of vampirism and how these representations of black female vampires in African American women's literature simultaneously negate and reinforce dominant, disparaging stereotypes of African American women. There are ramifications for all images that we consume, and the images of the black female vampire, whether in print or film, birth narratives and public perceptions, create ideals and tropes, and maintain the ability to either strengthen or destroy cultural pathologies.

[…]

The black female vampire, as I read her, assumes multiple contradictory notions of "self"; she is at once both and neither healer, nurturer, revolution-

1 Parker, *Black Female Vampires* xiv–xvi & xxxi.

2 Donna J. Haraway, "Universal Donors in a Vampire Culture: It's All in the Family. Biological Kinship Categories in the Twentieth-Century United States," in *Modest_Witness@Second_Millennium.FemaleMan©_Meets_OncoMouse™: Feminism and Technoscience* (New York: Routledge, 1997), p. 215. [Parker's note]

ary, victim, victimizer, vigilante and vixen. The African American novelists investigated in this book create their black female vampires as a way for African American women readers to view themselves wholly—in ways that reject the binary of either-or and embraces the binary of both-and. The vampire, as a variable of difference, encourages one to view difference as essential to the "self" and not something to be marginalized. Vampirism becomes a way for the narratives of construction of black female vampires to be interpreted as questioning and responding to the political forecasts for the environment in which they appear; it is not a stretch, then, to interpret the black female vampire in these respective novels as commentary on and an anticipation of the conservative backlash against social programs that clearly benefited marginalized women of color as well as commentary on the black nationalists' uncritical appropriation of the rhetoric of white patriarchal privilege and its adverse effect on black women.[1] Butler, Gomez, Banks and Cleage's construction of black female vampires explore and comment on these social politics and the ways the ruling elite's prejudices against African American women shape these policies.

It helps to be mindful of the term "vampire." When considering the term "vampire," it is helpful to view it as a socially constructed body that becomes a scapegoat for sexist, racist, and homophobic value systems, which are manifest in the mythology of the vampire. When I say "mythology of the vampire," I am not simply referring to the Western vampire that many of us are likely familiar with—basically Bram Stoker's *Dracula*. I am referring to African diasporic vampire figures like the *soucouyant*, *lougarou*, and *wazimamoto*.

As I explore what it means to be a black vampire in twentieth- and twenty-first-century African American women's literature, my use of the term "vampire" necessarily considers its multiple forms: the nineteenth-century notion of the vampire made popular by Stoker's *Dracula* (1897), the American and African appropriations of the Stoker-esque vampire, the incubus/succubus of Medieval literature and culture, and the soucouyant (or soucriat) of Caribbean folklore. I specifically say, "made popular" by Stoker because he was not, in fact, the first European to write about vampires, but his 1897 novel has been lauded as the quintessential vampire narrative, a narrative that has seen many film adaptations and literary interpretations.[2] The American prototype of the vampire,

1 These backlashes continued the legacy of what Linda Faye Williams calls "white skin privilege." Throughout *She Bites Back* I will only use "white skin privilege" when quoting Williams directly, but in my own discussion I will use "white privilege." [Parker's note]

2 Samuel Taylor Coleridge's "Christabel" (1797–1800), for example, is regarded as the first English poem to introduce the vampire trope; see J. Gordon Melton, *The Vampire Book: The Encyclopedia of the Undead* (Canton: Invisible Ink, 2010), 136. Stoker was likely influenced by vampire stories written by other English men, like *The Vampyre* (1819) written by John William Polidori, *Carmilla* (1874) by Joseph Sheridan Le Fanu and *Varney the Vampyre or The Feast of Blood* (1845–1847) by James Malcolm Rymer. According to Nina Auerbach and David J. Skal, Stoker was heavily influenced by Emily Gerard's *The Land Beyond the Forest: Facts, Figures, and Fancies from Transylvania* (1888), a collection of Transylvanian folklore that dealt with the paranormal—vampires, werewolves, witches and demons (Auerbach and Skal, *Dracula*, [(Norton Critical Edition, 1996,)] 212, note 2). [Parker's note]

modeled largely off of Stoker's Dracula, is that of a white male seducing and penetrating (the neck of) a young white girl. This model met with little variation until the 1970s and 1980s when white male vampires were more explicitly homoerotic and when black vampires first arrived in the films *Blacula* (1972), *Ganja and Hess* (1973), and *Scream, Blacula, Scream* (1973). In the early 1990s, white male vampires became more "sympathetic" with Joss Whedon's character Angel (performed by David Boreanaz) from the first three seasons of the popular television series *Buffy the Vampire Slayer* (1996–2003). Such "sympathy" extends to Edward Cullen from Stephanie Meyer's *Twilight* saga, Bill Compton from HBO's *True Blood* (2008–2014), Stefan and Damon Salvatore from the CW's television series *The Vampire Diaries* (2009–2017), and Elijah Michelson from the CW's *The Originals* (2013–2018).

Other forms of the vampire appear throughout Medieval, Caribbean, and African lore, and the common traits these vampire figures share are bloodsucking, a removal of life or life force, nocturnal visits, elements of disguise through shape shifting and boundary crossing, and the sexual connotation of each. In *Speaking with Vampires: Rumor and History in Colonial Africa* (2000), Luise White argues that vampire lore of East and Central Africa functions as etiological tales explaining rumors of exsanguination of Africans by other Africans hired by white colonialists. In this regard, the wazimamoto, a Swahili term for fireman, is linked to the African colonial experience and becomes a metaphor that translates into the Western conceptions of the vampire.[1] The incubus and succubus, male and female, are demons that are said to have paralyzed and attacked victims in their sleep by sexually enticing them and taking their energy via sex.[2] The incubi and succubi are most often considered demons or witches, and a "type" of vampire except that they do not drink blood; rather they sexually seduce and remove a person's energy or life force.[3] In *Things That Fly in the Night: Female Vampires in the Literature of Circum-Caribbean and African Diaspora* (2015), Giselle Liza Anatol traces the black female vampire figure—vampires, soucouyants, Ol'Hige, lougarou. Anatol posits that these black female vampire figures skin-shedding women that fly through the night, consume both the blood and energy of others, challenge patriarchal and heteronormative fears regarding non-normative female sexual activity, and disrupt racial and gendered social scripts. The soucouyant, popular in Caribbean folklore

1 Luise White, *Speaking with Vampires: Rumor and History in Colonial Africa* (Berkeley: University of California Press, 2000), 11. According to White, since the twentieth century, vampire stories in Africa circulated and identified European colonizers and their employment of African police officers and firefighters who captured other Africans as bloodsucking vampires. White discusses wazimamoto throughout her text. Depending on the location wazimamoto might refer to a fireman; other times it becomes a metaphor for property ownership and inheritance in Nairobi; and still other times wazimamota refers to blood donation centers (ibid., 133, 53, 78). [Parker's note]

2 Melton, *The Vampire Book*, 368–69. [Parker's note]

3 Ibid. [Parker's note]

(notably that of Trinidad and Dominica), is a witch vampire who lives by day as an old woman and by night as a shape shifter, traveling around as a red ball of fire entering people's homes.[1] Soucouyants suck the blood of their victims and if they take too much blood, the victims may die or turn into soucouyants themselves.

The consideration of each of these types of vampires is important for my consideration of what it means to be a vampire because the African American women writers who use black female vampires seem to borrow from all these traditions. Unlike Western vampires, none of the vampires in Butler's, Gomez's, or Cleage's fiction can transform humans into vampires with a single bite. Shori Matthews in *Fledgling* sneaks into houses at night to suck the blood of unsuspecting humans much like a soucouyant; Gilda in *The Gilda Stories* removes energy from her victims, but she provides them with memories to make up for her taking. To turn a human into a vampire, the humans must drink Gilda's blood in a ritual exchange. The Mayflower sisters in *Just Wanna Testify* do not drink blood but they seduce men, intend to use them for their sperm (life force), and intend to kill the men after conception. The lone exception is Banks's *The Vampire Huntress Legend* series. While Banks's vampires can transform humans into vampires, Banks's vampires have different types of bites—feeding bites, passion bites, elevation bites, mind-control bites, and turn bites—so they do not follow conventional, Western models of turning humans into vampires with a bite. Instead, Banks's vampires control the type of bite they deliver as well as the amount of pleasure or pain, life or death associated with the varying bite. Further, in Banks's fiction, there is a hierarchy among vampires, where only Council-level vampires or master-level vampires[2] can deliver the turn bite. However, bites from second- or third-generation vampires[3] will not turn a human into a vampire without a master vampire's permission; second- and third-generation bites only deliver pleasure to humans and later make humans sick. While the soucouyant, incubi, and wazimamoto may not

1 The implications of the soucouyant being a female are interesting in that the soucouyant is, in Caribbean folklore, associated with the monstrous and the grotesque. Caribbean writers Jean Rhys, Nalo Hopkinson, and David Chariandy, among others use the trope of the soucouyant in their works. Rhys in *Voyage in the Dark* (1968), Hopkinson in *Brown Girl in the Ring* (1998) and "Greedy Choke Puppy" in *Skin Folk (*2001), Chariandy in *Soucouyant* (2007). A study of the soucouyant as a metaphor for the "monstrous" Afro-Caribbean woman is explored in Anatol's *Things That Fly in the Night*. [Parker's note]

2 A council level vampire is a master vampire who is granted additional powers and one of five seats on the Vampire Council. The Vampire Council is the ruling body of Hell. [Parker's note]

3 In terms of vampire hierarchy, you have council-level vampires, master vampires, second-generation vampires, third-generation vampires and so on. Council-level vampire bites will turn a human into a vampire immediately. Master vampire bites will turn a human into a vampire after a three-day period. A human bitten and turned by a master vampire will become a "second-gen" vampire, and a second-gen vampire can only make third gens with a master's permission. As the vampire rank gets lower (from second to third, third to fourth, and so on), the abilities and strengths dilute, decrease, and eventually fade entirely from the blood stream. [Parker's note]

precisely fit Western conceptions of the vampire, they do share common traits. Whether intentional or not, a combination of these traits—Western vampire, soucouyant, incubi/succubi, and wazimamoto—influence Gomez's, Butler's, Banks's, and Cleage's construction of black female vampires.

Traditionally speaking, vampires embody "a source of erotic anxiety and corrupt desire";[1] they are monstrous, satiating themselves through human flesh, blood, and capital; they are exciting, drawing out suppressed sexual desires. If "every age embraces the vampire it needs,"[2] then it is fitting that the rhetoric of African American women as predators emerges from a distinctly American cultural tradition. As I state previously, when bearing in mind the term "vampire," it is important to understand it as a scapegoat for sexist, racist, and homophobic value systems, which are part and parcel of vampire mythology. [...]

As American society embraces the national narrative of African American women as predators or vampires through the stereotypes of the Welfare Queen, Sapphire, and Jezebel (among others), the appearance of black female vampires in literature written by African American women work to interrogate the culturally embedded "truths" that cast African American women as predatory. Thus, though the vampire is often a marker for what is "not normal" (though the *Twilight* saga suggests otherwise), the African American woman as predator becomes an embedded logic, a new truth, a new normal.

A two-pronged dichotomy emerges from the literary representations of black female vampires. On the one hand, black female vampires refute the widely held assumption that African American women are detrimental to the family unit and by extension the community. In *The Gilda Stories* and *Mind of My Mind*, for instance, black female vampires actively build families. Gilda forges communities largely (but not exclusively) composed of women, and in *Mind of My Mind*, Mary builds a family network and later a large community, bringing people together from all walks of life. [...] On the other hand, African American women's literary representations of black female vampires also reinforce the idea that African American women possess emasculatory, life-taking qualities, qualities perceived as threatening to all as evidenced in *Just Wanna Testify*. In *Just Wanna Testify*, black female vampires search for men to further their ancestral line, and once the men have served their purpose by impregnating the women, the vampires plan to kill the young men.

The presence of the black female vampire in African American women's literature is complex; the black female vampire possesses a "troubling mobility"[3] in challenging discourses of normativity and embodying difference while also

1 Veronica Hollinger and Joan Gordon, "Introduction," in *Blood Read: The Vampire as Metaphor in Contemporary Culture* (Philadelphia: University of Pennsylvania Press, 1997), 1. [Parker's note]

2 Nina Auerbach, *Our Vampires, Ourselves* (Chicago: University of Chicago Press, 1995), 145. [Parker's note]

3 Haraway, "Universal Donors," 215. [Parker's note]

feeding into perceptions of African American women as monstrous threats. The black female vampires in Butler, Gomez, Banks and Cleage's fiction inhabit and navigate multiple spaces, functioning, at times, as predatory and altruistic, as victims and victimizers, as vigilantes and damsels, or fragmented manifestations of any of these characterizations/constructs. The implications of such ambiguity reveal that perhaps little has changed since the publication of Stoker's (in)famous novel.

# ILLUSTRATIONS

## CHAPTER I.

MIDNIGHT.—THE HAIL-STORM.—THE DREADFUL VISITOR.—THE VAMPYRE.

The solemn tones of an old cathedral clock have announced midnight—that hour when all the superstitious fear with with which humanity, even in a partially educated state, is pervaded; and the hour when the feathery leaf falling from the ripe tree in autumn will produce an undefined fear—when the merest trifle will send the mind wandering in the land of spirits and of dreams—the air is thick and heavy, a strange, death-like stillness pervades all nature. Like the ominous calm which precedes some more than usually terrific outbreak of the elements, they seem to have paused even in their ordinary fluctuations, to gather a terrific strength for the great effort. A faint peal of thunder now comes from far off. Like a signal gun for the battle of the winds to begin, it appeared to awaken them from their lethargy, and one awful, warring hurricane swept over a whole city, producing more devastation in the four or five minutes it lasted, than would a half century of ordinary phenomena.

It was as if some giant had blown upon a toy town, and scattered the buildings before the hot blast of his terrific anger with

No. 1.

VARNEY THE VAMPYRE; OR, THE FEAST OF BLOOD. 153

FLORA ENCOUNTERS VARNEY IN THE SUMMER-HOUSE.

CHAPTER XXXIV.

THE THREAT.—ITS CONSEQUENCES.—THE RESCUE, AND SIR FRANCIS VARNEY'S

ness could be found in the whole expression of those diabolical features; and if he delayed making the attempt to strike terror into the heart of that unhappy, but beauti-

Illustrations from James Malcolm Rymer and Thomas Peckett Prest, *Varney the Vampire* (1847)

Illustration by David Henry Friston for Sheridan Le Fanu's, *Carmilla* (1872)

*Punch,* "The Irish Vampire" (1885)

*Punch*, "The English Vampire" (1885)

Edvard Munch, *Love and Pain/The Vampire* (1893)

Illustration from Mary Elizabeth Braddon's "The Good Lady Ducayne" (*The Strand Magazine*, 1896)

Cover image for 1919 edition of Bram Stoker's *Dracula*

Philip Burne-Jones, *The Vampire* (1897)

Max Ernst, *The Vampire's Kiss* (1934)

North Carolina newspaper illustration, “The Vampire That Hovers Over North Carolina” (1898)

Stills from F.W. Murnau's *Nosferatu* (1922), featuring Max Schreck

Stills from Tod Browning's *Dracula* (1931), featuring Bela Lugosi, Geraldine Dvorak, Dorothy Tree, and Cornelia Thaw

Still from William Crain's *Blacula* (1972), featuring William Marshall and Vonetta McGee

Anne Rice (author) and Ashley Marie Witter (illustrator), *Interview with the Vampire: Claudia's Story* (2012)

Hideyuki Kikuchi (author) and Yoshitaka Amano (illustrator), *Vampire Hunter D* (1983–present)

# BIBLIOGRAPHY

Abbott, Stacey. *Undead Apocalypse: Vampires and Zombies in the 21st Century.* Edinburgh UP, 2016.

Acocella, Joan. "In the Blood: Why Do Vampires Still Thrill." *The New Yorker,* 16 Mar. 2009.

Altner, Patricia. *Vampire Readings: An Annotated Bibliography.* Scarecrow Press, 1998.

Ambrose, Kala. *Spirits of New Orleans: Voodoo Curses, Vampire Legends, and the Cities of the Dead.* Clerisy Press, 2012.

Anatol, Giselle. *Things That Fly in the Night: Female Vampires in Literature of the Circum-Caribbean and African Diaspora.* Rutgers UP, 2015.

Antoni, Rita. "A Vampiric Relation to Feminism: The Monstrous-Feminine in Whitley Strieber's and Anne Rice's Gothic Fiction." *Americana: E-Journal of American Studies in Hungary,* vol. 4, no. 1, 2008.

Anyiwo, U. Melissa. "Introduction." *Race in the Vampire Narrative,* edited by U. Melissa Anyiwo, Sense Publishers, 2015, pp. 1–6.

Arata, Stephen D. "The Occidental Tourist: *Dracula* and the Anxiety of Reverse Colonization." *Victorian Studies,* vol. 33, no. 4, 1990, pp. 621–45.

Auerbach, Nina. *Our Vampires, Ourselves.* U of Chicago P, 1995.

Barger, Andrew. *The Best Vampire Stories 1800–1849: A Classic Vampire Anthology.* Bottletree Books, 2012.

*Blacula.* Directed by William Crain, Power Productions and American International Productions, 1972.

Bordo, Susan. *Unbearable Weight: Feminism, Western Culture, and the Body.* U of California P, 1993.

Brite, Poppy Z. (Billy Martin). *Lost Souls.* Dell, 1992.

Brock, Marilyn, editor. *Wollstonecraft to Stoker: Essays on Gothic and Victorian Sensation Fiction.* McFarland and Company, 2009.

Brown, Caitlin. "Feminism and the Vampire Novel." *The F-Word: Contemporary UK Feminism*, 8 Sept. 2009, https://thefword.org.uk/2009/09/feminism_aand_th/.

Carter, Margaret. "The Vampire as Alien in Contemporary Fiction." Gordon and Hollinger, pp. 27–44.

Case, Sue-Ellen. "Tracking the Vampire." *Differences: A Journal of Feminist Criticism*, vol. 3, no. 2, 1991, pp. 1–20.

Cohen, David. *The Psychology of Vampires*. Routledge, 2019.

Craft, Christopher. "'Kiss Me with Those Red Lips': Gender and Inversion in Bram Stoker's *Dracula*." *Representations*, vol. 8, Fall 1984, pp. 107–33.

Crawford, Heidi. "The Cultural-Historical Origins of the Literary Vampire in Germany." *Journal of Dracula Studies*, vol. 7, 2005, pp. 1–9.

———. *The Origins of the Literary Vampire*. Rowman and Littlefield, 2016.

Domínguez-Rué, Emma. "Sins of the Flesh: Anorexia, Eroticism and the Female Vampire in Bram Stoker's *Dracula*." *Journal of Gender Studies*, vol. 19, no. 3, 2010, pp. 297–308.

*Dracula*. Directed by Tod Browning, starring Bela Lugosi, Universal Pictures, 1931.

Frayling, Christopher. *Vampyres: Genesis and Resurrection from* Count Dracula *to* Vampirella. Thames and Hudson, 2016.

Freud, Sigmund. "The 'Uncanny' (1919)." *Imago*, vol. 5, 1919, reprinted in *Sammlung*, translated by Alix Strachey, 5th ed., https://web.mit.edu/allanmc/www/freud1.pdf.

Gelder, Ken. *Reading the Vampire*. Routledge, 1994.

Gibson, Matthew. "Jane Anne Cranstoun, Countess Purgstall: A Possible Inspiration for Le Fanu's 'Carmilla.'" *Le Fanu Studies*, vol. 2, no. 2, 2007.

Gomez, Jewelle. "Recasting the Mythology: Writing Vampire Fiction." Gordon and Hollinger, pp. 85–92.

Good, Abby. "'Teaching the Unfamiliar' Just Teach One." *Common-Place: The Journal of Early American Life*, https://jto.americanantiquarian.org/the-black-vampyre/teaching-the-unfamiliar/. Accessed 25 Oct. 2022.

Gordon, Joan. "Sharper Than a Serpent's Tooth: The Vampire in Search of Its Mother." Gordon and Hollinger, pp. 45–55.

Gordon, Joan, and Veronica Hollinger. *Blood Read: The Vampire as Metaphor in Contemporary Culture*. U of Pennsylvania P, 1997.

———. "Introduction: The Shape of Vampires." Gordon and Hollinger, pp. 1–7.

Groom, Nick. *The Vampire: A New History*. Yale UP, 2018.

Hallab, Mary Y. *Vampire God: The Allure of the Undead in Western Culture*. State U of New York, 2009.

Haraway, Donna J. *Modest_Witness@Second_ Millennium.FemaleMan©_ Meets_OncoMouse™: Feminism and Technoscience*. Routledge, 1997.

Heldreth, Leonard G., and Mary Pharr, editors. *The Blood Is the Life: Vampires in Literature.* Bowling Green State U Popular P, 1999.

*The Hunger.* Directed by Tony Scott, based on the novel by Whitley Strieber, MGM, 1983.

Johnson, Judith E. "Women and Vampires: Nightmare or Utopia?" *Kenyon Review*, vol. 15, no. 1, 1993, pp. 72–80.

Jung, Carl. "Archetypes of the Collective Unconscious." *The Archetypes and the Collective Unconsciousness*, translated by R.F.C. Hull, 2nd ed., Princeton UP, 1980, pp. 3–40.

Kent, Sarah. "'The Bloody Transaction': Black Vampires and the Afterlives of Slavery in *Blacula* and *The Gilda Stories.*" *The Journal of Popular Culture*, vol. 53, no. 3, 2020, pp. 739–59.

Latham, Rob. *Consuming Youth: Vampires, Cyborgs, and the Culture of Consumption.* U of Chicago P, 2002.

*Les Vampires.* www.lesvampires.org.

Lipman-Blumen, Jean. "Toward a Homosocial Theory of Sex Roles: An Explanation of the Social Institutions of Sex Segregation." *Signs*, vol. 1, no. 3, Spring 1976, pp. 15–31.

*The Lost Boys.* Directed by Joel Schumacher, Warner Bros, 1987.

Lumwe, Samuel D. "The Cosmology of Witchcraft in the African Context: Implications for Mission and Theology." *Digital Commons @ Andrews University, Journal of Adventist Mission Studies*, vol. 13, no. 1, 83–97.

Marx, Karl. *Capital.* Translated by B. Fowkes, vol. 1, Penguin, 1988.

Melton, J. Gordon. *The Vampire Book: The Encyclopedia of the Undead.* Visible Ink Press, 1994.

Moreno-Garcia, Silvia. *Certain Dark Things.* Nightfire, 2016.

Nixon, Nicola. "When Hollywood Sucks, or, Hungry Girls, Lost Boys, and Vampirism in the Age of Reagan." Gordon and Hollinger, pp. 115–28.

*The Only Lovers Left Alive.* Directed by Jim Jarmusch, Recorded Picture Company and Pandora Film, 2013.

Parker, Kendra R. *Black Female Vampires in African American Women's Novels, 1977–2011: She Bites Back.* Lexington Books, 2018.

Sedgwick, Eve Kosofsky. *Between Men: English Literature and Male Homosocial Desire.* Columbia UP, 1985.

Senf, Carol. "Daughters of Lilith: Women Vampires in Popular Literature." *The Blood Is the Life: Vampires in Literature*, edited by Leonard G. Heldreth and Mary Pharr, Bowling Green State U Popular P, 1999, pp. 199–216.

———. *The Vampire in 19th-Century English Literature.* U of Wisconsin P, 1988.

Smith, Felipe. *American Body Politics: Race, Gender, and Black Literary Renaissance.* U of Georgia P, 1998.

Stoker, Bram. *Dracula*. Edited by Glennis Byron, Broadview Press, 2000.

Swenson, Kristine. "The Menopausal Vampire: Arabella Kenealy and the Boundaries of True Womanhood." *Women's Writing*, vol. 10, issue 1, 2003, pp. 27–46.

*Twilight*. Directed by Catherine Hardwicke, based on the novel by Stephanie Meyers, Summit Entertainment, 2008.

Twitchell, James B. *Dreadful Pleasures: An Anatomy of Modern Horror*. Oxford UP, 1985.

*Underworld*. Directed by Len Wiseman, Sony Pictures, 2003.

White, Ed, and Duncan Faherty. "The Black Vampyre; A Legend of St. Domingo (1819) 'Uriah Derick D'Arcy.'" *Common Place: The Journal of Early American Life, Just Teach One*, vol. 15, Summer 2019, http://jto.common-place.org/just-teach-one-homepage/the-black-vampyre/.

White, Luis. *Speaking with Vampires: Rumor and History in Colonial Africa*. U of California P, 2000.

Zanger, Jules. "Metaphor into Metonymy: The Vampire Next Door." Gordon and Hollinger, pp. 17–26.

Zimmerman, Jess. "Hunger Makes Me." *Hazlitt*, https://hazlitt.net/feature/hunger-makes-me. Accessed 29 Sept. 2022.

# PERMISSIONS ACKNOWLEDGMENTS

Arata, Stephen D. From "The Occidental Tourist: Dracula and the Anxiety of Reverse Colonization," *Victorian Studies* 33, 4 (1990): 627–34. https://www.jstor.org/stable/3827794. Copyright © 1990 Indiana University Press. Reprinted by permission of the publisher, conveyed through Copyright Clearance Center, Inc.

Auerbach, Nina. "Introduction: Living with the Undead," from *Our Vampires, Ourselves*, University of Chicago Press, 1995. Copyright © 1995 The University of Chicago. Reprinted by permission of the publisher, conveyed through Copyright Clearance Center, Inc.

Brite, Poppy Z. (Billy Martin). From *Lost Souls.* Copyright © 1992 by Poppy Z. Brite. Reprinted by permission of Delacorte Press, an imprint of Random House, a division of Penguin Random House LLC. All rights reserved. Used in the United Kingdom by permission of Harold Ober Associates.

Butler, Octavia E. From *Fledgling.* Copyright © 2005 by Octavia E. Butler. Used in North America with the permission of The Permissions Company, LLC on behalf of Seven Stories Press, sevenstories.com. Used in the United Kingdom by permission of Headline Publishing Group, a division of Hachette UK (2022).

Carter, Angela. "The Lady of the House of Love," from *The Bloody Chamber and Other Stories*, Victor Gollancz, London, 1979. Copyright © 1979 Angela Carter. Reprinted with the permission of the author c/o Rogers, Coleridge & White Ltd., 20 Powis Mews, London W11 1JN.

Case, Sue-Ellen. "Tracking the Vampire," *Differences: A Journal of Feminist Cultural Studies* 3, 2 (1991): 1–20. Copyright © 1991 Brown University and Differences: A Journal of Feminist Cultural Studies. All rights reserved. Reprinted by permission of the copyright holder and the Publisher www.dukeupress.edu.

Craft, Christopher. From "'Kiss Me with Those Red Lips': Gender and Inversion in Bram Stoker's *Dracula*," *Representations* 8 (1984): 107–11. https://doi.org/10.2307/2928560. Copyright © 1984 The Regents of the University of California. Reprinted by permission of the University of California Press, conveyed through Copyright Clearance Center, Inc.

Dick, Philip K. "The Cookie Lady." Copyright © 1953 by Philip K. Dick. Used by permission of The Wylie Agency LLC.

Gomez, Jewelle. "Rosebud, Missouri: 1921," from *The Gilda Stories*. Copyright © 1991 by Jewelle Gomez. Used in North America with the permission of The Permissions Company, LLC on behalf of City Lights Books, citylights.com. Used outside North America by permission of SLL/Sterling Lord Literistic, Inc.

Hopkinson, Nalo. "Greedy Choke Puppy," published in *Dark Matter: A Century of Speculative Fiction from the African Diaspora*, ed. Sheree R. Thomas, Aspect/Warner Books, 2000. Copyright © 2000 Nalo Hopkinson. Reprinted by permission of Donald Maass Literary Agency (Brooklyn, NY).

Leiber, Fritz. "The Girl with the Hungry Eyes," from *The Girl with the Hungry Eyes and Other Stories*, Avon Publishing, 1949. Copyright © 1949 by Fritz Leiber. Reprinted by permission of Richard Curtis Associates, Inc., NY.

Matheson, Richard. "Drink My Blood," from *The Penguin Book of Vampire Stories*; originally published in *Imagination*, April 1951. Copyright © 1951 by Richard Matheson; renewed 1979 by Richard Matheson. Reprinted by permission of Don Congdon Associates, Inc.

Moore, C.L. "Shambleau," originally published in *Weird Tales*, Vol. 22, No. 5 (Nov. 1933). Copyright © renewed 1961 Catherine L. Moore. Reprinted by permission of Don Congdon Associates, Inc.

Moreno-Garcia, Silvia. "A Handful of Earth," published in *Expanded Horizons*, July 2011; reprinted in *Love & Other Poisons*, September 2014. Reprinted by permission of JABberwocky Literary Agency, Inc., NY.

Ngũgĩ wa Thiong'o. From *Devil on the Cross*, Heinemann African Writers Series, 1987. Copyright © 1982 Ngũgĩ wa Thiong'o. Used in North America by permission of Watkins Loomis Agency, Inc. Used outside North America by permission of Pearson Education Limited.

Parker, Kendra R. From "Introduction: The First Bite," in *Black Female Vampires in African American Women's Novels, 1977–2011: She Bites Back*, Lexington Books, 2019. Copyright © 2019 The Rowman & Littlefield Publishing Group, Inc. Reprinted by permission of the publisher, conveyed through Copyright Clearance Center, Inc.

Sakuraba, Kazuki. From *A Small Charred Face*, trans. Jocelyne Allen, Haikasoru, 2017. Copyright © 2014 Kazuki Sakuraba. Reprinted by permission of VIZ Media, LLC.

Senf, Carol A. "Daughters of Lilith: Women Vampires in Popular Literature," from *The Blood Is the Life: Vampires in Literature*, ed. Leonard G. Heldreth and Mary Pharr. Copyright © 1999 Bowling Green State University Popular Press. Reprinted by permission of the University of Wisconsin Press.

Yolen, Jane. "Mama Gone," from *Vampires: A Collection of Original Stories*, ed. Jane Yolen and Martin Greenberg, HarperCollins, 1991. Copyright © 1991 by Jane Yolen. Reprinted by permission of Curtis Brown, Ltd.

Zoboi, Ibi. "Old Flesh Song," published in *Dark Matter: Reading the Bones*, ed. Sheree R. Thomas, Aspect/Warner, 2005. Copyright © 2005 Ibi Zoboi. Reprinted by permission of Pippin Properties, Inc., NY, on behalf of the author.

## IMAGES

*Dracula* (1931), stills featuring Bela Lugosi; Geraldine Dvorak, Dorothy Tree, and Cornelia Thaw; directed by Tod Browning. Copyright © 1931 Universal Pictures Corporation. Used under license.

English Vampire ("Reply to *Punch*'s Irish Vampire"), by Richard Barratt, 1885. Call Number PD Pilot 1885 November 7 (A), Prints & Drawings Collection. Reproduced courtesy of the National Library of Ireland.

*Interview with the Vampire: Claudia's Story.* Text copyright © Anne O'Brien Rice and The Stanley Travis Rice, Jr. Testamentary Trust. Illustrations © Yen Press, LLC.

"*Punch, or the London Charivari.*—The Irish Vampire," by Sir John Tenniel, *Punch* magazine, Oct. 24, 1885. Used under license from British Library Board/TopFoto.

*Vampire Hunter D: Bloodlust* (2000), written/directed by Yoshiaki Kawjiri, produced by Madhouse, et al. Reprinted by permission of Tristone Entertainment Co., Ltd. (Tokyo, Japan).

"The Vampire That Hovers over North Carolina," by Norman Ethre Jennett, *News and Observer*, 1898. UNC Libraries, accessed October 23, 2023, https://exhibits.lib.unc.edu/items/show/2215.

*Volume III: The Court of the Dragon, a Week of Kindness or the Seven Deadly Elements*, by Max Ernst, 1934. Object no. 828.1964.C, The Louis E. Stern Collection, The Museum of Modern Art. Copyright © 2024 Artists Rights Society (ARS), New York/ADAGP, Paris. Used under license.

William Marshall in *Blacula* (1972), directed by William Crain. Copyright © 1972 American International Pictures. Used under license from Metro Goldwyn Mayer Studios.

## About the Publisher

The word "broadview" expresses a good deal of the philosophy behind our company. Our focus is very much on the humanities and social sciences—especially literature, writing, and philosophy—but within these fields we are open to a broad range of academic approaches and political viewpoints. We strive in particular to produce high-quality, pedagogically useful books for higher education classrooms—anthologies, editions, sourcebooks, surveys of particular academic fields and sub-fields, and also course texts for subjects such as composition, business communication, and critical thinking. We welcome the perspectives of authors from marginalized and underrepresented groups, and we have a strong commitment to the environment. We publish English-language works and translations from many parts of the world, and our books are available world-wide; we also publish a select list of titles with a specifically Canadian emphasis.

broadview press

The interior of this book is printed on 100% recycled paper.